❦

"ONE CAN NEVER HELP BEING born into perfection," I whispered.

He came close, wrapping an arm around my waist so that we faced each other. His nose tickled mine. He ran his fingers across my cheek so gently it seemed he was afraid I would break.

"No, I don't suppose you can," he breathed.

With his hand holding my face toward his, he lowered his lips to mine and gave me the faintest whisper of a kiss.

Something about the tentativeness of it made me feel beautiful. Without a word, I could understand how excited he was to have this moment, but then afraid at the same time. And deeper than any of that, I sensed that he adored me.

❦

THE SELECTION

KIERA CASS

An Imprint of HarperCollinsPublishers

HarperTeen is an imprint of HarperCollins Publishers.

The Selection
Copyright © 2012 by Kiera Cass

Library of Congress Cataloging-in-Publication Data
Cass, Kiera.
   The Selection / by Kiera Cass. — 1st ed.
        p.   cm.
   Summary: "Sixteen-year-old America Singer is living in
the caste-divided nation of Illéa, which formed after the war that
destroyed the United States. America is chosen to compete in
the Selection—a contest to see which girl can win the heart of
Illéa's prince—but all she really wants is a chance for a future with
her secret love, Aspen, who is a caste below her"— Provided by
publisher.
   ISBN 978-0-06-205994-9
   [1. Marriage—Fiction.   2. Contests—Fiction.   3. Social
classes—Fiction.   4. Princes—Fiction.   5. Love—Fiction.
6. Revolutionaries—Fiction.]   I. Title.
PZ7.C2685133Sel   2012   2011042113
[Fic]—dc23   CIP
                                                   AC

Typography by Sarah Hoy
16 17 18 19 20   CG/RRDH   40 39 38 37 36 35 34 33 32
❖
First paperback edition, 2013

Hi, Dad!
waves

CHAPTER 1

WHEN WE GOT THE LETTER in the post, my mother was ecstatic. She had already decided that all our problems were solved, gone forever. The big hitch in her brilliant plan was me. I didn't think I was a particularly disobedient daughter, but this was where I drew the line.

I didn't want to be royalty. And I didn't want to be a One. I didn't even want to *try*.

I hid in my room, the only place to avoid the chattering of our full house, trying to come up with an argument that would sway her. So far, I had a solid collection of my honest opinions . . . I didn't think there was a single one she would listen to.

I couldn't avoid her much longer. It was approaching dinnertime, and as the oldest child left in the house, cooking duties fell on me. I pulled myself out of bed and walked into the snake pit.

I got a glare from Mom but no words.

We did a silent dance through the kitchen and dining room as we prepared chicken, pasta, and apple slices, and set the table for five. If I glanced up from a task, she'd fix me with a fierce look as if she could shame me into wanting the same things she did. She tried that every so often. Like if I didn't want to take on a particular job because I knew the family hosting us was unnecessarily rude. Or if she wanted me to do a massive cleaning when we couldn't afford to have a Six come and help.

Sometimes it worked. Sometimes it didn't. And this was one area where I was unswayable.

She couldn't stand it when I was stubborn. But I got that from her, so she shouldn't have been surprised. This wasn't just about me, though. Mom had been tense lately. The summer was ending, and soon we'd be faced with cold. And worry.

Mom set down the pitcher of tea in the center of the table with an angry thud. My mouth watered at the thought of tea with lemon. But I would have to wait; it would be such a waste to have my glass now and then have to drink water with my meal.

"Would it kill you to fill out the form?" she said, no longer able to contain herself. "The Selection could be a wonderful opportunity for you, for all of us."

I sighed aloud, thinking that filling out that form might actually be something close to death.

It was no secret that the rebels—the underground colonies

that hated Illéa, our large and comparatively young country—made their attacks on the palace both violent and frequent. We'd seen them in action in Carolina before. One of the magistrates' houses was burned to the ground, and a handful of Twos had their cars vandalized. There was even a magnificent jailbreak once, but considering they only released a teenage girl who'd managed to get herself pregnant and a Seven who was a father to nine, I couldn't help thinking they were in the right that time.

But beyond the potential danger, I felt like it would hurt my heart to even consider the Selection. I couldn't help smiling as I thought about all the reasons I had to stay exactly where I was.

"These last few years have been very hard on your father," she hissed. "If you have any compassion at all, you might think of him."

Dad. Yeah. I really did want to help Dad. And May and Gerad. And, I supposed, even my mother. When she talked about it that way, there was nothing to smile about. Things had been strained around here for far too long. I wondered if Dad would see this as a way back to normal, if any amount of money could make things better.

It wasn't that our situation was so precarious that we were living in fear of survival or anything. We weren't destitute. But I guess we weren't that far off either.

Our caste was just three away from the bottom. We were artists. And artists and classical musicians were only three steps up from dirt. Literally. Our money was stretched as tight as a high wire, and our income was highly dependent on the changing seasons.

I remembered reading in a timeworn history book that all the major holidays used to be cramped into the winter months. Something called Halloween followed by Thanksgiving, then Christmas and New Year's. All back to back.

Christmas was still the same. It's not like you could change the birth date of a deity. But when Illéa made the massive peace treaty with China, the New Year came in January or February, depending on the moon. All the individual celebrations of thankfulness and independence from our part of the world were now simply the Grateful Feast. That came in the summer. It was a time to celebrate the forming of Illéa, to rejoice in the fact that we were still here.

I didn't know what Halloween was. It never resurfaced.

So at least three times a year, the whole family would be fully employed. Dad and May would make their art, and patrons would purchase them as gifts. Mom and I would perform at parties—me singing and her on piano—not turning down a single job if we could manage it. When I was younger, performing in front of an audience terrified me. But now I just tried to equate myself to background music. That's what we were in the eyes of our employers: meant to be heard and not seen.

Gerad hadn't found his talent yet. But he was only seven. He still had a little time.

Soon the leaves would change, and our tiny world would be unsteady again. Five mouths but only four workers. No guarantees of employment until Christmastime.

When I thought of it that way, the Selection seemed like a rope, something sure I could grab onto. That stupid letter could lift me out of the darkness, and I could pull my family along with me.

I looked over at my mother. For a Five, she was a little on the heavy side, which was odd. She wasn't a glutton, and it's not like we had anything to overeat anyway. Perhaps that's just the way a body looks after five children. Her hair was red, like mine, but full of brilliant white streaks. Those had appeared suddenly and in abundance about two years ago. Lines creased the corners of her eyes, though she was still pretty young, and I could see as she moved around the kitchen that she was hunched over as if an invisible weight rested on her shoulders.

I knew she had a lot to carry. And I knew that was why she had taken to being particularly manipulative with me. We fought enough without the extra strain, but as the empty fall quietly approached, she became much more irritable. I knew she thought I was being unreasonable now, to not even want to fill out a silly little form.

But there were things—important things—in this world that I loved. And that piece of paper seemed like a brick wall keeping me away from what I wanted. Maybe what I wanted was stupid. Maybe it wasn't even something I could have. But still, it was mine. I didn't think I could sacrifice my dreams, no matter how much my family meant to me. Besides, I had given them so much already.

I was the oldest one left now that Kenna was married and Kota was gone, and I did my best to contribute. We scheduled my homeschooling around my rehearsals, which took up most of the day since I was trying to master several instruments as well as singing.

But with the letter here, none of my work mattered anymore. In my mom's mind, I was already queen.

If I was smart, I would have hidden that stupid notice before Dad, May, and Gerad came in. But I didn't know Mom had it tucked away in her clothes, and mid-meal she pulled it out.

"'To the House of Singer,'" she sang out.

I tried to swipe it away, but she was too quick for me. They would find out sooner or later anyway, but if she did it like this, they'd all be on her side.

"Mom, please!" I pleaded.

"I want to hear!" May squealed. That was no surprise. My little sister looked just like me, only on a three-year delay. But where our looks were practically identical, our personalities were anything but. Unlike me, she was outgoing and hopeful. And currently very boy crazy. This whole thing would seem incredibly romantic to her.

I felt myself blush. Dad listened intently, and May was practically bouncing with joy. Gerad, sweet little thing, he just kept eating. Mother cleared her throat and went on.

"'The recent census has confirmed that a single woman between the ages of sixteen and twenty currently resides in your home. We would like to make you aware of an upcoming opportunity to honor the great nation of Illéa.'"

May squealed again and grabbed my wrist. "That's you!"

"I know, you little monkey. Stop before you break my arm." But she just held my hand and bounced some more.

"'Our beloved prince, Maxon Schreave,'" Mom continued, "'is coming of age this month. As he ventures into this new part of his life, he hopes to move forward with a partner, to marry a true Daughter of Illéa. If your eligible daughter, sister, or charge is interested in possibly becoming the bride of Prince Maxon and the adored princess of Illéa, please fill out the enclosed form and return it to your local Province Services Office. One woman from each province will be drawn at random to meet the prince.

"'Participants will be housed at the lovely Illéa Palace in Angeles for the duration of their stay. The families of each participant will be *generously compensated*'"—she drew out the words for effect—"'for their service to the royal family.'"

I rolled my eyes as she went on. This was the way they did it with sons. Princesses born into the royal family were sold off into marriage in an attempt to solidify our young relations with other countries. I understood why it was done—we needed allies. But I didn't like it. I hadn't had to see such a thing, and I hoped I never would. The royal family hadn't produced a princess in three generations. Princes, however, married women of the people to keep up the morale of our sometimes volatile nation. I think the Selection was meant to draw us together and remind everyone that Illéa itself was born out of next to nothing.

The idea of being entered into a contest for the whole country to watch as this stuck-up little wimp picked the most gorgeous and shallow one of the bunch to be the silent, pretty face that stood beside him on TV . . . it was enough to make me scream. Could anything be more humiliating?

Besides, I'd been in the homes of enough Twos and Threes to be sure I never wanted to live among them, let alone be a One. Except for the times when we were hungry, I was quite content to be a Five. Mom was the caste climber, not me.

"And of course he would love America! She's so beautiful," Mom swooned.

"Please, Mom. If anything, I'm average."

"You are not!" May said. "Because I look just like you, and *I'm* pretty!" Her smile was so wide, I couldn't contain my laughter. And it was a good point. Because May really was beautiful.

It was more than her face, though, more than her winning smile and bright eyes. May radiated an energy, an enthusiasm that made you want to be wherever she was. May was magnetic, and I, honestly, wasn't.

"Gerad, what do you think? Do you think I'm pretty?" I asked.

All eyes fell on the youngest member of our family.

"No! Girls are gross!"

"Gerad, please." Mom gave an exasperated sigh, but her heart wasn't in it. He was hard to get upset with. "America, you must know you're a very lovely girl."

"If I'm so lovely, how come no one ever comes by to ask me out?"

"Oh, they come by, but I shoo them away. My girls are too pretty to marry Fives. Kenna got a Four, and I'm sure you can do even better." Mom took a sip of her tea.

"His name is James. Stop calling him a number. And since when do boys come by?" I heard my voice getting higher and higher.

"A while," Dad said, making his first comment on all of this. His voice had a hint of sorrow to it, and he was staring decidedly at his cup. I was trying to figure out what upset him so much. Boys coming by? Mom and me arguing again? The idea of me not entering the contest? How far away I'd be if I did?

His eyes came up for the briefest of moments, and I suddenly understood. He didn't want to ask this of me. He wouldn't want me to go. But he couldn't deny the benefits if I managed to make it in, even for a day.

"America, be reasonable," Mom said. "We have to be the only parents in the country trying to talk our daughter into this. Think of the opportunity! You could be queen one day!"

"Mom. Even if I wanted to be queen, which I thoroughly don't, there are thousands of other girls in the province entering this thing. Thousands. And if I somehow was drawn, there would still be thirty-four other girls there, no doubt much better at seduction than I could ever pretend to be."

Gerad's ears perked up. "What's seduction?"

"Nothing," we all chorused back.

"It's ridiculous to think that, with all of that, I'd somehow manage to win," I finished.

My mother pushed her chair out as she stood and leaned across the table toward me. "Someone is going to, America. You have as good a chance as anyone else." She threw her napkin down and went to leave. "Gerad, when you finish, it's time for your bath."

He groaned.

May ate in silence. Gerad asked for seconds, but there weren't any. When they got up, I started clearing the table while Dad sat there sipping his tea. He had paint in his hair again, a smattering of yellow that made me smile. He stood, brushing crumbs off his shirt.

"Sorry, Dad," I murmured as I picked up plates.

"Don't be silly, kitten. I'm not mad." He smiled easily and put an arm around me.

"I just . . ."

"You don't have to explain it to me, honey. I know." He kissed me on my forehead. "I'm going back to work."

And with that I moved to the kitchen to start cleaning. I wrapped my mostly untouched plate under a napkin and hid it in the fridge. No one else left more than crumbs.

I sighed, heading to my room to get ready for bed. The whole thing was infuriating.

Why did Mom have to push me so much? Wasn't she happy? Didn't she love Dad? Why wasn't this good enough for her?

I lay on my lumpy mattress, trying to wrap my head

around the Selection. I guess it had its advantages. It would be nice to eat well for a while at least. But there was no reason to bother. I wasn't going to fall in love with Prince Maxon. From what I'd seen on the *Illéa Capital Report*, I wouldn't even like the guy.

It seemed like forever until midnight rolled around. There was a mirror by my door, and I stopped to make sure my hair looked as good as it had this morning and put on a little lip gloss so there'd be some color on my face. Mom was pretty strict about saving makeup for when we had to perform or go out in public, but I usually snuck some on nights like tonight.

As quietly as I could, I crept into the kitchen. I grabbed my leftovers, some bread that was expiring, and an apple and bundled it all up. It was painful to walk back to my room so slowly, now that it was late. But if I'd done it earlier, I would have just been antsy.

I opened my window and looked out into our little patch of backyard. There wasn't much of a moon out, so I had to let my eyes adjust before I moved. Across the lawn, the tree house stood barely silhouetted in the night. When we were younger, Kota would tie up sheets to the branches so it looked like a ship. He was the captain, and I was always his first mate. My duties mainly consisted of sweeping the floor and making food, which was dirt and twigs stuffed into Mom's baking pans. He'd take a spoonful of dirt and "eat" it by throwing it over his shoulder. This meant that I'd have to sweep again, but I didn't mind. I was just happy to be on the ship with Kota.

I looked around. All the neighboring houses were dark. No one was watching. I crawled out of the window carefully. I used to get bruises across my stomach from doing it the wrong way, but now it was easy, a talent I'd mastered over the years. And I didn't want to mess up any of the food.

I scurried across the lawn in my cutest pajamas. I could have left my day clothes on, but this felt better. I supposed it didn't matter what I wore, but I felt pretty in my little brown shorts and fitted white shirt.

It wasn't hard anymore to scale the slats nailed into the tree with only one hand. I'd developed that skill as well. Each step up was a relief. It wasn't much of a distance, but from here it felt like all the commotion from my house was miles away. Here I didn't have to be anyone's princess.

As I climbed into the tiny box that was my escape, I knew I wasn't alone. In the far corner, someone was hiding in the night. My breath sped; I couldn't help it. I set my food down and squinted. The person shifted, lighting an all but unusable candle. It wasn't much light—no one in the house would see it—but it was enough. Finally the intruder spoke, a sly grin spreading across his face.

"Hey there, gorgeous."

CHAPTER 2

I CRAWLED DEEPER INTO THE tree house. It wasn't much more than a five-by-five-foot cube; even Gerad couldn't stand up straight in here. But I loved it. There was the one opening to crawl into and then a tiny window on the opposite wall. I'd placed an old step stool in the corner to act as a desk for the candle, and a little rug that was so old it was barely better than sitting on the slats. It wasn't much, but it was my haven. *Our* haven.

"Please don't call me gorgeous. First my mom, then May, now you. It's getting on my nerves." By the way Aspen was looking at me, I could tell I wasn't helping my "I'm not pretty" case. He smiled.

"I can't help it. You're the most beautiful thing I've ever seen. You can't hold it against me for saying it the only time I'm allowed to." He reached up and cupped my face, and I looked deep into his eyes.

That was all it took. His lips were on mine, and I couldn't think about anything anymore. There was no Selection, no miserable family, no Illéa itself. There were only Aspen's hands on my back pulling me closer, Aspen's breath on my cheeks. My fingers went to his black hair, still wet from his shower—he always took showers at night—and tangled themselves into a perfect little knot. He smelled like his mother's homemade soap. I dreamed about that smell. We broke apart, and I couldn't help but smile.

His legs were propped open wide, so I sat sideways between them, like a kid who needed cradling. "Sorry I'm not in a better mood. It's just that . . . we got this stupid notice in the post today."

"Ah, yes, the letter." Aspen sighed. "We got two."

Of course. The twins had just turned sixteen.

Aspen studied my face as he spoke. He did that when we were together, like he was recommitting my face to memory. It had been over a week, and we both got anxious when it was more than a few days.

And I looked him over, too. No caste excluded, Aspen was, by far, the most attractive guy in town. He had dark hair and green eyes, and this smile that made you think he had a secret. He was tall, but not too tall. Thin, but not too thin. I noticed in the dim light that there were tiny bags under his eyes; no doubt he'd been working late all week. His black T-shirt was worn to threads in several places, just like the shabby pair of jeans he wore almost every day.

If only I could sit and patch them up for him. That was my great ambition. Not to be Illéa's princess. To be Aspen's.

It hurt me to be away from him. Some days I went crazy wondering what he was doing. And when I couldn't handle it, I practiced music. I really had Aspen to thank for me being the musician that I was. He drove me to distraction.

And that was bad.

Aspen was a Six. Sixes were servants and only a step up from Sevens in that they were better educated and trained for indoor work. Aspen was smarter than anyone knew and devastatingly handsome, but it was atypical for a woman to marry down. A man from a lower caste could ask for your hand, but it was rare to get a yes. And when anyone married into a different caste, they had to fill out paperwork and wait for something like ninety days before any of the other legal things you needed could be done. I'd heard more than one person say it was to give people a chance to change their minds. So us being this personal and out well past Illéa's curfew . . . we could both get in serious trouble. Not to mention the hell I'd get from my mother.

But I loved Aspen. I'd loved Aspen for nearly two years. And he loved me. As he sat there stroking my hair, I couldn't imagine entering the Selection.

"How do you feel about it? The Selection, I mean?" I asked.

"Okay, I guess. He's got to find a girl *somehow*, poor guy." I could hear the sarcasm. But I really wanted to know his opinion.

"Aspen."

"Okay, okay. Well, part of me thinks it's kind of sad. Doesn't the prince date? I mean, can he seriously not get *anyone*? If they try to wed the princesses to other princes, why don't they do the same for him? There's got to be some royal out there good enough for him. I don't get it. So there's that.

"But then . . ." He sighed. "Part of me thinks it's a good idea. It's exciting. He's going to fall in love in front of everyone. And I like that someone gets a happily ever after and all that. Anybody could be our next queen. It's kind of hopeful. Makes me think that I could have a happily ever after, too."

His fingers were tracing my lips. Those green eyes searched deep into my soul, and I felt that spark of connection that I'd only ever had with him. I wanted our happily ever after, too.

"So you're encouraging the twins to enter, then?" I asked.

"Yes. I mean, we've all seen the prince from time to time; he looks like a nice enough guy. A snot, no doubt, but friendly. And the girls are so eager; it's funny to watch. They were dancing in the house when I came home today. And no one can deny that it'd be good for the family. Mom's hopeful because we have two entries from the house instead of one."

That was the first good news about this horrible competition. I couldn't believe I'd been so self-absorbed that I hadn't thought about Aspen's sisters. If one of them went, if one of them won . . .

"Aspen, do you realize what that would mean? If Kamber or Celia won?"

He closed his hold tighter around me, his lips brushing my forehead. One hand moved up and down my back.

"It's all I've thought about today," he said. The gritty sound of his voice pushed out every other thought. All I wanted was for Aspen to touch me, kiss me. And that's exactly where the night would have gone, but his stomach growled and snapped me out of it.

"Oh, hey, I brought us a snack," I said lightly.

"Oh, yeah?" I could tell he was trying not to sound excited, but some of his eagerness came through.

"You'll love this chicken; I made it."

I found my little bundle and brought it to Aspen, who, to his merit, nibbled it all slowly. I took one bite of the apple so he would feel like it was for *us*, but then I set it down and let him have the rest.

Where meals were a worry at my house, they were a disaster at Aspen's. He had much steadier work than we did but got paid significantly less. There was never enough food for his family. He was the oldest of seven, and in the same way I'd stepped up to help as soon as I could, Aspen had stepped aside. He passed his share of the little food they had down to his siblings and to his mom, who was always tired from working. His dad had died three years ago, and Aspen's family depended on him for almost everything.

I watched with satisfaction as he licked the spices from the chicken off his fingers and tore into the bread. I couldn't imagine when he'd eaten last.

"You're such a good cook. You're going to make someone

very fat and happy one day," he said, his mouth half full with a bite of apple.

"I'm going to make *you* fat and happy. You know that."

"Ah, to be fat!"

We laughed, and he told me about life since the last time I'd seen him. He'd done some clerical work for one of the factories, and it was going to carry him through next week, too. His mom had finally gotten into a routine of house-cleaning for a few of the Twos in our area. The twins were both sad because their mom had made them drop their after-school drama club so they could work more.

"I'm going to see if I can pick up some work on Sundays, make a little more money. I hate for them to give up something they love so much." He said this with hope, like he really could do it.

"Aspen Leger, don't you dare! You work too hard as it is."

"Aw, Mer," he whispered into my ear. It gave me chill bumps. "You know how Kamber and Celia are. They need to be around people. They can't be cooped up cleaning and writing all the time. It's just not in their nature."

"But it's not fair for them to expect you to do it all, Aspen. I know exactly how you feel about your sisters, but you need to watch out for yourself. If you really love them, you'll take better care of their caregiver."

"Don't you worry about a thing, Mer. I think there are some good things on the horizon. I wouldn't be doing it forever."

But he would. Because his family would always need

money. "Aspen, I know you could do it. But you're not a superhero. You can't expect to be able to provide everything for everyone you love. You just . . . you can't do everything."

We were quiet for a moment. I hoped he was taking my words to heart, realizing that if he didn't slow down, he'd wear himself out. It wasn't anything new for a Six, Seven, or Eight to just die of exhaustion. I couldn't bear that. I pressed myself even closer to his chest, trying to get the image of it out of my head.

"America?"

"Yes?" I whispered.

"Are you going to enter the Selection?"

"No! Of course not! I don't want anyone to think I'd even *consider* marrying some stranger. I love *you*," I said earnestly.

"You want to be a Six? Always hungry? Always worried?" he asked. I could hear the pain in his voice, but also the genuine question: If I had to choose between sleeping in a palace with people waiting on me or the three-room apartment with Aspen's family, which one did I really want?

"Aspen, we'll make it. We're smart. We'll be fine." I willed it to be true.

"You know that's not how it'll be, Mer. I'd still have to support my family; I'm not the abandoning type." I squirmed a little in his arms. "And if we had kids—"

"*When* we have kids. And we'll just be careful about it. Who says we have to have more than two?"

"You know that's not something we can control!" I could hear the anger building in his voice.

I couldn't blame him. If you were wealthy enough, you could regulate having a family. If you were a Four or worse, they left you to fend for yourselves. This had been the subject of many an argument for us over the last six months, when we seriously started trying to find a way to be together. Children were the wild card. The more you had, the more there were to work. But then again, so many hungry mouths . . .

We fell quiet again, both unsure of what to say. Aspen was a passionate person; he tended to get a little carried away in an argument. He had gotten better about catching himself before he got too angry, and I knew that's what he was doing now.

I didn't want him to worry or be upset; I really thought we could handle it. If we just planned for everything we could, we'd make it through everything we couldn't. Maybe I was too optimistic, maybe I was just too far in love, but I really believed that anything Aspen and I wanted badly enough, we could make happen.

"I think you should do it," he said suddenly.

"Do what?"

"Enter the Selection. I think you should do it."

I glared at him. "Are you out of your mind?"

"Mer, listen to me." His mouth was right to my ear. It wasn't fair; he knew this distracted me. When his voice came, it was breathy and slow, like he was saying something romantic, though what he was suggesting was anything but. "If you had a chance for something better than this, and you didn't take it because of me, I'd never forgive myself. I couldn't stand it."

I let out my breath in a quick huff. "It's so ridiculous. Think of the thousands of girls entering. I won't even get picked."

"If you won't get picked, then why does it matter?" His hands were rubbing up and down my arms now. I couldn't argue when he did that. "All I want is for you to enter. I just want you to try. And if you go, then you go. And if you don't, then at least I won't have to beat myself up for holding you back."

"But I don't love him, Aspen. I don't even like him. I don't even *know* him."

"No one knows him. That's the thing, though, maybe you would like him."

"Aspen, stop. I love *you*."

"And I love you." He kissed me slowly to make his point. "And if you love me, you'll do this so I won't go crazy wondering what if."

When he made it about him, I didn't stand a chance. Because I couldn't hurt him. I was doing everything I could to make his life easier. And I was right. There was absolutely no way I'd get chosen. So I should just go through the motions, appease everyone, and when I didn't get picked, everyone would drop it.

"Please?" he breathed into my ear. The feeling sent chills down my body.

"Fine," I whispered. "I'll do it. But know now that I don't

want to be some princess. All I want is to be your wife."

He stroked my hair.

"You will be."

It must have been the light. Or the lack thereof. Because I swore his eyes welled up when he said that. Aspen had been through a lot, but I had seen him cry only once, when they whipped his brother in the square. Little Jemmy had stolen some fruit off a cart in the market. An adult would have had a brief trial and then, depending on the value of what was stolen, either been thrown in jail or sentenced to death. Jemmy was only nine, so he was beaten. Aspen's mom didn't have the money to take him to a proper doctor, so Jemmy had scars all up and down his back from the incident.

That night I waited by my window to see if Aspen would climb up into the tree house. When he did, I snuck out to him. He cried in my arms for an hour about how if he'd only worked harder, if he'd only done better, Jemmy wouldn't have had to steal. How it was so unfair that Jemmy had to hurt because Aspen had failed.

It was agonizing, because it wasn't true. But I couldn't tell him that; he wouldn't hear me. Aspen carried the needs of everyone he loved on his back. Somehow, miraculously, I became one of those people. So I made my load as light as I could.

"Would you sing for me? Give me something good to fall asleep to?"

I smiled. I loved giving him songs. So I settled in close and sang a quiet lullaby.

He let me sing for a few minutes before his fingers started moving absently below my ear. He pulled the neck of my shirt open wide and kissed along my neck and ears. Then he pulled up my short sleeve and kissed as far down my arm as he could reach. It made my breath hitch. Almost every time I sang, he did this. I think he enjoyed the sound of my raspy breathing more than the singing itself.

Before long we were tangled together on the dirty, thin rug. Aspen pulled me on top of him, and I brushed his scraggly hair with my fingers, hypnotized by the feel. He kissed me feverishly and hard. I felt his fingers dig into my waist, my back, my hips, my thighs. I was always surprised that he didn't leave little finger-shaped bruises all over me.

We were cautious, always stopping shy of the things we really wanted. As if breaking curfew wasn't bad enough. Still, whatever our limitations were, I couldn't imagine anyone in Illéa had more passion than we did.

"I love you, America Singer. As long as I live, I'll love you." There was some deep emotion in his voice, and it caught me off guard.

"I love you, Aspen. You'll always be my prince."

And he kissed me until the candle burned itself out.

It had to have been hours, and my eyes were heavy. Aspen never worried about his sleep, but he was always concerned about mine. So I wearily climbed down the ladder, taking my plate and my penny.

When I sang, Aspen ate it up, loved it. From time to time, when he had anything at all, he'd give me a penny to pay for my song. If he managed to scrounge up a penny, I wanted him to give it to his family. There was no doubt they needed every last one. But then, having these pennies—since I couldn't bear to spend them—was like having a reminder of everything Aspen was willing to do for me, of everything I meant to him.

Back in my room, I pulled my tiny jar of pennies out from its hiding spot and listened to the happy sound of the newest one hitting its neighbors. I waited for ten minutes, watching out the window, until I saw Aspen's shadow climb down and run down the back road.

I stayed awake a little while longer, thinking of Aspen and how much I loved him, and how it felt to be loved by him. I felt special, priceless, irreplaceable. No queen on any throne could possibly feel more important than I did.

I fell asleep with that thought securely etched in my heart.

CHAPTER 3

ASPEN WAS DRESSED IN WHITE. He looked angelic. We were in Carolina still, but there was no one else around. We were alone, but we didn't miss anyone. Aspen wove twigs to make me a crown, and we were together.

"America," Mom crowed, jarring me from my dreams.

She flicked on the lights, burning my eyes, and I rubbed my hands into them, trying to adjust.

"Wake up, America, I have a proposal for you." I looked over at the alarm clock. Just past seven in the morning. So that was . . . five hours in bed.

"Is it more sleep?" I mumbled.

"No, honey, sit up. I have something serious to discuss."

I worked myself into a sitting position, clothes rumpled and hair sticking out in strange directions. Mom clapped her hands over and over, as if it would speed up the process.

"Come on, America, I need you to wake up."

I yawned. Twice.

"What do you want?" I said.

"For you to submit your name for the Selection. I think you'd make an excellent princess."

It was way too early for this.

"Mom, really, I just . . ." I sighed as I remembered what I'd promised Aspen last night: that I would at least try. But now, in the light of day, I wasn't sure if I could make myself do it.

"I know you're opposed, but I figured I'd make a deal with you to see if you would change your mind."

My ears perked up. What could she possibly offer me?

"Your father and I spoke last night, and we decided that you're old enough to go on your jobs alone. You play the piano as well as I do, and if you'd try a little more, you'd be nearly flawless on the violin. And your voice, well, there's no one better in the province, if you ask me."

I smiled groggily. "Thanks, Mom. Really." I didn't particularly care to work alone, though. I didn't see how that was supposed to entice me.

"Well, that's not all. You can accept your own work now and go alone and . . . and you can keep half of whatever you make." She sort of grimaced as she said it.

My eyes popped open.

"*But* only if you sign up for the Selection." She was starting to smile now. She knew this would win me over, though I think she was expecting more of a fight. But how could I fight? I was already going to sign up, and now I could earn some money of my own!

"You know I can only agree to sign up, right? I can't make them pick me."

"Yes, I know. But it's worth a shot."

"Wow, Mom." I shook my head, still in shock. "Okay, I'll fill out the form today. Are you serious about the money?"

"Of course. Sooner or later you'd go out on your own anyway. And being responsible for your own money will be good for you. Only, don't forget your family, please. We still need you."

"I won't forget you, Mom. How could I, with all the nagging?" I winked, she laughed, and with that, the deal was done.

I took a shower as I processed everything that had happened in less than twenty-four hours. By simply filling out a form, I was winning the approval of my family, making Aspen happy, and earning the money that would help Aspen and me get married!

I wasn't so concerned about the money, but Aspen insisted we needed to have some savings of our own first. It cost a bit to do the legal stuff, and we wanted to have a very small party with our family after our wedding. I figured it wouldn't take very long for us to save for that once we decided we were ready, but Aspen wanted more. Maybe, finally, he'd trust that we wouldn't always be strapped if I did some serious work.

After my shower, I did my hair and put on the tiniest

bit of makeup to celebrate, then went to my closet and got dressed. There weren't a whole lot of options. Most everything was beige, brown, or green. I had a few nicer dresses for when we worked, but they were hopelessly behind in the fashion department. It was like that, though. Sixes and Sevens were almost always in denim or something sturdy. Fives mostly wore bland clothes, as the artists covered everything with smocks and the singers and dancers only really needed to look special for performances. The upper castes would wear khaki and denim from time to time to change up their looks, but it was always in a way that took the material to a whole new level. As if it wasn't enough that they could have pretty much whatever they wanted, they turned our necessities into luxuries.

I put on my khaki shorts and the green tunic top—by far the most exciting day clothes I owned—and looked myself over before going into the living room. I felt kind of pretty today. Maybe it was just the excitement behind my eyes.

Mom was sitting at the kitchen table with Dad, humming. They both looked up at me a couple of times, but even their stares couldn't bother me.

When I picked up the letter, I was a little surprised. Such high-quality paper. I'd never felt anything like it. Thick and slightly textured. For a moment the weight of the paper hit me, reminding me of the magnitude of what I was doing. Two words jumped into my head: *What if?*

But I shook the thought away and put pen to paper.

It was straightforward enough. I filled in my name, age,

caste, and contact information. I had to put my height and weight, hair, eye, and skin color, too. I was pleased to write that I could speak three languages. Most could speak at least two, but my mother insisted we learn French and Spanish, since those languages were still used in parts of the country. It also helped with the singing. There were so many pretty songs in French. We had to list the highest grade level we'd completed, which could vary immensely, since only Sixes and Sevens went to the public schools and had actual grade levels. I was nearly done with my education. Under special skills, I listed singing and all my instruments.

"Do you think the ability to sleep in counts as a special skill?" I asked Dad, trying to sound torn over the decision.

"Yes, list that. And don't forget to write that you can eat an entire meal in under five minutes," he replied. I laughed. It was true; I did tend to inhale my food.

"Oh, the both of you! Why don't you just write down that you're an absolute heathen!" My mother went storming from the room. I couldn't believe she was so frustrated— after all, she was getting exactly what she wanted.

I gave Dad a questioning look.

"She just wants the best for you, that's all." He leaned back in his chair, relaxing a bit before he started on the commissioned piece that was due by the end of the month.

"So do you, but you're never so angry," I noted.

"Yes. But your mother and I have different ideas of what's best for you." He flashed me a smile. I got my mouth from him—both the look and the tendency to say innocent things that got me into trouble. The temper was Mom's doing, but she was better at holding her tongue if it really mattered. Not me. Like right now . . .

"Dad, if I wanted to marry a Six or even a Seven, and he was someone I really loved, would you let me?"

Dad set his mug down, and his eyes focused on me. I tried not to give anything away with my expression. His sigh was heavy, full of grief.

"America, if you loved an Eight, I'd want you to marry him. But you should know that love can wear away under the stress of being married. Someone you think you love now, you might start to hate when he couldn't provide for you. And if you couldn't take care of your children, it'd be even worse. Love doesn't always survive under those types of circumstances."

Dad rested his hand on top of mine, drawing my eyes up to his. I tried to hide my worry.

"But no matter what, I want you to be loved. You deserve to be loved. And I hope you get to marry for love and not a number."

He couldn't say what I wanted to know—that I *would* get to marry for love and not a number—but it was the best I could hope for.

"Thanks, Dad."

"Go easy on your mother. She's trying to do the right thing." He kissed my head and went off to work.

I sighed and went back to filling out the application. The whole thing made me feel like my family didn't think I had any right to want something of my own. It bothered me, but I knew I couldn't hold it against them in the long run. We couldn't afford the luxury of wants. We had needs.

I took my finished application and went to find Mom in the backyard. She sat there, stitching up a hem as May did her schoolwork in the shade of the tree house. Aspen used to complain about the strict teachers in the public schools. I seriously doubted any of them could keep up with Mom. It was summer, for goodness' sake.

"Did you really do it?" May asked, bouncing on her knees.

"I sure did."

"What made you change your mind?"

"Mom can be very compelling," I said pointedly, though Mom was obviously not ashamed at all of her bribery. "We can go to the Services Office as soon as you're ready, Mom."

She smiled a little. "That's my girl. Go get your things, and we'll head out. I want to get yours in as soon as possible."

I went to grab my shoes and bag as I'd been instructed, but I stopped short at Gerad's room. He was staring at a blank canvas, looking frustrated. We kept rotating through options with Gerad, but none of them were sticking. One look at the battered soccer ball in the corner or the second-hand microscope we'd inherited as payment one Christmas, and it was obvious his heart just wasn't in the arts.

"Not feeling inspired today, huh?" I asked, stepping into his room.

He looked up at me and shook his head.

"Maybe you could try sculpting, like Kota. You have great

hands. I bet you'd be good at it."

"I don't want to sculpt things. Or paint or sing or play the piano. I want to play ball." He kicked his foot into the aging carpet.

"I know. And you can for fun, but you need to find a craft you're good at to make a living. You can do both."

"But why?" he whined.

"You know why. It's the law."

"But that's not fair!" Gerad pushed the canvas to the floor, where it stirred up dust in the light from his window. "It's not our fault our great-grandfather or whoever was poor."

"I know." It really seemed unreasonable to limit everyone's life choices based on your ancestors' ability to help the government, but that was how it all worked out. And I suppose I should just be grateful we were safe. "I guess it was the only way to make things work at the time."

He didn't speak. I breathed a sigh and picked up the canvas, setting it back into place. This was his life, and he couldn't just wipe it away.

"You don't have to give up your hobbies, buddy. But you want to be able to help Mom and Dad and grow up and get married, right?" I poked his side.

He stuck his tongue out in playful disgust, and we both giggled.

"America!" Mom called down the hall. "What's taking you so long?"

"Coming," I yelled back, and then turned to Gerad. "I know it's hard. It's just the way it is, okay?"

But I knew it wasn't okay. It wasn't okay at all.

Mom and I walked all the way to the local office. Sometimes we took the public buses if we were going too far or if we were working. It looked bad to show up sweaty at the house of a Two. They already looked at us funny anyway. But it was a nice day out, and the trip was just shy of being too long.

We obviously weren't the only ones trying to get our submission in right away. By the time we got there, the street in front of the Province of Carolina Services Office was packed with women.

Standing in line, I could see a number of girls from my neighborhood in front of me, waiting to go inside. The trail was nearly four people wide and wrapped halfway around the block. Every girl in the province was signing up. I didn't know whether to feel terrified or relieved.

"Magda!" someone called. My mother and I both turned at the sound of her name.

Celia and Kamber were walking up behind us with Aspen's mother. She must have taken the day off to do this. Her daughters were dressed up as neatly as they could afford, looking very tidy. It wasn't much, but they looked good no matter what they wore, just like Aspen. Kamber and Celia had his same dark hair and beautiful smiles.

Aspen's mother smiled at me, and I returned her grin. I adored her. I only got to talk to her every once in a while, but she was always nice to me. And I knew it wasn't because I was a step up from her; I'd seen her give clothes that didn't fit her kids anymore to families who had next to nothing. She was just kind.

"Hello, Lena. Kamber, Celia, how are you?" Mother greeted them.

"Good!" they sang in unison.

"You guys look beautiful," I said, placing one of Celia's curls behind her shoulder.

"We wanted to look pretty for our picture," Kamber announced.

"Picture?" I asked.

"Yes." Aspen's mom spoke in a hushed voice. "I was cleaning at one of the magistrates' houses yesterday. This lottery isn't much of a lottery at all. That's why they're taking pictures and getting lots of information. Why would it matter how many languages you spoke if it were random?"

That *had* struck me as funny, but I thought that was all information for after the fact.

"It appears to have leaked a little; look around. Lots of girls are way overdone."

I scanned the line. Aspen's mother was right, and there was a clear line between those who knew and those who didn't. Just behind us was a girl, obviously a Seven, still in her work clothes. Her muddy boots might not make the picture, but the dust on her overalls probably would. A few yards back another Seven was sporting a tool belt. The best I could say about her was that her face was clean.

On the other end of the spectrum, a girl in front of me had her hair up in a twist with little tendrils framing her face. The girl beside her, clearly a Two based on her clothes, looked like she was trying to drown the world in her cleavage. Several had on so much makeup, they looked kind of like clowns to me. But at least they were trying.

I looked decent, but I hadn't gone to any such lengths. Like the Sevens, I hadn't known to bother. I felt a sudden flutter of worry.

But why? I stopped myself and rearranged my thoughts.

I didn't want this. If I wasn't pretty enough, surely that was a good thing. I would at least be a notch below Aspen's sisters. They were naturally beautiful, and looked even lovelier with the little hints of makeup. If Kamber or Celia won, Aspen's whole family would be elevated. Surely my mother couldn't disapprove of me marrying a One just because he wasn't the prince himself. My lack of information was a blessing.

"I think you're right," Mom said. "That girl looks like she's getting ready for a Christmas party." She laughed, but I could tell she hated that I was at a disadvantage.

"I don't know why some girls go so over the top. Look at America. She's so pretty. I'm so glad you didn't go that route," Mrs. Leger said.

"I'm nothing special. Who could pick me next to Kamber or Celia?" I winked at them, and they smiled. Mom did, too, but it was forced. She must have been debating staying in the line or forcing me to run home and change.

"Don't be silly! Every time Aspen comes home from helping your brother, he always says the Singers inherited more

35

than their fair share of talent and beauty," Aspen's mother said.

"Does he really? What a nice boy!" my mother cooed.

"Yes. A mother couldn't ask for a better son. He's supportive, and he works so hard."

"He's going to make some girl very happy one day," my mother said. She was only half into the conversation as she continued to size up the competition.

Mrs. Leger took a quick look around. "Between you and me, I think he might already have someone in mind."

I froze. I didn't know if I should comment or not, unsure if either response would give me away.

"What's she like?" my mother asked. Even when she was planning my marriage to a complete stranger, she still had time for gossip.

"I'm not sure! I haven't actually met her. And I'm only guessing that he's seeing someone, but he seems happier lately," she replied, beaming.

Lately? We'd been meeting for nearly two years. Why only lately?

"He hums," Celia offered.

"Yeah, he sings, too," Kamber agreed.

"He sings?" I exclaimed.

"Oh, yeah," they chorused.

"Then he's definitely seeing someone!" my mother chimed in. "I wonder who she is."

"You've got me. But I'm guessing she must be a wonderful girl. These last few months he's been working hard—harder than usual. And he's been putting money away. I think he must be trying to save up to get married."

I couldn't help the little gasp that escaped. Lucky me, they all attributed it to the general excitement of the news.

"And I couldn't be more pleased," she continued. "Even if he's not ready to tell us who she is, I love her already. He's smiling, and he just seems satisfied. It's been hard since we lost Herrick, and Aspen's taken so much on himself. Any girl who makes him this happy is already a daughter to me."

"She'd be a lucky girl! Your Aspen is a wonderful boy," Mom replied.

I couldn't believe it. Here his family was, trying to make ends meet, and he was putting away money for me! I didn't know whether to scold him or kiss him. I just . . . I had no words.

He really *was* going to ask me to marry him!

It was all I could think about. *Aspen, Aspen, Aspen.* I went through the line, signed at the window to confirm that everything on my form was true, and took my picture. I sat in the chair, flipped my hair once or twice to give it some life, and turned to face the photographer.

I don't think any girl in all of Illéa could have been smiling more than me.

CHAPTER 4

IT WAS FRIDAY, SO THE *Illéa Capital Report* would be on at eight. We weren't exactly obligated to watch, but it was unwise to miss it. Even Eights—the homeless, the wandering—would find a store or a church where they could see the *Report*. And with the Selection coming up, the *Report* was more than a semi-requirement. Everyone wanted to know what was happening in that department.

"Do you think they'll announce the winners tonight?" May asked, stuffing mashed potatoes into her mouth.

"No, dear. Everyone who's eligible still has nine days to submit their applications. It'll probably be two more weeks until we know." Mom's voice was the calmest it had been in years. She was completely at ease, pleased to have gotten something she really wanted.

"Aw! I can't stand the wait," May complained.

She couldn't stand the wait? It was *my* name in the pot!

"Your mother tells me you had quite a long wait in line." I was surprised Dad wanted in on this conversation.

"Yeah," I said. "I wasn't expecting that many girls. I don't know why they're giving people nine more days; I swear everyone in the province has already gone in."

Dad chuckled. "Did you have fun gauging the competition?"

"Didn't bother," I said honestly. "I left that to Mom."

She nodded in agreement. "I did, I did. I couldn't help it. But I think America looked good. Polished but natural. You are *so* beautiful, honey. If they really are looking through instead of picking at random, you have an even better chance than I thought."

"I don't know," I hedged. "There was that girl who had on so much red lipstick she looked like she was bleeding. Maybe the prince likes that kind of thing."

Everyone laughed, and Mom and I continued to regale them with commentary on the outfits we'd noticed. May drank it all in, and Gerad just sat smiling between bites of dinner. Sometimes it was easy to forget that as long as Gerad had been able to really understand the world around him, things had been stressful in our house.

At eight we all piled into the living room—Dad in his chair, May next to Mom on the couch with Gerad on her lap, and me on the floor all stretched out—and turned the TV to the public access channel. It was the one channel you didn't have to pay to have, so even the Eights could get it if they had a TV.

The anthem played. Maybe it's silly, but I always loved our national anthem. It was one of my favorite songs to sing.

The picture of the royal family came into view. Standing at a podium was King Clarkson. His advisers, who had updates on infrastructure and some environmental concerns, were seated to one side, and the camera cut to show them. It looked like there would be several announcements tonight. On the left of the screen, the queen and Prince Maxon sat in their typical cluster of thronelike seats and elegant clothes, looking regal and important.

"There's your boyfriend, Ames," May announced, and everyone laughed.

I looked closely at Maxon. I guess he was handsome in his own way. Not at all like Aspen, though. His hair was a honey color, and his eyes were brown. He kind of looked like summertime, which I guess was attractive to some people. His hair was cropped short and neatly done, and his gray suit was perfectly fitted to him.

But he sat way too rigidly in his chair. He looked so uptight. His clean hair was too perfect, his tailored suit too crisp. He seemed more like a painting than a person. I almost felt bad for the girl who ended up with him. That would probably be the most boring life imaginable.

I focused on his mother. She looked serene. She sat up in her chair, too, but not in an icy way. I realized that, unlike the king and Prince Maxon, she hadn't grown up in the palace. She was a celebrated Daughter of Illéa. She might have been someone like me.

The king was already talking, but I had to know.

"Mom?" I whispered, trying not to distract Dad.

"Yes?"

"The queen . . . what was she? Her caste, I mean."

Mom smiled at my interest. "A Four."

A Four. She'd spent her formative years working in a factory or a shop, or maybe on a farm. I wondered about her life. Did she have a large family? She probably hadn't had to worry about food growing up. Were her friends jealous of her when she was chosen? If I had any really close friends, would they be jealous of me?

That was stupid. I wasn't going to be picked.

Instead I focused on the king's words.

"Just this morning, another attack in New Asia rocked our bases. It has left our troops slightly outnumbered, but we are confident that with the fresh draft next month will come lifted morale, not to mention a swelling of fresh forces."

I hated war. Unfortunately, we were a young country that had to protect itself against everyone. It wasn't likely this land would survive another invasion.

After the king gave us an update on a recent raid on a rebel camp, the Financial Team updated us on the status of the debt, and the head of the Infrastructure Committee announced that in two years they were planning to start work on rebuilding several highways, some of which hadn't been touched since the Fourth World War. Finally the last person, the Master of Events, came to the podium.

"Good evening, ladies and gentlemen of Illéa. As you all

know, notices to participate in the Selection were recently distributed in the mail. We have received the first count of submitted applications, and I am pleased to say that thousands of the beautiful women in Illéa have already placed their names in the lottery for the Selection!"

In the back corner Maxon shifted a little in his seat. Was he sweating?

"On behalf of the royal family, I would like to thank you for your enthusiasm and patriotism. With any luck, by the New Year we will be celebrating the engagement of our beloved Prince Maxon to an enchanting, talented, and intelligent Daughter of Illéa!"

The few advisers sitting there applauded. Maxon smiled but looked uncomfortable. When the applause died down, the Master of Events started up again.

"Of course, we will be having lots of programming dedicated to meeting the young women of the Selection, not to mention specials on their lives at the palace. We could not think of anyone more qualified to guide us through this exciting time than our very own Mr. Gavril Fadaye!"

There was another smattering of applause, but it came from my mom and May this time. Gavril Fadaye was a legend. For something like twenty years he'd done running commentary on Grateful Feast parades and Christmas shows and anything they celebrated at the palace. I'd never seen an interview with members of the royal family or their closest friends and family done by anyone but him.

"Oh, America, you could meet Gavril!" Mom crooned.

"He's coming!" May said, flailing her little arms.

Sure enough, there was Gavril, sauntering onto the set in his crisp blue suit. He was maybe in his late forties, and he always looked sharp. As he walked across the stage, the light caught on the pin on his lapel, a flash of gold that was similar to the forte signs in my piano music.

"Goooood evening, Illéa!" he sang. "I have to say that I am so honored to be a part of the Selection. Lucky me, I get to meet thirty-five beautiful women! What idiot wouldn't want my job?" He winked at us through the camera. "But before I get to meet these lovely ladies, one of which will be our new princess, I have the pleasure of speaking with the man of the hour, our Prince Maxon."

With that Maxon walked across the carpeted stage to a pair of chairs set up for him and Gavril. He straightened his tie and adjusted his suit, as if he needed to look *more* polished. He shook Gavril's hand and sat across from him, picking up a microphone. The chair was high enough that Maxon propped his feet on a bar in the middle of the legs. He looked much more casual that way.

"Nice to see you again, Your Highness."

"Thank you, Gavril. The pleasure is all mine." Maxon's voice was as poised as the rest of him. He radiated waves of formality. I wrinkled my nose at the idea of just being in the same room with him.

"In less than a month, thirty-five women will be moving into your house. How do you feel about that?"

Maxon laughed. "Honestly, it *is* a bit nerve-racking. I'm imagining there will be much more noise with so many guests. I'm looking forward to it all the same."

"Have you asked dear old dad for any advice on how he managed to get ahold of such a beautiful wife when it was his turn?"

Both Maxon and Gavril looked over to the king and queen, and the camera panned over to show them looking at each other, smiling and holding hands. It seemed genuine, but how would we know any better?

"I haven't actually. As you know, the situation in New Asia has been escalating, and I've been working with him more on the military side of things. Not much time to discuss girls in there."

Mom and May laughed. I suppose it was kind of funny.

"We don't have much time left, so I'd like to have one more question. What do you imagine your perfect girl would be like?"

Maxon looked taken aback. It was hard to tell, but he may have been blushing.

"Honestly, I don't know. I think that's the beauty of the Selection. No two women who enter will be exactly the same—not in looks or preferences or disposition. And through the process of meeting them and talking to them, I'm hoping to discover what I want, to find it along the way." Maxon smiled.

"Thank you, Your Highness. That was very well said. And I think I speak for all of Illéa when I wish you the best of luck." Gavril held out his hand for another shake.

"Thank you, sir," Maxon said. The camera didn't cut away quick enough, and you could see him looking over to his parents, wondering if he'd said the right thing. The next shot zoomed in on Gavril's face, so there was no way to see what their response was.

"I'm afraid that's all the time we have for this evening. Thank you for watching the *Illéa Capital Report*, and we'll see you next week."

With that, the music played and credits rolled.

"America and Maxon sitting in a tree," sang May. I grabbed a pillow and chucked it at her, but I couldn't help laughing at the thought. Maxon was so stiff and quiet. It was hard to imagine anyone being happy with such a wimp.

I spent the rest of the night trying to ignore May's teasing, and finally went to my room to be alone. Even the thought of being near Maxon Schreave made me uncomfortable. May's little jabs stayed in my head all night and made it difficult for me to sleep.

It was hard to pinpoint the sound that woke me, but once I was aware of it, I tried to survey my room in absolute stillness, just in case someone was there.

Tap, tap, tap.

I turned over slowly to face my window, and there was Aspen, grinning at me. I got out of bed and tiptoed to the door, shutting it all the way and locking it. I went back to the bed, unlocking and slowly opening my window.

A rush of heat that had nothing to do with summer swept

over me as Aspen climbed through the window and onto my bed.

"What are you doing here?" I whispered, smiling in the dark.

"I had to see you," he breathed into my cheek as he wrapped his arms around me, pulling me down until we were lying side by side on the bed.

"I have so much to tell you, Aspen."

"Shhh, don't say a word. If anyone hears, there'll be hell to pay. Just let me look at you."

And so I obeyed. I stayed there, quiet and still, while Aspen stared into my eyes. When he had his fill of that, he went to nuzzling his nose into my neck and hair. And then his hands were moving up and down the curve of my waist to my hip over and over and over. I heard his breathing get heavy, and something about that drew me in.

His lips, hidden in my neck, started kissing me. I drew in sharp breaths. I couldn't help it. Aspen's lips traveled up my chin and covered my mouth, effectively silencing my gasps. I wrapped myself around him, our rushed grabbing and the humidity of the night covering us both in sweat.

It was a stolen moment.

Aspen's lips finally slowed, though I was nowhere near ready to stop. But we had to be smart. If we went any further, and there was ever evidence of it, we'd both be thrown in jail.

Another reason everyone married young: Waiting is torture.

"I should go," he whispered.

"But I want you to stay." My lips were by his ears. I could smell his soap again.

"America Singer, one day you will fall asleep in my arms every night. And you'll wake up to my kisses every morning. And then some." I bit my lip at the thought. "But now I have to go. We're pushing our luck."

I sighed and loosened my grip. He was right.

"I love you, America."

"I love you, Aspen."

These secret moments would be enough to get me through everything coming: Mom's disappointment when I wasn't chosen, the work I'd have to do to help Aspen save, the eruption that was coming when he asked Dad for my hand, and whatever struggles we'd go through once we were married. None of it mattered. Not if I had Aspen.

CHAPTER 5

A WEEK LATER, I BEAT Aspen to the tree house.

It took a bit of work to get the things I wanted up there in silence, but I managed. I rearranged the plates one last time as I heard someone climbing the tree.

"Boo."

Aspen started and laughed. I lit the new candle I'd purchased just for us. He crossed the tree house to kiss me, and after a moment, I started talking about all that had happened during the week.

"I never got to tell you about the sign-ups," I said, excited about the news.

"How'd it go? Mom said it was packed."

"It was crazy, Aspen. You should have seen what people were wearing! And I'm sure you know that it's less of a lottery than they're claiming. So I was right all along. There are far more interesting people to choose in Carolina than me, so this was all a big nothing."

"All the same, thank you for doing it. It means a lot to me." His eyes were still focused on me. He hadn't even bothered looking around the tree house. Drinking me in, like always.

"Well, the best part is that since my mother had no idea I'd already promised you, she bribed me to sign up." I couldn't contain my smile. This week families had already started throwing parties for their daughters, sure that they would be the one chosen for the Selection. I'd sung at no less than seven celebrations, packing two into a night for the sake of getting my own paychecks. And Mom was true to her word. It felt liberating to have money that was mine.

"Bribed you? With what?" His face was lit with excitement.

"Money, of course. Look, I made you a feast!" I pulled away from him and started grabbing plates. I'd made too much dinner on purpose to save him some, and I'd been baking pastries for days. May and I both had a terrible addiction to sweets anyway, and she was jubilant that this was how I was choosing to spend my money.

"What's all this?"

"Food. I made it myself." I was beaming with pride at my efforts. Finally, tonight, Aspen could be full. But his smile faded as he took in plate after plate.

"Aspen, is something wrong?"

"This isn't right." He shook his head and looked away from the treats.

"What do you mean?"

"America, I'm supposed to be providing for you. It's humiliating for me to come here and have you do all this for me."

"But I give you food all the time."

"Your little leftovers. You think I don't know better? I don't feel bad about taking something you don't want. But to have you—*I'm* supposed to—"

"Aspen, you give me things all the time. You provide for me. I have all my pen—"

"Pennies? You think bringing that up *now* is a good idea? Don't you know how much I hate that? That I love to hear you sing but can't really pay you when everyone else does?"

"You shouldn't pay me at all! It's a gift. Anything of mine you want you can have!" I knew we needed to be careful to keep our voices down. But at the moment I didn't care.

"I'm not some charity case, America. I'm a man. I'm supposed to be a provider."

Aspen put his hands in his hair. I could see his breaths coming fast. Just like always, he was thinking his way through the argument. But this time, there was something different in his eyes. Instead of his face growing focused, it fell into confusion one millimeter at a time. My anger faded quickly as I saw him there, looking so lost. I felt guilty instead. I had meant to spoil him, not humiliate him.

"I love you," I whispered.

He shook his head.

"I love you, too, America." But he still wouldn't look at

me. I picked up some of the bread I'd made and put it in his hand. He was too hungry not to take a bite.

"I didn't mean to hurt you. I thought it would make you happy."

"No, Mer, I love it. I can't believe you did all this for me. It's just . . . you don't know how much it bothers me that I can't do this for you. You deserve better." Mercifully, he kept eating as he spoke.

"You've got to stop thinking of me that way. When it's just you and me, I'm not a Five and you're not a Six. We're just Aspen and America. And I don't want anything in the world but you."

"But I can't stop thinking that way." He looked at me. "That's how I was raised. Since I was little, it was 'Sixes are born to serve' and 'Sixes aren't meant to be seen.' My whole life, I've been taught to be invisible." He grabbed my hand in a viselike grip. "If we're together, Mer, you're going to be invisible, too. And I don't want that for you."

"Aspen, we've talked about this. I know that things will be different, and I'm prepared. I don't know how to make it any clearer." I put my hand on his heart. "The moment you're ready to ask, I'm ready to say yes."

It was terrifying to put myself out there like that, to make it absolutely clear how deep my affections ran. He knew what I was saying. But if making myself vulnerable meant he'd be brave, I'd endure it. His eyes searched mine. If he was looking for doubt, he was wasting his time. Aspen was the one thing I was sure of.

"No."

"What?"

"No." The word felt like a slap across the face.

"Aspen?"

"I don't know how I fooled myself into ever thinking this would work." He ran his fingers through his hair again, like he was trying to get all the thoughts he'd ever had about me out of his head.

"But you just said you loved me."

"I do, Mer. That's the point. I can't make you like me. I can't stand the thought of you hungry or cold or scared. I can't make you a Six."

I felt the tears coming. He didn't mean that. He couldn't. But before I could tell him to take it back, Aspen was already moving to crawl out of the tree house.

"Where . . . where are you going?"

"I'm leaving. I'm going home. I'm sorry I did this to you, America. It's over now."

"What?"

"It's over. I won't come around anymore. Not like this."

I started crying. "Aspen, please. Let's talk about this. You're just upset."

"I'm more upset than you know. But not at you. I just can't do this, Mer. I can't."

"Aspen, please . . ."

He pulled me in tight and kissed me—really kissed me— one last time. Then he disappeared into the night. And because this country is the way it is, because of all the rules that had kept us in hiding, I couldn't even call out after him. I couldn't tell him I loved him one more time.

As the next few days passed, I knew my family could tell that something was wrong, but they must have assumed I was nervous about the Selection. I wanted to cry a thousand times, but held it back. I just pushed on to Friday, hoping that everything would go back to normal after the *Capital Report* broadcast the names.

I dreamed it up in my head. How they would announce Celia or Kamber, and my mother would be disappointed, but not as disappointed as she would have been if it was a stranger. Dad and May would be excited for them; our families were close. I knew Aspen had to be thinking about me like I'd been thinking about him. I bet he'd be over here before the program was over, begging me for forgiveness and asking for my hand. It would be a little premature, since there was nothing guaranteed for the girls, but he could capitalize on the general excitement of the day. It would probably smooth a lot of things over.

In my head, it worked out perfectly. In my head, everyone was happy . . .

It was ten minutes until the *Report* came on, and we were all in place early. I couldn't imagine we were alone in not wanting to miss a second of this announcement.

"I remember when Queen Amberly was chosen! Oh, I knew from the beginning she would make it." Mom was making popcorn, as if this were a movie.

"Did you go in the lottery, Mama?" Gerad asked.

"No, sweetie, Mama was two years too young for the cut-off. But lucky me, I got your father instead." She smiled and winked.

Whoa. She must have been in a good mood. I couldn't remember the last time she was that affectionate toward Dad.

"Queen Amberly is the best queen ever. She's so beautiful and smart. Every time I see her on TV, I want to be just like her," May said with a sigh.

"She is a good queen," I added quietly.

Finally eight o'clock rolled around, and the national emblem rose on the screen along with the instrumental version of our anthem. Was I actually trembling? I was so ready for this to be over.

The king appeared and gave a brief update on the war. The other announcements were also short. It seemed like everyone there was in a good mood. I guessed this must be exciting for them, too.

Finally the Master of Events came up and introduced Gavril, who walked straight over to the royal family.

"Good evening, Your Majesty," he said to the king.

"Gavril, always good to see you." The king was border-line giddy.

"Looking forward to the announcement?"

"Ah, yes. I was in the room yesterday as a few were drawn; all very lovely girls."

"So you know who they are already?" Gavril exclaimed.

"Just a few, just a few."

"Did he happen to share any of this information with you, sir?" Gavril turned to Maxon.

"Not at all. I'll see them when everyone else does," Maxon replied. You could see he was trying to hide his nerves.

I realized my palms were sweating.

"Your Majesty," Gavril went over to the queen. "Any advice for the Selected?"

She smiled her serene smile. I didn't know what the other women looked like when she went through the Selection, but I couldn't imagine anyone being as graceful and lovely as her.

"Enjoy your last night as an average girl. Tomorrow, no matter what, your life will be different forever. And it's old advice, but it's good: Be yourself."

"Wise words, my queen, wise words. And with that, let us reveal the thirty-five young ladies chosen for the Selection. Ladies and gentlemen, please join me in congratulating the following Daughters of Illéa!"

The screen changed to the national emblem. In the upper right-hand corner, there was a small box with Maxon's face, to see his reactions as the pictures went across the monitor. He would already be making decisions about them, the way we all would.

Gavril had a set of cards in his hands, ready to read out the names of the girls whose worlds, according to the queen, were about to change forever.

"Miss Elayna Stoles of Hansport, Three." A photo of a

tiny girl with porcelain skin popped up. She looked like a lady. Maxon beamed.

"Miss Tuesday Keeper of Waverly, Four." A girl with freckles appeared. She looked older, more mature. Maxon whispered something to the king.

"Miss Fiona Castley of Paloma, Three." A brunette with smoldering eyes this time. Maybe my age, but she seemed more . . . experienced.

I turned to Mom and May on the couch. "Doesn't she seem awfully—"

"Miss America Singer of Carolina, Five."

I whipped my head back around, and there it was. The picture of me just after I'd found out Aspen was saving up to marry me. I looked radiant, hopeful, beautiful. I looked like I was in love. And some idiot thought that love was for Prince Maxon.

Mom screamed by my ear, and May jumped up, sending popcorn everywhere. Gerad got excited too and started dancing. Dad . . . it's hard to say, but I think he was secretly smiling behind his book.

I missed what Maxon's expression was.

The phone rang.

And it didn't stop for days.

CHAPTER 6

THE NEXT WEEK WAS FULL of officials swarming into our house to prepare me for the Selection. There was an obnoxious woman who seemed to think I'd lied about half my application, followed by an actual palace guard who came to go over security measures with the local soldiers and give our home a once-over. Apparently I didn't have to wait until getting to the palace to worry about potential rebel attacks. Wonderful.

We got two phone calls from a woman named Silvia—who sounded very perky and businesslike at the same time—wanting to know if we needed anything. My favorite visitor was a lean, goateed man who came to measure me for my new wardrobe. I wasn't sure how I felt about wearing dresses that were as formal as the queen's all the time, but I was looking forward to a change.

The last of these visitors came on Wednesday afternoon, two days before I was to leave. He was in charge of going over all the official rules with me. He was incredibly skinny with greasy black hair that was smoothed back, and he kept sweating. Upon entering the house, he asked if there was someplace private we could talk. That was my first clue that something was going on.

"Well, we can sit in the kitchen, if that's all right," Mom suggested.

He dabbed his head with a handkerchief and looked over at May. "Actually, anyplace is fine. I just think you might want to ask your younger daughter to leave the room."

What could he possibly say that May couldn't hear?

"Mama?" she asked, sad to be missing out.

"May, darling, go and work on your painting. You've been neglecting your work a bit this last week."

"But—"

"Let me walk you out, May," I offered, looking at the tears welling up in her eyes.

When we were down the hall and no one could hear, I pulled her in for a hug.

"Don't worry," I whispered. "I'll tell you everything tonight. Promise."

To her credit, she didn't blow our cover by jumping up and down as usual. She merely nodded somberly and went away to her little corner in Dad's studio.

Mom made tea for Skinny, and we sat at the kitchen table to talk. He had a stack of papers and a pen laid out next to another folder with my name on it. He arranged his information neatly and spoke.

"I'm sorry to be so secretive, but there are certain things I need to address that are unfit for young ears."

Mom and I exchanged a quick glance.

"Miss Singer, this is going to sound harsh, but as of last Friday, you are now considered property of Illéa. You must take care of your body from here on out. I have several forms for you to sign as we go through this information. Any failure to comply on your part will result in your immediate removal from the Selection. Do you understand?"

"Yes," I said warily.

"Very good. Let's start with the easy stuff. These are vitamins. Since you are a Five, I'll assume that you may not always have access to necessary nutrition. You must take one of these every day. You're on your own now, but at the palace, you'll have someone to help you." He passed a large bottle across the table to me, along with a form I had to sign to say that I had received it.

I had to stop myself from laughing. Who needs help taking a pill?

"I have with me the physical from your doctor. Not much of a worry there. You seem to be in excellent health, although he said you haven't been sleeping well?"

"Umm, I mean . . . just with the excitement, it's been a little hard to sleep." It was almost the truth. The days were whirlwinds of palace preparation, but at night, when I was still, I thought of Aspen. It was the one time I couldn't avoid him coming into my mind, and it appeared he wasn't eager to leave.

"I see. Well, I can have some sleep aids here tonight if you need them. We want you well rested."

"No, I don't—"

"Yes," Mom interrupted. "Sorry, honey, but you look exhausted. Please, get her the sleep aids."

"Yes, ma'am." Skinny made another note in my file. "Moving on. Now, I know this is personal, but I've had to discuss it with every contestant, so please don't be shy." He paused. "I need confirmation that you are, in fact, a virgin."

Mom's eyes nearly popped out. So this was why May had to leave.

"Are you serious?" I couldn't believe they'd send someone out to do this. At least send a woman . . .

"I'm afraid so. If you're not, we need to know that immediately."

Eww. And with my mother in the room. "I know the law, sir. I'm not stupid. Of course I am."

"Consider, please. If you are found to be lying . . ."

"For goodness' sake, America's never even had a boyfriend!" Mom said.

"That's right." I grabbed that rope, hoping it would end this discussion.

"Very good. I'll just need you to sign this form to confirm your statement."

I rolled my eyes but obeyed. I was glad Illéa existed, considering that this very land had nearly been turned to rubble, but these regulations were starting to make me feel like I was suffocating, like there were invisible chains keeping me down. Laws about who you could love, forms about your virginity being intact; it was infuriating.

"I need to go over the rules with you. They are very straightforward, and you shouldn't have a hard time complying. If you have any questions, just speak up."

He looked up from his stack of forms and made eye contact with me.

"I will," I mumbled.

"You cannot leave the palace of your own accord. You have to be dismissed by the prince himself. Even the king and queen cannot force you out. They can tell the prince they do not approve of you, but he makes every decision on who stays and who leaves.

"There is no set timeline for the Selection. It can be over in a matter of days or stretch into years."

"Years?" I asked in horror. The thought of being gone that long set me on edge.

"Not to worry. The prince is unlikely to let it go for very long. This is a moment for him to show his decisiveness, and allowing the Selection to drag on doesn't look good. But should he choose to take it that way, you will be required to stay for as long as the prince needs to make his choice."

My fear must have shown on my face because Mom reached over and patted my hand. Skinny, however, was unfazed.

"You do not arrange your times with the prince. He will

seek you out for one-on-one company if he wants it. If you are in a larger social setting and he is present, that is different. But you do not go to him without invitation.

"While no one expects you to get along with the other thirty-four contestants, you are not to fight with them or sabotage them. If you are found laying hands on another contestant, causing her stress, stealing from her, or doing anything that might diminish her personal relationship with the prince, it is in his hands whether or not to dismiss you on the spot.

"Your only romantic relationship will be with Prince Maxon. If you are found writing love notes to someone here or are caught in a relationship with another person in the palace, that is considered treason and is punishable by death."

Mom rolled her eyes at that one, though that might be the only rule that worried me.

"If you are found breaking any of Illéa's written laws, you will receive the punishment tied to that offense. Your status as one of the Selected does not put you above the law.

"You must not wear any clothes or eat any food that is not specifically provided for you by the palace. This is a security issue and will be strictly enforced.

"On Fridays you will be present for all *Capital Report* broadcasts. On occasion, but always with warning, there will be cameras or photographers in the palace, and you will be courteous and allow them to see your lifestyle with the prince.

"For each week you stay at the palace, your family will be

compensated. I will give you your first check before I leave. Also, should you not stay at the palace, an aide will help you adjust to your life after the Selection. Your aide will assist you with final preparations before you leave for the palace, as well as help you seek new housing and employment afterward.

"Should you make it to the top ten, you will be considered an Elite. Once you reach that status, you will be required to learn about the particular inner workings of the life and obligations you would have as a princess. You are not permitted to seek out such details before that time.

"From this moment on, your status is a Three."

"A Three?" Mom and I both exclaimed.

"Yes. After the Selection, it's hard for girls to go back to their old lives. Twos and Threes do fine, but Fours and below tend to struggle. You are a Three now, but the rest of your family remain Fives. Should you win, you and your entire family become Ones as members of the royal family."

"Ones." The word was faint on Mom's lips.

"And should you go to the end, you will marry Prince Maxon and become the crowned princess of Illéa and take on all the rights and responsibilities of that title. Do you understand?"

"Yes." That part, as big as it sounded, was the easiest to bear.

"Very good. If you could just sign this form saying you've heard all the official rules, and Mrs. Singer, if you could just sign this form saying you received your check, please."

I didn't see the sum, but it made her eyes well. I was miserable at the idea of leaving, but I was sure if I went there only to be sent back the next day, this check alone would provide us with enough money for a very comfortable year. And when I got back, everyone would want me to sing. I'd have plenty of work. But would I be allowed to sing as a Three? If I had to pick one of the career paths of a Three, I think I'd teach. Maybe I could at least help others learn music.

Skinny collected his forms and stood to leave, thanking us for our time and for the tea. I would have to interact with only one more official before I left, and that would be my aide: the person who would guide me through getting from my house to the send-off to the airport. And then . . . then I'd be on my own.

Our guest asked if I would show him to the door, and Mom consented, as she wanted to start dinner. I didn't like being alone with him, but it was a short walk.

"One more thing," Skinny said with his hand on the door. "This isn't exactly a rule, but it would be unwise of you to ignore it. When you are invited to do something with Prince Maxon, you do not refuse. No matter what it is. Dinner, outings, kisses—more than kisses—anything. Do not turn him down."

"Excuse me?" Was the same man who made me sign a form affirming my purity suggesting that I let Maxon have it if he wanted it?

"I know it sounds . . . unbecoming. But it would not

behoove you to reject the prince under any circumstances. Good evening, Miss Singer."

I was disgusted, revolted. The law, Illéan law, was that you were to wait until marriage. It was an effective way of keeping diseases at bay, and it helped keep the castes intact. Illegitimates were thrown into the street to become Eights, and the penalty for being discovered, either by a person or through pregnancy, was jail time. If someone was even suspicious, you could spend a few nights in a cell. True, it restricted me from being intimate with the one person I loved, and that had bothered me. But now that Aspen and I were over, I was glad I'd been forced to save myself.

I was infuriated. Hadn't I just signed a form saying I'd be punished if I broke Illéan law? I wasn't above the rules; that was what he'd said. But apparently the prince was. And I felt dirty, lower than an Eight.

"America, honey, it's for you," Mom sang. I'd heard the doorbell myself but was in no rush to answer it. If this was another person asking for an autograph, I didn't think I'd be able to handle it.

I walked down the hall and turned the corner. There, with a handful of wildflowers, was Aspen.

"Hello, America." His voice was restrained, almost professional.

"Hello, Aspen." Mine was weak.

"These are from Kamber and Celia. They wanted to wish you luck." He closed the distance between us and gave me the flowers. Flowers from his sisters, not from him.

"That's awfully sweet!" Mom exclaimed. I had almost forgotten she was in the room.

"Aspen, I'm glad you're here." I tried to sound as removed as he had. "I've made a mess trying to pack. Could you help me clean?"

With my mom there, he had to accept. As a general rule, Sixes didn't turn down work. We were the same in that way.

He exhaled through his nose and nodded once.

Aspen followed me down the hall. I thought about how many times I'd wanted just this: for Aspen to walk in my house and come to my room. Could the circumstances have been any worse?

I pushed open the door to my room and Aspen laughed out loud.

"Did you let a dog do your packing?"

"Shut up! I had a little trouble finding what I was looking for." In spite of myself, I smiled.

He went to work, setting things upright and folding shirts. I helped, of course.

"Aren't you taking any of these clothes?" he whispered.

"No. They dress me from tomorrow on out."

"Oh. Wow."

"Were your sisters disappointed?"

"No, actually." He shook his head in disbelief. "The moment they saw your face, the whole house erupted. They're crazy about you. My mom in particular."

"I love your mom. She's always really nice to me."

A few minutes passed in silence as my room went slowly back to normal.

"Your picture . . . ," he began, "was absolutely beautiful."

It hurt to have him tell me I was beautiful. It wasn't fair. Not after everything he'd done.

"It was for you," I whispered.

"What?"

"It's just . . . I thought you were going to be proposing soon." My voice was thick.

Aspen was quiet for a moment, choosing his words.

"I'd been thinking about it, but it doesn't matter anymore."

"It does. Why didn't you tell me?"

He rubbed his neck, deciding.

"I was waiting."

"For what?" What could possibly be worth waiting for?

"For the draft."

That *was* an issue. It was hard to know whether to wish to be drafted or not. In Illéa, every nineteen-year-old male was eligible for it. Soldiers were chosen at random twice a year, to catch everyone within six months of their birthday. You served from the time you were nineteen until you were twenty-three. And it was coming soon.

We'd talked about it, of course, but not in a realistic way. I guess we both hoped that if we ignored the draft, it would ignore us, too.

It was a blessing in that being a soldier meant you were an automatic Two. The government trained you and paid you for the rest of your life. The drawback was you never knew where you would go. They sent you away from your province, for sure. They assumed you were more likely to be lenient with people you knew. You might end up at the palace or in some other province's local police force. Or you might end up in the army, shipped off to war. Not very many men sent into battle made it home.

If a man wasn't married before the draft, he'd almost always wait. You'd be separated from your wife for four years, at the very best. At the worst, she'd be a young widow.

"I just . . . I didn't want to do that to you," he whispered.

"I understand."

He straightened up, trying to change the subject. "So what are you taking to the palace?"

"A change of clothes to wear whenever they finally kick me out. Some pictures and books. I've been told I won't need my instruments. Anything I want will be there already. So that little bag there, that's it."

The room was tidy now, and that backpack seemed huge for some reason. The flowers he'd brought looked so bright on my desk compared to the drab things I owned. Or maybe it was just that everything seemed paler now . . . now that it was over.

"That's not much," he noted.

"I've never needed very much to be happy. I thought you knew that."

He closed his eyes. "Stop it, America. I did the right thing."

"The right thing? Aspen, you made me believe we could do it. You made me love you. And then you talked me into this damn contest. Do you know they're practically shipping me off to be one of Maxon's playthings?"

He whipped his head around to face me. "What?"

"I'm not allowed to turn him down. Not for *anything*."

Aspen looked sick, angry. His hands clenched up into fists. "Even . . . even if he doesn't want to marry you . . . he could . . . ?"

"Yes."

"I'm sorry. I didn't know." He took a few deep breaths. "But if he does pick you . . . that'll be good. You deserve to be happy."

That was it. I slapped him. "You idiot!" I whisper-yelled at him. "I hate him! I loved you! I wanted you; all I ever wanted was you!"

His eyes welled up, but I couldn't care. He'd hurt me enough, and now it was his turn.

"I should go," he said, and started heading to the door.

"Wait. I didn't pay you."

"America, you don't have to pay me." He went to leave again.

"Aspen Leger, don't you dare move!" My voice was fierce. And he stopped, finally paying attention to me.

"That'll be good practice for when you're a One." If it hadn't been for his eyes, I would have thought it was a joke, not an insult.

I just shook my head and went to my desk, pulling out all

the money I'd earned by myself. I put every last bit of it in his hands.

"America, I'm not taking this."

"The hell you aren't. I don't need it and you do. If you ever loved me at all, you'll take it. Hasn't your pride done enough for us?" I could feel a part of him shut down. He stopped fighting.

"Fine."

"And here." I dug behind my bed, pulled out my tiny jar of pennies, and poured them into his hand. One rebellious penny that must have been sticky stayed glued to the bottom. "Those were always yours. You should use them."

Now I didn't have anything of his. And once he spent those pennies out of desperation, he wouldn't have anything of mine. I felt the hurt coming up. My eyes got wet, and I breathed hard to keep the sobs back.

"I'm sorry, Mer. Good luck." He shoved the money and the pennies into his pockets and ran out.

This wasn't how I thought I'd cry. I was expecting huge, jarring sobs, not slow, tiny tears.

I started to put the jar on a shelf, but I noticed that little penny again. I put my finger in the jar and got it unstuck. It rattled around in the glass all by itself. It was a hollow sound, and I could feel it echo in my chest. I knew, for better or for worse, I wasn't really free of Aspen, not yet. Maybe not ever. I opened the backpack, put in my jar, and sealed it all away.

May snuck into my room, and I took one of those stupid pills. I fell asleep holding her, finally feeling numb.

CHAPTER 7

THE NEXT MORNING, I DRESSED myself in the uniform of the Selected: black pants, white shirt, and my province flower— a lily—in my hair. My shoes I got to pick. I chose worn-out red flats. I figured I should make it clear from the start that I wasn't princess material.

We were set to leave for the square shortly. Each of the Selected was getting a send-off in her home province today, and I wasn't looking forward to mine. All those people staring while I did nothing more than stand there. The whole thing already felt ridiculous, as I had to be driven the two short miles for security reasons.

The day began uncomfortably. Kenna came with James to send me off, which was kind of her, considering she was pregnant and tired. Kota came by, too, though his presence added more tension than ease. As we walked from our house to the car we'd been provided, Kota was by far the slowest, letting the few photographers and well-wishers who were there get a good look at him. Dad just shook his head.

May was my only solace. She held my hand and tried to inject some of her enthusiasm into me. We were still linked when I stepped into the crowded square. It seemed like everyone in the province of Carolina came out to see me off. Or just see what the big deal was.

Standing on the raised stage, I could see the boundaries between the castes. Margareta Stines was a Three, and she and her parents were staring daggers at me. Tenile Digger was a Seven, and she was blowing kisses. The upper castes looked at me like I'd stolen something that was theirs. The Fours on down were cheering for me—an average girl who'd been elevated. I became aware of what I meant to everyone here, as if I represented something for all of them.

I tried to focus in on those faces, holding my head high. I was determined to do this well. I would be the best of us, the Highest of the Lows. It gave me a sense of purpose. America Singer: the champion of the lower castes.

The mayor spoke with a flourish.

"And Carolina will be cheering on the beautiful daughter of Magda and Shalom Singer, the new Lady America Singer!"

The crowd clapped and cheered. Some threw flowers.

I took in the sound for a moment, smiling and waving, and then went back to surveying the crowd, but this time for a different purpose.

I wanted to see his face one more time if I could. I didn't know if he would come. He told me I looked beautiful yesterday but was even more distant and guarded than he had been in the tree house. It was over, and I knew that. But you don't love someone for almost two years and then turn it off overnight.

It took a few passes of the crowd before I found him. I immediately wished I hadn't. Aspen was standing there with Brenna Butler in front of him, casually holding her around the waist and smiling.

Maybe some people could turn it off overnight.

Brenna was a Six and about my age. Pretty enough, I supposed, though she didn't look a bit like me. I guessed she'd get the wedding and life he'd been saving for with me. And apparently the draft didn't bother him so much anymore. She smiled at him and walked away to her family.

Had he liked her all along? Was she the girl he saw every day and was I the girl who fed him and showered him with kisses once a week? It occurred to me that maybe all the time he omitted in our stolen conversations wasn't simply long, boring hours of inventory.

I was too angry to cry.

Besides, I had admirers here who wanted my attention. So, without Aspen even knowing that I'd seen him, I went back to those adoring faces. I put my smile back on, bigger than ever, and started waving. Aspen would not have the satisfaction of breaking my heart anymore. He'd put me here, and I would just have to take advantage of it.

"Ladies and gentlemen, please join me in sending off America Singer, our favorite Daughter of Illéa!" the mayor called. Behind me, a small band played the national anthem.

More cheers, more flowers. Suddenly the mayor was at my ear.

"Would you like to say something, dear?"

I didn't know how to say no without being rude. "Thank you, but I'm so overwhelmed, I don't think I could."

He cupped my hands in his. "Of course, dear girl. Don't you worry, I'll take care of everything. They'll train you for this kind of thing at the palace. You'll need it."

The mayor then told the gathered crowd of my attributes, slyly mentioning that I was very intelligent and attractive for a Five. He didn't seem too bad a guy, but sometimes even the nicer members of the upper castes were condescending.

I caught Aspen's face once more as my eyes swept the crowd. He looked pained. It was the polar opposite of the face he'd worn with Brenna a few minutes ago. Another game? I broke my gaze.

The mayor finished speaking, and I smiled and everyone cheered, as if he'd just given the most inspiring speech known to man.

And suddenly it was time to say good-bye. Mitsy, my aide, told me to say my farewells quietly and briefly, and then she'd escort me back to the car that would take me to the airport.

Kota hugged me, telling me he was proud of me. Then, not so subtly, he told me to mention his art to Prince Maxon.

I wiggled out of that embrace as gracefully as I could.

Kenna was crying.

"I barely see you as it is. What will I do when you're gone?" she cried.

"Don't worry. I'll be home soon enough."

"Yeah, right! You're the most beautiful girl in Illéa. He'll love you!"

Why did everyone think it all came down to beauty? Maybe it did. Maybe Prince Maxon didn't need a wife to speak to, just someone to look pretty. I actually shivered, considering that as my future. But there were many girls much more attractive than me going.

Kenna was hard to hug over her pregnant belly, but we managed. James, who I really didn't know that well, hugged me, too. Then it was Gerad.

"Be a good boy, okay? Try the piano. I'll bet you're amazing. I expect to hear it all when I come home."

Gerad just nodded, abruptly sad. He threw his tiny arms around me.

"I love you, America."

"I love you, too. Don't be sad. I'll be home soon."

He nodded again, but crossed his arms to pout. I'd had no idea he'd take my leaving this way. It was the exact opposite of May. She was bouncing on her toes, absolutely giddy.

"Oh, America, you're going to be the princess! I know it!"

"Oh, hush! I'd rather be an Eight and stay with you any day. Just be good for me, and work hard."

She nodded and bounced some more, and then it was time for Dad, who was close to tears.

"Daddy! Don't cry." I fell into his arms.

"Listen to me, kitten. Win or lose, you'll always be a princess to me."

"Oh, Daddy." I finally started to cry. That was all it took to unleash the fear, the sadness, the worry, the nerves—the one sentence that meant none of it mattered.

If I came back used and unwanted, he'd still be proud of me.

It was too much to bear, to be loved that much. I'd be surrounded by scores of guards at the palace, but I couldn't imagine a place safer than my father's arms. I pulled away and turned to hug Mom.

"Do whatever they tell you. Try to stop sulking and be happy. Behave. Smile. Keep us posted. Oh! I just knew you'd turn out to be special."

It was meant to be sweet, but it wasn't what I needed to hear. I wished she could have said that I was already something special to her, like I was to my father. But I guessed she would never stop wanting more for me, more from me. Maybe that's what mothers did.

"Lady America, are you ready?" Mitsy asked. My face was away from the crowd, and I quickly wiped away my tears.

"Yes. All ready."

My bag was waiting in the shiny white car. This was it. I started to walk to the edge of the stage to the stairs.

"Mer!"

I turned. I'd know that voice anywhere.

"America!"

I searched and found Aspen's flailing arms. He was pushing the crowd aside, people protesting at his not-so-gentle shoves.

Our eyes met.

He stopped and stared. I couldn't read his face. Worry? Regret? Whatever it was, it was too late. I shook my head. I was done with Aspen's games.

"This way, Lady America," Mitsy instructed from the bottom of the stairs. I gave myself a quick second to absorb my new name.

"Good-bye, sweetheart," my mother called.

And I was led away.

CHAPTER 8

I WAS THE FIRST ONE to the airport, and I was beyond terrified. The giddy excitement of the crowd had faded, and now
I was faced with the horrific experience of flying. I would
be traveling with three other Selected girls, and I tried to
get control of my nerves. I really didn't want to have a panic
attack in front of them.

I'd already memorized the names, faces, and castes of all
the Selected. It started as a therapeutic exercise, something
to calm me down. I did the same thing with memorizing
scales and bits of trivia. Originally, I had been looking for
friendly faces, girls I might want to spend time with while
I was there. I'd never really had a friend. I'd spent most of
my childhood playing with Kenna and Kota. Mom did all
my schooling, and she was the only person I worked with.
When the older siblings moved on, I dedicated myself to

May and Gerad. And Aspen . . .

But Aspen and I were never just friends. From the moment I became truly aware of him, I was in love with him.

Now he was holding some other girl's hand.

Thank goodness I was alone. I couldn't have handled the tears in front of the other girls. It ached. *I* ached. And there was nothing I could do.

How in the hell did I get here? A month ago, I was sure of everything in my life, and now any little piece of familiarity was gone. New home, new caste, new life. All because of a stupid piece of paper and a picture. I wanted to sit and cry, to mourn for everything I'd lost.

I wondered if any of the others girls were *sad* today. I imagined that everyone except for me was celebrating. And I at least needed to look like I was too, because everyone would be watching.

I braced myself for all that was coming, and I made myself be brave. As for everything I was leaving behind, I decided I'd do just that: leave him behind. The palace would be my sanctuary. I'd never think or say his name again. He wasn't allowed to come with me there—my own rule for this little adventure.

No more.

Good-bye, Aspen.

About half an hour later, two girls in white shirts and black pants just like mine walked through the doors with their own aides hauling their bags. They were both smiling, confirming my thought that I was the only one of the Selected who might be depressed today.

It was time to follow through on my promise. I put on a smile and stood to shake their hands.

"Hi," I said brightly. "I'm America."

"I know!" said the girl on the right. She was a blonde with brown eyes. I recognized her immediately as Marlee Tames of Kent. A Four. She didn't bother with my extended hand; she moved in for an immediate hug.

"Oh!" I exhaled. I hadn't expected that. Though Marlee was one of the girls whose faces seemed genuine and friendly, Mom had been telling me for the last week to look at these girls as enemies, and her offensive thinking had leaked into my own. So here I was expecting at the very best a cordial welcome from the girls who were prepared to fight me to the death for someone I didn't want. Instead I was embraced.

"I'm Marlee and this is Ashley." Yes, Ashley Brouillette of Allens, Three. She had blond hair, too, but much lighter than Marlee's. And her eyes were very blue, which looked delicate in her peaceful face. She seemed fragile next to Marlee.

They were both from the North; I guessed that was why they came together. Ashley gave a neat little wave and smiled, but that was it. I wasn't sure if she was shy or if she was already trying to figure us out. Maybe it was that she was a Three by birth and knew to behave better.

"I love your hair!" Marlee gushed. "I wish I'd been born with red hair. It makes you look so alive. I hear that people with red hair have bad tempers. Is that true?"

Despite my rotten day, Marlee's manner was so vivacious that my smile grew wider. "I don't think so. I mean, I can have a bad temper at times, but my sister is a redhead, and she's as sweet as can be."

With that we settled into an easy conversation about what got us mad and what always fixed our moods. Marlee liked movies, and so did I, though I rarely got to see them. We talked about actors who were unbearably attractive, which seemed strange since we were off to be Maxon's pack of girl-friends. Ashley giggled every once in a while but never more than that. If she was asked a direct question, she'd give a brief answer and go back to her guarded smile.

Marlee and I got along easily, and it gave me hope that maybe I'd come out of this with a friend to show for it. Though we talked for probably half an hour, the time flew by. We wouldn't have stopped talking except for the distinct sound of high heels clicking across the floor. Our heads all turned in unison, and I heard Marlee's mouth open with a pop.

There, walking toward us, was a brunette with sunglasses on. She had a daisy in her hair, but it had been dyed red to match her lipstick. Her hips swayed as she walked, and each fall of her three-inch heels accentuated her confident stride. Unlike Marlee and Ashley, she didn't smile.

But it wasn't because she was unhappy. No, she was focused. Her entrance was meant to inspire intimidation. And it worked on ladylike Ashley, who I heard breathe an

"Oh, no" as the new girl walked closer.

This person, who I recognized as Celeste Newsome of Clermont, Two, didn't bother me. She assumed we were fighting for the same thing. But you can't be pushed if it's something you don't want.

Celeste finally reached us, and Marlee squeaked out a hello, trying to be friendly even in the midst of intimidation. Celeste merely looked her over and sighed.

"When do we leave?" she asked.

"We don't know," I answered without a hint of fear. "You've been holding up the show."

She didn't like that at all, and I got a once-over from her. She wasn't impressed.

"Sorry, quite a few people wanted to see me off. I couldn't help it." She smiled wide, as if it was obvious she was meant to be worshipped.

And I was about to surround myself with girls like this. Great.

As if on cue, a man appeared through the door to our left.

"I hear all four of our Selected girls are here?"

"We sure are," Celeste replied sweetly. The man sort of melted a little, you could see it in his eyes. Ah. So this was her game.

The captain paused a moment and then snapped to. "Well. Ladies, if you'll just follow me, we'll get you on the plane and off to your new home."

The flight, which was really only terrifying during the takeoff and landing, lasted a few short hours. We were offered movies and food, but all I wanted to do was look out the window. I watched the country from above, amazed at just how big it all was.

Celeste chose to sleep through the flight, which was a small mercy. Ashley had a foldout desk set up and was already writing letters about her adventure. That was smart of her to pack paper. I bet May would love to hear about this part of the journey, even though it didn't include the prince.

"She's so elegant," Marlee whispered to me, tilting her head toward Ashley. We were sitting across from each other in plush seats in the very front of the small plane. "From the moment we met, she's been nothing but proper. She's going to be tough competition," she said with a sigh.

"You can't think about it that way," I answered. "Yes, you're trying to make it to the end, but not by beating someone else. You've just got to be you. Who knows? Maybe Maxon would prefer someone more relaxed."

Marlee thought that over. "I guess that's a good point. It's hard to not like her. She's awfully kind. And so beautiful." I nodded in agreement. Marlee's voice dropped to a whisper. "Celeste, on the other hand . . ."

I widened my eyes and shook my head. "I know. It's only been an hour, and I'm already looking forward to her going home."

Marlee covered her mouth to hide a laugh. "I don't want to talk badly about anyone, but she's so aggressive. And Maxon's not even around yet. I'm a little nervous about her."

"Don't be," I assured her. "Girls like that? They'll take

themselves out of the competition."

Marlee sighed. "I hope so. Sometimes I wish . . ."

"What?"

"Well, sometimes I wish that the Twos had an idea about what it felt like to be treated the way they treat us."

I nodded. I'd never really thought of myself being on the same level as a Four, but I guess we were in a similar place. If you weren't a Two or Three, it was just varying shades of bad.

"Thanks for talking to me," she said. "I was worried that everyone would just be out for themselves, but you and Ashley have been really nice. Maybe this will be fun." Her voice lifted with hope.

I wasn't so sure, but I smiled back. I had no reason to shun Marlee or be rude to Ashley. The other girls might not be so laid-back.

When we landed, the air was silent as we walked the distance from the plane to the terminal with guards at our side. But once the doors were opened, we were met with ear-shattering screams.

The terminal was full of people jumping and cheering. A path had been cleared for us with a golden carpet lined with coordinating rope barriers. At regular intervals along this channel were guards, looking around anxiously and poised to strike at the first hint of danger. Surely there were more important things they should be doing?

Luckily, Celeste was in front, and she started waving. I knew immediately that that was the right response, not the cowering I had been considering. And since the cameras were there to catch our every move, I was doubly glad I hadn't been leading the pack.

The crowd was wild with joy. These would be the people we lived the closest to, and they were all looking forward to catching the first glimpses of the girls coming to town. One of us would be their queen someday.

I turned my head a dozen times in a matter of seconds as people called my name from all over the packed terminal. There were signs with my name on them, too. I was amazed. Already there were people here—people not in my caste or from my province—who hoped it would be me. I felt a little roll of guilt in my stomach that I would let them all down.

I dropped my head for a moment and saw a little girl pressed up against the railing. She couldn't have been more than twelve years old. In her hands was a sign that said RED-HEADS RULE! with a little crown painted in the corner and tiny stars everywhere. I knew I was the only redhead in the competition, and I noticed that her hair and mine were very nearly the same shade.

The girl wanted an autograph. Beside her, someone wanted a photograph, and beside him someone wanted to shake my hand. So I went practically down the entire line, turning around once or twice to talk to people on the other side of the carpet, too.

I was the last one to leave, making the other girls wait at least twenty minutes for me. Quite honestly, I probably wouldn't have left as soon as I did except the next plane of

Selected girls was coming in, and it seemed rude to overlap their time.

Getting into the car, I saw Celeste roll her eyes, but I didn't care. I was still sort of in awe of how I'd adjusted so quickly to something that had frightened me only moments before. I had made it through my good-byes, meeting the first girls, my flight, and interacting with our mob of fans. All without doing anything embarrassing.

I thought about the cameras following me in the terminal and pictured my family watching my entrance on TV. I hoped they'd be proud.

CHAPTER 9

EVEN AFTER THE SUBSTANTIAL GREETING party at the airport, the roads leading up to the palace were lined with masses of people calling out their well-wishes. The sad thing was that we weren't allowed to roll down the windows to acknowledge them. The guard in the front said to think of ourselves as extensions of the royal family. Many adored us, but there were people out there who wouldn't be above hurting us to hurt the prince. Or the monarchy itself.

I was stuck next to Celeste in the car—a special one that had two rows of seats facing each other in the back and darkened windows—with Ashley and Marlee sitting together in front of us. Marlee beamed as she stared out the windows, and it was obvious why. Her name was on several of the signs. It would be impossible to count how many admirers she had.

Ashley's name was sprinkled in there, too, almost as much as Celeste's, and far more than mine. Ashley, ever the lady, took not being a runaway favorite in stride. Celeste, I could see, was irritated.

"What do you think she did?" Celeste whispered in my ear, as Marlee and Ashley spoke to each other of home.

"What do you mean?" I whispered back.

"To be so popular. You think she bribed someone?" Her cold eyes focused in on Marlee as if she was weighing her worth in her head.

"She's a Four," I said doubtfully. "She wouldn't have the means to bribe someone."

Celeste sucked her teeth. "Please. A girl has more than one way she can pay for what she wants," she said, and pulled away to look out the window.

It took me a moment to understand what she was suggesting, and it didn't sit well with me. Not because it was obvious that someone as innocent as Marlee would never think about sleeping with someone to get ahead—or even consider breaking a law—but because it was becoming clear that life at the palace might be more vicious than I had imagined.

I didn't have a very good view coming up to the palace, but I noticed the walls. They were a pale yellow stucco and very, very high. Guards were placed on top at either side of the wide gate that swung open as we approached. Inside we were greeted with a long gravel drive that circled a fountain and led to the front doors, where officials waited to welcome us.

With barely more than a hello, two women took me by the arms and ushered me inside.

"So sorry to rush, miss, but your group is running late," one said.

"Oh, I'm afraid that's my fault. I got a little too chatty at the airport."

"Talking to the crowds?" the other asked in surprise.

They exchanged a look I didn't understand before they started calling out locations as we passed.

The dining room was to the right, they told me, and the Great Room was to the left. I caught a glimpse of sprawling gardens out the glass doors and wished I could stop. Before I could even process where we were going, they pulled me into a huge room full of bustling people.

A swarm parted, and I saw rows of mirrors with people working on girls' hair and painting their nails. Clothes hung on racks, and people were shouting things like "I found the dye!" and "That makes her look pudgy."

"Here they are!" I saw a woman coming up to us, clearly the person in charge. "I'm Silvia. We spoke on the phone," she said as a means of introduction, then immediately went to work. "First things first. We need 'before' pictures. Come over here," she commanded, pointing us to a chair in the corner in front of a backdrop. "Don't mind the cameras, ladies. We'll be doing a special on your makeovers, since every girl in Illéa's going to want to look like you by the time we're done today."

Sure enough, teams of people with cameras were

wandering around the room, zooming in on girls' shoes, and interviewing them. Once the pictures were done, Silvia began shouting orders. "Take Lady Celeste to station four, Lady Ashley to five . . . and it looks like they just finished up at ten. Take Lady Marlee there, and Lady America to six."

"So here's the thing," a short, dark-haired man said, pulling me over to a seat with a six on the back. "We need to talk about your image." He was all business.

"My image?" Wasn't I just me? Wasn't that what got me here?

"How do we want to make you look? With that red hair, we can make you quite the temptress, but if you want to play that kind of thing down, we can work that out, too," he said matter-of-factly.

"I'm not changing everything about me to cater to some guy I don't even know." *Or like*, I added in my head.

"Oh, my. Do we have an individual here?" he sang, as if I were a child.

"Aren't we all?"

The man smiled at me. "Fine, then. We won't change your image, we'll just enhance it. I need to polish you up a bit, but your aversion to all things fake might just be your greatest asset here. Hold on to that, honey." He patted me on the back and walked away, sending a group of women swarming my way.

I didn't realize that when he said "polish," he meant it literally. I had women scrub my body because I apparently couldn't be trusted to do a good enough job on my own. Then every exposed bit of skin was covered with lotions and oils that left me smelling like vanilla, which according to the girl who applied them was one of Maxon's favorite smells.

After they were done making me smooth and supple, attention was turned to my nails. They were trimmed and buffed and the tough little pieces of skin around them were miraculously smoothed away. I told them I'd prefer not to have my nails painted, but they looked so disappointed that I told them they could do my toes. The one girl picked a nice neutral shade, so it wasn't too bad.

The team of people who worked on my nails left me for another girl, and I sat quietly in my chair, waiting for the next round of beautification. A camera crew came past, zooming in on my hands.

"Don't move," a woman ordered. She squinted at my hand. "Do you even have anything on your nails?"

"No."

She sighed, got her shot, and moved on.

I heaved a heavy sigh myself. Out of the corner of my eye, I saw a jerking motion just to my right. I looked and saw a girl staring into nowhere while her leg bounced up and down under a large cape they'd draped over her.

"You okay?" I asked.

My voice shocked her out of her trance. She sighed. "They want to dye my hair blond. They said it would look better with my skin tone. I'm just nervous, I guess."

She gave me a tight smile, and I returned it. "You're Sosie, right?"

"Yeah." She smiled in earnest then. "And you're America?" I nodded. "I heard you came in with that Celeste girl. She's terrible!"

I rolled my eyes. Since we'd arrived, every few minutes the entire room could hear Celeste yelling at some poor maid to bring her something or to get out of her way.

"You have no idea," I muttered, and we both giggled. "Listen, I think your hair's very pretty." It was, too. Not too dark, not too light, and very full.

"Thanks."

"If you don't want to change it, you shouldn't have to."

Sosie smiled, but I could tell she wasn't completely sure if I was trying to be friendly or hold her back. Before she could say anything, teams of people came to work on us, directing one another so loudly there was no way for us to finish talking.

My hair was washed, conditioned, hydrated, and smoothed. It was long and all one length when I came in—my mom usually cut it, and that was the best she could do—but by the time they were done, it was several inches shorter and had layers. I liked those; they made my hair catch the light in interesting ways. Some girls got things called highlights, and others, like Sosie, had the color changed completely. But my attendants and I all agreed that mine should go untouched in that department.

A very pretty-looking girl did my makeup. I instructed

her to go light, and it was nice. Lots of the other girls looked a little older or younger or just nicer after the makeup. I still looked like me when I was done. Of course, so did Celeste, since she insisted upon piling it on.

I'd gone through most of this process in a robe, and once they were done fixing me up, I was led over to the racks of clothes. My name was hanging above a bar holding a week's worth of dresses. I guessed princesses-in-training didn't wear pants.

The one I ended up in was a cream color. It fell off my shoulders, fit snugly at my waist, and hit just at my knees. The girl helping me into it called it a day dress. She told me that my evening dresses were already in my room, and the rest of these would go up there as well. Then she placed a silver pin near the top of my dress. My name glittered across it. Finally she put me into shoes she called kitten heels and sent me back to the corner so I could take my "after" shot. From there I was ordered to one of four little stations lined up against the wall. Each had a chair with a backdrop and a camera sitting in front of it.

I sat down as instructed and waited. A woman came up with a clipboard of information in her hand and asked me to be patient while she found my papers.

"What's this for?" I asked.

"The makeover special. We'll be airing one about your arrivals tonight, the makeovers are on Wednesday, and then Friday you'll do your first *Report*. People have seen your pictures and know a little bit about what was on your applications," she said as she located her papers and placed them on the top of her clipboard. Then she laced her fingers together and continued. "But we want to make them really pull for you. And that won't happen unless they can get to know you. So we'll just do a little interview here, and you do your best on the *Reports*, and then don't be shy when you see us around the palace. We aren't here every day, but we'll be around."

"Okay," I said meekly. I really didn't want to talk to camera crews. It all felt so intrusive.

"So, America Singer, yes?" she asked just seconds after a red light lit up on the top of the camera.

"Yes." I tried to push the nerves out of my voice.

"I have to be honest, you don't look like you changed too much to me. Can you tell us what happened in your make-over today?"

I thought. "They put layers in my hair. I like that." I ran my fingers through the red strands, feeling how soft my hair was after professional care. "And they covered me in vanilla lotion. I kind of smell like dessert," I said, sniffing my arm.

She laughed. "It is lovely. And that dress really suits you."

"Thanks," I said, looking down at my new clothes. "I don't typically wear a lot of dresses, so this is going to take a little getting used to."

"That's right," my interviewer said. "You're one of only three Fives in the Selection. How has this experience been so far?"

I searched my head for something that would describe how

everything had felt today. From my disappointment in the square to the sensation of flying to the comfort of Marlee.

"Surprising," I said.

"I imagine there will be more surprising days to come," she commented.

"I hope they're at least a little calmer than today," I said with a sigh.

"How do you feel about your competition so far?"

I swallowed. "The girls are all really nice." With one glaring exception.

"Mm-hmm," she said, seeing through my answer. "So how do you feel about the way your makeover turned out? Worried about anyone else's look?"

I considered that. To say no sounded snotty, to say yes sounded needy. "I think the staff has done a great job bringing out each girl's individual beauty."

She smiled and said, "All right, I think that'll be enough."

"That's all?"

"We have to fit thirty-five of you into an hour and a half, so that will be plenty."

"Okay." That wasn't so bad.

"Thank you for your time. You can head over to that couch over there, and you'll be taken care of."

I stood and went to sit on the large circular couch in the corner. Two girls I had yet to meet were sitting there, talking quietly. I looked around the room and saw someone announcing that the last batch was heading in. A new flurry began around the stations. I was focused on it and almost didn't notice Marlee sit down beside me.

"Marlee! Look at your hair!"

"I know. They put extensions in it. Do you think Maxon will like it?" She looked genuinely worried.

"Of course! What guy doesn't like a gorgeous blonde?" I said with a playful smile.

"America, you're so nice. All those people at the airport loved you."

"Oh, I was just being friendly. You met people, too," I countered.

"Yeah, but not half as many as you."

I lowered my head, a little embarrassed for being complimented over something that seemed so obvious. When I looked up, I turned to the other two girls sitting with us. Emmica Brass and Samantha Lowell and I hadn't been introduced, but I knew who they were. I did a double take. They were looking at me funny. Before I had time to guess why, Silvia, the woman from earlier, approached us.

"All right, girls, are we all ready?" She checked her watch and looked at us expectantly. "I'm going to give you a quick tour and take you to your assigned rooms."

Marlee clapped her hands, and the four of us rose to leave. Silvia told us the space we were currently using to get pampered was the Women's Room. Usually the queen, her maids, and the handful of other female family members entertained themselves there.

"Get used to that room—you'll be spending a lot of time there. Now, on your way in you passed the Great Room, which is generally used for parties and banquets. If there were too many more of you ladies here, that's where you'd be taking your meals. But the regular dining room is large enough to meet your needs. Let's take a quick step in there."

We were shown where the royal family ate, at a table alone. We would be seated at long tables to either side, so the setup looked like a very stiff U. Our places were currently assigned, set with elegant place markers. I would be sitting next to Ashley and Tiny Lee, who I'd seen go through the Women's Room earlier, and across from Kriss Ambers.

We left the dining hall and continued on down a set of stairs and saw the room used to broadcast the *Illéa Capital Report*. Back upstairs our guide pointed down a hall where the king and Maxon spent most of their time working. That area was off-limits to us.

"Another thing that is off-limits: the third floor. The royal family has their private rooms up there, and any sort of intrusion will not be tolerated. Your rooms are all located on the second floor. You will inhabit a large portion of the guest rooms. Not to worry, though; we still have room for any visitors coming through.

"These doors here go out to the back garden. Hello, Hector, Markson." The two guards at the doors gave her a quick nod. It took me a moment to recognize that the large archway to our right was the side door to the Great Room, meaning the Women's Room was just around the corner. I was proud of myself for figuring that out. The palace was kind of like an opulent maze.

"You are not to go outside under any circumstances," Silvia continued. "During the day, there will be times when you can go into the garden, but not without permission. This is merely a safety restriction. Try as we may, rebels have gotten within the grounds before."

A chill went down my body.

We rounded a corner and walked up the massive stairs to the second floor. The carpets felt so lush under my shoes, like I was sinking an inch every time I took a step. High windows let in light, and it smelled like flowers and sunshine. Large paintings hung on the walls, depicting the kings of the past and a few renderings of old American and Canadian leaders. At least, that's what I guessed they were. They didn't wear any crowns.

"Your things are already in your rooms. If the decor is unsuitable, just tell your maids. You each have three, and they are already in your rooms, too. They will help with any unpacking you might have and will help you get dressed for dinner.

"Before dinner tonight, you will meet in the Women's Room for a special screening of the *Illéa Capital Report*. Next week, you'll all be on the show yourselves! Tonight you'll get to see some of the footage they've taken of you leaving your homes and arriving here. It promises to be very special. You should know that Prince Maxon hasn't seen anything yet today. He'll see what all of Illéa will see tonight, and then you will officially meet him tomorrow.

"You girls will all be having dinner as a group, so you will be able to meet one another, and then, tomorrow, the games begin!"

I gulped. Too many rules, too much structure, too many people. I just wanted to be alone with a violin.

We moved across the second floor, dropping off Selected girls at their rooms. Mine was tucked around a corner in a little hallway with Bariel, Tiny, and Jenna. I was glad it wasn't quite in the middle of things, like Marlee's room was. Maybe I'd have a little privacy like this.

Once Silvia left, I opened my door to the excited gasps of three women. One was sewing in a corner, and the others were cleaning an already perfect room. They scurried over and introduced themselves as Lucy, Anne, and Mary, but I forgot which was which almost immediately. It took quite a bit of convincing to get them to leave. I didn't want to be rude since they were so eager to serve, but I needed time alone.

"I just need a little nap. I'm sure you've had a long day, too, getting ready and all. The best thing you could do is let me rest, get some rest yourselves, and please come wake me up when it's time to go downstairs."

There was a flurry of thanks and bows, which I tried to discourage, and then I was alone. It didn't help. I tried to stretch out on my bed, but every part of my body pulled tight, refusing to let me get comfortable in a place that was so obviously not meant for me.

There was a violin in the corner, as well as a guitar and a gorgeous piano, but I couldn't bring myself to bother with them. My backpack was securely fastened, waiting at the foot of my bed, but that felt like too much work, too. I knew they'd set special things for me in my closet and drawers and bathroom, but I didn't feel like exploring.

I just lay there, still. It felt like only a few moments before my maids quietly tapped on my door. I let them in and, as strange as it was, let them dress me. They were just so excited to be helpful, I couldn't ask them to leave again.

They pulled parts of my hair back with delicate pins and freshened my makeup. The dress—which, along with the rest of my wardrobe, had been created by their hands—was deep green and floor length. Without those tiny heels again I'd stumble all over it. Silvia knocked on my door promptly at six to take me and my three neighbors down the hall. We waited in the foyer by the stairway for everyone to come and then marched down to the Women's Room. Marlee spotted me, and we walked together.

The sound of thirty-five pairs of heels on the marble stairs was the music of some elegant stampede. There were a few murmurs, but most girls were silent. I noticed as we passed the dining room that the doors were closed. Was the royal family in there now? Perhaps taking in one last meal as the three of them?

It seemed strange that we were their guests but hadn't met a single one of them yet.

The Women's Room had changed since we left. The mirrors and racks were all gone, and tables and chairs dotted the floor along with some very comfortable-looking couches.

Marlee looked at me and inclined her head toward one of the couches, and we sat there together.

Once we were all settled the TV was turned on, and we watched the *Report*. There were the same announcements as ever—budget updates for projects, progress of the war, and another rebel attack in the East—and then the last half hour was Gavril making commentary over footage of our day.

"Here Miss Celeste Newsome says good-bye to her many admirers in Clermont. It took this lovely young lady more than an hour to break away from her fans."

I saw Celeste smile smugly as she watched herself on-screen. She was sitting next to Bariel Pratt, who had hair straight as a bone and so pale blond it looked white as it fell to her waist. There was no mild way to put it: Her breasts were huge. They crept out of her strapless dress, tempting anyone to try and ignore them.

Bariel was beautiful, but in a typical way. It was similar to Celeste's style. I wasn't sure exactly how, but the image of them side by side prompted the thought, *Keep your enemies closer.* I think they'd singled each other out right away as the other's strongest competition.

"The others from the Mideast were just as popular. Ashley Brouillette's quiet, refined demeanor sets her apart immediately as a lady. As she carries herself through the crowd, she wears a humble, beautiful expression not too different from the face of the queen herself."

"And Marlee Tames of Kent was all bubbles as she departed today, singing the national anthem with her send-off band."

Pictures of Marlee smiling and embracing people from her home province flashed across the screen. "She's an immediate favorite of several people we interviewed today."

Marlee reached over and squeezed my hand. That settled it; I was pulling for Marlee.

"Also traveling with Miss Tames was America Singer, one of only three Fives who made it into the Selection." They made me look better than I felt in the moment. All I remembered was searching the crowds, sad. But the footage they chose of me searching made me appear mature and caring. The image of me hugging my father was touching, beautiful.

Still, it was nothing compared to the images of me in the airport. "But we know castes mean nothing in the Selection, and it seems Lady America is not to be overlooked. Upon landing in Angeles, Lady Singer was the crowd darling at the airport, stopping to take pictures, sign autographs, and simply speak to anyone there. Miss America Singer is not afraid to get her hands dirty, a quality that many believe our next princess needs."

Nearly everyone turned to look at me. I could see it in their eyes, the same look I'd gotten from Emmica and Samantha. Suddenly those stares made sense. My intentions didn't matter. They didn't know I didn't want this. In their eyes, I was a threat. And I could see they wanted me gone.

CHAPTER 10

I KEPT MY HEAD DOWN at dinner. In the Women's Room I could be brave because Marlee was beside me, and she just thought I was nice. But here, sandwiched between people whose hate I could feel radiating off in waves, I was a coward. I looked up from my plate once to see Kriss Ambers twirling her fork menacingly. And Ashley, who was so lady-like, had her lips pouted and didn't speak to me. I just wanted to escape to my room.

I didn't understand why it was all so important. So the people seemed to like me, so what? They were outranked in here; their little signs and cheers didn't matter.

After everything was said and done, I didn't know whether to feel honored or annoyed.

I focused my energies on the food. The last time I'd had steak was for Christmas a few years ago. I knew Mom did her best, but it was nothing like this. So juicy, so tender, so flavorful. I wanted to ask someone else if this wasn't the best steak they'd ever had. If Marlee had been nearby, I would have. I took a tentative peek around the room. Marlee was chattering quietly with the people around her.

How did she manage to do that? Hadn't that same clip declared her one of the immediate favorites? How did she get people to talk to her?

Dessert was an assortment of fruits in vanilla ice cream. It was like I'd never eaten before. If this was food, what had I been putting in my mouth up to this point? I thought of May and her equal love for all things sweet. She would have loved this. I bet she would have excelled here.

We weren't allowed to leave dinner until everyone had finished, and after that we were under strict orders to go straight to bed.

"You'll be meeting Prince Maxon in the morning, and you'll want to look your best," Silvia instructed. "He is someone in this room's future husband, after all."

A few girls sighed at the thought.

The click and clack of shoes up the stairs was quieter this time around. I couldn't wait to get out of mine. Out of the dress, too. I had one set of clothes from home in my backpack and was debating putting them on just to feel like myself for a moment.

We dispersed at the top of the stairs, each girl heading off to her own room. Marlee pulled me aside.

"Are you okay?" she asked.

"Yes. It's just that some of the girls were looking at me funny during dinner." I tried not to come across as whiny.

"They're just a little nervous because everyone liked you so much," she said, waving off their behavior.

"But the people liked you, too. I saw the signs. Why weren't the girls being mean to you?"

"You haven't spent a whole lot of time with groups of girls, have you?" She was smiling slyly, like I should know what was happening.

"No. Just my sisters mostly," I confessed.

"Homeschooled?"

"Yes."

"Well, I get tutored with a bunch of other Fours back home, all girls, and they each have their ways of getting under other people's skin. See, it's all about knowing the person, figuring out what will bug them the most. Lots of girls give me backhanded compliments, or little remarks, things like that. I know I come across as bubbly, but I'm shy underneath that, and they think they can wear me down with words."

I scrunched my forehead. They did that on purpose?

"For you, someone kind of quiet and mysterious—"

"I'm not mysterious," I interrupted.

"You are a little. And sometimes people don't know whether to interpret silence as confidence or fear. They're looking at you like you're a bug so maybe you'll feel like you are one."

"Huh." That kind of made sense. I wondered what I was

doing, if I was picking away at others' insecurities somehow. "What do you do? When you want to get the best of them, I mean?"

She smiled. "I ignore it. I know one girl at home who gets so irritated when she can't bother you, she just ends up sulking. So don't worry," she said. "All you have to do is not let them know they're getting to you."

"They're not."

"I almost believe you . . . but not quite." She laughed a little, a warm sound that evaporated in the quiet hallway. "Can you believe we meet him in the morning?" she asked, moving on to more important things in her eyes.

"No, actually, I can't." Maxon seemed like a ghost haunting the palace—implied but never really there.

"Well, good luck tomorrow." And I could tell she meant it.

"Better luck to you, Marlee. I'm sure Prince Maxon will be more than pleased to meet you." I squeezed her hand one time.

She smiled in a way that was both excited and timid and walked off to her room.

When I got to mine, Bariel's door was still open, and I heard her muttering something to a maid. She caught sight of me and slammed the door in my face.

Thanks for that.

My maids were there, of course, waiting to help me wash and undress. My nightgown, a flimsy little green thing, had been laid out for me on the bed. Kindly, none of them had touched my bag.

They were efficient but purposeful. They obviously had this end-of-the-day routine down, but they didn't rush through it. I suppose the effect was meant to be soothing, but I was ready to have them gone. I couldn't speed them up as they washed my hands and unlaced my dress and pinned my silver name tag to my silken nightgown. And as they did all these things that made me incredibly self-conscious, they asked questions. I tried to answer them without being rude.

Yes, I'd finally seen all the other girls. No, they weren't very talkative. Yes, dinner was fantastic. No, I wouldn't meet the prince until tomorrow. Yes, I was very tired.

"And it would really help me wind down if I could have some time alone," I added to the end of that last answer, hoping they would take the hint.

They looked disappointed. I tried to recover.

"You're all very helpful. I'm just used to spending time alone. And I've been swarmed with people today."

"But Lady Singer, we're supposed to help you. It's our job," the head girl said. I'd figured out that she was Anne. Anne seemed to be on top of things, Mary was easygoing, and Lucy I guessed was just shy.

"I really do appreciate you all, and I'll definitely want your help getting started tomorrow. But tonight, I just need to unwind. If you want to be helpful, some time to myself would be good for me. And if you're all rested, I'm sure it will make things better in the morning, right?"

They looked at one another. "Well, I suppose so," Anne acquiesced.

"One of us is supposed to stay here while you sleep. In case you need something." Lucy looked nervous, like she was afraid of whatever decision I would make. She seemed to have little tremors now and then, which I guessed was her shyness coming to the surface.

"If I need anything, I'll ring the bell. It'll be fine. Besides, I won't be able to rest knowing someone's watching me."

They looked at one another again, still a little skeptical. I knew one way to stop this, but I hated using it.

"You're supposed to obey my every command, right?"

They nodded hopefully.

"Then I command you all to go to bed. And come help me in the morning. Please."

Anne smiled. I could tell she was starting to get me.

"Yes, Lady Singer. We'll see you in the morning." They curtsied and quietly left the room. Anne gave me one last look. I supposed I wasn't quite what she had been expecting. She didn't seem too upset about it, though.

Once they were gone, I stepped out of my fancy slippers and stretched my toes on the floor. It felt good, natural, to be barefoot. I went to unpack my things, which was quick. I kept my change of clothes tucked in the bag and stored it in my massive closet. I surveyed the dresses as I did so. There were only a few. Enough to get me through a week or so. I assumed this was the same for everyone. Why make a dozen dresses for a girl who might leave the next day?

I took the few photos I had of my family and stuck them in the edge of my mirror. It stretched so high and wide, I could look at the pictures without having anything interrupt my view of myself. I had a small box of personal trinkets—earrings and ribbons and headbands I loved. They'd probably look incredibly plain here, but they were all so personal that I'd had to have them with me. The few books I'd brought found their way to the helpful shelf near the doors that opened to my balcony.

I peeked out the entry to the balcony and saw the garden. There was a maze of paths with fountains and benches. Flowers blossomed everywhere, and each hedge was perfectly trimmed. Past this obviously manicured piece of land was a short, open field and then a massive forest. It stretched back so far that I couldn't tell if it was entirely closed in by palace walls. I wondered for a moment why it existed and then debated the last article from home that I held in my hand.

My tiny jar with its rattling penny. I rolled it in my hands a few times, listening to the penny skate around the edges of the glass. Why had I even brought this? To remind myself of something I couldn't have?

That tiny thought—that this love I had been building in a quiet, secret place for years was really beyond my reach now—made my eyes well up. On top of all the tension and excitement of the day, it was just too much. I didn't know where the jar's permanent place here would be, but for the moment I set it on the table by my bed.

I dimmed the lights, crawled up on top of the luxurious blankets, and stared at my jar. I let myself be sad. I let myself think of *him*.

How had I lost so much in such a short period of time? It would seem like leaving your family, living in some foreign place, and being separated from the person you love should be events that take years to roll into place, not just a day.

I wondered what exactly he had wanted to tell me before I left. The only thing I could deduce was that he didn't feel comfortable saying it out loud. Was it about *her*?

I stared at the jar.

Maybe he was trying to say he was sorry? I had given him a sound scolding last night. So perhaps that was it.

That he'd moved on? Well, I could see that pretty clearly myself, thank you very much.

That he *hadn't* moved on? That he still loved me?

I shut the thought down. I couldn't let that hope build in me. I needed to hate him right now. That anger would keep me going. Staying as far away from him as I could for as long as possible was half my reason for being here.

But the hope ached. And with the hope came home-sickness, wishing May was sneaking into my bed like she sometimes did. And then fear that the other girls wanted me gone, that they might keep trying to make me feel small. And then nervousness at being presented to the nation on television for as long as I was here. And terror that people might try to kill me just to make a political statement. It all came at me too fast for my dizzy head to compute after such a long day.

My vision got blurry. I didn't even register that I'd started crying. I couldn't breathe. I was shaking. I jumped up and ran to the balcony. I was so panicked, it took me a moment to open the latch, but I did. I thought the fresh air would be enough, but it wasn't. My breaths were still shallow and cold.

There was no freedom in this. The bars of my balcony caged me in. And I could still see the walls around the palace, high with guards atop the points. I needed to be outside the palace, and no one was going to let that happen. Desperation made me feel even weaker. I looked at the forest. I'd bet I couldn't see anything but greenery from there.

I turned and bolted. I was a little unsteady with the tears in my eyes, but I managed to get out the door. I ran down the one hallway I knew, not seeing the art or the drapery or golden trim. I barely noticed the guards. I didn't know my way around the palace, but I knew if I got down the stairs and turned the right way, I'd see the massive glass doors that led to the garden. I just needed the doors.

I ran down the grand stairwell, my bare feet making slapping sounds on the marble. There were a few more guards along the way, but no one stopped me. That is, until I actually found the place I was looking for.

Just like earlier, two men were stationed at either side of the doors, and when I tried to run for them, one of them stepped in my way, the spearlike staff in his hand barring me from the exit.

"Excuse me, miss, you need to go back to your room," he said with authority. Even though he wasn't speaking loudly, his voice seemed thunderous in the still of the elegant hallway.

"No . . . no. I need . . . outside." The words were tangled; I couldn't breathe right.

"Miss, you need to get back to your room now." The second guard was taking steps toward me.

"Please." I started gasping. I thought I might faint.

"I'm sorry . . . Lady America, is it?" He found my pin. "You need to go back to your room."

"I . . . I can't breathe," I stammered, falling into the guard's arms as he moved close enough to push me away. His staff fell to the ground. I feebly clawed at him, feeling woozy with the effort.

"Let her go!" This was a new voice, young but full of authority. My head half turned, half fell in its direction. There was Prince Maxon. He looked a little odd, thanks to the angle my head was hanging at, but I recognized the hair and the stiff way he stood.

"She collapsed, Your Majesty. She wanted to go outside." The first guard looked nervous as he explained. He would be in terrible danger if he damaged me. I was the property of Illéa now.

"Open the doors."

"But—Your Majesty—"

"Open the doors and let her go. Now!"

"Right away, Your Highness." The first guard went to work, pulling out a key. My head stayed in its strange position as I heard the sound of keys clanking against one another and then one sliding into the lock. The prince looked at me warily as I tried to stand. And then the sweet smell of fresh air pulsed through me, giving me all the motivation I needed. I pulled myself out of the guard's arms and ran like a drunk into the garden.

I was staggering quite a bit, but I didn't care if I looked less than graceful. I just needed to be outside. I let myself feel the warm air on my skin, the grass beneath my toes. Somehow even things in nature seemed to be bred into something extravagant here. I meant to go all the way into the trees, but my legs only carried me so far. I collapsed in front of a small stone bench and sat there, my fine green nightgown in the dirt, and my head resting in my arms on the seat.

My body didn't have the energy to sob, so the tears that came were quiet. Still, they took all my focus. How did I get here? How had I let this happen? What would become of me here? Would I ever get back any piece of the life I'd had before this? I just didn't know. And there wasn't a damn thing I could do about any of it.

I was so consumed with my thoughts that I didn't realize I wasn't alone until Prince Maxon spoke.

"Are you all right, my dear?" he asked me.

"I am *not* your dear." I looked up to glare at him. There would be no mistaking the disgust in my tone or eyes.

"What have I done to offend you? Did I not just give you the very thing you asked for?" He was genuinely confused by my response. I suppose he expected us to adore him and thank our lucky stars for his existence.

I stared him down without fear, though the effect was probably weakened by my tearstained cheeks.

"Excuse me, dear, are you going to keep crying?" he asked, sounding very put out by the thought.

"Don't call me that! I am no more dear to you than the thirty-four other strangers you have here in your cage."

He walked closer, not seeming at all offended by my loose speech. He just looked . . . thoughtful. It was an interesting expression on his face.

His walk was graceful for a boy, and he looked incredibly comfortable as he paced around me. My bravery melted a little in the face of how awkward this was. He was fully dressed in his sharp suit, and I was cowering and half-naked. As if his rank didn't threaten me enough, his demeanor did. He must have had plenty of experience dealing with unhappy people; he was exceptionally calm as he answered.

"That is an unfair statement. You are all dear to me. It is simply a matter of discovering who shall be the dearest."

"Did you really just use the word 'shall'?"

He chuckled. "I'm afraid I did. Forgive me, it's a product of my education."

"Education," I muttered, rolling my eyes. "Ridiculous."

"I'm sorry?" he asked.

"It's ridiculous!" I yelled, regaining some of my courage.

"What is?"

"This contest! The whole thing! Haven't you ever loved anyone at all? Is this how you want to pick a wife? Are you really so shallow?" I shifted on the ground a little. To make things easier for me, he sat on the bench so I wouldn't have to twist. I was too upset to be thankful.

"I can see how I would appear that way, how this whole thing could seem like it's nothing more than cheap entertainment. But in my world, I am very guarded. I don't meet very many women. The ones I do are daughters of diplomats, and we usually have very little to discuss. And that's when we manage to speak the same language."

Maxon seemed to think that was a joke, and he laughed lightly. I wasn't amused. He cleared his throat.

"Circumstances being what they are, I haven't had the opportunity to fall in love. Have you?"

"Yes," I said matter-of-factly. As soon as the word came out, I wished I could steal it back. That was a private thing, none of his business.

"Then you have been quite lucky." He sounded jealous.

Imagine that. The one thing I could hold over the head of the Prince of Illéa, the very thing I was here to forget.

"My mother and father were married this way and are quite happy. I hope to find happiness, too. To find a woman that all of Illéa can love, someone to be my companion and to help entertain the leaders of other nations. Someone who will befriend my friends and be my confidante. I'm ready to find my wife."

Something in his voice struck me. There wasn't a trace of sarcasm. This thing that seemed like little more than a game show to me was his only chance for happiness. He couldn't try with a second round of girls. Well, maybe he could, but how embarrassing. He was so desperate, so hopeful. I felt my distaste for him lessen. Marginally.

"Do you really feel like this is a cage?" His eyes were full of compassion.

"Yes, I do." My voice came out quiet. I quickly added, "Your Majesty."

"I've felt that way more than once myself. But you must admit, it is a very beautiful cage."

"For you. Fill your beautiful cage with thirty-four other men all fighting over the same thing. See how nice it is then."

He raised his eyebrows. "Have there really been arguments over me? Don't you all realize I'm the one doing the choosing?"

"Actually, that was unfair. They're fighting over two things. Some fight for you, others fight for the crown. And they all think they've already figured out what to say and do so your choice will be obvious."

"Ah, yes. The man or the crown. I'm afraid some cannot tell the difference." He shook his head.

"Good luck there," I said dryly.

It was quiet for a moment in the wake of my sarcasm. I looked up at him out of the corner of my eye, waiting for him to speak. He gazed at an unfixed point in the grass, concern marking his face. It seemed this thought had been plaguing him. He took a breath and turned back to me.

"Which do you fight for?"

"Actually, I'm here by mistake."

"Mistake?"

"Yes. Sort of. Well, it's a long story. And now . . . I'm here.

And I'm not fighting. My plan is to enjoy the food until you kick me out."

He laughed out loud at that, actually doubling over and slapping his knee. It was a bizarre mix of rigidity and calm.

"What are you?" he asked.

"I'm sorry?"

"A Two? Three?"

Wasn't he paying attention at all? "Five."

"Ah, yes, then food would probably be good motivation to stay." He laughed again. "I'm sorry, I can't read your pin in the dark."

"I'm America."

"Well, that's perfect." Maxon looked off into the night and smiled at nothing in particular. Something in all this was amusing to him. "America, my dear, I do hope you find something in this cage worth fighting for. After all this, I can only imagine what it would be like to see you actually try."

He came down from the bench to crouch beside me. He was too close. I couldn't think right. Maybe I was a little star-struck or still feeling shaky from my crying episode. Either way I was too shocked to protest when he took my hand.

"If it would make you happy, I could let the staff know you prefer the garden. Then you can come out here at night without being manhandled by the guard. I would prefer if you had one nearby, though."

I wanted that. Freedom of any kind sounded heavenly, but he needed to be absolutely sure of my feelings.

"I don't . . . I don't think I want anything from you." I pulled my fingers from his loose grip.

He was a little taken aback, hurt. "As you wish." I felt more regret. Just because I didn't like the guy didn't mean I wanted to hurt him. "Will you be heading inside soon?"

"Yes," I breathed, looking at the ground.

"Then I'll leave you with your thoughts. There will be a guard near the door waiting for you."

"Thank you, um, Your Majesty." I shook my head. How many times had I addressed him wrongly in this conversation?

"Dear America, will you do me a favor?" He took my hand again. He was persistent.

I squinted at him, not sure of what to say. "Maybe."

His smile returned. "Don't mention this to the others. Technically, I'm not supposed to meet you until tomorrow, and I don't want anyone getting upset. Though I wouldn't call you yelling at me anything close to a romantic tryst, would you?"

It was my turn to smile. "Not at all!" I took a deep breath. "I won't tell."

"Thank you." He took the hand he was holding and lowered his lips to it. When he pulled away, he gently placed my hand in my lap. "Good night."

I looked at the warm spot on my hand, stunned for a moment. Then I turned to watch Maxon as he walked away, giving me the privacy I'd wanted all day.

CHAPTER 11

IN THE MORNING I WOKE not to the sound of the maids coming in—though they had—or my bath being drawn—though it was. I woke to the light coming through my window as Anne gently pulled back the rich, heavy curtains. She hummed a quiet song to herself, absolutely happy with her task.

I wasn't ready to move. It had taken me a long time to come down from getting so worked up, and even more time to relax after I'd realized exactly what that conversation in the garden would mean for me. If I got a chance, I would apologize to Maxon. It would be a miracle if he let me get that far.

"Miss? Are you awake?"

"Noooo," I moaned into the pillow. I hadn't had nearly enough sleep, and the bed was far too comfortable. But Anne,

Mary, and Lucy laughed at my groan, which was enough to make me smile and decide to start moving.

These girls would probably be the easiest for me to get along with in the palace. I wondered if they could become confidantes of some kind, or if training and protocol would render them completely unable to even share a cup of tea with me. Though I was a born Five, I was covered with Threeness now. And if they were maids, that made them all Sixes. But that was fine with me. I did enjoy the company of Sixes.

I moved slowly into the monstrous bathroom, every step echoing against the vastness of tile and glass. In the long mirrors I saw Lucy eyeing the dirt stains on my nightgown. Then Anne's careful eyes caught them. Then Mary's. Thankfully, none of them asked any questions. Yesterday I thought they had been prying with all their inquiries, but I was wrong. They were obviously overly concerned with my comfort. Questions about what I was doing outside my room—let alone the palace—would only be awkward.

All they did was remove the gown with care and usher me toward the bath.

I wasn't used to being naked around other people—not even Mom or May—but there seemed to be no way around it. These three would be dressing me for as long as I was here, so I would have to bear it until I left. I wondered what would happen to them when I was gone. Would they get assigned to other girls who would need more attention as the competition drew on? Did they already have other jobs in the palace they were temporarily excused from? It seemed rude to ask what they used to do or imply that I was leaving soon, so I didn't.

After my bath, Anne dried my hair, pulling half up with ribbons I'd brought from home. They were blue and just so happened to accent the flowers in one of the day dresses my maids had created for me, so that was what I wore. Mary did my makeup, which was just as light as the day before, and Lucy rubbed lotion into my arms and legs.

There was an array of jewelry to choose from, but I asked for my box instead. There was a tiny necklace with a songbird on it that my dad had given me, and it was silver so it matched my name pin. I did take a pair of earrings from the royal store, but they were probably the smallest ones in the collection.

Anne, Mary, and Lucy looked me over and smiled at the results. I took that as a sign I was decent enough to leave for breakfast. With bows and smiles, they wished me well as I went to leave. Lucy's hands were trembling again.

I went into the upstairs foyer where we had all met yesterday. I was the first one there, so I took to a small sofa to wait for the rest. Slowly, others started to trickle in. I quickly noticed a theme. Every one of the girls looked phenomenal. They had their hair pulled up in intricate braids or curls, away from their faces. The makeup was meticulously done, dresses pressed to perfection.

I had probably chosen my plainest dress for the first day, and everyone else's had something sparkly on it. I saw two girls walk into the foyer and realize they were wearing almost the exact same dress. They both turned back around to change. Everyone wanted to stand out, and they all did in their own ways. Even me.

Everyone here looked like a One. I looked like a Five in a nice dress.

I thought it had taken me a long time to get ready, but it took the other girls much, much longer. Even when Silvia came to escort us downstairs, we still had to wait for Celeste and Tiny, who, true to her name, had to have her dress taken in.

Once we were all assembled, everyone started to move toward the stairs. There was a gilded mirror on the wall, and we all turned to take one last peek as we descended. I caught a glimpse of myself next to Marlee and Tiny. I looked positively plain.

But at least I looked like me, and that was a minor consolation.

We went downstairs expecting to be taken into the dining room, where we had been told we would be eating. But instead we were taken into the Great Room, where individual tables and chairs had been set up in rows, all with plates, glasses, and silverware. There wasn't any food, though. Not even a hopeful smell. In the front corner, tucked away in a small nook, I noticed a small set of couches. A few cameramen, stationed around the room, filmed our arrival.

We filed in, sitting wherever we wanted as there were no place cards here. Marlee was in the row in front of me, and Ashley sat to my right. I didn't bother to take in anyone else. It seemed like several people had made at least one ally, just as I had in Marlee. Ashley had chosen her seat beside me, so I assumed she wanted my company. Still, she didn't speak. Maybe she was upset over the news reports last night. Then again, she was quiet when we met. Maybe it was just her nature. I figured the worst she could do was not answer back, so I decided to at least acknowledge her.

"Ashley, you look lovely."

"Oh, thank you," she said quietly. We both checked to make sure the camera crews were far away. Not that this was private, but who wanted them around for everything? "Isn't it fun to wear all this jewelry? Where's yours?"

"Umm, it was too heavy for me. I decided to go light instead."

"It is heavy! I feel like I have twenty pounds on my head. Still, I couldn't pass it up. Who knows how long any of us will stay?"

That was funny. Ashley had seemed quietly confident from the very beginning. With the way she looked and carried herself, she was prime princess material. It seemed strange that she would doubt herself.

"But don't you think you'll win?" I asked.

"Of course," she whispered. "But it's rude to say so!" She winked at me, which made me giggle.

Yet another mistake on my part. That giggle caught the attention of Silvia, who was walking in the door.

"Tsk-tsk. A lady never raises her voice above a gentle whisper."

Every murmur hushed. I wondered if the cameras had caught my mistake, and my cheeks filled with warmth.

"Hello again, ladies. I hope you all had a restful first night in the palace, because now our work begins. Today I will begin to instruct you on conduct and protocol, a process that will continue for the duration of your stay. Please know that I will be reporting any missteps on your part to the royal family.

"I know it sounds harsh, but this isn't a game to be taken lightly. Someone in this room will be the next princess of Illéa. It is no small task. You must endeavor to elevate yourselves, no matter your previous station. You will become ladies from the ground up. And this very morning, you will receive your first lesson.

"Table manners are very important, and before you can eat in front of the royal family, you must be aware of certain etiquette. The faster we get through this little lesson, the sooner you get to have your breakfasts, so faces forward, please."

She began explaining how we would be served from the right, which glass was for what beverage, and to never, ever reach for a pastry with our hands. Always use the tongs. Hands were to rest in our lap when not in use, napkin draped underneath. We weren't to speak unless spoken to. Of course, we could talk quietly to our neighbors, but always at a level befitting the palace. She eyed me seriously as she gave that last note.

Silvia went on and on in her elegant tone, taunting my

stomach. Even if they were small, I was used to getting my three meals at home. I needed food. I was getting a bit grumpy when we heard a knock at the door. Two guards stepped away, and in came Prince Maxon.

"Good morning, ladies," he called.

The lift in the room was tangible. Backs straightened, locks of hair were tossed over shoulders, and hems were rearranged. I looked not at Maxon, but Ashley, whose chest was moving fast. She stared in such a way that I felt embarrassed for noticing.

"Your Majesty," Silvia said with a low curtsy.

"Hello, Silvia. If you don't mind, I would like to introduce myself to these young women."

"Of course." She bowed again.

Prince Maxon surveyed the room and found me. Our eyes met for a moment, and he smiled. I wasn't expecting that. I was thinking that he'd probably changed his opinion of how to act toward me in the night, and I'd be called out in front of everyone for my behavior. But maybe he wasn't mad at all. Maybe he found me entertaining. He had to get incredibly bored around here. Whatever the reason, that brief smile led me to believe that maybe this wasn't going to be such a terrible experience after all. I settled into the decision I couldn't make last night and hoped Prince Maxon would hear out my apology.

"Ladies, if you don't mind, one at a time I'll be calling you over to meet with me. I'm sure you're all eager to eat, as am I. So I won't take up too much of your time. Do forgive me if I'm slow with names; there are quite a few of you."

There was a low rumble of giggles. Quickly, he went over to the girl in the front row on the far right and escorted her over to the couches. They spoke for a few minutes, then both rose. He bowed to her, she curtsied back. She went back to her table, spoke to the girl beside her, and it happened all over again. These conversations lasted only a few minutes and were spoken in hushed voices. He was trying to get a feel for each girl in less than five minutes.

"I wonder what he wants to know," Marlee turned and asked.

"Maybe he wants to know which actors you think are the most handsome. Keep your mental list ready," I whispered back. Marlee and Ashley both chuckled at that.

We weren't the only ones talking. Around the room voices lifted like gentle hums, as we tried to distract ourselves until it was our turn. Not to mention the cameramen were hopping around, asking girls about their first day in the palace, how they liked their maids, and things like that. When they stopped by Ashley and me, I let her do all the talking.

I kept looking over to the couches as each of the Selected were interviewed. Some were calm and ladylike, others fidgeted in excitement. Marlee blushed wildly as she walked over to Prince Maxon, and beamed when she walked back. Ashley straightened her dress several times, like a nervous little tic of her hands.

I was near sweating when she came back, meaning it was my turn to go. I took a deep breath and steadied myself. I was about to ask for a monumental favor.

He stood and went to read my pin as I approached. "America, is it?" he said, a smile playing on his lips.

"Yes, it is. And I know I've heard your name before, but could you remind me?" I wondered if opening with a joke was a bad idea, but Maxon laughed and motioned for me to sit.

He leaned in and whispered, "Did you sleep well, my dear?"

I didn't know what my face looked like in response to that name, but Maxon's eyes glittered with amusement.

"I am still not your dear," I replied, but with a smile. "But yes. Once I calmed down, I slept very well. My maids had to pull me out of bed, I was so cozy."

"I am glad you were comfortable, my . . . America," he corrected himself.

"Thank you," I said. I fidgeted with a piece of my dress for a moment, trying to think of how to say this right. "I'm very sorry I was mean to you. I realized as I was trying to fall asleep that even though this is a strange situation for me, I shouldn't blame you. You're not the reason I got swept up in all this, and the whole Selection thing isn't even your idea. And then, when I was feeling miserable, you were nothing but nice to me, and I was, well, awful. You could have thrown me out last night, and you didn't. Thank you."

Maxon's eyes were tender. I bet every girl before me had already melted because he'd given them a look like this. I would have been bothered that he looked at me that way, but it was obviously just part of his nature. He ducked his head for a moment. When he looked at me again, he leaned forward, resting his elbows on his knees as if he wanted me to understand the importance of what was coming next.

"America, you have been very up front with me so far. That is a quality that I deeply admire, and I'm going to ask you to be kind enough to answer one question for me."

I nodded, a little afraid of what he wanted to know. He leaned in even closer to whisper. "You say you're here by mistake, so I'm assuming you don't want to be here. Is there any possibility of you having any sort of . . . of loving feelings toward me?"

I couldn't help but fidget a little. I genuinely didn't want to hurt his feelings, but I couldn't beat around the bush on this.

"You are very kind, Your Majesty, and attractive, and thoughtful." He smiled at that. In a low voice I added, "But for very valid reasons, I don't think I could."

"Would you explain?" His face hid it well, but I could hear the disappointment caused by my immediate rejection. I guessed he wasn't used to that.

It wasn't something I wanted to share, but I didn't think anything else would make him understand. In an even lower whisper than I'd used before, I told him the truth.

"I . . . I'm afraid my heart is elsewhere." I could feel my eyes getting wet.

"Oh, please don't cry!" Maxon's whisper was marked with a genuine worry. "I never know what to do when women cry!"

That made me laugh, and any threat of tears retreated for the moment. The relief on his face was unmistakable.

"Would you like me to let you go home to your love today?" he asked. It was obvious that my preference for some-one else bothered him, but instead of choosing to be angry, he showed compassion. The gesture made me trust him.

"That's the thing. . . . I don't want to go home."

"Really?" He ran his fingers through his hair, and I had to laugh again at how lost he seemed.

"Could I be perfectly honest with you?"

He nodded.

"I need to be here. My family needs me to be here. Even if you could let me stay for a week, that would be a blessing for them."

"You mean you need the money?"

"Yes." I felt bad admitting it. It must have seemed like I was using him. In truth, I guess I was. But there was more to it. "And there are . . . certain people"—I looked up at him—"at home who I can't bear to see right now."

Maxon nodded his head in understanding but did not speak.

I hesitated. I guessed the worst that could happen now was being sent home anyway, so I continued. "If you would be willing to let me stay, even for a little while, I'd be willing to make a trade," I offered.

His eyebrows shot up. "A trade?"

I bit my lip. "If you let me stay . . ." This was going to sound so stupid. "All right, well, look at you. You're the prince. You're busy all day, what with helping run a country and all, and you're supposed to find time to narrow thirty-five, well, thirty-four girls, down to one? That's a lot to ask, don't you think?"

He nodded. I could see his genuine exhaustion at the thought.

"Wouldn't it be much better for you if you had someone on the inside? Someone to help? Like, you know, a friend?"

"A friend?" he asked.

"Yes. Let me stay, and I'll help you. I'll be your friend." He smiled at the words. "You don't have to worry about pursuing me. You already know that I don't have feelings for you. But you can talk to me anytime you like, and I'll try and help. You said last night that you were looking for a confidante. Well, until you find one for good, I could be that person. If you want."

His expression was affectionate but guarded. "I've met nearly every woman in this room, and I can't think of one who would make a better friend. I'd be glad to have you stay."

My relief was inexpressible.

"Do you think," Maxon asked, "that I could still call you 'my dear'?"

"Not a chance," I whispered.

"I'll keep trying. I don't have it in me to give up." And I believed him. It was annoying to think he'd press that issue.

"Did you call all of them that?" I nodded my head toward the rest of the room.

"Yes, and they all seemed to like it."

"That is the exact reason why I don't." And I stood.

Maxon was chuckling as he rose with me. I would have scowled, but it actually was kind of funny. He bowed, I curtsied, and I went back to my seat.

I was so hungry that it felt like an eternity until he'd gone through the last rows. But finally the last girl was back in her seat, and I was eagerly anticipating my first breakfast at the palace.

Maxon walked to the center of the room. "If I have asked you to remain behind, please stay in your seats. If not, please proceed with Silvia here into the dining hall. I will join you shortly."

Asked to stay? Was that a good thing?

I stood, as did most of the girls, and started walking. He must just want some special time with those girls. I saw that Ashley was one of them. No doubt she was special, a born princess by the looks of her. The rest were girls I hadn't managed to meet. Not that they had wanted to meet me. The cameras lingered behind to capture whatever special moment was about to occur, and the rest of us moved on.

We walked into the banquet room and there, looking more majestic than even I could imagine, were King Clarkson and Queen Amberly. Also in the room, more camera crews swarmed to catch our first meeting. I hesitated, wondering if we should all go back to the door and be invited in. But most everyone else—if somewhat hesitantly—kept walking. I walked quickly to my chair, hoping I hadn't drawn attention to myself.

Silvia walked in not two seconds later and took in the scene.

"Ladies," she said, "I'm afraid we didn't get this far. Whenever you enter a room where the king or queen is present, or if they should enter a room you are in, the proper thing to do is curtsy. Then when you are addressed, you may rise and take your seat. All together, shall we?" And we all curtsied in the direction of the head table.

"Welcome, girls," the queen said. "Please take your seats, and welcome to the palace. We're pleased to have you." There was something pleasant about her voice. It was calm in the same way her expression was, but not lifeless by any means.

As Silvia had said, the servers came to our right to pour orange juice into our glasses. Our plates came covered on large trays, and the butlers lifted the covers off right in front of us. I was hit in the face with a fragrant blast of steam from my pancakes. Mercifully, the murmurs of awe across the room covered my growling stomach.

King Clarkson blessed our food, and we all began to eat. A few minutes later, Maxon walked in to take his seat, but before we could move, he called out.

"Please don't rise, ladies. Enjoy your breakfasts." He walked up to the head table, kissed his mother on the cheek, gave his father a firm pat on the back, and settled into his own chair just to the king's left. He made a few comments to the closest butler, who laughed quietly, and then dug into his own plate.

Ashley didn't come. Or any of the other girls. I looked around, confused, counting to see how many were missing. Eight. Eight girls were not here.

It was Kriss, sitting across from me, who answered the question in my eyes.

"They're gone," she said.

Gone? Oh. Gone . . .

I couldn't imagine what they had done in less than five minutes to displease Maxon, but I was suddenly grateful I'd chosen to be honest.

Just like that, we were down to twenty-seven.

CHAPTER 12

THE CAMERAS DID A LAP around the room and left to let us enjoy our breakfast in peace, getting one last shot of the prince before they departed.

I was a little thrown off by the sudden elimination, but Maxon didn't seem too distressed. He ate his food without a care, and as I watched I realized I should eat my own breakfast before it got cold. Again, it was almost too delicious. The orange juice was so pure that I had to take smaller sips just to absorb it. The eggs and bacon were heaven, and the pancakes were perfectly done, not too thin like the ones I made at home.

I heard lots of little sighs all around me and knew I wasn't the only one enjoying the food. Remembering to use the tongs, I picked up a strawberry tart from the basket in the center of the table. As I did so, I looked around the room to see how the other Fives were enjoying their meals. That was when I noticed that I was the only Five left.

I didn't know if Maxon was aware of that information—he barely seemed to know our names—but it was strange they were both gone. If I had been another stranger to Maxon when I walked into that room, would I have been kicked out, too? I mulled this over as I bit into the strawberry tart. It was so sweet and the dough was so flaky, every millimeter of my mouth was engaged, taking over the rest of my senses entirely. I didn't mean to make the little moan, but it was by far the best thing I had ever tasted. I took another bite before I even swallowed the first.

"Lady America?" a voice called.

The other heads in the room turned to the voice, which belonged to Prince Maxon. I was shocked that he'd address me, or any of us, so casually and in front of the others.

What was worse than being called out so unexpectedly was that my mouth was full of food. I covered my mouth with my hand and chewed as quickly as I could manage. It couldn't have been more than a few seconds, but with so many eyes on me, it felt like an eternity. I noted Celeste's smug face as she watched me. I must have looked like an easy kill in her eyes.

"Yes, Your Majesty?" I replied as soon as I had most of it swallowed.

"How are you enjoying the food?" Maxon seemed on the verge of laughter, either from my bewildered expression or because he'd brought up a detail from our very first and highly unauthorized conversation.

I tried to stay calm myself. "It's excellent, Your Majesty. This strawberry tart . . . well, I have a sister who loves sweets more than I do. I think she'd cry if she tasted this. It's perfect."

Maxon swallowed a bite of his own breakfast and leaned back in his chair. "Do you really think she would cry?" He seemed exceedingly amused at the idea. He did have strange feelings toward women and crying.

I thought about it. "Yes, actually, I do. She doesn't have much of a filter when it comes to her emotions."

"Would you wager money on it?" he asked quickly. I noticed the heads of every girl turning back and forth between us like they were watching a game of tennis.

"If I had any to bet, I certainly would." I smiled at the idea of betting over someone else's tears of joy.

"What would you be willing to barter instead? You seem to be very good at striking deals." He was enjoying this little game. Fine. I'd play.

"Well, what do you want?" I posed. Then I wondered what in the world I could offer someone who had everything.

"What do *you* want?" he countered.

Now that was a fascinating question. Almost as interesting as thinking about what I could offer Maxon was what he could offer me. He had the world at his disposal. So what did I want?

I wasn't a One, but I was living like I was. I had more

food than I could finish and the most comfortable bed I could imagine. People were waiting on me hand and foot, whether I liked it or not. And if I needed anything, all I had to do was ask.

The only thing I really wanted was something that made this place feel like less of a palace. If my family were running around somewhere, or if I wasn't so done up. I couldn't ask for my family to visit. I'd only been here a day.

"If she cries, I want to wear pants for a week," I offered.

Everyone laughed, but in a quiet, polite way. Even the king and queen seemed to find my request amusing. I liked the way the queen looked at me, like I was less of a foreigner to her now.

"Done," Maxon said. "And if she doesn't, you owe me a walk around the grounds tomorrow afternoon."

A walk on the grounds? That was it? It didn't seem like anything special to me. I remembered what Maxon had said last night, that he was guarded. Maybe he didn't know how to just ask a girl for time alone. Maybe this was his way of navigating something very alien to him.

Someone next to me made a disapproving sound. Oh. I realized that if I lost, I'd be the first person to officially get time one-on-one with the prince. Part of me wanted to renegotiate, but if I was going to be helpful—as I'd promised him—I couldn't brush off his first attempts at trying to date.

"You drive a hard bargain, sir, but I accept."

"Justin?" The butler he had spoken to earlier stepped forward. "Go make a parcel of strawberry tarts and send it to the lady's family. Have someone wait while her sister tastes it, and let us know if she does, in fact, cry. I'm most curious about this."

Justin nodded and was off.

"You should write a note to send with it, and tell your family you're safe. In fact, you all should. After breakfast, write a letter to your families, and we'll make sure they receive them today."

Everyone smiled and sighed, happy to finally be included in the goings-on. We finished the rest of our breakfast and went to write our letters. Anne found me some stationery, and I wrote a quick letter to my family. Even though things had gotten off to a very awkward start, the last thing I wanted was for them to worry. I tried to sound breezy.

> Dear Mom, Dad, May, and Gerad,
>
> I miss you all so much already! The prince wanted us to write home and let our families know we were safe and well. I am both. The plane ride was a little scary, but it was fun in a way, too. The world looks so small from up so high!
>
> They've given me lots of wonderful clothes and things, and I have three sweet maids who help me get dressed and clean for me and tell me where to go. So even if I get totally confused, they always know just where I'm supposed to be and help me get there on time.
>
> The other girls are mostly shy, but I think I might have a friend. You remember Marlee from Kent? I met

her on the way over to Angeles. She's very bright and
friendly. If I have to come home anytime soon, I'm
hoping she makes it to the end.

I have met the prince. The king and queen, too. They're
even more regal in person. I haven't spoken to them
yet, but I did talk to Prince Maxon. He's a surprisingly
generous person . . . I think.

I have to go, but I love you and miss you, and I'll write
again as soon as I can.

Love,
America

I didn't think there was anything shocking in there, but I could have been wrong. I was imagining May reading it over and over again, finding hidden details about my life in the words. I wondered if she'd read this before she ate the pastries.

P.S. May, don't these strawberry tarts just make you
want to cry?

There. That was the best I could do.

Apparently, it wasn't good enough. A butler knocked on my door that evening with an envelope from my family and an update.

"She didn't cry, miss. She said they were so good she could have—as you suggested—but she did not actually cry. His Majesty will come and get you from your room around five tomorrow. Please be ready."

I wasn't so upset about losing, but I seriously would have enjoyed the pants. At least, if I couldn't have that, I had letters. I realized that this was the first time I'd been parted from my family for more than a few hours. We weren't wealthy enough to go on trips, and since I didn't really have friends growing up, I'd never even spent the night away. If only there was a way I could get letters every day. I supposed it could be done, but it would have to be so expensive.

I read Dad's first. He went on and on about how beautiful I looked on TV and how proud he was of me. He said I shouldn't have sent three boxes of tarts, because May was going to get spoiled. Three boxes! For goodness' sake.

He went on to say that Aspen had been at the house helping with paperwork, so he'd taken a box home to his family. I didn't know how to feel about that. On the one hand, I was glad they would have something so decadent to eat. On the other, I just imagined him sharing some with his new girlfriend. Someone he could spoil. I wondered if he was jealous of Maxon's gift, or if he was glad to be rid of my attention.

I lingered on those lines much longer than I meant to.

Dad closed by saying he was pleased I'd made a friend. Said I always was slow in that department. I folded the letter up and ran my finger over his signature on the outside. I'd never noticed how funny he signed his name before.

Gerad's letter was short and to the point. He missed me, he loved me, and please send more food. I laughed out loud at that.

Mom was bossy. Even in print I could hear her tone, smugly congratulating me on already earning the prince's affections—she had been informed that I was the only one to get gifts to send home—and telling me firmly to keep up whatever I was doing.

Yeah, Mom, I'll just keep telling the prince that he has absolutely no shot with me and offend him as often as I can. Great plan.

I was glad I'd saved May's for last.

Her letter was absolutely giddy. She admitted how jealous she was that I was eating like that all the time. She also complained that Mom was bossing her around more. I knew how that felt. The rest was a barrage of questions. Was Maxon as cute in person as he was on TV? What was I wearing now? Could she come and visit the palace? Did Maxon have a secret brother who would be willing to marry her one day?

I giggled and embraced my collection of letters. I'd have to make the effort to write back soon. There had to be a telephone around here somewhere, but so far no one had made us aware of it. Even if I had one in my room, it would probably be overkill to call home daily. Besides, these letters would be fun to hold on to. Proof I'd really been here when this whole place would be a memory.

I went to bed with the comforting knowledge that my family was doing well, and that warmth lulled me into a sound sleep that was only hitched by a twinge of nerves at being alone with Maxon again. I couldn't quite pin down the reason, but I hoped it was all for nothing.

"For the sake of appearances, would you please take my arm?" Maxon asked as he escorted me from my room the next day. I was a little hesitant, but I did.

My maids had already put me in my evening dress: a little blue thing with an empire waist and capped sleeves. My arms were bare, and I could feel the starched fabric of Maxon's suit against my skin. Something about it all made me uncomfortable. He must have noticed, because he tried to distract me.

"I'm sorry she didn't cry," he said.

"No you're not." My joking tone made it clear I wasn't too upset about losing.

"I've never gambled before. It was nice to win." His tone was slightly apologetic.

"Beginner's luck."

He smiled. "Perhaps. Next time we'll try to make her laugh."

I instantly started running scenarios through my mind. What from the palace would make May just die with laughter?

Maxon could tell I was thinking about her. "What's your family like?"

"What do you mean?"

"Just that. Your family must be very different from mine."

"I'd say so." I laughed. "For one, no one wears their tiaras to breakfast."

Maxon smiled. "More of a dinner thing at the Singer house?"

"Of course."

He chuckled quietly. I was starting to think maybe Maxon wasn't nearly the snob I'd suspected he was.

"Well, I'm the middle child of five."

"Five!"

"Yeah, five. Most families out there have lots of kids. I'd have lots if I could."

"Oh, really?" Maxon's eyebrows were raised.

"Yes," I answered. My voice was low. I couldn't quite say why, but that seemed like a very intimate detail about my life. Only one other person had really known about it.

I felt a spasm of sadness but shoved it away.

"Anyway, my oldest sister, Kenna, is married to a Four. She works in a factory now. My mom wants me to marry at least a Four, but I don't want to have to stop singing. I love it too much. But I guess I'm a Three now. That's really weird. I think I'm going to try to stay in music if I can.

"Kota is next. He's an artist. We don't see much of him these days. He did come to see me off, but that's about it.

"Then there's me."

Maxon smiled effortlessly. "America Singer," he announced, "my closest friend."

"That's right." I rolled my eyes. There was no way I could actually be his closest friend. At least not yet. But I had to admit, he was the only person I'd ever really confided in who wasn't family or someone I was in love with. Well,

Marlee, too. Could it be the same way for him?

Slowly we moved down the hallway and toward the stairs. He didn't appear to be in any sort of rush.

"After me there's May. She's the one who sold me out and didn't cry. Honestly, I was robbed; I can't believe she didn't cry! But yeah, she's an artist. I . . . I adore her."

Maxon examined my face. Talking about May softened me a bit. I liked Maxon well enough, but I didn't know how far I wanted to let him in.

"And then Gerad. He's the baby; he's seven. He hasn't quite figured out if he's into music or art yet. Mostly he likes to play ball and study bugs, which is fine except that he can't make a living that way. We're trying to get him to experiment more. Anyway, that's everyone."

"What about your parents?" he pressed.

"What about *your* parents?" I replied.

"You know my parents."

"No, I don't. I know the public image of them. What are they really like?" I pulled on his arm, which was quite a feat. Maxon's arms were huge. Even beneath the layers of his suit, I could feel the strong, steady muscles there. Maxon sighed, but I could tell I didn't really exasperate him at all. He seemed to like having someone pester him. It must be sad to grow up in this place without any siblings.

He started thinking about what he was going to say as we stepped into the garden. The guards all wore sly smiles as we passed. Just past them a camera crew waited. Of course they would want to be present for the prince's first date. Maxon

shook his head at them, and they retreated indoors immediately. I heard someone curse. I wasn't particularly looking
forward to being followed around by cameras, but it seemed
strange to dismiss them.

"Are you all right? You seem tense," Maxon noted.

"You get confused by crying women, I get confused by
walks with princes," I said with a shrug.

Maxon laughed quietly at that but said no more. As we
moved west, the sun was blocked by the massive forest on
the grounds, though it was still early in the evening. The
shade crept over us, creating a tent of darkness. When I'd
sought isolation the other night, this was where I wanted to
be. We truly seemed alone now. We walked on, away from
the palace and out of earshot of the guards.

"What about me is so confusing?"

I hesitated but said what I felt. "Your character. Your intentions. I'm not sure what to expect out of this little stroll."

"Ah." He stopped walking and faced me. We were very
close to each other, and in spite of the warm summer air, a
chill ran down my spine. "I think you can tell by now that
I'm not the type of man to beat around the bush. I'll tell you
exactly what I want from you."

Maxon took a step closer.

My breath caught in my throat. I'd just walked into the
very situation I feared. No guards, no cameras, no one to
stop him from doing whatever he wanted.

Knee-jerk reaction. Literally. I kneed His Majesty in the
thigh. Hard.

Maxon let out a yell and reached down, clutching himself as I backed away from him. "What was that for?"

"If you lay a single finger on me, I'll do worse!" I promised.

"What?"

"I said, if you—"

"No, no, you crazy girl, I heard you the first time." Maxon grimaced. "But just what in the world do you mean by it?"

I felt the heat run through my body. I'd jumped to the worst possible conclusion and set myself up to fight something that obviously wasn't coming.

The guards ran up, alerted by our little squabble. Maxon waved them away from an awkward, half-bent position.

We were quiet for a while, and once Maxon was over the worst of his pain, he faced me.

"What did you think I wanted?" he asked.

I ducked my head and blushed.

"America, what did you think I wanted?" He sounded upset. More than upset. Offended. He had obviously guessed what I'd assumed, and he didn't like that one bit. "In public? You thought . . . for heaven's sake. I'm a gentleman!"

He started to walk away but turned back.

"Why did you even offer to help if you think so little of me?"

I couldn't even look him in the eye. I didn't know how to explain I had been prepped to expect a dog, that the darkness and privacy made me feel strange, that I'd only ever been alone with one other boy and that was how we behaved.

"You'll be taking dinner in your room tonight. I'll deal

with this in the morning."

I waited in the garden until I knew all the others would be in the dining hall, and then I paced up and down the hallway before I went into my room. Anne, Mary, and Lucy were beside themselves when I came in. I didn't have the heart to tell them I hadn't spent the whole time with the prince.

My meal had been delivered and was waiting on the table by the balcony. I was hungry now that I wasn't distracted by my own humiliation. But my long absence wasn't the reason my maids were in a tizzy. There was a very large box on the bed, begging to be opened.

"Can we see?" Lucy asked.

"Lucy, that's rude!" Anne chided.

"They dropped it off the moment you left! We've been wondering ever since!" Mary exclaimed.

"Mary! Manners!" Anne scolded.

"No, don't worry, girls. I don't have any secrets." When they came to kick me out tomorrow, I'd tell my maids why.

I gave them a weak smile as I pulled at the big red bow on the box. Inside were three pairs of pants. A linen set, another that was more businesslike but soft to the touch, and a glorious pair made from denim. There was a card resting on top with the Illéa emblem on it.

You ask for such simple things, I can't deny you. But for my sake, only on Saturdays, please. Thank you for your company.
Your friend,
Maxon

CHAPTER 13

I DIDN'T REALLY HAVE THAT much time to feel ashamed or worried, all things considered. When my maids dressed me the next morning without a hint of worry, I assumed my presence downstairs would be welcome. Even allowing me to come down to breakfast showed a hint of kindness in Maxon I hadn't been expecting: I got a last meal, a last moment as one of the beautiful Selected.

We were halfway through breakfast before Kriss worked up the courage to ask me about our date.

"How was it?" she asked quietly, the way we were meant to speak at mealtimes. But those three small words made ears all up and down the table perk up, and everyone within hearing distance was paying attention.

I took a breath. "Indescribable."

The girls looked at one another, clearly hoping for more.

"How did he act?" Tiny asked.

"Umm." I tried to choose my words carefully. "Not at all how I expected he would."

This time, little murmurs went down the table.

"Are you being like that on purpose?" Zoe interjected. "If you are, it's awfully mean."

I shook my head. How could I explain this? "No, it's just that—"

But I was spared trying to form an answer by the confusing noises coming down the hallway.

The shouts were strange. In my very short time at the palace, not a single sound had registered as anything close to loud. Beyond that, there was a kind of music to the click of the guards' shoes on the floor, the massive doors opening and closing, the forks touching the plates. This was complete and absolute mayhem.

The royal family seemed to understand it before the rest of us.

"To the back of the room, ladies!" King Clarkson yelled, and ran over to a window.

Girls, confused but not wanting to disobey, slowly moved toward the head table. The king was pulling down a shade, but it wasn't the typical light-filtering kind. It was metal and squealed into place. Beside him Maxon came and drew down another. And beside Maxon the lovely and delicate queen was racing to pull down the next.

That was when the wave of guards made it into the dining hall. I saw a number of them lining up outside the room just before the monstrous doors were closed, bolted, and secured with bars.

"They're inside the walls, Majesty, but we're holding them back. The ladies should leave, but we're so close to the door—"

"Understood, Markson," the king replied, cutting off the sentence.

It didn't take more than that for me to comprehend. There were rebels inside the grounds.

I'd figured it would come. This many guests in the palace, so many preparations going on. Surely someone would miss something somewhere and let our safety slip. And even if there were no easy way in, this would be an excellent time to mount a protest. At its barest of bones, the Selection was kind of disturbing. I was sure the rebels hated it along with everything else about Illéa.

But whatever their opinion, I wasn't going down quietly.

I pushed my chair back so quickly it fell over, and I ran to the closest window to pull down the metal shade. A few other girls who understood how threatened we were did the same.

It took me only a moment to get the thing down, but locking it into place was a little more difficult. I had just managed to get the latch right when something crashed into the metal plate from outside the palace, sending me screaming backward until I tripped over my fallen chair and tumbled to the ground.

Maxon appeared immediately.

"Are you hurt?"

I did a quick evaluation. I'd probably have a bruise on my hip, and I was scared, but that was the worst of it.

"No, I'm fine."

"To the back of the room. Now!" he ordered as he helped me off the ground. He raced down the hall, snatching up girls who had begun to freeze up in fear and ushering them to the back corner.

I obeyed, running to the back of the room, toward the clusters of girls huddled together. Some of them were weeping; others were staring into space in shock. Tiny had fainted. The most reassuring sight was King Clarkson talking intently to a guard along the back wall, just far away enough that the girls wouldn't hear. He had one arm wrapped protectively around the queen, who stood quietly and proudly beside him.

How many times had she survived attacks now? We got reports that these happened several times a year. That had to be unnerving. The odds were getting slimmer and slimmer for her . . . and her husband . . . and her only child. Surely, eventually, the rebels would figure out the right alignment of circumstances to get what they wanted. Yet she stood there, her chin set, her still face wearing a quiet calm.

I surveyed the girls. Did any of them have the strength it would take to be the queen? Tiny was still unconscious in someone's arms. Celeste and Bariel were making conversation. I knew what Celeste looked like at ease, and this wasn't it. Still, compared to the others, she hid her emotions well.

Others were near hysterics, whimpering on their knees. Some had mentally shut down, blocking out the entire ordeal. Their faces were blank, and they absently wrung their hands, waiting for it to end.

Marlee was crying a little, but not so much that she looked like a wreck. I grabbed her arm and pulled her upright.

"Dry your eyes and stand up straight," I barked into her ear.

"What?" she squeaked.

"Trust me, do it."

Marlee wiped her face on the side of her gown and stood up a little taller. She touched her face in several places, checking for smudged makeup, I guessed. Then she turned and looked at me for approval.

"Good job. Sorry to be so bossy, but trust me on this one, okay?" I felt bad ordering her around in the middle of something so distressing, but she had to look as calm as Queen Amberly. Surely Maxon would want that in his queen, and Marlee had to win.

Marlee nodded her head. "No, you're right. I mean, for the time being, everyone is safe. I shouldn't be so worried."

I nodded back to her, though she was most assuredly wrong. *Everyone* was not safe.

Guards waited on edge by the massive doors as heavy things were thrown against wall and windows again and again. There wasn't a clock in here. I had no idea how long this attack was lasting, and that only made me more anxious. How would we know if they got inside? Would it only be once they started banging on the doors? Were they already inside and we just didn't know it?

I couldn't take the worry. I stared at a vase of ornate flowers—none of which I knew the names of—and bit away at one of my perfectly manicured nails. I pretended that those flowers were all that mattered in the world.

Eventually Maxon came by to check on me, as he had with the others. He stood beside me and stared at the flowers, too. Neither of us really knew what to say.

"Are you doing all right?" he finally asked.

"Yes," I whispered.

He paused a moment. "You seem unwell."

"What will happen to my maids?" I asked, voicing my greatest worry. I knew I was safe. Where were they? What if one of them had been walking down the hall as the rebels made their way in?

"Your maids?" he asked in a tone that implied I was an idiot.

"Yes, my maids." I looked into his eyes, shaming him into acknowledging that only a choice minority of the throngs who lived in the palace were actually being protected. I was on the verge of tears. I didn't want them to come, and I was breathing rapidly trying to keep my emotions at bay.

He looked into my eyes and seemed to understand that I was only one step up from being a maid myself. That wasn't the reason for my worry, but it did seem strange that a lottery was the main difference between someone like Anne and me.

"They should be hiding by now. The help have their

own places to wait. The guards are very good about getting around quickly and alerting everyone. They ought to be fine. We usually have an alarm system, but the last time they came through, the rebels thoroughly dismantled it. They've been working on fixing it, but . . ." Maxon sighed.

I looked at the floor, trying to quiet all the worries in my head.

"America," he begged.

I turned to Maxon.

"They're fine. The rebels were slow, and everyone here knows what to do in an emergency."

I nodded. We stood there quietly for a minute, and I could tell he was about to move on.

"Maxon," I whispered.

He turned back, a little surprised to be addressed so casually.

"About last night. Let me explain. When they came to prep us, to get us ready to come here, there was a man who told me that I was never to turn you down. No matter what you asked for. Not ever."

He was dumbfounded. "What?"

"He made it sound like you might ask for certain things. And you said yourself that you hadn't been around many women. After eighteen years . . . and then you sent the cameras away. I just got scared when you got that close to me."

Maxon shook his head, trying to process all this. Humiliation, rage, and disbelief all played across his typically even-tempered face.

"Was everyone told this?" he asked, sounding appalled at the idea.

"I don't know. I can't imagine many girls would need such a warning. *They're* probably waiting to pounce on you," I noted, nodding my head toward the rest of the room.

He gave a dark chuckle. "But you're not, so you had absolutely no qualms about kneeing me in the groin, right?"

"I hit your thigh!"

"Oh, please. A man doesn't need that long to recover from a knee to the thigh," he replied, his voice full of skepticism.

A laugh escaped me. Thankfully, Maxon joined in. Just then another mass hit the windows, and we stopped in unison. For a moment I had forgotten where I was.

"So how are you handling a roomful of crying women?" I asked.

There was a comical bewilderment in his expression. "Nothing in the world is more confusing!" he whispered urgently. "I haven't the faintest clue how to stop it."

This was the man who was going to lead our country: the guy rendered useless by tears. It was too funny.

"Try patting them on the back or shoulder and telling them everything is going to be fine. Lots of times when girls cry, they don't want you to fix the problem, they just want to be consoled," I advised.

"Really?"

"Pretty much."

"It can't possibly be that simple." Intrigue and doubt played in his voice.

"I said most of the time, not all the time. But it would probably work for a lot of the girls here."

He snorted. "I'm not so sure. Two have already asked if I'll let them leave if this ever ends."

"I thought we weren't allowed to do that." I shouldn't have been surprised, though. If he had agreed to let me stay on as a friend, he couldn't be too concerned with technicalities. "What are you going to do?"

"What else can I do? I won't keep someone here against her will."

"Maybe they'll change their minds," I offered hopefully.

"Maybe." He paused. "What about you? Have you been scared off yet?" he asked almost playfully.

"Honestly? I was convinced you were sending me home after breakfast anyway," I admitted.

"Honestly? I had considered that myself."

There was a quiet smile between us. Our friendship—if I could even call it that—was obviously awkward and flawed, but at least it was honest.

"You didn't answer me. Do you want to leave?"

Another something hit the wall, and the idea sounded appealing. The worst attack I'd gotten at home was Gerad trying to steal my food. The girls here didn't care for me, the clothes were stifling, people were trying to hurt me, and the whole thing felt uncomfortable. But it was good for my family and nice to be full. Maxon did seem a bit lost, and I'd get to stay away from *him* for a little bit longer. And who knew, maybe I could help pick out the next princess.

I looked Maxon in the eye. "If you're not kicking me out, I'm not leaving."

He smiled. "Good. You'll need to tell me more tricks like this shoulder-patting thing."

I smiled back. Yes, it was all wrong, but some good would come out of this.

"America, could you do me a favor?"

I nodded.

"As far as anyone knows, we spent a lot of time together yesterday evening. If anyone asks, could you please tell them that I'm not . . . that I wouldn't . . ."

"Of course. And I really am sorry about everything."

"I should have known that if any girl was going to disobey an order, it would be you."

A collection of heavy objects hit the wall at once, making a handful of girls scream.

"Who are they? What do they want?" I asked.

"Who? The rebels?"

I nodded.

"Depends on who you ask. And which group you're talking about," he answered.

"You mean there's more than one?" That made the entire experience much worse. If this was one group, what could two or more do together? As far as I knew, a rebel was a rebel was a rebel, but Maxon made it sound like some could be worse than others. "How many are there?"

"Two generally, the Northerners and the Southerners. The Northerners attack much more frequently. They're closer.

They live in the rainy patch of Likely near Bellingham, just north of here. No one really wants to live there—it's practically all ruins—so they've made it a home of sorts, though I guess they travel. The traveling is one theory of mine—one no one listens to. But they're far less likely to break in, and when they do the results are . . . tame almost. I'd guess that this is a Northern job right now," he said over the din.

"Why? What makes them so different from the Southerners?"

Maxon seemed to hesitate, unsure if this information was something I should know. He looked around to see if anyone could hear us. I looked around, too, and saw that several people were watching us. In particular, Celeste looked like she was trying to set me on fire with her eyes. I didn't keep eye contact for long. Still, even with all the onlookers, no one was close enough to hear. When Maxon came to the same conclusion, he leaned in to whisper.

"Their attacks are much more . . . lethal."

I shivered. "Lethal?"

He nodded. "They only come about once or twice a year, as best I can tell from the aftermath. I think that everyone here is trying to protect me from the statistics, but I'm not stupid. People die when they come. The trouble is, both groups look alike to us—dingy, mostly men, lean but strong, no sort of emblem as far as we can tell—so we don't know what we're getting until it's all over."

I looked around the room. A lot of people were in danger if Maxon was wrong and they happened to be Southerners.

I thought of my poor maids again.

"But I still don't understand. What do they want?"

Maxon shrugged. "The Southerners appear to want us demolished. I don't know why, but I'm guessing some dissatisfaction or another, tired of living on the fringes of society. I mean, they're not even Eights technically, since they have no part in the social network. But the Northerners are a bit of a mystery. Father says they just want to bother us, disrupt our governing, but I don't think so." He looked rather proud for a moment. "I have another theory about that as well."

"Do I get to know it?"

Maxon hesitated again. I guessed this time it wasn't so much out of fear of scaring me, but perhaps not being taken seriously.

He came close again and whispered, "I think they're looking for something."

"What?" I wondered.

"That I don't know. But it's always the same around here after the Northerners come. Guards are knocked out, injured, or tied up, but never killed. It's like they just don't want to be followed around. Though some people get taken with them, and that's a bit disturbing. And then the rooms— well, all the ones they can get into—they're a mess. Every drawer pulled out, shelves searched, carpet upturned. Lots of things get broken. You wouldn't believe the number of cameras I've replaced over the years."

"Cameras?"

"Oh," he said bashfully. "I like photography. But despite

all that, they don't end up taking much. Father thinks my idea is rubbish, of course. What could a bunch of illiterate barbarians be looking for? Still, I think there must be something."

It was intriguing. If I was penniless and knew how to break into the palace, I think I'd take every piece of jewelry I could find, anything I could sell. These rebels must have something in mind beyond a mere political statement or their day-to-day survival in mind when they came here.

"Do you think it's silly?" Maxon asked, bringing me out of my wonderings.

"No, not silly. Confusing, but not silly."

We shared a small smile. I realized that if Maxon had simply been Maxon Schreave and not Maxon, future king of Illéa, he would be the kind of person I would have wanted to be my next-door neighbor, someone to talk to.

He cleared his throat. "I suppose I should finish my rounds."

"Yes, I imagine there are quite a few ladies wondering what's taking you so long."

"So, *buddy*, any suggestions as to whom I should speak with next?"

I smiled and looked behind me to make sure my candidate for princess was still holding it together. She was.

"See the blond girl over there in the pink? That's Marlee. Sweetheart, very kind, loves movies. Go."

Maxon chuckled and walked in her direction.

⊰⋅⊱

The time in the dining hall felt like an eternity, but the attack had only lasted a little over an hour. We found out later that no one had actually gotten inside the palace, just inside the grounds. The guards didn't shoot at the rebels until they tried for the main doors, which accounted for the bricks—bricks that had been gouged out of the palace walls—and rotten food being thrown at the windows for so long.

In the end, two men got too close to the doors, shots were fired, and they all fled. If Maxon's labels were correct, I would assume these were Northerners.

They kept us tucked away for a little while longer, searching the perimeter of the palace. When everything was as it should be, we were released to our rooms. I walked arm in arm with Marlee. Despite holding it together downstairs, the strain of the attack had exhausted me, and I was glad to have someone to distract me from it.

"He let you have the pants anyway?" she asked. I had started talking about Maxon as soon as I could, eager to know how their conversation had gone.

"Yeah. He was very generous about it all."

"I think it's charming that he's a good winner."

"He is a good winner. He's even gracious when he's gotten the raw end of things." Like a knee to the royal jewels, for example.

"What do you mean?"

"Nothing." I didn't want to explain that one. "What did you two talk about today?"

"Well, he asked me if I'd like to see him this week." She blushed.

"Marlee! That's great!"

"Hush!" she said, looking around, though the rest of the girls had already ascended the stairs. "I'm trying not to get my hopes up."

We were quiet for a minute before she burst.

"Who am I kidding? I'm so excited I can barely stand it! I hope he won't take too long to call on me."

"If he's already asked, I'm sure he'll follow through soon. I mean, after he finishes running the country for the day, that is."

She laughed. "I can't believe this! I mean, I knew he was handsome, but I wasn't sure how he'd behave. I was worried he'd be . . . I don't know, stuffy or something."

"Me, too. But he's actually . . ." What was Maxon actually? He was sort of stuffy, but not in a way that was as off-putting as I'd imagined. Undeniably a prince, but still so . . . so . . . "Normal."

Marlee wasn't looking at me anymore. She'd lost herself in a daydream as we walked. I hoped that this image of Maxon that she was building was one he could deliver. And that she would be the kind of girl he wanted. I left her at her door with a small wave and went on to my room.

My thoughts of Marlee and Maxon flew out of my head as soon as I opened the door. Anne and Mary were crouched around a very distressed Lucy. Her face was red with tears falling down her cheeks; her usual tiny trembles were full-on shakes, racking her entire body.

"Calm down now, Lucy, everything's fine," Anne was whispering as she stroked Lucy's messy hair.

"Everything is over now. No one was hurt. You're safe, dear," Mary cooed, holding a twitching hand.

I was too shocked to speak. This moment was Lucy's private struggle, not meant for my eyes. I went to back out of my room, but Lucy caught me before I could back away.

"S-s-sorry, Lady, Lady, Lady . . . ," she stammered. The others looked up with anxious expressions.

"Don't trouble yourself. Are you all right?" I asked, closing the door so no one else would see.

Lucy tried to start again, but couldn't form the words. Her tears and the shaking were overwhelming her little body.

"She'll be fine, miss," Anne interceded. "It takes a few hours, but she calms down once everything's quiet. If it stays bad, we can take her to the hospital wing." Anne dropped her voice. "Only Lucy doesn't want that. If they think you're unfit, they hide you down in the laundry rooms or the kitchen. Lucy likes being a maid."

I didn't know who Anne thought she was hiding her voice from. We were all surrounding Lucy, and she could hear those words clearly, even in her state.

"P-p-please, miss. I don't—I don't—I . . . ," she tried.

"Hush. No one's turning you in," I told her. I looked to Anne and Mary. "Help me get her on the bed."

With the three of us it should have been easy, but Lucy was writhing so that her arms and legs would slip from our hands. It took quite a bit of effort to get her settled. Once we tucked her under the covers, the comfort of the bed seemed to do more than our words could. Lucy's shudders became slower, and she stared vacantly at the canopy above the bed.

Mary sat on the edge of the bed and started humming a tune, reminding me all too much of the way I would baby May when she was sick. I pulled Anne into a corner, far away from Lucy's ears.

"What happened? Did someone get through?" I asked. I would expect to be told if that were the case.

"No, no," Anne assured me. "Lucy always gets like this when the rebels come. Just talking about them will send her into a crying fit. She . . ."

Anne looked down to her polished black shoes, trying to decide if she should tell me something. I didn't want to pry into Lucy's life, but I did want to understand. She took a deep breath and started.

"Some of us were born here. Mary was born in the castle, and her parents are still here. I was an orphan, taken in because the palace needed staff." She straightened her dress, as if she could rub off this piece of her history that seemed to bother her. "Lucy was sold to the palace."

"Sold? How can that be? There aren't slaves here."

"Not technically, no, but that doesn't mean it doesn't happen. Lucy's family needed money for an operation for her mother. They gave their services over to a family of Threes in exchange for the money. Her mother never got better, they never made their way out of the debt, so Lucy and her father had been living with this family for ages. From what I understand, it wasn't much better than living in a barn with the way they were kept.

"The son had taken a liking to Lucy, and I know sometimes it doesn't matter what caste you're in, but Six to Three is quite a jump. When his mother discovered his intentions for Lucy, she sold her and her father to the palace. I remember when she came. Cried for days. They must have been terribly in love."

I looked over at Lucy. At least in my case, one of us got to make the decision. She had no choice when it came to losing the man she loved.

"Lucy's dad works in the stables. He's not very fast or strong, but he's incredibly dedicated. And Lucy is a maid. I know it might seem silly to you, but it's an honor to be a maid in the palace. We are the front line. We are the ones deemed fit enough and smart enough and attractive enough to be seen by anyone who comes to call. We take our positions seriously, and with reason. If you screw up, you're put in the kitchen, where your fingers are working all day, and the clothes are baggy. Or you chop firewood or rake the grounds. It's no small thing to be a maid."

I felt stupid. In my mind, they were all Sixes. But there were rankings even within that, statuses that I didn't understand.

"Two years ago, there was an attack on the palace in the middle of the night. They got the guards' uniforms, and everyone was confused. It was such disarray, no one knew who to attack or defend, and people slipped through holes in the lines . . . it was terrifying."

I shuddered just thinking about it. The dark, the confusion, the wide expanse of the palace. Compared to this morning, it sounded like the work of Southerners.

"One of the rebels got ahold of Lucy." Anne ducked her eyes for a minute. She spoke her next lines quietly. "I'm not sure they have very many women with them, if you catch my meaning."

"Oh."

"I didn't see this myself, but Lucy told me that this man was covered in grime. She said he kept licking her face."

Anne cringed away from the thought. My stomach heaved, threatening to bring up my breakfast. It was positively revolting, and I could see how someone who'd already been as scarred as Lucy would break under that kind of attack.

"He was dragging her off somewhere, and she was screaming as loud as she could. In the commotion, it was hard to hear her cries. But another guard came around the corner, a real one. He took aim and fired a bullet right through the man's head. The rebel fell to the ground, pinning Lucy. She was covered in blood."

I covered my mouth. I couldn't imagine delicate little Lucy going through all that. No wonder she reacted this way.

"She was treated for some cuts, but no one ever really saw to her mind. She's a little jittery now but tries to hide it as best she can. And it's not just for her sake, but her father's. He's so proud that his daughter is good enough to be a maid. She doesn't want to let him down. We try to keep her calm, but every time the rebels come, she thinks it's going to be worse. Someone's going to take her this time, hurt her, kill her.

"She's trying, miss, but I'm not sure how much more of this she can stand."

I nodded, looking over to Lucy in the bed. She had closed her eyes and fallen asleep, even though it was still quite early.

I spent the rest of the day reading. Anne and Mary cleaned things that weren't dirty. We all stayed quiet while Lucy recovered.

I promised myself that, if I could help it, Lucy wouldn't have to go through that again.

CHAPTER 14

As I predicted, the girls who had asked to go home changed their minds once everything had settled down. None of us knew exactly who had wanted out, but there were some—Celeste in particular—who were determined to find out. For the time being we remained at twenty-seven girls.

The attack was so inconsequential, according to the king, that it barely warranted notice. However, since camera crews had been making their way in that morning, some of it was aired live. Apparently the king wasn't pleased about that. It made me wonder just how many attacks the palace suffered through that we never heard about. Was it far less safe here than I'd thought?

Silvia explained that if the attack had been much worse, we would have all been able to call our families and tell them we were safe. As it was, we were instructed to write letters home instead.

I wrote that I was well and that the attack probably seemed worse than it was and that the king had us all kept safely tucked away. I urged them not to worry about me and told them that I missed them and handed the letter off to a helpful maid.

The day after the attack passed without incident. I had planned on going down to the Women's Room to talk up Maxon to the others, but after seeing Lucy so shaken, I chose to keep to my room.

I didn't know what my three maids busied themselves with while I was away, but when I was in the room, they played card games with me and let pieces of gossip slip into the conversation.

I learned that for every dozen people I saw in the palace, there were a hundred or more behind them. The cooks and laundresses I knew about, but there were also people whose sole job was to keep the windows clean. It took a solid week for the team to get them all done, by the end of which the dust would find its way past the palace walls and cling to the clean glass, and they'd have to be washed all over again. There were also jewelers hidden away, making pieces for the family and gifts for visitors, and teams of seamstresses and buyers keeping the royal family—and now us—immaculately clothed.

I learned other things, too. The guards they thought were the cutest and the horrid new design of a dress the head maid was making the staff wear for the holiday parties. How some in the palace were taking bets on which Selected girl might win and that I was in the top ten picks. A baby of one of the cooks was sick beyond hope, which made Anne tear up a bit. This girl happened to be a close friend of hers, and the couple had been waiting so long for a child.

Listening to them and joining in when I had something worth saying, I couldn't imagine anything more entertaining happening downstairs and was glad to have such company. The mood in my room was a quiet and happy one.

The day had been so nice, I stayed up there the day after as well. This time, we kept the doors open to both the hallway and the balcony, and the warm air filtered in and wrapped itself around us. It seemed to do particularly wonderful things for Lucy, and I wondered how often she actually got to step outside.

Anne made a comment about how this was all inappropriate—me sitting with them, playing games with the doors open—but let it drop almost immediately. She was quickly getting over trying to make me the lady it seemed I ought to be.

We were in the middle of a game of cards when I noticed a figure out of the corner of my eye. It was Maxon, standing at the open door, looking amused. As our eyes met, I could see that his expression was clearly asking what in the world I was doing. I stood, smiling, and walked over to him.

"Oh, sweet Lord," Anne muttered as she realized the prince was at the door. She immediately swept the cards into a sewing basket and stood, Mary and Lucy following suit.

"Ladies," Maxon said.

"Your Majesty," she said with a curtsy. "Such an honor, sir."

"For me as well," he answered with a smile.

The maids looked back and forth to one another, flattered. We were all silent for a moment, not quite sure what to do.

Mary suddenly piped up. "We were just leaving."

"Yes! That's right," Lucy added. "We were—uh—just . . ." She looked to Anne for help.

"Going to finish Lady America's dress for Friday," Anne concluded.

"That's right," Mary said. "Only two days left."

They slowly circled us to get out of the room, huge smiles plastered on their faces.

"Wouldn't want to keep you from your work," Maxon said, following them with his eyes, completely fascinated with their behavior.

Once in the hall, they gave awkwardly mistimed curtsies and walked away at a feverish pace. Immediately after they rounded the corner, Lucy's giggles echoed down the corridor, followed by Anne's intense hushing.

"Quite a group you have," Maxon said, walking into my room, surveying the space.

"They keep me on my toes," I answered with a smile.

"It's clear they have affection for you. That's hard to find." He stopped looking at my room and faced me. "This isn't what I imagined your room would look like."

I raised an arm and let it fall. "It's not really my room, is it? It belongs to you, and I just happen to be borrowing it."

He made a face. "Surely they told you that changes could be made? A new bed, different paint."

I shrugged. "A coat of paint wouldn't make this mine. Girls like me don't live in houses with marble floors," I joked.

Maxon smiled. "What does your room at home look like?"

"Um, what did you come for exactly?" I hedged.

"Oh! I had an idea."

"About?"

"Well," he started, continuing to walk around the room, "I thought that since you and I don't have the typical relationship that I have with the other girls, maybe we should have . . . alternative means of communication." He stopped in front of my mirror and looked at the pictures of my family. "Your little sister looks just like you," he said, amused by this observation.

I walked deeper into my room. "We get that a lot. What was that about alternative communication?"

Maxon finished up with the pictures and moved toward the piano in the back. "Since you are supposed to be helping me, being my friend and all," he continued with a pointed look at me, "perhaps we shouldn't be relying on the traditional notes sent through maids and formal invitations for dates. I was thinking something a little less ceremonial."

He picked up the sheet music on top of the piano. "Did you bring these?"

"No, those were here. Anything I really want to play, I can do from memory."

His eyebrows rose. "Impressive." He moved back in my direction without finishing his explanation.

"Could you please stop poking around and complete an entire thought?"

Maxon sighed. "Fine. What I was thinking was that you and I could have a sign or something, some way of communicating that we need to speak to each other that no one else would catch onto. Perhaps rubbing our noses?" Maxon ran a finger back and forth just above his lips.

"That looks like your nose is stopped up. Not attractive."

He gave me a slightly perplexed look and nodded. "Very well. Perhaps we could simply run our fingers through our hair?"

I shook my head almost immediately. "My hair is almost always pulled up with pins. It's nearly impossible to get my fingers through it. Besides, what if you happen to be wearing your crown? You'd knock it off your head."

He shook a thoughtful finger at me. "Excellent point. Hmmm." He passed me, continuing to think, and stopped near the table by my bed. "What about tugging your ear?"

I considered. "I like it. Simple enough to hide, but not so common we could mistake it for something else. Ear tugging it is."

Maxon's attention was fixated on something, but he

turned to smile at me. "I'm glad you approve. The next time you want to see me, simply tug your ear, and I'll come as soon as I'm able. Probably after dinner," he concluded with a shrug.

Before I could ask about me coming to him, Maxon strolled across the room with my jar in his hand. "What in the world is this about?"

I sighed. "That, I'm afraid, is beyond explanation."

Friday arrived, and with that came our debut on the *Illéa Capital Report*. It was something that was required of us, but at least this week all we had to do was sit there. With the time difference, we'd go on at five, sit through the hour, and then go off to dinner.

Anne, Mary, and Lucy took extra care in dressing me. The gown was a deep blue, hovering near purple. It was fitted through my hips, and fanned out in satiny smooth waves behind me. I couldn't believe I was touching something so beautiful. Button after button was fastened up my back, and my maids put pins bedecked with pearls in my hair. They added tiny pearl earrings and a necklace made of wire so thin and pearls so far apart they looked like they floated on my skin, and I was done.

I looked in the mirror. I still looked like me. It was the prettiest version of myself I'd seen so far, but I knew that face. Ever since my name had been drawn, I'd feared I would become something unrecognizable—covered in layers of makeup and so hung down with jewelry that I'd have to dig out of it for weeks to find myself again. So far, I was still America.

And, exactly like myself, I found that I was covered in a sheen of sweat as I walked down to the room where they recorded messages at the palace. They'd told us to be there ten minutes early. Ten minutes meant fifteen to me. It meant more like three to someone like Celeste. So the arrival of the girls was staggered.

Hordes of people were swarming around, putting the last touches on the set—which now held rows of tiered seating for the Selected. The council members who I recognized from years of watching the *Report* were there, reading over their scripts and adjusting their ties. The Selected crowd were checking themselves in mirrors and tugging at their extravagant dresses. It was a flurry of activity.

I turned and caught the briefest of moments in Maxon's life. His mother, the beautiful Queen Amberly, pushed some stray hairs back into place. He straightened his jacket and said something to her. She gave a reassuring nod, and Maxon smiled. I would have watched a little longer, but Silvia, in all her glory, came to escort me into place.

"Just head over to the risers, Lady America," she said. "You may sit anywhere you like. So you know, most of the girls have already claimed the front row." She looked sorry for me, as if she were delivering bad news.

"Oh, thank you," I said, and went happily to take a seat in the back.

I didn't like climbing the little steps with a snug dress and such strappy shoes. (Were the shoes really necessary? No one was even going to see my feet.) But I managed. When I saw Marlee come in, she smiled and waved and came to sit right next to me. It meant a great deal to me that she chose a place beside me as opposed to a spot in the second row. She was faithful. She'd make a great queen.

Her dress was a brilliant yellow. With her blond hair and sun-kissed skin, she looked like she was radiating light into the room.

"Marlee, I love that dress. You look fantastic!"

"Oh, thank you." She blushed. "I thought it might be a bit too much."

"Not at all! Trust me, it's perfect on you."

"I've wanted to speak to you, but you've been missing. Do you think we could talk tomorrow?" she asked in a whisper.

"Of course. In the Women's Room, right? It's Saturday," I said in a matched tone.

"Okay," she answered excitedly.

Just in front of us, Amy turned around. "I feel like my pins are falling out. Can you guys check them?"

Without a word, Marlee put her slim fingers in the curls of Amy's hair and checked for loose pins. "That feel better?"

Amy sighed. "Yes, thank you."

"America, is there lipstick on my teeth?" Zoe asked. I turned to my left and found her smiling maniacally, exposing all her pearly whites.

"No, you're good," I answered, seeing out of the corner of my eye that Marlee was nodding in confirmation.

"Thanks. How is he so calm?" Zoe asked, pointing over at Maxon, who was talking to a member of the crew. She then bent down and put her head between her legs and started doing controlled breathing.

Marlee and I looked at each other, eyes wide with amusement, and tried not to laugh. It was hard if we looked at Zoe, so we surveyed the room and chatted about what others were wearing. There were several girls in seductive reds and lively greens, but no one else in blue. Olivia had gone so far as to wear orange. I'd admit that I didn't know that much about fashion, but Marlee and I both agreed that someone should have intervened on her behalf. The color made her skin look kind of green.

Two minutes before the cameras turned on, we realized it wasn't the dress making her look green. Olivia vomited into the closest trash can very loudly and collapsed on the floor. Silvia swooped in, and a fuss was made to wipe the sweat off her and get her into a seat. She was placed in the back row with a small receptacle at her feet, just in case.

Bariel was in the seat in front of her. I couldn't hear what she muttered to the poor girl from where I was, but it looked like Bariel was prepared to injure Olivia should she have another episode near her.

I guessed that Maxon had seen or heard some of the commotion, and I looked over to see if he was having any sort of reaction to it all. But he wasn't looking toward the disturbance; he was looking at me. Quickly—so quickly it would look like nothing but scratching an itch to anyone else—Maxon reached up and tugged on his ear. I repeated the action back, and we both turned away.

I was excited to know that tonight, after dinner, Maxon would be stopping by my room.

Suddenly the anthem music was playing, and I could see the national emblem on tiny screens around the room. I shifted to sit up straighter. All I could think was that my family was going to see me tonight, and I wanted them to be proud.

King Clarkson was at the podium speaking about the brief and unsuccessful attack on the palace. I wouldn't have called it unsuccessful. It managed to scare the daylights out of most of us. Announcement after announcement came, and I tried to be aware of everything they said, but it was hard. I was used to watching this on a comfy couch with bowls of popcorn and family commentary.

Many of the announcements tied into the rebels, placing blame for certain things on their shoulders. The roads being built in Sumner were behind schedule because of the rebels, and the number of local officers in Atlin was down because they'd been sent to help with a rebel-caused disturbance in St. George. I had no idea either of those things had happened. Between everything I'd heard and seen growing up and what I'd learned since coming to the palace, I began to wonder just how much we knew about the rebels. Maybe I just didn't understand, but I didn't think they could be blamed for everything that was wrong with Illéa.

And then, as if he had appeared out of thin air, Gavril

was walking on set after being introduced by the Master of Events.

"Good evening, everyone. Tonight I have a special announcement. The Selection has been going for a week now and eight ladies have already gone home, leaving twenty-seven beautiful women for Prince Maxon to choose from. Next week, by hook or by crook, the majority of the *Illéa Capital Report* will be dedicated to getting to know these amazing young women."

I felt the little beads of sweat pooling on my temple. Sit here and look nice . . . I could do that. But answer questions? I knew I wasn't going to win this little game; that wasn't the issue. I just really, really didn't want to look like a moron in front of the entire country.

"Before we get to the ladies, tonight let's take a moment with the man of the hour. How are you tonight, Prince Maxon?" Gavril said, walking across the stage. Maxon had been ambushed. He didn't have a microphone or prepared answers.

Just before Gavril's microphone reached Maxon's face, I caught his eye and gave him a wink. That tiny action was enough to make him smile.

"I'm very well, Gavril, thank you."

"Are you enjoying your company so far?"

"Yes! It's been a pleasure getting to know these ladies."

"Are they all the sweet, gentle ladies they appear to be?" Gavril asked. Before Maxon replied, the answer brought a smile to my face. Because I knew that it was yes . . . sort of.

179

"Umm . . ." Maxon looked past Gavril at me. "Almost."

"Almost?" Gavril asked, surprised. He turned to us. "Is someone over there being naughty?"

Mercifully, all the girls let out light giggles, so I blended in. The little traitor!

"What exactly did these girls do that isn't so sweet?" Gavril asked Maxon.

"Oh, well, let me tell you." Maxon crossed his legs and got very comfortable in his chair. It was probably the most relaxed I'd ever seen him, sitting there poking fun at me. I liked this side of him. I wished it would come out more often. "One of them had the nerve to yell at me rather forcefully the first time we met. I was given a very severe scolding."

Above Maxon's head, the king and queen exchanged a glance. It seemed they were hearing this story for the first time, too. Beside me the girls were looking at one another, confused. I didn't get it until Marlee said something.

"I don't remember anyone yelling at him in the Great Room. Do you?"

Maxon seemed to have forgotten that our first meeting was meant to be a secret. "I think he's talking it up to make it funnier. I did say some serious things to him. I think he might mean me."

"A scolding, you say? Whatever for?" Gavril continued.

"Honestly, I wasn't really sure. I think it was a bout of homesickness. Which is why I forgave her, of course." Maxon was loose and easy now, talking to Gavril as if he were the only person in the room. I'd have to tell him later how wonderful he did.

"So she's still with us, then?" Gavril looked over at the collection of girls, grinning widely, and then returned to face his prince.

"Oh, yes. She's still here," Maxon said, not letting his eyes wander from Gavril's face. "And I plan on keeping her here for quite a while."

CHAPTER 15

DINNER WAS DISAPPOINTING. NEXT WEEK I'd have to tell my maids to leave some room in the dress for me to eat.

In my room, Anne, Mary, and Lucy waited to help me out of my gown, but I explained that I'd need to stay in it a little bit longer. Anne figured it out first—that Maxon was coming to see me—because I was always eager to get out of the binding clothes.

"Would you like us to stay later tonight? It's no problem," Mary said just a little too hopefully. After the calamity of Maxon visiting earlier this week, I decided sending them out as early as possible was the best way to go. Besides, I couldn't bear to have them watching me until he showed up.

"No, no. I'm fine. If I have a problem with the dress later, I'll ring."

They reluctantly backed out the door and left me to wait

for Maxon. I didn't know how long he'd be, and I didn't want to start a book and have to stop, or sit down at the piano only to hop right back up. I ended up just lounging on the bed, waiting. I let my mind wander. I thought of Marlee and her kindness. I realized that, besides a few small details, I knew very little about her. Still, I trusted that her actions toward me were in no way fake. And then I thought of the girls who were all too fake. I wondered if Maxon could tell the difference.

It seemed like Maxon's experience with women was so great and so small at once. He was gentlemanly enough, but when he got too close, he came undone. It was like he knew how to treat a lady, he just didn't know how to treat a date.

It was quite a contrast to Aspen.

Aspen.

His name, his face, his memory hit me so quickly it was hard to process. Aspen. What was he doing now? It was getting close to curfew in Carolina. He'd still be at work, if he had a job today. Or maybe out with Brenna, or whoever else he'd decided to start spending his time with since we broke up. Part of me ached to know . . . part of me wanted to crumble just thinking about it.

I looked over to my jar. I picked it up and felt the penny slide around, so lonely.

"Me, too," I whispered. "Me, too."

Was it stupid of me to keep this? I'd given back everything else, so why save one little penny? Would this be all I had left? A penny in a jar to show my daughter one day, to tell her about my first boyfriend—the one no one knew about?

I didn't have time to dwell on my worries. Maxon's firm knock came only minutes later. I found myself running to the door.

I drew it open in a big sweep, and Maxon looked surprised to see me.

"Where in the world are your maids?" he asked, surveying my room.

"Gone. I send them off when I come back from dinner."

"Every day?"

"Yes, of course. I can take my clothes off by myself, thank you."

Maxon raised his eyebrows and smiled. I blushed. I hadn't meant it to come out like that.

"Grab a wrap. It's chilly out."

We walked down the hall. I was still a little distracted by my thoughts, and I knew by now that Maxon wasn't great with starting conversations. I had looped my hand around his arm almost immediately, though. I was glad that there was a sort of familiarity there.

"If you insist on not keeping your maids around, I'm going to have to post a guard outside your door," he said.

"No! I don't like being babysat."

He chuckled. "He'd be *outside*. You wouldn't even know he was there."

"I would too," I complained. "I'd sense his presence."

Maxon made a playfully exhausted sigh. I was so busy arguing, I didn't hear the whispers until they were practically in front of us. Celeste, Emmica, and Tiny were heading past us toward their rooms.

"Ladies," Maxon said, and gave a small head nod.

I supposed it was foolish to think no one would see us together. I felt my face heat up, but I wasn't sure why.

The girls all curtsied and carried on their way. I looked over my shoulder at them as we went toward the stairs. Emmica and Tiny looked curious. Within minutes, they would be telling others about this. I would be cornered tomorrow for sure. Celeste was staring daggers at me. I was sure she thought I had personally wronged her.

I turned away and said the first thing that came to mind.

"I told you the girls who got nervous about the attack would end up staying." I didn't know exactly who had asked to leave, but rumors pointed to Tiny as being one. She had fainted. Someone else had said Bariel, but I knew that was a lie. You'd have to pry the crown out of her cold dead hands first.

"You can't imagine what a relief that was." He sounded sincere.

It took me a moment to think of how to respond, as that wasn't quite what I was expecting, and I was very focused on not falling. I didn't know how to take steps down very well while holding on to someone else. The heels didn't help. At least if I slipped, he would grab me.

"I would have thought it would be helpful in a way," I said as we made it to the first floor and I found my footing again. "I mean, it has to be complicated to pick one person out of all these girls. If the circumstances weeded some out for you, shouldn't that make it easier?"

Maxon shrugged. "I suppose it should. But it didn't feel that way at all, I assure you." He looked hurt. "Good evening, sirs," he greeted the guards, who opened the doors to the garden without the slightest hesitation. Maybe I would have to take Maxon up on that offer to have them know I liked to go outside. The idea of being able to escape so easily was appealing.

"I don't understand," I said as he led me to a bench—our bench—and let me sit facing the lights of the palace. He took a seat with his body facing the opposite direction, so that we were sort of turned in toward each other. It was an easy way to talk.

He looked hesitant about sharing, but he took a breath and spoke. "Maybe I was just flattering myself, thinking I'd be worth some sort of risk. Not that I'd wish that on anyone!" he clarified. "I don't mean that. It just . . . I don't know. Don't you all see everything *I'm* risking?"

"Umm, no. You're here with your family to give you advice, and we all live around your schedule. Everything about your life stays the same, and ours changed overnight. What in the world could you possibly be risking?"

Maxon looked shocked.

"America, I might have my family, but imagine how embarrassing it is to have your parents watch as you attempt to date for the first time. And not just your parents—the whole country! Worse than that, it's not even a normal style of dating.

"And living around my schedule? When I'm not with you all, I'm organizing troops, making laws, perfecting budgets . . . and all on my own these days, while my father watches me stumble in my own stupidity because I have none of his experience. And then, when I inevitably do things in a way he wouldn't, he goes and corrects my mistakes. And while I'm trying to do all this work, you—the girls, I mean—are all I can think about. I'm excited and terrified by the lot of you!"

He was using his hands more than I'd ever seen, whipping them in the air and running them through his hair.

"And you think my life isn't changing? What do you think my chances might be of finding a soul mate in the group of you? I'll be lucky if I can just find someone who'll be able to stand me for the rest of our lives. What if I've already sent her home because I was relying on some sort of spark I didn't feel? What if she's waiting to leave me at the first sign of adversity? What if I don't find anyone at all? What do I do then, America?"

His speech had started out angered and impassioned, but by the end his questions weren't rhetorical anymore. He really wanted to know: What was he going to do if no one here was even close to being someone he could love? Though that didn't even seem to be his main concern; he was more worried that no one would love him.

"Actually, Maxon, I think you will find your soul mate here. Honestly."

"Really?" His voice charged with hope at my prediction.

"Absolutely." I put a hand on his shoulder. He seemed to be comforted by that touch alone. I wondered how often people simply touched him. "If your life is as upside down as you say it is, then she has to be here somewhere. In my experience, true love is usually the most inconvenient kind." I smiled weakly.

He seemed happy to hear those words, and they consoled me as well. Because I believed them. And if I couldn't have love of my own, the best I could do was help Maxon find it himself.

"I hope you and Marlee hit it off. She's incredibly sweet."

Maxon made a strange face. "She seems so."

"What? Is something wrong with sweet?"

"No, no. Sweet is good."

He didn't elaborate.

"What do you keep looking for?" he asked suddenly.

"What?"

"You can't seem to keep your eyes in one place. I can tell that you're paying attention, but you seem to be looking for something."

I realized he was right. All through his little speech, I'd scanned the garden and the windows and even the towers along the walls. I was getting paranoid.

"People . . . cameras . . ." I shook my head as I looked into the night.

"We're alone. There's just the guard by the door." Maxon pointed to the lone figure in the palace lamplight. He was right, no one had followed us out, and the windows were all lit up but vacant. I'd seen that already through my scanning, but it helped to have it confirmed.

I felt my posture relax a little.

"You don't like people watching you, do you?" he asked.

"Not really. I prefer being below the radar. That's what I'm used to, you know?" I traced the patterns carved into the perfect block of stone beneath me, not meeting his eyes.

"You'll have to adjust to that. When you leave here, eyes will be on you for the rest of your life. My mom still talks to some of the women she was with when she went through the Selection. They're all viewed as important women. Still."

"Great," I moaned. "Just one more thing I can't wait to go home to."

Maxon's face was apologetic, but I had to look away. I was freshly reminded of how much this stupid competition was costing me, how my idea of normal was never coming back. It didn't seem fair. . . .

But I checked myself again. I shouldn't take it out on Maxon. He was as much a victim in this as the rest of us, though in a very different way. I sighed and looked back to him. I saw his face set as he decided something.

"America, could I ask you something personal?"

"Maybe," I hedged. He gave me a humorless smile.

"It's just . . . well, I can tell that you really don't like it here. You hate the rules and the competition and the attention and the clothes and the . . . well, no, you like the food." He smiled. I did, too. "You miss your home and your family . . .

and I suspect other people very, very much. Your feelings are incredibly close to the surface."

"Yeah." I rolled my eyes. "I know."

"But you're willing to be homesick and miserable *here* instead of going home. Why?"

I felt the lump rise in my throat, and I pushed it back down.

"I'm not miserable . . . and you know why."

"Well, sometimes you seem okay. I see you smiling when you talk to some of the other girls, and you seem very content at meals, I'll give you that. But other times you just look so sad. Would you tell me why? The whole story?"

"It's just another failed love story. It's nothing big or exciting. Trust me." *Please don't push me. I don't want to cry.*

"For better or for worse, I'd like to know one true love story besides my parents', one that was outside these walls and the rules and the structure. . . . Please?"

The truth was I'd carried the secret for so long, I couldn't imagine putting it into words. And it hurt so much to think of Aspen. Could I even say his name out loud? I took a deep breath. Maxon was my friend now. He tried so hard to be nice to me. And he'd been so honest with me. . . .

"In the world out there"—I pointed past the vast walls—"the castes take care of one another. Sometimes. Like my father has three families who buy at least one painting every year, and I have families that always pick me to sing at their Christmas parties. They're our patrons, see?

"Well, we were sort of patrons to his family. They're Sixes.

When we could afford to have someone help clean or if we needed help with the inventory, we always called his mother. I knew him when we were kids, but he was older than me, closer to my brother's age. They always played rough, so I avoided them.

"My older brother, Kota, he's an artist like my dad. A few years back this one metal sculpture piece that he'd been working on for years sold for a massive amount of money. You may have heard of him."

Maxon mouthed the words *Kota Singer*. The seconds passed, and I saw the connection click in his brain.

I brushed my hair off my shoulders and braced myself.

"We were really excited for Kota; he'd worked really hard on that piece. And we needed that money so badly at the time, the whole family was elated. But Kota kept almost all the money for himself. That one sculpture catapulted him; people started calling for his work every day. Now he has a waiting list a mile long and charges through the roof because he can. I think he might be a little addicted to the fame. Fives rarely get that kind of notice."

Our eyes met in a very significant moment, and I thought again of how I was past ever going unnoticed again, whether I wanted to be or not.

"Anyway, after the calls started coming, Kota decided to detach himself from the family. My older sister had just gotten married, so we lost her income. Then Kota starts making real money, and he up and leaves us." I put my hands on Maxon's chest to emphasize my point. "You don't do that.

You don't just leave your family. Sticking together . . . it's the only way to survive."

I saw the understanding in Maxon's eyes. "He kept it all for himself. Trying to buy his way up?"

I nodded. "He's got his heart set on being a Two. If he was happy being a Three or Four, he could have bought that title and helped us, but he's obsessed. It's stupid, really. He lives more than comfortably, but it's that damn label he wants. He won't stop until he gets it."

Maxon shook his head. "That could take a lifetime."

"As long as he dies with a Two on his gravestone, I guess he doesn't care."

"I take it you're not close anymore?"

I sighed. "Not now. But at first I thought that I'd just misunderstood something. I thought that Kota was moving out to be independent, not to separate himself from us. In the beginning, I was on his side. When Kota got his apartment and studio set up, I went to help him. And he called the same family of Sixes we always did and their eldest son was available and eager and worked with Kota a few days helping set things up."

I paused, remembering.

"So there I was, just pulling things out of boxes . . . and there he was. Our eyes met, and he didn't seem so old or rough anymore. It had been awhile since we'd seen each other, you know? We weren't kids anymore.

"The whole day I was there, we would *accidentally* touch each other as we moved things around. He would look at me or smile, and I felt like I was really alive for the first time. I just . . . I was crazy about him."

My voice finally broke, and some of the tears I'd been longing to shed came out.

"We lived pretty close to each other, so I'd take walks during the day just in case I might get to see him. Whenever his mother came by to help, sometimes he'd show up too. And we'd just watch each other—that's all we could do." I let out a tiny sob. "He's a Six and I'm a Five, and there are laws . . . and my mother! Oh, she would have been furious. No one could know."

I was moving my hands a little spastically, the stress of all the secret-keeping coming to the surface.

"Soon, there were little anonymous notes left taped to my window telling me I was beautiful or that I sang like an angel. And I knew they were from him.

"The night of my fifteenth birthday, my mom threw a party and his family was invited. He cornered me and gave me my birthday card and told me to read it when I was alone. When I finally got to it, it didn't have his name or even a 'Happy Birthday' on the inside. It just said, 'Tree house. Midnight.'"

Maxon's eyes widened. "Midnight? But—"

"You should know that I break Illéa curfew regularly."

"You could have landed yourself in jail, America." He shook his head.

I shrugged. "Back then, it seemed inconsequential. That first time, I felt like I was flying. Here he was, figuring out a way for us to be alone together. I just couldn't believe he wanted to be alone with *me*.

"That night I waited up in my room and watched the tree house in my backyard. Near midnight, I saw someone climb up. I remember I actually went to brush my teeth again, just in case. I crept out my window and up the tree. And he was there. I just . . . I couldn't believe it.

"I don't remember how it started, but soon we were confessing how we felt about each other, and we couldn't stop laughing because we were so happy the other one felt the same way. And I just couldn't be bothered to worry about breaking curfew or lying to my parents. And I didn't care that I was a Five and he was a Six. I didn't worry about the future. Because nothing could matter as much as him loving me . . .

"And he did, Maxon, he did. . . ."

More tears. I clutched my chest, feeling Aspen's absence like I never had. Saying it out loud only made it more real. There was nothing to do but finish the story.

"We dated in secret for two years. We were happy, but he was always worried about us sneaking around and how he couldn't give me what he thought I deserved. When we got the notice about the Selection, he insisted that I sign up."

Maxon's mouth dropped open.

"I know. It was so stupid. But it would have hung over him forever if I didn't try. And I honestly, *honestly* thought that I would never get chosen. How could I?"

I raised my hands in the air and let them fall. I was

still baffled by it all.

"I found out from his mom that he'd been saving up to marry some mystery girl. I was so excited. I made him a little surprise dinner, thinking I could coax the proposal out of him. I was so ready.

"But when he saw all the money that I'd spent on him, it upset him. He's very proud. He wanted to spoil me, not the other way around, and I guess he saw then that he'd never be able to. So he broke up with me instead. . . .

"One week later, my name got called."

I heard Maxon whisper something unintelligible.

"The last time I saw him was at my send-off," I choked. "He was with another girl."

"WHAT?" Maxon shouted.

I buried my head in my hands.

"The thing is, it drives me crazy because I know other girls are after him, they always were, and now he has no reason to turn them down. Maybe he's even with the girl from my send-off. I don't know. And I can't do anything about it. But the thought of going home and watching it . . . I just can't, Maxon. . . ."

I wept and wept, and Maxon didn't rush me. When the tears finally started to slow, I spoke.

"Maxon, I hope you find someone you can't live without. I really do. And I hope you never have to know what it's like to have to try and live without them."

Maxon's face was a shallow echo of my own pain. He looked absolutely brokenhearted for me. More than that, he looked angry.

"I'm sorry, America. I don't . . ." His face shifted a little. "Is this a good time to pat your shoulder?"

His uncertainty made me smile. "Yes. Now would be a great time."

He seemed as skeptical as he'd been the other day, but instead of just patting my shoulder, he leaned in and tentatively wrapped his arms around me.

"I only really ever hug my mother. Is this okay?" he asked.

I laughed. "It's hard to get a hug wrong."

After a minute, I spoke again. "I know what you mean, though. I don't really hug anyone besides my family."

I felt so drained after the long day of dressing and the *Report* and dinner and talking. It was nice to have Maxon just hold me, sometimes even patting my hair. He wasn't as lost as he seemed. He patiently waited for my breathing to slow, and when it did, he pulled back to look at me.

"America, I promise you I'll keep you here until the last possible moment. I understand that they want me to narrow the Elite down to three and then choose. But I swear to you, I'll make it to two and keep you here until then. I won't make you leave a moment before I have to. Or the moment you're ready. Whichever comes first."

I nodded.

"I know we just met, but I think you're wonderful. And it bothers me to see you hurt. If he were here, I'd . . . I'd . . ." Maxon shook with frustration, then sighed. "I'm so sorry, America."

He pulled me back in, and I rested my head on his broad shoulder. I knew Maxon would keep his promises. So I settled into perhaps the last place I ever thought I'd find genuine comfort.

CHAPTER 16

WHEN I WOKE THE NEXT MORNING, my eyelids felt heavy. As I rubbed the tiny ache out of them, I felt glad that I'd told Maxon everything. It seemed so funny that the palace—the beautiful cage—was the one place I could actually let myself be open about everything I'd been feeling.

Maxon's promise settled in during the night, and I felt sure that I'd be safe here. This whole process of Maxon whittling down thirty-five women to one was going to take weeks, maybe months. Time and space were just what I needed. I couldn't be sure I'd ever get over Aspen. I'd heard my mom talk about your first love being the one that sticks with you. But maybe I'd be able to just feel normal sooner rather than later with this time in between us.

My maids didn't ask about my puffy eyes, they just made them less swollen. They didn't question my mess of hair, they just smoothed it. And I appreciated that. It wasn't like home, where everyone saw that I was sad and didn't do anything about it. Here I could feel that they were all worried about me and whatever it was I was going through. In response they handled me with extreme care.

By midmorning I was ready to start my day. It was Saturday, so there was no routine or schedule, but it was the one day a week we were all required to stay in the Women's Room. The palace saw guests on Saturdays, and we had been warned that people might want to meet us. I wasn't too excited about it, but at least I got to wear my new jeans for the first time. Of course, they were the best-fitting pair of pants I'd ever owned. I hoped that since Maxon and I were on such good terms, he'd let me keep them after I left.

I went downstairs slowly, a little tired from a late night. Before I even got to the Women's Room, I heard the buzz of talking girls, and when I walked in, Marlee grabbed me and pulled me toward two chairs in the back of the room.

"There you are! I've been waiting for you," she said.

"Sorry, Marlee. I had a long night and slept in."

She turned to look at me, probably noting the leftover sadness in my voice, but sweetly decided to focus on my jeans. "Those look fantastic."

"I know. I've never felt anything like them." My voice lifted a bit. I decided to go back to my old rule: Aspen wasn't allowed here. I pushed him away and focused on my second-favorite person in the palace. "Sorry to keep you waiting. What did you want to talk about?"

Marlee hesitated. She bit her lip as we sat down. There was no one else around. She must have a secret.

"Actually, now that I think of it, maybe I shouldn't tell you. Sometimes I forget that we're competing against each other."

Oh. She had secrets of the Maxon variety. This I had to hear.

"I know just how you feel, Marlee. I think we could become really close friends. I can't bring myself to think of you as an enemy, you know?"

"Yeah. I think you're so sweet. And the people love you. I mean, you're probably going to win. . . ." She seemed a little defeated at the idea.

I had to will myself not to wince or laugh at those words.

"Marlee, can I tell you a secret?" My voice was full of gentle truth. I hoped she would believe my words.

"Of course, America. Anything."

"I don't know who will win this whole thing. Really, it could be anyone in this room. I guess everyone thinks that it'll be them, but I already know that if it can't be me, I'd want it to be you. You seem generous and fair. I think you'd be a great princess. Honestly." It was almost all the truth.

"I think you're smart and personable," she whispered. "You'd be great, too."

I bowed my head. It was sweet of her to think so highly of me. I felt a bit uncomfortable when people talked about me that way, though . . . May, Kenna, my maids . . . it was hard to believe how many people thought I'd be a good princess.

Was I the only one who saw how flawed I was? I was unrefined. I didn't have it in me to be bossy or overly organized. I was selfish and had a horrible temper, and I didn't like being in front of people. And I wasn't brave. You had to be brave to take this job. And that's what this was. Not just a marriage, but a position.

"I feel that way about a lot of the girls," she confessed. "Like everyone has some quality that I don't that would make them better than me."

"That's the thing, Marlee. You could probably find something special about everyone in this room. But who knows exactly what Maxon is looking for?"

She shook her head.

"So let's not worry about that. You can tell me anything you want to. I'll keep your secrets if you keep mine. I'll pull for you, and if you want to, you can pull for me. It's nice to have friends here."

She smiled, then looked around the room, checking to make sure no one could hear us.

"Maxon and I had our date," she whispered.

"Yeah?" I asked. I knew I seemed overly eager, but I couldn't help it. I wanted to know if he'd managed to be any less stiff around her. And I wanted to know if he liked her.

"He sent a letter to my maids and asked if he could see me on Thursday." I smiled as Marlee spoke and thought of how the day before he'd done that, Maxon and I had decided to eliminate those formalities. "I sent one back saying yes, of course, like I'd ever turn him down! He came to get me, and we walked around the palace. We got to talking about movies, and it turns out we like a bunch of the same ones. So we went downstairs to the basement. Have you seen the movie theater down there?"

"No." I'd never actually been in a movie theater, and I couldn't wait for her to describe it.

"Oh, it's perfect! The seats are wide and they recline and you can even pop some popcorn—they have a popper. Maxon stood there and made a batch just for us! It was so cute, America. He measured the oil wrong and the first batch burned. He had to call someone to come and clean it up and try again."

I rolled my eyes. Smooth, Maxon, real smooth. At least Marlee seemed to think it was endearing.

"So we watched the movie, and when we got to the romantic part at the end, he held my hand! I thought I'd faint. I mean, I'd taken his arm when we walked, but that's just what you're supposed to do. Here he was taking my hand. . . ." She sighed and fell back into her chair.

I giggled out loud. She looked completely smitten. Yes, yes, yes!

"I can't wait for him to visit me again. He's just so handsome, don't you think?" she asked.

I paused. "Yeah, he's cute."

"Come on, America! You have to have noticed those eyes and his voice. . . ."

"Except when he laughs!" Just remembering Maxon's laugh had me grinning. It was cute but awkward. He pushed his breaths out, and then made a jagged noise when he inhaled, almost like another laugh in itself.

"Yes, okay, he does have a funny laugh, but it's cute."

"Sure, if you like the lovable sound of an asthma attack in your ear every time you tell a joke."

Marlee lost it and doubled over in laughter.

"All right, all right," she said, coming up for air. "You have to think there's something attractive about him."

I opened my mouth and shut it two or three times. I was tempted to take another jab at Maxon, but I didn't want Marlee to see him in a negative light. So I thought about it.

What was attractive about Maxon?

"Well, when he lets his guard down, he's okay. Like when he just talks without checking his words or you catch him just looking at something like . . . like he's really looking for the beauty in it."

Marlee smiled, and I knew she'd seen that in him, too.

"And I like that he seems genuinely involved when he's there, you know? Like even though he's got a country to run and a thousand things to do, it's like he forgets it all when he's with you. He just dedicates himself to what's right in front of him. I like that.

"And . . . well, don't tell anyone this, but his arms. I like his arms."

I blushed at the end. Stupid . . . why hadn't I just stuck to the general good things about his personality? Luckily, Marlee was happy to pick up the conversation.

"Yes! You can really feel them under those thick suits,

can't you? He must be incredibly strong," Marlee gushed.

"I wonder why. I mean, what's the point of him being that strong? He does deskwork. It's weird."

"Maybe he likes to flex in front of the mirror," Marlee said, making a face and flexing her own tiny arms.

"Ha, ha! I bet that's it. I dare you to ask him!"

"No way!"

It sounded like Marlee had had a great time. I wondered why Maxon seemed so reluctant to mention that last night. Based on his reaction, it seemed like they hadn't been together at all. Maybe he was shy?

I looked around the room and saw that more than half the girls seemed tense or unhappy. Janelle, Emmica, and Zoe were listening intently to something Kriss was saying. Kriss was smiling and animated, but Janelle's face was tight with worry, and Zoe was biting her nails. Emmica was absently kneading a spot just below her ear, as if she was in pain. Beside them the mismatched pair of Celeste and Anna sat having another intense discussion. True to her usual form, Celeste looked incredibly smug as she spoke. Marlee noted my staring and clarified what was happening.

"The grumpy ones are the girls he hasn't been out with yet. He told me I was his second date on Thursday alone. He's trying to spend time with everyone."

"Really? You think that's it?"

"Yeah. I mean, look at you and me. We're fine, and it's because he's seen us both one-on-one. We know he liked us enough to see us and not kick us out right afterward. It's getting around who he's spent time with and who he hasn't. They're worried he's waiting on them because he isn't interested, and that once he does see them, he'll just let them go."

Why hadn't he told me any of this? Weren't we friends? A friend would talk about this. He'd seen at least a dozen girls based on their smiles. We'd spent the better part of the evening together last night, and all he did was make me cry. What kind of friend held those kinds of secrets while making me spill all my own?

Tuesday, who had been listening to Camille with an anxious expression on her face, got up from her seat and looked around the room. She found Marlee and me in the corner and quickly walked over.

"What did you guys do on your date?" she asked abruptly.

"Hi, Tuesday," Marlee said cheerfully.

"Oh, hush!" she cried, and turned back to me. "Come on, America, spill."

"I told you."

"No. The one last night!" A maid came to the corner and offered us tea, which I was prepared to take, but Tuesday shooed her away.

"How . . . ?"

"Tiny saw you together and told," Marlee said, trying to explain Tuesday's mood. "You're the only one he's been alone with twice. A lot of the girls who haven't seen him yet were complaining. They don't think it's right. But it's not your fault if he likes you."

"It's completely unfair," Tuesday whined. "I haven't seen

him outside of mealtimes, not even in passing. What in the world did you two do?"

"We . . . uh . . . we went back to the gardens. He knows I like it outside. And we just talked." I felt nervous, like I was in trouble. Tuesday's face was so intense, I looked away. When I did, I saw that a few girls at nearby tables were listening in.

"You just talked?" she asked skeptically.

I shrugged. "That's it."

Tuesday huffed and went to Kriss's table, urging her to tell her story over again, quite energetically. I, however, was stunned.

"Are you okay, America?" Marlee asked, snapping me back into reality.

"Yes. Why?"

"You just look upset." Marlee's brow furrowed in concern.

"Nope. Not upset. Everything's great."

Suddenly, in a move so swift I would have missed it if they weren't so close, Anna Farmer—a Four who worked land for a living—reached up and slapped Celeste across the face.

Several people gasped, including myself. Those who missed it turned around and asked what had happened, most notably Tiny, whose high voice pierced the quiet left in the room.

"Oh, Anna, no," Emmica said with a sigh.

The moment after it happened, Anna slowly comprehended what she'd just done. She would probably be sent home; we weren't supposed to physically assault another Selected. Emmica started tearing up while Anna sat in stunned silence. They were both farm girls and had bonded early on. I couldn't imagine how I'd feel if it was Marlee suddenly leaving.

Anna, who I'd only met in passing, had always struck me as an effervescent creature. I knew there was nothing in her that would naturally seek to harm another person. During a large part of the rebel attack, she'd been on her knees in prayer.

Undoubtedly, she had been provoked, but no one was sitting within earshot to prove that. It would be Anna's word against Celeste's as far as any exchange of words went, but Celeste would have a roomful of people who could back up that she'd been hit. Maxon would presumably be urged to send Anna home as an example to the others.

Tears welled in Anna's eyes as Celeste whispered something to her and swiftly left the room.

Anna was gone before dinner.

CHAPTER 17

"Who was the president of the United States during the Third World War?" Silvia quizzed us.

This was one I didn't know, and I averted my eyes, hoping Silvia wouldn't call on me. Luckily, Amy raised her hand and answered. "President Wallis."

We were in the Great Room again, starting the week with a history lesson. Well, more like a history test. This was one of those areas where it always seemed that what people knew was varied, both as far as what was fact and just how informed they were. Mom always taught us orally when it came to history. We had pages and worksheets to master for English and math, but when it came to the stories that made up our past, there was very little that I knew for sure was truth.

"Correct. President Wallis was the president before the Chinese assault and continued leading the United States throughout the war," Silvia confirmed. I thought the name to myself. *Wallis, Wallis, Wallis.* I really wanted to remember this to tell May and Gerad when I went home, but we were learning so much, it was hard to keep it all straight. "What was their motivation for invading? Celeste?"

She smiled. "Money. The Americans owed them a lot of money and couldn't pay them back."

"Excellent, Celeste." Silvia gave her a doting smile. How did Celeste wrap people around her finger like that? It was so irritating. "When the United States couldn't repay their massive debt, the Chinese invaded. Unfortunately for them, this didn't get them any money, as the United States was beyond bankruptcy. However, it did gain them American labor. And when the Chinese took over, what did they rename the United States?"

I raised my hand, along with a few others. "Jenna?" Silvia called.

"The American State of China."

"Yes. The American State of China had the appearance of its original country, but was merely a facade. The Chinese were pulling strings behind the scenes, influencing any major political happenings, and steering legislation in their favor." Silvia walked through the desks slowly. I felt like a mouse in the sights of a hawk that was circling ever closer.

I looked around the room. A few people seemed confused. I thought that part was common knowledge.

"Does anyone have anything they'd like to add?" Silvia asked.

Bariel piped up. "The Chinese invasion prompted several countries, particularly those in Europe, to align themselves with one another and make alliances."

"Yes," Silvia replied. "However, the American State of China had no such friends at the time. It took them five years to regroup, and they could barely handle that, let alone trying to forge alliances." She tried to express the hardship through an exhausted look. "The ASC planned to fight back against China but was then faced with another invasion. What country attempted to occupy the ASC then?"

Lots of hands went up this time. "Russia," someone said without waiting to be called on. Silvia looked around for the offender, but couldn't pinpoint the source.

"Correct," she said, slightly unhappily. "Russia tried to expand in both directions and failed miserably, but this failure on their part provided the ASC with an opportunity to fight back. How?"

Kriss raised her hand and answered. "The entirety of what was North America banded together to fight Russia, since it seemed clear they had their eyes on more than just the ASC. And fighting Russia was easier because China was attacking them as well for attempting to steal their territory."

Silvia smiled proudly. "Yes. And who headed up the assault against Russia?"

The whole room shouted out the answer: "Gregory Illéa!" Some girls even clapped.

Silvia nodded. "And that led to the founding of the country. The alliances the ASC acquired had formed a united front, and the United States's reputation was so damaged, no one wanted to readopt that name. So a new nation was formed under Gregory Illéa's name and leadership. He saved this country."

Emmica raised her hand, and Silvia acknowledged her. "In some ways, we're kind of like him. I mean, we get to serve our country. He was just a private citizen who donated his money and knowledge. And he changed everything," she said with wonder.

"That is a beautiful point," Silvia said. "And exactly like him, one of you will be elevated to royalty. For Gregory Illéa, he became a king as his family married into a royal family, and for you, it will be marrying into this one." Silvia had moved herself to awe, so when Tuesday raised her hand, it took her a moment to acknowledge it.

"Umm, why is it that we don't have any of this in a book? So we could study?" There was a hint of irritation in her voice.

Silvia shook her head. "Dear girls, history isn't something you study. It's something you should just know."

Marlee turned to me and whispered, "But clearly we don't." She smiled at her own joke, and then focused again on Silvia.

I thought about that, how we all knew different things or had to guess at the truth. Why weren't we given history books?

I remembered a few years ago when I went into Mom and Dad's room, since Mom said I could choose what I wanted to read for English. As I went through my options, I spotted a thick, ratty book in the back corner and pulled it out. It was a U.S. history book. Dad came in a few minutes later, saw what I was reading, and said it was okay, so long as I never told anyone about it.

When Dad asked me to keep a secret, I did so without question, and I loved looking through all those pages. Well, the ones that were still legible. Lots had been torn out, and the edge of the book looked like it might have been burned, but that's where I saw a picture of the old White House and learned about the way holidays used to be.

I never thought to question the lack of truth until it had been placed in front of me. Why did the king just let us guess?

The flashbulbs went off again, capturing Maxon and Natalie smiling brightly.

"Natalie, bring your chin down just a touch, please. That's it." The photographer snapped another picture, filling the room with light. "I think that will do. Who's next?" he called.

Celeste came in from the side, a general group of maids still swarming around her before the photographer started up again. Natalie, still beside Maxon, said something and kicked up her foot flirtatiously behind her. He responded quietly, and she giggled as she walked away.

We'd been told after yesterday's history lesson that this photo shoot was merely for the amusement of the public, but

I couldn't help thinking that there was some actual weight to it. Someone had written an editorial in a magazine about the look of a princess. I didn't get to read the article myself, but Emmica and some of the others did. According to her, it was about Maxon needing to find someone who actually looked regal and photographed well with him, someone who would look nice on a stamp.

And now we were all lined up in identical cream-colored, cap-sleeved, drop-waist dresses with a heavy red sash across our shoulders, taking pictures with Maxon. The photos would be printed in the same magazine, and the magazine staff was going to make picks. I was kind of uncomfortable with it all. This was the thing I'd been bothered about since the beginning, that Maxon was looking for nothing more than a pretty face. Now that I'd met him, I was sure that wasn't true, but it got to me that people thought that Maxon was like that.

I sighed. Some of the girls were walking around, munching on no-drip foods and chatting, but the majority, including myself, were standing around the perimeter of the set erected in the Great Room. A huge golden tapestry that reminded me of the drop cloths Dad used at home was hung up against a wall and spilled across the floor. A small couch was off to one side and a pillar was on the other. In the middle the Illéan emblem stood, giving the whole silly thing an air of being patriotic. We watched as each Selected paraded across the space to be photographed, and many who watched were whispering things they liked and didn't or what they were planning for themselves.

Celeste walked up to Maxon with a sparkle in her eyes, and he smiled as she approached. The moment she reached him, she put her lips to his ear and whispered something. Whatever it was, Maxon leaned his head back with laughter and nodded, agreeing with her little secret. It was strange to see them like that. How could someone who got along so well with me do the same with someone like her?

"All right, miss, just face the camera and smile, please," the photographer called, and Celeste immediately complied.

She turned herself toward Maxon and placed a hand on his chest, tilted her head down, and gave an expert smile. She seemed to understand how to use the lighting and set to her best advantage and kept moving Maxon over a few inches or insisting on changing their pose. Where some of the girls took their time and made their turn with Maxon last—particularly those who still hadn't secured a date— Celeste appeared to want to show her efficiency instead.

In a bolt of speed, she was done, and the photographer called for the next girl. I was so busy watching Celeste run her fingers down Maxon's arm as she exited that a maid had to gently remind me it was my turn.

I gave my head a tiny shake and willed myself to focus. I gathered up my dress in my hands and walked toward Maxon. His eyes shifted from Celeste to me, and maybe I imagined it, but his face seemed to brighten a bit.

"Hello, my dear," he sang.

"Don't even start," I warned, but he merely chuckled and

reached his hands out.

"Hold on a moment. Your sash is crooked."

"Not surprised." The darn thing was so heavy, I could feel it shifting every time I stepped.

"I suppose that'll do," he said jokingly.

I fired back, "In the meantime, they ought to hang you up with the chandeliers." I poked at the glittering medals across his chest. His uniform, which looked almost like something the guards would wear, only far more elegant, also had golden things on his shoulders and a sword hanging off his hip. It was a bit much.

"Look at the camera, please," the photographer called. I looked up and saw not just his eyes but the faces of all the other girls watching, and my nerves shot up.

I wiped my moist hands on my dress and exhaled.

"Don't be nervous," Maxon whispered.

"I don't like everyone looking at me."

He pulled me very close and put his hand on my waist. I went to step back, but Maxon's arm held me securely to him. "Just look at me like you can't stand me." He squinted into a mock pout, which made me crack up.

The camera flashed at just that second, capturing us both laughing.

"See," Maxon said. "It's not so bad."

"I guess." I was still tense for a few minutes as the photographer shouted out instructions and Maxon shifted from a close embrace to a loose one, or turned me so my back was against his chest.

"Excellent," the photographer said. "Could we get a few on the lounge?"

I was feeling better now that it was half over, and I sat next to Maxon with the best posture I could muster. Every once in a while, he'd poke or tickle me, making my smile grow bigger until it burst into laughter. I hoped the photographer was catching the moments just before my face scrunched together, otherwise this whole thing was going to be a disaster.

From the corner of my eye, I noticed a waving hand, and a moment later Maxon turned as well. A man in a suit was standing there, and he clearly needed to speak to the prince. Maxon nodded, but the man hesitated, looking to him and then to me, evidently questioning my presence.

"She's fine," Maxon said, and the man came over and knelt before him.

"Rebel attack in Midston, Your Majesty," he said. Maxon sighed and dropped his head wearily. "They burned acres of crops and killed about a dozen people."

"Where in Midston?"

"The west, sir, near the border."

Maxon nodded slowly and looked as if he was adding this piece of information to others in his head. "What does my father say?"

"Actually, Your Majesty, he wanted your thoughts."

Maxon seemed taken aback for a split second, then spoke. "Localize troops in the southeast of Sota and all along Tammins. Don't go as far south as Midston, it'd be a waste. See if we can intercept them."

The man stood and bowed. "Excellent, sir." As swiftly as he'd come, he vanished.

I knew we were supposed to get back to the pictures, but Maxon didn't seem nearly so interested in it all now.

"Are you all right?" I asked.

He nodded somberly. "Just all those people."

"Maybe we should stop," I suggested.

He shook his head, straightened up, and smiled, placing my hand in his. "One thing you must master in this profession is the ability to appear calm when you feel anything but. Please smile, America."

I raised myself up and gave a shy smile to the camera as the photographer clicked away. In the middle of those last few frames, Maxon squeezed my hand tight, and I did the same to his. In that moment, it felt like we had a connection, something true and deep.

"Thank you very much. Next, please," the photographer sang.

As Maxon and I stood, he held on to my hand. "Please don't say anything. It's imperative you're discreet."

"Of course."

The click of a pair of heels coming toward us reminded me that we weren't alone, but I kind of wanted to stay. He gave my hand one last squeeze and released me, and as I walked away, I considered several things. How nice it felt that Maxon trusted me enough to let me know this secret, and how it had sort of felt like we were alone for a moment. Then I thought about the rebels, and how the king was usually quick to point out their sedition, but I was supposed to keep this news to myself. It didn't quite make sense.

"Janelle, my dear," Maxon said as the next girl approached. I smiled to myself at the tired endearment. He lowered his voice, but I still heard. "Before I forget, are you free this afternoon?"

Something kind of knotted in my stomach. I guessed it was a late batch of nerves.

"She must have done something terrible," Amy insisted.

"That's not what she made it sound like," Kriss countered.

Tuesday pulled on Kriss's arm. "What did she say again?"

Janelle had been sent home.

This particular elimination was crucial for us to understand, because it was the first one that was isolated and not caused by rule breaking. She had done something wrong, and we all wanted to know what it was.

Kriss, whose room was across from Janelle's, had seen her come in and was the only person she'd spoken to before she left. Kriss sighed and retold the story for the third time.

"She and Maxon had gone hunting, but you knew that," she said, waving her hand around like she was trying to clear her thoughts. Janelle's date really had been common knowledge. After the photo shoot yesterday, she gushed about their plans to anyone who would listen.

"That was her second date with Maxon. She's the only one who got two," Bariel said.

"No, she isn't," I mumbled. A few heads turned, acknowledging my statement. It was true, though. Janelle was the only girl to have two dates with Maxon besides me. Not that I was counting.

Kriss continued. "When she came back, she was crying. I asked her what was wrong, and she said she was leaving, that Maxon had told her to go. I gave her a hug because she was so upset and asked her what happened. She said she couldn't tell me about it. I don't understand that. Maybe we're not allowed to talk about why we're eliminated?"

"That wasn't in the rules, was it?" Tuesday asked.

"No one said anything to me about it," Amy replied, and several others shook their heads in confirmation.

"But what did she say then?" Celeste urged.

Kriss sighed again. "She said that I'd better be careful of what I say. Then she pulled away and slammed the door."

The room went quiet a moment, considering. "She must have insulted him," Elayna said.

"Well, if that's why she left, then it isn't fair, since Maxon said that *someone* in this room insulted him the first time they met," Celeste complained.

People started looking around the room, trying to discover the guilty party, perhaps in an effort to get them—me— kicked out as well. I gave a nervous glance to Marlee, and she sprang into action.

"Maybe she said something about the country? Like the policies or something?"

Bariel sucked her teeth. "Please. How boring must that date have been for them to start talking policy? Has anyone in here actually talked to Maxon about anything related to running the country?"

No one answered.

"Of course you haven't," Bariel said. "Maxon's not looking for a coworker, he's looking for a wife."

"Don't you think you're underestimating him?" Kriss objected. "Don't you think Maxon wants someone with ideas and opinions?"

Celeste threw her head back and laughed. "Maxon can run the country just fine. He's trained for it. Besides, he has teams of people to help him make decisions, so why would he want someone else trying to tell him what to do? If I were you, I'd start learning how to be quiet. At least until he marries you."

Bariel sidled up beside Celeste. "Which he won't."

"Exactly," Celeste said with a smile. "Why would Maxon bother with some brainiac Three when he could have a Two?"

"Hey!" Tuesday cried. "Maxon doesn't care about numbers."

"Of course he does," Celeste replied in a tone someone would use with a child. "Why do you think everyone below a Four is gone?"

"Still here," I said, raising my hand. "So if you think you've got him figured out, you're wrong."

"Oh, it's the girl who doesn't know when to shut up," Celeste said in mock amusement.

I balled my fist, trying to decide if it would be worth hitting her. Was that part of her plan? But before I could move at all, Silvia burst through the door.

"Mail, ladies!" she called out, and the tension in the room flew away.

We all stopped, eager to get our hands on what Silvia was carrying. We'd been at the palace nearly two weeks now, and with the exception of hearing from our families on the second day, this was our first real contact from home.

"Let's see," Silvia said, looking through stacks of letters, completely oblivious to the almost-argument that had taken place not seconds ago. "Lady Tiny?" she called as she looked around the room.

Tiny raised her hand and walked forward. "Lady Elizabeth? Lady America?"

I practically ran forward and snatched the letter out of her hand. I was so hungry for words from my family. As soon as it was in my clutches, I retreated to a corner for a few moments to myself.

> Dear America,
> I can't wait for Friday to come. I can't believe you're going to get to talk to Gavril Fadaye! You have all the luck.

I certainly didn't feel lucky. Tomorrow night we were all getting grilled by Gavril, and I had no idea what he would ask us. I felt sure I'd make an idiot out of myself.

> It'll be nice to hear your voice again. I miss you singing around the house. Mom doesn't

do it, and it's been so quiet since you left. Will you wave to me on the show?

How's the competition going? Do you have lots of friends there? Have you talked to any of the girls who left? Mom is saying all the time now that it's not a big deal if you lose anymore. Half those girls who went home are already engaged to the sons of mayors or celebrities. She says someone will take you if Maxon doesn't. Gerad is hoping you marry a basketball player instead of a boring old prince. But I don't care what anybody says. Maxon is so gorgeous!

Have you kissed him yet?

Kissed him? We'd only just met. And there'd be no reason for Maxon to kiss me anyway.

I bet he's the best kisser in the universe. I think if you're a prince, you have to be!

I have so much more to tell you, but Mom wants me to go paint. Write me a real letter soon. A long one! With lots and lots of details!

I love you! We all do.

May

So the eliminated girls were already getting snatched up by wealthy men. I didn't realize being the castoff of a future king made you a commodity. I walked around the perimeter of the room, thinking over May's words.

I wanted to know what was going on. I wondered what had really happened with Janelle and was curious if Maxon had another date tonight. I really wanted to see him.

My mind was racing, searching for a way to simply speak to him. As I thought, I stared at the paper in my hands.

The second page of May's letter was almost completely blank. I tore off a piece of it as I wandered. Some girls were still buried in pages of letters from their families, and others were sharing news. After a lap I stopped by the Women's Room guest book and picked up the pen.

I scribbled quickly on my scrap of paper.

Your Majesty—

Tugging my ear. Whenever.

I walked outside the room as if I were simply going to the bathroom and looked up and down the hall. It was empty. I stood there, waiting, until a maid rounded the corner with a tray of tea in her hands.

"Excuse me?" I called to her quietly. Voices carried in these great halls.

The girl curtsied in front of me. "Yes, miss?"

"Would you happen to be going to the prince with that?"

She smiled. "Yes, miss."

"Could you please take this to him for me?" I held out my little folded-up note.

"Of course, miss!"

She took it eagerly and walked away with a newfound

energy. No doubt she would unfold it as soon as she was out of sight, but I felt secure in its odd phrasing.

These hallways were captivating, each one more ornate than my entire house. The wallpaper, the gilt mirrors, the giant vases of fresh flowers all so beautiful. The carpets were lavish and immaculate, the windows were sparkling, and the paintings on the walls were lovely.

There were some paintings by artists I knew—van Gogh, Picasso—and some I didn't. There were photographs of buildings I had seen before. There was one of the legendary White House. Compared to the pictures and what I'd read in my old history book, the palace dwarfed it in size and luxury, but I still wished it was around to see.

I walked farther down the hall and came upon a portrait of the royal family. It looked old; Maxon was shorter than his mother in this picture. He towered over her now.

In the time I'd been at the palace, I had only ever seen them together at dinners and the *Illéa Capital Report* airing. Were they very private? Did they not like all these strange young girls in their house? Were they only all here because of blood and duty? I didn't know what to make of this invisible family.

"America?"

I turned at the sound of my name. Maxon was jogging down the hall toward me.

I felt like I was seeing him for the first time.

He had his suit coat off, and the sleeves were rolled up on his white shirt. His blue tie was loosened at the neck, and his hair that was always slicked back was bouncing around a bit as he moved. In stark contrast to the person in uniform yesterday, he looked more boyish, more real.

I froze. Maxon came up to me and grabbed my wrists.

"Are you okay? What's wrong?" he pressed.

Wrong?

"Nothing. I'm fine," I replied. Maxon let out a breath I didn't realize he was holding.

"Thank goodness. When I got your note, I thought you were sick or something happened to your family."

"Oh! Oh, no. Maxon, I'm so sorry. I knew that was a stupid idea. I just didn't know if you'd be at dinner, and I wanted to see you."

"Well, what for?" he asked. He was still looking me over with a furrowed brow, as if he was making sure nothing was broken.

"Just to see you."

Maxon stopped moving. He looked into my eyes with a kind of wonder.

"You just wanted to see me?" He looked happily surprised.

"Don't be so shocked. Friends usually spend time together." My tone added the *of course*.

"Ah, you're cross with me because I've been engaged all week, aren't you? I didn't mean to neglect our friendship, America." Now he was back to the businesslike Maxon.

"No, I'm not mad. I was just explaining myself. You look busy. Go back to work, and I'll see you when you're free." I noticed he was still holding on to my wrists.

"Actually, do you mind if I stay a few minutes? They're having a budget meeting upstairs, and I detest those things." Without waiting for an answer, Maxon pulled me over to a short, plush sofa halfway down the hall that rested underneath a window, and I giggled a little as we sat. "What's so funny?"

"Just you," I said, smiling. "It's cute to see that your job bugs you. What's so bad about the meetings, anyway?"

"Oh, America!" he said, facing me again. "They go round and round in circles. Father does a good job at calming the advisers, but it's so hard to push the committees in any given direction. Mom is always on Father to give more to the school systems—she thinks the more educated you are, the less likely you are to be a criminal, and I agree—but Father is never forceful enough to get them to take away from other areas that could manage perfectly with lower funds. It's infuriating! And it's not like I'm in command, so my opinion is easily overlooked." Maxon propped his elbows on his knees and rested his head in his hands. He looked tired.

So now I could see a bit of Maxon's world, but it was just as unimaginable as ever. How could you deny the voice of your future sovereign?

"I'm sorry. On the plus side, you'll have more of a say in the future." I rubbed his back, trying to encourage him.

"I know. I tell myself that. But it's so frustrating when we could change things now if they'd only listen." His voice was a little hard to hear when it was directed at the carpet.

"Well, don't be too discouraged. Your mom is on the

right path, but education alone won't fix anything."

Maxon raised his head. "What do you mean?" It almost sounded like an accusation. And rightly so. Here was an idea that he'd been championing, and I'd just squashed it. I tried to backpedal.

"Well, compared to the fancy-pants tutors someone like you has, the education system for Sixes and Sevens is terrible. I think getting better teachers or better facilities would do them a world of good. But then what about the Eights? Isn't that caste responsible for most of the crimes? They don't get any education. I think if they felt they had something, anything at all, it might encourage them.

"Besides . . ." I paused. I didn't know if this was something a boy who'd grown up with everything handed to him could grasp. "Have you ever been hungry, Maxon? Not just ready for dinner, but *starving*? If there was absolutely no food here, nothing for your mother or father, and you knew that if you just took something from people who had more in a day than you'd have in your whole life, you could eat . . . what would you do? If they were counting on you, what wouldn't you do for someone you loved?"

He was quiet for a moment. Once before—when we'd talked about my maids during the attack—we'd kind of acknowledged the wide gap between us. This was a far more controversial topic of discussion, and I could see him wanting to avoid it.

"America, I'm not saying that some people don't have it hard, but stealing is—"

"Close your eyes, Maxon."

"What?"

"Close your eyes."

He frowned at me but obeyed. I waited until his eyes were shut and his face looked relaxed before I started.

"Somewhere in this palace, there is a woman who will be your wife."

I saw his mouth twitch, the beginnings of a hopeful smile.

"Maybe you don't know which face it is yet, but think of the girls in that room. Imagine the one who loves you the most. Imagine your 'dear.'"

His hand was resting next to mine on the seat, and his fingers grazed mine for a second. I shied away from the touch.

"Sorry," he mumbled, looking my way.

"Keep 'em closed!"

He chuckled and went back to his original position.

"This girl? Imagine that she depends on you. She needs you to cherish her and make her feel like the Selection didn't even happen. Like if you were dropped on your own out in the middle of the country to wander around door to door, she's still the one you would have found. She was always the one you would have picked."

The hopeful smile began to settle. More than settle, it started to sag.

"She needs you to provide for her and protect her. And if it came to a point where there was absolutely nothing to eat, and you couldn't even fall asleep at night because the sound of her stomach growling kept you awake—"

"Stop it!" Maxon stood quickly. He walked across the hall and stayed there for a while, facing away from me.

I felt a little awkward. I hadn't realized this would make him so upset.

"Sorry," I whispered.

He nodded his head but continued to look at the wall. After a moment he turned around. His eyes were searching mine, sad and questioning.

"Is it really like that?" he asked.

"What?"

"Out there . . . does that happen? Are people hungry like that a lot?"

"Maxon, I—"

"Tell me the truth." His mouth settled into a firm line.

"Yes. That happens. I know of families where people give up their share for their children or siblings. I know of a boy who was whipped in the town square for stealing food. Sometimes you do crazy things when you're desperate."

"A boy? How old?"

"Nine," I breathed with a shiver. I could still remember the scars on Jemmy's tiny back, and Maxon stretched his own back as if he felt it all himself.

"Have you"—he cleared his throat—"have you ever been like that? Starving?"

I ducked my head, which was a giveaway. I really didn't want to tell him about that.

"How bad?"

"Maxon, it will only upset you more."

"Probably," he said with a grave nod. "But I'm only starting to realize how much I don't know about my own country. Please."

I sighed.

"We've been pretty bad. Most times if it gets to where we have to choose, we keep the food and lose electricity. The worst was when it happened near Christmas one year. It was very cold, so we were all wearing tons of clothes and watching our breath inside the house. May didn't understand why we couldn't exchange gifts. As a general rule, there are never any leftovers at my house. Someone always wants more."

I watched his face grow pale and realized I didn't want to see him upset. I needed to turn this around, make it positive.

"I know the checks we've gotten over the last few weeks have really helped, and my family is very smart about money. I'm sure they've already tucked it away so it'll stretch out for a long time. You've done so much for us, Maxon." I tried to smile at him again, but his expression remained unchanged.

"Good God. When you said you were only here for the food, you weren't kidding, were you?" he asked, shaking his head.

"Really, Maxon, we've been doing pretty well lately. I—" But I couldn't finish my sentence.

Maxon came over and kissed my forehead.

"I'll see you at dinner."

As he walked away, he straightened his tie.

CHAPTER 18

MAXON HAD SAID HE WOULD see me at dinner, but he wasn't there. The queen entered alone. We made our delicate bows as she took her seat, and then settled in ourselves.

I looked around the room to find the empty chair, assuming he was on a date, but everyone was here.

I had spent the afternoon replaying what I'd said to Maxon. No wonder I'd never had any friends. I was shockingly bad at it.

Just then Maxon and the king walked in. Maxon had his suit coat back on, but his hair was still a handsome mess. He and the king had their heads together as they walked. We hurried to stand. Their conversation was animated. Maxon was using his hands to express things and the king was nodding, acknowledging his son's words but looking a little put out. When they reached the head table, King Clarkson gave

Maxon a heavy pat on the back, his expression stern.

As the king turned to face us all, his face suddenly flooded with enthusiasm. "Oh, goodness, dear ladies, please sit." He kissed the queen on her head and sat himself.

But Maxon remained standing.

"Ladies, I have an announcement." Every eye focused in. What could he possibly have for us?

"I know you were all promised compensation for your participation in the Selection." His voice was full of a ringing authority that I had only really heard once—the night he let me into the garden. He was much more attractive when he was using his status for a purpose. "However, there have been some new monetary allocations. If you are a natural Two or a Three, you will no longer be receiving financing. Fours and Fives will continue to receive compensation, but it will be slightly less than what it has been so far."

I could see some of the girls had their mouths open in shock. Money was part of the deal. Celeste, for example, was fuming. I guessed if you had a lot of money, you got used to the idea of collecting it. And the thought that someone like me would be getting anything she wasn't probably got under her skin.

"I do apologize for any inconvenience, but I will explain this all tomorrow night on the *Capital Report*. And this is a nonnegotiable situation. If anyone has a problem with this new arrangement and no longer wants to participate, you may leave after dinner."

He sat down and started talking again to the king, who seemed more interested in his dinner than Maxon's words. I was a little disheartened that my family would be receiving less money, but at least we were still getting some. I tried to focus on my dinner, but mostly I was wondering what this meant, and I wasn't alone. Murmurs went up around the room.

"What do you think that's about?" Tiny asked quietly.

"Maybe it's a test," Kriss offered. "I bet there are some people here who are only in it for the money."

As I listened to her, I saw Fiona nudge Olivia and nod her head toward me. I turned away so she wouldn't know I saw.

The girls offered up theories, and I kept watching Maxon. I tried to catch his attention so I could tug my ear, but he didn't look my way.

Mary and I were alone in my room. Tonight I'd face Gavril—and the rest of the nation—on the *Illéa Capital Report*. Not to mention the other girls would be right there the whole time, watching one another and mentally critiquing. Saying I was nervous was a gross understatement. I fidgeted while Mary listed some possible questions, things she thought the public would want to know.

How was I enjoying the palace? What was the most romantic thing Maxon had done for me? Did I miss my family? Had I kissed Maxon yet?

I eyed Mary when she asked me that one. I'd been throwing out answers to the questions, trying not to think too hard. But I could tell she'd asked that one out of genuine curiosity. The smile on her face proved it.

"No! For goodness' sake." I tried to sound mad, but it was too funny to be upset about. I ended up smirking. And that made Mary giggle. "Oh, just . . . why don't you clean something!"

She laughed outright, and before I could tell her to stop, Anne and Lucy burst through the doors with a garment bag.

Lucy was looking more excited than I'd seen her since the moment I'd walked in the first day, and Anne seemed quietly devious.

"What's this about?" I asked as Lucy stopped in front of me to give a buoyant curtsy.

"We finished your dress for the *Report*, miss," she replied.

My brow wrinkled together. "A new one? Why not the blue one in the closet? Didn't you just finish that one? I love it."

The three of them exchanged looks.

"What did you do?" I asked, pointing at the bag Anne was hanging up on the hook near the mirror.

"We talk to all the other maids, miss. We hear a lot of things," Anne began. "We know that you and Lady Janelle are the only two who got more than one date with His Majesty, and from what we understand, there might be a link between you two."

"How so?" I asked.

"From what we've heard," Anne continued, "the reason she was asked to leave is because she said some rather unkind things about you. The prince did not agree and dismissed her immediately."

"What?" I put a hand to my mouth, trying to hide my shock.

"We're sure you're his favorite, miss. Most everyone says so." Lucy sighed happily.

"I think you've been misinformed," I told them. Anne shrugged with a smile on her face, not concerned at all with my opinion.

Then I remembered where this had started. "What does any of this have to do with my dress?"

Mary came over to Anne and began unzipping the long bag, revealing a stunning red dress that shimmered in the fading light falling through the window.

"Oh, Anne," I said, absolutely awestruck. "You've outdone yourself."

She acknowledged my praise with a nod of her head. "Thank you, miss. We all worked on it, though."

"It's beautiful. But I still don't understand what this has to do with anything you said."

Mary pulled the dress out of the bag, airing it out, while Anne continued. "As I said, many people around the palace think you're the prince's favorite. He says kind things about you and prefers your company above the others'. And it seems the other girls have noticed."

"What do you mean?"

"We go down to a workroom to do most of the sewing on your dresses. There are stores of material and a place to make shoes, and the other maids are in there, too. Everyone requested a blue dress for tonight. All the maids think it's because you wear that color almost daily, and the others are trying to copy you."

"It's true," Lucy chimed in. "Lady Tuesday and Lady Natalie didn't put on any of their jewelry today. Just like you."

"And most of the ladies are requesting simpler dresses, like the ones you prefer," Mary stated.

"That still doesn't explain why you made me a red dress."

"To make you noticeable, of course," Mary answered. "Oh, Lady America, if he really likes you, you have to keep standing out. You've been so generous with us, especially Lucy." We all looked over to Lucy, who nodded in agreement and said, "You—you're good enough to be the princess. You'd be amazing."

I hunted for a way to get out of this. I hated being the center of attention.

"But what if everyone else is right? What if the reason Maxon likes me is because I'm not as over the top as everyone else, and then you go and put me in something like that and it ruins it all?"

"Every girl needs to shine once in a while. And we've known Maxon most of his life. He would love this." Anne spoke with such assurance that I felt there was nothing I could do.

I didn't know how to explain to them that the notes he sent me, the time he'd spent with me, meant nothing other than friendship between us. I couldn't tell them. It would deflate their happiness, and besides, I needed to keep up appearances if I wanted to stay. And I did. I needed to stay.

"Okay, let's try it on," I conceded with a sigh.

Lucy jumped up and down with excitement until Anne reminded her that it wasn't proper. I slid the silky dress over my head, and they stitched a handful of places they hadn't quite finished. Mary's skilled hands held my hair in various ways to see which looked best with the dress, and within half an hour, I was ready.

The set was arranged a little differently tonight for our special show. The thrones for the royal family were off to one side as always, and our seats were on the opposite side again. But the podium was off center, leaving the space focused on two tall chairs. A microphone was resting on one for us to take when we spoke to Gavril. I got queasy just thinking about it.

Sure enough, the room was full of dresses in every shade of blue. Some of them fell closer to green, others closer to purple, but it was clear there was a theme. I felt immediately uncomfortable. I caught Celeste's eye right away and decided to just stay away from her until I absolutely had to go over to the seats.

Kriss and Natalie walked past, having just checked their makeup one last time. They both looked a little unhappy, though sometimes it was hard to tell with Natalie. Kriss at least looked somewhat different from the crowd as well. Her blue dress was melting into white, like delicate strands of ice were weaving their way to the floor.

"You look stunning, America," she said in a way that was slightly more an accusation than praise.

"Thanks. That dress is gorgeous."

She ran her hands down her torso, straightening imaginary wrinkles. "Yeah, I liked it, too."

Natalie ran her hand across one of the capped sleeves on my dress. "What's that material? It's really going to shine under the lights."

"I have no idea, actually. We don't get a lot of the nice stuff as Fives," I said with a shrug. I looked down at the fabric. I'd had at least one other dress made from the same type of cloth, but I hadn't bothered learning the name.

"America!"

I looked up to see Celeste standing right beside me. Smiling.

"Celeste."

"Could you come with me for just one moment? I need some help."

Without waiting for an answer, she pulled me away from Kriss and Natalie and around the heavy blue curtain that was the backdrop of the *Report* studio.

"Take off your dress," she ordered as she started unzipping her own.

"What?"

"I want your dress. Take it off. Ugh! Damn hook," she said, still trying to get out of her clothes.

"I'm not taking off my dress," I said, and went to leave. I didn't get very far, though, as Celeste buried her nails into my arm and jerked me back.

"Ouch!" I cried, grabbing my arm. It looked like there would be marks but hopefully no blood.

"Shut up. Take off the dress. Now."

I stood there, my face set, refusing to budge. Celeste was just going to have to get over not being the center of Illéa.

"I could take it off for you," she offered coldly.

"I'm not afraid of you, Celeste," I said as I crossed my arms. "This dress was made for me, and I'm going to wear it. Next time you pick out your clothes, maybe you should try being yourself instead of me. Oh, wait, but maybe then Maxon would see what a brat you are and send you home, huh?"

Without a second of hesitation, she reached up and ripped one of my sleeves off and walked away. I gasped in outrage but was too stunned to do anything more. I looked down and saw a tattered scrap of fabric dangling pathetically in front of me. I heard Silvia calling for everyone to come to their seats, so I walked around the side of the curtain as bravely as I could manage.

Marlee had saved me a seat beside her, and I saw the shocked look on her face as I came into view.

"What happened to your dress?" she whispered.

"Celeste," I explained in disgust.

Emmica and Samantha, who were sitting in front of us, turned around.

"She tore your dress?" Emmica asked.

"Yes."

"Go to Maxon and turn her in," she pleaded. "That girl's a nightmare."

"I know," I said with a sigh. "I'll tell him next time I see him."

Samantha looked sad. "Who knows when that will be? I thought we'd get to spend more time with him."

"America, lift your arm," Marlee instructed. She expertly tucked my tattered sleeve into the side of my dress as Emmica plucked away a few stray threads. You couldn't even tell anything had happened to it. As for the nail marks, well, at least they were on my left arm and away from the camera.

It was almost time to start. Gavril was flipping through notes as the royal family came in at last. Maxon had on a dark blue suit with a pin of the national emblem on his lapel. He looked sharp and calm.

"Good evening, ladies," he sang with a smile.

A chorus of "Majesty" and "Highness" fell over him.

"Just so you know, I'll be giving one brief announcement and then introducing Gavril. It'll be a nice change; he's always introducing me!" He chuckled, and we all followed. "I know some of you are probably a little nervous, but you have no need to be. Please, just be yourselves. The people want to know you." Our eyes met a few times while he was talking, but nothing long enough for me to read him. He didn't seem to notice the dress. My maids would be disappointed.

He walked over to the podium, calling out "Good luck" over his shoulder.

I could tell something was going on. I assumed this announcement of his would be related to what he'd told us yesterday, but I still couldn't guess at what it all meant. Maxon's little mystery distracted me, and I wasn't so nervous anymore. I felt all right as the anthem played and the camera settled squarely on Maxon's face. I'd been watching the *Report* since I was a child. Maxon had never addressed the country before, not like this. I wished I could have told him good luck, too.

"Good evening, ladies and gentlemen of Illéa. I know that tonight is an exciting night for us all as the country gets to finally hear from the twenty-five remaining women in the Selection. I can't begin to express how excited I am for you to meet them. I'm sure you will all agree that any one of these amazing young ladies would be a wonderful leader and future princess.

"But before we get to that, I'd like to announce a new project I am working on that is of great importance to me. Having met these ladies, I've been exposed to the wide world outside our palace, a world that I rarely get to see. I've been told of its remarkable goodness and made aware of its unimaginable darkness. Through speaking to these women, I've embraced the importance of the masses outside these walls. I have been woken to the suffering of some of our lower castes, and I intend to do something about it."

What?

"It will be at least three months before we can set this up properly, but around the new year, there will be public

241

assistance for food in every Province Services Office. Any Five, Six, Seven, or Eight may go there any evening for a free, nutritious meal. Please know that these women before you have all sacrificed some or all of their compensation to help fund this important program. And while this assistance may not be able to last forever, we will keep it running as long as we can."

I kept trying to swallow up the gratitude, the awe, but a few tears leaked out. I was still aware enough of what was coming next to worry about my makeup but so appreciative that it was no longer the top priority.

"I feel that no good leader can let the masses go unfed. Most of Illéa is comprised of these lower castes, and we have overlooked these people far too long. That is why I am moving forward and why I am asking others to join me. Twos, Threes, Fours . . . the roads you drive on don't pave themselves. Your houses aren't cleaned by magic. Here is your opportunity to acknowledge that truth by donating at your local Province Services Office."

He paused. "By birth you have been blessed, and it is time to acknowledge that blessing. I will have further updates as this project progresses, and I thank you all for your attention. But now, let's get to the real reason you all tuned in tonight. Ladies and gentlemen, Mr. Gavril Fadaye!"

There was a smattering of applause from everyone in the room, though it was obvious not everyone was enthusiastic about Maxon's announcement. The king, for instance, was clapping but without excitement, though the queen was radiant with pride. The advisers also seemed torn about whether or not this was a good idea.

"Thank you so much for that introduction, Your Majesty!" Gavril announced as he ran onto the set. "Very well done! If this whole prince thing doesn't work out, you should consider a job in entertainment."

Maxon laughed out loud as he walked to his seat. The cameras were focused on Gavril now, but I watched Maxon and his parents. I didn't understand why their reactions were mixed.

"People of Illéa, do we have a treat for you! This evening we'll be getting the inside scoop from each of these young women. We know you've been dying to meet them and hear how things are coming along with our Prince Maxon, so tonight . . . we're just going to ask! Let's get started with"— Gavril looked at his note cards—"Miss Celeste Newsome of Clermont!"

Celeste moved sinuously from her seat in the top row and down the steps. She actually kissed Gavril on both cheeks before she sat down. Her interview was predictable, and so was Bariel's. They tried to be sexy, bending forward a lot to get clear shots down their dresses. It looked fake. I watched their faces in the monitors as they kept glancing at Maxon and winking. Every once in a while, like when Bariel tried to smoothly lick her lips, Marlee and I made brief eye contact and then had to look away so we wouldn't laugh.

Others were more composed. Tiny's voice matched her name, and she seemed to fold in on herself as the interview progressed. But I knew she was sweet and hoped that Maxon wouldn't count her out just because she wasn't a great public speaker. Emmica was poised, as was Marlee, the main difference being that Marlee's voice was so full of excitement and enthusiasm it flew higher and higher as she talked.

Gavril asked a variety of questions, but there were two that seemed to pop up with everyone: "What do you think of Prince Maxon?" and "Are you the girl who yelled at him?" I wasn't looking forward to telling the country that I had chided the future king. Thank goodness that, as far as anyone knew, I'd behaved that way only once.

Everyone was proud to say they weren't the girl who'd yelled at him. Then every single girl thought that Maxon was nice. That was almost always the word: nice. Celeste said that he was handsome. Bariel said he was quietly powerful, which I thought sounded creepy. A few girls were asked if Maxon had kissed them yet. They all blushed and said no. After the third or fourth no, Gavril turned on Maxon.

"Haven't you kissed any of them yet?" he asked, shocked.

"They've only been here two weeks! What kind of man do you think I am?" Maxon replied. He said it lightheartedly but seemed to squirm in his seat a little. I wondered if he'd ever kissed anyone.

Samantha had just finished saying she was having a wonderful time, and then Gavril called me. The other girls applauded as I stood, like we had for everyone. I gave Marlee a nervous smile. I focused on my feet as I walked over, but once I got into the chair, I found it was easy to look right past Gavril's shoulder at Maxon. He gave me a little wink as I picked up the microphone. I felt instantly calmer. I didn't have to win anyone over.

I shook Gavril's hand and sat down across from him. Up close, I could finally see the pin on his lapel. It obviously lost its detail through the camera, but now I saw that it wasn't just the lines and curls of a forte sign, but a small X was engraved in the middle, making the whole thing look almost like a star. It was beautiful.

"America Singer. That's an interesting name you have there. Is there a story behind it?" Gavril asked.

I sighed in relief. This was an easy one.

"Yes, actually. While my mom was pregnant with me, I kicked a lot. She said she had a fighter on her hands, so she named me after the country that fought so hard to keep this land together. It's odd, but to her credit, she was right— we've been fighting ever since."

Gavril laughed. "She sounds like a feisty woman herself."

"She is. I get a lot of my stubbornness from her."

"So you're stubborn, then? Have a bit of a temper?"

I saw Maxon covering his mouth with his hands, laughing. "Sometimes."

"If you have a temper, would you happen to be the one who yelled at our prince?"

I sighed. "Yes, it was me. And right now, my mother is having a heart attack."

Maxon called out to Gavril, "Get her to tell the whole story!"

Gavril whipped his head back and forth quickly. "Oh! What's the whole story?"

I tried to glare at Maxon, but the whole situation was so silly, it didn't quite work.

"I got a little . . . claustrophobic the first night, and I was desperate to get outside. The guards wouldn't let me through the doors. I was actually about to faint in this one guard's arms, but Prince Maxon was walking by and made them open the doors for me."

"Aw," Gavril said, tilting his head to one side.

"Yes, and then he followed to make sure I was all right. . . . But I was stressed out, so when he spoke to me, I basically ended up accusing him of being stuck-up and shallow."

Gavril chuckled deeply at this. I looked past him to Maxon, who was shaking with laughter. But the more embarrassing thing was that the king and queen were laughing along with him. I didn't turn to look at the girls, but I heard some of them giggling, too. Well, good. Maybe now they would finally stop seeing me as any sort of threat. I was just someone Maxon found entertaining.

"And he forgave you?" Gavril asked in a slightly more sober tone.

"Oddly enough." I shrugged.

"Well, since the two of you are on good terms again, what sort of activities have you been doing together?" Gavril was back to business.

"We usually just go for walks around the garden. He knows I like it outside. And we talk." It sounded pathetic after what some of the other girls had said. Trips to the theater, going hunting, horseback riding—those were impressive next to my story.

But I suddenly understood why he had been speed dating over the last week. The girls needed something to tell Gavril, so he had to provide it. It still seemed weird that he hadn't mentioned any of it to me, but at least I knew why he had been away.

"That sounds very relaxing. Would you say the garden is your favorite thing about the palace?"

I smiled. "Maybe. But the food is exquisite, so . . ."

Gavril laughed again.

"You are the last Five left in the competition, yes? Do you think that hurts your chances of becoming the princess?"

The word sprang from my lips without thought. "No!"

"Oh, my! You do have a spirit there!" Gavril seemed pleased to have gotten such an enthusiastic response. "So you think you'll beat out all the others, then? Make it to the end?"

I thought better of myself. "No, no. It's not like that. I don't think I'm better than any of the other girls; they're all amazing. It's just . . . I don't think Maxon would do that, just discount someone because of their caste."

I heard a collective gasp. I ran over the sentence in my head. It took me a minute to catch my mistake: I'd called him Maxon. Saying that to another girl behind closed doors was one thing, but to say his name without the word "Prince" in front of it was incredibly informal in public.

And I'd said it on live television.

I looked to see if Maxon was angry. He had a calm smile on his face. So he wasn't mad . . . but I was embarrassed. I blushed fiercely.

"Ah, so it seems you really have gotten to know our prince. Tell me, what do you think of *Maxon*?"

I had thought of several answers while I was waiting for my turn. I was going to make fun of his laugh or talk about the pet name he wanted his wife to call him. It seemed like the only way to save the situation was to get back the comedy. But as I lifted my eyes to make one of my comments, I saw Maxon's face.

He really wanted to know.

And I couldn't poke fun at him, not when I had a chance to say what I'd really started to think now that he was my friend. I couldn't joke about the person who'd saved me from facing absolute heartbreak at home, who fed my family boxes of sweets, who ran to me worried that I was hurt if I asked for him.

A month ago, I had looked at the TV and seen a stiff, distant, boring person—someone I couldn't imagine anyone loving. And while he wasn't anything close to the person I did love, he was worthy of having someone to love in his life.

"Maxon Schreave is the epitome of all things good. He is going to be a phenomenal king. He lets girls who are supposed to be wearing dresses wear jeans and doesn't get mad when someone who doesn't know him clearly mislabels him." I gave Gavril a keen look, and he smiled. And behind him, Maxon looked intrigued. "Whoever he marries will be a lucky girl. And whatever happens to me, I will be honored to be his subject."

I saw Maxon swallow, and I lowered my eyes.

"America Singer, thank you so much." Gavril went to shake my hand. "Up next is Miss Tallulah Bell."

I didn't hear what any of the girls said after me, though I stared at the two seats. That interview had become way more personal than I'd intended it to be. I couldn't bring myself to look at Maxon. Instead I sat there replaying my words again and again in my head.

The knock on my door came around ten. I flung it open, and Maxon rolled his eyes.

"You really ought to have a maid in here at night."

"Maxon! Oh, I'm so sorry. I didn't mean to call you that in front of everyone. It was so stupid."

"Do you think I'm mad at you?" he asked as he walked in and shut the door. "America, you call me by my name so often, it was bound to slip out. I wish it had been in a slightly more private setting," he said with a sly smile, "but I don't hold that against you at all."

"Really?"

"Of course, really."

"Ugh! I felt like such an idiot tonight. I can't believe you made me tell that story!" I slapped him on the side gently.

"That was the best part of the whole night! Mom was

really amused. In her day the girls were more reserved than even Tiny, and here you are calling me shallow . . . she couldn't get over it."

Great. Now the queen thought I was a misfit, too. We walked across my room and ended up on the balcony. There was a small, warm breeze blowing the scent of the thousands of flowers in the garden toward us. A full moon shone down on us, adding to the lights around the palace, and it gave Maxon's face a mysterious glow.

"Well, I'm glad you're so amused," I said, running my fingers across the railing.

Maxon hopped up to sit on the railing, looking very relaxed. "You're always amusing. Get used to it."

Hmm. He was almost being funny.

"So . . . about what you said . . . ," he started tentatively.

"Which part? The part about me calling you names or fighting with my mom or saying food was my motivation?" I rolled my eyes.

He laughed once. "The part about me being good . . ."

"Oh. What about it?" Those few sentences suddenly seemed more embarrassing than anything else I'd said. I ducked my head down and twisted a piece of my dress.

"I appreciate you making things look authentic, but you didn't need to go that far."

My head snapped up. How could he think that?

"Maxon, that wasn't for the sake of the show. If you had asked me a month ago what my honest opinion of you was, it would have been very different. But now I know you, and

I know the truth, and you are everything I said you were. And more."

He was quiet, but there was a small smile on his face.

"Thank you," he finally said.

"Anytime."

Maxon cleared his throat. "He'll be lucky, too." He got down from his makeshift seat and walked to my side of the balcony.

"Huh?"

"Your boyfriend. When he comes to his senses and begs you to take him back," Maxon said matter-of-factly.

I had to laugh. No such thing would happen in my world.

"He's not my boyfriend anymore. And he made it pretty clear he was done with me." Even I could hear the tiny bit of hope in my voice.

"Not possible. He'll have seen you on TV by now and fallen for you all over again. Though, in my opinion, you're still much too good for the dog." Maxon spoke almost as if he was bored, like he'd seen this happen a million times.

"Speaking of which!" he said a bit louder. "If you don't want me to be in love with you, you're going to have to stop looking so lovely. First thing tomorrow I'm having your maids sew some potato sacks together for you."

I hit his arm. "Shut up, Maxon."

"I'm not kidding. You're too beautiful for your own good. Once you leave, we'll have to send some of the guards with you. You'll never survive on your own, poor thing." He said all this with mock pity.

"I can't help it." I sighed. "One can never help being born into perfection." I fanned my face as if being so pretty was exhausting.

"No, I don't suppose you can help it."

I giggled. I didn't notice for a moment that Maxon didn't seem to think it was funny.

I stared out at the garden and saw out of the corner of my eye that Maxon was looking at me. His face was incredibly close to mine. When I turned to ask just what he was looking at, I was surprised to see that he was close enough to kiss me.

I was even more surprised when he did.

I pulled away quickly, taking a step. Maxon stepped back as well.

"Sorry," he mumbled, blushing.

"What are you doing?" I asked in a shocked whisper.

"Sorry." He was slightly turned away, obviously embarrassed.

"Why did you do that?" I put my hand to my mouth.

"It's just . . . with what you said earlier, and then seeking me out yesterday . . . just the way you acted . . . I thought maybe your feelings had changed. And I like you, I thought you could tell." He turned to face me. "And . . . Oh, was it terrible? You don't look happy at all."

I tried to wipe whatever expression I had off my face. Maxon looked mortified.

"I'm so sorry. I've never kissed anyone before. I don't know what I'm doing. I'm just . . . I'm sorry, America." He breathed a heavy sigh and ran his hand through his hair a few times, leaning against the railing.

I didn't expect it, but a warmth filled me.

He'd wanted his first kiss to be with me.

I thought about the Maxon I knew now—the man full of compliments, the man prepared to give me the winnings of a bet I lost, the man who forgave me when I hurt him both physically and emotionally—and discovered that I didn't mind that at all.

Yes, I still had feelings for Aspen. I couldn't undo that. But if I couldn't be with him, then what was holding me back from being with Maxon? Nothing more than my preconceived ideas of him, which were nothing close to who he was.

I stepped up to him and rubbed my hand across his forehead.

"What are you doing?"

"I'm erasing that memory. I think we can do better." I pulled my hand down and propped myself up beside him, facing toward my room. Maxon didn't move . . . but he did smile.

"America, I don't think you can change history." All the same, his expression looked hopeful.

"Sure we can. Besides, who'd ever know about it but you and me?"

Maxon looked at me for a moment, clearly wondering if this was really okay. Slowly, I saw a cautious confidence creep into his face as he looked into my eyes. We stayed that way for a moment before I could remember just what I had said.

"One can never help being born into perfection," I whispered.

He came close, wrapping an arm around my waist so that we faced each other. His nose tickled mine. He ran his fingers across my cheek so gently it seemed he was afraid I would break.

"No, I don't suppose you can," he breathed.

With his hand holding my face toward his, Maxon lowered his lips to mine and gave me the faintest whisper of a kiss.

Something about the tentativeness of it made me feel beautiful. Without a word, I could understand how excited he was to have this moment, but then afraid at the same time. And deeper than any of that, I sensed that he adored me.

So this was what it felt like to be a lady.

After a moment, he pulled back and asked, "Was that better?"

I could only nod. Maxon looked like he was on the verge of doing a backflip. There was a similar feeling in my chest. That was so unexpected. This was all too quick, too strange. The confusion must have shown on my face, because Maxon got serious.

"May I say something?"

I nodded again.

"I'm not so stupid as to believe that you've completely forgotten about your former boyfriend. I know what you've gone through and that you're not exactly here under the normal circumstances. I know you think there are others here more suited for me and this life, and I wouldn't want you to rush into trying to be happy with any of this. I just . . . I just want to know if it's possible . . ."

It was a hard question to answer. Would I be willing to live a life I'd never wanted? Would I be willing to watch as he kindly tried to date the others to be sure he wasn't making a mistake? Would I be willing to take on the responsibility that he had as a prince? Would I be willing to love him?

"Yes, Maxon," I whispered. "It's possible."

CHAPTER 19

I TOLD NO ONE WHAT had happened between Maxon and
me, not even Marlee or my maids. It felt like a wonderful
secret that I could revisit in the middle of one of Silvia's boring lessons or another long day in the Women's Room. And
to be honest, I thought about our kisses—both the awkward
and the sweet—more often than I expected I would.

I knew I wasn't just going to fall in love with Maxon
overnight. I knew my heart wouldn't let me. But I suddenly
found myself in a place where that was something I might
want. So I thought about the possibility quietly in my head,
though I was tempted to blurt out my secret more than once.

Particularly three days later when Olivia announced to
the half-full Women's Room that Maxon had kissed her.

I couldn't believe how shattered I felt. I caught myself looking at Olivia and wondering what was so special about her.

"Tell us everything!" Marlee insisted.

Most of the other girls were curious as well, but Marlee was the most enthusiastic. In the short time since she and Maxon had their last date, her interest in everyone else's progress seemed to be growing. I couldn't tell what was behind the shift, and I wasn't quite brave enough to ask.

Olivia didn't need encouragement. She sat down on one of the couches and fanned out her dress. It looked like she was practicing to be the princess. I felt like telling her that one kiss didn't mean she was winning.

"I don't want to go into all the details, but it was quite romantic," she gushed, tucking her chin into her chest. "He took me to the roof. There's this place that's kind of like a balcony, but it looks like it's used for the guards. I couldn't tell. We could look out over the wall, and the whole city was just glittering as far as we could see. He didn't really say anything. He just pulled me in and kissed me." Her whole body contracted with joy.

Marlee sighed. Celeste looked like she was ready to break something. I sat there.

I kept telling myself that I shouldn't care so much, that this was all part of the Selection. And who's to say that I'd really want to end up with Maxon anyway? Honestly, I ought to consider myself lucky. It was clear Celeste's malice had a new target, and after that whole episode with my dress—which I realized I'd forgotten to mention to Maxon—I was glad to see her move on.

"Do you think she's the only one he's kissed?" Tuesday

whispered in my ear. Kriss, who was standing beside me, heard her concerns and piped in.

"He wouldn't just kiss anyone. She must be doing something right," Kriss lamented.

"What if he's kissed half the room and people are keeping quiet about it? Maybe it's part of their strategy," Tuesday wondered.

"I don't think anyone who kept quiet would necessarily consider that a strategy," I countered. "Maybe they're just private."

Kriss sucked in a breath. "What if Olivia telling us all this is just some game? Now we're all worried, and it's not as if any of us would actually ask Maxon if he'd kissed her. There's no way to tell if she's lying or not."

"Do you think she would do that?" I asked.

"If she did, I wish I'd thought of it first," Tuesday said longingly.

Kriss sighed. "This is much more complicated than I thought it would be."

"Tell me about it," I mumbled.

"I like almost everyone in this room, but when I hear about Maxon doing something with someone else, I just want to figure out how I can do one better than her," she confessed. "I don't like feeling competitive toward you all."

"It's kind of like what I was telling Tiny the other day," Tuesday said. "I know she's a little on the timid side, but she's very ladylike and I think she'd make a great princess. I can't be mad at her if she has more dates than me, even if

I want the crown myself."

Kriss and I met eyes for a second, and I could tell we were both thinking the same thing. She said *crown*, not *him*. But I let it drop, because the other part of her little speech struck on something familiar. "Marlee and I talk about that all the time. How we can see great qualities in each other."

We all exchanged looks, and something felt different. Suddenly I didn't feel so jealous of Olivia or even so at odds with Celeste. We were all going through this in a different way, and maybe even for different reasons, but we were at least going through it together.

"Maybe Queen Amberly was right," I said. "The only thing to do is be yourself. I'd rather have Maxon send me home for being myself than keep me for being like someone else."

"That's true," Kriss said. "And in the end, thirty-four people have to go. If I was the last one standing, I'd want to know I had everyone else's support, so we should try to be supportive, too."

I nodded, knowing she was right. I was confident that I could do that.

Just then Elise burst into the room, followed by Zoe and Emmica. She was usually very slow and calm, and never raised her voice. Today, however, she turned her head and squealed at us.

"Look at these combs!" she cried, pointing to two beautiful hair ornaments that were covered in what looked like thousands of dollars' worth of precious stones. "Maxon gave them to me. Aren't they beautiful?"

This set the room into a new flurry of excitement and disappointment, and my newborn confidence disappeared.

I tried not to be disappointed. After all, hadn't I received gifts? Hadn't I been kissed? But as the room filled with girls and the stories were retold, I found myself wanting to just go hide. Maybe today would be a good day to spend with my maids.

As I was considering leaving the room, Silvia came in, looking slightly frazzled and excited at the same time.

"Ladies!" she called out, attempting to quiet us. "Ladies, are you all here?"

We sang our yeses back to her.

"Thank goodness for that," she said, settling down. "I know this is very late notice, but we've just learned the king and queen of Swendway are coming to visit in three days, and as you all know, we have relations in their royal family. Also, the queen's extended family will be coming in to meet you at the same time, so we're going to have quite a full house. We have very little time to get ready, so clear your afternoons. Lessons in the Great Room immediately after lunch," she said, and turned to leave.

You would have thought the palace staff had months to plan. Giant tented pavilions were set up in the gardens, with food and wine stations scattered about the lawn. The number of guards out was higher than usual, and they were joined by several Swendish soldiers the king and queen had brought with them. I guess even they knew how at risk the palace was.

There was a tent with thrones set up for the king, queen, and Maxon as well as the king and queen of Swendway. The Swendish queen—whose name I couldn't pronounce to save my life—was almost as beautiful as Queen Amberly and seemed to be a dear friend to her. They were all settled comfortably under that tent except for Maxon, who was busy making rounds with all the girls and the extended members of his family.

Maxon looked thrilled to see his cousins, even the little ones who kept tugging on his suit coat and running away. He had one of his many cameras out and was chasing the children with it, snapping away. Nearly all the Selected girls were watching him in adoration.

"America," someone called. I turned to my right to see Elayna and Leah talking to a woman who looked almost identical to the queen. "Come and meet the queen's sister." There was something in Elayna's tone that I couldn't quite name but made me nervous about joining them.

I walked over and curtsied to the lady, who cackled and said, "Stop that, honey. I'm not the queen here. I'm Adele, Amberly's older sister." She extended a hand, which I took, and she hiccuped as we shook. The woman had a slight accent, and something about her was comforting in the way that coming home feels. She was curvaceous and held a near-empty glass of wine that, based on the heavy look in her eyes, was not her first.

"Where are you from? I love your accent," I said. Some of the other girls from the South sounded similar, and their voices seemed incredibly romantic to me.

"Honduragua. Right by the coast. We grew up in the tiniest house," she said, making a space the size of an inch between her finger and thumb. "And look at her now. Look at me," she said, motioning down to her dress. "Such a change."

"I live in Carolina, and my parents took me to the coast once. I loved it," I replied.

"Oh, no, no, no, child," she said, waving her hand about. Elayna and Leah looked like they were holding in laughter. Clearly they didn't think the queen's sister should be quite so familiar. "The beaches in middle Illéa are trash compared to the ones down south. You have to go see one day."

I smiled and nodded, thinking that I'd love to see more of the country, but it was doubtful I ever would. Shortly after, one of Adele's many children came up to her and pulled her away, and Elayna and Leah burst into laughter.

"Isn't she hilarious?" Leah said.

"I don't know. She seems friendly," I replied with a shrug.

"She's vulgar," Elayna replied. "You should have heard all the things she said before you came up."

"What was so bad about her?"

"You'd think she'd have picked up a few lessons in decorum over the years. How did Silvia not get ahold of her?" Leah said with a sneer.

"Need I remind you, she was raised as a Four. Same as you," I shot back.

Her smug expression faltered, and she seemed to remember that she and Adele weren't so different. Elayna, however, was a natural Three and kept on talking.

"You can bet, if I win, my family will either be trained or deported. I wouldn't let any of them embarrass me like that."

"What was so embarrassing?" I asked.

Elayna sucked her teeth. "She's drunk. The queen and king of Swendway are here. She ought to be caged."

I decided that was enough and walked away to get some wine of my own. Once I had a glass, I looked around and honestly couldn't find a single place I wanted to settle. The whole reception was beautiful and interesting and completely aggravating.

I thought about what Elayna had said. If I ended up living in the palace, would I expect my family to change? I looked at the children running around, the people huddled together catching up. Wouldn't I want Kenna to be exactly who she was, want her children enjoying all this no matter how they behaved?

How much would living at the palace change me?

Would Maxon want me to change? Was that why he was off kissing other girls? Because there was something not quite right about me?

Was the rest of the Selection going to feel this irritating?

"Smile."

I turned, and Maxon snapped a picture of me. I bounced back in surprise. That unexpected picture wore out the last of my patience, and I turned away.

"Something wrong?" Maxon asked, lowering the camera. I shrugged.

"What's going on?"

"I just don't feel like being a part of the Selection today," I answered curtly.

Unfazed, Maxon stepped closer and lowered his voice. "Need someone to talk to? I could tug my ear right now," he offered.

I sighed and tried to put a polite smile on my face. "No, I just need to think." I went to leave.

"America," he said quietly. I stopped and turned. "Have I done something?"

I hesitated. Should I ask about him kissing Olivia? Should I tell him how tense I was feeling around the girls now that things had changed between us? Should I tell him how I didn't want to change myself or my family to be a part of this? I was about to let everything spill out when a shrill voice called from behind us.

"Prince Maxon?"

We turned, and Celeste was standing there, talking to the queen of Swendway. It was clear she wanted to have this conversation with Maxon on her arm. She waved, inviting him over.

"Why don't you run along?" I said, my annoyance leaking into my voice again.

Maxon looked at me. The expression on his face reminded me that this was part of the deal. I was expected to share.

"Careful with that one." I gave Maxon a quick curtsy and walked away.

I made my way toward the palace, and along the way noticed Marlee sitting alone. I didn't even want to be with her right now, but I noticed she was parked on a bench near the back wall of the palace in the brutally hot sun, her closest companion a young, silent guard stationed just a few yards away.

"Marlee, what are you doing? Get under a tent before you burn your skin."

She gave me a polite smile. "I'm happy here."

"No, really," I said, putting a hand around her arm. "You'll look like my hair. You should—"

Marlee jerked her hand out of my grip, but spoke gently. "I want to stay here, America. I prefer it."

There was a tension in her face she was trying to mask. I was sure she wasn't upset with me, but something was going on.

"Fine. Try to get some shade soon, though. Sunburns hurt," I said, attempting to cover my frustration, and walked toward the palace.

Once inside, I decided to go to the Women's Room. I couldn't be gone for too long, and at least that room would be empty. But when I went in, I found Adele sitting near the window and watching the scene unfold outside. She turned when I entered and gave me a small smile.

I walked over and sat next to her. "Hiding?"

She smiled. "Kind of. I wanted to meet you all and see my

sister again, but I hate it when these things turn into state functions. They make me tense."

"I'm not such a fan myself. I couldn't imagine doing things like this all the time."

"I bet," she said lazily. "You're the Five, right?"

The way she said it, it wasn't an insult. More like she was asking if I was in the club. "Yeah, that's me."

"I remembered your face. You were sweet at the airport. It's the kind of thing she would have done," she said, nodding out the window toward the queen. She sighed. "I don't know how she does it. She's stronger than most people know." I watched her pick up a wineglass and sip away.

"She does seem strong, but ladylike, too."

Adele beamed. "Yes, but it's more than that. Look at her now."

I watched the queen. I noticed her eyes were trained across the lawn. I followed her gaze, and she was watching Maxon. He was speaking to the queen of Swendway next to Celeste while one of his cousins clung to his leg.

"He would have been a great brother," she said. "Amberly had three miscarriages. Two before him, one after. She still thinks about it, she tells me so. And then I have six kids. I feel guilty every time I show up."

"I'm sure she doesn't think of it that way. I'll bet she's excited every time you visit," I assured her.

She turned. "You know what makes her happy? You do. Do you know what she sees out there? A daughter. She knows that when this is all over, she'll have two children."

I turned from Adele to look at the queen again. "You think so? She seems a little distant. I haven't even spoken to her yet."

Adele nodded. "Just you wait. She's terrified of becoming attached to all of you just to watch you leave. Once it's a smaller group, you'll see."

I looked at the queen again. And then at Maxon. Back to the king. And then to Adele.

So much went through my head. How families are families, no matter their castes. How mothers all have their own worries to bear. How I really didn't hate any of the girls here, no matter how wrong they might be. How everyone out there must be putting on a brave face for some reason or another. And finally, how Maxon had made me a promise.

"Excuse me. I have someone I need to talk to."

She sipped her wine and happily waved me away. I ran out of the room, and back into the blinding sun of the gardens. I searched around for a moment and found that Maxon's young cousin had begun chasing him around a shrub. I smiled and approached slowly.

Finally Maxon stopped, waving his hands in the air, admitting his defeat. As he laughed, he turned and saw me, his smile still wide on his face. When our eyes met, his smile faded. He searched my face, looking for a sign of my mood.

I bit my lip and looked down. It was clear that caring about what happened to me as a member of the Selection would mean processing a lot of other feelings that I hadn't been prepared for. However I took them in, I had to try not to force them out on other people, especially Maxon.

I thought about the queen—hosting visiting leaders, family members, a gaggle of girls all at once. She managed events and backed causes. She assisted her husband, her son, and the country. And underneath it all, she was a Four who held her own heartbreaks and never let her former rank or current aches keep her from doing it all.

I looked beneath my eyelashes at Maxon and smiled. He slowly smiled back, and whispered something to the little boy, who immediately turned and ran away. He reached up and tugged his ear. And I did the same.

CHAPTER 20

THE QUEEN'S FAMILY STAYED A few days, and the visitors from Swendway an entire week. They did a segment on the *Report* discussing international relations and movements toward more peace for both nations.

It was now a month into my stay at the palace, and I was completely at home. My body was comfortable in the new climate. The warmth of the palace was heavenly, like a holiday. September was almost over, and it got very cool in the evenings, but it was much warmer than home. The sights of this giant space were no longer a mystery. The sounds of heeled shoes on marble, crystal glasses clinking, guards marching—they were starting to become as normal as the refrigerator humming or Gerad kicking a soccer ball up against the house.

Meals with the royal family and times in the Women's

Room were staples in my routine, but the middle moments of my days were always new. I spent a lot of time working on music; the instruments at the palace were far superior to the ones I had at home. I had to admit, they were making me spoiled. The quality of the sound was unimaginably better. And the Women's Room had gotten a little more exciting, as the queen had shown up at least twice now. She hadn't really spoken to anyone yet, but she sat in a comfortable chair with her maids at her side, watching as we read or conversed.

In general, the animosity had settled as well. We were getting used to one another. We finally found out the magazine's top picks for our photographs. I was shocked to see I was one of the front-runners. Marlee was in the top spot, with Kriss, Tallulah, and Bariel close behind. Celeste didn't talk to Bariel for days upon hearing this, but eventually everyone let it pass.

What still seemed to bring the most tension were the bits of information tossed around. Whoever had been with Maxon recently couldn't help but gush about their little interlude. The way everyone spoke, it seemed as if Maxon was going to be choosing six or seven wives. But not everyone was shining in this experience.

For instance, Marlee had more than a few dates with Maxon, which put everyone on edge. Still, she never came across as excited as she had after their very first one.

"America, if I tell you this, you have to swear not to tell a soul," she said as we walked in the garden. I knew it was something serious. She'd waited until we got away from the listening ears in the Women's Room and far beyond the eyes of the guards.

"Of course, Marlee. Are you all right?"

"Yes, I'm fine. I just . . . I need your opinion on something." Her face was heavy with worry.

"What's wrong?"

She bit her lip. "It's Maxon. I'm not sure it's going to work out." She looked down.

"What makes you think that?" I asked, concerned.

"Well, for starters, I don't . . . I don't *feel* anything, you know? No spark, no connection."

"Maxon can be a little shy is all. You have to give him time." This was true. I was surprised she didn't know that about him.

"No, I mean, I don't think *I* like *him*."

"Oh." That was something very different. "Have you tried?" What a stupid question.

"Yes! So hard! I keep waiting for a moment to come when he'll say or do something to make me feel like we have something in common, but it never happens. I think he's handsome, but that's not enough to build a whole relationship on. I don't even know if he's attracted to me. Do you have any idea what kind of things he, you know, likes?"

I thought about it. "No, actually. We've never talked about what he's looking for in the physical department."

"And that's another thing! We never talk. He talks on and on to you, but we never seem to have anything to say. We spend a lot of our time quietly watching something or playing cards."

She looked more worried by the minute.

"Sometimes we're quiet together, too. Sometimes we just sit and say nothing. Besides, feelings like that don't always happen overnight. Maybe you're both just taking it slow." I tried to sound reassuring—Marlee looked like she was on the verge of tears.

"Honestly, America, I think the only reason I'm still here is because the people like me so much. I think their opinions matter to him."

That thought hadn't occurred to me, but it sounded plausible. Long ago, I'd dismissed their opinion, but Maxon loved his people. They'd have more of a hand in choosing the next princess than they would know.

"And besides," she whispered, "everything between us feels so . . . empty."

Then the tears came.

I sighed and hugged her. Truthfully, I wanted her to stay, to be here with me, but if she didn't love Maxon . . .

"Marlee, if you don't want to be with Maxon, I think you need to tell him."

"Oh, no, I don't think I can."

"You have to. He doesn't want to marry someone who doesn't love him. If you don't have any feelings for him, he needs to know."

She shook her head. "I can't just ask to leave! I need to stay. I couldn't go home . . . not now."

"Why, Marlee? What's keeping you here?"

For a moment, I wondered if Marlee and I shared the same dark secret. Maybe there was someone she needed distance from, too. The only difference in our situations was that Maxon knew about mine. I wanted her to say it! I wanted to know I wasn't the only one who'd ended up here out of some ridiculous circumstances.

But Marlee's tears stopped almost as quickly as they started. She sniffed a few times and straightened up. She smoothed out her day dress, squared her shoulders, and turned to face me. She pulled a strong, warm smile to her face and spoke.

"You know what? I bet you're right." She started to back away. "I'm sure if I just give it some time, it'll all work out. I have to go. Tiny's expecting me."

Marlee half ran back to the palace. What in the world had come over her?

The next day, Marlee avoided me. The day after that, too. I made a point of sitting in the Women's Room at a safe distance and making sure to acknowledge her whenever we crossed paths. I wanted her to know that she could trust me; I wouldn't make her talk.

It took four days for her to give me a sad, knowing smile. I just nodded. It seemed that would be all there was to say about whatever was going on in Marlee's heart.

That same day, while I was sitting in the Women's Room, Maxon called for me. It would be a lie to say I wasn't absolutely giddy when I ran out the door and into his arms.

"Maxon!" I breathed, falling into him. When I stepped

back, he sort of fumbled a moment, and I knew why. The day we'd left the Swendway reception and went inside to talk, I confessed what a hard time I was having dealing with the way I felt. And I asked him not to kiss me until I was more certain. I could tell he was hurt, but he nodded and hadn't broken his promise yet. It was just too hard to decipher those feelings when he acted like he was my boyfriend, but clearly wasn't.

There were still twenty-two girls here after Camille, Mikaela, and Laila had been sent home. Camille and Laila were simply incompatible and left with very little fanfare. Mikaela got so homesick she burst into heaving sobs during breakfast two days later. Maxon escorted her from the room, patting her shoulder the whole way. He seemed fine with letting them go, and was happy to focus on his other prospects, myself included. But he and I both knew it would be foolish of him to invest his heart completely in me when even I wasn't sure where mine was.

"How are you today?" he asked, stepping back.

"Perfect, of course. What are you doing here? Aren't you supposed to be working?"

"The president of the Infrastructure Committee is sick, so the meeting was postponed. I'm free as a bird all afternoon." His eyes were gleaming. "What do you want to do?" he asked, holding his arm out for me.

"Anything! There's so much of the palace I still haven't seen. There are horses here, right? And the movie theater. You still haven't taken me there."

"Let's do that. I could use something relaxing. What kinds of movies do you like best?" he asked as we started walking toward where I guessed the stairwell to the basement was.

"Honestly, I don't know. I don't get to watch a lot of movies. But I like romantic books. And comedies, too!"

"Romance, you say?" He raised his eyebrows like he was up to no good. I had to laugh.

We turned a corner and continued to talk. As we approached, a mass of the palace guard pulled to the side of the hall and saluted. There had to be more than a dozen men standing in the hallway. I was used to them by now. Even the sight of a collection that big couldn't distract me from the fun time I was about to have with Maxon.

What did stop me was when I heard the gasp that escaped someone's mouth as we passed. Maxon and I both turned.

And there was Aspen.

I gasped, too.

A few weeks ago, I'd heard some administrator in the palace talk about the draft in passing. I had wondered about Aspen, but seeing as I was running late to one of Silvia's many lessons, I didn't really have a chance to speculate much.

So he'd been taken by the draft after all. Of all the places he could have gone . . .

Maxon caught on. "America, do you know this young man?"

It had been more than a month since I'd seen Aspen, but this was the person I'd spent years committing to memory, the person who still visited my dreams. I would know him anywhere. He looked a little bigger, like he'd been fed, really fed, and was working out a lot. His scraggly hair had been cut short, practically all gone. And I was used to seeing him in secondhand clothes that were barely being held together by threads, and here he was in one of the brilliant, fitted uniforms of the palace guard.

He was alien and familiar at once. So many of the things around him seemed wrong. But those eyes . . . those were Aspen's eyes.

My eyes fell to the name tag on his uniform: OFFICER LEGER.

I doubted a second had passed.

I kept myself composed enough that no one saw the storm raging inside—a miracle in and of itself. I wanted to touch him, kiss him, scream at him, demand he leave my sanctuary. I wanted to melt away and disappear, but I felt so very *here*.

None of it made sense.

I cleared my throat. "Yes. Officer Leger comes from Carolina. He's actually from my hometown." I smiled at Maxon.

No doubt Aspen would have heard us laughing as we rounded the corner, would have noted that my arm was still draped on the prince's. Let him make of that what he would.

Maxon seemed excited for me. "Well, how about that! Welcome, Officer Leger. You must be happy to see your Champion Girl again." Maxon held his hand out, and Aspen shook it.

Aspen's face was like a stone. "Yes, Your Majesty. Very much so."

What did that mean?

"I'm sure you're pulling for her, too," Maxon encouraged as he winked at me.

"Of course, Your Majesty." Aspen bowed his head a bit.

And what did *that* mean?

"Excellent. Since America is from your home province, I can't think of a better man in the palace to leave her with. I'll make sure you're put on her guard rotation. This girl of yours refuses to keep a maid in her room at night. I've tried to tell her. . . ." Maxon shook his head at me.

Aspen finally seemed to relax a bit. "I'm not surprised by that, Your Majesty."

Maxon smiled. "Well, I'm sure you all have a busy day ahead of you. We'll just be off. Good day, officers." Maxon gave a quick nod and pulled me away.

It took all the strength in my body not to look back.

In the dark of the theater, I tried to figure out what to do. Maxon had made it clear from the night I'd told him about Aspen that he hated anyone who would treat me with so little care. If I told Maxon that the man he'd just assigned to watch over me was that very person, would he punish him somehow? I wouldn't put it past him. He'd invented an entire support system for the country based on my stories of being hungry.

So I couldn't tell him. I wouldn't tell him. Because as mad as I was, I loved Aspen. And I couldn't bear him being hurt.

Then should I leave? The ambivalence pulled at my heart. I could escape Aspen, get away from his face—a face that would torture me every day when I saw it and knew it was no longer mine. But if I left, I'd have to leave Maxon, too. And Maxon was my closest friend, maybe even more. I couldn't just go. Besides, how would I explain it without telling him Aspen was here?

And my family. Maybe the checks they got were smaller, but at least they were getting them. May had written saying that Dad was promising our best Christmas ever this year, but I was sure that came with the stipulation that another Christmas might never be as good. If I left, who could say how much money my past fame would bring for my family? We had to save up as much as we could now.

"You didn't like that one, did you?" Maxon asked nearly two hours later.

"Huh?"

"The movie. You didn't laugh or anything."

"Oh." I tried to remember one little piece of information, a single scene that I could say I'd enjoyed. Nothing registered. "I think I'm just a little out of it today. Sorry you wasted your afternoon."

"Nonsense." Maxon waved away my lackluster attitude. "I just enjoy your company. Though perhaps you should take a nap before dinner. You're looking a little pale."

I nodded. I was considering going to my room and never coming back out.

CHAPTER 21

IN THE END, I DECIDED against hiding in my room. Instead I chose the Women's Room. Usually I darted in and out all day, visiting libraries, taking walks with Marlee, or even heading back upstairs to visit my maids. But now I was using the Women's Room like a cave. No men, not even guards, were allowed inside without the queen's express permission. It was perfect.

Well, it was perfect for three days. With this many girls, it was only a matter of time until someone had a birthday. Kriss's was on Thursday. I guessed she'd mentioned it to Maxon—who seemed to never pass up an opportunity to give someone something—and the outcome was a mandatory party for all the Selected. As a result, Thursday was a mad rush of girls in and out of one another's rooms, asking what they were wearing or guessing at how grand it would be.

It didn't appear that gifts were required, but I figured I'd do something nice for her all the same.

On the day of the party, I donned one of my favorite day dresses and grabbed my violin. I crept down to the Great Room, looking around corners before I committed to walking on. Once I made it to the room, I did another sweep, surveying the guards who lined the walls. Mercifully, Aspen was nowhere to be seen, and I had to chuckle at the presence of so many men in uniform. Were they expecting a riot or something?

The Great Room was decorated beautifully. Special vases hung on the wall, displaying huge arrangements of yellow and white flowers, and similar bouquets sat in bowls around the room. Windows, stretches of wall, and pretty much anything that didn't move was draped in garlands. A few small tables had been set out, and they were covered with bright linens. Little bits of glittering confetti sparkled on the tabletops. Ornate bows adorned the backs of chairs.

In one corner, a massive cake that matched the colors of the room waited to be cut. Next to it, a small table held a few gifts for the birthday girl.

A string quartet was set up against the wall, effectively making my attempt at a gift meaningless, and a photographer wandered the room, capturing moments for the public eye.

The mood in the room was playful. Tiny—who had so far only managed to get close to Marlee—was talking to Emmica and Jenna and looking more animated than I'd ever seen her. Marlee hovered near a window, looking like one of the many guards dotting the wall. She made no effort to leave her chosen spot but stopped anyone who passed by to chat. A group of Threes—Kayleigh, Elizabeth, and Emily—all turned and waved and smiled. I returned the gesture. Everyone seemed so friendly and happy today.

Except for Celeste and Bariel. Usually they were inseparable, but today they were on opposite ends of the room, with Bariel speaking to Samantha, and Celeste sitting alone at a table, clutching a crystal glass of deep red liquid. I'd obviously missed something between yesterday's dinner and this afternoon.

I gripped my violin case again and walked toward the back of the room to see Marlee.

"Hi, Marlee. This is something, isn't it?" I asked, setting down the violin.

"It sure is." She hugged me. "I hear Maxon's coming by later to wish Kriss a happy birthday in person. Isn't that sweet? I'll bet he has a present, too."

Marlee went on in her typical enthusiastic way. I still wondered what her secret was, but I trusted her enough to bring up the subject if she really needed to talk about it. We spoke of little nothings for a few minutes until we heard a general clamor at the front end of the room.

Marlee and I both turned, and while she remained calm, I was completely deflated.

Kriss's dress choice had been incredibly strategic. Here we all were in day dresses—short, girlish things—and she was in a floor-length gown. But the length meant little. It was that her dress was a creamy, almost white color. Her hair was done up with a row of yellow jewels pinned into a line across the front in a very subtle resemblance to a crown. She looked mature, regal, bridal.

Even though I wasn't entirely sure where my heart was, I felt a pang of jealousy. None of us would ever get a similar moment. No matter how many parties or dinners came and went, it would be rather pathetic to try to copy Kriss's look. I saw Celeste's hand—the one that wasn't clutching her drink—ball into a fist.

"She looks really pretty," Marlee commented wistfully.

"Better than pretty," I replied.

The party continued on, and Marlee and I mostly crowd-watched. Surprisingly—and suspiciously—Celeste clung to Kriss, talking up a storm as Kriss circled the room, thanking everyone for coming, even though we really had no choice.

Eventually she made it to the back corner where Marlee and I were standing, soaking up the warm sun from the windows. Marlee, true to form, threw her arms around Kriss.

"Happy birthday!" she squealed.

"Thank you!" Kriss replied, returning Marlee's affection and enthusiasm.

"So you're nineteen today, right?" Marlee asked.

"Yes. I couldn't think of a better way to celebrate. I'm so glad they're taking pictures. My mother will love this! Even though we do pretty well, we've never had money to have something like this. It's so beautiful!" she gushed.

Kriss was a Three. There weren't nearly as many limits to her life as mine, but I'd imagine anything close to this scale would be hard to justify.

"It is impressive," Celeste commented. "For my birthday last year, I had a black and white party. Any trace of color, and you weren't even allowed in the door."

"Wow," Marlee whispered, obvious envy in the tiny word.

"It was fantastic. Gourmet food, dramatic lighting, and the music! Well, we flew in Tessa Tamble. You've heard of her?"

It was impossible not to know Tessa Tamble. She had at least a dozen hit songs. Sometimes we saw videos of hers on TV, though that was frowned on by Mom. She thought we were infinitely more talented than anyone like Tessa, and it irked her to no end that she had fame and money when we didn't for doing essentially the same thing.

"She's my favorite!" Kriss exclaimed.

"Well, Tessa's a dear friend of the family, so she came in and did a concert for my party. I mean, we couldn't have a bunch of dreary Fives sucking all the life out of the room."

Marlee gave me a quick sideways glance. I could tell she was feeling embarrassed for me.

"Oops," Celeste added, looking at me. "I forgot. I meant no offense."

The sticky sweetness of her voice was infuriating. Once again I was tempted to hit her. . . . Better not to push it.

"None taken," I replied, as composed as I possibly could. "Exactly what do you do as a Two, Celeste? I mean, I've never heard your music on the radio."

"I model," she answered in a tone that implied I should have known that. "Haven't you seen my ads?"

"Can't say I have."

"Oh, well, you are a Five. I guess you can't afford the magazines anyway."

It hurt because it was true. May loved to sneak peeks at magazines when we managed to go by a store, but there was absolutely no reason for us to buy them.

Kriss, taking on the role of host again, switched directions.

"You know, America, I've been meaning to ask what your focus was as a Five."

"Music."

"You should play for us sometime!"

I sighed. "Actually, I brought my violin to play for you today. I thought it would make a nice gift, but you've already got a quartet, so I figured—"

"Oh, play for us!" Marlee begged.

"Please, America, it's my birthday!" Kriss echoed.

"But they've already given you a—" It didn't matter how I protested. Kriss and Marlee had already shushed the quartet and made everyone come to the back of the room. Some girls fanned their dresses out and sat on the floor, while others pulled a few chairs toward the corner. Kriss stood in the middle of the crowd, clutching her hands with excitement, as Celeste stood by, holding the crystal glass she had yet to take a sip from.

As the girls settled themselves, I prepped the violin. The quartet of young men who had been playing walked over to support me, and the few waitstaff who had been buzzing about the room became still.

I took a deep breath and brought the violin to my chin. "For you," I said, looking at Kriss.

I let the bow hover above the strings for a moment, closed my eyes, and then let the music come.

For a while, there was no wicked Celeste, no Aspen lurking in the palace, no rebels trying to invade. There wasn't anything but one perfect note stringing itself to the next in such a way they seemed afraid they might get lost in time without one another. But they did hold together, and as they floated on, this gift that was meant to be something for Kriss became something for me.

I might be a Five, but I wasn't worthless.

I played the song—as familiar as my father's voice or the smell of my room—for a few brief, beautiful moments, and then let it come to its unavoidable end. I gave the bow one last sweep across the strings and lifted it into the air.

I turned to find Kriss, hoping she'd enjoyed her gift, but I didn't even see her face. Behind the crowd of girls, Maxon had walked in. He was in a gray suit with a box under his arm for Kriss. The girls were kindly applauding, but I couldn't register the sound. All I saw was that Maxon wore a handsome, awestruck expression, which slowly turned into a smile, a smile for no one but me.

"Your Majesty," I said with a curtsy.

The other girls all clambered to their feet to greet Maxon. In the midst of this, I heard a shocked squeal.

"Oh, no! Kriss, I'm so sorry."

A few girls had gasped in the same direction, and as Kriss turned my way I saw why. Her beautiful dress was stained down the front from Celeste's punch. It looked like Kriss had been stabbed.

"I'm sorry, I just turned too fast. I didn't mean to, Kriss. Let me help you." To the average person, Celeste's tone probably sounded sincere, but I could see through it.

Kriss covered her mouth as she started to cry, then ran from the room, which ended the party. To his credit, Maxon went after her, though I really wished he had stayed.

Celeste was pleading her case to anyone who would listen, saying it was a complete accident. Tuesday was nodding, saying she saw the whole thing, but there were so many rolling eyes and sagging shoulders from the rest that her support was pointless. I quietly put my violin away and went to leave.

Marlee grabbed my arm. "Someone should do something about her."

If Celeste could move someone as lovely as Anna to violence, or think it was acceptable to try and take the dress off my back, or make someone as good as Marlee come close to anger, then she really was too much for the Selection.

I had to get that girl out of the palace.

CHAPTER 22

"I'M TELLING YOU, MAXON, IT wasn't an accident." We were in the garden again, passing time until the *Report*. It had taken me a whole day to get a chance to speak with him.

"But she looked mortified, and she was so apologetic," he countered. "How could it not have been an accident?"

I sighed. "I'm telling you. I see Celeste every day, and that was her sneaky way of ruining Kriss's moment in the spotlight. She's so competitive."

"Well, if she was trying to take my attention from Kriss, she failed. I spent nearly an hour with the girl. Rather pleasant time I had, too."

I didn't want to hear about that. I knew that there was something small and tenuous between us, and I didn't want to deal with anything that might change it. Not until I knew how I felt about it myself.

"Then what about Anna?" I asked.

"Who?"

"Anna Farmer? She hit Celeste, and you kicked her out, remember? I know Anna had to have been provoked."

"Did you hear Celeste say something?" He sounded skeptical.

"Well . . . no. But I knew Anna, *and* I know Celeste. I'm telling you, Anna was not the type of person to head straight to violence. Celeste must have said something heartless to her for her to have reacted that way."

"America, I'm aware that you spend more time with the girls than I do, but how well can you really know them? You like to hide in your room or the libraries. I daresay you're more familiar with your maids' personalities than any of the Selected."

He was probably right, but I wouldn't back down. "That's not fair. I was right about Marlee, wasn't I? Don't you think she's nice?"

He made a face. "Yes . . . she is nice, I suppose."

"Then why won't you believe me when I say that what Celeste did was a calculated move?"

"America, it's not that I think you're lying. I'm sure, to you, it seemed that way. But Celeste was sorry. And she's been nothing but gracious with me."

"I'll bet she has," I muttered under my breath.

"That's enough," Maxon said with a sigh. "I don't want to talk about the others right now."

"She tried to take my dress, Maxon," I complained.

"I said I don't want to talk about her," he said fiercely.

That was all I was going to take. I huffed and lifted my arms in the air just to drop them with a thud against my legs. I was so frustrated I wanted to scream.

"If you're going to act this way, I'm going to find someone who does want my company." He walked off.

"Hey!" I called.

"No!" He turned back on me and spoke more forcefully than I'd ever imagined he could. "You forget yourself, Lady America. It would do you well to remember that I am the crown prince of Illéa. For all intents and purposes, I am lord and master of this country, and I'll be damned if you think you can treat me like this in my own home. You don't have to agree with my decisions, but you *will* abide by them."

He turned and left, either not seeing or caring that I had tears in my eyes.

I didn't look his way through dinner, but it was difficult to do during the *Report*. I caught him looking at me twice, and both times he tugged his ear. I didn't return the action. I didn't want to talk to him right now. I could only assume I'd be scolded more anyway, and I didn't need that.

I walked up to my room afterward so upset with Maxon I couldn't think clearly. Why wouldn't he listen to me? Did he think I was a liar? Even worse, did he think Celeste was above lying?

Maybe Maxon was just a typical guy, and Celeste was a beautiful girl, and in the end that would be what won out. For all his talk about wanting a soul mate, maybe all he wanted was a bedmate.

And if that was the kind of person he was, why was I even bothering with this? Stupid, stupid, stupid! I kissed him! I told him I'd be patient! And for what? I just—

I turned the corner to my room, and there was Aspen, waiting outside my door. All my rage melted away into a strange uncertainty. Guards, as a rule, kept their eyes forward and stayed at attention, but he was looking at me with an unreadable expression.

"Lady America," he whispered.

"Officer Leger."

Though it wasn't his job, he leaned over to open my door for me. I walked past slowly, almost afraid to turn my back on him, almost afraid he wasn't real. As much as I'd tried to keep him out of my head and my heart, I just wanted him to be with me in that moment. As I passed, I heard him inhale just next to my hair. It gave me a chill.

He fixed me with another stare and slowly closed the door.

Sleep was pointless. I tossed for hours as thoughts of Maxon's stupidity and Aspen's closeness battled in my head. I didn't know what to do about anything. My reflections were so consuming, I didn't even realize that I'd been mulling them over until well past two in the morning.

I sighed. My maids were going to have to work extra hard to make me look good tomorrow.

Suddenly I saw a light from the hallway. So quietly it felt like I was dreaming it, Aspen cracked open the door, walked in, and shut it behind him.

"Aspen, what are you doing?" I whispered as he crossed the room. "You'll be in so much trouble if you're caught in here!"

He continued to walk silently.

"Aspen?"

He stopped in front of my bed and quietly laid the staff he was holding on the ground. "Do you love him?"

I looked into Aspen's deep eyes, barely visible in the dark. For a split second, I didn't know what to say.

"No."

He ripped back my blankets in a move both graceful and violent. I should have protested, but I didn't. His hand was behind my head, pushing my face to his. He kissed me feverishly, and every good thing in the world fell into place. He didn't smell like his homemade soap anymore, and he was stronger than he used to be, but every move, every touch was familiar.

"They'll kill you for doing this," I breathed in a brief moment when his lips traveled to my neck.

"If I don't, I'll die anyway."

I tried to work up the will to tell him to stop, but I knew any attempts would be halfhearted. A thousand things about this moment felt wrong—that we were breaking so many rules, that as far as I knew Aspen had another girlfriend, that Maxon and I had some sort of feelings for each other—but I couldn't care. I was so angry with Maxon, and Aspen felt so comforting, I just let his hands travel up and down my legs.

I marveled at how different it felt. We'd never had so much space before.

Even with the distraction, I could feel everything else swarming in my head. I was angry with Maxon, angry with Celeste, even angry with Aspen. Hell, I was angry with Illéa. As we kissed on and on, I started crying.

Aspen kissed me through it, and soon some of the tears were his, too.

"I hate you, you know?" I said.

"I know, Mer. I know."

Mer. When he touched me like that, called me that name, I felt like I was a world away. Upset as I was, Aspen felt like home.

We went on for nearly fifteen minutes before he remembered himself.

"I have to get back, the guard doing rounds will be expecting me."

"What?"

"There are guards who do rounds at random. I might have twenty minutes, I might have an hour. If it's a short round, I have less than five minutes."

"Hurry!" I urged, hopping up with him to help him straighten his hair.

He grabbed his staff, and we ran across the floor together. Before he opened the door, he pulled me in to kiss me again. It felt like pure sunlight was traveling down my veins.

"I can't believe you're here," I said. "How did you end up on the palace guard?"

He shrugged. "Turns out I'm a natural. They fly everyone to this training place in Whites. America, it was covered in snow! Nothing like the flurries we get back home. All the new guards are fed and trained and tested. There are shots, too. Don't know what's in them, but I grew really fast. I'm a solid fighter, and I'm smart. I tested the highest in our class."

I smiled with pride. "Not surprised by that at all." I kissed him again. Aspen had always been too good to lead the life of a Six.

He opened the door and checked the hallway. It looked empty.

"I have so much to tell you. We need to talk," I whispered.

"I know. And we will. It's going to take some time, but I'll be back. Not tonight. I don't know when, but soon." He kissed me again, so hard it almost hurt.

"I missed you," he whispered into my mouth, and went back to his post.

I walked back to my bed in a daze. I couldn't believe what I'd just done. Part of me—a very upset part—felt like Maxon deserved this. If he wanted to spare Celeste and humiliate me, then I certainly wouldn't be a part of the Selection much longer. If she could find a way around the rules, there was nothing to stop me anymore. Problem solved.

Suddenly worn out, I fell asleep in moments.

CHAPTER 23

THE NEXT MORNING, I WOKE feeling a little guilty. Frightened even. Just because I didn't return Maxon's ear tug didn't mean he couldn't come to my room any time he wanted. We so easily could have been caught. If anyone had any idea what I'd done . . .

It was treason. And there was only one way the palace dealt with treason.

But another part of me didn't care. In the hazy moments of waking, I relived every look in Aspen's eyes, every touch, every kiss. I missed that so badly.

I wished we'd had more time to talk. I really needed to know what Aspen was thinking, though last night had given me some clues. It was just so unbelievable—after trying so hard to not want him—that *he* might still want *me*.

It was Saturday, and I was supposed to go to the Women's

Room, but I just couldn't stand it. I needed to think, and I knew that wouldn't happen in the endless chatter floating downstairs. When my maids came, I told them I had a headache and would be staying in bed.

They were so helpful, bringing me food and cleaning the room as quietly as possible, that I almost felt bad for lying to them. I had to, though. I couldn't face the queen and the girls and possibly Maxon while my mind was so solidly fixated on Aspen.

I closed my eyes but did not sleep. I tried to clear up just how I felt. Before I got very far, though, there was a knock at the door. I rolled over, catching Anne's face as she silently asked if she should answer it. I sat up quickly, straightened my hair, and gave her a nod.

I prayed that it wouldn't be Maxon— I was afraid he'd be able to read my crimes on my face—but I wasn't prepared to see Aspen's face walking through my door. I felt myself sit up taller and hoped my maids didn't notice.

"Pardon me, miss," he said to Anne. "I'm Officer Leger. I'm here to speak to Lady America about some security measures."

"Of course," she said, smiling brighter than usual and gesturing for Aspen to enter. In the corner I saw Mary nudge Lucy, who let out a tiny giggle.

When he heard the sound, Aspen turned toward them and tipped his hat. "Ladies."

Lucy ducked her head and Mary's cheeks looked redder than my hair, but they didn't answer. Anne, though she also seemed taken by Aspen's good looks, was put together enough to speak at least.

"Shall we leave, miss?"

I considered this. I didn't want to seem too obvious, but some privacy would be nice.

"Only for a moment. I'm sure Officer Leger won't need me for long," I decided, and they whisked right out of the room.

Once they had disappeared behind the door, Aspen spoke. "You're wrong, I'm afraid. I'm going to be needing you for a very long time." He winked at me.

I shook my head. "I still can't believe you're here."

Wasting no time, Aspen took off his hat and sat on the edge of my bed, setting his hands so our fingers just barely touched. "I never thought I'd count the draft as a blessing, but if it gives me the chance to apologize to you, I'll be forever grateful."

I was stunned into silence.

Aspen looked deep into my eyes. "Please forgive me, Mer. I was so, so stupid, and I've regretted that night in the tree house since the second I climbed down the ladder. I was too stubborn to say anything and then your name got called . . . I didn't know what to do." He stopped for a second. It looked like he had tears in his eyes. Was it possible that Aspen had been crying for me the way I'd been crying for him? "I'm still so in love with you."

I bit my lip, holding back my tears. I needed to be sure of one thing before I could even think about this.

"What about Brenna?"

His face fell. "What?"

I gave an unsteady breath. "I saw you two together in the square when I was leaving. Is that over?"

Aspen squinted his face in concentration then burst into laughter. He covered his mouth with his hands and fell backward on the bed before popping up and asking, "Is that what you think? Oh, Mer, she fell. She tripped and I caught her."

"Tripped?"

"Yeah, the square was so full, people were standing on top of one another. She fell into me and made a joke about being a klutz, which you know is true for Brenna even on a good day." I thought about the time she seemed to just fall off the sidewalk for no apparent reason. Why hadn't this occurred to me before? "As soon as I could get free, I was rushing to the stage."

I remembered those moments, Aspen's desperate attempt to get close to me. He hadn't been faking at all. I smiled. "And just what were you planning on doing once you got there?"

He shrugged. "I didn't actually think it out that far. I was considering begging you to stay. I was prepared to make an idiot out of myself if it meant you wouldn't get in that car. But then you looked so mad . . . and I get why you were." He let out a sigh. "I just couldn't do it. Besides, maybe you'd be happy here." He looked around the room at all the beautiful things that were temporarily considered mine. I could see how he would think that.

"Then," he continued, "I thought that I could win you

over once you came home." His voice seemed suddenly tinged with worry. "I was sure you'd want out and come home as soon as you could. But . . . you didn't."

He paused to look at me, but mercifully, didn't ask just how close Maxon and I were. He'd seen some of it already, but he didn't know that we kissed or had secret signals, and I didn't want to have to explain that.

"Then there was the draft, and I figured it would be unfair to even think about writing. I could die out here. I didn't want to try to make you love me again and then . . ."

"Love you again?" I asked incredulously. "Aspen, I never stopped."

In a swift but gentle move, Aspen leaned in and kissed me. He put his hand to my cheek, holding me to him, and every minute of the last two years flooded my body. I was so grateful they weren't lost.

"I'm so sorry," he mumbled between kisses. "I'm so sorry, Mer."

He pulled away to look at me, a small smile on his perfect face, his eyes asking exactly what I was thinking: What do we do now?

Just then, the door opened, and I was horror-struck as my maids took in Aspen's closeness.

"Thank goodness you're back!" he said to them as he pushed his hand more firmly against my cheek before moving it to my forehead. "I don't think you have a temperature, miss."

"What's wrong?" Anne asked, worry falling over her

face as she raced to my bedside.

Aspen stood. "She started saying that she felt funny, something about her head."

"Is your headache worse, miss?" Mary asked. "You look so pale!"

I bet I did. No doubt every drop of blood had dashed away from my face the moment they saw us together. But Aspen, so cool under pressure, had fixed it in a split second.

"I'll get the medicine," Lucy piped in, scurrying to the bathroom.

"Forgive me, miss," Aspen said as my maids went to work. "I don't wish to disturb you any more. I'll come back when you're feeling better."

In his eyes I could see the same face I'd kissed a thousand times in the tree house. The world around us was completely new, but our connection was the same as ever.

"Thank you, officer," I said weakly.

He went to leave, giving me a small bow.

Soon my maids were all stirring around me, trying to heal a sickness that wasn't even there.

My head didn't ache, but my heart did. The longing for Aspen's arms was so familiar, it was like it never left.

I woke to a hard shake on my shoulders from Anne in the middle of the night.

"Wha—?"

"Please, miss, you have to get up!" Her voice was frantic, worn with terror.

"What's wrong? Are you hurt?"

"We're under attack. We have to get you to the base-ment."

My mind was groggy; I couldn't be sure I was hearing her right. But I noticed behind her that Lucy was already crying.

"They're inside?" I asked in disbelief.

Lucy's fearful wail was all the confirmation I needed.

"What do we do?" I asked. A sudden adrenaline spike woke me up, and I jumped out of bed. As soon as I was standing, Mary was pushing my feet into shoes and Anne was putting a robe on me. All I could think was *North or South? North or South?*

"There's a passage here in the corner. It'll take you straight to the safe room in the basement. The guards are there wait-ing. The royal family should already be there and most of the girls, too. Hurry, miss." Anne pulled me out into the hall-way and pushed on a section of wall. It turned, like a hidden passage from some mystery novel. Sure enough, behind the wall, a stairwell awaited me. As I stood there, Tiny bolted from her room and scurried down the passage.

"Okay, let's go," I said. Anne and Mary gaped at me. Lucy was shaking to the point she could barely stand. "Let's go," I repeated.

"No, miss. We go somewhere else. You have to hurry before they get here. Please!"

I knew at best they'd be injured if they were found; at worst they'd die. I couldn't bear them being hurt. Maybe I was a little cocky, but if Maxon had gone out of his way to do everything he'd done thus far, maybe they would matter to him if they mattered to me. Even if we were fighting. Perhaps it was too much generosity to bank on, but I wasn't leaving them here. The fear made me move faster. I grabbed Anne's arm and pushed her in. She stumbled and couldn't stop me as I grabbed Mary and Lucy.

"Move!" I told them.

They started walking, but Anne was protesting the whole way. "They won't let us in, miss! This place is just for the family. . . . They'll just make us leave!" But I didn't care what she said. Whatever their hiding place was, there was no way it would be as safe as wherever the royal family was staying.

The stairwell was lit every few yards, but even so I nearly fell a few times in my haste to move. My mind was blinded with worry. How far had the rebels penetrated before? Did they know these pathways to safety existed? Lucy was half-paralyzed, and I tugged her down to keep us together.

I couldn't tell how long it took for us to reach the bottom, but finally the tiny pathway opened up to a man-made cavern. I could see other stairways and other girls, everyone running behind what looked to be a two-foot-thick door. We ran up to our safe place.

"Thank you for delivering this girl. You can leave," a guard said to my maids.

"No! They're with me. They're staying," I said with authority.

"Miss, they have their own places to be," he countered.

"Fine. They don't go in, I don't go in. I'm sure Prince Maxon will appreciate knowing that my absence is your doing. Let's go, ladies." I pulled on Mary and Lucy's hands. Anne was shocked into stillness.

"Wait! Wait! Fine, go inside. But if anyone has an issue with it, it's on your hands."

"Not a problem," I said. I turned the girls and walked into the safe room with my head held high.

There was a clamor of activity inside. Some girls were huddled together crying, others were in prayer. I saw the king and queen sitting alone, surrounded by more guards. Beside them, Maxon was holding Elayna's hand. She looked a little shaken but obviously felt calmer with him touching her. I looked at the royal family's position . . . so close to the door. I wondered if it was like a captain going down with his ship. They'd do everything to keep this place afloat, but if it went down, they'd be the first ones to drown.

Their little group saw my entrance and noted the company I was keeping. I took in the confused expressions on their faces, nodded once, and continued to walk with my head high. I figured so long as I looked sure of myself, no one would question me.

I was wrong.

I took three more steps and Silvia walked up. She looked incredibly calm. This was all obviously old news for her.

"Good. Some help. Girls, you will immediately get to the water stores in the back and begin serving refreshments to the royal family and the ladies. Get going, now," she commanded.

"No." I turned to Anne and gave her my first real order. "Anne, please take some refreshments to the king, queen, and prince and then come join me." I faced Silvia. "The rest can fend for themselves. They chose to leave their maids alone, they can get their own damn water. Mine will be sitting with me. Come, ladies."

I knew we were close enough to the royals that they would have heard me. In my quest to have a level of authority, I'd spoken a little too loudly. But I didn't care if they thought I was rude. Lucy was more frightened than most of the people in this room. She was trembling head to foot, and there was no way I'd have her serving people half her equal in goodness in her state.

Perhaps it was all my years as a big sister, but I just had to keep these girls safe.

We found a little space in the back of the room. Whoever usually kept this place ready must not have been prepared for the influx the Selection would cause, because there weren't nearly enough chairs in here. But I saw the stores of food and water and could tell they would get us through months down here, if the need arose.

It was a funny little array of people. Obviously, several officials had been up working through the night, and they were in suits. Maxon himself was still dressed. But nearly all the girls were in their thin nightgowns that helped you sleep in the warmth of the rooms upstairs. Not all of them had been able to get a robe on in their haste to leave. I was even a little chilly under mine.

Many of the girls had piled themselves toward the front of the room. Obviously, they'd be the first to die if someone got through the door. But if they didn't, think of all the time spent right in front of Maxon! A few were closer to where we were, and most of them were in a similar state as Lucy—shaking, tearful, and petrified with worry.

I pulled Lucy under an arm and Mary cuddled her from the other side. There wasn't anything to say about the situation that was pleasant, so we stayed quiet, listening to the clamor of the room. The jangle of voices reminded me of the first day here, when they were giving us makeovers. I closed my eyes and pictured that action with the sound in an attempt to make myself as calm as I appeared.

"Are you okay?"

I looked up and there was Aspen, glorious in his uniform. His tone was very official, and he didn't seem shaken by the situation at all. I sighed.

"Yes, thank you."

We were quiet for a moment, watching people get settled in the room. Mary had obviously been exhausted—she was already asleep and leaning heavily on Lucy's side. Lucy was fairly calm, all things considered. She'd stopped crying and just sat there looking at Aspen with a kind of wonder in her eyes.

"It was good of you to bring your maids. Not everyone would be so kind to people considered beneath them," he said.

"Castes never meant that much to me," I said quietly. He

gave me the smallest smile.

Lucy took in a breath like she was going to ask Aspen a question, but a loud yelling coursed through the chamber. A guard on the far end of the room was barking instructions for us to all silence ourselves.

Aspen walked away, which was good. I feared someone would be able to see something.

"That was the same guard from earlier, wasn't it?" Lucy asked.

"Yes, it was."

"I've seen him guarding your door lately. He's awfully friendly," she commented.

I was sure Aspen would speak to my maids as kindly as he spoke to me when they crossed his path. They were Sixes, after all.

"He's very handsome," she added.

I smiled and contemplated saying something, but that same guard instructed us to be quiet. After a few jagged edges of conversation dulled away, an eerie hush fell over the room.

The silence was worse than any sound. Without a single sense to guide me, my imagination took over, producing horrific scenes in my head: rooms demolished, a string of bodies, a merciless army only feet from the door. I found myself clutching the girls nearer to me, as if we could protect one another from whatever would come.

The only stirring was Maxon walking around to check on each of the girls. When he got to our corner, only Lucy was awake with me, and every once in a while, we'd have a quick conversation in breathed words, reading each other's lips. As Maxon approached, he smiled at the pile of people leaning on me. In that moment, I could see no anger left from our argument, though I really wanted to resolve it. Instead, I saw his grateful smile, simply happy that I was okay. A wave of guilt went through me. . . . What had I gotten myself into?

"Are you well?" he asked.

I nodded. He looked at Lucy and leaned across me to speak to her. I inhaled. Maxon didn't smell like anything that could be bottled. Not like cinnamon or vanilla or even, I remembered quickly, like homemade soap. He had his own smell, a mix of chemicals that burned out from him.

"And you?" he asked Lucy.

She nodded, too.

"Are you surprised to find yourself down here?" He smiled at Lucy, making light of what was an unimaginable situation.

"No, Your Majesty. Not with her." Lucy nodded in my direction.

Maxon turned to look at me, and his face was incredibly close. I felt uncomfortable. Too many people could see us; Aspen included. But the moment passed quickly, and he turned back to Lucy.

"I know what you mean." Maxon smiled again. He looked like he might say more, but then changed his mind and moved to stand.

I quickly grabbed his arm and whispered, "North or South?"

"Do you remember the photo shoot?" he breathed.

Shocked, I nodded. These rebels were making their way northwest, burning crops and slaughtering people along the way. *Intercept them*, he'd said. These rebels, these murderers, had been slowly coming for us all this time, and we couldn't stop them. They were killers. They were Southerners.

"Tell no one." He left, moving on to Fiona, who was holding herself and crying quietly.

I practiced breathing slowly, trying to imagine ways I could escape if they got to us, but I was fooling myself. If the rebels managed to get down here, it was all over. There was nothing to do but wait.

The hours crept on. I had no idea what time it was, but people who had dozed off had woken up, and those of us who had powered through the time were starting to wilt.

Finally, the door opened as some guards left to investigate. More time passed as the palace was swept, and eventually they returned.

"Ladies and gentlemen," one of the guards called, "the rebels have been subdued. We are asking that everyone please return to their rooms via the back stairs. There's quite a mess and scores of injured guards. It's better if you all bypass the main rooms and halls until they can be cleared. If you are a member of the Selection, please proceed to your room and stay there until further notice. I've spoken with the cooks, and food will be brought to you within the hour. I'm going to need all medical personnel to report with me to the hospital wing."

With that, people stood and started moving like nothing had happened. Some people even looked bored. Except for the faces of people like Lucy, it seemed everyone took the attack in stride, as if it were to be expected.

My room had been ransacked. Mattress on the floor, dresses pulled out of the closet, the pictures of my family torn up on the ground. I looked around for my jar, and it was still intact with its penny inside, just hidden under the bed. I tried not to cry, but my eyes kept welling up. It wasn't that I was afraid, though I was. I just didn't like that an enemy had put their hands all over my things, had ruined them.

It took quite a while to set things right, since we were all so tired. We managed, though. Anne even found some tape so I could put my pictures back together. I sent my maids to bed the moment I got my tape. Anne protested, but I wouldn't have any of it. Now that I'd found my ability to command, I wasn't afraid to use it.

Once I was alone, I let myself cry. The fear, even though it had mostly passed, still had a hold on me.

I pulled out the jeans that Maxon had given me and my one shirt from home and put them on. I felt a little more normal this way. My hair was messy from the events of the night and most of the morning, so I pulled it up into a casual little bun on the top of my head, pieces falling down around my face.

I set the fragments of pictures on the bed, trying to figure out which ones went together. It was like having four puzzles' worth of pieces all in the same box. I had managed to put only one together when there was a knock at the door.

Maxon, I thought. *Please be Maxon.* I threw the door open hopefully.

"Hello, dearie." It was Silvia. She had a little pout on her face that I supposed was meant to be a consolation. She scuttled right past me into my room, then turned and took in what I was wearing.

"Oh, don't tell me you're leaving, too," she whined. "Honestly, it was nothing." She wiped the whole incident away with her hand.

I wouldn't call it nothing. Couldn't she tell I'd been crying?

"I'm not leaving," I said, tucking a hair behind my ear. "Are others going home?"

She sighed. "Yes, three so far. And Maxon, dear boy, told me to let anyone who wants to leave go home. Arrangements are being made as we speak. It's so funny. It was as if he knew girls would be leaving. If I were in your position, I'd think twice before leaving over all this nonsense."

Silvia started walking around my room, taking in the decor. Nonsense? What was wrong with this woman?

"Did they take anything?" she asked casually.

"No, ma'am. They made a mess, but nothing's missing as far as I can tell."

"Very good." She walked over to me and handed me a tiny portable phone. "This is the safest line in the palace.

You need to call your family and tell them you're fine. Don't take too long, now. I still have a few girls to see."

I marveled at the tiny object. I'd never actually held a portable phone. I'd seen them before in the hands of Twos and Threes, but I never thought I'd get to use one. My hands trembled with excitement. I was going to hear their voices!

I dialed the number eagerly. After everything that had happened, it actually brought a smile to my face. Mom picked up after two rings.

"Hello?"

"Mom?"

"America! Is that you? Are you okay? Some guard called to tell us we might not be able to get ahold of you for a few days, and we knew those damn rebels had gotten through. We've been so scared." She started crying.

"Oh, don't cry, Mom. I'm safe." I looked over at Silvia. She looked bored.

"Hold on." There was a bit of movement.

"America?" May's voice was thick with tears. She must have had the worst day.

"May! Oh, May, I miss you so much!" I felt the tears rising again.

"I thought you were dead! America, I love you. Promise me you won't die," she wailed.

"I promise." I had to smile at such a vow.

"Will you come home? Can't you? I don't want you there anymore." May was practically begging.

"Come home?" I asked.

I felt so many things. I missed my family, and I was tired of hiding from rebels. I was getting more and more confused over my feelings for Aspen and Maxon, and I didn't know how to handle them. The easiest thing to do would be to leave. But still.

"No, May, I can't come home. I have to stay here."

"Why?" May moaned.

"Because," I said simply.

"Because why?"

"Just . . . because."

May was quiet for a moment, thinking. "Are you in love with Maxon?" For a minute I heard the boy-crazy May that I was used to. She'd be fine.

"Umm, I don't know about that, but—"

"America! You're in love with Maxon! Oh my gosh!" I heard Dad yelling, "What?" in the background and then Mom's "Yes, yes, yes!"

"May, I never said—"

"I knew it!" May just laughed and laughed. Just like that, all her fears of losing me vanished.

"May, I have to go. The others need the phone. But I just wanted you all to know that I'm okay. I'll write you soon, I promise."

"Okay, okay. Tell me about Maxon! And send more treats! I love you!" she yelled.

"I love you, too. Bye."

I hung up the phone before she could ask for anything

else. The moment her voice was gone, though, I missed her more than I had before.

Silvia was swift. She had the phone out of my hand in a matter of seconds and was walking to the door.

"There's a good girl," she said, and disappeared down the hall.

I certainly didn't feel good. But I knew that once I figured out how to set things right with Aspen and Maxon, I would.

CHAPTER 24

AMY, FIONA, AND TALLULAH were gone within hours. I wasn't sure if the speed was due to the efficiency of Silvia or the nerves of the girls. We dropped to nineteen, and it suddenly felt like this was all moving quickly. Still, I couldn't have predicted how much faster it would become.

The Monday after the attacks, we returned to our routine. Breakfast was as delicious as ever, and I wondered if there would come a time when I wouldn't appreciate these amazing meals.

"Kriss, isn't this divine?" I asked as I bit into a piece of star-shaped fruit. I'd never seen it before I came to the palace. Kriss's mouth was full, but she nodded in agreement. I felt a warm sense of sisterhood this morning. Now that we had survived a major rebel attack together, it felt like these small bonds had sealed into something unbreakable. Beside

Kriss, Emily was passing me honey. Next to me, Tiny was asking where my songbird necklace came from with admiration in her eyes. The atmosphere was that of my family dinners a few years ago, before Kota turned into a jerk and we lost Kenna to a husband: full, bright, chatty.

I suddenly knew, just as Maxon had said his mother had done, that I would contact these girls down the road. I would want to know who everyone married and send them Christmas cards. And in twenty-some-odd years, if Maxon had a son, I'd call to ask them about their favorite girls in the new Selection. And we'd remember everything we'd gone through and laugh about it as if it had been an adventure, not a competition.

Oddly enough, the only person in the room who appeared to be distressed was Maxon. He didn't touch his food but instead gazed up and down the rows of girls with a clear look of concentration on his face. Every once in a while, he paused midthought and seemed to debate with himself over something, and then moved on.

When he came to my row, he caught me looking at him and gave me a weak smile. Except for the quick interlude last night, we hadn't spoken since our argument, and there were things that needed to be said. This time, I needed to be the initiator. With an expression that said it was a request, not a demand, I tugged my ear. His expression remained strained, but he tugged his ear, too.

I sighed with relief and found my eyes moving toward the doors of the massive room. As I'd suspected, another pair of eyes was looking my way. I'd noticed Aspen when I entered, but I tried not to acknowledge him. I supposed it was impossible to ignore someone you've loved that much.

Maxon stood up. The sudden movement made his chair screech in a way that drew our collective attention. As we all turned toward him, he looked like he wished he could sit back down unnoticed. Realizing that wasn't an option, he spoke instead.

"Ladies," he said with a bow of his head. He looked genuinely pained. "I'm afraid that after yesterday's attack, I've been forced to seriously reconsider the operation of the Selection. As you know, three ladies asked to leave yesterday, and I obliged. I wouldn't want anyone here against their will. Furthermore, I don't feel comfortable keeping anyone in the palace, facing this constant threat of danger, when I feel confident that we don't have any sort of future together."

Around the room, the confusion changed to a clear and unhappy understanding.

"He's not . . . ," Tiny whispered.

"Yes, he is," I replied.

"Though it grieves me to do this, I have discussed the matter with my family and a few close advisers and have decided to go ahead and narrow the Selection down to the Elite. However, instead of ten, I've decided to send all but six of you home," Maxon stated in a businesslike tone.

"Six?" Kriss gasped.

"That's not fair," Tiny breathed, already starting to cry.

I looked around the room as the hum of complaints rose

and fell. Celeste braced herself, as if she could fight for a spot. Bariel had closed her eyes and crossed her fingers, perhaps hoping that image would garner her some sympathy. Marlee, who had admitted that she didn't care for Maxon, looked incredibly tense. Why did she want to stay so badly?

"I don't wish to draw this out unnecessarily, so only the following ladies will be staying. Lady Marlee and Lady Kriss."

Marlee breathed out a sigh of relief and put a hand to her chest. Kriss did a happy, fidgety dance in her chair and looked at the girls around her, expecting us to be happy. And I was until I realized that two of the six spots were already gone. With a disagreement hanging between Maxon and me, would he send me home? Did he not see any future with me? Did I want him to? What would I do if I had to go?

This whole time, the power had been in my hands as to when I would leave. I was abruptly aware of how important it was to me to stay.

"Lady Natalie and Lady Celeste," he continued, looking at them both in turn. I cringed at Celeste's name. He couldn't keep her and not me. I could hardly believe he was keeping her at all. But was that a sign I was going? We'd fought about her very presence here.

"Lady Elise," he said, and the room inhaled a breath, awaiting the final name. I realized Tiny and I were squeezing each other's hands.

"And Lady America." Maxon looked over at me, and I felt every muscle in my body relax. Tiny started bawling immediately, and she wasn't alone. Maxon let out a long sigh.

"To everyone else, I'm incredibly sorry, but I hope you all trust me when I say that I meant this to be a good thing for you. I don't want to raise anyone's hopes for no reason and risk your life in the process. If anyone who is leaving wants to speak to me, I'll be in the library down the hall, and you may visit me as soon as you've finished eating."

Maxon walked out of the room as quickly as he could without running. I watched him until he crossed in front of Aspen, and then my attention was diverted. Aspen's face was confused, and I knew why. I'd told him I didn't love Maxon, so he would have assumed I meant next to nothing to Maxon as well. So why would I be so tense about staying or going? And why would Maxon want to keep me around?

Before a second had passed, Emmica and Tuesday were running after Maxon, no doubt looking for an explanation. Some girls were in tears, obviously heartbroken, and it fell on those of us remaining to comfort them.

It was unbearably awkward. Tiny ended up swatting away my hands and running out of the room. I hoped she wouldn't hold any bitter feelings against me.

People left within minutes, no longer hungry. I didn't linger myself, unable to handle the outpouring of emotion. As I passed Aspen, he whispered "tonight." I gave a tiny nod and went on my way.

The rest of the morning was odd. I'd never really had friends that I would miss. All the occupied rooms on the second floor were open, and girls scurried in and out, passing notes and gathering addresses. We cried together and laughed together, and by the afternoon, the palace had turned into a far more serious place than it was when we came.

No one was left in my little wing of the hall, so there was no sound of maids rushing to and fro, or of doors closing. I sat at my table, reading a book as my maids dusted. I wondered if the palace always felt this lonely. The emptiness made me miss my family.

Suddenly a knock came at the door. Anne rushed to get it, looking at me to make sure I was prepared for a visitor. I gave her a small nod.

When Maxon came into the room, I jumped to my feet.

"Ladies," he said, looking to my maids. "We meet again."

They curtsied and giggled. He acknowledged them and turned his eyes to me. I hadn't realized how eager I was to see him. I stood by the table in a daze.

"Do forgive me, but I need to speak with Lady America. Would you give us a moment?"

There was more curtsying and giggling, and Anne asked— with a tone that implied near worship of the prince—if she could bring him anything. Maxon declined, and they left us. He had his hands in his pockets. We were silent for a while.

"I thought you might not keep me," I finally admitted.

"Why?" he asked, sounding honestly confused.

"Because we fought. Because everything between us is weird. Because . . ." *Because even though you're dating five other women, I think I'm cheating on you*, I thought.

Maxon closed the distance between us slowly, choosing

his words as he walked. When he finally reached me, he picked up my hands in his and explained everything.

"First, let me say I'm sorry. I shouldn't have yelled at you." His voice was completely sincere. "It's just that some of the committees and my father are already pressuring me in this, and I truly want to be able to make the decision for myself. It was frustrating to run into another situation where my opinion wasn't being taken seriously."

"Another situation?" I asked.

"Well, you've seen my choices. Marlee is a favorite with the people, and that cannot be overlooked. Celeste is a very powerful young woman, and she comes from an excellent family to align ourselves with. Natalie and Kriss are charming girls, both very agreeable and favorites of some in my family. Elise happens to have relations in New Asia. Since we're trying to end this damn war, that is something to take into consideration. I've been debated down and cornered from every side on this decision."

There was no explanation for me, and I almost didn't ask for it. I knew that we were friends first and that I had no political uses at all. But I needed to hear the words so I could make the decision for myself. I couldn't look him in the eye.

"And why am I still here?" My voice was barely above a whisper. I was sure this was going to hurt. In the pit of my stomach I was sure I was only still here because he was too good to break his promise.

"America, I thought I'd made myself clear," Maxon said

calmly. He let out a patient sigh and used his hand to nudge up my chin. When I was finally looking into his eyes, he confessed.

"If this were a simpler matter, I'd have eliminated everyone else by now. I know how I feel about you. Maybe it's impulsive of me to think I could be so sure, but I'm certain I would be happy with you."

I blushed. I could feel tears rising, but I blinked them away. The expression on his face was so adoring, I didn't want to miss it.

"There are moments when I feel like you and I have broken down every last wall, and then others when I think you only want to stay for convenience. If I knew for sure that I, and I alone, was your motivation . . ."

He paused and shook his head, as if the end of his sentence was something he couldn't let himself want.

"Would I be wrong in saying that you're still unsure of me?"

I didn't want to hurt him, but I had to be honest. "No."

"Then I have to hedge my bets. You may decide to leave, and I will let you go if you do. In the meantime, I have to find a wife. I'm trying to make the best decision I can within the boundaries I've been given, but please, don't doubt for a moment that I care for you. Deeply."

I couldn't hold back the tears anymore. I thought about Aspen and what I'd done, and I felt so ashamed.

"Maxon?" I sniffed. "Can you . . . can you ever forgive—?" I didn't get to finish my confession. He came even closer and started sweeping the tears off my face with his strong fingers.

"Forgive what? Our stupid little fight? It's already forgotten. Your feelings being a little slower than mine? I'm prepared to wait," he said with a shrug. "I don't think there's anything you could do that I couldn't forgive. Need I remind you of the knee to my groin?"

I couldn't help but laugh. Maxon chuckled once, then became suddenly serious.

"What's wrong?" I asked.

He shook his head. "They were so fast this time." Maxon's voice was full of an aggravated wonder at the talents of the rebels. I suddenly wondered how close to disaster I had come by trying to save my maids.

"I'm getting more and more worried, America. North or South, they're getting exceptionally determined. It seems they won't stop until they get what they want, and we haven't the faintest clue what it is." Maxon looked confused and sad. "I feel like it's only a matter of time until they destroy someone important to me."

He looked into my eyes.

"You know, you still have a choice in this. If you're afraid to stay, you should say so." He paused, thinking. "Or if you don't think you can love me at all, it would be kinder to tell me now. I'll let you go on your way, and we can part as friends."

I wrapped my arms around him, resting my head against his chest. Maxon seemed both comforted and surprised by the gesture. It took only a second for him to wrap his arms securely around me.

"Maxon, I'm not completely sure what we are, but we're definitely more than friends."

He let out a sigh. With my head there against his chest, I could faintly make out the sound of his heart beating through his suit coat. It seemed to be rushing. His hand, gentle as ever, reached to cup my cheek. As I looked into his eyes, I felt that unnameable feeling that was growing between us.

With his eyes, Maxon asked for something we'd both agreed to wait on. I was glad he didn't want to wait anymore. I gave him a tiny nod, and he bridged the small gap between us, kissing me with unimaginable tenderness.

I felt a smile underneath his lips, and it lingered for a long time after.

CHAPTER 25

I FELT A NUDGE ON my arm. It was dark and either very late or very early. For a fraction of a second, I thought that there'd been yet another attack. Then I knew I was wrong because of the single word used to wake me.

"Mer?"

My back was to Aspen, and I took a moment to steady myself before I faced him. In my head, I knew that there were things that needed to be set right between us. I hoped my heart would let me say them.

I rolled over and caught Aspen's bright green eyes and knew this would be difficult. Then I noticed that he'd left the door to my room open.

"Aspen, are you crazy?" I whispered. "Close the door."

"No, I've thought this out. With the door open, I can tell anyone who comes by that I heard a noise and was checking on you, which is my job. No one would suspect a thing."

It was simple and brilliant. I nodded my head in under-standing. "Okay."

I turned on the small lamp on my bedside table to make it clear to any passersby that we weren't hiding anything. I noticed that the clock said it was past three in the morning.

Aspen was obviously pleased with himself. His smile, the same one that used to greet me in the tree house, was wide.

"You kept it," he said.

"Huh?"

Aspen pointed down to my bedside table, where the jar sat with its lone penny.

"Yeah," I said. "I just couldn't bring myself to get rid of it."

His expression grew more and more hopeful. He turned to look at the door, as if checking quickly that no one was there. Then he bent down to kiss me.

"No," I said quietly, pulling away. "You can't do that."

The look in his eyes warred between confusion and sad-ness, and I feared that everything I was about to say was only going to make things worse.

"Did I do something wrong?"

"No," I said adamantly. "You've been wonderful. I've been so happy to see you again and to know that you still love me. It's changed everything."

He smiled. "Good. Because I do love you, and I'm plan-ning on making sure you never have a reason to doubt it."

I squirmed. "Aspen, whatever we were, or are right now,

we can't be that here."

"What do you mean?" he asked, shifting his weight.

"I'm part of the Selection right now. I'm here for Maxon, and I can't date you or whatever this is while it's still going on." I started fidgeting with a bit of my comforter.

He thought a moment. "So were you lying to me? When you said you never stopped loving me?"

"No," I assured him. "You've been in my heart the whole time. You're the reason things have been going as slow as they are. Maxon likes me, but I can't let myself really care about him because of you."

"Well, great," he said sarcastically. "Glad to know you'd be fine dating him if I wasn't around."

Underneath the anger, I could see he was heartbroken, but it wasn't my fault it turned out this way.

"Aspen?" I asked quietly, getting him to look at me. "When you left me in the tree house, you crushed me."

"Mer, I said I—"

"Let me finish." He huffed, then was silent. "You took away my dreams, and the only reason I'm here is because you insisted I sign up."

He shook his head, irritated at the truth.

"I've been trying to put myself back together, and Maxon really cares about me. You mean so much to me, you know you do. But I'm part of this now, and I'd be stupid to not let myself see what happens."

"So you're choosing him over me?" he asked miserably.

"No, I'm not choosing him *or* you. I'm choosing me."

That was the truth at the core of everything. I didn't know what I wanted yet, and I couldn't let myself be swayed by what was easy or what someone else thought was right. I had to give myself time to decide what was best for me.

Aspen mulled this over for a moment, still not happy with what I was saying. Finally he smiled.

"You know I'm not giving up, right?" His tone was an obvious challenge, and I grinned in spite of myself. It was true that Aspen was not the type to admit defeat.

"This really isn't a good place to try to fight for me. Your determination is a dangerous trait here."

"I'm not afraid of that *suit*," he scoffed.

I rolled my eyes, amused at being on this end of the relationship. I'd always been worried about someone stealing Aspen. I felt guilty about how refreshing it was to see him worried about someone stealing me for a change.

"Okay. You said you didn't love him . . . but you must like him a little to be willing to stay, right?"

I ducked my head. "I do," I said with a tiny nod. "He's more than I ever imagined he was."

He considered that for a moment, soaking it in.

"I guess that means I'll have to fight harder than I thought," he said, heading for the hall. Then he turned and gave me another wink. "Goodnight, Lady America."

"Goodnight, Officer Leger."

The door clicked shut, and the sense of peace was overwhelming. Since the Selection had started, I'd been worrying that it was something that was going to ruin my life. But in this moment, I couldn't think of a time that felt more right.

Too soon, my maids bustled in. Anne pulled back the curtains, and as the light fell on me, it felt like this was truly my first day at the palace.

The Selection was no longer something that was simply happening to me, but something I was actively a part of. I was an Elite. I pulled back the covers and leaped into the morning.

END OF BOOK ONE

ACKNOWLEDGMENTS

OKAY, JUST IN CASE YOU'RE really busy or tired because you stayed up late finishing, I want to thank you first for reading my book. For reals, I love you. Thanks.

Now, to the people who made this happen. Well, actually, let's go back a bit more.

As always, I thank God for words. I'm so glad I don't have to try to communicate this story to you with my antennae or something. Words are so delicious, and I'll be forever happy they exist.

Callaway: Oat bananas! Thanks for supporting me and being generally awesome.

Guyden: Thank you for sharing Mommy with the friends in her head.

Loads of love to my mom, dad, and little brother for encouraging me to be strange. Also, hugs and love to my mom, dad, and little brother-in-law for being such incredible cheerleaders. Between the six of you, I've been engulfed in excitement, and I'm so grateful for all of you.

Thank you to the gang at [nlcf] and to the FTW Crew for celebrating with me along the way. Hugs!

Thanks to Mary—the first person to read *The Selection*

ever—for thinking it was cool, and to Liz and Michelle for being the thoughtful, rational, in-depth readers that I am not. The book is better because of you guys. Also, I think you are awesome.

Thank you to Ashley Brouillette for making a great video and earning her name a spot in the book. Bravo, miss! I also have to say thanks to Elizabeth O'Brien, Emily Arnold, and Kayleigh Poulin for hanging out with me when I was a nerd. Thanks for letting me use your names as well.

Other names I borrowed: Jenna, Elise, Mary, Lucy, Gerad, Amy, etc. Thanks for popping into my mind when I had no idea what to type. Yay!

Elana Roth: You are a rock goddess of an agent, and I cannot thank you enough for taking a chance on me even though I'm really, really awful on the phone. Still can't figure out what possessed you. Also, thanks for letting me hug you. Love!

To Caren and Colleen at JLA, thanks for being there and generally rocking.

Erica Sussman: You are so dang cool. For realzies. It's kind of amazing how well you get America and how fun you are to work with. I adore you and your purple pen. Thank you for never making this feel like work.

Tyler, you sassy girl, I feel your energy in everything. Thanks for all your work.

Dear Everyone at HarperTeen: Umm, THANK YOU! You were a dream I didn't dare speak aloud, and I'm honored to be one of your authors and appreciate all of your work for me. From cover art to marketing to just the way you communicate with me, everything has been better than I could have ever hoped for. Thank you. Truly.

Jeannette, Catherine, Kati, Ciara, Christina, the ladies at Guy's daycare, and anyone I might have missed: Thank you for watching Guyden at various times so I could work. It meant so much to me to know I wasn't alone in this.

And, if you made it all the way through this, thanks again to you! Some of you have been with me from the first time I sat in front of a camera and said "Hello Interwebs." Some of you read *The Siren* or found me on Twitter. Some of you just saw the pretty girl on the cover of the book and decided to pick it up. However and whenever you found me, thank you for reading my book. I hope it made you all kinds of happy.

READ ON FOR A SNEAK PEEK AT

35 GIRLS CAME TO THE PALACE. ONLY 6 REMAIN.

THE ELITE

A SELECTION NOVEL

KIERA CASS

New York Times BESTSELLING AUTHOR

CHAPTER 1

THE ANGELES AIR WAS QUIET, and for a while I lay still, listening to the sound of Maxon's breathing. It was getting harder and harder to catch him in a truly calm and happy moment, and I soaked up the time, grateful that he seemed to be at his best when he and I were alone.

Ever since the Selection had been narrowed down to six girls, he'd been more anxious than he was when the thirty-five of us arrived in the first place. I guessed he thought he'd have more time to make his choices. And though it made me feel guilty to admit it, I knew I was the reason why he wished he did.

Prince Maxon, heir to the Illéa throne, liked me. He'd told me a week ago that if I could simply say that I cared for him the way he did for me, without anything holding me back, this whole competition would be over. And sometimes

I played with the idea, wondering how it would feel to be Maxon's alone.

But the thing was, Maxon wasn't really mine to begin with. There were five other girls here—girls he took on dates and whispered things to—and I didn't know what to make of that. And then there was the fact that if I accepted Maxon, it meant I had to accept a crown, a thought I tended to ignore if only because I wasn't sure what it would mean for me.

And, of course, there was Aspen.

He wasn't technically my boyfriend anymore—he'd broken up with me before my name was even drawn for the Selection—but when he showed up at the palace as one of the guards, all the feelings I'd been trying to let go of flooded my heart. Aspen was my first love; when I looked at him . . . I was his.

Maxon didn't know that Aspen was in the palace, but he did know that there was someone at home that I was trying to get over, and he was graciously giving me time to move on while attempting to find someone else he'd be happy with in the event I couldn't ever love him.

As he moved his head, inhaling just above my hairline, I considered it. What would it be like to simply love Maxon?

"Do you know the last time I really looked at the stars?" he asked.

I settled closer to him on our blanket, trying to keep warm in the cool Angeles night. "No idea."

"A tutor had me studying astronomy a few years ago. If

you look closely, you can tell that the stars are actually different colors."

"Wait, the last time you looked at the stars was to *study* them? What about for fun?"

He chuckled. "Fun. I'll have to pencil in some between the budget consultations and infrastructure committee meetings. Oh, and war strategizing, which, by the way, I am terrible at."

"What else are you terrible at?" I asked, running my hand across his starched shirt. Encouraged by the touch, Maxon drew circles on my shoulder with the hand he had wrapped behind my back.

"Why would you want to know that?" he asked in mock irritation.

"Because I still know so little about you. And you seem perfect all the time. It's nice to have proof you're not."

He propped himself up on an elbow, focusing on my face. "You *know* I'm not."

"Pretty close," I countered. Little flickers of touch ran between us. Knees, arms, fingers.

He shook his head, a small smile on his face. "Okay, then. I can't plan wars. I'm rotten at it. And I'm guessing I'd be a terrible cook. I've never tried, so—"

"Never?"

"You might have noticed the teams of people keeping you up to your neck in pastries? They happen to feed me as well."

I giggled. I helped cook practically every meal at home. "More," I demanded. "What else are you bad at?"

He held me close, his brown eyes bright with a secret. "Recently I've discovered this one thing. . . ."

"Tell."

"It turns out I'm absolutely terrible at staying away from you. It's a very serious problem."

I smiled. "Have you really tried?"

He pretended to think about it. "Well, no. And don't expect me to start."

We laughed quietly, holding on to each other. In these moments, it was so easy to picture this being the rest of my life.

The rustle of leaves and grass announced that someone was coming. Even though our date was completely acceptable, I felt a little embarrassed and sat up quickly. Maxon followed suit as a guard made his way around the hedge to us.

"Your Majesty," he said with a bow. "Sorry to intrude, sir, but it's really unwise to stay out this late for so long. The rebels could—"

"Understood," Maxon said with a sigh. "We'll be right in."

The guard left us alone, and Maxon turned back to me. "Another fault of mine: I'm losing patience with the rebels. I'm tired of dealing with them."

He stood and offered me his hand. I took it, watching the sad frustration in his eyes. We'd been attacked twice by the rebels since the start of the Selection—once by the simply disruptive Northerners and once by the deadly Southerners—and even with my brief experience, I could understand his exhaustion.

Maxon was picking up the blanket and shaking it out, clearly not happy that our night had been cut short.

"Hey," I said, urging him to face me. "I had fun."

He nodded.

"No, really," I said, walking over to him. He moved the blanket to one hand to wrap his free arm around me. "We should do it again sometime. You can tell me which stars are which colors, because I seriously can't tell."

Maxon gave me a sad smile. "I wish things were easier sometimes, normal."

I moved so I could wrap my arms around him, and as I did so, Maxon dropped the blanket to return the gesture. "I hate to break it to you, Your Majesty, but even without the guards, you're far from normal."

His expression lightened a bit but was still serious. "You'd like me more if I was."

"I know you find it hard to believe, but I really do like you the way you are. I just need more—"

"Time. I know. And I'm prepared to give you that. I only wish I knew that you'd actually want to be with me when that time was over."

I looked away. That wasn't something I could promise. I weighed Maxon and Aspen in my heart over and over, and neither of them ever had a true edge. Except, maybe, when I was alone with one of them. Because, at that moment, I was tempted to promise Maxon that I would be there for him in the end.

But I couldn't.

"Maxon," I whispered, seeing how dejected he looked at my lack of an answer. "I can't tell you that. But what I can tell you is that I *want* to be here. I *want* to know if there's a possibility for . . . for . . ." I stammered, not sure how to put it.

"Us?" Maxon guessed.

I smiled, happy at how easily he understood me. "Yes. I want to know if there's a possibility for us to be an us."

He moved a lock of hair behind my shoulder. "I think the odds are very high," he said matter-of-factly.

"I think so, too. Just . . . time, okay?"

He nodded, looking happier. This was how I wanted to end our night, with hope. Well, and maybe one more thing. I bit my lip and leaned into Maxon, asking with my eyes.

Without a second of hesitation, he bent to kiss me. It was warm and gentle, and it left me feeling adored and somehow aching for more. I could have stayed there for hours, just to see if I could get enough of that feeling; but too soon, Maxon backed away.

"Let's go," he said in a playful tone, pulling me toward the palace. "Better get inside before the guards come for us on horseback with spears drawn."

As Maxon left me at the stairs, the tiredness hit me like a wall. I was practically dragging myself up to the second floor and around the corner to my room when, suddenly, I was quite awake again.

"Oh!" Aspen said, surprised to see me, too. "I think it makes me the worst guard ever that I assumed you were in your room this whole time."

I giggled. The Elite were supposed to sleep with at least one of their maids on watch in the night. I really didn't like that, so Maxon insisted on stationing a guard by my room in case there was an emergency. The thing was, most of the time that guard was Aspen. It was a strange mix of exhilaration and terror knowing that nearly every night he was right outside my door.

The lightness of the moment faded quickly as Aspen grasped what it meant that I hadn't been safely tucked in my bed. He cleared his throat uncomfortably.

"Did you have a good time?"

"Aspen," I whispered, looking to make sure no one was around. "Don't be upset. I'm part of the Selection, and this is just how it is."

"How am I supposed to stand a chance, Mer? How can I compete when you only ever talk to one of us?" He made a good point, but what could I do?

"Please don't be mad at me, Aspen. I'm trying to figure all this out."

"No, Mer," he said, gentleness returning to his voice. "I'm not mad at you. I *miss* you." He didn't dare say the words aloud, but he mouthed them. *I love you.*

I melted.

"I know," I said, placing a hand on his chest, letting myself forget for a moment all that we were risking. "But that doesn't change where we are or that I'm an Elite now. I need time, Aspen."

He reached up to hold my hand in his and nodded. "I can give you that. Just . . . try to find some time for me, too."

I didn't want to bring up how complicated that would be, so I gave him a tiny smile before gently pulling my hand away. "I need to go."

He watched me as I walked into my room and shut the door behind me.

Time. I was asking for a lot of it these days. I hoped that if I had enough, everything would somehow fall into place.

CHAPTER 2

"No, no," Queen Amberly answered with a laugh. "I only had three bridesmaids, though Clarkson's mother suggested I have more. I just wanted my sisters and my best friend, who, coincidentally, I'd met during my Selection."

I peeked over at Marlee and was happy to find she was looking at me, too. Before I arrived at the palace, I had assumed that with this being such a high-stakes competition, there'd be no way any of the girls would be friendly. Marlee had embraced me the first time we met, and we'd been there for each other from that moment on. With a single almost-exception, we'd never even had an argument.

A few weeks ago, Marlee had mentioned that she didn't think she wanted to be with Maxon. When I'd pushed her to explain, she clammed up. She wasn't mad at me, I knew that, but those days of silence before we'd let it go were lonely.

"I want seven bridesmaids," Kriss said. "I mean, if Maxon chooses me and I get to have a big wedding."

"Well, I won't have bridesmaids," Celeste said, countering Kriss. "They're just distracting. And since it would be televised, I want all eyes on me."

I fumed. It was rare that we all got to sit and talk with Queen Amberly, and here Celeste was, being a brat and ruining it.

"I'd want to incorporate some of my culture's traditions into my wedding," Elise added quietly. "Girls back in New Asia use a lot of red in their ceremonies, and the groom has to bring gifts to the bride's friends to reward them for letting her marry him."

Kriss piped up. "Remind me to be in your wedding party. I love presents!"

"Me, too!" Marlee exclaimed.

"Lady America, you've been awfully quiet," Queen Amberly said. "What do you want at your wedding?"

I blushed because I was completely unprepared to comment.

There was only one wedding I'd ever imagined, and it was going to take place at the Province of Carolina Services Office after an exhausting amount of paperwork.

"Well, the one thing I've thought about is having my dad give me away. You know when he takes your hand and puts it in the hand of the person you marry? That's the only part

I've ever really wanted." Embarrassingly enough, it was true.

"But everyone does that," Celeste complained. "That's not even original."

I should have been mad that she called me out, but I merely shrugged. "I want to know that my dad completely approves of my choice on the day it really matters."

"That's nice," Natalie said, sipping her tea and looking out the window.

Queen Amberly laughed lightly. "I certainly hope he approves. No matter who it is." She added the last words quickly, catching herself in the middle of implying that Maxon would be my choice.

I wondered if she thought that, if Maxon had told her about us.

Shortly after, the wedding talk died down, and the queen left to go work in her room. Celeste parked herself in front of the large television embedded in the wall, and the others started a card game.

"That was fun," Marlee said as we settled in at a table together. "I'm not sure I've ever heard the queen talk so much."

"She's getting excited, I think." I hadn't mentioned to anyone what Maxon's aunt had told me about how Queen Amberley tried many times for another child and failed. Adele had predicted that her sister would warm up to us once the group was smaller, and she was right.

"Okay, you have to tell me: Do you honestly not have any other plans for your wedding or did you just not want to share?"

"I really don't," I promised. "I have a hard time picturing a big wedding, you know? I'm a Five."

Marlee shook her head. "You *were* a Five. You're a Three now."

"Right," I said, remembering my new label.

I was born into a family of Fives—artists and musicians who were generally poorly paid—and though I hated the caste system in general, I liked what I did for a living. It was strange to think of myself as a Three, to consider embracing teaching or writing as a profession.

"Stop stressing," Marlee said, reading my face. "You don't have anything to worry about yet."

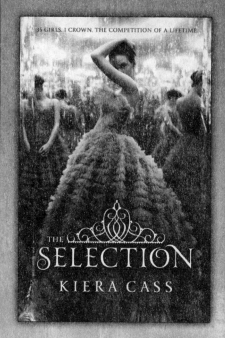

HE LEANED DOWN, LIPS MEETING mine, holding them there. Then his lips parted and closed and parted again. I drew a breath in the moment between kisses, sensing he would come back again. He did, and thank goodness, because I hadn't been kissed like this before and I needed more.

The few times I'd kissed boys were rushed, sloppy moments hiding in a coatroom or behind a statue. But this, with so much air around us and no one coming to check on me . . . it was different.

I leaned into him, and he brought up his free hand and cupped my cheek. He held my lips to his for what felt like forever before pulling back.

ALSO BY KIERA CASS

THE HEIR

KIERA CASS

An Imprint of HarperCollinsPublishers

HarperTeen is an imprint of HarperCollins Publishers.

The Heir
Copyright © 2015 by Kiera Cass
All rights reserved. Printed in the United States of America.
No part of this book may be used or reproduced in any manner
whatsoever without written permission except in the case of brief
quotations embodied in critical articles and reviews. For information
address HarperCollins Children's Books, a division of HarperCollins
Publishers, 195 Broadway, New York, NY 10007.
www.epicreads.com

Library of Congress Control Number: 2015933400
ISBN 978-0-06-234986-6

Typography by Sarah Hoy
16 17 18 19 20 CG/RRDH 10 9 8 7 6 5 4 3 2 1

First paperback edition, 2016

To Jim and Jennie Cass.
For lots of reasons, but mostly for making Callaway.

THE HEIR

CHAPTER 1

I COULD NOT HOLD MY breath for seven minutes. I couldn't even make it to one. I once tried to run a mile in seven minutes after hearing some athletes could do it in four but failed spectacularly when a side stitch crippled me about halfway in.

However, there was one thing I managed to do in seven minutes that most would say is quite impressive: I became queen.

By seven tiny minutes I beat my brother Ahren into the world, so the throne that ought to have been his was mine. Had I been born a generation earlier, it wouldn't have mattered. Ahren was the male, so Ahren would have been the heir.

Alas, Mom and Dad couldn't stand to watch their firstborn be stripped of a title by an unfortunate but rather lovely set of breasts. So they changed the law, and the people rejoiced, and I was trained day by day to become the next ruler of Illéa.

What they didn't understand was that their attempts to make my life fair seemed rather *unfair* to me.

I tried not to complain. After all, I knew how fortunate I was. But there were days, or sometimes months, when it felt like far too much was piled on me, too much for any one person, really.

I flipped through the newspaper and saw that there had been yet another riot, this time in Zuni. Twenty years ago, Dad's first act as king was to dissolve the castes, and the old system had been phased out slowly over my lifetime. I still thought it was completely bizarre that once upon a time people lived with these limiting but arbitrary labels on their backs. Mom was a Five; Dad was a One. It made no sense, especially since there was no outward sign of the divisions. How was I supposed to know if I was walking next to a Six or a Three? And why did that even matter?

When Dad had first decreed that the castes were no more, people all over the country had been delighted. Dad had expected the changes he was making in Illéa to be comfortably in place over the course of a generation, meaning any day now everything should click.

That wasn't happening—and this new riot was just the most recent in a string of unrest.

"Coffee, Your Highness," Neena said, setting the drink on my table.

"Thank you. You can take the plates."

I scanned the article. This time a restaurant was burned to the ground because its owner refused to promote a waiter to a position as a chef. The waiter claimed that a promotion had been promised but was never delivered, and he was sure it was because of his family's past.

Looking at the charred remains of the building, I honestly didn't know whose side I was on. The owner had the right to promote or fire anyone he wanted, and the waiter had the right not to be seen as something that, technically, didn't exist anymore.

I pushed the paper away and picked up my drink. Dad was going to be upset. I was sure he was already running the scenario over and over in his head, trying to figure out how to set it right. The problem was, even if we could fix one issue, we couldn't stop every instance of post-caste discrimination. It was too hard to monitor and happening far too often.

I set down my coffee and headed to my closet. It was time to start the day.

"Neena," I called. "Do you know where that plum-colored dress is? The one with the sash?"

She squinted in concentration as she came over to help.

In the grand scheme of things, Neena was new to the palace. She'd only been working with me for six months, after my last maid fell ill for two weeks. Neena was acutely attuned to my needs and much more agreeable to be around, so I kept her on. I also admired her eye for fashion.

Neena stared into the massive space. "Maybe we should reorganize."

"You can if you have the time. That's not a project I'm interested in."

"Not when I can hunt down your clothes for you," she teased.

"Exactly!"

She took my humor in stride, laughing as she quickly sorted through gowns and pants.

"I like your hair today," I commented.

"Thank you." All the maids wore caps, but Neena was still creative with her hairdos. Sometimes a few thick, black curls would frame her face, and other times she twisted back strands until they were all tucked away. At the moment there were wide braids encircling her head, with the rest of her hair under her cap. I really enjoyed that she found ways to work with her uniform, to make it her own each day.

"Ah! It's back here." Neena pulled down the knee-length dress, fanning it out across the dark skin of her arm.

"Perfect! And do you know where my gray blazer is? The one with the three-quarter sleeves?"

She stared at me, her face deadpan. "I'm definitely rearranging."

I giggled. "You search; I'll dress."

I pulled on my outfit and brushed out my hair, preparing for another day as the future face of the monarchy. The outfit was feminine enough to soften me but strong enough that I'd be taken seriously. It was a fine line to walk, but I did it every day.

Staring into the mirror, I talked to my reflection.

"You are Eadlyn Schreave. You are the next person in line

to run this country, and you will be the first girl to do it on your own. No one," I said, "is as powerful as you."

Dad was already in his office, brow furrowed as he took in the news. Other than my eyes, I didn't look much like him. Or Mom, for that matter.

With my dark hair, oval-shaped face, and a hint of a tan that lingered year round, I looked more like my grandmother than anyone else. A painting of her on her coronation day hung in the fourth-floor hallway, and I used to study it when I was younger, trying to guess at how I would look as I grew. Her age in the portrait was near to mine now, and though we weren't identical, I sometimes felt like her echo.

I walked across the room and kissed Dad's cheek. "Morning."

"Morning. Did you see the papers?" he asked.

"Yes. At least no one died this time."

"Thank goodness for that." Those were the worst, the ones where people were left dead in the street or went missing. It was terrible, reading the names of young men who'd been beaten simply for moving their families into a nicer neighborhood or women who were attacked for trying to get a job that in the past would not have been open to them.

Sometimes it took no time at all to find the motive and the person behind these crimes, but more often than not we were faced with a lot of finger-pointing and no real answers. It was exhausting for me to watch, and I knew it was worse for Dad.

"I don't understand it." He took off his reading glasses and rubbed his eyes. "They didn't want the castes anymore. We took our time, eliminated them slowly so everyone could adjust. Now they're burning down buildings."

"Is there a way to regulate this? Could we create a board to oversee grievances?" I looked at the photo again. In the corner, the young son of the restaurant owner wept over losing everything. In my heart I knew complaints would come in faster than anyone could address them, but I also knew Dad couldn't bear doing nothing.

Dad looked at me. "Is that what you would do?"

I smiled. "No, I'd ask my father what he would do."

He sighed. "That won't always be an option for you, Eadlyn. You need to be strong, decisive. How would you fix this one particular incident?"

I considered. "I don't think we can. There's no way to prove the old castes were why the waiter was denied the promotion. The only thing we can do is launch an investigation into who set the fire. That family lost their livelihood today, and someone needs to be held responsible. Arson is not how you exact justice."

He shook his head at the paper. "I think you're right. I'd like to be able to help them. But, more than that, we need to figure out how to prevent this from happening again. It's become rampant, Eadlyn, and it's frightening."

Dad tossed the paper into the trash, then stood and walked to the window. I could read the stress in his posture. Sometimes his role brought him so much joy, like visiting the schools he'd worked tirelessly to improve or seeing communities flourish in the war-free era he'd ushered in. But those instances were becoming few and far between. Most days he was anxious about the state of the country, and he had to fake his smiles when reporters came by, hoping that his sense of calm would somehow spread to everyone else. Mom helped shoulder the burden, but at the end of the day the fate of the country was placed squarely on his back. One day it would be on mine.

Vain as it was, I worried I would go gray prematurely.

"Make a note for me, Eadlyn. Remind me to write Governor Harpen in Zuni. Oh, and put to write it to Joshua Harpen, not his father. I keep forgetting he was the one who ran in the last election."

I wrote his instructions in my elegant cursive, thinking how pleased Dad would be when he looked at it later. He used to give me the worst time over my penmanship.

I was grinning to myself when I looked back at him, but my face fell almost immediately when I saw him rubbing his forehead, trying so desperately to think of a solution to these problems.

"Dad?"

He turned and instinctively squared his shoulders, like he needed to act strong even in front of me.

"Why do you think this is happening? It wasn't always like this."

He raised his eyebrows. "It certainly wasn't," he said, almost to himself. "At first everyone seemed pleased. Every time we removed a new caste, people held parties. It's only been in the last few years, since all the labels have officially been erased, that it's gone downhill."

He stared back out the window. "The only thing I can think is that those who grew up with the castes are aware of how much better this is. Comparatively, it's easier to marry or work. A family's finances aren't capped by a single profession. There are more choices when it comes to education. But those who are growing up without the castes and are still running into opposition . . . I guess they don't know what else to do."

He looked at me and shrugged. "I need time," he muttered. "I need a way to put things on pause, set them right, and press play again."

I noted the deep furrow in his brow. "Dad, I don't think that's possible."

He chuckled. "We've done it before. I can remember. . . ."

The focus in his eyes changed. He watched me for a moment, seeming to ask me a question without words.

"Dad?"

"Yes."

"Are you all right?"

He blinked a few times. "Yes, dear, quite all right. Why don't you get to work on those budget cuts. We can go over your ideas this afternoon. I need to speak with your mother."

"Sure." Math wasn't a skill that came to me naturally, so I had to work twice as long on any proposals for budget cuts or financial plans. But I absolutely refused to have one of Dad's advisers come behind me with a calculator to clean up my mess. Even if I had to stay up all night, I always made sure my work was accurate.

Of course, Ahren was naturally good at math, but he was never forced to sit through meetings about budgets or rezoning or health care. He got off scot-free by seven stupid minutes.

Dad patted me on the shoulder before dashing out of the room. It took me longer than usual to focus on the numbers. I couldn't help but be distracted by the look on his face and the unmistakable certainty that it was tied to me.

CHAPTER 2

AFTER WORKING ON THE BUDGET report for a few hours, I decided I needed a break and retreated to my room to get a hand massage from Neena. I loved those little bits of luxury in my day. Dresses made to my exact measurements, exotic desserts flown in simply because it was Thursday, and an endless supply of beautiful things were all perks; and they were easily my favorite parts of the job.

My room overlooked the gardens. As the day shifted, the light changed to a warm, honey color, brightening the high walls. I focused on the heat and Neena's deliberate fingers.

"Anyway, his face got all funny. It was kind of like he disappeared for a minute."

I was trying to explain Dad's out-of-character departure this morning, but it was hard to get it across. I didn't even know if he found Mom or not, as he never came back to the office.

"Do you think he's sick? He does seem tired these days." Neena's hands worked her magic as she spoke.

"Does he?" I asked, thinking that Dad didn't seem tired exactly. "He's probably just stressed. How could he not be with all the decisions he has to make?"

"And someday that will be you," she commented, her tone a mix of genuine worry and playful amusement.

"Which means you will be giving me twice as many massages."

"I don't know," she said. "I think in a few years I might like to try something new."

I scrunched my face. "What else would you do? There aren't many positions better than working in the palace."

There was a knock on the door, and she didn't have a chance to answer the question.

I stood, throwing my blazer back on to look presentable, and gave a nod to Neena to let my guests in.

Mom came around the door, smiling, with Dad contentedly trailing her steps. I couldn't help but notice it was always this way. At state events or important dinners, Mom was beside Dad or situated right behind him. But when they were just husband and wife—not king and queen—he followed her everywhere.

"Hi, Mom." I walked over to hug her.

Mom tucked my hair behind my ear, smiling at me. "I like this look."

I stood back proudly and smoothed out my dress with my hands. "The bracelets really set it off, don't you think?"

She giggled. "Excellent attention to detail." Every once in

a while Mom let me pick out jewelry or shoes for her, but it was rare. Mom didn't find it as much fun as I did, and she didn't rely on the extras for beauty. In her case, she really didn't need it. I liked that she was classic.

Mom turned and touched Neena's shoulder. "You're excused," she said quietly.

Neena instantly curtsied and left us alone.

"Is something wrong?" I asked.

"No, sweetheart. We simply want to speak in private." Dad held out a hand and ushered us all to the table. "We have an opportunity to talk to you about."

"Opportunity? Are we traveling?" I adored traveling. "Please tell me we're finally going on a beach trip. Could it just be the six of us?"

"Not exactly. We wouldn't be going somewhere so much as having visitors," Mom explained.

"Oh! Company! Who's coming?"

They exchanged glances, then Mom continued talking. "You know that things are precarious right now. The people are restless and unhappy, and we cannot figure out how to ease the tension."

I sighed. "I know."

"We're seeking a way to boost morale," Dad added.

I perked up. Morale boosting typically involved a celebration. And I was always up for a party.

"What did you have in mind?" I started designing a new dress in my head and dismissed it almost as quickly. That wasn't what needed my attention at the moment.

"Well," Dad started, "the public responds best to something positive with our family. When your mother and I were married, it was one of the best seasons in our country. And do you remember how people threw parties in the street when they found out Osten was coming?"

I smiled. I was eight when Osten was born, and I'd never forget how excited everyone got just over the announcement. I heard music playing from my bedroom practically until dawn.

"That was marvelous."

"It was. And now the people look to you. It won't be long before you're queen." Dad paused. "We thought that perhaps you'd be willing to do something publicly, something that would be exciting for the people but also might be very beneficial to you."

I narrowed my eyes, not sure where this was going. "I'm listening."

Mom cleared her throat. "You know that in the past, princesses were married off to princes from other countries to solidify our international relations."

"I did hear you use the past tense there, correct?"

She laughed, but I wasn't amused. "Yes."

"Good. Because Prince Nathaniel looks like a zombie, Prince Hector dances like a zombie, and if the prince from the German Federation doesn't learn to embrace personal hygiene by the Christmas party, he shouldn't be invited."

Mom rubbed the side of her head in frustration. "Eadlyn, you've always been so picky."

Dad shrugged. "Maybe that's not a bad thing," he said, earning a glare from Mom.

I frowned. "What in the world are you talking about?"

"You know how your mother and I met," Dad began.

I rolled my eyes. "Everyone does. You two are practically a fairy tale."

At those words their eyes went soft, and smiles washed over their faces. Their bodies seemed to tilt slightly toward each other, and Dad bit his lip looking at Mom.

"Excuse me. Firstborn in the room, do you mind?"

Mom blushed as Dad cleared his throat and continued. "The Selection process was very successful for us. And though my parents had their problems, it worked well for them, too. So . . . we were hoping. . . ." He hesitated and met my eyes.

I was slow to pick up on their hints. I knew what the Selection was, but never, not even once, had it been suggested as an option for any of us, let alone me.

"No."

Mom put up her hands, cautioning me. "Just listen—"

"A Selection?" I burst out. "That's insane!"

"Eadlyn, you're being irrational."

I glared at her. "You promised—*you promised*—you'd never force me into marrying someone for an alliance. How is this any better?"

"Hear us out," she urged.

"No!" I shouted. "I won't do it."

"Calm down, love."

"Don't talk to me like that. I'm not a child!"

Mom sighed. "You're certainly acting like one."

"You're ruining my life!" I ran my fingers through my hair and took several deep breaths, hoping it would help me think. This couldn't happen. Not to me.

"It's a huge opportunity," Dad insisted.

"You're trying to shackle me to a stranger!"

"I told you she'd be stubborn," Mom muttered to Dad.

"Wonder where she gets that from," he shot back with a smile.

"Don't talk about me like I'm not in the room!"

"I'm sorry," Dad said. "We just need you to consider this."

"What about Ahren? Can't he do it?"

"Ahren isn't going to be the future king. Besides, he has Camille."

Princess Camille was the heir to the French throne, and a few years ago she'd managed to bat her lashes all the way into Ahren's heart.

"Then make them get married!" I pleaded.

"Camille will be queen when her time comes, and she, like you, will have to ask her partner to marry her. If it was Ahren's choice, we'd consider it; but it's not."

"What about Kaden? Can't you have him do it?"

Mom laughed humorlessly. "He's fourteen! We don't have that kind of time. The people need something to be excited about now." She narrowed her eyes at me. "And, honestly, isn't it time you look for someone to rule beside you?"

Dad nodded. "It's true. It's not a role that should be shouldered alone."

"But I don't want to get married," I pleaded. "Please don't

make me do this. I'm only eighteen."

"Which is how old I was when I married your father," Mom stated.

"I'm not ready," I urged. "I don't want a husband. Please don't do this to me."

Mom reached across the table and put her hand on mine. "No one would be doing anything to you. You would be doing something for your people. You'd be giving them a gift."

"You mean faking a smile when I'd rather cry?"

She gave me a fleeting frown. "That has always been part of our job."

I stared at her, silently demanding a better answer.

"Eadlyn, why don't you take some time to think this over?" Dad said calmly. "I know this is a big thing we're asking of you."

"Does that mean I have a choice?"

Dad inhaled deeply, considering. "Well, love, you'll really have thirty-five choices."

I leaped up from my chair, pointing toward the door.

"Get out!" I demanded. "Get! Out!"

Without another word they left my room.

Didn't they know who I was, what they'd trained me for? I was Eadlyn Schreave. No one was more powerful than me.

So if they thought I was going down without a fight, they were sadly mistaken.

CHAPTER 3

I DECIDED TO TAKE DINNER in my room. I didn't feel like seeing my family at the moment. I was irate with all of them. At my parents for being happy, at Ahren for not picking up the pace eighteen years ago, at Kaden and Osten for being so young.

Neena circled me, filling my cup as she spoke. "Do you think you'll go through with it, miss?" she asked.

"I'm still trying to figure a way out."

"What if you said you were already in love with somebody?"

I shook my head as I poked at my food. "I insulted my three most likely candidates right in front of them."

She set a small plate of chocolates in the middle of the table, guessing correctly that I'd probably want those more than the caviar-garnished salmon.

"Perhaps a guard then? Happens to the maids often enough," she suggested with a giggle.

I scoffed. "That's fine for them, but I'm not that desperate."

Her laughter faded.

I saw immediately that I had offended her, but that was the truth. I couldn't settle for any old person, let alone a guard. Even considering it was a waste of time. I needed a way out of this whole situation.

"I don't mean it like that, Neena. It's just that people expect certain things from me."

"Of course."

"I'm done. You can go for the night; I'll leave the cart in the hallway."

She nodded and left without another word.

I grazed on the chocolates before completely giving up on the food and slipped into my nightgown. I couldn't reason with Mom and Dad right now, and Neena didn't understand. I needed to talk to the only person who might see my side, the person who sometimes felt like he was half of me. I needed Ahren.

"Are you busy?" I asked, cracking open his door.

Ahren was sitting at his desk, writing. His blond hair was end-of-the-day messy, but his eyes were far from tired, and he looked so much like the pictures of Dad when he was younger it was eerie. He was still dressed from dinner but had taken off his coat and tie, settling in for the evening.

"Knock, for goodness' sake."

"I know, I know; but it's an emergency."

"Then get a guard," he snapped back, returning to his papers.

"That's already been suggested," I muttered to myself. "I'm serious, Ahren; I need your help."

Ahren peeked over his shoulder at me, and I could see he was already planning to give in. He used his foot to push out the seat next to him casually. "Step into my office."

Sitting, I sighed. "What are you writing?"

He quickly piled papers on top of the one he'd been working on. "A letter to Camille."

"You know you could simply phone her."

He grinned. "Oh, I will. But then I'll send her this, too."

"That makes no sense. What could you possibly have to talk about that would fill an entire phone call and a letter?"

He tilted his head. "For your information, they serve different purposes. The calls are for updates and to see how her day went. The letters are for the things I can't always say out loud."

"Oh, really?" I leaned over, reaching for the paper.

Before I could even get close, Ahren's hand gripped my wrist. "I will murder you," he vowed.

"Good," I shot. "Then you can be the heir, and you can go through a Selection and kiss your precious Camille goodbye."

He scrunched his forehead. "What?"

I slumped back into my chair. "Mom and Dad need to

boost morale. They've decided that, for the sake of Illéa," I said in mock patriotism, "I need to go through a Selection."

I was expecting abject horror. Perhaps a sympathetic hand on my shoulder. But Ahren threw back his head and laughed.

"Ahren!"

He continued to howl, pitching himself forward and hitting his knee.

"You're going to wrinkle your suit," I warned, which only made him laugh harder. "For goodness' sake, stop it! What am I supposed to do?"

"As if I know! I can't believe they think this would even work," he added, his smile still not fading.

"What's that supposed to mean?"

He shrugged. "I don't know. I guess I thought, if you ever did get married, it'd be down the line. I think everyone assumed that."

"And what is *that* supposed to mean?"

The warm touch I'd been hoping for finally came as he reached for my hand. "Come on, Eady. You've always been independent. It's the queen in you. You like to be in charge, do things on your own. I didn't think you'd partner up with anyone until you at least got to reign for a while."

"Not like I really had a choice in the first place," I mumbled, tilting my head to the floor but still looking to my brother.

He gave me a little pout. "Poor little princess. Don't want to rule the world?"

I swatted his hand away. "Seven minutes. It should have

been you. I'd much rather sit alone and scribble away instead of do all that stupid paperwork. And this ridiculous Selection nonsense! Can't you see how dreadful this is?"

"How did you get roped into this anyway? I thought they'd done away with it."

I rolled my eyes again. "It has absolutely nothing to do with me. That's the worst part. Dad's facing public opposition, so he's trying to distract them." I shook my head. "It's getting really bad, Ahren. People are destroying homes and businesses. Some have died. Dad isn't completely sure where it's coming from, but he thinks it's people our age, the generation that grew up without castes, causing most of it."

He made a face. "That doesn't make sense. How could growing up without those restrictions make you upset?"

I paused, thinking. How could I explain what we could only really guess at? "Well, I grew up being told I was going to be queen one day. That was it. No choice. You grew up knowing you had options. You could go into the military, you could become an ambassador, you could do plenty of things. But what if that wasn't really happening? What if you didn't have all the opportunities you thought you would?"

"Huh," he said, following. "So they're being denied jobs?"

"Jobs, education, money. I've heard of people refusing to let their kids get married because of old castes. Nothing is happening the way Dad thought it would, and it's nearly impossible to control. Can we force people to be fair?"

"And that's what Dad's trying to figure out now?" he asked, skeptical.

"Yes, and I'm the smoke-and-mirror act diverting their attention while he comes up with a plan."

He chuckled. "That makes much more sense than you suddenly being romantically inclined."

I cocked my head. "Let it go, Ahren. So I'm not interested in marriage. Why does that matter? Other women can stay single."

"But other women aren't expected to produce an heir."

I hit him again. "Help me! What do I do?"

His eyes searched mine, and I knew, as easily as I could read any emotion in him, that he saw I was terrified. Not irritated or angry. Not outraged or repulsed.

I was scared.

It was one thing to be expected to rule, to hold the weight of millions of people in my hands. That was a job, a task. I could check things off lists, delegate. But this was much more personal, one more piece of my life that ought to be mine but wasn't.

His playful smile disappeared, and he pulled his chair closer to mine. "If they're looking to distract people, maybe you could suggest other . . . opportunities. A possible marriage isn't the only choice. That said, if Mom and Dad came to this conclusion, they might have already exhausted every other option."

I buried my head in my hands. I didn't want to tell him I tried to offer up him as an alternative or that I thought Kaden might even be acceptable. I sensed he was right, that the Selection was their last hope.

"Here's the thing, Eady. You'll be the first girl to hold the throne fully in her own right. And people expect a lot from you."

"Like I don't already know that."

"But," he continued, "that also gives you a lot of bargaining power."

I raised my head marginally. "What do you mean?"

"If they really need you to do this, then negotiate."

I sat up straight, my mind running around in circles, trying to think of what I could ask for. There might be a way to get through this quickly, without it even ending in a proposal.

Without a proposal!

If I spoke fast enough, I could probably get Dad to agree to practically anything so long as he got his Selection out of it.

"Negotiate!" I whispered.

"Exactly."

I stood up, grabbed Ahren by his ears, and planted a kiss on his forehead. "You are my absolute hero!"

He smiled. "Anything for you, my queen."

I giggled, shoving him. "Thanks, Ahren."

"Get to work." He waved me toward the door, and I suspected he was actually more eager to get back to his letter than he was for me to come up with a plan.

I dashed from the room, heading to my own to fetch some paper. I needed to think.

As I rounded the corner, I ran smack into someone, falling backward onto the carpet.

"Ow!" I complained, looking up to see Kile Woodwork, Miss Marlee's son.

Kile and the rest of the Woodworks had rooms on the same floor as our family, a singularly huge honor. Or irritation, depending on how one felt about the Woodworks.

"Do you mind?" I snapped.

"I wasn't the one running," he answered, picking up the books he'd dropped. "You ought to be looking where you're going."

"A gentleman would offer his hand right now," I reminded him.

Kile's hair flopped across his eyes as he looked over at me. He was in desperate need of a cut and a shave, and his shirt was too big for him. I didn't know who I was more embarrassed for: him for looking so sloppy or my family for having to be seen with such a disaster.

What was especially irritating was that he wasn't always so scruffy, and he didn't have to be now. How hard would it be to run a brush through his hair?

"Eadlyn, you've never thought I was a gentleman."

"True." I pulled myself up without help and brushed off my robe.

For the last six months I had been spared Kile's less-than-thrilling company. He'd gone to Fennley to enroll in some accelerated course, and his mother had been lamenting his absence ever since the day he left. I didn't know what he was studying, and I didn't particularly care. But he was back now, and his presence was another stressor on an ever-growing list.

"And what would make such a lady run like that in the first place?"

"Matters you are far too dim to comprehend."

He laughed. "Right, because I'm such a simpleton. It's a miracle I manage to bathe myself."

I was about to ask if he did bathe, because he looked like he'd been running away from anything that resembled a bar of soap.

"I hope one of those books is a primer on etiquette. You seriously need a refresher."

"You're not queen yet, Eadlyn. Take it down a notch." He walked away, and I was furious with myself for not getting the last word.

I pressed on. There were bigger problems in my life right now than the state of Kile's manners. I couldn't waste my time quibbling with people or being distracted by anything that couldn't put the Selection to death.

CHAPTER 4

"I WANT TO BE CLEAR," I said, sitting down in Dad's office. "I have no desire to get married."

He nodded. "I understand that you don't want to get married today, but it was always something you'd have to do, Eadlyn. You're obligated to continue the royal line."

I hated it when he talked about my future like that, like sex and love and babies weren't happy things but duties performed to keep the country running. It took every speck of joy out of the prospect.

Of all the things in my life, shouldn't those be the real pleasures, the best parts?

I shook the worry away and focused on the task at hand.

"I understand. And I agree that it's important," I replied diplomatically. "But weren't you ever worried when you went through your Selection that no one in the pool was right for you? Or that maybe they were there for the wrong reason?"

His lips hitched up in a smile. "Every waking moment, and half the time I slept."

He'd told me a handful of vague stories about one girl who'd been so pliable he could hardly stand her and another who had tried to manipulate the process at every turn. I didn't know many names or details, and that was fine with me. I had never liked to imagine Dad possibly falling in love with anyone but Mom.

"And don't you think that as the first woman to fully control the crown, there should be . . . some standards set for who might rule beside me?"

He tilted his head. "Go on."

"I'm sure there's some sort of vetting process in place to make sure an actual psychopath doesn't make his way into the palace, yes?"

"Of course." He grinned as if this wasn't a valid concern.

"But I don't trust just anyone to do this job with me. So"—I sighed deeply—"I will agree to go through with this ridiculous stunt if you make me a few tiny promises."

"It's not a stunt. It's had an excellent track record. But please, dear girl, tell me what you want."

"First, I want the contestants to have the freedom to leave of their own free will. I won't have someone feeling obligated to stay if they don't care for me or the life they'd have to lead in the palace."

"I fully agree to that," he said forcefully. Seemed like I had touched a nerve.

"Excellent. And I know you might be opposed to the idea, but if by the end of this I can't find anyone suitable, then we call the whole thing off. No prince, no wedding."

"Ah!" he said, leaning forward in his chair and pointing a calculating finger at me. "If I allow that, you'll turn them all away the first day. You won't even try!"

I paused, thinking. "What if I guaranteed you a timeline? I would keep the Selection running for, say, three months and weigh my options for at least that amount of time. After then, if I haven't found a suitable match, all the contestants are released."

He ran his hand across his mouth and shifted in his chair a little before pressing his eyes into mine. "Eadlyn, you know how important this is, don't you?"

"Of course," I replied instantly, very aware of how serious this was. I sensed one wrong move would set my life on a course I could never correct.

"You need to do this and do it well. For everyone's sake. Our lives, all of them, are given over in service to our people."

I looked away. If anything, it felt like Mom, Dad, and I were the trinity of sacrifice here, with the others doing as they pleased.

"I won't let you down," I promised. "You do what you must. Make your plans, find a way to appease our public, and I will give you an acceptable window of time to pull it all together."

His eyes darted toward the ceiling in thought. "Three months? And you swear you'll try?"

I held up my hand. "I give you my word. I'll even sign something if you like, but I can't promise you I'll fall in love."

"Wouldn't be so sure if I was you," he said knowingly. But I wasn't him, and I wasn't Mom. No matter how romantic he thought this was, all I could think of were the thirty-five loud, obnoxious, weird-smelling boys who were about to invade my home. Nothing about that sounded magical.

"It's a deal."

I stood, practically ready to dance. "Really?"

"Really."

I took his hand and sealed my future with a single shake. "Thank you, Dad."

I left the room before he could see how big my smile was. I had already been running through how I could get most of the boys to leave of their own volition. I could be intimidating when I needed to be or find ways to make the palace a very unwelcoming environment. I also had a secret weapon in Osten, who was the most mischievous of us all and would help me if I asked him to, probably with minimal persuasion.

I admired the thought of a common boy feeling brave enough to face the challenge of becoming a prince. But no one was going to tie me down before I was ready, and I was going to make sure those poor suckers knew what they were signing up for.

They kept the studio cold, but once the lights came on, we might as well have been in an oven for all the good it did. I'd learned years ago to keep my clothing choices for the *Report* airy, which was why my dress tonight fell off my shoulders. My look was classy, as always, but not something that would subject me to a heatstroke.

"That's the perfect dress," Mom commented, pulling at the little ruffles on the sleeves. "You look lovely."

"Thank you. So do you."

She smiled as she continued to straighten my dress. "Thank you, sweetheart. I know you're feeling a little overwhelmed, but I think a Selection will be good for everyone. You're alone a lot, and it's something we would have to think about eventually, and—"

"And it will make the people happy. I know."

I tried to hide the misery in my voice. We had technically moved past selling off the royal daughters, but . . . this didn't feel that different. Didn't she get that?

Her eyes moved from the gown to my face. Something in them told me she was sorry.

"I know you feel like this is a sacrifice; and it's true that when you live a life of service, there are many things you do, not because you want to, but because you must." She swallowed. "But through this I found your father, and I found my closest friends, and I learned that I was stronger than I ever thought I could be. I know about the agreement you made with your dad, and if this ends without you finding the right person, so be it. But please, let yourself experience something here. Sharpen yourself, learn something. And try not to hate us for asking you to do it."

"I don't hate you."

"You at least considered it when we proposed this," she said with a grin. "Didn't you?"

"I'm eighteen. I'm genetically encoded to fight with my parents."

"I don't mind a good fight so long as you still know how much I love you in the end."

I reached to hug her. "And I love you. Promise."

She held me for a moment, then pulled away, smoothing my dress to make sure I was still immaculate before she went to find Dad. I walked to take my seat next to Ahren, who wiggled his eyebrows at me teasingly. "Looking good, sis. Practically bridal."

I swung my skirt and sat down gracefully. "One more word and I will shave your head in your sleep."

"I love you, too."

I tried not to smile but failed. He just always knew.

The room filled with the palace household. Miss Lucy sat alone, as General Leger was on rounds, and Mr. and Mrs. Woodwork sat behind the cameras with Kile and Josie. They were the Woodworks' only children, and I knew Miss Marlee meant the world to Mom, so I kept it to myself that I thought her kids were the absolute worst. Kile wasn't as obnoxious as Josie, but, in all the years I'd known him, he'd never made anything remotely close to an interesting conversation. So help me, if I ever got a bad case of insomnia, I'd hire him to sit in my room and talk. Problem solved. And Josie . . . I didn't have words for how wretched that girl was.

Dad's advisers filed in, bowing as they came. There was only one woman in Dad's cabinet, Lady Brice Mannor. She was lovely and petite, and I was never sure how someone so demure managed to stay afloat in the political arena. I'd never heard her raise her voice or get angry, but people listened to her. The men didn't listen to me unless I was stern.

Her presence made me curious though. What would happen if I, as queen, made my entire board of counselors women?

That might be an interesting experiment.

The chairmen and advisers delivered their announcements and updates, and finally, Gavril turned to me.

Gavril Fadaye had slicked-back silver hair but a very handsome face. He'd been talking recently about retirement, but after an announcement this big, he'd have to stick around a bit longer.

"Tonight, Illéa, to conclude our program, we have some very exciting news. And there is no one better to deliver it than our future queen, the beautiful Eadlyn Schreave."

He swept his hand grandly in my direction, and I smiled widely as I walked across the carpeted stage to polite applause.

Gavril gave me a quick embrace and a kiss on each cheek. "Princess Eadlyn, welcome."

"Thanks, Gavril."

"Now, I have to be honest. It feels like only yesterday I was announcing the birth of you and your brother Ahren. I can't believe it's been more than eighteen years!"

"It's true. We're all grown up." I looked toward my family, sharing a warm gaze.

"You're on the edge of making history. I think all of Illéa is eager to see what you'll do a few years down the road when you become queen."

"That'll certainly be an exciting time, but I'm not sure I want to wait that long to make history." I gave him a playful nudge with my elbow, and he mocked surprise.

"Why don't you tell us what you have in mind, Your Highness?"

I squared my shoulders in front of camera C and smiled. "Our great country has gone through many changes over the years. In my parents' lifetimes alone we've seen the rebel forces within our country practically run into extinction, and though we still face challenges, the caste system no longer divides our people along imaginary lines. We live in an era of extraordinary freedom, and we wait with anticipation to see our nation become everything it possibly can."

I remembered to smile and speak articulately. Years of lessons on how to address an audience had drilled the proper technique into me, and I knew I was hitting every last point I was meant to as I delivered my announcement.

"And that's great . . . but I'm still an eighteen-year-old girl." The small audience of guests and advisers giggled. "It gets a little boring when you spend the majority of the day in an office with your dad. No offense, Your Majesty," I added, turning to Dad.

"None taken," he called back.

"And so I've decided it's time for a change of pace. It's time to search, not just for someone to be a coworker with me in this very demanding job, but for a partner to walk with me through life. To do that, I'm hoping Illéa will indulge my deepest wish: to have a Selection."

The advisers gasped and muttered. I saw the shocked faces of the staff. It became clear that the only person who was already in on this was Gavril, which surprised me.

"Tomorrow, letters will be sent to all the eligible young men in Illéa. You'll have two weeks to decide whether you would like to compete for my hand. I realize, of course, that this is uncharted territory. We've never had a female-run Selection before. Still, even though I have three brothers, I'm very excited to meet another prince of Illéa. And I'm hoping that all of Illéa will celebrate with me."

I gave a small curtsy and retreated to my seat. Mom and Dad were beaming proudly at me, and I tried to tell myself that their reaction was enough, though I felt like my blood was trembling in my veins. I couldn't help but think I'd missed something, that there was a gaping hole in the net I'd set up to catch myself.

But there was nothing I could do. I'd just thrown myself off the ledge.

CHAPTER 5

I KNEW WE HAD AN arsenal of staff working at the palace, but I was convinced the majority of them had been in hiding until today. As the announcement of this unexpected Selection spread, it wasn't simply the maids and butlers running around in preparation, but people I'd never even seen before.

My daily workload of reading reports and sitting in on meetings shifted as I became the focal point of the Selection preparations.

"This is slightly less expensive, Your Highness, but it is still incredibly comfortable and would work well with the existing decor." A man held out a very large swatch of fabric, which he draped over the previous two options.

I touched it, enchanted by the texture of cloth as I usually was, though this was clearly not intended to be worn.

"I'm not sure I understand why we're doing this," I confessed.

The man, one of the palace decorators, pressed his lips together. "It has been suggested that some of the guest rooms are a bit feminine and that your suitors might be more comfortable in something like this," he said, pulling out yet another option. "We can make a room look entirely different with a simple bedspread," he assured me.

"Fine," I said, thinking it was a little unnecessary to get this worked up over some sheets. "But do I need to make this decision?"

He smiled kindly. "Your fingerprints will be all over this Selection, miss. Even if you don't choose, people will assume you did. We might as well get your authority on all things."

I stared at the fabric, more than a little exhausted thinking about how all these silly details would point back to me. "This one." I chose the least-expensive option. It was a deep green and would be perfectly acceptable for a three-month stay.

"Very wise, Your Highness," the decorator complimented. "Now, should we consider adding new art as well?" He clapped his hands, and a stream of maids walked in carrying paintings. I sighed, knowing my afternoon was lost.

The following morning I was summoned to the dining hall. Mom came with me, but Dad couldn't be pulled away from his work.

A man I assumed was our head chef bowed to us, not able to go very low because of his wide stomach. His face was closer to red than white, but he didn't sweat, which made me think that all the years in the kitchen had simply steamed him.

"Thank you for joining us, Your Majesty, Your Highness. The kitchen staff has been working day and night to find appropriate options for the first dinner once your suitors arrive. We want to serve seven courses, obviously."

"Of course!" Mom replied.

The chef smiled at her. "Naturally, we would like your approval for the final menu."

I groaned internally. A true seven-course meal could take six hours from the first sip of a cocktail to the final bite of chocolate. How long would it take to sample several different options for each course?

About eight hours, it turned out, and I had a dreadful stomachache for the rest of the day, which made me less than enthusiastic when someone came asking about music selections for the evening of the first dinner.

The hallways were like crowded streets, and every corner of the palace was noisy with speedy preparations. I endured it as best I could until Dad stopped me in passing one day.

"We were thinking about making a special room for the Selected. What do you think about—"

"Enough!" I sighed, exasperated. "I don't care. I have no idea what a boy would like in a recreational space, so I suggest you ask someone with some testosterone. And as for me, I'll be in the garden."

Dad could tell I was near a breaking point, and he let

me pass without a fight. I was thankful for the momentary respite.

I lay on my stomach in my bikini on a blanket in the open stretch of grass that spread out just before the forest. I wished, as I had so many times before, that we had a pool. I was pretty good at getting my way, but Dad never budged on the pool issue. When the palace was mine, that was the first thing on the agenda.

I sketched dresses in my book, trying to relax. As the sun warmed me, the quick scratch of my pencil blended with the sound of rustling leaves, making a lovely, tranquil song. I mourned the loss of peace in my life. *Three months,* I recited. *Three months, and then everything goes back to normal.*

A piercing laugh polluted the stillness of the garden. "Josie," I muttered to myself. Shading my eyes, I turned and saw her walking toward me. She was with one of her friends, an upper-class girl she'd chosen to associate with specifically because the company in the palace wasn't enough for her.

I closed my book, hiding my designs, and turned onto my back simply to take in the sun.

"It will be a good experience for everyone," I heard Josie remark to her friend. "I don't get to interact with boys very often, so it'll be nice to have an opportunity to talk to some. One day, when my wedding is arranged, I'd like to be able to carry on a conversation."

I rolled my eyes. If I thought I'd have the slightest attachment to these boys, it would have bothered me that she thought they were here for her. Then again, Josie thought everything existed for her. And the idea that she was so important that her marriage would need to be arranged on her behalf was comical. She could marry anyone off the street and no one would care one way or the other.

"I hope I'll be able to visit during the Selection," her friend replied. "It'll be so fun!"

"Of course, Shannon! I'll make sure all my friends get to come often. It'll be valuable for you as well."

How kind of her to offer up my home and events as learning opportunities for her little buddies. I took a deep breath. I needed to focus on relaxing.

"Eadlyn!" Josie cried, spotting me.

I groaned, then raised a hand to acknowledge her, hoping the silence would convey my wish for privacy.

"How excited are you for the Selection?" she yelled, continuing over.

I wasn't going to holler like a farmhand, so I said nothing. Eventually, Josie and her friend were standing above me, blocking the sun.

"Didn't you hear me, Eadlyn? Aren't you excited for the Selection?"

Josie never addressed me properly.

"Of course."

"Me, too! I think it'll be exciting to have all the company."

"You won't have any company," I reminded her. "These boys are *my* guests."

She tipped her head like I was stating the obvious. "I

know! But it'll still be nice to have more people around."

"Josie, how old are you?"

"Fifteen," she answered proudly.

"I thought so. If you really want to, I'm sure you could get out and meet people of your own accord now. You're certainly old enough."

She smiled. "I don't think so. That's not exactly appropriate."

I didn't want to get into this argument again. *I* was the one who couldn't pick up and leave the palace without warning. Security sweeps, proper announcements, and protocol reviews were all necessary before I could even consider it.

Also, I constantly had to be aware of the company I kept. I couldn't be seen with just anyone. An unflattering picture wasn't simply taken; it was documented, stored, and resurrected whenever the newspapers needed to criticize me. I had to be relentlessly on my toes to avoid anything that could possibly tarnish my image, my family's image, or the country at large.

Josie was a commoner. She didn't have any such restrictions.

Not that it stopped her from acting like she did.

"Well, at least you have some company for today, then. If you two don't mind, I'm trying to rest."

"Certainly, Your Highness." Her friend bowed her head. Okay, she wasn't too bad.

"I'll see you at dinner!" Josie was a little too enthusiastic about it.

I tried to lull myself back into relaxation, but Josie's piercing voice kept finding its way over to me, and I eventually scooped up my blanket and sketches, and headed inside. If I couldn't enjoy myself here, I might as well figure out something else to do.

After being so exposed to the bright Angeles sun, the palace halls looked like twilight as I waited for my eyes to adjust. I blinked hard, trying to make out the face of the person coming toward me. It was Osten, carrying two notebooks as he rushed down the hall.

He shoved the books into my arms. "Hide these in your room, okay? And if anyone asks, you haven't seen me."

As quickly as he appeared, he vanished. I sighed, knowing that even attempting to comprehend would be pointless. I sometimes couldn't stand the pressure placed on me from being born first, but thank goodness it was me and not Osten. Every time I tried to imagine him at the helm, it gave me a headache.

I flipped through the notebooks, curious as to what he was plotting. Turned out they weren't his at all. They were Josie's. I recognized her babyish handwriting, and, if that hadn't given it away, the sheets of her and Ahren's names in hearts made it all too obvious. It wasn't just Ahren's name though. A few pages later she was in love with all four members of Choosing Yesterday, a popular band, and just after that it was some actor. Anyone with any sort of clout would do, it seemed.

I decided to set the books on the floor by the doors to the

garden. Whatever Osten had planned, there was no way it would be as distressing as her stumbling across them when she came inside, with no clue as to how they'd gotten there or who had seen them.

For someone who prided herself on being so close to the royal family, she really should have learned a lesson or two in discretion by now.

When I got to my room, Neena was at the ready, grabbing my blanket to place in the wash. I threw something on, not really in the mood to think about my outfit too much today. As I was about to fix my hair, I noticed some files on the table.

"Lady Brice dropped those off for you," Neena said.

I stared at the folders. Though it was my first piece of actual work in a week, I couldn't be bothered. "I'll get to them later," I promised, knowing that I probably wouldn't. I'd maybe look at them tomorrow. Today was mine.

I pinned back my hair, double-checked my makeup, and went to look for Mom. I could use the company, and I felt pretty confident that she wouldn't ask me to pick out furniture or food.

I found her alone in the Women's Room. A plaque beside the door declared that the space was actually titled the Newsome Library, but I'd never heard anyone call it by that name except for Mom on occasion. It was the space where the women congregated, so the original label seemed more practical, I supposed.

I could tell Mom was in there before I even opened the

door because I heard her playing the piano, and her sound was unmistakable. She loved to tell the story of how Dad made her pick out four brand-new pianos, each with various attributes, after they were married. They were placed all over the palace. One was in her suite, a second in Dad's, one here, and another in a largely unused parlor on the fourth floor.

I was still jealous of how easy she made it look. I remembered her warning me that one day time would take the dexterity out of her hands, and she'd only be able to plunk away at one or two keys at a time. So far time had failed.

I tried to be quiet, but she heard me all the same.

"Hello, darling," she called, pulling her fingers away from the keys. "Come sit with me."

"I didn't mean to interrupt." I walked across the room, settling next to her on the bench.

"You didn't. I was clearing my head, and I feel much better now."

"Is something wrong?"

She smiled distractedly and rubbed her hand over my back. "No. Just the everyday wear and tear of the job."

"I know what you mean," I said, running my fingers along the keys, not actually making any sound.

"I keep thinking that I've gotten to a point where I've seen it all, where I've mastered everything about being queen. No sooner do I think it than everything changes. There are . . . Well, you have enough to worry about today. Let's not bother with it."

With some work she pasted a smile back onto her face, and while I wanted to know what was troubling her—because, in the end, all those troubles also fell on me—she was right. I simply couldn't deal with it today.

It seemed she hardly could either.

"Do you ever regret it?" I asked, seeing the sadness in her eyes despite her efforts. "Entering the Selection and ending up queen?"

I was grateful she didn't just immediately say yes or no but actually considered the question.

"I don't regret marrying your father. I sometimes wonder about the life I would have had without the Selection, or if I had still come to the palace but lost. I think I would have been fine. Not unhappy exactly, but not aware of what else there could have been for me. But the path to him was a difficult one, mostly because I didn't want to walk it."

"At all?"

She shook her head. "It wasn't my idea to enter the Selection."

My mouth fell open. She'd never told me that. "Whose was it?"

"That's not important," she answered quickly. "But I can tell you that I understand your reservations. I think the process will teach you a lot about yourself. I hope you'll trust me on this."

"It'd be a lot easier to trust you if I knew you were doing this for me and not to buy yourself some peace." The words came out sharper than I meant them to.

She took a deep breath. "I know you think this is selfish, but you'll see. One day the welfare of the country will be on your shoulders, and you'll be surprised at what you'd try in order to keep it all from crumbling. I never thought we'd have another Selection, but plans change when that much is demanded of you."

"Plenty is demanded of me now," I shot back.

"One, watch your tone," she warned. "And two, you only see a fraction of the work. You have no idea how much pressure is placed on your father."

I sat there, silent. I wanted to leave. If she didn't like my tone, then why did she push me?

"Eadlyn," she began quietly. "The timing of this happened to fall when it did. But, honestly, sooner or later I would have done something."

"What do you mean?"

"You seem shut off in a way, disconnected from your people. I know you're constantly worried about the demands you will face as queen, but it's time you see the needs of others."

"You don't think I do that now?" Did she see what I did all day?

She pressed her lips together. "No, honey. Not if it comes before your comfort."

I wanted to scream at her, and at Dad, too. Sure, I took shelter in long baths or a drink with dinner. I didn't think that was too much to ask for considering what I sacrificed.

"I didn't realize you thought I was so flawed." I stood, turning away.

"Eadlyn, that's not what I'm saying."

"It is. That's fine." I made my way to the door. The accusation filled me with so much rage I could barely stand it.

"Eadlyn, darling, we want you to be the best queen you can be, that's all," she pleaded.

"I will," I answered, one foot in the hallway. "And I certainly don't need a boy to show me how to do that."

I tried to calm myself before walking away. It felt like the universe was plotting against me, its arms taking turns swatting me down. I repeated in my head that it was only three months, only three months . . . until I heard someone crying.

"Are you sure?" It sounded like General Leger.

"I talked with her this morning. She decided to keep it." Miss Lucy pulled in a jagged breath.

"Did you tell her that we could give that baby everything? That we had more money than we could ever spend? That we'd love it, no matter its faults?" General Leger's words fell out in a whispered rush.

"All that and more," Miss Lucy insisted. "I knew there was a huge chance of the baby being born with mental issues. I told her we'd be able to tend to any need he had, that the queen herself would see to it. She said she talked with her family, and they agreed to help her, and that she never really wanted to let the baby go in the first place. She only looked into adoption because she thought she'd be alone. She apologized, like that could fix it."

Miss Lucy sniffed as if she was trying to quiet her sobs. I

drew close to the corner of the passage, listening

"I'm so sorry, Lucy."

"There's nothing to be sorry for. It's not your fault." She said those words kindly, bravely. "I think we need to accept that it's over. Years of treatments, so many miscarriages, *three* failed adoptions . . . we just need to let it go."

There was a long silence before General Leger answered. "If that's what you think is best."

"I do," she said, her voice sounding assertive, before she sank into tears again. "I still can't believe I'll never be a mother."

A second later her cries were muffled, and I knew her husband had pulled her to his chest, trying to comfort her as best he could.

All these years I had thought the Legers had chosen to be a childless couple. Miss Lucy's struggles had never made it into conversation when I was in the room, and she seemed content enough to play with us as children and send us on our way. I'd never considered that it might have been an unfortunate circumstance thrust on them.

Was my mother right? Was I not as observant or caring as I thought? Miss Lucy was one of my favorite people in the world. Shouldn't I have been able to see how sad she was?

CHAPTER 6

THIRTY-FIVE MASSIVE BASKETS SAT IN the office, filled with what must have been tens of thousands of entries, all left in their envelopes to protect the gentlemen's anonymity. I tried to give off an air of eager anticipation for the sake of the camera, but I felt like I might vomit into one of those baskets at any given moment.

That would be one way to narrow the pool.

Dad placed a hand on my back. "All right, Eady. Just walk to each basket and select an envelope. I'll hold them for you so your hands don't get full. Then we'll open them live tonight on the *Report*. It's that easy."

For something so simple, it seemed incredibly daunting. Then again, I'd felt overwhelmed since we announced the Selection, so this shouldn't have been a surprise.

I adjusted my favorite tiara and smoothed out my iridescent

gray dress. I wanted to make sure I looked positively radiant today, and when I'd checked my reflection before heading downstairs, even I was a little intimidated by the girl in the mirror.

"So I literally select each one myself?" I whispered, hoping the cameras weren't watching too closely.

He gave me a tiny smile and spoke softly. "It's a privilege I never had. Go ahead, love."

"What do you mean?"

"Later. Go on now." He gestured toward the piles and piles of entries.

I took a deep breath. I could do this. No matter what people were hoping for, I had a plan. And it was foolproof. I would walk away from this unscathed. Just a few months of my life—nothing, in the grand scheme of things—and then I'd go back to the work of becoming queen. Alone.

So why are you stalling?

Shut up.

I walked to the first basket, with a label declaring the contestants were all from Clermont. I pulled one from the side, cameras flashed, and the handful of people in the room actually applauded. Mom wrapped her arm around Ahren in excitement, and he sneakily made a face at me. Miss Marlee sighed with delight, but Miss Lucy was absent. Osten was missing, too, which was no surprise, but Kaden stood by, observing the whole thing with interest.

I used different techniques for different bins. On one, I plucked the envelope from the very top. On the next, I buried my arm to fish out my choice. The onlookers seemed incredibly amused when I got to Carolina, Mom's home province, picked up two envelopes, and weighed them in my hands for a few seconds before dropping one back in.

I placed the last entry in Dad's hands, and there was more clapping and camera flashes. I gave what I hoped was an enthusiastic smile before the reporters all exited the room, off to give their exclusive stories. Ahren and Kaden left, joking as they went, and Mom gave me a quick kiss on the head before she followed them. We were speaking again but didn't have much to say.

"You did marvelously," Dad said once we were alone, a genuine tone of awe in his voice. "Really, I understand how nerve-racking this can feel, but you were wonderful."

"How do you know though?" I placed my hands on my hips. "If you didn't pick out the entries yourself?"

He swallowed. "You've heard the broad strokes of how your mother and I found each other. But there are tiny details that are best left in the drawer. The only reason I am telling you this is because I think it will help you to see how fortunate you are."

I nodded, not sure where he was going.

He took a breath. "My Selection wasn't a farce, but it wasn't that far off. My father chose all the contestants by hand, picking young women with political alliances, influential families, or enough charm to make the entire country worship the ground they walked on. He knew he had to make it varied enough to seem legit, so there were three

Fives thrown into the mix but nothing below that. The Fives were meant to be little more than throwaways to keep anyone from being suspicious."

I realized my mouth was gaping open and shut it immediately. "Mom?"

"Was meant to be gone almost immediately. Truth be told, she barely made it past my father's attempts to sway my opinion or remove her himself. And look at her now." His whole face changed. "Though it was hard for me to imagine, she is even more beloved as queen than my mother. She has made four beautiful, intelligent, strong children. And she has been the source of every happiness in my life."

He flipped idly through the envelopes in his hands. "I'm not sure if fate or destiny is real. But I can tell you that sometimes the very thing you've been hoping for will walk through the door, determined to fend you off. And still, somehow, you will find that you are enough."

Until then I'd never had a reason to doubt that I'd seen the whole picture of my parents' love story. But between Dad's confession that Mom wasn't even supposed to be a choice and Mom's revelation that she didn't want to be a part of the choosing in the first place, I wondered how they had managed to find each other at all.

It was clear from Dad's expression, he could barely believe it himself.

"You're going to do great, you know?" he said, beaming proudly.

"What makes you think so?"

"You're like your mother, and my mother, too. You're determined. And, perhaps most important, you don't like to fail. I know this will all work out, if only because you'll refuse to allow it to go any other way."

I nearly told him, nearly confessed I had come up with pages of ideas to drive these boys away. Because he was right: I didn't want to fail. But for me, failure meant having my life led by someone else.

"I'm sure everything will turn out just as it should," I said, a whisper of regret hanging in my voice.

He lifted a hand and placed it on my cheek. "It usually does."

CHAPTER 7

IN THE STUDIO, THE SET was slightly rearranged. Typically, Ahren and I were the only ones who sat on camera with my parents, but tonight Kaden and Osten were given seats onstage as well.

Dad's officials were in a cluster of seats on the opposite side, and in the middle a bowl waited with all the envelopes I'd picked earlier. Beside it was an empty bowl for me to place them in as they were opened. I had reservations about reading out the names myself, but at least it gave the appearance of control. I liked that.

Behind the cameras, seats were filled with other members of our household. General Leger was there, kissing Miss Lucy on her forehead and whispering something to her. It had been a few days since I'd overheard their conversation, and I still felt awful for her. Of all the people in the world who ought to be parents, it was the Legers. And of all the people in the world who ought to have the ability to fix things, it was the Schreaves.

Still, I was lost as to how to help.

Miss Marlee was shushing Josie, probably for laughing at a joke Josie made herself that lacked any level of humor. I'd never understand how someone so wonderful had birthed such awful people. My favorite tiara? The one I was wearing? It was only my favorite because Josie bent my first favorite and lost two stones out of the second. She wasn't even supposed to touch them. Ever.

Beside her, Kile was reading a book. Because, clearly, everything going on in our country and home was too boring for him. What an ingrate.

He peeked up from his book, saw me watching, made a face, and went back to reading. Why was he even here?

"How are you feeling?" Mom was suddenly beside me, her arm around my shoulder.

"Fine."

She smiled. "There's no way you're fine. This is terrifying."

"Why, yes, yes it is. How kind of you to subject me to such a delightful thing."

Her giggle was tentative, testing to see if we were on good terms again.

"I don't think you're flawed," she said quietly. "I think you're a thousand wonderful things. One day you'll know what it's like to worry for your children. And I worry for you more than the others. You're not just any girl, Eadlyn. You're *the* girl. And I want everything for you."

I wasn't sure what to say. I didn't want for us to fight right now, not with something this big coming. Her arm was still on my shoulder, so I wrapped mine around her back, and she kissed my hair, just under my tiara.

"I feel very uncomfortable," I confessed.

"Just remember how the boys are feeling. This is huge for them as well. And the country will be so pleased."

I concentrated on my breathing. Three months. Freedom. A piece of cake.

"I'm proud of you," she said, giving me a final squeeze. "Good luck."

She walked away to greet Dad, and Ahren strode toward me, smoothing out his suit. "I cannot believe this is actually happening," he said, genuine excitement coloring his tone. "I'm really looking forward to the company."

"What, is Kile not enough for you?" I darted my eyes at him again, and he still had his nose buried.

"I don't know what you have against Kile. He's really smart."

"Is that code for boring?"

"No! But I'm excited to meet different people."

"I'm not." I crossed my arms, partly frustrated, partly protecting myself.

"Aww, come on, sis. This is going to be fun." He surveyed the room and dropped his voice to a whisper. "I can only imagine what you have in store for those poor saps."

I tried to suppress my smile, but I was anticipating watching them squirm.

He picked up one of the envelopes and bopped me on the nose with it. "Get ready now. If you have a basic grasp of the English language, you should manage this part just fine."

"Such a pain," I said, punching his arm. "I love you."

"I know you do. Don't worry. This is going to be easy."

We were instructed to take our seats, and Ahren threw the envelope back down, taking my hand to walk me to my place. The cameras started rolling, and Dad began the *Report* with an update about an approaching trade agreement with New Asia. We worked so closely with them now, it was hard to imagine a time we were actually at war. He touched on the growing immigration laws, and all his advisers spoke, including Lady Brice. It simultaneously felt like it dragged on forever and passed in an instant.

When Gavril announced my name, it took me a second to remember exactly what I was supposed to be doing. But I stood and walked across the stage, and assumed my place in front of the microphone.

I flashed a smile and looked straight into the camera, knowing every TV in Illéa was on tonight. "I'm sure you're all as excited as I am, so let's skip ceremony and get right to what everyone is dying to hear. Ladies and gentlemen, here are the thirty-five young men invited to participate in this groundbreaking Selection."

I reached into the bowl and pulled out the first envelope. "From Likely," I read, pausing to open it, "Mr. MacKendrick Shepard."

I held up his photograph, and the room applauded as I set it in the other bowl and moved back for the next entry.

"From Zuni . . . Mr. Winslow Fields."

There was a smattering of applause after every name.

Holden Messenger. Kesley Timber. Hale Garner. Edwin Bishop.

It felt like I had opened at least a hundred envelopes by the time my hands reached for the final one. My cheeks hurt, and I was hoping Mom wouldn't judge me if I skipped dinner and ate alone in my room. I really thought I'd earned it.

"Ah! From Angeles." I ripped at the paper, pulling out the final entry. I knew my smile must have faltered, but really, it couldn't be helped. "Mr. Kile Woodwork."

I heard the reactions around the room. Several gasps, a handful of laughs, but, most obviously, I could hear Kile's reaction. He dropped his book.

I pulled in a breath. "There you have it. Tomorrow, advisers will be sent out to begin prepping these thirty-five candidates for the adventure before them. And, in one short week, they will arrive at the palace. Until then, join me in congratulating them."

I began the applause, the room followed, and I retreated to my seat, trying not to look as sick as I felt.

Kile's name being in there shouldn't have shaken me the way it did. At the end of the day, none of those boys stood a chance. But something about this felt wrong.

The second Gavril finished signing off, everyone erupted. Mom and Dad walked to the Woodworks. I followed right behind them, Josie's laughter acting as a homing beacon.

"I didn't do it!" Kile insisted. As I approached, our eyes met. I could see he was as upset as I was.

"Does that even matter?" Mom said. "Anyone of age is allowed to put his name in."

Dad nodded. "That's true. It's a bit of a strange situation, but there's nothing illegal about it."

"But I don't want to be a part of this." Kile looked at Dad imploringly.

"Who put your name in?" I asked.

Kile shook his head. "I don't know. It has to be a mistake. Why would I enter when I don't want to compete?"

Mom's eyes were on General Leger, and it looked almost like they were smiling. But there wasn't anything funny about this.

"Excuse me!" I protested. "This is unacceptable. Is anyone going to do anything about it?"

"Pick someone else," Kile offered.

General Leger shook his head. "Eadlyn announced your name in front of the country. You're the candidate from Angeles."

"That's right," Dad agreed. "Reading the names publicly makes it official. We can't replace you."

Kile rolled his eyes. He did that a lot. "Then Eadlyn can eliminate me the first day."

"And send you where?" I asked. "You're already home."

Ahren chuckled. "Sorry," he said, noticing our glares. "That's not going to sit well with the others."

"Send me away," Kile offered, sounding thrilled.

"For the hundredth time, Kile, you're not leaving!" Miss

Marlee said in the firmest voice I'd ever heard her use. She put her hand to her temple, and Mr. Carter wrapped an arm around her, speaking into her ear.

"You want to go somewhere else?" I asked, incredulous. "Isn't a palace good enough for you?"

"It's not mine," he said, raising his voice. "And quite frankly, I'm tired of it. I'm over the rules, I'm over being a guest, and I'm so over your bratty attitude."

I gasped as Miss Marlee thwacked her son over the head.

"Apologize!" she commanded.

Kile pressed his lips together, looking at the ground. I crossed my arms. He wasn't leaving until I got an apology. I'd get it one way or another.

Finally, after a forceful shake of his head, he muttered it under his breath.

I looked away, hardly impressed with his efforts.

"We'll move forward as planned," Dad said. "This is a Selection, just like any of the others. It's about choices. Right now, Kile is one option of many, and Eadlyn could certainly do worse."

Thanks, Dad. I quickly checked Kile's expression. He was staring at the floor, seeming embarrassed and angry.

"For now I think we should all get some food and celebrate. This is a very exciting day."

"That's right," General Leger agreed. "Let's eat."

"I'm tired," I said, turning. "I'll be in my room."

I didn't wait for approval. I didn't owe anyone anything after tonight. I was giving them everything they wanted.

CHAPTER 8

I AVOIDED EVERYONE OVER THE weekend, and no one seemed bothered by it, not even Mom. With the names out there, the Selection felt that much more real, and I was saddened by the dwindling days of solitude.

The Monday before the candidates arrived, I finally rejoined humanity and made my way to the Women's Room. Miss Lucy was there, seeming back to her usual, cheerful self. I kept wishing I could do something to help her. I knew a puppy wasn't a person, but so far my only idea was to get her a pet.

Mom was talking to Miss Marlee, and they waved me over the moment I was through the doorway.

Miss Marlee put her hand on mine as I sat. "I wanted to explain about Kile. He doesn't want to leave because of you. He's been talking about going for a long time, and I thought the semester away would put an end to it. I can't bear to let him go."

"You'll have to let him make his own choice sooner or later," Mom urged. Funny, since she was the one trying to marry her daughter to a stranger.

"I don't understand it. Josie never talks about leaving."

I rolled my eyes. Of course she doesn't.

"But what can you do? You can't force him to stay." Mom poured a cup of tea and set it in front of me.

"I'm hiring another tutor. This one has hands-on experience and can give Kile more than a book could, so I think I've bought some more time. I keep hoping—"

Aunt May burst into the room, looking as if she stepped out of a magazine. I bolted over to her and gave her a bone-crushing hug.

"Your Highness," she greeted.

"Shut up."

She laughed and pulled me back, grasping me by both shoulders and looking into my eyes. "I want to hear everything about the Selection. How are you feeling? Some of those pictures were cute. Are you already in love?"

"Not even close," I replied with a laugh.

"Well, give 'em a few days."

That's how it was with Aunt May. A new love every few months or so. She treated the four of us—and our cousins, Astra and Leo—like we were her kids since she never settled down herself. I particularly enjoyed her company, and the palace always felt more exciting when she was here.

"How long are you staying?" Mom asked, and May held my hand as we crossed back to her.

"Leaving again Thursday."

I gasped.

"I know. I'm going to miss all the excitement!" She pouted at me. "But Leo has a game Friday afternoon, and Astra's dance recital is on Saturday, and I promised I'd be there. She's really coming along," Aunt May said, turning to Mom. "You can tell her mother was an artist."

They shared a smile. "I wish I could go," Mom lamented.

"Why don't we?" I suggested, picking up some cookies for my tea.

Aunt May gave me a questioning look. "You do realize you already have plans for this weekend, right? Big plans? Life-changing plans?"

I shrugged. "I'm not too worried about missing them."

"Eadlyn," Mom reprimanded.

"Sorry! It's just overwhelming. I like the way things are now."

"Where are the pictures?" May asked.

"In my room, on my desk. I'm trying to learn the names, but I haven't gotten very far yet."

May waved her arm at a maid. "Dearie, will you go up to the princess's room and grab the stack of Selection candidates' forms off her desk?"

The maid beamed and curtsied, and I suspected she'd be thumbing through the pile on her way down.

Mom leaned in toward her sister. "I just want to remind

you that, one, they're off-limits, and, two, even if they weren't, you're twice their age."

Miss Marlee and I laughed, while Miss Lucy only smiled. She was much easier on Aunt May than the rest of us.

"Don't tease her," Miss Lucy protested. "I'm sure she has the best intentions."

"Thank you, Lucy. This isn't for me; it's for Eadlyn!" she vowed. "We're going to help her get a head start."

"That's not really how it works." Mom leaned back, drinking her tea with an air of superiority.

Miss Marlee laughed loudly. "This from you! Do we need to remind you of *your* head start?"

"What?" I asked, shocked. How many details had my parents omitted from their story? "What does she mean?"

Mom put down her tea and held up a hand defensively. "I accidentally ran into your father the night before the Selection started, and, I will have you know," she said, more to Miss Marlee than to me, "I could easily have been kicked out for that. It wasn't exactly the first impression you hope for."

I sat there gaping. "Mom, exactly how many rules did you break?"

Her eyes darted up as if she was trying to tally them. "Okay, you know what, go through the pictures all you want; you win."

Aunt May laughed with delight, and I tried to memorize the way her head sloped gracefully to one side and her eyes sparkled. Everything about her was so effortlessly glamorous, and I adored her with a love close to what I held for my mother. While I felt a little slighted by Josie being my closest female playmate growing up, Mom's circle of friends more than made up for it. Aunt May's spirit, Miss Lucy's kindness, Miss Marlee's buoyancy, and Mom's strength were invaluable, and more enlightening than any class I ever took.

The maid came back, placing the pile of forms and pictures in front of me. To my surprise, it was Miss Marlee who grabbed the first handful of applications to graze through. Aunt May was close behind, and while Mom didn't pick up any herself, she did lean over Miss Marlee's shoulder to peek. Miss Lucy looked like she was trying not to be curious but in the end had a pile in her own lap as well.

"Oh, he looks promising." Aunt May shoved a picture in front of me. I stared into a set of dark eyes embedded deep in ebony skin. His hair was cropped short, and he wore a bright smile. "Baden Trains, nineteen, from Sumner."

"He's handsome," Mom gushed.

"Well, obviously," May agreed. "And with a last name like Trains, he probably comes from a family of Sevens. It says here he's in his first year studying advertising. That means either he or someone in his family is very determined."

"True," Miss Marlee agreed. "That's no small feat."

I pulled a couple of the forms over, picking through them.

"So how are you feeling?" Aunt May asked. "Is everything ready to go?"

"I think so." I flipped over an application, scanning for something that might seem remotely interesting. I just didn't care. "For a while everyone was in such a tizzy I thought it might never end. It looks like all the rooms are finished, the food calculations have been made, and now that the list is official, travel arrangements should be done by tomorrow."

"You sound positively thrilled," May teased, poking me.

I sighed, then looked pointedly at Mom. "You might as well know, this isn't completely about me."

"What do you mean, honey?" Miss Lucy asked, setting her pile of papers on her lap, looking between Mom and me with concern.

"Of course we're hoping Eadlyn will find someone worthy of settling down with," Mom began shrewdly. "But as it happens, this is coming at a time when we were in need of a plan to calm the unrest over the castes."

"Ames!" May said. "Your daughter is a decoy?"

"No!"

"Yes," I muttered. Aunt May rubbed my back, and it made me feel so much better to have her there.

"Sooner or later, we would have needed to look at suitors, and this isn't binding. Eadlyn has an agreement with Maxon that if she doesn't fall in love, then the whole thing is off. However, yes, Eadlyn is doing her job as a member of the royal family by creating a little . . . diversion while the population cools down and we investigate what more we could do. And, might I add, it's working."

"It is?" I asked.

"Haven't you looked at the papers? You're the center of everything right now. Local papers are interviewing their candidates, and some provinces are holding parties, hoping their suitor will be the winner. Magazines are talking about possible front-runners, and I saw a segment on the news last night about a few girls who were forming fan clubs and wearing shirts with the names of their favorites plastered all over them. The Selection has consumed the entire country."

"It's true," Miss Marlee confirmed. "Kile living in the palace is no longer a secret."

"Have they also discovered he has no interest in participating?" I asked, more irritation in my voice than I intended. Miss Marlee wasn't to blame for this whole debacle.

"No," she answered with a laugh. "Again, though, that has nothing to do with you."

I smiled back. "Miss Marlee, you heard Mom. He doesn't need to worry. I think Kile and I already know we wouldn't be that great of a match, and there's a chance I'll walk away from this without a fiancé anyway." A one hundred percent chance, to be more accurate. "Don't worry about him hurting my feelings, because I'm just seeing how it goes," I replied, as if this was normal, bringing in a slew of boys for me to pick from. "I'm not upset."

"You said it's taken over everything," May began, concerned. "Do you think it will last?"

"I think it'll hold things off long enough for the people to forget some of the unhappiness that's been so prevalent lately and for us to come up with a way to address issues if they pop up again." Mom sounded confident.

"*When* they pop up," I corrected. "My life might be

exciting for a while, but eventually people will start worrying about themselves again." I went back to looking at the pictures, almost pitying these boys. They had no chance of winning and no idea they were part of a public distraction.

"This is strange," I said, picking up one of the applications. "I don't want to be judgmental, but look at this. I caught three different spelling mistakes on this one."

Mom took the form. "It's possible he was nervous."

"Or an idiot," I offered.

May chuckled.

"Don't be so harsh, sweetie. It's scary on their end, too." Mom handed me the form, and I clipped it back to a picture of a boy with a very innocent face and a head full of wild blond curls.

"Wait, are you scared?" Aunt May asked, worry on my behalf coating her voice.

"No, of course not."

Her expression relaxed back into its normal, beautiful, carefree state. "Can't imagine you being scared of anything." She winked at me.

It was comforting that at least one of us thought so.

CHAPTER 9

WHEN THEY STARTED POURING IN, I fled to my room, sketching in the sunlight on my balcony. Too many boisterous laughs and overly enthusiastic greetings. I wondered how long that camaraderie would last. This was a competition, after all. I mentally added finding ways to pit them against one another to my to-do list.

"I think we should put my hair up, Neena. I want to look mature today."

"Excellent choice, my lady." She scrubbed at my nails. "Any thoughts on a dress?"

"I'm thinking evening gown. Black would do nicely."

She chuckled. "Looking to scare them?"

I couldn't hold back my sly smile. "Only a little."

We giggled together, and I was glad to have her with me. I was going to need her soothing words and calming touches over the next few weeks.

After my hair was dry, we braided and knotted it up like a crown, which only made my tiara look better. I found the black dress I'd worn for a New Year's Eve party last year. It was covered in lace and fitted to the knee before it flared out to the floor. An oval of skin was exposed across my back, and the tiny butterfly sleeves set low across my shoulders. I had to admit it looked even more beautiful in the sun than it did under candles.

My clock struck one, and I made my way downstairs. We had converted one of the libraries on the fourth floor into a Men's Parlor so the Selected could gather and relax during their time in the palace. It was about the same size as the Women's Room and had plenty of places to sit, lots of books, and two televisions.

I was heading to that area of the palace now. We had decided that the suitors would be brought out one at a time to greet me and then escorted to the Men's Parlor to get to know one another.

I saw a cluster of people down the hallway, including my parents and General Leger, and made my way toward them, trying not to let my nerves show. Dad looked stunned and Mom covered her mouth as I approached.

"Eadlyn . . . you seem so grown up." She sighed as she touched my cheek and shoulder and hair, not fixing anything, just checking.

"Probably because I am."

She nodded to herself, tears in her eyes. "You look the

part. I never really thought I passed for a queen, but you . . . wholly perfect."

"Stop it, Mom. You're completely adored. You and Dad brought peace to the country. I haven't done anything."

She placed a finger under my chin. "Not yet. But you're too determined to accomplish nothing."

Before I could respond, Dad approached us. "Ready?"

"Yes," I answered, steadying myself. That wasn't the pep talk I'd been envisioning. "I don't intend to eliminate anyone just yet. I figure everyone deserves at least a day."

Dad smiled. "I think that's wise."

I took a breath. "All right, then. Let's begin."

"Do you want us to stay or go?" Mom asked.

I considered. "Go. For now, anyway."

"As you wish," Dad said. "General Leger and a few guards will be nearby. If you need anything, simply ask. We want you to have a wonderful day."

"Thank you, Daddy."

"No," he said, embracing me, "thank you."

He pulled away and offered his arm to Mom. They walked off, and I felt like I could see their happiness glowing simply in the way they moved.

"Your Highness," General Leger said gently. I turned to see his smiling face. "Nervous?"

I shook my head slightly, almost convincing myself. "Bring the first one out."

He nodded before making eye contact with a butler down the hall. A boy walked out of one of the libraries, straightening his cuff links as he approached. He was lean and a little on the short side, but he had a pleasant enough face.

He stopped in front of me, bowing. "Fox Wesley, Your Highness."

I tilted my head in greeting. "A pleasure."

He took in a breath. "You are so beautiful."

"So I've been told. You can go now." I swept my arm across my body, pointing to the Men's Parlor.

Fox furrowed his eyebrows before giving me another bow and leaving.

The next boy was in front of me, tipping his head to greet me.

"Hale Garner, Your Highness."

"Welcome, sir."

"Thank you so much for letting us into your home. I hope to prove myself worthy of your hand more and more each day."

I cocked my head curiously. "Really? And how will you do that today?"

He smiled. "Well, today I would let you know I come from an excellent family. My father used to be a Two."

"Is that all?"

Undeterred, he went on. "I think it's pretty impressive."

"Not as impressive as having a father who used to be a One."

His face faltered.

"You may go."

He bowed and started to walk away. After a few steps he looked back. "I'm sorry to have offended you, Your Highness."

And his face was so sad that I nearly told him he hadn't. But that wouldn't fall in line with my plan for the day.

A parade of endlessly unmemorable boys crossed my path. A little past the halfway point, Kile came through the line, stopping in front of me. For once his hair was styled in such a way that I could actually see his eyes.

"Your Highness," he greeted.

"It's 'Royal Pain in the Ass' to you, sir."

He chuckled.

"So, how have they been treating you? Your mom says the papers spilled that you lived at the palace."

He shook his head in shock. "I thought that it would be an immediate invitation to be pummeled by a bunch of jealous meatheads, but it turns out, most of them see me as an asset."

"Oh?"

"They assume I know everything about you already. I've been bombarded with questions all morning."

"And what are you telling them, exactly?"

He smirked, his smile slightly crooked. "What a pleasure you are, of course."

"Right." I rolled my eyes, not believing him for a second. "You can go ahead—"

"Listen, I want to tell you I'm sorry again. For calling you bratty."

I shrugged. "You were upset."

He nodded, accepting that excuse. "Still, it's unfair all the same. I mean, don't get me wrong, you are exceedingly spoiled." He shook his head. "But you're tough because you have to be. You're going to be queen, and while I've seen things unfold in the palace, I've never actually had the weight of your work on me. It's not fair for me to judge."

I sighed. The polite thing would be to thank him. So, fine, I would be polite. "Thank you."

"Sure."

There was a long pause.

"Umm, the Men's Parlor is that way," I said, pointing.

"Right. See you later, I guess."

I smiled to myself, noticing as he left that he held a notebook in the hand he'd kept behind his back. Kile looked better than usual thanks to the mandatory makeover, but he was still an annoying little bookworm.

It was clear that the gentleman after him was anything but.

His caramel-colored hair was brushed back, and he walked with his hands in his pockets, as if he'd strolled down these halls before. His demeanor actually threw me for a second. Was he here to meet me, or was I here to meet him?

"Your Majesty," he greeted silkily as he sank into a bow.

"Highness," I corrected.

"No, no. It's just Ean."

He cocked one cheek up into a smile.

"That was awful," I said with a laugh.

"It was a risk I had to take. There are thirty-four other guys here. How else was I supposed to get you to remember me?"

His gaze was intent, and if I hadn't dealt with so many politicians in my life, I might have been charmed.

"Very nice to meet you, sir."

"And you, Your Highness. Hope to see you soon."

He was followed by a boy with a drawl so thick I had to really focus to catch his words. Another asked when he was going to be paid. There was one who was sweating so much I had to call over a butler to give me a towel for my hand once he left, and the one after him blatantly stared at my chest for the entirety of our meeting. It was an ongoing pageant of disasters.

General Leger came to my side. "In case you've lost count, this is the last one."

I threw back my head in relief. "Thank. Goodness!"

"I don't think your parents will want to ask you for a follow-up, but you should go to them when you're done."

I gave him a look. "If you insist."

He chuckled. "Go easy on them. Your father has a lot to deal with right now."

"*He's* got a lot to deal with? Did you see that one guy sweat?!"

"Can you blame him? You're the princess. You have the capacity to sentence him to death, if you wanted."

General Leger had these sparkling green eyes that shimmered with mischief, one of those men who grew even more handsome as he aged. I knew it for a fact because Miss Lucy once showed me a picture of their wedding day, and he seriously only got better looking. Sometimes, if he was tired or if the weather was bad, he walked with a limp, but it never slowed him. Maybe it was because I knew how much Miss Lucy loved him, but he always seemed like a safe place. If I hadn't been nervous about him siding with Mom and Dad, I would have asked for his advice on how to get these boys to plead to go home. Something in his eyes made me think he'd know exactly how to do it.

"A few of them make me uneasy," I confessed. The smooth words, the leering eyes. Even though I grew up knowing I was special, I didn't like being looked at as a prize.

His expression grew sympathetic. "It's a strange situation, I know. But you never have to be alone with anyone you don't like, you're free to dismiss someone for nothing more than a feeling, and even the dumbest of them wouldn't be stupid enough to hurt you," he promised. "Trust me; if someone did, I'd make sure they never walked again."

He gave me a wink before moving away and signaling for the final contestant to be brought out.

I was a bit confused when it wasn't one person but two. The first was dressed in a crisp suit, but the second wore only a button-up shirt. The slightly drabber one walked a few steps behind the other, his eyes trained on the floor. The first was nothing but smiles, and it looked like someone had tried to tame his hair and failed.

"Hello, Highness," he greeted, his voice thick with an accent I couldn't identify. "How are you?"

Confused but disarmed by his incredibly warm smile, I answered, "I'm well. It's been a long day. I'm sure it has been for you, too."

Behind him, the other boy leaned forward and whispered

something in garbled words I couldn't understand.

The first nodded. "Oh, yes, yes, but . . . eets nice to meeting you." He used his hands as he spoke, trying to get the words across with his gestures.

I leaned in, not understanding, and somehow hoping a closer proximity would clear up his accent. "Excuse me?"

The boy behind him spoke up. "He says it's a pleasure to meet you."

I squinted, still confused.

"My name ees Henri." He bowed in greeting, and I could see in his face that he meant to do this earlier and forgot.

I didn't want to be rude, so I nodded my head in acknowledgment. "Hello, Henri."

He lit up at the sound of his name, and he stood there, looking back and forth between the gentleman behind him and me.

"I can't help but notice your accent," I remarked in what I hoped was a friendly tone. "Where do you come from?"

"Umm, Swend—?" he began, but turned to the guest with him.

He nodded, carrying on in Henri's place. "Sir Henri was born in Swendway, so he has a very strong Finnish accent."

"Oh," I replied. "And does he speak much English?"

Henri piped up. "English, no, no." He didn't seem embarrassed though. Instead he laughed it off.

"How are we supposed to get to know each other?"

The translator turned to Henri. "*Miten saat tuntemaan toisensa?*"

Henri pointed to the translator, who answered, "Through me, it seems."

"Okay. Well. Umm." I wasn't prepared for this. Was it rude for me to dismiss him? Interacting with these people one-on-one was going to be awkward enough. I wasn't prepared for a third person.

In that instant Henri's application popped back into my mind. That was why some of the words were spelled wrong. He was guessing at them.

"Thank you. It's very nice to meet you, too, Henri."

He smiled at his name, and I got the feeling the rest of the words didn't even matter. I couldn't send him away.

"The Men's Parlor is over here."

Henri bowed as his translator mumbled the instructions, and they walked away together.

"General Leger," I called, burying my face in my hands.

"Yes, Your Highness."

"Tell Dad I'll update him in an hour. I need to take a walk."

CHAPTER 10

WE MADE IT THROUGH THE first day, the first dinner, and the first evening without further incident. As the cameras circled the dining hall, I could hear the men working them sigh in boredom. I didn't address anyone in the group, and the boys themselves seemed too nervous even to speak to one another.

I could hear Dad's thoughts as clearly as if they were my own.

This is dull! No one will want to see this! How will this buy us a single second let alone three months?

He glanced over at me a few times, begging me with his eyes to do something, anything, to make this worth enduring. I was at war with myself. I didn't want to fail him, but any warmth on my part today would set a bad precedent. They needed to know that I wasn't going to fawn over them.

I told myself not to worry. In the morning everything would change.

The following day the boys were dressed in their best, ready for the parade. An army of people swarmed on the front lawn, ready to prep us to go beyond the gates.

Dad was proud of this idea, my biggest contribution to the Selection so far. I thought it would be exciting to have a short parade, something never done before. I felt certain this would give everyone something to talk about.

"Good morning, Your Highness," one of the boys greeted. I remembered Ean in an instant, and after yesterday it was no surprise he was the first one to speak to me.

"And to you." I walked on, not slowing, though many of the others bowed or called my name. I only stopped to be briefed by one of the guards heading up the process.

"It's a short loop, Your Highness. At under ten miles an hour, it should take twenty to thirty minutes to make our way around. Guards are lining the route for good measure, but everyone is so excited, it should be a very fun event."

I clasped my hands calmly in front of me. "Thank you, officer. I appreciate your work to make this happen."

He pressed his lips together, attempting to hide his proud smile. "Anything for you, Your Highness."

He went to walk away, but I called him back. The officer puffed out his chest, so pleased to be needed again. I looked around at the swarm of young men, dazed by their number, trying to make the smartest choice.

I saw Henri's wild hair blowing in the wind and smiled to myself. He stood on the outside of a group, listening to what they were saying and nodding, though I was sure he couldn't understand anything going on around him. I didn't see his translator and wondered if Henri had banished him for the day.

I searched again, hunting . . . and found one boy who really knew how to wear a suit. It wasn't that he looked like a model but more like he understood the fine art of tailoring and had set his butler to work immediately on his choice for the day. Also, I couldn't get over his two-toned shoes. Thank goodness I remembered his name.

"When I'm up there, I'd like Mr. Garner on one side and Mr. Jaakoppi on the other, please."

"Certainly, Your Highness. I'll take care of it."

I turned and looked at the float. They'd taken the frame of one of the Christmas floats and adorned it with thousands of summer blooms. It was festive and beautiful, and the scent of the flowers permeated the air. I inhaled, and the clean, sweet smell soothed every piece of me.

Over the walls I could hear the shouts of people who had lined up for this moment. Whatever ways I'd failed last night would be more than forgotten today.

"All right, gentlemen." General Leger's voice boomed over the din. "I need you all to line up along the path, and we'll get you up safely."

Mom was in the back with Dad, who had picked up a few stray flowers that had blown off the float and stuck them in her hair. She looked at him with absolute adoration as he stepped away with his camera.

He circled the group, snapping pictures. He got plenty of the boys, some of the fountain, and a couple of me.

"Dad!" I whispered, a little embarrassed.

He winked and backed away, still taking shots but in a less obvious way.

"Your Highness," General Leger said, placing a hand on my back. "We're going to send you up last. I heard you wanted Henri and Hale beside you, is that right?"

"Yes."

"Good picks. They're polite ones. Okay, we'll be ready to go in a moment."

He walked over to my mother and relayed something to her. She seemed uneasy, but General Leger made motions with his hands, attempting to reassure her. Dad was a little harder to read from here. Either he wasn't bothered at all, or he was hiding it very well.

The boys were led up the hidden ladder, and I paced as I waited for my turn. Along the wall, mixed in with a few guards and guests, I noticed Henri's translator standing, arms crossed, watching the scene. He bit at a fingernail, and I shook my head, walking over.

"Don't do that," I started, trying to be firm without being rude. "You don't want the cameras to catch you with your fingers in your mouth, do you?"

He whipped his hand down immediately. "I'm sorry, Your Highness."

"Not going up there?" I nodded toward the massive float.

He smiled. "No, Your Highness. I think Henri can wave without interpretation." Still, I felt the nerves buzzing around him.

"He'll be right beside me," I assured him. "I'll try to make sure he knows what's going on."

The translator let out a massive sigh. "That makes this far less distressing. And he's going to be so excited. He talks about you every waking moment."

I laughed. "Well, it's hardly been a day. I'm sure it'll pass."

"I don't think so. He's in awe of you, of everything, really. The experience alone is big for him. His family has worked hard to establish themselves, and that he finds himself in a place where he can have even a second of your attention . . . he's so happy."

I looked up at Henri, straightening his tie as he waited on the front of the float. "Is that what he told you?"

"Not in so many words. He's aware of how fortunate he is, and he sees so many good things in you. He goes on and on."

I smiled sadly. It would have been nice if he could say as much to me. "Were you born in Swendway, too?"

He shook his head. "No. First generation to be born in Illéa. But my parents are trying to hold on to our old customs and things, so we live in a small Swendish community in Kent."

"Like Henri?"

"Yes. They're becoming more and more common. When Henri was Selected, his family put out a call for a reliable translator, and I submitted my résumé, flew to Sota, and now I have a new job."

"So you've only known Henri for . . . ?"

"A week. But we've already spent so much time together and get along so well, I feel like I've known him for years." He spoke with a sweet affection, brotherly in a way.

"I feel so rude—I don't even know your name."

He bowed. "I'm Erik."

"Erik?"

"Yes."

"Huh. I expected something a bit different."

He shrugged. "Well, that's the closest translation."

"Your Highness?" General Leger called, and that was my cue.

"I'll watch out for him," I promised, scurrying over to the float.

The ladder was a challenge. I had to conquer it while wearing heels and holding my dress with one hand, which meant I had to let go of one rung before grabbing the next, and I was particularly proud of myself for managing that on my own.

I brushed back my hair as I went to take my place. Henri turned to me immediately.

"Hello today, Your Highness." His blond curls were lifted by the breeze, and he smiled brightly.

I touched his shoulder. "Good morning, Henri. Call me Eadlyn."

He scrunched his face, a little confused. "Say to you Eadlyn?"

"Yes."

He gave me a thumbs-up, and I patted myself on the back for putting him beside me. In seconds he left me smiling. I leaned behind Henri, looking between the others to find Erik on the ground and gave him a thumbs-up, too. He smiled and put a hand over his heart like he was relieved.

I faced Hale. "How are you today?"

"Good," he said tentatively. "Listen, I wanted to apologize again for yesterday. I didn't mean to—"

I waved my hand, stopping him. "No, no. As I'm sure you can imagine, this is a bit stressful for me."

"Yes. I wouldn't want to be in your shoes."

"I *would* want to be in yours!" I exclaimed, looking down. "I love these!"

"Thank you. Do they work all right with the tie? I like to experiment, but I'm starting to second-guess."

"No. You make it all work."

Hale beamed, thrilled to be past his first impression and on to the second.

"So, it was you who said you'd prove yourself to me each day, yes?"

"Indeed it was." He seemed pleased I remembered.

"And how will you do that today?"

He considered. "If you feel the slightest bit unsteady, my hand is here for you. And I promise not to let you fall."

"I like that one. You think you've got it bad, try this in heels."

"We're opening the gates!" someone called. "Hold on!"

I waved good-bye to Mom and Dad, then grabbed on to the bar surrounding the top of the float. It wasn't too far of a drop if someone fell, but for the five of us across the front, there was a chance we'd get flattened by the float if we did. Hale and Henri were steady, just as I'd hoped, but plenty of the others clapped or shouted out self-encouragements. Burke, for one, kept yelling "We've got this!" even though all he really had to do was stand and wave.

The moment the gates opened, the cheering erupted. As we rounded the corner, I could see the first camp of cameras filming every second. Some people had signs supporting their favorite Selected boy or were waving the Illéan flag.

"Henri, look!" I said, leaning into him and pointing to a sign with his name on it.

He took a moment to understand. Then when he finally saw his name, he gasped. "Hey!" He was so excited, he lifted my hand off his shoulder and kissed it. Had anyone else done that it might have been unwelcome, but from him, the gesture felt so innocent, I wasn't bothered at all.

"We love you, Princess Eadlyn," someone called, and I waved in the direction of the sound.

"Long live the king!"

"Bless you, Princess!"

I mouthed my thanks to them for their support, and I felt encouraged. It wasn't every day that I saw my people face-to-face, heard their voices, and sensed how they needed us. I knew they loved me, of course. I was going to be their queen. But typically, when I did leave the palace, the focus was on Mom or Dad. It felt amazing to have so much of the affection finally centered on me. Maybe I could be as beloved as my father.

The parade went on, with people calling our names and throwing flowers. It was turning out to be the spectacle I'd hoped. I couldn't have asked for anything better, until we reached the final stretch of the route.

Something hit me that was clearly not a flower. I looked to see a runny egg dripping down my dress and onto my bare legs. After that, half a tomato hit me, then something else I couldn't identify.

I dropped down, covering myself with my arms.

"We need jobs!" someone shrieked.

"The castes still live!"

I peeked out and saw a cluster of people protesting and hurling their rotten food at the float. Some held angry signs they must have hidden from the guards until now, and others threw disgusting words at me, calling me things that I'd never imagined even the worst of people saying.

Hale dropped down and lay in front of me, wrapping an arm around my shoulder. "Don't worry, I've got you."

"I don't understand," I mumbled.

Henri got down on one knee, trying to hit anything that came near us, and Hale guarded me without wavering, even though I heard him grunt and felt him clench up when he was hit with something heavy.

I recognized General Leger's voice shouting at the Selected to get down. As soon as everyone was low and secure, the float sped up, moving faster than it was probably designed to. People who actually cared about the parade booed as we hurtled past them, stealing their opportunity to catch a glimpse of the whole entourage.

I heard the float hit the gravel of the palace driveway, and the instant we came to a stop I pulled back from Hale and jumped to my feet. I hurried to the ladder and worked my way down.

"Eadlyn!" Mom cried.

"I'm fine."

Dad stood in shock. "Love, what happened?"

"Hell if I know." I stormed off, humiliated. As if the whole thing wasn't embarrassing enough, the sad eyes of everyone around me made it even worse.

Poor thing, their expressions seemed to say. And I hated their pity more than I hated the people who thought this was acceptable.

I scurried through the palace, head down, hoping no one would stop me. It wasn't my lucky day, of course, because as I rounded onto the landing of the second floor, Josie was there.

"Ew! What happened to you?"

I didn't answer, moving even faster. Why? What had I done to deserve this?

Neena was cleaning when I walked in. "Miss?"

"Help," I whimpered before bursting into tears.

She came over and embraced me, getting my mess all over her pristine uniform. "Hush now. We'll clean you up. You get undressed, and I'll start the bath."

"Why would they do this to me?"

"Who did it?"

"My people!" I answered in pain. "My subjects. Why would they do this?"

Neena swallowed, disappointed for my sake. "I don't know."

I wiped at my face and makeup, and something green came off on my hand. The tears fell again.

"Let me start that bath."

She scurried away, and I stood there, helpless.

I knew the water would get rid of the mess, and I knew it would take away the smell, but no amount of scrubbing would ever wash away this memory.

Hours later I was scrunched up on a chair in Dad's sitting room, bundled in my coziest sweater. Despite the heat, my clothes were my only armor at the moment, and the layers made me feel safe. Mom and Dad were both drinking something a little stronger than wine—a rare occasion—though it didn't appear to be doing much for their nerves.

Ahren knocked but came in before anyone answered the door. Our eyes met, and I rushed across the room, throwing my arms around him.

"Sorry, Eady," he said, kissing my hair.

"Thanks."

"Glad you could come, Ahren." Dad was looking at some of the stills from the parade that the photographers had provided him, stacking them on top of several of today's papers.

"Of course." He put his arm around my shoulder and walked me to my seat, going to stand with Dad while I curled back up into a ball.

"I still can't believe this happened," Mom said, reaching the bottom of her glass. I could see her weighing in her head whether or not to have another. She decided against it.

"Me either," I mumbled, still suffering under the surge of hatred those people felt for me. "What did I do?"

"Nothing," Mom assured me, coming to sit beside me. "They're mad at the monarchy, not you. Today your face was the one they could see, and that's the one they attacked. It could have been any of us."

"I felt so certain a Selection would lift their mood. I thought they would delight in this." Dad stared at the pictures, still shocked.

We sat silent for a while. He'd been so wrong.

"Well," Ahren started. "They might have if it wasn't Eadlyn."

We all gaped at him.

"Excuse me?" I nearly started crying all over again, pained by his cruel words. "Mom just said it could have been you or her or anyone. So why are you blaming me?"

He pursed his lips, looking around the room. "Fine. We'll talk about this. If Eadlyn was a typical girl, one who wasn't raised to be in control all the time, this would probably look different. But pick up any of those papers," he said, gesturing to the pile. Dad did. "In general she comes across as distant, and every picture from last night's dinner is uncomfortable to look at. You're nearly scowling in some of them."

"If you were in my shoes, you'd know how hard this is."

Ahren rolled his eyes at me. More than anyone, he knew I wasn't intending to pick a mate in the next few months.

Mom left me and peeked over Dad's shoulder. "He's right. On your own, you look like an island, and with the Selected there's no chemistry, no romance."

"Listen, I'm not performing for anyone. I refuse to act all dopey over a bunch of boys to entertain people." I crossed my arms, determined.

Two days in and this was already a disaster. I knew it wouldn't work, and now I was stuck in this humiliating situation. Could they dare ask me to sink further into shame for the sake of something that clearly wasn't going to help?

The room went silent, and, foolishly, I thought for a moment that I'd won.

"Eadlyn." I looked at Dad, trying not to be moved by the pleading in his eyes. "You promised me three months. We're trying hard to brainstorm on our end, but we can't extinguish that fire if we're dealing with new ones. I need you to try."

In that moment I saw something I hadn't really noticed before: his age. Dad wasn't old by any stretch of the word, but he had done more in his lifetime than most people twice his age could even hope for. He was in a constant state of sacrifice—for Mom, for us, for his people—and he was exhausted.

I swallowed, knowing that I'd need to find a way to look like I cared about the Selection, if only for his sake. "I assume you know how to get in touch with the press?"

Dad nodded. "Yes. We have trusted photographers and journalists on call."

"Get a few cameras in the Men's Parlor tomorrow morning. I'll take care of this."

CHAPTER 11

THE NEXT MORNING I SKIPPED breakfast with my family so I could compose myself. I didn't want anyone seeing how rattled yesterday had left me, and I felt like I was building a shield around myself, one steady breath at a time.

Neena was humming as she tidied my room, and it was one of the best things. Not only was she gentle with me after I came in yesterday, she didn't ask a single question or bring up the topic again. I didn't have to worry about her, which was why she couldn't leave the palace one day. What about me?

"I think it's a pants day, Neena," I called.

She stopped humming. "More black?"

"At least a little." We shared a smile as she handed me my tight black pants, which I paired with heels that would kill me by noon. I pulled on a flowy shirt and a vest, and found a tiara with jewels that matched the shirt. I was ready.

I decided that I was going to do exactly what Dad had done with his Selection. On his first day he sent home at least six girls. I was planning to eliminate nearly twice as many. Certainly weeding out all the unlikely candidates would show how seriously I was taking this process, that the outcome was important to me.

I wished there was a way to do this without the cameras, but they were a necessary evil. I had a mental list prepared, and I knew vaguely what I wanted to say; but if I made a mistake with reporters present, it would be just as bad as yesterday . . . meaning I needed to be perfect.

Because the Women's Room was considered the property of the queen, any male had to ask permission before entering. The Men's Parlor had been thrown together for my convenience, so no such formality stood, and I was able to complete a rather dazzling entrance by pulling the double doors open and letting the rush of wind blow back my hair.

The Selected all hurried to face me, some jumping to their feet or pulling themselves away from the reporters accompanying the cameras.

I passed Paisley Fisher, noticing that he audibly gulped as I stopped. Smiling, I placed a hand on his shoulder.

"You can go."

He glanced at the people beside him. "Go?"

"Yes, go. As in, thank you for your participation, but your presence at the palace is no longer required."

When he lingered, I leaned in, breathing my instructions.

"The longer you stay, the more embarrassing it becomes. You should leave."

I pulled back, noting the marked anger in his eyes as he slowly left the room.

I couldn't figure out why he was so vexed. It wasn't as if I'd kicked him or shouted. I internally praised myself for getting rid of someone so childish and tried to remember my list. Who was next? Oh . . . this one was well deserved.

"Blakely, isn't it?"

"Ye—" His voice squeaked and he started again. "Yes, Your Highness."

"When we met, you couldn't stop staring at my breasts." His face went pale, as if he seriously thought he was so subtle no one would notice. "Make sure you get an equally satisfactory look at my backside as you leave."

I made sure to address him loud enough that the cameras and the other boys would hear. Hopefully his humiliation would prevent others from thinking they could behave similarly. He ducked his head and left the room.

I stopped in front of Jamal. "You can leave." Next to him, Connor was breaking out into a sweat again. "You can join him."

They shared a confused look and left together, shaking their heads.

I came upon Kile next. Unlike most of the others, he didn't avert his eyes. On the contrary, he stared into mine, and I could see him pleading for me to end his misery and get him out of here.

I might have if I didn't think his mother would kill me—as I would surely have to make him leave the palace—and if I hadn't seen his name on the most signs yesterday. Of course, Kile was the hometown pick, so maybe the crowd was biased. Still, I couldn't get rid of him. Not yet.

Beside him, Hale swallowed. I remembered how he'd protected me during the parade, knowing he'd taken hits that were intended for me, some of which had seemed rather painful.

I came near and spoke softly. "Thank you for yesterday. You were very brave."

"It was nothing," he assured me. "Though the suit couldn't be saved."

He said it jokingly, trying to make the whole thing seem like less of an issue than it was.

"Shame."

I lowered my eyes and continued walking. I didn't think the cameras would have picked up the conversation, but I knew they'd see our smiles. I wondered what would be made of that.

"Issir," I said to a slick-haired, gangly young man. "No. Thank you."

He didn't even question it. He blushed and fled as quickly as he could.

I heard a mumbling and wondered who would dare to speak right now. As I whipped my head around, I saw Henri's translator relaying the scene in Henri's ear as quickly and quietly as he could. Henri's eyes were stressed, but when he finished listening, he looked up at me and smiled. He had such a goofy little grin and his hair curled in a way that he looked like he was playing a game while standing still.

Ugh. I had intended to end his suffering and send him home, but he looked far too pleased to be here. Some of them had to stay anyway, and Henri was harmless.

I simply flicked my hand as I passed Nolan and announced to Jamie that his request for a payout was the most offensive way to introduce himself.

I continued to stalk around the room, checking to make sure I covered everyone I wanted gone. The reactions of the spared boys ranged from interesting to bizarre. Holden kept swallowing, waiting for the bomb to drop, while Jack smiled in a strange way, almost as if he found this all entertaining or exciting. I finally came up to Ean, who didn't look away but chose to wink at me.

I noticed he was sitting alone, with only a leather-bound journal and pen to keep him company. Not here to make friends it seemed.

"A wink is a bit bold, don't you think?" I asked quietly.

"What princess would want a man by her side who wasn't bold?"

I raised an eyebrow, amused. "You're not at all worried about being overconfident, are you?"

"No. It's who I am. And I don't intend to hide anything from you."

There was something almost frightening about his presence, but I liked that he had the nerve to be real. I noted the camera coming to hover behind him, trying to capture my expression, and I shook my head at him, suppressing a smirk. I moved on, adding Arizona, Brady, Pauly, and MacKendrick to the ranks of the evicted. If I'd counted correctly, that was eleven gone.

Once the eliminated had all left, I went to the door, turning to face the remaining candidates. "If you're still here, that means you've done something between our first meeting and now to impress me or have at least had the common sense not to offend me." Some smiled, probably thinking of Blakely, while others stood there stunned. "I want to encourage you all to be deliberate, because I take this very seriously. This isn't a game, gentlemen. This is my life."

I pulled the doors shut behind me and heard the flurry of activity pick up in my wake. Some laughed or sighed, while someone simply repeated "Oh, my goodness, oh, my goodness" again and again. The reporters' voices rose above them all, encouraging them to recount their feelings on the first elimination. Letting out a long breath, I walked away feeling confident. I'd taken a decisive step, and Dad could rest easy now, knowing the Selection was properly under way and that I wouldn't let him down.

To make up for the lackluster first evening and the complete absence of interaction after the parade yesterday, the boys were invited that night to a predinner tea to meet the household and, of course, speak with me, their beloved would-be bride. Mom and Dad were there, along with Ahren, Kaden, and Osten. Josie came with the Woodworks—who were working very hard not to hover over their son—and Miss Lucy was circling the room, not really speaking to anyone but looking lovely. She never seemed to care for crowds.

I'd changed into a gown for dinner and put on another pair of toe-destroying heels. I was still riding my post-elimination buzz, so pleased to be making steps to help Dad. It dwindled quickly though as Ahren walked toward me with a warning glare in his eyes.

"What in the world did you do to them?" he asked accusingly.

"Nothing," I vowed. "I held an elimination. I wanted to show everyone that this was important to me. Like Dad."

Ahren pressed his palm into his forehead. "Have you had your nose buried in reports all day?"

"Of course I have," I replied. "You might not have noticed, but that's kind of my job."

Ahren leaned in. "The clips on the news have painted you to be a black widow. Your face was smug as you kicked them out. And you got rid of a third of them, Eadlyn. That doesn't make the candidates look important. It makes them look disposable." I could feel the blood draining from my face as Ahren continued in a whisper. "Two of them have asked in the most circumspect and quiet ways possible if there was a chance that you prefer women."

I let out a sound that wasn't quite a laugh. "Of course, because the only way I could possibly like men is if I bowed down at their feet?"

"This isn't the time to make a stand, Eadlyn. You need to be gracious."

"Pardon me, Your Highness?"

Ahren and I both turned at the sound of our title, and I found myself with a reporter in my face, her eyes and smile bordering on manic.

"I hate to interrupt, but I was wondering if I could have a brief interview with the princess before my deadline." The reporter showed her teeth again, and I couldn't stop myself from feeling I was about to be eaten alive either figuratively or literally.

"She'd be happy to," Ahren offered, kissing my forehead as he disappeared.

My pulse sped. I hadn't prepared myself for this. But of all the things that could happen right now, I refused to let the public see me sweat.

"Your Highness, you eliminated eleven suitors today. Do you think this cut was a bit drastic?"

I squared my shoulders and gave her a sweet grin. "I can certainly see why some might think that," I answered generously, "but this is a very important decision. I don't think it would be wise to spend time on young men who are rude or unimpressive. I'm hoping with a smaller pool, I'll be able to get to know these gentlemen much better."

I scanned the words in my head. Nothing humiliating or incriminating in there.

"Yes, but why were you so harsh? For a few you simply said 'no' or flicked your hand."

I tried not to let the worry show on my face. At the time those things had seemed kind of funny.

"When my father is stern, no one chastises him. I don't think it's fair that when I act similarly, I'm seen as cruel. I'm making a huge decision, and I'm trying to be wise about it." While I wanted to scream those words, I said them with the voice I'd been trained to use in interviews, and I even managed to smile through most of it.

"But one of them cried after you left the room," she informed me.

"What?" I asked, worrying that my face was growing paler by the second.

"One of the Selected cried when the elimination ended. Do you think that's a normal response or that you maybe elicited it by being severe with them?"

I swallowed, scrambling for anything to say. "I have three brothers. They all cry, and I can assure you, the reasons rarely make sense to me."

She chuckled. "So you don't think you were too hard on them?"

I knew what she was doing, digging at the same question until I snapped. She was very close to getting the better of me.

"I can't imagine what it would be like on the other end of the Selection process and to be removed so early on. But, besides my father, no one here knows what it's like to be on this side of it either. I'm going to do my best to find a worthy husband. And if that man can't handle a harsh word or two, he definitely wouldn't make it as a prince. Trust me on that!" I reached out and touched her arm, as if this was gossip or a joke. It was a disarming technique.

"Speaking of suitors, I hope you'll excuse me. I need to go spend some time with them."

She opened her mouth to ask another question, but I turned away, holding my head high. I didn't know what to do. I couldn't go straight to the drinks, I couldn't unleash every swear word I knew into the air, and I couldn't run into the arms of my parents. I had to look content, so I walked around the room, smiling and batting my lashes at the boys as I passed them.

I noticed those small things alone made them grin at me or change their posture. Instead of retreating, their expressions softened, and I could see these tiny moments of gentleness were erasing their memories of this morning in the Men's Parlor already. I wished with everything I had that the public would let it slide as quickly as the boys did.

I figured eventually one of them would be brave enough to speak to me. And it turned out that person was Hale.

"So, we're at a tea party," he said, falling into step beside me. "What kind of tea does the princess like best?"

He sipped from his own cup, smiling shyly.

Hale had an effortless warmth about him, similar to Miss Marlee, and it was easy to hold a conversation with him. At the moment, I was more grateful he was the first one to approach me than he could have ever guessed. He'd rescued me twice now.

"It depends on my mood. Or the season. Like I can't seem to enjoy a white tea during the winter. But black tea is a good staple."

"Agreed." Hale stood there, nodding.

"I heard someone cried after I left today. Is that true?"

Hale's eyes widened and he let out a whistle. "Yeah, it was Leeland. I thought he'd broken a bone or something. Took us nearly an hour to calm him down."

"What happened?"

"You happened! You come in, prowling around the room, eliminating people at random. I guess he has a timid disposition, and you really shook him."

I spotted Leeland standing alone in a corner. If I was sincerely looking for a husband, he'd be gone already. I was a little surprised he hadn't asked to leave.

"I think it came out more callously than I'd intended."

Hale laughed once. "You don't have to be callous at all. We all know who you are and what you can do. We respect that."

"Tell that to the guy who asked when he was getting paid," I muttered.

He didn't have a response for that, and I felt bad for bringing our conversation to a halt.

"So, what is it today?" I asked, trying to regain my composure.

"I'm sorry?"

"How are you proving yourself to me today?"

He smiled. "Today it's my promise never to bring you white tea in the winter." He didn't say good-bye or bow but walked away, seeming hopeful.

Over his shoulder, Baden caught my eye. My first impression of him had nothing to do with our initial conversation. I only saw him as the boy Aunt May thought had promise.

I could tell he was debating whether or not to walk over. I looked down at the floor and peeked his way from under my lashes. I felt foolish trying to play this part, but it worked and he started to cross the floor. I thought back to the interviewer, musing over how funny it was that I'd been taught plenty of disarming techniques for interviews or negotiations, but when it came to boys, I was left to figure it out alone.

Baden looked eager to speak to me, but we were both shocked when another boy coming from a different direction arrived at us at the exact same moment.

"Gunner," Baden greeted. "How are you enjoying the party?"

"It's excellent. I was just coming to thank Her Highness for hosting it. It's been a pleasure to meet your younger brothers."

"Oh, dear. What did they do?"

Baden laughed, and Gunner tried to suppress a smile. "Osten is awfully . . . energetic."

I sighed. "I blame my parents. It seems that by the time you get to your fourth child, your desire to instill certain values goes out the window."

"I like him though. Hope he'll be around."

"It's hard to say. Osten's the hardest to keep tabs on. Even his nanny—whom he *despises*, by the way—can't keep up with him. Either he's causing chaos or he's hiding."

Baden jumped in. I wondered if he was trying to flirt or just seem brave. "Those two moods are so different! Is everyone in your family like that?"

I knew what he was asking: Was I the kind of girl who aimed to find solace or cause a stir with no in between? "Unquestionably."

Baden nodded. "Good to know. I'll buy a shield and some binoculars."

And, darn it, I giggled. I didn't mean to, but I did. I tried not to be upset for letting my guard down. Hopefully it would make for some good pictures. I curtsied and continued around the space.

I saw Henri across the room, Erik shadowing his every step. When our eyes met, he began walking my way immediately, grinning from ear to ear.

"Hello! *Hyvää iltaa!*" He kissed my cheek, which, again, would have been shocking from anyone else.

"He says 'Good evening.'"

"Oh um . . . *heevat eelah?*" I mumbled, attempting to duplicate his words.

He chuckled as I butchered his language. "Good, good!" Was he always this cheerful?

I turned to Erik. "How bad was it really?"

His tone was kind, but he wasn't going to lie. "I'm sorry to say, there is no way I could have even guessed at what that was."

I smiled, genuinely. The pair of them were so unassuming,

and considering how alienated Henri must have felt, that was saying something.

Before I could continue the conversation, Josie was beside me. "Great party, Eadlyn. You're Henri, right? I've seen your picture," she said in a rush, sticking her hand out to greet him.

He must have been confused, but he accepted the gesture all the same.

"I'm Josie. Eadlyn and I are practically sisters," she gushed.

"Except that we're not related at all," I added.

Erik tried to convey everything to Henri quickly and quietly, which distracted Josie.

"Who are you?" she asked. "I don't remember seeing your picture."

"I'm Sir Henri's translator. He only speaks Finnish."

Josie looked incredibly disappointed. I realized then that she must have come over because she found Henri attractive. He certainly seemed younger than most of the others and did have that happy-go-lucky air about him, which she must have thought suited her better than me.

"So . . . ," she began, "how does he, like, even live?"

Without even checking with Henri, Erik spoke up. "If you're practically Her Highness's sister, then I'm sure the palace has afforded you an excellent education. So, of course you know the relations between Illéa and Swendway are old and strong, drawing many Swendish people to settle here, making small communities, and vice versa. It's not difficult at all."

I pressed my lips together, trying not to grin at how articulately he put Josie in her place.

Josie nodded. "Oh, of course. Umm . . ." And that was as hard as she was willing to try. "Excuse me."

"I'm sorry," I whispered once she was out of earshot. "It has nothing to do with you two. She's just terrible."

"No offense taken," Erik replied honestly. He conversed back and forth for a moment with Henri in Finnish, presumably catching him up on what just happened.

"Pardon me. I need to speak with someone, but I'll see you at dinner." I curtsied and left them, searching for any sort of retreat.

I'd been totally thrown off by that interview earlier, and I was proud that I pulled myself back together in the aftermath. But Josie had the ability to ruffle me without fail.

I saw Mom alone and rushed over to her, hoping for some solace. Instead I was greeted by a glare similar to Ahren's when I'd first come in.

"Why didn't you tell us that was what you were going to do?" she asked quietly, holding a smile as if nothing was wrong.

I did the same as I answered. "I thought it would be good. That's what Dad did."

"Yes, but he did it on a much smaller scale and privately. You put their shame on display. No one will admire you for that."

I huffed. "I'm sorry. Really. I didn't realize."

She put an arm around me. "I don't mean to be hard on

you. We know you're trying." Just then a photographer came up to get a candid photo of us talking. I wondered what the headline for that one would be? Something about the Selected teaching the Selector maybe.

"What am I supposed to do now?"

She looked around the room, double-checking that no one could hear. "Just . . . consider a little romance. Nothing scandalous, for goodness' sake," she added quickly. "But watching you fall in love . . . that's what the people want to see."

"I can't *make* that happen. I can't—"

"America, dear," Dad called. It looked like Osten had spilled something on himself, and Mom rushed over to lead him away.

I would have bet money that whatever just happened was a deliberate attempt on Osten's part to get out of the room.

I stood there alone, trying to be inconspicuous as I scanned the room. Too many strangers. Too many eyes watching and waiting for me to perform. I was ready for the Selection to be over about four hours ago. I took a deep breath. Three months would buy me freedom. I could do this. I had to.

I walked across the room deliberately, knowing who I needed to speak to. Once I found him, I leaned in and spoke in his ear.

"Come to my room. Eight o'clock sharp. Tell no one."

CHAPTER 12

I PACED AS I WAITED for the knock to come. Kile was really the only person I could trust with this task, though I was loath to ask him. I was prepared to strike a bargain, but I wasn't sure what I could offer him yet. I felt confident he'd have his own ideas.

The raps on the door were quiet, and I could almost hear the question in them: *What am I doing here?*

I pulled the door open and there, right on time, was Kile.

"Your Highness," he said with a comical bow. "I've come to sweep you off your feet."

"Hardy har. Get in here."

Kile walked in and surveyed my shelves. "Last time I was in your room, you had a collection of wooden ponies."

"Outgrew that."

"But not being a bossy tyrant?"

"Nope. Just like you didn't outgrow being an insufferable bookworm."

"Is this how you win over all your dates?"

I smirked. "More or less. Sit down. I have a proposition for you."

He spotted the wine I'd provided and wasted no time in pouring himself a glass. "You want some?"

I sighed. "Please. We'll both need it."

He paused, eyeing me before continuing. "Now I'm nervous. What do you want?"

I took my glass, trying to remember how I wanted to explain this to him. "You know me, Kile. You've known me my whole life."

"True. In fact, I was thinking yesterday that I have a vague recollection of you running around in nothing but a diaper. It was a good look."

I rolled my eyes and tried not to laugh. "Anyway. You, to some degree, understand my personality, who I am when the cameras aren't rolling."

He sipped, contemplating my words. "I think I understand you when they're on as well, but please continue."

I hadn't thought about that, how he'd seen me go through the many phases of growing up, both on and off screen. There was a switch I had to flip when I was on display, and he knew it. "The Selection wasn't my idea, but it's something I need to put my best effort into. I think I am, personally. But the public expects me to be a giddy little girl next to all of you, and I don't think I can do that. I can't act stupid."

"Actually—"

"Don't!"

He smiled wickedly and took another sip of his wine.

"You're such a pain. Why am I even bothering?"

"No, go on, you don't want to act stupid." He set down his glass and leaned forward.

I took a breath, hunting for the words again. "They want romance, but I'm not prepared to behave like that publicly, at least not when I haven't truly connected with someone. Still, I need to give them something."

I ducked my head and peeked up at him from under my lashes.

"Like what exactly?"

"A kiss."

"A kiss?"

"Just a little one. And you're the only person I can ask, because you'd know it wasn't real and things wouldn't get complicated. And I'm willing to give you something in return."

He raised his eyebrows. "What?"

I shrugged. "Whatever you want, really. Within reason. I can't offer you a country or anything."

"Could you talk to my mom? Help get me out of here?"

"And go where, exactly?"

"Anywhere." He sighed desperately. "My mom . . . I don't know what happened that made her so crazy loyal to your parents, but she's got it in her head that this is our home for-ever. Do you know how much work it took for me to get out of here and take that one accelerated course?

"I want to travel, I want to build, I want to do more than read about things. Sometimes I think one more day behind these walls might kill me."

"I get that," I whispered, not thinking. I straightened up. "I can make it happen. As soon as an opportunity becomes available, I will help convince your parents that you need to leave the palace."

He paused a second, then threw back the rest of his wine. "One kiss?"

"Just one."

"When?"

"Tonight. There will be a photographer waiting down the hall at nine. Hopefully very well hidden, because I'd like to pretend he isn't there."

Kile nodded. "Fine. One kiss."

"Thank you."

We sat in silence, watching the hands on the clock. After three minutes I couldn't take it anymore.

"What do you mean you want to build things?"

He lit up. "That's what I study. Architecture and design. I like dreaming up structures, figuring out how to make them and, sometimes, how to make them particularly beautiful."

"That's . . . actually really interesting, Kile."

"I know." He gave one of his crooked smiles, just like his dad's, and it was fun to see how excited he was about it. "Do you want to see?"

"See what?"

"Some of my designs. I have them in my room. My old one, not my Selected one, so they're just down the hall."

"Sure." I took one last sip of wine and followed him out. Except for a guard or two, the hallway was empty as Kile and I made our way to his room.

He opened the door and flicked on the lights, and I had to stop myself from gasping.

He. Was. A. Mess!

His bed wasn't made, there were clothes amassed in a corner, and several dirty plates were piled on his side table.

"I know what you're thinking. How does he keep it so immaculate?"

"You read my mind," I said, trying not to appear completely repulsed. At least it didn't smell bad.

"About a year ago I asked the staff to stop cleaning for me. I do it myself. But the Selection kind of caught me off guard, so I just left it how it was."

He started kicking objects under his bed and trying to pull the things within his reach a little straighter.

"Why don't you let them clean?"

"I'm a grown man. I can take care of myself."

I didn't think he meant that as a dig at me, but it stung all the same.

"Anyway, this is my work space."

In the far corner of the room the walls were covered in pictures and posters of everything from skyscrapers to mud huts. His desk was overflowing with prints he'd drawn up, and models built from wooden scraps and thin strips of metal.

"Did you make all these?" I asked, gently touching a structure that slightly twisted as it went upward.

"Yep. Concept, design. I'd love to create real buildings one day. I'm studying, but there's only so much I can learn without getting my hands on things, you know?"

"Kile . . ." I took in all of it: the colors and lines, the amount of time and thought that must have gone into each of them. "This is amazing."

"It's just me fooling around."

"No, don't do that. Don't make it seem like less than it is. I could never do something like this."

"Sure you could." He went over and pulled out a ruler shaped like a *T* and laid it over something he was already working on. "See, it's just a matter of looking at the lines and doing the math."

"Ugh, more math. I do enough of that as it is."

He laughed. "But this is fun math."

"Fun math is an oxymoron."

Kile and I moved to his couch, and we went through a few books of his favorite architects, studying their styles. He seemed particularly interested in how some worked with the land around them and others worked against it. "I mean, look at that!" he said enthusiastically after nearly every page.

I couldn't believe it had taken me all these years to see this side of him. He tucked himself inside a shell, shutting himself away from others here because the palace had trapped *him*. Behind the books and the snippy remarks there was a curious, engaging, and sometimes very charming person.

I felt like I'd been lied to. Was someone going to pop around the corner and tell me Josie was really a saint?

Eventually Kile looked down to his watch. "It's ten after nine."

"Oh. We should go then." But I didn't want to get up. Kile's messy room was one of the most comfortable places I'd ever been.

"Yeah." Kile closed the book and put it back on the shelf. Even though that corner was as haphazard as the rest of the room, I could see the care he took with it.

I waited for him by the door, suddenly nervous.

"Here," he said, offering his hand. "It's the end of a date, right?"

I placed my hand in his. "Thanks. For showing me your work, and for doing this. I promise to pay you back."

"I know."

He opened the door and walked me down the hall. "When do you think we last held hands?" I wondered out loud.

"Probably a game of red rover or something."

"Probably."

We were quiet as we headed toward my room. When we reached it, I turned back to Kile and watched as he swallowed.

"Nervous?" I whispered.

"Nah." He smiled, but he also fidgeted. "So . . . goodnight."

Kile leaned down, lips meeting mine, holding them there. Then his lips parted and closed and parted again. I drew a breath in the moment between kisses, sensing he would come back again. He did, and thank goodness, because I hadn't been kissed like this before and I needed more.

The few times I'd kissed boys were rushed, sloppy moments hiding in a coatroom or behind a statue. But this, with so much air around us and no one coming to check on me . . . it was different.

I leaned into Kile, still holding him, and he brought up his free hand and cupped my cheek. He held my lips to his for what felt like forever before pulling back.

And even when he did pull away, his nose stayed right against mine, so close that when he whispered, I could smell what was left of the wine on his breath.

"Do you think that was enough?"

"I . . . um . . . I don't know."

"Just to be sure."

He pressed his mouth to mine again, and I was so surprised to get another kiss like that, it felt like my bones were turning into mush. I wrapped my fingers up into his hair, shocked at myself for having the urge to hold him in that pose all night.

He pulled back again, looking into my eyes, and there was something different. Was he feeling that funny warmth creep into his arms and chest and head, too?

"Thank you," I murmured.

"Any time. I mean"—he shook his head, laughing at himself—"you know what I mean."

"Goodnight, Kile."

"Goodnight, Eadlyn." He gave me a quick kiss on the cheek before heading toward the stairs that led back to his temporary quarters.

I watched him go and told myself that the only reason I was smiling like that was because the cameras were hidden somewhere, not because of anything Kile Woodwork had done.

CHAPTER 13

"So, I think I managed to distract everyone for a while."
I held on to Ahren's arm as we walked through the garden.

"I'll say." Ahren made a smart little face at me, and I
fought the urge to hit him. "How was it?"

At that I really did hit him. "You pig! A lady never tells."

"Well, is a real lady meant to be photographed kissing her
suitor in the dark?"

I shrugged. "Either way, it worked."

The pictures of Kile and me were gobbled up like food,
just as predicted. It felt a little strange that this was what
people were hungry for, but it didn't really matter as long as
they were satisfied. The reactions to the kiss ranged though.
A handful of the papers thought it was sweet, but the majority of them were displeased that I was so willing to give up a
kiss this early in the competition.

One of the gossip magazines even had a back and forth with two of their biggest reporters over whether I was loose for giving such a kiss or if it was sweet because I'd known Kile since birth. I tried to shrug it off. There would be other things to talk about soon enough.

"I dug a few pages in," I said, turning back to Ahren. "Not a single report of post-caste discrimination."

"So, what are your plans for today? Going to make the boys cry again?"

I rolled my eyes. "It was only one. And, I don't know. Maybe I won't visit them today."

"Nope," Ahren blurted, moving us to a new path. "So help me, Eadlyn, if I have to drag you by your hair through this I will, but you've actually got to participate in the Selection."

I let my arm slip away from his. "I can't help feeling there's no way it was this hard for Dad."

"Have you asked him?"

"No, and I don't think I can. Just recently both he and Mom have been giving me more details, thinking it might be helpful. I feel like they must have held those things close to them for a reason, and it seems rude to ask. Besides, I don't know that any two people in this situation would handle it the exact same way, and I really don't want to know if Dad cared about anyone besides Mom."

"Isn't that a strange thought?" He sat on a nearby stone bench. "Some other woman could have been our mother!"

"No," I countered, joining him. "We only exist because

they found each other. Any other combination would not have created the two of us."

"You're messing with my head, Eady."

"Sorry. This situation is throwing me off." I traced my finger around the stone. "I mean, I get why the concept sounds appealing. That somewhere out there, my perfect match could be waiting for me, and by chance I could pull his name and meet him and fall madly in love. But then there's the feeling of being a prize horse, that I'm being judged more so than usual. And when I look at all these boys, they seem foreign in comparison to the type of people I generally encounter, and I don't think I like it. The whole thing makes me feel unsettled."

Ahren was quiet for a while, and I could see he was carefully choosing words, which made me nervous.

I wasn't sure if that was a twin thing or a bond exclusive to Ahren and me, but it was almost physical when we were at odds. It felt like a rubber band pulling tight between us.

"Listen, Eady, I know this might have been the wrong way to go about it, but I do think it's good for you to have someone in your life. I've been with Camille a long time, and even if everything ended tomorrow, I'd be a better person because of her. There are some things you don't learn about yourself until you let someone else into the most intimate places of your heart."

"How can you two even manage to do that? You spend almost all of your time apart."

He grinned. "She's my soul mate. I know it."

"I don't think soul mates are real," I said, examining my shoes. "You happened to meet a French princess because you only ever meet royalty, and you like her more than anyone else. Your true soul mate could be milking a cow right now, and you'd never know."

"You're always so down on her." His tone made the invisible rubber band stretch again.

"I'm simply discussing possibilities."

"In the meantime, you have dozens of possibilities in front of you and refuse to look at them."

I snorted. "Did Dad put you up to this?"

"No! I think you should look at this with an open mind. You're one of the most isolated people in the country, but that doesn't mean your walls have to be up all the time. You need to experience a romantic relationship at least once in your life."

"Hey! I've experienced romantic relationships!"

"A picture in the paper does not count as a relationship," he said heatedly. "Neither does making out with Leron Troyes at that Christmas ball in Paris."

I gasped. "How do you know about that?"

"Everyone knows about that."

"Even Mom and Dad?"

"Dad doesn't know. Well, unless Mom told him, because I'm positive she does."

I buried my face and made some screechy sound that encapsulated my complete humiliation.

"All I'm saying is, this could be good for you."

That line pushed all the shame out of my body and replaced it with rage.

"Everyone keeps saying that: it might be good for me. What does that even mean? I'm smart and beautiful and strong. I don't need to be rescued."

Ahren shrugged. "Maybe not. But you never know if one of them might need to be."

I stared at the grass, considering that. I shook my head. "What are you doing, Ahren? What's with the sudden change of heart? I thought you were on my side."

I saw a flicker of something in his eyes before he pushed it away and put an arm around me. "I am, Eadlyn. You, Mom, and Camille are the most important women in my life. So please understand me when I say that sometimes I wonder how happy you are."

"I'm happy, Ahren. I'm the princess. I have everything."

"I think you're mistaking comfort for joy."

His words vaguely reminded me of my recent chat with Mom.

Ahren rubbed my arm and stood, brushing off his suit. "I promised Kaden I'd help with his French lesson. Just think about all this, okay? Maybe I'm wrong. It certainly wouldn't be the first time." We shared a smile.

I nodded. "I'll think about it."

He gave me a wink. "Go on a date or something. You need to get a life."

I stood outside the door to the Men's Parlor pacing, worrying I was wasting time. After my talk with Ahren, I really should have gone straight to the office. Truthfully, I was looking forward to getting back to the normal monotony of shuffling papers. But his words, above anyone else's, made me wonder if I should at least try. And not the fake trying I was planning for the cameras, but genuine effort.

I told myself that I would have to date them eventually anyway. It was the bare minimum of what I'd need to do. It didn't mean I was choosing anyone; I was just keeping my promise to Dad and doing what the people expected.

Sighing, I handed the envelope to the butler. "Okay, go ahead."

He bowed before he left, and I waited outside.

I'd decided I wasn't going to barge into the Men's Parlor again. I wanted the Selected to be on their toes, but everyone needed a retreat now and then. I knew that better than anybody.

A moment later the butler returned, holding the door as Hale stepped out. Two things passed through my head as he approached. First, I wondered what Kile would think, which, admittedly, was odd. Second, it was obvious Hale still didn't know what to make of me, because he was very cautious as he came to a stop about two feet away and bowed. "Your Highness."

I clasped my hands in front of me. "You may call me Eadlyn."

There was a hint of a smile in his eyes. "Eadlyn."

No one in the world is as powerful as you.

"I was wondering if you'd like to join me for dessert tonight after dinner."

"Just you and me?"

I sighed. "Was there someone else you wanted to invite? Do you need a translator as well?"

"No, no!" he said, a real smile coming across his face. "I'm just . . . pleasantly surprised, I guess."

"Oh." It was a pathetic response to such a sweet admission, but I simply wasn't prepared.

Hale stood there, his hands jammed in his pockets, beaming, and it was hard to think of him as another person I'd just send home.

"Umm, anyway, I'll come by your room about twenty minutes after dinner, and we'll go to one of the parlors upstairs."

"Sounds great. See you tonight."

I started walking. "See you tonight."

I was a little bothered because I was looking forward to it now. His anticipation was kind of cute. But worse than the feeling that the Selection was getting to me was the triumphant look on Hale's face when he caught me peeking back at him.

CHAPTER 14

WOULD IT BE STRANGE IF I changed dresses between dinner and dessert? Was he going to change clothes? I'd been wearing tiaras for the last few days, but was it inappropriate if I wore one on a date?

On a date.

This was too far out of my comfort zone. I felt so vulnerable, which I couldn't understand. I had interacted with plenty of young men. I did have that spectacular interlude with Leron at that Christmas party, and Jamison Akers fed me a strawberry lip-to-lip hidden behind a tree at a picnic. I'd even made it through last night with Kile, though that was nothing close to a real date.

I had met all thirty-five of the Selected candidates and stood tall through every minute. Not to mention, I helped run an entire country. Why was one date with one boy making me so anxious?

I decided that, yes, I would change, and I put on a yellow dress that was longer in the back than in the front, which I paired with a navy belt so it looked a little less I'm-ready-for-the-garden-party and a little more let's-go-out. And no tiara. Why had I even considered it?

I gave my reflection a once-over and reminded myself that *he* was trying to win *me* over, not the other way around.

I jumped at the knock on the door. I still had five minutes! And I was supposed to go to him! He was throwing off my entire preparation strategy, and so help me, I'd send him away and start all over again if I had to.

Without waiting for an answer, Aunt May poked her head in, Mom smiling right behind her.

"Aunt May!" I ran over and crushed her in a hug. "What are you doing here?"

"I figured you could use some extra support, so I came back."

"And I'm here to make this whole thing more awkward than it has to be," Mom promised with a smile.

I laughed nervously. "I'm not used to this. I don't know what to do."

Aunt May cocked an eyebrow. "According to the papers, you're doing very well."

I blushed. "That was different. It wasn't an actual date. It didn't mean anything."

"But this does?" she asked, her voice gentle.

I shrugged. "It's not the same."

"I know everyone says this," Mom began, pushing back my hair, "but it's the best advice I can give you: be yourself."

That was easier said than done. Because, who was I really? One half of a set of twins. The heir to a throne. One of the most powerful people in the world. The biggest distraction in the country.

Never just daughter. Never just girl.

"Don't take any of this too seriously." Aunt May fixed her own hair in the mirror before turning back to me. "You should just enjoy yourself."

I nodded.

"She makes a good point," Mom agreed. "It's not as if we want you to choose someone today. You have time here, so have fun meeting some new people. Goodness knows, that's a rarity for you."

"True. It just feels awkward. I'm going to be alone with him, and then he'll tell all the other guys about it, and then we'll have to talk about it on TV."

"It sounds harder than it is. Most of the time it's funny," Mom insisted.

I tried to imagine teenage her, blushing and talking about her dates with Dad. "So you didn't mind it?"

She pursed her lips together, studying the ceiling as she thought. "Well, it was harder in the beginning. I was very hesitant to be the center of attention. But you're brilliant at that, so treat this like any other party or event you'd give an interview about."

May looked at her. "It's not exactly like a post–Grateful Feast recap," she pointed out before focusing on me, "but your mother is right about you being better in the spotlight.

She was embarrassing at your age."

"Thanks, May." Mom rolled her eyes.

"Any time."

I chuckled, wishing briefly that I had just one sister. Mom's other sister, Aunt Kenna, died years ago of a heart condition. Uncle James was a simple man, so he didn't want to raise Astra and Leo in the palace even though we offered several times. We kept in touch, of course, but Astra and I were very different girls. Still, I remembered all too clearly the way Mom had spent a week in bed holding May and Grandma Singer after Kenna passed away. More and more I wondered if losing a sister was like Mom losing part of herself. I knew it would feel like that for me if anything happened to Ahren.

Aunt May elbowed Mom, and they shared a smile. They never really fought, not over anything that truly mattered, and the two of them soothed my worries.

They were right. This was nothing.

"You're going to do great," Mom said. "You don't know how to fail." She gave me a wink, and I felt myself stand taller.

I checked the clock. "I should go. Thanks for coming," I said, taking Aunt May's hand.

"No problem." I hugged her at the door, and then headed downstairs.

When I got to Hale's room, I paused and drew in a deep breath before I knocked. He answered, not his butler, and he seemed thrilled to see me.

"You look fantastic," he said.

"Thank you," I answered, smiling in spite of myself. "So do you."

He'd changed, too, which made me feel much more comfortable, and I liked what he'd done with himself. His tie was gone, and he had his top button undone. Between that and the vest, he looked . . . well, he looked cute.

Hale tucked his hands into his pockets. "So where are we going?"

I pointed down the hall. "This way, up to the fourth floor."

He rocked on his feet a few times then hesitantly held out his arm for me. "Lead the way."

"All right," I began as we walked toward the stairs. "I know the basic facts. Hale Garner, nineteen years old, Belcourt. But those entry forms are a little cut and dried, so what's your story?"

He chuckled. "Well, I too am the oldest in my family."

"Really?"

"Yes. Three boys."

"Ugh, I feel bad for your mother."

He smiled. "Eh, she doesn't mind. We remind her of Dad, so when one of us is a little too loud or laughs at something he would have, she'll sigh and say we're just like him."

I was afraid to ask, but I wanted to be clear. "Are your parents divorced?" I asked, doubting that was the case.

"No. He passed away."

"I'm sorry," I said, feeling mortified that I'd indirectly insulted his memory.

"It's okay. Not one of those things you know without being told."

"Can I ask when he died?"

"About seven years ago. I know this will sound weird, but sometimes I'm jealous of my youngest brother. Beau was about six when it happened, and he remembers Dad, but not the way I do, you know? Sometimes I wish I didn't have so much to miss."

"I'd be willing to bet he's jealous of you for the opposite reason."

He gave me a sad smile. "I never thought about that."

We turned up the main stairs, focusing on our steps. When we got to the landing on the fourth floor, I started again.

"What does your mother do?"

Hale swallowed. "Right now she's working as a secretary at the local university. She . . . well, it's been hard for her to hold down a good job, but she likes this one, and she's had it for a long time. I just realized I began that sentence with 'right now' because I was used to her switching a lot, but she hasn't done that for a while.

"Like I said when we met, my dad was a Two. He was an athlete. Went in for a surgery on his knee, but there was a clot and it made its way to his heart. Mom had never worked a day in her life—between her parents and Dad she was taken care of. After we lost him, all she was good at was being a basketball player's wife."

"Oh, no."

"Yeah."

I was so grateful when we came upon the parlor. How had

Dad managed this? How did he sift through all those girls, testing them to find his wife? Getting to know one person was already wearing me out, and we weren't even five minutes into our first date.

"Wow," Hale whispered, admiring the setup.

From the fourth-floor parlors at the front of the palace you could just barely look out over the walls. Angeles in the evening let out a beautiful glow, and I'd asked for the parlor lights to be dimmed so we could really see it.

There was a small table in the middle of the room that had various cakes on it, and a dessert wine was waiting on the side. I'd never tried to set up a romantic evening before, but I thought I did a good job for my first try.

Hale pulled out my chair before joining me at the table.

"I didn't know what you liked, so I got several. These are chocolate, obviously," I said, pointing to the dozens of tiny cakes. "Then lemon, vanilla, and cinnamon."

Hale stared at the piles of treats in front of us like I'd actually given him something huge. "Listen, I don't want to be rude," he said, "but if there's anything you want, you should grab it now, because there's a serious chance I will demolish these."

I laughed. "Help yourself."

He picked up one of the chocolate cakes and popped the whole thing into his mouth. "Mmmmmmm."

"Try the cinnamon. It'll change your life."

We kept eating for a while, and I thought maybe this would be enough for one night. We'd moved into very safe territory; I could talk about desserts for hours! But then, without warning, he started talking about his life again.

"So my mom works at the university, but I work with a tailor in town."

"Oh?"

"Yeah, I'm very interested in clothes. Well, I am now anyway. Right after Dad died it was harder to get new things, so I learned to hide the rips in my brothers' shirts or let out a hem as they grew. Then Mom had a pile of dresses she was hoping to sell to get some money, and I took two pieces and combined them to make something new for her. It wasn't perfect, but I was good enough at it that I could probably get a job.

"So I read a lot and study what Lawrence does—he's my boss. Every now and then he'll let me take projects on my own. I guess that's what I'll do down the line."

I smirked. "You're definitely one of the more put-together guys in the group."

He smiled bashfully. "It's easy when I've got so much to work with. My butler is great, so he's helped me with making sure the fit on everything is impeccable. I don't think he appreciates all my pairings, but I want to look like a gentleman while still looking like myself, if that makes any sense."

I nodded enthusiastically as I swallowed a bit of cake. "Do you know how hard it is when you love jeans but you're a princess?"

He chuckled. "But you balance it so well! I mean, they plaster your outfits across every magazine, so I've seen plenty.

Your style is very individual."

"You think so?" I felt encouraged. Criticism was heavy these days, and that one scrap of praise was like water in the desert.

"Definitely!" he gushed. "I mean, you dress like a princess but then kind of not. I wouldn't be surprised if you were actually the ringleader of an all-girl mafia."

I spit out my wine all over the table, which made Hale burst into laughter.

"I'm so sorry!" I felt my cheeks burning. "If Mom saw that, I'd get the worst lecture."

Hale wiped the tears from his eyes and leaned forward. "Do they really lecture you? I mean, aren't you basically running the country?"

I shrugged. "Not really. Dad does most of the work. I just shadow him."

"But that's a formality at this point, right?"

"How do you mean?" My words must have come out harsher than I meant, because the laughter in his eyes disappeared instantly.

"I'm not trying to insult him or anything, but lots of people say he looks tired. I've heard some people speculate all the time on when you'll be ascending."

I looked down. Did people really talk about Dad being tired?

"Hey," Hale said, grabbing my attention again. "I'm really sorry. I was only trying to talk. I didn't mean to make you upset."

I shook my head. "No, you're fine. I'm not sure what got

to me. Maybe thinking about doing this without Dad."

"It's so funny to hear you call the king 'Dad.'"

"But that's who he is!" I found myself smiling again. Something about the way Hale talked made everything feel calmer, brighter. I liked that.

"I know, I know. Okay, so back to you. Besides being the most powerful woman in the world, what do you do for fun?"

I ate another piece of cake to hide how big my grin was. "It may or may not surprise you that I am also very into fashion."

"Oh, really?" he replied sarcastically.

"I sketch. A lot, actually. I've tried my hand at the things my parents like as well. I know a bit about photography, and I can play the piano a little. But I always come back to my sketchbook."

I knew I was smiling. Those pages with their scribbles of colored pencils were one of my safest places in the world.

"Could I see them?"

"What?" I crossed my ankles and sat up straighter.

"Your sketches. Could I see them sometime?"

No one saw my sketches. I only ever showed designs to my maids when I had to since I didn't do any of the construction. But for every one I shared, there were a dozen I hid, things I knew I could never wear. I thought about those pieces, each of them stored in my head or on paper, as if keeping them secret was the only way they could possibly be mine.

I knew he didn't understand my sudden silence or why I

held tightly to the arms of my chair. Hale asking that question, assuming he was welcome in that world, made me feel like he had somehow seen me—really seen me—and I didn't like it.

"Excuse me," I said, standing. "I think I had a little too much wine."

"Do you need help?" he asked, standing as well.

"No, please stay and enjoy yourself." I moved as quickly as I could.

"Your Highness!"

"Goodnight."

"Eadlyn, wait!"

In the hallway I moved much faster, unable to express my relief when he didn't follow me.

CHAPTER 15

I FULLY BELIEVED MY CURRENT state was not my fault, not even in the slightest. I knew who to point the finger at, and they were all other Schreaves. I blamed Mom and Dad for not being able to get the country under control and forcing me into this situation, and I blamed Ahren for trying to get me to consider these boys in the first place.

I was going to be queen, and a queen could be many things . . . but vulnerable wasn't one of them.

Last night's interlude with Hale made me sure of several things. First, I was right about the Selection. There was no way I could possibly find a companion under these circumstances, and I considered it miraculous that anyone had in the past. Forced openness with scores of strangers could not be good for one's soul.

Second, if I ever did get married, the chances of me

having a passionate, enduring love for that person were slim. Love did nothing but break down defenses, and I could not afford that. I already gave so much affection to my family that I knew they were my weakness, Dad and Ahren in particular. It was hard to imagine doing that to myself on purpose.

Ahren knew his words could sway me, knew how much I loved him. That was why, above the others, I wanted to throttle him after my date.

I went down to breakfast, walking with determined steps as if nothing had changed. I was still in control, and a bunch of silly boys were not going to take over my world. My plan for today was to get back to work. There had been far too many distractions lately, and I needed to focus. Dad talked about me finding someone to help me do my job, but so far all they were managing to do was make it harder.

Ahren and Osten sat next to Mom, and I took my place between Dad and Kaden. Even from the opposite side of the table I could hear Osten chewing.

"You all right, sis?" Kaden asked, pausing between heaping spoonfuls of oatmeal.

"Of course."

"You look a little stressed."

"You would, too, if you were going to run the country," I teased.

"Sometimes I think about that," he said, getting all serious. "Like, what if a disease swept over all of Illéa, and you and Mom and Dad and Ahren got sick and died. Then I'd be in charge and have to figure out everything on my own."

In my periphery I saw Dad lean forward, listening to his son. "That's a little morbid, Kaden."

Kaden shrugged. "It's always good to plan ahead."

I propped my chin on my hand. "So what would be King Kaden's first order of business?"

"Vaccinations, obviously."

I chuckled. "Good call. And after that?"

He considered. "I think I'd try to meet people. Nonsick people, so I could know what they need me to do. It probably looks a little different out there than it does in here."

Dad nodded. "That's pretty smart, Kaden."

"I know." And Kaden went back to eating, his imaginary rule at an end. Lucky him.

I picked at my food, surreptitiously looking over at Dad. Yes, I'd noticed him looking tired the other night, but that was a one-time thing. Sure, he needed glasses these days, and he had laugh lines surrounding his eyes, but that didn't translate into being worn-out. What did Hale know?

I peeked around the room. The boys were speaking to one another in hushed tones. I saw Ean chatting with Baden. Burke had spilled something on his tie and was trying to remove it discreetly and failing. My eyes passed over Hale, happy he wasn't looking in my direction at the moment.

At the back of the far table I saw Henri and Kile. Erik was translating patiently, and based on all three of their expressions, they were having a pretty good conversation.

I was engrossed. I tried for a minute to figure out what

they were talking about but to no avail. I sat there staring at Kile, watching his hands. It was funny to see the way they gestured to others and gripped a fork when I knew how well they held a pencil for sketching. Or—even better—pulled back hair for a kiss.

Eventually Kile caught me staring and gave me a little nod and a smile. Henri noticed him looking, and he turned in his chair to give me a wave. I bowed my head in acknowledgment, hoping no one noticed my blush. Henri turned back immediately to say something to Erik, who passed it on to Kile, who raised his eyebrows and nodded. I knew they were talking about me, and I couldn't help but wonder if Kile had shared certain details of our kiss.

Aunt May might be the only person I could spill all the little details of that kiss to without being completely horrified. I'd be lying if I said that moment in the hall hadn't crossed my mind several times since it happened.

Ahren stood, kissing Mom on her cheek before he turned to leave.

"Wait, Ahren, I need to talk to you," I said, standing as well.

"See you in a bit, sweetie?" Dad asked, glancing at me.

"I'll be up shortly. I promise."

Ahren held out his arm for me, and we walked together from the room. I could feel how we drew attention. It was like an energy that followed me nearly everywhere I went. I often reveled in that feeling.

"What do you want to talk about?"

I spoke through my smile. "I'll tell you once we're in the hall."

His step faltered. "Uh-oh."

When we rounded the corner, I pulled back and whacked him on the shoulder.

"Ow!"

"I went on a date last night, and it was awful, and I blame you personally."

Ahren rubbed his arm. "What happened? Was he mean?"

"No."

"Did he . . ." He lowered his voice. "Did he try to take advantage of you?"

"No." I crossed my arms.

"Was he rude?"

I sighed. "Not exactly, but it was . . . awkward."

He threw both of his arms up in exasperation. "Well, of course it was. If you saw him again, it would be better. That's the point. It takes time to get to know someone."

"I don't want him to get to know me! I don't want any of them to get to know me!"

His face fell into a confused scowl. "I always thought that you were the one person in the world I would understand no matter what. I thought you'd always understand me, too. But you tease me for being in love, and when the opportunity to find someone falls into your lap, you hate it."

I pointed a finger at his chest. "Wasn't it you who said this made no sense for me? Weren't you looking forward to how I'd make them squirm? I thought you and I both agreed this was a joke. And now, suddenly, you're the Selection's biggest cheerleader."

The hallway was painfully silent. I waited for Ahren to argue with me, or at least to explain.

"Sorry I let you down. But I think this is about more than a date. You need to figure out why you're so scared."

I raised myself to my full height. "I'm the next queen of Illéa. I'm scared of nothing."

He backed away. "Keep saying that, Eadlyn. See if it fixes the problem."

Ahren didn't get too far down the hall though. Josie had friends over this morning, and the whole lot of them basically melted at the sight of his face. I recognized one of them from the day in the garden and only remembered her because she had addressed me correctly.

I watched as they gave shy grins and ducked their heads. Ahren, to his credit, was polite as always.

"Josie has said your mastery of literature is very impressive," one of the girls said.

Ahren looked away. "She's exaggerating. I do love to read, and I write a little, but nothing worth sharing."

Another girl stepped forward. "I doubt that's true. I bet our tutor would be happy to have you come teach us sometime. I'd love to hear your thoughts on a few of the books we've been reading."

Josie clasped her hands together. "Oh, yes, please, Ahren. Won't you come teach us?"

Her friends giggled at her casually using his first name, a

habit from growing up beside him.

"I'm afraid I have far too much to do at the present. Perhaps another time. You ladies have a wonderful day." He bowed kindly and continued down the hall, and the girls didn't even wait until he was out of earshot to start giggling like idiots.

"He's so handsome," one said, ready to burst with adoration.

Josie sighed. "I know. He's so sweet to me, too. We took a walk together the other day, and he was saying that he thinks I'm one of the prettiest girls he's ever met."

I couldn't take it anymore. I barged past them, not slowing down. "You're too young for him, and he has a girlfriend, Josie. Let it go."

I rounded up the stairs to go to the office. I knew I'd feel better once I did something manageable, something I could check off a list.

"See," Josie said, not bothering to lower her voice. "I told you she was awful."

CHAPTER 16

WORK DIDN'T MAKE ME FEEL better. I was still very unsettled about last night with Hale, and any time Ahren and I fought, it was like I lost my equilibrium. The whole planet was off its axis. Adding Josie's ridiculous comments to the mix was the cherry on top.

My head was swarming with other people's words and my own questions, and I was positive the day was going to end up being a waste.

"You know," Dad said, peeking up from his work. "I got distracted early on, too. It gets easier to manage as the group gets smaller."

I smiled. Fine, let him think I had a crush. "Sorry, Dad."

"Not at all. Do you need me to cover your work for you today? Take the afternoon off?"

I straightened my papers. "No, that's not happening. I'm perfectly capable."

"I wasn't doubting you, love. I just—"

"I've already taken so much time away from work for this. I don't want to neglect my duties. I'm fine."

I didn't mean to sound so snippy with him.

"All right." He adjusted his glasses and started reading again. I tried to do the same.

What did Ahren mean, it was more than the date that upset me? I knew why I was mad. And since when had I given him a hard time about Camille? Sure, I didn't talk to her very much, but that was because we didn't have a lot in common. I didn't dislike the girl.

I shook my head, focusing on the papers.

"It would be fine if you needed to clear your head," Dad offered again. "You could go spend some time with one of the Selected and come back after lunch. Besides, you'll want to have something to talk about on the *Report*."

I felt a flurry of emotions, trying to figure out how I would discuss how exposed I'd felt after my date with Hale . . . or how stunned I felt after my kiss with Kile. Trying to balance the conflicting feelings around those two moments was dizzying without adding anything else.

"I went on a date last night, Dad. Isn't that enough?"

He swallowed as he thought. "Eventually you need to start alerting us when you have dates. A few pictures from some of them would be good for everyone. And I think you need at least one more date before Friday."

"Really?" I whined.

"Do something you enjoy. You're treating it like work."

"That's because it is!" I protested with an incredulous laugh.

"It can be fun, Eadlyn. Give it a chance." He looked at me over his glasses, almost like he was daring me.

"Fine. One date. That's all you get, old man," I teased.

He chuckled. "Old man is right."

Dad went back to his papers, satisfied. I sat there, peeking furtively at him from my desk. He stretched often, rubbing the back of his neck, and even though there weren't any urgent tasks today, he ran his hands through his hair as if he was troubled.

Now that Hale had put it in my head, I was going to be watching him often.

I decided to make Baden my next target. Maybe Aunt May knew something, because Baden didn't come in brashly or, conversely, like he was trying to hide. When someone else stole a moment that should have been solely his at the tea party, he didn't make a fuss. And when I approached him for time alone, he turned the focus back to me.

"You play the piano, right?" Baden asked when I invited him on a date.

"I do. Not as well as my mother, but I'm pretty proficient."

"I play the guitar. Maybe we could make some music."

It wasn't anything I would have thought of. Perhaps music would mean less talking, though, and I was all up for that.

"Sure. I'll secure the Women's Room for us."

"Am I even allowed in there?" he asked skeptically.

"When you're with me, yes. And I'll make sure it's empty.

My favorite piano in the palace is there. Do you need a guitar?"

He smirked. "Nah. I brought my own."

Baden ran a hand over his cropped hair, seeming very relaxed. I was still attempting to come across as distant and impenetrable, but I could tell there were a handful of guys who weren't bothered by my attitude at all, and Baden was one of them.

"What are the chances of the room being empty now?" he asked.

I smiled at his enthusiasm. "High, actually, but I have work to do."

He bent down, his eyes devilish. "But don't you always have work to do? I bet you could stay up till three in the morning if you had to."

"True, but—"

"And it'll all still be there when you get back."

I clasped my hands and considered it. "I'm really not supposed to . . ."

He started chanting slowly. "Skip it, skip it, skip it!"

My lips were pressed together, trying to hide my smile. Really, I ought to tell someone. I was going to have yet another undocumented date . . . but maybe I deserved one more. *Next week,* I bargained with myself. *After this* Report, *I'll worry about the cameras.*

"Go get your guitar," I said, caving.

"Two minutes!" He bolted down the hall, and I shook my head. I hoped he wouldn't tell everyone I was an utter pushover.

I walked to the Women's Room, expecting to find it empty. Except for Miss Marlee sitting alone in a corner reading, I was right.

"Your Highness," she greeted. It was one of those funny things. Plenty of people called me that, but when Mom's friends said it, they might as well have been calling me pumpkin or kiddo or baby. I didn't mind it, but it was always kind of strange.

"Where's Mom?"

She closed her book. "Migraine. I went to see her, and she made me leave. Any sound was excruciating."

"Oh. I was supposed to be having a date right now, but maybe I should go check on her."

"No," she insisted. "She needed rest, and both your parents would be pleased for you to have a date."

I considered. If she was really feeling that bad, maybe it would be better to wait.

"Umm, all right. Well, would it be okay if I used the room? Baden and I are going to make music." I squinted. "I mean that literally, by the way."

She giggled and stood. "That's no problem at all."

"Is it weird for you?" I asked suddenly. "That Kile is a part of this? That you know I'm about to go on a date with someone who isn't him? Is it, you know, okay?"

"It was quite a shock to see you two on the front page of every paper," she said, shaking her head like she couldn't fathom how it had happened. Then she came close, as if we were trying to keep a secret. "But you forget your parents aren't the only ones here who've been through a Selection."

I felt like a downright idiot. Why hadn't I thought of that?

"I remember watching your father scramble to find time for everyone, trying to please those around him while searching for someone who'd be a good partner. And it's even harder for you, because it's bigger than that. You're making history while trying to divert attention. Saying it's tough is an understatement."

"True," I admitted, my shoulders sagging under the weight of it all.

"I don't know how you and Kile ended up . . . umm . . . in that position, but I'd be surprised if he made it to the top of your list. All the same, I'm thankful to you."

I was taken aback. "Why? I haven't done anything."

"You have," she contradicted. "You're giving your parents time, which is very generous of you. But you're giving me time, too. I'm not sure how much longer I can keep him here."

A knock came at the door.

I turned. "That'll be Baden."

She placed a hand on my shoulder. "You stay put. I'll let him in."

"Oh!" Baden exclaimed when Miss Marlee opened the door for him.

She chuckled. "Don't worry, I'm on my way out. She's waiting for you."

Baden looked past her to find me, smiling the entire time. He looked so triumphant, so pleased to be alone together.

"Is that it?" he asked, pointing just behind me.

I spun, taking in the piano. "Yes. The tone on this one is wonderful, and this room has great acoustics."

He followed me, and I could hear his guitar case bump into his leg or a couch as he navigated through the maze of seats.

Without asking, he found an armless chair and pulled it up beside the piano. I trilled my fingers over the keys, doing a quick scale.

Baden tuned his guitar, which was dark and worn. "How long have you been playing?"

"As long as I can remember. I think Mom sat me down next to her as a toddler, and I just went along with whatever she did."

"People have always said your mother was a fantastic musician. I think I heard her play on TV once, for a Christmas program or something."

"She always plays a lot at Christmastime."

"Her favorite time of the year?" he guessed.

"In a way, sure, but in others, no. And she usually plays when she's worried or sad."

"How do you mean?" He tightened a string, finishing his preparations.

"Oh, you know," I hedged. "Holidays can be stressful." I didn't feel right exposing Mom's memories, losing her father and sister during the same time of year, not to mention a horrific attack that nearly stole my father.

"I can't imagine being sad at Christmastime here. If she

was poor, I could see why she'd be anxious."

"Why?"

He smiled to himself. "Because it's hard to watch all your friends getting piles of gifts when you don't get any."

"Oh."

He took the stab at our social differences in stride, not getting mad or calling me a snob, which some might have done. I examined Baden, trying to learn more. The guitar was old, but it was hard to make a call about his financial status while he wore palace-issued clothes. I remembered what Aunt May said about his last name.

"You're in college, right?" I asked.

He nodded. "Well, it's on hold for now. Some of my professors were thrown off, but most of them are letting me send assignments back to finish the semester from here."

"That's really impressive."

He shrugged. "I know what I want. So I'm willing to do whatever it takes to get it."

I gave him a curious smirk. "How does the Selection fit into that?"

"Wow, no holding back there." Again, no anger. He almost treated it as a joke.

"It's a fair question, I think." I started playing one of the classics Mom had taught me. Baden knew the song and joined in. I'd never considered how it would sound with strings.

The music won, and we dropped the conversation. But we didn't stop communicating. He watched my eyes, and

I studied his fingers. I'd never played with anyone before other than Mom, and I was engaged in a way I didn't know I could be.

We played on with no more than two or three missteps across the entire song. Baden was beaming as we finished.

"I only know a handful of classics. Some Beethoven and Debussy, mostly."

"You're so talented! I've never imagined songs like that on a guitar."

"Thanks." He was only the slightest bit bashful. "To answer your question, I'm here because I want to get married. I haven't dated much, but when this opportunity came up, I thought it might be worth a try. Am I in love with you? Well, not today. I'd like to know if I could be though."

Something about his tone made me trust he was being completely transparent. He was trying to find a mate, and I was someone he would never have met if he hadn't put his name in for the drawing.

"I'd like to make you a promise, if that's okay," he offered.

"What kind of promise?"

He plucked at a few strings. "A promise about us."

"If you're vowing to give me your unwavering devotion, it's still too soon."

Baden shook his head. "No, that's not in my plan."

"Okay, then. I'm listening." His fingers outlined a slightly familiar melody, not a classic, but something I knew. . . . I couldn't pinpoint it.

"If you found that I wasn't a reasonable choice for you, you'd send me home so you could focus on your other options. What I want to promise you is this: if I can tell that you're not the right one for me, I'll tell you. I don't want either of us to waste our time."

I nodded. "I'd appreciate that."

"Good," he said smartly, then began bellowing: "Well she walks up in the room with that smile, smile, smile and those legs that go on for a mile, mile, mile! Eyes searching the room for a little fun!"

I laughed, finally recognizing the tune he was playing. It was a Choosing Yesterday song that I sang in the bath more often than I cared to admit.

"I can't look away from her face, face, face until she starts dancing to that bass, bass, bass! I can't help it, that girl is number one!"

I joined in on the piano, giggling a little too hard to get all the notes right for the chorus. But we both sang along, botching up the melody and having too much fun to care.

"Oh, she can't be more than seventeen, but she's all grown up if you know what I mean. She's the prettiest thing that I've ever seen, yeah, she's my"—*BAM BAM!*—"she's my, she's my queen!"

I kept up with Baden through most of the song, even though I really only had experience with classical music.

"Why are you bothering with college? You should be touring," I cheered.

"That's my backup plan if the prince thing doesn't pan out." He was so candid, so real. "Thanks for playing hooky for me."

"No problem. I should get back to work though."

"That was the shortest date in history!" he complained.

I shrugged. "You would have had more time if you waited until tonight."

He huffed. "Fine. Lesson learned."

I pulled the cover back over the keys as he placed his guitar in its case. "You should take that to the others," I said. "I bet they'd get a kick out of trying to play."

"What, my guitar? No, no, no. This is my baby!" I watched as he gently petted the shabby case. "If someone broke this, I'd be devastated. My dad got it for me, and it was hard earned. I try to take good care of it."

"I'm like that with my tiaras."

"*Pffff!*" Baden laughed outright at me.

"What?"

He took his time, covering his eyes and shaking his head. "Tiaras!" he finally said. "You really are a princess, huh?"

"Did you think the last eighteen years were a clever trick?"

"I like that, you know? That you protect your tiaras like I do my guitar. I like that that's your thing."

I pushed the door open, leading us into the hallway. "Good. Because they're beautiful."

He smiled. "Thanks for spending some time with me."

"Thank *you*. It was a pleasure."

There was a pause. "So do we shake or hug or what?"

"You may kiss my hand," I replied, extending an arm.

He took it. "Until next time."

Baden kissed me quickly, bowed, and headed toward his room. I walked away thinking of how Aunt May would say she told me so as soon as I saw her again.

★ ★ ★

I knew I'd be the focal point of the *Report*. Typically, I didn't mind giving speeches or updates. But tonight was going to be different. One, this would be the first time I faced the public since the parade, and two, I knew they'd want to hear about Kile.

I wore red. I felt strong in red. And I pulled my hair up, hoping I'd come across as mature.

Aunt May hovered in the background, winking at me, while Mom helped Dad with his tie. I heard one of the boys yelp and turned to see Alex holding something sharp in his hand. He was rubbing his backside like he'd sat on it. I hunted, finding Osten in a corner trying desperately not to laugh aloud.

With all the company, the room felt crowded, adding to my discomfort, which was why I jumped when someone called my name, even though it was hardly above a whisper.

"I'm sorry, Your Highness," Erik said.

"No, I'm just a little on edge. How can I help you?"

"I hate to bother you, but I wasn't sure who to ask. Where is it most convenient for me to sit so I can translate for Henri?"

I shook my head. "How rude, I didn't even think about that. Um, here, follow me."

I escorted Erik to the stage manager, and we placed Henri in the back row of the stadium-style chairs. Erik was given a seat behind him that was low enough so he wouldn't be seen but close enough that Henri would be able to hear him.

I stayed by them until they were settled. Henri gave a

thumbs-up, and Erik turned to thank me.

"I'll make sure to go to the stage manager next time so I won't bother you. I apologize."

"It's fine, really. I want you to be comfortable, the both of you."

Erik bowed his head and smiled shyly. "You don't need to worry about my comfort, Your Highness. I'm no suitor."

"Eadlyn! Eadlyn, where are you?" Mom called.

I turned from Erik, running around to the front. "Here, Mom."

She placed a hand on her heart like it had been racing. "I couldn't find you. I thought maybe you were backing out on us," she said quietly as I approached.

"Calm down, Mom," I replied, grabbing her hand. "I'm not perfect, but I'm no coward."

Tonight's *Report* centered around the women. Mom gave an update on province-run aid systems, encouraging others to follow the example set by three northern provinces that were helping the homeless by donating food as well as free classes on topics like managing finances and interviewing skills. Lady Brice spoke about a drilling proposal that would affect a large chunk of central Illéa. It would benefit the country as a whole, but those six provinces would have to approve it by a vote first. And then, of course, all eyes went to the boys.

Gavril stepped onto the stage, looking as dashing as ever, and I could see a bit of a spring in his step. This was the fifth Selection Illéa had witnessed, and he had overseen three of them. We all knew he'd find a replacement once this was over, but he seemed so pleased that this would be his final role for the royal family.

"Of course, ladies and gentlemen, we will be dedicating a lot of airtime to the charming young men of the Selection. For now, how about we say hello to a few of them?"

Gavril strode across the floor, looking for someone in particular. I wondered if he was having as hard a time memorizing their names as I was.

"Sir Harrison," he began, stopping in front of a sweet-faced boy with dirty-blond hair and dimples.

"A pleasure," Harrison greeted.

"How are you enjoying the palace?"

He beamed. "It's beautiful here. I've always wanted to come up to Angeles, so that alone has been a real treat."

"Any challenges so far?" Gavril prodded.

Harrison shrugged. "I was worried that it would be all-out fistfights from dawn till dusk with the princess on the line," he said, gesturing over to me. I instantly arranged a smile on my face, knowing a camera would zoom in on me at any second. "But the other guys have been great."

Gavril slid the microphone to the boy next to him. "What about you? And can you remind us of your name?"

"It's Fox. Fox Wesley," he answered. Fox had a bit of a tan, but, unlike me, I could see that he wasn't born with it. He must spend a lot of time outside. "Honestly, and I hope I'm not alone here, so far the biggest challenge is mealtimes. They set out at least a dozen forks for each of us."

A few people chuckled, and Gavril nodded. "You have

to wonder where we could possibly store so much cutlery."

"It's crazy," mumbled the boy behind Fox.

"Oh, Sir Ivan, yes?" Gavril stretched to put the mic in front of him.

"Yes, sir. Happy to meet you."

"And you as well. How are you managing at mealtimes?"

Ivan held both hands in front of him as if this was very serious. "My current approach is using one fork for each bite and then making a pile of them in the middle of the table. It's working so far."

The room laughed even more at Ivan's ridiculous answer, and Gavril stepped away from the group, turning to the cameras.

"Clearly, we have an extremely entertaining pool of candidates here. So why don't we take a moment to speak with the young lady who somehow has to narrow it down to only one? Ladies and gentlemen, Her Royal Highness, Princess Eadlyn Schreave."

"Go get 'em," Ahren whispered as I pushed myself out of my seat and crossed the floor, embracing dear Gavril.

"Always nice to see you, Your Highness," he said as I sat in the chair opposite him center stage.

"And you, Gavril."

"So here we are, one week into the first-ever female-led Selection. How would you say it's going?"

I gave an award-winning smile. "I think it's going well. Of course, I still have work to do each day, so we're off to a fairly slow start."

Gavril glanced back over his shoulder. "Judging by the thinning crowd, I wouldn't say it's that slow."

Batting my eyes, I giggled. "Yes, about a third of the gentlemen invited to the palace have been eliminated. I have to trust my gut, and between our initial meetings and the information I've been given, I feel very confident about my choices."

Gavril inclined his head. "It sounds like you're using more of your head than your heart at the moment."

I fought the blush. I couldn't tell how well I'd done, but I refused to touch my face to check.

"Would you suggest that I fall in love with thirty-five young men at once?"

He raised his eyebrows. "Well, when you put it that way . . ."

"Exactly. I only have one heart, and I'm saving it."

I heard sighs around the room, and I felt I'd gotten away with something. How many more lines could I dream up over the following months to keep everyone entertained and at bay? Then I realized, I hadn't planned those words. I really felt them, and they escaped under pressure.

"It seems you may have let your heart lead the way at least once," he said knowingly. "I have a picture to prove it."

I watched as a huge picture of me and Kile was displayed, and the room erupted with hoots and claps.

"Could we get him down here for a moment? Where's Sir Kile?"

He hopped up from his place and sat on a chair next to me.

"Now, this is a very unique position for me," Gavril began, "because I've known both of you your entire lives."

Kile laughed. "I was thinking about this the other day. My mom said I crawled on set once as a baby, and you held me for the closing of the *Report*."

Gavril's eyes widened. "That's true! I'd forgotten all about that!"

I looked at Kile, giggling at this new story. That must have happened before I was born.

"So, from the pictures, it looks like perhaps a childhood friendship is growing into something more?"

Kile stared at me, and I shook my head. No way was I going first on this.

He finally caved. "Honestly, I don't think either of us ever thought about the other as a possibility until we were forced to."

Our families laughed boisterously.

"Although, if he had gotten a haircut years ago, I might have considered it," I teased.

Gavril shook his head at us. "Everyone's dying to know: how was this infamous kiss?"

I knew it was coming, but I was mortified. This was much worse than I imagined it would be, having my private life on display.

Mercifully, Kile addressed it. "I think I can speak for both of us when I say it was a surprise. And while it was special, I don't think we're going to put too much stock in it. I mean, I've been spending time with these other guys, and so many of them would make a wonderful prince."

"Really? And would you agree with that, Princess? Have you had one-on-one time with anyone else this week?"

It felt like Gavril's words were on a delay. I didn't hear them until I'd processed everything Kile had just said. Did he mean that? Did he not feel anything at all? Or was he only saying that to maintain some level of privacy?

I snapped back into the moment and nodded enthusiastically. "Yes, a few."

Gavril eyed me. "And?"

"And they were very nice." I wasn't really in the mood for this in the first place, and Kile had made me doubt sharing anything at all.

"Hmm," Gavril said, turning to the group of the Selected. "Maybe we'll get some more information out of the gentlemen in question. Sir Kile, you may head back to your seat. Now, who were the lucky men?"

Baden raised his hand, followed by Hale.

"Come on down, gentlemen."

Gavril started applauding and the room joined in as Hale and Baden approached and yet another chair was brought in. I considered myself pretty intelligent, but I could not think of a way to beg them to keep their mouths shut without actually using words.

Only then did I realize how easily Kile managed to do just that. I supposed there was something to be said for knowing each other forever.

"Now, what's your name again, sir?" Gavril asked.

"Hale Garner." He pressed down his tie, though it was already in place.

"Oh, yes. So, what can you tell us about your date with the princess?"

Hale gave me a shy smile, then turned back to Gavril. "Well, I can tell you that our princess is as smart and gracious as I always believed she was. Umm, and that we do have a few things in common. We're both the oldest children in our families, and it was fun to talk about my work as a tailor with such a well-dressed young lady. I mean, she looks like a million bucks."

I ducked my head, trying to take the compliment playfully while staying on my toes.

"But beyond that, I hope you'll forgive me if I keep most of the details to myself," Hale added.

Gavril made a face. "You're not going to tell us anything?"

"Well, dating and falling in love are typically private things. It's kind of weird to talk about at this stage."

"Perhaps we'll get more out of the next gentleman," Gavril said impishly to the cameras. "Remind us of your name again?"

"Baden Trains."

"And what did you and the princess do?"

"We played music. Princess Eadlyn is as talented as her mother."

I heard Mom's "aww" in the background.

"And?"

"And she's a lovely dancer, even when she's sitting down. Just so everyone knows, the princess is very up-to-date on current music." Baden laughed and a few people joined in.

"And?" Gavril pressed.

"And I kissed her hand . . . and I'm hoping for more kisses in the future."

I wanted to die. For some reason Baden's request for a kiss was much more embarrassing than talking about one that had already happened with Kile.

The room made encouraging noises again, and I could see Gavril was trying to milk this. Unfortunately for him, there really weren't any more juicy details. Kile was the only one with anything remotely shocking to share, and that had already been soaked up.

"You look so disappointed, Gavril," I remarked quickly.

He made a little pout. "I'm simply excited for you, Your Highness, and want to know everything that's happening. And if we could ask our millions of viewers, I'm sure they'd agree."

"Well, don't worry. You, and all of Illéa, will be happy to know that tomorrow I will be hosting a small party for the Selected and members of the palace household. Cameras will be there for the entire event, so everyone will get to peek inside the Selection process."

The room burst into applause again. I could see Josie practically floating out of her chair, she was so excited.

Gavril sent Hale and Baden back to their seats with the others before launching into questions again.

"What kind of party can we expect tomorrow, Your Highness?"

"We'll be out in the gardens, enjoying the sun and

spending time getting to know one another."

"That sounds like a wonderful plan. Very relaxing."

"Well, it will be, except for one tiny detail," I added, pinching my fingers in the air.

"And what is that?"

"After the party there will be an elimination."

Murmurs filled the room, and I knew, regardless of how the public felt about me, meeting the boys tonight would make them curious about who stayed and who left.

I continued, hushing the crowd with my words. "It could be one person, it could be three. . . . I don't know. So, gentlemen," I said, turning back to the Selected, "come prepared."

"I can't wait to see how this all turns out, and I'm positive it will be a wonderful event. Now, one final question before we call it a night."

I sat up taller. "Go for it."

"What are you looking for in a husband?"

What was I looking for? My independence. Peace, freedom . . . a happiness I thought I had until Ahren questioned it.

I shrugged. "I'm not sure anyone knows what they're looking for until they find it."

CHAPTER 17

HOW DID JOSIE GET HER hands on another one of my tiaras? I'd just about had it with her. She was going to parade around in front of the cameras in her best dress and my tiara pretending she was royal for the millionth time in her life.

I made eye contact and smiled at people as I passed, but I didn't stop to talk to anyone until I found Kile. He was standing with Henri again, sipping iced tea and watching a game of badminton. Henri bowed right away.

"Hello today, Your Highness," he said, his accent making the words sound brighter.

"Hello, Henri. Kile."

"Hi, Eadlyn."

I might have been imagining there was something different about Kile's voice, but for maybe the first time ever, I wanted to hear him speak. I shook my head, focusing.

"Kile, could you please go talk to your sister?"

The contentment in his eyes quickly turned to frustration. "Why? What'd she do this time?"

"She's taken yet another one of my tiaras."

"Don't you have, like, a thousand of those?"

I huffed. "That's hardly the point. It's mine, and she shouldn't be wearing it. When she walks around like that, she gives the impression that she's royal when she's not. It's inappropriate. Could you please talk to her about her behavior?"

"When did I become the person who did all these favors for you?"

My eyes darted over to Henri and Erik, who didn't know about the arrangement behind our kiss. They didn't seem to catch on.

"Please?" I asked in a hushed voice.

His eyes softened, and I saw a little of the person he showed me in his room, someone sweet and engaging. "Fine. But Josie just likes attention. I don't think she's doing it to be mean."

"Thank you."

"I'm going. Be right back."

He stomped off as Erik conveyed what was happening to Henri.

Henri cleared his throat before speaking, his words ending on strange pitches. "How are you today, Your Highness?"

I wasn't completely sure if I should try to go through Erik or not. . . . I went with Henri. "Very good. You?"

"Good, good," he replied cheerfully. "I to enjoy . . . umm." He turned and conveyed the rest of his comment to Erik.

"He thinks the party is great, and he likes the company."

I wasn't sure if he meant Kile or me, but either way, it was nice of him to say.

"So when did you move over from Swendway?"

Henri was nodding his head as if to confirm he was from Swendway but not actually answering the question. Erik whispered over to him quickly, and Henri gave him a lengthy reply that was translated for me.

"Henri emigrated to Illéa last year when he was seventeen. He comes from a family of cooks, which is what he does back home. They make food from their homeland and generally interact with others who also came from Swendway and only speak Finnish. He has a younger sister who is working very hard on her English, but it's a difficult language."

"Wow. That was a lot to keep up with," I said to Erik.

He waved his hand. "I try."

I could guess how hard Erik's work was, but I appreciated his modesty. I turned to Henri. "We'll have to spend some time together soon. Where we can talk easier."

Erik passed that on to Henri, who nodded vigorously. "Yes, yes!"

I giggled. "Until then."

The lawn was full of the Selected. General Leger had Miss Lucy on his arm as he spoke with a handful of boys by a fountain, and Dad was making his rounds, occasionally clapping someone on the back and saying hello before whisking off again. Mom was sitting in a chair under a parasol, and I wasn't sure if it was charming or unsettling that several of the Selected were buzzing around her.

It was a delightful party. People were playing games, there was lots of food, and a string quartet was performing under a canopy. The cameras zoomed around capturing it all, and I hoped this would be enough to calm the people. I had no idea whether Dad was closer to having a plan for how to soothe the country permanently.

In the meantime, I had to find a way to eliminate at least one person after today, and have a good enough reason to make it seem believable.

Kile sneaked up on me. "Here you go." He held my tiara in his hands.

"I can't believe she gave it up."

"It took some convincing, but I reminded her that if she made a scene at this event, Mom probably wouldn't let her come to another one. That was enough to get her to take it off. So here."

"I can't take it," I said, keeping my hands together.

"But you just asked for it," he complained.

"I don't want it on her, but I also can't carry it around. I have things to do."

He shifted his weight, clearly vexed. It was kind of nice to be on this side of the irritating.

"So, what, I have to hold on to it for the rest of the day?"

"Not the *whole* day. Just until we go inside, and then I can take it."

Kile shook his head. "You're really unbelievable."

"Hush. Go enjoy the party. But first, wait, we have to take off this tie."

He looked down as I started tugging. "What's wrong with my tie?"

"Everything," I said. "Everything in the universe is wrong with this tie. I bet we could find world peace if we burned it."

I got it unknotted and wrapped it up in my hand.

"That's so much better." I placed the wadded fabric in his palm, grabbed the tiara from his other hand, and placed it on his head. "That really works with your hair."

He smirked, his eyes staring into mine with amusement. "So, since you don't want your tiara now, maybe I could give it back to you tonight. I could come by your room, if you like." Kile bit his lip, and all I could think about was how soft they were.

I swallowed, understanding the unspoken question. "That would be fine," I answered, fighting a blush. "Maybe around nine?"

"Nine." Kile nodded and backed away.

So he was just being discreet on the *Report*! I furrowed my brow in thought. Or maybe he was simply planning to pass his time kissing me. Or maybe he'd been deeply in love with me since he was seven and was only now finding the courage to stop teasing me and say so. Or maybe—

Ean walked up and laced his arm through mine.

"Oh!" I gasped.

"You look upset. Whatever that little boy said to upset you, don't give it another thought."

"Sir Ean," I greeted, impressed with how calm he was around me. "How can I help you?"

"By taking a walk with me, of course. I still haven't gotten a chance to speak with you just the two of us."

Ean's caramel-colored hair looked almost golden in the sun, and while he didn't have the same cutting-edge style Hale did, he looked smarter in his suit than most of the others. Some men simply didn't look good in them.

"Well, you have me alone now. What would you like to talk about?"

He smirked. "Mostly, I'm curious about you. I've always thought of you as very independent, so I was surprised that you would start looking for a husband so young. Based on seeing you on the *Report* and all the specials on your family, I thought you'd take your time."

He knew. He was so calm in his assessment, I was sure he knew this was all for show.

"It's true; I'd planned to wait. But my parents are so blissfully in love, I thought this might be worth trying."

Ean examined me. "Do you feel like any one of these candidates truly has what it takes to be your partner?"

I raised my eyebrows. "Do you think so little of yourself?"

He stopped walking, and we faced each other. "No, but I think very highly of you. And I can't see you deigning to settle before you've really lived."

It seemed impossible that a stranger could see so much, especially considering the lengths I took to guard my thoughts and feelings. How closely had Ean been watching me all these years?

"People can change," I replied vaguely.

He nodded. "They can, I suppose. But if you ever find yourself feeling . . . lost in this competition, I'd be happy to help you in any way I could."

"And how exactly would you help me?"

Ean gently escorted me back toward the crowd. "I think that's a conversation for another day. But know that I am here for you, Your Highness."

He stared deep into my eyes, as if he thought that all my secrets would spill out if he held my gaze long enough. I found myself needing to take some deep breaths once we finally broke eye contact.

"It's a lovely day."

I looked up, and one of the Selected was standing there. I was completely blanking on his name.

"Yes, it is. Are you having a good time?" Oh, please, what was his name?

"I am." He had a very friendly face and a pleasant warmth to his voice. "I just won a round of croquet. Do you play?"

"A little." How was I going to figure this out? "Do you play a lot back home?"

"Nah. Not really. Up in Whites, it's mostly winter sports."

Whites! . . . Nope, still didn't have it.

"If I'm honest, I'm a bit more of an indoor girl."

"Well, then you'd love Whites," he said with a laugh. "I only get out when I have to."

"Excuse me."

Whites Boy and I turned to the newcomer. This one I knew.

"I'm sorry, Your Highness, but I was hoping I could steal you away for a moment."

"Certainly, Holden." I took his arm. "Nice talking to you," I said to Whites Boy, who looked a bit forlorn.

"I hope that wasn't too rude of me," Holden said as we wandered away.

"Not at all."

We moved slowly, and he seemed comfortable, like he'd walked with a princess dozens of times.

"I don't want to keep you. I only wanted to tell you that I admired the way you cut people last week."

I was taken aback. "Really?"

"Absolutely! I admire a woman who knows what she wants, and I like that you're assertive. My mother is the head of a lab back in Bankston. I know how hard it is to run something that small, so the pressure you must be under is hard for me to imagine. But you do it well, and I like that. I just wanted you to know."

I stepped back. "Thank you, Holden." He nodded, and I walked away, lost in thought.

This entire situation only confirmed what I knew to be true: If I came in sweet and gentle, no one would take me seriously. If I had kindly tapped people on the shoulder and hugged them on their way out, would Holden have admired me less? The whole thing was—

"Oh!" I fell to the side, only missing the ground because of a pair of steady arms.

"Your Highness." Hale clutched my arms, helping to pull me up. "I'm so sorry, I didn't see you."

I heard the click of a camera nearby and pushed my cheeks up into a smile.

"Laugh," I said through my teeth.

"Huh?"

"Help me up and laugh it off." I giggled, and after a moment Hale gave a few chuckles.

"What was that about?" He kept the smile on his face.

I straightened my dress as I explained. "The camera crews are watching."

He glanced to the side.

"Don't," I urged, and he faced me again.

"Yikes. Are you always on the lookout like that?"

This time my laugh was genuine. "Basically."

His smiled faded. "Is that why you ran away the other night?"

My face became serious as well. "I'm sorry. I wasn't feeling well."

"First you run, and then you lie." He shook his head, disappointed.

"No."

"Eadlyn," he whispered. "That wasn't easy for me. I don't

like talking about my dad dying or my mom having a hard time keeping a job or my family losing our status. That was difficult for me to share. And when we started really talking about you, you left me."

That prickling, naked feeling came over me again.

"I sincerely apologize, Hale."

He studied my face. "I don't think you mean that." I swallowed, nervous. "But I like you all the same."

I looked up at him, mesmerized by that possibility.

"When you're ready to talk—to really talk—I'll be here. Unless, of course, you come in and ninja eliminate me like you did those other guys."

I laughed awkwardly. "I don't think that'll happen again."

"I hope not." Hale stared, and I didn't like that his eyes felt like they could dig several layers beneath my skin. "Glad your dress didn't get stained. Would have been a pity."

He went to leave, but I grabbed his arm. "Hey. Thank you. For being reserved on the *Report*."

He grinned. "Something every day, remember?"

CHAPTER 18

"ALL RIGHT, YOUR HIGHNESS, WHENEVER you're ready."

The makeup girl did a last check, and I corrected my posture, reviewing the names in my head. I nodded, and the light on the camera turned red, telling me we were filming.

"You've seen the extravagant tea party, you heard about the delicious food, and you saw all the breathtaking fashion; but who did you think should be eliminated?

"Yes, Sir Kile looked somewhat less than manly in my tiara, and Sir Hale nearly swept me off my feet . . . in a bad way," I concluded with a grin. "But, after much deliberation, the two Selected leaving us today are Kesley Timber from Whites and Holden Messenger from Bankston.

"How is your favorite doing? Dying to learn more about the remaining contestants? Hungry for more Selection-related news? Tune in to the *Report* each Friday night for updates from me and the gentlemen themselves, and don't forget to look out for exclusive programs dedicated to the Selection exclusively on the Public Access Channel."

I held my smile a few seconds longer.

"Cut!" the director called. "Excellent. Sounded perfect to me, but let's do one more for good measure."

"Sure. When will this go out?"

"They'll edit all the footage from this afternoon's party tonight and get it on air tomorrow, so this should be out on Monday."

I nodded. "Great. One more time?"

"Yes, Your Highness, if you don't mind."

I swallowed and went over my speech again before pulling myself up into the exact same pose.

At ten past nine I heard the knock on my door, and I skipped over to answer it. Kile was there, leaning against the door-frame, tiara in hand.

"I heard you were missing this," he said jokingly.

"Come in, loser."

He passed through the doorway, looking around again as if I redecorated my room daily. "So am I getting cut yet?"

I grinned. "No, it's Kesley and Holden. Don't let that spill though. I can't send them away until after the garden party airs."

"That won't be a problem. Neither of them really speaks to me anyway."

"No?" I asked as he handed me my tiara.

"I've heard they thought me being a part of the Selection was unfair. And then seeing our kiss plastered everywhere sealed that opinion."

I placed the tiara on the shelf with the others. "Made a good call then, didn't I?"

He chuckled. "Oh, I brought you another present."

"I love presents!"

"You'll hate this one, trust me." He reached into his pocket and pulled out that spectacular disaster of a tie.

"I figured if you were having a bad day, you could take it to the garden and burn it. Get your aggression out on something that won't cry. Unlike Leeland."

"I wasn't *trying* to make him cry."

"Sure you weren't."

I smiled, taking the wound-up fabric from his hand. "I actually really like this present. It assures me that no human will be forced to wear it ever again."

Looking over at him, at his hitched-up smile, I was able to push away everything for a minute. It felt like the Selection wasn't even happening just then. I was a girl with a boy. And I knew what I wanted to do with that boy.

I dropped the tie on the floor and put a hand on his chest. "Kile Woodwork, do you want to kiss me?"

He let out a whistle. "Not shy at all, are you?"

"Stop it. Yes or no?"

He pursed his lips, pretending to think it over. "I wouldn't mind it."

"And you understand that me kissing you doesn't mean I actually like you and that I would never, ever marry you?"

"Thank goodness."

"Right answer."

I wrapped my hand around his head, pulling him to me, and an instant later his arms were around my waist. It was the perfect balm for a long day. Kile's kisses were direct and slow, and he made it impossible for me to think about much else.

We toppled onto the bed, holding each other as we laughed.

"Of all the things I thought would happen when my name was called, I never dreamed I'd ever kiss you."

"I never dreamed you'd be good at it."

"Hey," he said, "I've had a bit of practice."

I propped myself up on my elbow. "Who was your last kiss?"

"Caterina. When the Italian family visited in August, right before I left."

"That doesn't surprise me at all."

Kile shrugged, not ashamed in the slightest. "What can I say? They're very friendly."

"Friendly," I repeated, rolling my eyes. "That's one word for it."

He chuckled. "What about you?"

"Ask Ahren. Apparently everyone already knows."

"Leron Troyes?"

"How did *you* find out?"

We lay there, laughing so much we were nearly crying. I played with a button on his shirt, and he twirled a piece of my hair between kisses, and the world shrank to just the two of us.

"I've never seen you like this," he commented. "I didn't know it could be so easy to make you smile."

"It's not. You must be in rare form today."

Kile wrapped an arm around me and placed his face inches from mine. "How are you feeling? I know this has got to be a crazy time for you."

"Don't," I whispered.

"Don't what?"

"Don't ruin this. I like having you here, but I'm not in need of a soul mate. You can be quiet and go back to kissing me, or you can leave."

He rolled onto his back, silent for a few minutes. "Sorry. I just wanted to talk."

"And you can. But not about you, not about me, and definitely not about you and me together."

"But it seems like you must be lonely. How in the world do you deal with all this?"

I huffed, standing and pulling him to his feet. "If I need advice, I talk to my parents. If I need a friendly ear, I have Ahren. You were helping for a minute, and then you had to start with the questions."

I turned him around and pushed him toward the door. "Do you realize how unhealthy that is?" he asked

"Are you the model of adult behavior? You can't even get

your mother to cut the apron strings."

Kile rounded back, staring me down. I was sure his anger was reflected in my face. I waited for him to scold me again, as he'd done a thousand times growing up. But his eyes softened, and before I knew it, his hand was at the base of my neck, pulling me to him.

He crushed his lips to mine, and I simultaneously hated and adored him for it. All I could think of was the way his mouth moved and how I seemed so fragile in his hands. The passion slowed, until the kisses were so soft they tickled.

When Kile finally pulled away, he kept his fingers teasingly close to my hair, rubbing the skin absentmindedly.

"You are so spoiled, and you are so obnoxious . . . but I'm here." With a final kiss, he opened the door and left.

I gazed around my room, dizzy with confusion. Why was he trying to get me to open up when he clearly couldn't stand me? And I didn't like him either! Sometimes he could be just as bratty as Josie.

I went toward my closet to get ready for bed and saw his ugly tie on the floor. I'd be doing everyone a favor if I threw it away now.

Maybe I would set it on fire the next time I was having a particularly wretched day. For now I tucked it into a drawer.

My thoughts the next morning were a mess. I kept wondering what Kile's goal was last night. And I couldn't shake off how it made me feel similar to when Hale asked too many questions. They were such different people with vastly different understandings of me, yet they'd both quickly figured out how to make me back away. Would all the boys be like that? Was that something they all knew how to do?

"Neena?" I pulled the brush through my hair, trying to tame it as my maid walked behind me in the steam-filled bathroom, picking up the pajamas I'd left on the floor.

"Yes, Your Highness?" She caught my eyes in the mirror as we spoke.

"I feel like it's been a while since we've talked about your boyfriend. What's his name again?"

A smile crept up on her face. "Mark. Why do you ask?"

"I'm surrounded by a million boys. Just wondering how it is when you only have to deal with one."

She shook her head at me. "One boy on a string is a wonderful thing," she said, her happiness forcing me to smile along with her. "He's doing great. He finally got into a university, and he's studying all the time. I get a call from him maybe once or twice a week. It's not much, but we both have pretty full schedules."

"I do need constant supervision," I said with a wink.

"Amen."

"Does he mind much? That you're far away and busy?"

She straightened the clothes looped over her arm. "No. His program is very demanding, so for now it's actually helpful."

I leaned my head to one side, continuing to brush. "That's interesting. What's he studying?"

"Mark is a chemist. He's studying biochemistry, specifically."

My eyes widened. "Really? Such a range in your professions."

She frowned. "There's no caste system anymore, Your Highness. People can date and marry anyone they want to."

I turned away from the mirror to look at her directly. "That's not what I mean. It's simply intriguing to me the dynamic you must have. You have my laundry in your arms, and he might cure a disease. Those are two incredibly different roles in the world."

Neena swallowed and dropped everything on the ground. "I won't be doing your laundry forever. I made a choice to come here, and I can leave whenever I like."

"Neena!"

"I don't feel well," she said abruptly. "I'll send someone else up to help you."

She didn't even curtsy.

"Neena, I was simply talking!"

The door slammed, and I looked after her, shocked that she so shamelessly left without permission. I hadn't meant to offend her. I was merely curious, and that one observation didn't even begin to touch on the things I truly wanted to ask about.

I finished my hair and makeup on my own. When the substitute maid showed up, I sent her away. Just because Neena was in a bad mood didn't mean she could get out of her work. I could take care of myself, and she could clean tomorrow.

I picked up the applications for the remaining boys in

the Selection. Whether I liked it or not, I knew what was expected of me. All I needed was to find situations that kept things as close to the surface as possible.

Ean was certainly captivating, but his charisma was almost too overwhelming. I wasn't sure I was prepared to spend time alone with him. Edwin was harmless enough. I pulled out Apsel's sheet and looked it over. Nothing extraordinary there. I was tempted to send him home for being so bland, but after the reaction over the first elimination, I didn't think I could get away with that. Kile's form came up next, but he was a no at the moment. Winslow was, I hated to say it, considerably unattractive. The more and more I looked at him, the easier it was to see. I didn't think I had a type, but he made me wonder if I had an anti-type. Ivan . . . was this the guy who smelled vaguely of chlorine?

Near the bottom of the pile, Jack Ranger's picture jumped out at me. I had caught him staring at me a few times at the party, but we hadn't spoken. I took that to mean he might still be intimidated enough for me to get through an evening together without him leaving me feeling as unpleasant as some of the others had.

I wrote a note out on my stationery inviting him to watch a movie with me tonight. That was an easy enough date. No unnecessary talking. I'd have a butler deliver it to him once Jack had joined the others. I was planning always to announce dates by sending a letter into or drawing the boys out of the room. That should make things interesting.

I sped through breakfast, ready to work. Looking at these

endless requests and bills and budgets and proposals wasn't exactly my favorite thing, but it kept me busy, and I liked having my mind occupied all day. My nights and weekends for the next three months would belong to those boys, but the rest of the time I had a different job to do.

"Eadlyn, dear," Dad said, taking a break for some tea. "I didn't get to tell you, but I thought the garden party was a success. I saw some of the stories in the papers this morning, and it was very well covered."

"I glanced at a few myself. And I caught a little of the special they did, and it all looked nicely done." I stretched in my chair, achy from sitting still.

He smiled. "Indeed. I think you should try to do another event like that soon—something with the group that people can see."

"Something that might have an elimination afterward?"

"If you think that would help."

I walked over to his desk, pouring myself some of his tea. "I think it adds something. Like people might be more interested if their favorite might be on the line."

He considered that. "Interesting. Any thoughts on how it would be structured?"

"No, but I thought, since we're supposed to be looking for a prince here, it might be good to test them on the things they would need to know as a prince. History or policy. I think there's a way to make it playful, kind of like a game show maybe?"

He laughed. "The public would eat that up."

I sipped my tea. "See, I have great ideas. I don't need a prince."

"Eadlyn, you could run the world on your own if you needed to. That's not the point," he said with a chuckle.

"We'll see."

CHAPTER 19

I STOPPED BY JACK'S ROOM after dinner, and he was waiting for me outside the door. That was kind of strange, but I figured his nerves had gotten the best of him.

"Good evening, Jack," I said, approaching.

"Your Highness," he replied with a bow.

"You can call me Eadlyn."

He smiled. "Great. Eadlyn."

There was an awkward silence as I waited for him to offer his arm. He simply stood there, his smile tight but his eyes animated. When I finally gave up on him figuring it out, I pointed toward the stairs. "It's this way."

"Super." Then he started walking ahead of me, even though he didn't know the way.

"No, Jack. We need to turn here." I said the same thing maybe three or four times as we traveled, and he never apologized. He simply went where I told him as if he'd been planning to go that way all along. I did my best to let his missteps slide. With a handful of boys already mentally lined up for the next elimination, I didn't want a reason to add Jack to that list.

The palace went up four stories, but it went down much farther. The *Report* was filmed on the sub-one floor, and there was a storage area as well as the theater. The staff and guards also had rooms on the first and second sublevels, but their quarters weren't connected to the theater wing. There was also a monstrous safe room beneath all of that. I'd only had to go there twice that I remembered: once during a drill when I was three and once when the last string of rebels attacked us shortly after.

It was strange to think about it. The rebels were gone, but now we were faced with different pockets of people fighting the monarchy. I almost wished the rebels still existed. At least we could put a name to that. At least back then we knew exactly who we were fighting.

I shook my head, coming back to the situation at hand. I was on a date. As I remembered that fact, I chided myself. Dad would have wanted a camera here for this. Oh, well. Next time.

"So, I hope you like movies."

"I do," Jack replied enthusiastically.

"Good. I do as well, but it's not always possible for me to go out to the theater. We have access to a few new films downstairs, though our options are limited. Chances are we'll have something good."

"That's great." It was strange, this fine line he was walking between being rude and polite. I wondered if he simply didn't know how many mistakes he was making.

A butler had already made us popcorn, and I used the remote to scroll through our options.

"How about *Eye of the Beholder*?" I suggested. The brief description hinted at romance and drama, as did the poster image.

"That sounds okay. Any action in that one?"

"I don't think so. There is in *Black Diamonds*." The picture was dark and brooding, with the silhouette of a man with a gun off to one side. It wasn't something I'd have seen of my own volition.

"Yeah! That sounds good."

"We have other choices," I said, trying to make my way back to the menu.

"But this is what I want to watch. It won't be too scary. And if it is, you can snuggle up next to me."

I made a face, wondering if I should have given Apsel more consideration. The seats in our theater were wide and very soft. The only way I could snuggle up to anyone would be to squish myself into his seat, which was not going to happen. Also, I'd rather be scarred for life than admit to being afraid.

Then again, that wasn't what I was worried about with this movie. It simply didn't seem worth watching.

I sighed, feeling a little overrun. Again, it was as if he

wasn't aware of how foolish he was acting. I let it go, thinking I'd need to tell Dad that the boys as a whole required more etiquette training, and started the movie.

Long story short, Main Guy's dad was killed by Bad Guy. Main Guy spends his life tracking down Bad Guy, but Bad Guy slips from his grasp several times. Main Guy sleeps with Super Blonde. Super Blonde disappears. Main Guy kills Bad Guy, and Super Blonde shows up again. Oh, and some things explode.

Jack seemed to enjoy it, but I was bored. If Super Blonde had killed someone, I might have cared a little more.

But at least we didn't have to talk.

When the credits rolled, I used the remote to raise the lights.

"So, what did you think?" he asked, his eyes bright with excitement.

"It was okay. Definitely seen better."

The movie seemed to leave him hyperanimated. "But the effects were incredible!"

"Sure, but the story was tired."

He squinted his eyes. "I liked it."

"All right."

"Does that make you upset?"

I made a face. "No. It just means you have bad taste."

He laughed, a dark sound that was more foreboding than friendly. "I love it when you do that."

"Do what?" I stood and took my popcorn bowl to the counter, leaving it for the staff.

"I've been waiting all night for a little of your attitude."

"Excuse me?"

"I've been hoping you'd get mad or snippy." He brought his bowl over, too. "When you cleared out the Men's Parlor the day after the parade? That was great. I mean, I don't want to go home, but I wouldn't be devastated if you yelled at me."

I stared at him. "Jack, you do realize we've hardly spoken to each other, and in the first conversation we have, you reveal that my anger turns you on. Do you see how this might be a lapse in judgment on your part?"

He broke into a smile, undeterred. "I thought you'd appreciate my honesty. I have the feeling you get irritated easily, and I want you to know that doesn't bother me. I actually like it."

Jack reached for my hand, and I ripped it away. "You thought wrong. This date is over. Goodnight."

He caught up to me, grabbing me again. I didn't want to admit how scared I was, but I could feel the icy strands of fear pulsing through my veins. He was bigger than me, and he seemed to enjoy a fight.

"Don't run off," he said silkily. "I'm only trying to tell you that I think I could be a good fit for you, an easy match." He ran his fingers down my cheek and under my jaw. His breathing was speeding up, and I knew I couldn't waste time. I had to get out of here now.

I squinted my eyes. "And I'm only trying to tell you that if you don't remove your hand, you will be dead before you could be a match for anyone."

"Hot." He smirked, seeming to think I was enjoying this. "This is a fun little game."

"Let. Me. Go."

He loosened his hand, but I could still see the wild excitement in his eyes. "This was fun. Let's do it again soon."

I went for the stairs, praying he wouldn't chase me. From this second forward, there would be cameras on every. Single. Date.

When I made my way breathlessly to the first floor, I found a pair of officers and ran straight to them.

"Your Highness," the first gasped as I fell into his arms.

"Get him out of here!" I insisted, pointing toward the stairs. "Jack! Get him out of my house!"

The guards let me go, sprinting to capture him, and I cowered on the floor, petrified.

"Eadlyn?"

Just behind me, Ahren was approaching. I let out a cry and bolted into his embrace.

"What happened? Are you hurt?"

"It was Jack," I stammered. "He grabbed my arm. He touched me." I shook my head, trying to understand how it escalated so quickly, only then seeing it hadn't been fast at all.

He was often watching me, never approaching, quietly biding his time. Even tonight his moves were slow, watching my rising frustration with a reserved thrill of energy, enjoying the building tension until the moment of release.

"He kept saying strange things, and the way he looked at me . . . Ahren, I've never been so scared."

We both turned at the uproar coming up the stairs. The two guards were wrestling with Jack, getting him up to the landing. Once his eyes fell on me, he began snarling.

"You liked it!" he insisted. "You were coming on to me!"

Grabbing my hand, Ahren pulled me over to Jack, though my instinct was to run in the other direction. He planted me right in front of Jack's face.

"Knock his lights out, Eadlyn," Ahren commanded. I stared up at him, thinking it was a joke. But the rage in his eyes told me otherwise.

I was tempted. I couldn't retaliate when people called me names or criticized my clothes. I couldn't go back to the parade and tell all those people how foolishly they'd acted. But here, for once, I could take revenge on someone who'd truly wronged me.

I might have done it if it wasn't for Jack's wicked grin, like he hoped I would, like he'd dream about the touch later. Sex and violence were connected in his head, and to give him one was close to giving the other.

"I can't," I whispered.

Jack gave a fake pout. "You sure, sweetie? I wouldn't mi—"

I'd never seen Ahren throw a punch before. It was almost as shocking as Jack's limp body after my brother's fist forced his head to whip back at an awkward angle.

Ahren grunted, holding his hand. "That hurts! Ow, that really hurts!"

"Let's get you to the hospital wing," I urged, pointing Ahren down the hall.

"Your Highness, should we take him with you?"

I looked at Jack's limp form, noting the rise and fall of his chest.

"No. Get him on a plane, conscious or not."

I piled into Ahren's bed with him on one side and Kaden on the other. Ahren was flexing his wrapped fingers, which were badly bruised.

"Does it hurt?" Kaden asked, seeming more excited than worried.

"A little, but I'd do it all over again in a second."

I smiled up at my twin, so grateful for him.

"If I had been there," Kaden started, "I'd have challenged him to a duel."

I giggled as Ahren reached across me to ruffle his hair. "Sorry, buddy, it all happened too quickly for me to think of that."

Kaden shook his head. "All those years of sword-fighting lessons for nothing."

"You were always better than me anyway," Ahren said as Osten came in without knocking, a phone to his ear.

"If you had only practiced more!" Kaden chastised.

Osten landed on the bed chatting into the phone. "Yeah, yeah. Okay, hold on." He turned the receiver away and looked to me. "Eady, where was that Jack guy from anyway?"

I tried to remember his form. "Paloma, I think."

Kaden nodded. "It was Paloma."

"Awesome." Osten spoke into the phone again. "Did you hear that? I'll be in touch."

He hung up and slid the phone into his pocket as we all stared at him.

I laughed. "I'd usually try to stop whatever you're doing, but I'm not even going to ask."

"I think that's for the best."

I looked around at all my brothers, so caring and smart and puckish. So many times I'd hated them for not being older than me, for forcing me into a role I never wanted. Tonight, maybe for the first time, I loved them for exactly who they were. Kaden was distracting, Ahren had defended me, and Osten . . . well, he'd help in his own way.

Osten had left the door open, and Mom and Dad walked in to find all their children together.

Mom seemed happy to see her family safe, but Dad was shaken.

He put one hand on his hip and gestured with the other. "Everyone okay?"

"Slightly spooked," I admitted.

"And a little bruised," Ahren added.

Dad swallowed, taking us all in. "Eadlyn, I'm so sorry. I don't know how he slipped through the cracks. I thought the applications were vetted, and I had no idea . . ."

He stopped, looking as though he was close to tears.

"I'm all right, Daddy."

He nodded but didn't speak.

Mom stepped forward, taking over. "We'd like to put some guidelines in place. Perhaps have a guard nearby on any dates from here on out, or have all dates in a public area."

"That or have photographers. I think that would help, too." I cursed myself again for not remembering earlier.

"Excellent idea, sweetie. We want to keep this safe."

"Which reminds me," Dad said, under control again. "How do you want to proceed with Jack? Should we cover this up? Press formal charges? Personally, I'd like to tear him limb from limb, but that's really up to you."

I smiled. "No charges, but let's not cover it up. Let everyone know exactly what kind of man he is. That will be punishment enough."

"Very wise," Ahren agreed.

Dad folded his arms, considering. "If that's what you want, that's what we'll do. I've been told he's on his way home now, and that will be the end of it."

"Thank you."

Dad put his arm around Mom, and they turned to leave, Mom taking one last look at all of us.

"By the way," Dad said, glancing over his shoulder, "while I agree with the sentiment behind throwing him out without seeing if he regained consciousness, if he *had* died, that would have looked really bad."

I pressed my lips together, but I knew my eyes were smiling. "Fine. No more carelessly tossing people out through the gates."

"And more sword fights!" Kaden yelled.

While Ahren and I laughed, our parents shook their heads. "Goodnight. Don't stay up too late," Mom warned.

And we didn't mean to, but we did end up talking for a long time. I eventually fell asleep with Kaden's back pressed against mine, Ahren's arm under my head, and Osten holding on to one of my feet.

I woke early the next morning, well before the others, and smiled at my brothers, my protectors. The sister in me wanted to stay. But the princess in me got up and went to prepare for the new day.

CHAPTER 20

WHILE WE SAT AT THE breakfast table the next morning, I found myself looking over the boys, searching for signs that anyone else might be like Jack. I kept thinking that if I'd paid more attention those first few days, I'd have been able to see there was something off about him.

Then my eyes passed over some of the others I'd gotten to know, like Hale and Henri. Even Erik's presence was a welcome one. After meeting them, I couldn't let one boy make me fearful of all the others. And in truth, I really didn't have the privilege of being fearful.

So I pulled myself together, remembering who I was. I couldn't run scared.

As the meal drew to a close, I stood, commanding their attention. "Gentlemen, I have a surprise for you. In fifteen minutes, please come meet me in the studio for a little game."

Some laughed and others clapped, but they didn't know what was waiting for them. I almost felt bad. I left the room before them, going to make sure my dress and hair looked right for filming.

Shortly thereafter, the boys filed in, all of them seeming a little stunned by the set.

I sat in front, a bit like a schoolteacher, while they each had a stool with a paper and marker and a large, cartoonish name tag like the ones I'd seen on TV game shows.

"Welcome, gentlemen!" I sang. "Please come find your seat."

The cameras were already rolling, capturing the nervous smiles and confused head shaking as they found their places and stuck on their tags.

"Today we're having a pop quiz on all things Illéa. We'll be discussing history, foreign affairs, and domestic policies. When you get an answer right, one of the maids standing by," I said, motioning to the ladies waiting in the wings, "will come and put a gold check mark sticker on you. Get one wrong, and they'll bring a black X."

The boys chuckled with excitement and anxiety, looking at the baskets of stickers.

"Don't worry, this is all for fun. But I will be using this information to help decide my next elimination. If you get the most wrong, it doesn't mean you're automatically out . . . but I'm watching," I teased, pointing a finger at them.

"First question," I announced. "This is an important one! When is my birthday?"

There were several laughs as the boys bent their heads,

scribbling answers and peeking at their neighbors' answers.

"Okay, hold up your signs," I ordered, and gawked humorously at the range of dates.

Kile, of course, knew it was April 16, and he had plenty of company, but there were only a few who knew the year as well.

"You know what, I'm going to go ahead and give this to anyone who got April at all."

"All right!" Fox called enthusiastically, and Lodge and Calvin high-fived in the back. The maids crossed the stage, and boys who got an X wailed comically but took the stickers without sulking.

"Here's one with lots of potential answers. Who would you consider Illéa's greatest allies?"

Some correctly guessed France, Italy, and New Asia, while Henri held up Swendway, followed by several exclamation points.

Julian's sign had several arrows drawn up to his face and had *ME* written in large letters.

I pointed at him. "Wait, wait, wait! What does that even mean?" I asked, trying to suppress a smile.

His grin was huge as he shrugged. "I just think I'd be a really great friend."

I shook my head. "Ridiculous." But I didn't think I came off sounding as reproachful as I meant to.

A maid raised her hand on the side of the stage. "So does he still get an X or . . . ?"

"Oh, that's an X!" I assured her, and the boys chuckled, even Julian.

Most correctly named August Illéa as Dad's partner in eradicating the rebel forces, and they all knew the history of the Fourth World War. By the time we got to the end, I was pleased that the majority of them were so well-informed.

"Let me see. Who has the most checks?" The maids helped me count across the rows, which was very efficient since they had handed out the points. "Hale has six. So do Raoul and Ean. Bravo, gentlemen!"

I clapped, and the others joined in before realizing what was next.

"Okay, and now, who has the most X marks?"

The maids quickly pointed to the back corner, where poor Henri was covered with black.

"Oh, no, Henri!" I yelled with a laugh, trying to communicate how little stock I took in the game.

I really had hoped to weed out someone this way, but I knew Henri's lack of information came from living in the country for only a year or a misunderstanding of the questions in translation.

"Who else do we have? Burke and Ivan . . . not too terrible." They had each done pretty badly but still had three correct answers over Henri. At least it confirmed my lack of excitement over Ivan.

"Thank you all for indulging me this morning, and I will keep this information in mind as I continue to narrow down suitors in the next few weeks. Congratulations on being so intelligent!" I applauded them, and they patted one another on the back as the cameras powered down.

"Before you go, gentlemen, I have one last question; and it comes from some very recent history, so you all had best get it right."

They nervously murmured among themselves, ready for the challenge.

"If you know the answer, feel free to just shout it out. Ready? When is it acceptable to put your hands on me without my permission?"

I stared at them all, stone-faced, daring a single one of them to laugh. They exchanged glances with one another, but it was only Hale who was brave enough to answer.

"Never," he called out.

"That is correct. You'd all do well to remember that. Jack Ranger was let off easy, with nothing more than a punch to his face from my brother and the shame of his ejection. If another one of you attempts to touch me without my consent, you will be caned or worse. Are we clear?"

The room was still.

"I'll take that as a yes."

I walked away, hoping my words would linger after me. The game was over, and they couldn't be left doubting that.

After lunch Dad was a little late getting into the office, which was rare. So I was alone when Lady Brice came knocking on the door.

"Your Highness," she greeted. "Is your father not here yet?"

"No. Not sure what's holding him up."

"Hmm." She tidied the stack of papers in her arms, thinking. "I really needed to speak with him."

Lady Brice looked so young sometimes. She was much older than me, of course, but not quite Dad's age. I never really knew what to make of her. Not that I disliked her or anything, but I always wondered why she was the only woman Dad worked with.

"Anything I could help you with?" I offered.

She looked down, thinking it over. "I'm not sure how widely he'd want to share this information, so I don't think so. Sorry."

I smiled, knowing she meant it. "No problem. Lady Brice, can I ask you a question? You're very smart and kind. Why haven't you ever married?"

She giggled a little. "I am married. To this job! It means a lot to me, and I'd rather do it well than seek out a spouse."

I rolled my eyes. "Amen to that."

"I know you understand. And the only people I ever get to see are the other advisers, and I don't think I'd want to be in a relationship with any of them. So I'll just keep working."

I nodded. "I respect that. I think people assume women aren't happy without a husband and children, but you seem quite satisfied."

She shrugged. "I think about it. I might adopt one day. I do think motherhood is an honor. And not everyone does it well."

The hint of bitterness in her tone made me think she was

referring to her own mother, but I didn't want to ask about specifics.

"I know. I'm fortunate to have such a wonderful one."

She sighed, melting a little. "Your mom is a natural. In a way, she was like a second mother to me when I was younger, and I learned a lot from her."

I squinted. "I didn't realize you'd been around the palace that long." I tried to remember if there was a time when I hadn't seen her in the hallways, though I'd never paid much attention to the advisers until I hit thirteen and started working with Dad in earnest. Perhaps I simply didn't notice.

"Yes, miss. I've been here almost as long as you," she replied with a laugh. "Your parents are far too generous."

Eighteen years was a long time to hold a position in the palace, especially as an adviser. Dad switched most people in and out every five to eight years based on recommendations and the mood of the country. What kept Lady Brice in her place for so long?

I studied her as she swept her hair over her shoulder and smiled. Had Dad let her stay because she was attractive? No. I felt guilty for even thinking Dad could be capable of being that shallow or selfish.

"Well, I'm sorry I can't help you, but I'll tell Dad you came by."

"Thanks, Your Highness. It's not terribly urgent, so there's no rush. You have a good day."

"You, too."

She curtsied and left, and I watched the door long after she was gone, curious about this woman I'd apparently known all my life without realizing it. I shrugged it away, turning back to my papers. Between the Selection and work, there was no room in my head for Lady Brice.

CHAPTER 21

DINNER THAT NIGHT WAS PLEASANT because I could tell the boys had learned from Jack's mistake. They all sat a little taller as I entered, nodding their heads as I passed, and I sensed that, once again, I'd regained control.

Dad looked a little calmer as well, though I could tell he hadn't quite let go of all his worry. Ahren leaned across the table to give me a conspiratorial wink, and it was almost like this terrible thing had made life a little better.

Dad had suggested that I try to make conversation with the boys at dinner, but calling out over all those people felt rude. I didn't think I could do that, at least not in a way that felt natural. I knew that, even with what I'd gone through, I was expected to get back out there. Instead of talking, I looked at my options. . . .

Of all the boys left, Ean struck me as the most intimidating.

Not because he seemed violent in any way, but because of that constant pride and calmness that hung around him, like an earthquake couldn't make him move if he didn't want it to.

So maybe going out with him next would conquer a fear in some way. There was no way he was as impervious as he seemed. We'd simply need to do something in the open and make sure the photographers came.

As if he could read my thoughts, Ean looked up at me at that very second, and I turned away, pretending to be engrossed with my brother.

I noticed Kaden was reading a newspaper beneath the table.

"What's that article about?" I asked.

He answered without looking away, like he was trying to finish his day's work before the end of dinner. "A collection going around in an area in Midston. They're raising money for a girl to go to art school. She's talented, but she can't afford to study on her own. She says . . . hold on. Here it is. 'I come from a line of Threes. My family thinks it's beneath me to study art, even though the castes no longer exist. It's hard. I remind them that the queen was born a Five, and she's brilliant. They won't pay for my schooling, so I'm asking for help to pursue my dreams.'

"Look at the picture of her paintings. They aren't bad."

I grew up with a deep appreciation for art, and while her work wasn't an aesthetic I particularly cared for, I could see she was talented.

"They're good. It's so silly. The point of getting rid of the castes was so people could have the choice of whatever profession they wanted, and they're not even using it. It's almost like they don't want it to work."

"Setting up a system to allow something doesn't mean people will do it."

"Obviously," I commented coldly, sipping my drink.

"The key is to make them understand that. Do you remember Mom showing us those old history books and how the United States had that paper"—he paused to think of the name—"the Declaration of Independence? And it said the people were allowed to pursue happiness. But no person making that document could actually hand over happiness."

I smiled. "You're too smart."

"I'd take that as a compliment, but last week you were caught kissing Kile in the dark."

"Oh, ha ha ha," I said, tempted to stick out my tongue at him. "It's not like my opinion ever mattered much anyway."

"Are you going to marry Kile?"

I nearly choked. "No!"

Kaden laughed wildly, making most of the room look our way.

"I take it back," I said, dabbing my lips. "You are a singularly gifted idiot!"

I stood, flicking Kaden's ear as I passed. "Hey!"

"Thanks for being there for me, Kaden. You're a great brother."

He rubbed at his ear, still grinning. "I try."

Marry Kile, I thought, doing my best not to burst out laughing again. If he could continue to be discreet, the chances of me kissing Kile again were very, *very* high . . . but I couldn't imagine actually being married to him.

I wasn't sure I could imagine being married to any of these boys.

I wasn't sure I could imagine being married at all. . . .

I slowed, looking at some of their faces as I passed. What would it be like to fall asleep next to Hale? Or to have Baden slip a ring on my finger?

I tried to picture it and couldn't. I remembered Ahren mentioning that some of the Selected asked him if it was possible I liked girls, but even thinking about that made me laugh. I knew that wasn't what was stopping me from genuinely being able to connect with a boy . . . but I sensed now that something was. It wasn't simply a desire to be independent; there was a wall around me, and I wasn't completely sure why.

But wall or no wall, I'd made a promise.

When I got to Ean, I paused.

"Mr. Cabel?"

He stood and bowed. "Yes, Your Highness."

"Do you ride horses?"

"I do."

"Would you like to accompany me on a ride tomorrow?"

A wicked glint came into his eye. "I would."

"Excellent. See you then."

★ ★ ★

I chose to wear a dress and do the whole thing sidesaddle. It wasn't my favorite way to ride, but I thought a touch of femininity would add to the purpose of the afternoon.

When I walked out to the stables, Ean was waiting for me, saddling his horse.

"Ean!" I called as I approached.

He lifted his head and waved. He was very handsome, the kind of person I thought people expected to see next to me. Every action of his was controlled, and I was determined to match him and not let myself be anxious.

"Are you ready?" he asked.

"Almost. I need to grab my saddle." I walked past him into the stalls.

"Is that what you're going to wear?"

I whipped back around. "I can do more in ten minutes wearing this dress than most men can do all day wearing pants."

He laughed. "I don't doubt it."

Butterscotch was at the back, in a slightly wider stall than most of the others. A princess's horse deserved some space and a good view.

I prepped her and walked back to Ean. "If you don't mind, we're going to take some photos in the garden first."

"Oh. No, that's fine."

We took our horses by the reins and walked them around to the garden. A man with a camera was there, snapping shots of the sky or trees as he waited. When he saw us, he came over.

"Your Highness," he greeted, shaking my hand. "I'm Peter. I thought it'd be nice to get a few pictures of the two of you together."

"Thank you." I petted Butterscotch. "Where do you want us?"

Peter looked around. "If you can put the horses by a tree, I think a couple of shots in front of this fountain would look nice."

I let go of Butterscotch, knowing she wouldn't run. "Come on," I said warmly.

Once he had tied his horse to a branch, I took his hands. Peter wasted no time. Ean and I smiled and looked shyly away from each other, and this little walk was documented in pictures. We stood in front of the fountain, sat against a shrub, and even took a couple of pictures in front of the horses.

When Peter announced that would be plenty, I nearly threw my arms up in celebration. He walked off rather quickly, grabbing his bags and double-checking his camera. I looked around, and as promised, we weren't completely alone. Guards lined the palace walls, and a few workers moved around the grounds, tending the grass and paths.

"Here, Butterscotch!" I walked up to her, and she flicked her tail.

Ean masterfully mounted his horse, and I was happy that he was as competent as he'd led me to believe.

"Forgive me, but that seemed a bit staged," Ean said as we trotted toward the edge of the lawn.

"I know. But allowing them to capture staged moments means that I get to keep the candid moments private."

"Interesting. So, was that scene with Kile staged or private, then?"

I smirked. Wow, he was quick.

"Last time we spoke, it sounded like you had something you wanted to talk about," I reminded him.

"I do. I want to be honest with you. But that will require you being completely honest with me. Can you do that?"

Looking into his face, I wasn't sure I could give him what he asked for. Not today.

"That depends."

"On?"

"Many things. I don't tend to divulge my soul to people I've only known two weeks."

We trotted on for a few minutes in silence.

"Favorite food?" he asked, a satisfied smile on his face.

"Do mimosas count?"

He chuckled. "Sure. What else . . . favorite place you've ever visited?"

"Italy. Partly for the food and partly for the company. If they come here, you have to meet the royal family. They're too much fun."

"I'd like that. Okay, favorite color?"

"Red."

"Power color. Nice."

He stopped quizzing me for a moment, and we continued on our path around the palace. It was kind of peaceful. We passed the front gates, and the gardeners stopped their work and bowed as we went by. Once we were out of their hearing, Ean brought his horse closer to mine.

"I could be very wrong, but I'm going to take a guess at some things about you."

"Go ahead," I dared.

He hesitated. "Hold on. Let's stop over here."

Along the palace wall there was a lone bench, and we pulled up to it.

I hopped off Butterscotch and sat on the small space with Ean.

"Your Highness."

"Eadlyn."

"Eadlyn." He swallowed, showing the first chink in his super-confident armor. "I get the feeling that the Selection isn't something you truly wanted to do."

I said nothing.

"If it was, perhaps it's not what you thought it would be, and now you're in a situation you don't particularly like. Most women would die to have dozens of men at their beck and call, but you come across as distant."

I smiled kindly. "I told you. I don't open up to people I just met."

He shook his head. "I've seen you on the *Report* for years. You seem above something like this."

I inhaled deeply, unsure what to say.

"I come to you with an offer. You may not need it at all, but I want to present the option all the same."

"What could you, sir, offer to your future queen?"

He smiled, seeming sure of himself again. "A way out."

It was risky to ask what he meant, but I couldn't help being curious. "How?"

"I would never hold you down. I would never hold you back. I wouldn't even ask you to love me. If you choose me, you can have a marriage free of conventional restraints. Make me your king, and you would be free to reign however you see fit."

I brushed out my dress. "You would never be king."

He tilted his head comically. "Not your type?"

I rolled my eyes. "That's neither here nor there. Any man who married me would never be king. He would be a prince consort, as no one can hold a title higher than mine."

"I'd take that."

I leaned on the arm of the bench. "Out of curiosity, why make such an offer? You're very charismatic, quite handsome. I'd assume you could have a marriage filled with happiness, which makes me wonder why you would commit yourself to one you just admitted would be loveless."

He nodded. "That's a fair question. Personally, I believe love to be overrated."

I couldn't help but smile.

"I come from a large family. Six children. I've managed to scrape by, but I don't want to live that life forever. The chance at a comfortable life with an agreeable woman is better than anything else I can hope for."

"Agreeable?" I raised an eyebrow. "Is that it?"

He chuckled. "I like you. You are yourself at all costs. I certainly don't consider marrying a clever, beautiful, powerful woman settling. And I can offer you the means to an end if you find no one suitable in this group. Honestly, I can tell you, the majority of these guys are jokes. And you can give me something I've never had."

I considered. So far the Selection hadn't been anything I'd expected. It had opened with people assaulting me with food, complaining about my first elimination, and judging my kiss with Kile. Even though I was just figuring out that, for me, there was something inherently unappealing about getting married, I couldn't help but wonder if I'd take someone simply for the sake of making Dad happy. Every time I looked into his eyes, I was more and more aware of how tired he seemed.

I loved my dad.

But I also loved myself.

And I would have to live with me much longer.

"You don't have to say yes or no," Ean said, drawing me back to the moment. "I'm simply saying that I'm here if you need me."

I nodded. "I can't say if I'll even consider it." I stood. "For now let's continue our ride. I don't get to see my Butterscotch nearly enough."

And we did ride for quite a while longer, but Ean didn't speak much. It was comfortable in a way not to be burdened with the need to make conversation. Ean would take my silence gratefully. I wondered if that could last, if he would eventually tire of that kind of life.

For the time being I studied him. Handsome, proud, straightforward. His confidence didn't hinge on my approval, and I knew I wouldn't worry about receiving his. I could possibly be married without actually *feeling* like I was. . . .

He might be a very attractive suitor, indeed.

CHAPTER 22

I SENT EAN IN SHORTLY thereafter, and he didn't protest at all, maybe proving right away that he would be as compliant as I needed him to be. It was certainly an interesting proposition, though I'd have to get much further along in this process before I could know if I'd need to use it or not.

Too soon, I had to get ready for dinner, so I put Butterscotch away and took a brush to my boots. I wasn't terribly dirty. "Night, night," I whispered to my horse, slipping her a piece of sugar before heading back to the palace.

"Eadlyn!" someone called as I entered the palace.

It was Kile. He was talking with Henri, Erik, Fox, and Burke. He gave the others a sign to wait for him and jogged down the hall to me.

"Hey," he said, his crooked smile settling on his face. He looked a little nervous.

"How are you?"

"Good. I was talking with some of the guys, and we have a proposal for you."

I sighed. "Another one?"

"Huh?"

"Nothing." I shook my head to clear it. "Should I come speak to them now?"

"Well, yeah, but I wanted to ask you something first."

"Sure."

Kile stuffed his hands in his pockets. "Are we okay?"

I squinted. "Kile, you realize you're not actually my boyfriend, right?"

He chuckled. "Yeah, I do. But, I don't know, I liked having someone to show my designs to and laugh with, and I wanted to come check on you after I heard about Jack, but I was afraid you wouldn't want to talk about it. Then I was afraid that staying away would make you upset, too. Do you know how difficult you are?"

"I'd forget, but you keep reminding me!" I teased.

Kile fidgeted. "I'll ease up. But seriously, are we okay?"

I watched as he bit his lip, and I had to fight myself from daydreaming about them. He said he was here for me, so I hoped, maybe, I'd get to feel those lips again.

"Yes, Kile. We're okay. Don't worry so much."

"All right. Come over here. I think you're going to like this idea."

We turned and walked down to the cluster of boys waiting. Henri immediately kissed my hand.

"Hello today," he greeted, making me laugh.

"Hello, Henri. Burke, Fox. Hi, Erik."

"Your Highness," Burke began. "Maybe this is a little out of line, but we were thinking that the Selection is a very challenging time for you."

I chuckled. "You have no idea."

Fox smiled. He and Burke looked a little comical next to each other. Burke was so burly, and he was so lean. "It has to be crazy. You have your work to do, and then you need to find time to do solo dates or try to get around to everyone at a party. It seems exhausting."

"So we had an idea," Kile said. "Could the four of us do something with you this week?"

This was completely brilliant. "Yes!" I exclaimed. "That would be great. Any ideas on what to do?"

"We were thinking about cooking together." Burke's face was so happy, I couldn't say no, even though that was exactly what I wanted to do.

"Cooking?" I said, a fake smile plastered on my face.

"Come on," Kile urged. "It'll be fun."

I exhaled nervously. "All right. Cooking. How about tomorrow night?"

"Perfect!" Fox said quickly, like he was worried I'd change my mind.

"Okay. Thursday, six o'clock. I'll meet you in the foyer, and we can walk to the kitchens together." This was going to be a nightmare. "If you'll excuse me, I have to get ready for dinner."

I headed upstairs wondering if there was any way to make this better. I doubted it.

"Neena," I called, walking into my room.

"Yes, miss?"

"Can you start a bath? I need one before dinner."

"Certainly."

I wrestled with my boots and flung off my dress. Besides the simple giving and responding to orders, we hadn't spoken much lately, and I had to admit, it was hard on me. My room was my retreat, the place I rested and sketched and hid from the world. Neena was a part of that, and her being upset with me set everything off-kilter.

I walked into the bathroom, happy to find that she was dropping pieces of lavender into the tub without me asking.

"Neena, you're a mind reader."

"I try," she said slyly.

I moved cautiously, not wanting to anger her again. "Have you heard from Mark recently?"

It seemed she couldn't help her smile. "Yes, just yesterday."

"What did you say he studied again?" I slipped into the warm water, already feeling better.

"Biochemistry." She looked down. "I admit, he uses plenty of words I don't understand when he tells me about it, but I get the idea of what he means."

"I wasn't trying to imply I thought you were stupid, Neena. I was curious. I thought that was obvious." Biochemistry. Something about that rang a bell.

She sighed and dropped more lavender into the bath. "It

came out much harsher than that."

"There are boys here from very different walks of life than mine. I can hardly stand to be in the same room with some of them. It was intriguing that the two of you do such varied jobs and still manage to share common ground."

She shook her head. "We work. It's not something you can figure out on paper. Some people are meant to be together."

I leaned back in the tub. If there was no way to explain anything, then why bother? I thought again of Ean's offer and Kile's worry and Hale's questions. I couldn't believe how murky everything had become. I barely understood my own feelings anymore. I knew I wanted my independence, and the idea of any man coming up behind me trying to fix my work or do it for me was unacceptable. Then I thought of Dad's gray hairs, slowly mixing in with the blond, and wondered how far I'd go to make his life easier.

It was strange. Basically, every boy downstairs was an option, if I really had to choose one. And each of them could easily hurl my world into a new trajectory. I didn't like that. I wanted to be in charge of my path. I wondered if that was the reason for putting a fence around myself, if it was the worry that anyone who crossed it would take away my control.

But maybe that control was an illusion. Even if I passed on all the Selected boys, would someone eventually come along and make me not even care about control? Would he cause me to hand it over willingly?

It seemed impossible, something I certainly couldn't have

imagined happening a few weeks ago.

There were still plenty of reasons to keep my guard up, and I knew I would. Still, I didn't think I'd be able to ignore the way these boys were affecting me much longer.

CHAPTER 23

I WAITED NERVOUSLY IN THE palace foyer. I wasn't sure about what I was wearing—what did people wear to cook?—or how to fake expertise in the kitchen or how to disperse attention evenly among four suitors.

And while I knew having a photographer there was both good for publicity and personal safety, the idea of someone documenting this night did not make me feel any less jittery.

I pulled at my shirt, which was rather plain in case I got dirty, and touched my hair, making sure it was still in place. The clock showed the boys were four minutes late, and I was getting antsy.

Just as I was about to send a butler to fetch them, I heard the echo of voices in the hallway. Kile rounded the corner first. Burke was right beside him, clearly trying to buddy up to the alleged leader of the pack. Fox was with Henri, both smiling quietly. Not far behind, Erik walked with his hands tucked behind him. His presence was necessary, but I sensed he felt a little out of place as the sole nonparticipant in a group date.

Kile rubbed his hands together. "You ready to eat?"

"Eat, yes. Cook? We'll see how that goes." I tried to hide my worry with a smile, but I think Kile knew.

"So is it true you two have known each other your whole lives?" Burke asked. It was so abrupt, I didn't know how to respond.

"Trust me, you've got the better end of the deal," Kile replied smoothly, elbowing him in the ribs.

"It's true," I confirmed. "It's like Kile said on the *Report*: I never considered him boyfriend material until I was forced to. He's like family."

Everyone laughed, and I realized how true that was. It annoyed me whenever Josie told people she was like my sister, but I did know both her and Kile better than I knew my cousins.

"The kitchen is this way," I said, pointing past them to the dining hall. "The staff knows we're coming, so let's go cook."

Kile shook his head at my fake enthusiasm but said nothing.

We walked to the back of the dining hall and rounded a partition. There was a wide dumbwaiter the staff used to bring up carts of food next to a stairwell that led to the main kitchen. Burke rushed to my side quickly, offering his arm as we traveled down the wide steps.

"What do you want to cook tonight?" he asked.

I wondered if my face showed my shock. I really thought someone else would be providing the ideas.

"Oh, I'm kind of up for whatever," I hedged.

"Let's make courses," Kile suggested. "An appetizer, an entrée, and a dessert."

"That sounds good," Fox agreed.

Erik piped up from the back. "Henri and I will do dessert, if that's all right."

"Sure," Kile answered.

I could smell the dinner that was being prepared for the rest of the palace. I couldn't pinpoint everything, but there was a delicious hint of garlic in the air, and I suddenly had a new reason to hate this date: I had to postpone actually eating.

In a low-ceilinged room, a dozen people with their hair pulled back tightly or tucked under scarves were running around, tossing vegetables into pots of steaming water or double-checking the seasonings of the sauces. Despite the fact that there was still a meal to finish preparing for everyone in the palace, the staff had cleared half of the space for us to use.

A man in a tall chef's hat approached us. "Your Highness. Will this be enough room?"

"More than enough, thank you."

I remembered his face from a few weeks ago when he'd presented me with the sample ideas for the first dinner. I'd been so annoyed at the time, Mom did most of the choosing, and I hadn't even thought to thank him. Looking around and seeing how much work was going into a single meal, I felt ashamed of myself.

"*Missä pidät hiivaa?*" Henri asked politely.

My eyes went to Erik, who spoke up. "Pardon me, sir, but where do you keep your yeast?"

Fox and Burke giggled, but I remembered what Erik had told me once and what was crudely worded on Henri's own application: he was a cook.

The chef waved Henri down, and he and Erik followed him closely, trying to chat. The chef was clearly excited to have someone with some experience in the room. The other boys . . . not so much.

"Okay, so . . . let's go see what's in the fridge." Fox hesitantly led the way to one of several large refrigerators along the wall. I looked at the organized contents—parchment-wrapped meats labeled in pencil, the four different types of milk we used, and the various sauces or starters prepped and stored ahead of time—and knew I was way out of my league.

I heard a click and turned to see the photographer had arrived.

"Just pretend I'm not here!" she whispered cheerfully.

Kile grabbed some butter. "You always need butter," he assured me.

I nodded. "Good to know."

Burke found a pile of something on the counter. He turned to the chef. "What is this?"

"Phyllo paper. You can make dozens of things with that. Melt some of that butter, and I'll get you some recipes."

Kile gave me a face. "See?"

"How do we want to decide who works together?" Burke asked, obviously hoping I'd simply go with him.

"Rock, paper, scissors?" Fox suggested.

"That's fair," Kile agreed. He and Fox went up against each other first, and though no one said it one way or the other, they knew the losers would be stuck with each other.

Kile beat both Fox and Burke. Fox took it in stride, but Burke had no talent at masking his emotions. The two of them picked an appetizer to make together—asparagus wrapped with prosciutto and phyllo—while Kile and I were left staring at some chicken, trying to figure out what to do with it.

"So, what's step one?" I asked.

"I cooked plenty when I was away in Fennley, but I need a recipe at least. I bet those books would help." We walked over to a cupboard that contained dozens of cookbooks. Most of them had markers hanging in multiple places, and there were piles of note cards next to them with more ideas.

As Kile flipped through the pages, I played with the jars of herbs. The kitchen made me think of what a scientist's lab would look like, only with food. I opened some, inhaling them or feeling the texture.

"Smell this," I insisted, holding up a jar to Kile.

"What's that?"

"Saffron. Doesn't it smell delicious?"

He smiled at me and went straight to the back of the book he was holding. "Aha!" he said, turning forward to find his page. "Saffron chicken. Want to give that a try?"

"Sure." I clutched the jar in my hand like it was my big contribution to the night.

"All right. Saffron chicken . . . so, let's preheat the oven."

I stood next to him, staring at the buttons and dials. Probably the ovens in normal people's homes didn't look like this, but this massive, industrial setup seemed like it might launch a satellite if we touched the wrong thing. We looked at the stove like it might give us some instructions if we waited long enough.

"Should I get more butter?" I asked.

"Shut up, Eadlyn."

The chef walked past and mumbled, "Dial on the left, three fifty."

Kile reached over and turned it as if he knew what to do the whole time.

I glanced toward Fox and Burke. Burke was clearly acting as their leader and loudly giving orders. Fox didn't seem to mind at all, laughing and joking without being obnoxious. They peeked back over at us several times, Burke sneaking in a wink now and then. Past them, Erik and Henri were working quietly, with Erik doing a minimal amount of labor, only assisting when Henri asked for it.

Henri's sleeves were rolled up and he'd gotten some flour

on his pants, and I kind of loved that he didn't seem to care about it. Erik was a little messy himself, and he didn't bother wiping any of it off either.

I looked at Kile, who was buried in the cookbook. "I'll be right back."

"Sure." As I walked away, I heard him quietly try to get the chef's attention.

"Looking good, boys," I said, pausing by Fox.

"Thanks. This is actually kind of soothing. I never cooked much at home, nothing like this anyway. But I'm looking forward to trying it." Fox's hands stuttered for a moment, trying to find his rhythm again.

"This will be the best asparagus you've ever had," Burke promised.

"I can't wait," I replied, moving to the far end of the table.

Erik looked up, greeting me with a smile. "Your Highness. How's our dinner looking?"

"Very bad indeed," I promised. He chuckled and told Henri the state of our poor supper.

Their hands were covered in dough, and I could see bowls of cinnamon and sugar waiting to be used. "This looks promising though. Do you cook as well, Erik?"

"Oh, not professionally. But I live on my own, so I cook for myself, and I love all the traditional Swendish foods. This is a favorite."

Erik turned to Henri, and I could tell they were talking about food because Henri was alight with excitement.

"Oh, yeah! Henri was just saying there's this soup he has

when he's sick. It's got potatoes and fish, and, oh, I miss my mother just thinking about it."

I smiled, trying to imagine Erik alone trying to master his mother's meals and Henri in the back of a restaurant already having conquered every recipe in his family's memory. I kept worrying that Erik felt like an outcast. He certainly worked to separate himself from the Selected. He dressed differently, walked at a slower pace, and even carried himself a little lower. But watching him here, interacting with Henri, who was too kind for me to dismiss, I was so grateful for his presence. He brought a little piece of home to a situation twice removed from Henri's idea of normal.

I stepped away, allowing them to work, and went back to my station. Kile had collected some ingredients in my absence. He was dicing garlic on a wooden brick next to a bowl of something that looked like yogurt.

"There you are," he greeted. "Okay, crush those saffron threads and then mix them in the bowl."

After a moment of blank staring, I picked up the tiny bowl and mallet I assumed was meant for thread crushing and started pressing. It was a strangely satisfying exercise. Kile did most of the work, smothering the chicken with the yogurt mix and throwing it in the oven. The other teams were at various stages of prep as well, and in the end, the dessert was ready first, followed by the appetizer, and our entrée pulled up the rear.

Realizing belatedly that Kile and I should have made something to go with our chicken, we decided to use the wrapped asparagus as a side, all laughing at how poorly we'd planned this.

The whole lot of us crowded around one end of the long table. I was sandwiched between Burke and Kile, with Henri across from me and Fox at the head. Erik was slightly removed but still clearly enjoying the company.

Honestly, I was, too. Cooking made me nervous because it was totally foreign to me. I didn't know how to cut or sauté or anything, and I despised failing or looking foolish. But the majority of us had limited experience, and instead of it becoming a stressor, it became a joke, making this one of the most relaxed meals I'd ever had. No formal place settings, no assigned seats; and since nearly all the china was in use for our very full house, we were using plain plates that looked so old, the only reason they could possibly still be here was sentimentality.

"Okay, since they were supposed to be the appetizer, I think we should try the asparagus first," Kile insisted.

"Let's do it." Burke speared his asparagus and took a bite, and we all followed. It appeared the results were inconsistent. Henri nodded approvingly, but mine tasted awful. I could tell Fox's was bad as well based on his poorly concealed grimace.

"That . . . that is the worst thing I've ever tasted," Fox said, trying to chew.

"Mine's good!" Burke said defensively. "You're probably just not used to eating such quality food."

Fox ducked his head, and I gathered something I wouldn't

have known otherwise: Fox was poor.

"Can I try a bite of yours?" I whispered to Henri, using my hands and happy to find he understood without Erik's help.

"Do you mind?" Fox replied quietly, and I pretended to be too focused on the food to hear him. And Henri's piece actually was much better. "Who's to say it's not because of your cooking?"

"Well, maybe if I had a better partner," Burke snapped.

"Hey, hey, hey!" Kile insisted. "There's no way yours could be worse than ours."

I giggled, trying to break the tension. I could feel Burke's anger like an actual, physical thing hanging in the air, and I wanted nothing more than to return to the relaxed feeling we had when we'd sat down.

"All right," I said with a sigh. "I think the first thing we need to do is cut each piece of chicken in half to make sure it's cooked through. I seriously don't want to kill anyone."

"Are you doubting me?" Kile asked, offended.

"Definitely!"

I took a tentative bite . . . and it was pretty good. It wasn't undercooked; in fact, some of the edges were a little dry where the paste hadn't covered it all. But it was edible! Considering that I'd only done a fraction of the work, I was maybe a little too proud.

We ate, sharing pieces of the asparagus that hadn't turned out too bad, though I genuinely worried I might be sick later.

Finally, I'd had enough. "I'm ready for dessert!"

Henri chuckled in understanding and went over to where his pastries were cooling on a rack. With careful movements, only using the edges of his fingers even though the rolls seemed firm, he transferred them all to a plate and set them in front of us.

"Is *korvapuusti*," he said, giving the dish a name. Then, taking my hand, he gave me a very important speech; I could tell by the intensity in his eyes. I wished so badly that I could understand him on my own.

When he finished, Erik smiled and turned to me.

"*Korvapuusti* is one of Henri's favorite things to prepare as well as eat. He says that if you do not like it, you should send him home tonight, for he's sure your relationship could not survive if you aren't as in love with this as he is."

Fox laughed at my shocked face, but Henri nodded, assuring me he meant it.

I took a deep breath and picked up one of the delicately rolled pastries. "Here goes nothing."

Right away I could taste the cinnamon. There was something else in there that reminded me of grapefruit . . . but I knew that wasn't it. It was deliciously sweet, but more than it being a fantastic recipe, I could tell it was made by a fantastic *chef.* Henri had poured himself into this. And I was willing to bet part of that was for me . . . but I thought it was mostly for himself, that he couldn't allow himself to make it anything less than incredible.

I was blown away. "It's perfect, Henri."

The others grabbed pieces and shoved them into their mouths, grunting in approval.

"My mom would be dying right now. She has such a sweet tooth!" I said.

Kile was nodding with his eyes wide. He knew how she was about desserts. "This is great, Henri. Nice job to you, too, Erik."

Erik shook his head. "I barely helped."

"Was this rigged?" Burke asked, his mouth half full with the pastry.

We all looked at him, confused.

"I mean, I came up with this idea, and then Henri jumped in on it just to show the rest of us up."

His face was turning red, and that feeling of unease was filling the room again.

Fox put a hand on his shoulder. "Calm down, man. It's just a cinnamon roll."

Burke shrugged it off and threw the rest of his dessert across the room. "I would have done way better if you weren't there screwing me up the whole time!"

Fox made a face. "Hey, you were the one standing there talking about how hot she was when you should have been watch—"

Burke threw a punch that knocked Fox back several steps. I sucked in a breath, frozen. Fox came back at him, and I was pushed to the floor by Burke's arm pulling back for another punch.

"WHOA!" Kile jumped over me and started pulling at

Burke, while Henri was yelling at Fox in Finnish. After everything with Jack, my new instinct was to get back up and throw a punch. No one was going to hurt me and get away with it. And I might have tried if it wasn't for one thing.

Erik, the quiet observer, had launched himself over the table to pick me up.

"Come," he said.

I wasn't particularly a fan of obeying orders. But he said it so urgently, I followed.

CHAPTER 24

ERIK RUSHED ME UP THE stairs and into the dining hall. Everyone else in the palace was in the middle of their dinner, and the room felt too loud.

"Eadlyn?" Daddy called, but Erik kept me moving, somehow knowing that I couldn't bear to stay there. He only paused when we got to the end of the room, and just long enough to pass along the problem.

"Pardon me, officer, some of the Selected are in a fight in the kitchen. It's very physical, and it looked to be escalating."

"Thank you." The officer motioned to two other guards, and they followed him as he ran toward the fray.

I realized I was hugging myself, both frightened and enraged. Erik gently placed a hand on my back and ushered me away. My parents were calling after me, but I couldn't deal with that many people right now, surrounding me, asking questions.

He slowed and asked me quietly, "Where do you want to go?"

"My room."

"Lead the way."

He didn't touch me exactly, except for the occasional brush against my back, which made me realize he must have kept his hand there the whole time, inches away from me, just in case. I pushed open my door, and Neena was inside, polishing the table, filling the room with the scent of lemons.

"My lady?"

I held up a hand.

"Maybe go get her some tea?" Erik offered.

She nodded and rushed away.

I walked over to my bed and took a few deep breaths. Erik stood there, calm and silent.

"I've never seen anything like that," I confessed. He got down on a knee so he was level with me. "My father has never so much as swatted my hand, and he's always taught us to seek peaceful resolutions. Ahren and I gave up trying to fight each other before we could really talk."

I remembered this all with a laugh.

"When we were down there, all I could think about was how I ran from Jack. Burke knocked me to the ground, and this time I was going to fight back, but I just realized I'd have no idea how to do it."

Erik smiled. "Henri says, when you're upset, the look in your eyes is as strong as a punch. You're not powerless."

I ducked my head, thinking of how I told myself over and

over that no one in the world was as powerful as me. There was truth to it, sure. But if Jack had pinned me to the ground or Burke had turned his fists on me, my crown would have done me no good until after the fact. I could punish, but I couldn't prevent.

"You know, boy or girl, I think aggression is a sign of weakness. I'm always more impressed when people can end something with words." His eyes were seeing another place and time when he went on. "Maybe that's why language became so important to me. My father, he always used to say 'Eikko, words are weapons. They are all you need.'"

"Ayco?" I asked.

He grinned, a little embarrassed. "E-I-K-K-O. Like I said, Erik is the closest in English."

"I like it. Really."

He turned his attention back to me, looking at my arms. "Are you hurt?"

"Oh . . . umm, I don't think so." I felt a little sore from hitting the ground, but it was nothing serious. "I just can't believe how fast it happened."

"I don't want to excuse either of them at all—that was unacceptable—but I hear the guys talking, and they're stressed. They all want to impress you, but they have no idea how to do it, considering who you are. Some talk about trying to undermine others without getting caught. A few are working out at every turn to be physically superior. I understand that it's a lot of pressure, and that's probably why Burke snapped. But that will never make it okay."

"I'm so sorry you have to be around that."

He shrugged. "It's fine. Mostly I just stick with Henri and Kile, sometimes Hale, and they're good company. Not that I'd ever try to choose for you, but the three of them are a pretty safe place to start."

I smiled. "I think you're right." Though I hadn't spent one-on-one time with everyone yet, I already knew Hale was a good guy. And seeing Henri so excited about his food tonight, about this part of his life, gave me a glimpse of the person behind the barrier. And Kile . . . well, I didn't know what to make of Kile, but he was a better companion than I'd given him credit for.

"Would you tell Henri for me how wonderful his food was? I could tell how important it was to him, and I admire his passion."

"I will. Happily."

I extended my hand and he gave me his, resting them both on my knee. "Thank you so much for this. You really went above and beyond tonight, and I'm so thankful you were here."

"It's the least I could do."

I tilted my head, really looking at him. It felt like something had just happened, but I didn't know what it was.

Erik, without knowing me, had done so much right. He pulled me away before I made the situation worse, got me to solitude before I lost control of my emotions, and stayed with me, listening to my worries and making everything better with his words. There were scores of people on call, ready to do whatever I asked.

It was so funny to me that with him I didn't even have to ask.

"I won't forget this, Eikko. Not ever."

There was a tiny lift of a smile at the sound of his given name, and he squeezed my hand ever so slightly.

I remembered the feeling of my first date with Hale, how I felt when I was sure he'd peeled everything back and had seen the real me. This time, I felt like I was on the other side of that, looking past duty and worry and rank, seeing the true heart of a person.

And his was so beautiful.

Neena came back in carrying a tray, and Erik and I ripped our hands apart.

"Are you all right, my lady?"

"Yes, Neena," I promised her, standing. "There was a fight, but Erik got me away. I'm sure the guards will come with a report soon. In the meantime I just need to calm down."

"The tea will help. I got some chamomile, and we'll get you into something comfortable before you need to report anywhere," Neena said, already making my night easier by planning it.

I turned back to Erik, who was standing by the door. He bowed deeply.

"Goodnight, Your Highness."

"Goodnight."

He walked away quickly, and Neena came over, handing

me a cup of tea. The strange thing was, my hands were already so warm.

About an hour later I met Mom and Dad in the office to discuss what'd happened.

"Sir Fox looks pretty bad," a guard relayed. "Sir Henri tried to pull him away, but Sir Burke was practically unstoppable. Both Sir Henri and Sir Kile got some marks simply from trying to separate them."

"How bad?" I asked.

"Sir Henri has a bruise on his chest and a cut just above his eye. Sir Kile's lip was busted open, and there aren't any big scars besides that, but he feels sore from trying to contain Sir Burke."

"You can stop calling him 'Sir'!" Dad insisted. "Burke is leaving right now! The same for Fox!"

"Maxon, reconsider. Fox didn't do anything," Mom urged. "I agree it was inappropriate, but don't make that choice on Eadlyn's behalf."

"I will!" he yelled. "We did this to bring our people joy, to give our daughter a chance at the same happiness we have. And since it began, she's been assaulted twice! I will NOT have monsters like that under my roof!" He finished his speech, slamming his fist into a side table, knocking his tea onto the floor.

I stiffened, gripping the arms of my chair. "Daddy, stop," I pleaded, my words hushed with fear I might somehow make it worse.

He looked over his shoulder at me, as if he only now realized Mom and I were still in the room. His eyes instantly softened, and he turned away, shaking his head.

After a deep breath he straightened his suit and spoke to the guard. "Before anything continues, I expect thorough background checks on each of the Selected. Do it secretively and use whatever means possible. If anyone has so much as gotten into a squabble in grade school, I want them gone."

Calm again, he sat beside Mom. "I unconditionally insist that Burke leaves. That's not up for debate."

"But what about Fox?" Mom asked. "It sounds like he didn't really instigate anything."

Dad shook his head. "I don't know. The idea of letting anyone involved stay seems like very poor judgment."

Mom leaned her head on Dad's shoulder. "Once upon a time I was involved in a fight during the Selection, and you let me stay. Imagine how things would have been if you hadn't."

"Mom, you got into a fight?" I asked, dumbfounded.

"It's true," Dad confirmed, sighing.

Mom smiled. "I actually still think about the other girl often. She turned out to be quite lovely."

Dad huffed, his tone begrudging. "Fine. Fox can stay, but only if Eadlyn thinks he might be someone she'd have a chance at happiness with."

Their eyes settled on me, and I was confused about so many things at once, I felt positive it read on my face. I turned to the guard. "Thank you for your update. Have

Burke escorted from the premises and tell Fox I'll speak with him shortly. You can go now."

Once he left the room, I rose from my chair, trying to compose my thoughts.

"I'm not going to ask about that fight, though, for the life of me, I cannot figure out why you two have withheld so much about your Selection from me and have only decided to share some of the bigger bits and pieces now. And *after* I've faced something you've already experienced."

They sat there guiltily.

"Mom met you before she was supposed to," I accused, pointing to Dad. "Your candidates were all planted by your father. . . . Maybe you could have given me a heads-up about how to deal with a fight two weeks ago."

I crossed my arms, exhausted.

"I promised you three months, and I'm going to give you that," I said, taking in their worried expressions. "I'll go on dates and let people take pictures so we have something to print in the papers and to talk about on the *Report*. But you two seem to think that if I stick this out, I'm magically going to fall in love."

I stood there, shaking my head. "That's not going to happen. Not for me."

"It could," Mom whispered tenderly.

"I know I'm disappointing you, but it's not what I want. And these boys are fine, but . . . some of them make me uncomfortable, and I don't think they can handle the pressure of this position. I'm not going to handcuff myself to a weight for the sake of a distracting headline."

Dad stood. "Eadlyn, that's not what we want either."

"Then please"—I raised my hands in front of me, guarding myself—"stop pressuring me to fall for people I never wanted here in the first place."

I clasped my hands together. "This whole situation has been awful. I've had people throw food at me in public; others have judged me over a kiss. One boy touched me against my will, and another flung me to the ground. For all the effort I put in to make things right, the papers have had a field day with the constant shame."

They exchanged a concerned glance.

"When I said I'd help distract people, I didn't think it would be this degrading."

"Sweetheart, we were never trying to hurt you." Mom looked heartbroken, close to tears.

"I know, and I'm not mad. I just want my freedom. If this is what I have to do in order to get that, then I will. If you want your distraction, I'll deliver. But please don't place all those expectations on me. I don't want to let you down any more than I have already."

CHAPTER 25

I KNOCKED ON FOX'S DOOR, kind of hoping he wouldn't answer. It had been a draining night, and I wanted to go hide under my blankets.

Of course, his butler opened the door and pulled it so far back that Fox saw me before I could be announced.

He looked as bad as I'd been told. One eye was swollen and surrounded by varying shades of purple, and the opposite side of his head was covered in a bandage, as well as the knuckles across his right hand.

"Eadlyn!" he said, hopping up off his bed, then wincing and grabbing his ribs. "Sorry. I meant Your Highness."

"You can go," I said hurriedly to the butler as I rushed over to Fox.

"Sit," I urged. "Shouldn't you still be in the hospital wing?"

He shook his head as he settled down again. "I've been medicated, and they thought I'd rest better in my own room."

"How are you feeling?" I asked, though I could tell he was in pain.

"Besides the bruises?" he asked. "Humiliated."

"Can I join you?" I asked, pointing to the spot beside him on the edge of bed.

"Of course."

I sat, not sure where to start. I didn't want to send him home now, partly out of charity. I peeked at Burke's and Fox's applications before going to see Dad, and Fox had actually hinted at a lot about his home life on his form. Typically, I was looking for mutual interests or things we could talk about, so I'd missed some important details about him.

Living in Clermont, he worked as a lifeguard at the beach, which explained the sun-kissed skin and overly blond hair. I got the feeling that it wasn't paying enough to support the rest of his family, though that situation was a little unclear on paper. His mother wasn't living at home, but I didn't know if that meant she had passed or not. I also could see his father was terminally ill, so I doubted he was contributing to the finances.

Furthermore, if I'd paid attention at all, I would have noticed how much fuller his cheeks looked compared to the picture on his form now that he was getting fed properly.

I wanted him to stay. I wanted him to keep his stipend. I wanted him to steal some of the things from his room when he left and sell them when he got home.

But asking him to stay meant giving him hope.

"Listen," he started, "I understand if you have to send me home. I do. I don't want to leave, but I know the rules. I just . . . I don't want to leave with you thinking I'm like Burke or Jack. Try not to think poorly of me when I go, okay?"

"I won't. I don't."

Fox looked over and gave me a sad grin. "I never got to tell you so many things. Like how I wish I could command a room like you. It's so impressive. Or how your eyes sparkle when you make a joke. It's really pretty."

"Do they do that? Wait, do I make jokes?"

He chuckled. "Yeah. I mean, they're mostly subtle, but you give it away with your eyes. And I can see how pleased you are when you're teasing us. Like at the quiz the other day."

I smiled. "That was fun. Tonight was fun, too, up until the end."

"I'll never forget your face when you bit into that asparagus."

I pressed my lips together, pretty sure that his expression and mine had been similar. What made it better was that I knew how hard he'd tried, and he still wasn't upset over it. The only thing hurting him now was this worry that I'd remember him as something less than a gentleman.

"Fox, I'm going to ask you some questions, and I need you to be completely honest with me. If I think you're lying at all, that's it. You'll be gone within the hour."

He swallowed, the silliness of the last few moments fading from his face. "You have my word."

I nodded, believing him. "All right. Would you tell me about your dad?"

He huffed, clearly not expecting the conversation to head in this direction. "Umm, he's sick, which I guess you know. He's got cancer. He's still functioning pretty well. Like he's working, but it's only part-time right now. He needs a lot of sleep.

"When he got sick my mom left, so . . . I really don't want to talk about her, if that's okay."

"That's okay."

He looked at the floor as he continued. "I've got a brother and a sister, and they go on and on about her like she's coming back, but I know that's not happening. If she did, then *I'd* leave."

"We really don't have to talk about her, Fox."

"Sorry. You know, I thought the hardest part about coming here would be the distance, but what's so bad it almost hurts is seeing you with your family." He scratched at his hair with his good hand. "Your parents are still in love, and your brothers look at you like you're heaven on earth, and I wish I had that. I don't have anything close."

I put a hand on his back. "We're not perfect. I promise. And it sounds like you and your dad have something special."

"We do." He glanced over at me. "I didn't mean to get

like that. I don't talk about my family a lot."

"That's fine. I have other questions."

He sat up straight again, and I could see the pain of the action. I pulled my hand away and rolled my eyes. "Actually, I just realized this might be a hard one, too."

He smiled. "Go ahead anyway."

"Okay . . . did you come here for me or to get away from them?"

Fox paused, his eyes dead set on mine. "Both. I love my dad. I can't tell you how much he means to me, and I don't mind taking care of him, really. But it's also kind of tiring. It's been like a holiday here most of the time. I also think my brother and sister are starting to appreciate what I do, which is validating in a way.

"And then, there's you." He shook his head. "Look, you know I live paycheck to paycheck. And I come from a broken family. I realize I'm nothing special," he said, placing his hand on his chest. Then he suddenly got shy. "But, you know, I've watched you my whole life, and I've always thought you were so sharp and beautiful. I don't know if I stand the smallest chance of getting to be with you . . . but I had to at least put my name in. I don't know; I just thought if I could get here, I'd find a way to show you that I could be worth taking a chance on.

"And then I got in a fight." He shrugged. "So I guess that's how it ends."

I hated the disappointment in his voice. I didn't *want* to care. I knew that letting him get closer to me would end badly. I couldn't explain why I knew, but I was sure that if I allowed any of these boys to cross into a certain level of intimacy, it would be disastrous. So why—*why*—couldn't I keep them from getting closer?

"I have another question."

"Sure," he replied, defeated.

"What's it like to work on the beach all day?"

He didn't try to fight the smile. "It's wonderful. There's something kind of fascinating about the ocean. It's almost like it has different moods on different days. Like, sometimes the water is so still and other times it's wild. And I'm so glad Angeles is warm all the time, or I don't think I could have handled it."

"I love the weather here, too, but I don't get to go to the beach very often. Mom and Dad don't like it, and people end up swarming Ahren and me if we go just the two of us. It's kind of a pain."

He poked me gently. "If you ever come to Clermont, look me up. You can rent a private beach and swim and lounge to your heart's content."

I sighed dreamily. "That sounds perfect."

"I'm serious. It's the least I could do."

I looked at my hands and back to Fox's hopeful face. "How about this? If you make it to, say, the top three, we can go out there together and rent a beach, and maybe I could meet your dad."

His face froze in shock as he understood what that meant. "I'm not going home?"

"Tonight wasn't your fault. And I appreciate you being honest about your motivations. So, how about you stay a little longer, and we'll see how it goes?"

"I'd love that."

"All right then." I stood, feeling so many things. Before tonight Fox was hardly a draw for me, and now I was looking forward to seeing him around the palace. "Forgive me for dashing off, but there's a lot to take care of before the morning."

"I can imagine," he said, walking beside me to the door. "Thank you, Your Highness, for giving me a chance."

"That's all you wanted, right?" I smiled. "And you really can call me Eadlyn."

He grinned and used his good hand to pick up mine. He placed the gentlest kiss across the ridges of my fingers. "Goodnight, Eadlyn. And thank you again."

I gave him a quick nod before I scurried from the room. That was one issue taken care of . . . but tomorrow there would be a thousand more.

The photographer had done such a remarkable job of blending into the background, I didn't realize she was still there when the fight broke out. Burke and Fox were front-page news, and the headline proclaimed that the first was ejected while the second was spared. There were other pictures, too. Me, standing next to Kile, grinding saffron, and again beside Erik as he translated something to Henri. But they were all overshadowed by the animalistic rage on Burke's face as he threw himself at Fox.

I bypassed that photo for the smaller ones with the others, tearing them out to save. I wasn't sure why. I ended up tucking them into the drawer next to Kile's catastrophe of a tie.

I walked into breakfast feeling the weight of everyone's stares. Typically that wasn't an issue for me, but between all the boys being overcurious about the fight and my parents' worried eyes, I was buried beneath all the unspoken words.

I wondered if maybe I'd said too much last night, or if it had come off as me accusing them. I meant to explain how hurtful and draining this process had been, not to blame them for it. Still, as little as I wanted to participate, I knew I'd done what I'd promised. Burke's fists had overshadowed everything else in the country, at least for today.

"What happened?" Kaden whispered.

"Nothing."

"Liar. Mom and Dad have been messed up all morning."

I peeked over. Dad kept rubbing the spot over his eyebrow, and Mom was trying to fool everyone by moving the food around her plate.

I sighed. "It's grown-up stuff. You wouldn't understand."

He rolled his eyes. "Don't talk to me like that, Eadlyn. I'm fourteen, not four. I read all the papers, and I pay attention at the *Report*s. I speak more languages than you, and I'm learning all the things you have without anyone making me do it. Don't act like you're better than me. I'm a prince."

I sighed. "Yes, but I will be queen," I corrected, sipping my coffee. I really didn't need this right now.

"And your name will be in a history book one day, and some bored ten-year-old will memorize it for a test and then forget all about you. You have a job, just like everybody in the world. Stop acting like it makes you more or less than anyone else."

I was left speechless. Was that what Kaden really thought about me?

Was that what *everyone* thought about me?

I had intended to be strong today, to show Mom and Dad that I really was going to follow through and prove to the boys that things like last night could not break me. But Kaden's words made me—and all my efforts—seem worthless.

I stood up to leave, trying to think of what I'd need to grab from the office. I certainly couldn't work there today.

"Hey, Eadlyn, wait up."

It was Kile, jogging to catch up with me. I hadn't even looked at him when I went into the dining hall this morning. His lip was a little swollen, but he seemed okay otherwise.

"Are you all right?" he asked.

I nodded my head . . . then I shook it. "I really don't know."

He put his hands on my shoulders. "Everything's okay."

I was so overwhelmed, I pressed my lips into his, knowing that would make everything else stop for a minute.

"Ow!" he cried, backing away.

"Sorry! I just—"

He grabbed me by the wrist and swung me into the nearest

room, slammed the door, and pushed me against the wall. He kissed me harder than I'd kissed him, apparently not bothered by his lip so much if he knew what was coming.

"What's this all about?" he breathed.

"I don't want to think. Just kiss me."

Without a word, Kile drew me to him, his hands lost in my hair. I grabbed fistfuls of his shirt, holding on to him tightly.

And it worked. As we swayed together, everything else stopped mattering for a little while. His lips moved from my mouth and onto my neck. These kisses were different than before. They were aggressive and demanding, pulling all my focus. Without thinking about it, I dragged his shirt upward.

He laughed devilishly into my cheek. "Okay, if clothes are coming off, we really ought to go to a room. And you should probably know my middle name."

"Is it Ashton? Arthur? I feel like it starts with an *A*."

"Not even close."

I sighed, letting go of his clothes. "Fine."

He leaned back, his arms still around my waist, smirking at me. "Are you all right? I know last night was kind of scary."

"I just didn't expect it. It was asparagus. . . . He literally punched someone over a vegetable."

Kile laughed. "See, this is why you stick with butter."

"Oh, you and your stupid butter." I shook my head, tracing a finger down his chest. "I'm really sorry about your lip. Does anything else hurt?"

"My stomach. He elbowed me a few times trying to get free, but I'm surprised I didn't get it worse. Henri's eye looks painful. Glad he didn't get hit an inch lower."

I grimaced, thinking about how bad it could have been. "Kile, would you have kicked them both out? If you were in my position?"

"I think I would have even had to consider Henri and me if I were you," he replied.

"But you both tried to stop it."

He raised a finger. "True. You know that because you were there. But the others have seen the papers, and the pictures make it look like we were all involved."

"So keeping Fox, Henri, and you makes it seem as if you got away with something?"

"And that maybe others could, too."

"This day just gets worse." I sighed, running my fingers through my hair and propping myself up against the wall.

"Is my kissing that bad?"

I started laughing, thinking back to the other night in my room. It had seemed so alien when Kile wanted to talk to me, but I wasn't completely sure why I thought that now. I could have had a new outlet, a new perspective this whole time.

"Why haven't we really talked before? It's so easy."

He shrugged. "You're the one in charge here. What do you think?"

I looked down, embarrassed to say it. "I think I held Josie against you. The constant imitation drives me crazy."

"I think I held the palace against you. It's our parents' fault, not yours, but I lumped you in since you were going to be queen."

"I can understand that."

"And I know what you mean about Josie. But it's hard for her, growing up in your shadow."

I couldn't deal with adding Josie to the growing list of things I felt guilty about. I straightened my clothes, knowing that going to work would distract me. "Let's do something soon. Not a date, just spending some time together."

That crooked smile spread across his face. "I'd like that."

He started tucking his shirt back in, and I fought the blush that I could feel on my cheeks. How had I gotten so out of control?

"And, listen," he said. "Don't let this stuff get you down. You're bigger than the Selection."

"Thanks, Kile." I kissed his cheek and left, heading to my room.

I remembered how angry I was when I saw his name come up the day of the drawing, like I was being cheated somehow. Now I didn't care how that form ended up in the pile; I was just glad it did.

I hoped that he felt the same way.

CHAPTER 26

TONIGHT WAS GOING TO BE a challenge. Yes, the pictures with Ean looked fantastic in print, and yes, the little game show clips came off as charming, but I wondered if Gavril would feel obligated to ask about Jack's and Burke's dismissals instead of focusing on the remaining candidates.

What was worse was that I wasn't sure I had much to tell about the boys as it was. Dad was entering his security sweep, so unless the guards moved quickly, I wouldn't have any dates this week . . . meaning nothing to share on next week's *Report*. Tonight had to matter, and I wasn't sure how to do it.

I couldn't shake the feeling that something was off, like I was missing some key piece of information that would make the Selection process better.

It wasn't an absolute disaster in my eyes, if only because

I got to know Kile, Henri, Hale, and Fox. But as far as the public knew, nearly everything was going down in flames.

Even though I'd only glanced at the paper that day for a millisecond, I remembered the way I looked shrinking down on the parade float. Worse than that, I could still see people on the sidelines pointing and laughing. We'd kicked out two candidates this week alone for misconduct, and in their wake every romantic gesture had been completely overshadowed.

It looked so, so bad.

I sat in my room, sketching, trying to organize my thoughts. There had to be a way to spin this, to turn it into something good.

My pencil zipped across the page, and it felt like each time a line straightened out, so did a problem. I'd probably have to skip talking about my previous dates this week. Bringing up one would require me to bring up them all, and I didn't want to rehash Jack's hands on me.

But maybe, instead of events, I could talk about what I knew of the boys. There was enough to praise, and if I came across as enamored by their talents, it would make sense to be confused about who to choose. It wasn't that the Selection was falling apart; it was that there were too many good choices.

By the time I had a plan, I also had a beautiful design. The dress came up into a halter, was very fitted, and ended mid-thigh. Over it I drew a sheer, long bubble of a skirt that made it look modest. The colors I'd used—a burgundy for the dress and a golden brown for the overskirt—gave it a delicious autumnal feeling.

I could imagine how I'd style my hair with it. I even knew what jewelry would look best.

As I looked at it, though, I knew this gown was more suited for a starlet than a princess. In my eyes, it was gorgeous without end, but I worried about other people's opinions. More than any other season of my life, they really mattered now.

"Oh, miss!" Neena said, catching a glimpse of the drawing in passing.

"You like it?"

"It's the most glamorous thing I've ever seen."

I stared at the gown. "Do you think I could get away with wearing this on the *Report*?"

She made a face as if I should already know. "You're basically covered from head to toe, and as long as you don't plan on coating it in rhinestones, I don't see why not."

I petted the paper like I could almost really touch it.

"Should I get started?" Neena asked, a hint of excitement in her voice.

"Actually, could you take me down to the workroom? I think I'd like to help make this one. I want it for tonight."

"I'd be thrilled," Neena said. I grabbed my book and followed her into the hallway, more excited than I'd ever been.

It was worth the marathon of cutting and sewing when I walked in for the *Report* and the first thing I saw was the out-and-out envy in Josie's eyes. I'd worn a pair of golden heels and curled my hair so it fell loosely over my shoulders, and it was possibly the most beautiful I'd ever felt. The blatant stares from the Selected only confirmed I was particularly lovely tonight, and I was so bewildered, I had to turn my back on them to suppress my grin.

It was then that I felt something was off. There was a pang of tension that seemed to be floating through the room, and it was far more powerful than the pride over my dress or the sense of admiration coming from the boys. It was so weighty, it nearly gave me a chill.

I looked around, searching for a clue. Mom and Dad were in a corner, trying to be discreet. I could tell by Dad's tensed brow and Mom's gestures that something was wrong. What I wasn't sure of was if I could go talk to them. Was a few days of silence enough?

"Hey!" Baden had snuck up on me.

"Hi."

"Did I startle you?"

I focused politely. "No, I'm fine. A little lost in thought. Do you need something?"

"Well, I was wondering if I could invite you out for dinner or something this week? Maybe another jam session?" He strummed an invisible guitar, biting his smiling lip.

"That's sweet, but traditionally, I'm supposed to do the asking."

He shrugged. "So? Didn't that cooking thing happen because those guys invited you?"

I squinted, trying to remember. "Maybe technically."

"So, since I didn't grow up in the palace, I can't ask, but Kile can?"

"I assure you, Kile has less of an advantage than you'd imagine," I answered with a laugh, thinking of all the years of frustration.

Baden stood there, silent and unbelieving. "Sure."

I was completely shocked when he walked away, hands in his pocket and footsteps steady. Had I done something rude? I was being honest. And I hadn't actually turned him down.

I tried to shake off the snub, focusing on my duty for the evening: being charming and gracious, and trying to convince everyone that I was falling in love.

Dad passed me, and I gently grabbed his arm. "What's wrong?"

He shook his head and patted my hand. "Nothing, darling."

The lie shook me more than Baden's dismissal. People whirred around the room, giving commands and checking notes. I heard Josie laugh, and someone shush her immediately after. The boys talked to one another, all a little too loud to be considered appropriate. Baden was sulking next to Henri, ignoring everyone, and I pressed my hands to my stomach, calming myself.

Next to Henri, just offstage in the dark, I saw a waving hand. It was Erik, standing on the sideline, waiting to take his hidden seat. Once he had my attention, he gave me a thumbs-up, but the expression on his face let me know it was a question. I shrugged. He pressed his lips together, then mouthed the word *sorry*. I gave him a tight smile and a thumbs-up back, which wasn't quite right but was the only thing I could do. Erik shook his head at me, and I was strangely comforted. At least someone seemed to understand how I was feeling.

Taking a deep breath, I went over to sit between Mom and Ahren.

"Something's wrong," I whispered to him.

"I know."

"Do you know what it is?"

"Yes."

"Will you tell me?"

"Later."

I sighed. How was I supposed to perform with worry hanging over my head?

The updates were dispensed, and Daddy spoke briefly, though I couldn't concentrate on anything he was saying. All I could see were the lines of stress around his eyes, the way his shoulders wore the strain of whatever was troubling him.

Partway through, Gavril stepped toward the middle of the set and announced that he had a few questions for the Selected, and I watched them all straighten their ties or cuffs and move into more assertive stances in their chairs.

"So, let's see . . . Sir Ivan?" On the near side of the first row, Ivan raised his hand, and Gavril faced him.

"How are you enjoying the Selection so far?"

He chuckled. "I'd be enjoying it more if I could manage to get to see the princess one-on-one." Ivan winked at me, and I felt my face set on fire.

"I imagine the princess has a hard time getting to everyone," Gavril said graciously.

"For sure! I'm not complaining, just being hopeful," he added, still chortling like this was all a joke.

"Well, maybe you can press Her Royal Highness tonight and sway her into making time for you. Tell us: what do you think the most important job of a future prince would be?"

Ivan's laughing stopped. "I don't know. I think just being good company is important. Princess Eadlyn is forced into lots of relationships for work, and I think it would be nice to be one of the people she always wanted to be around. Just for, you know, fun."

I tried not to roll my eyes. You *are* a forced relationship, honey.

"Interesting," Gavril commented. "What about you, Sir Gunner?"

Gunner was a bit on the short side, and he looked almost petite sitting beside the gangly Ivan. He tried to straighten himself, but it was no use.

"I think any future prince should be prepared to be available. You've already mentioned the princess's busy schedule, so anyone in her life should try to put himself in a position to be helpful. Of course, I don't know what that looks like yet, but it's important to think of how your life and priorities might change."

Gavril made an approving face, and Dad clapped, which led others to follow. I joined in, but it felt strange. This was a legitimate question, and I wasn't sure I liked it being turned into entertainment.

"Sir Kile, you've lived in the palace your whole life," Gavril said, walking across the stage. "How do you think your life might change were you to become prince?"

"I'd definitely need to focus more on my hygiene."

"*Pfffft!*" I covered my mouth, so embarrassed, but I couldn't stop laughing.

"Oh! Sounds like someone over there agrees."

Behind Kile, Henri belatedly joined in the laughter. Of course, he'd heard the comment on a delay. Gavril noticed him and moved back.

"Sir Henri, yes?" Henri nodded, but I could see the pure terror in his eyes. "What's your opinion on all this? What do you think a future prince's most important role might be?"

He tried not to let his fear show as he leaned to the side to hear Erik. Once he understood he nodded.

"Oh, oh, yes. The preence should being for preensess . . . ummm . . ."

I stood. I couldn't bear it. "Henri?" I called. All eyes turned to me, and I waved him over to come join me in the middle of the set. He carefully came down from his seat. "And Erik? You, too."

Henri waited for his friend to come around from behind the set. Erik looked nervous, not prepared to be in the spotlight; but Henri mumbled something to him with a smile, and he eased as they found their way with Gavril to the front.

I linked my arm around Henri's, and Erik stood just behind him, going into shadow mode.

"Gavril, Sir Henri was raised in Swendway. His first language is Finnish, so he requires a translator." I motioned to Erik, who gave a quick bow, ready to go back into obscurity. "I'm sure Henri would be happy to answer your question, but I think it would be much easier without Erik hiding behind the risers."

Henri smiled as Erik conveyed all this to him, and I felt strangely proud when he reached across and gently squeezed my arm.

Pausing to collect himself, Henri gave his answer. I could see he was thinking about his words, and even though he'd been thrown off, he was deliberate as he spoke. Finally, he came to a finish and all eyes fell on Erik.

"He says that any future prince should remember that it isn't simply one role to fill but several. Husband, consultant, friend, and dozens more. He would need to be prepared to study and work as hard as Her Highness and be ready to set his ego aside to serve." Erik put his hands behind his back, and I could see he was trying to remember the last of Henri's words. "And he would also need to understand that there is a weight she carries that he never could and be ready to sometimes just be a clown."

I giggled, happy to see Henri's huge smile when Erik was done. The entire room erupted in applause, and I got up on tiptoes to whisper in his ear.

"Good, good."

He beamed. "Good, good?"

I nodded.

"Your Highness, this is an extraordinary complication in the Selection process," Gavril gasped. "How do you manage?"

"Right now, with two things: patience and Erik."

There was a smattering of laughter across the room.

"But how could this work? At some point it would have to change."

This was the first time in my life that I'd ever wanted to run over, grab my chair, and fling it across the room at Gavril Fadaye.

"Yes, probably, but there are certainly worse things than a language barrier."

"Could you give us some examples?"

I motioned for Henri and Erik to go sit down, and worked very hard not to laugh at how quickly Erik moved. Henri gave me an affectionate smile as he left, and that inspired me.

"Well, since this began with Henri, let me use him as an example. We have to work hard to communicate, but he's an incredibly kind person. Whereas Jack and Burke spoke perfect English but behaved rather poorly."

"Yes, we all saw the story of Burke's fight, and let me say, I'm happy to see you were unharmed by that outburst."

Uninjured? Sure. Unharmed? That was questionable. But no one would want to hear about that.

"Yes, but they seem to be the exception, not the rule. There are so many candidates I could brag about."

"Oh? Well, don't let me stop you!"

I smiled and peeked back to the boys. "Sir Hale has incredible taste and works as a tailor. I would not be surprised to see all of Illéa covered in his designs one day."

"I love that dress!" he called.

"I made it!" I yelled back, unable to contain my pride.

"Perfection."

"See," I said, turning back to Gavril. "Told you he had good taste." I looked around again. "Of course, I've already mentioned Sir Baden's musical skills, but they're worth bringing up again. He's so talented."

Baden gave a quick nod, and, if he was still irritated, he was covering it well.

"Sir Henri, I've discovered, is an amazing cook. And it takes a lot to impress me in that department because, as you know, the palace chefs could rival anyone in the world. So trust me when I say you're jealous of me because I've gotten to taste his food."

More laughter filled the studio, and I caught a glimpse of Dad in a monitor looking so, so delighted.

"Sir Fox . . . now, some might not be aware of what a valuable skill this is, but he has the ability to make the best out of any situation. The Selection can be stressful, and yet he is always looking at the bright side. He's a pleasure to be around."

I shared a gaze with Fox, and, even with the gash on his head and his bruised eye showing slightly through the makeup, he looked as far from menacing as possible. I was glad I'd let him stay.

"Anyone else?" Gavril questioned, and I scanned the boys. Yes, there was one more.

"Most people have a hard time believing that I don't know Sir Kile backward and forward because we've lived in the same place our whole lives, but it's true. The Selection has allowed me to get to know him much better, and I've now learned that he's a very promising architect. If we ever needed a second palace built, he's the first person I'd call."

There were some sweet sighs around the room at the idea of childhood friends finally becoming possible lovers.

"Although, I can confirm, he needs help in the hygiene department," I added, sending the room into laughs again.

"It sounds like these are some truly amazing young men!" Gavril called, beginning another round of applause for them.

"Absolutely."

"So, if you're so impressed, I have to ask: has anyone got a special place in your heart just yet?"

I found myself fiddling with my hair. "I don't know."

"Oh, ho!"

I giggled, looking down. This wasn't real . . . was it?

"Does it happen to be anyone you mentioned?"

I slapped his arm playfully. "Oh, my gosh, Gavril!"

He snickered, as did most of the room. I fanned myself with a hand and turned back to him.

"The truth is, it's still difficult to talk about this so publicly, but I'm hoping to have more to say in the future."

"That's wonderful news, Your Highness. Let me join all of Illéa in wishing you luck as you look for your partner."

"Thank you." I nodded my head modestly and casually peeked over at Dad.

The expression on his face was one of disbelief, almost as if he was optimistic. It was bittersweet for me, to feel so unsure about the whole thing but to see that even the slightest glimmer of possibility took so much worry out of his eyes.

For now, that would be enough.

CHAPTER 27

"IT'S BAD."

I lay on Ahren's bed, curled in a ball while he sat upright, telling me everything Mom and Dad didn't want to.

"Just say it."

He swallowed. "It always seems to start in the poorer provinces. They're not rebelling, not like when Mom and Dad were kids. . . . It's more like they're uprising."

"What does that mean exactly?"

"They're rallying to end the monarchy. No one is getting what they want out of the caste dissolution, and they think we don't care."

"Don't care?" I asked, astonished. "Dad's running himself ragged trying to fix it. I'm dating strangers for them!"

"I know. And I have no idea where that performance tonight came from, but that was spectacular." I made a smart face, acknowledging the praise, but I was starting to question just how much of tonight was planned and how much was genuine. "But even then, what are we supposed to do? Perform forever?"

"Ha!" I scoffed. "As if you'd ever be asked to perform. It would always be me, and I can't. I feel like I'm suffocating as it is."

"We could all step down," he suggested. "But then what would happen? Who would take over? And if we don't step down, will they run us out?"

"Do you think they'd do that?" I breathed.

He stared into the distance. "I don't know, Eady. People have done far worse things when they're hungry or tired or unwaveringly poor."

"But we can't feed everyone. We can't make everyone earn the same amount of money. What do they want from us?"

"Nothing," he said honestly. "They just want more for themselves. I can't say I blame them, but the people are confused. They think their lives are in our hands, but they're not."

"They're in their own."

"Exactly."

We sat in silence for a long time, considering what this meant for us. Truthfully, though, I knew it would hit me harder than anyone else if the people followed through on this. I didn't know how things like this happened, but governments changed. Kingdoms rose and fell; entire ideologies took over, shoving others to the side. Could I be brushed into the gutter?

I shivered, trying to imagine a life like that.

"They already threw food at me," I murmured.

"What?"

"I've been so stupid," I answered, shaking my head. "I've grown up believing that I was adored . . . but the people don't love me. Once Mom and Dad step down, I can't imagine there would be anything preventing the country from getting rid of me."

It was a tangible thing, like I was being held aloft by this idea, and now that I knew it was a lie, my body felt heavier.

Ahren's face grew worried. I waited for him to contradict me, but he couldn't. "You can make them love you, Eadlyn."

"I'm not as charming as you or as clever as Kaden or as adorably rambunctious as Osten. There's nothing that special about me."

He whacked his head on his headboard as he groaned. "Eadlyn, you're joking, right? You're the first female heir. You're unlike anything this country has ever known. You just have to learn how to use that, to remind them who you are."

I'm Eadlyn Schreave, and no one in the world is as powerful as me.

"I don't think they'd like me if they knew who I really was."

"If you're going to whine, I'll kick you out."

"I'll have you flogged."

"You've been threatening me with that since we were six."

"One day it'll happen. Heed my warning."

He chuckled. "Don't worry, Eady. The chances of people organizing enough to do anything are slim. They're venting.

Once they get this out of their system, things will go back to normal, you'll see."

I nodded and sighed. Maybe I was fretting for nothing, but I could still hear the hateful yelling during the parade, and I could still see the hateful remarks from my kiss with Kile. This certainly wouldn't be the last we heard about abolishing the monarchy.

"Don't tell Mom and Dad I know, okay?"

"If you insist."

I hopped up and kissed Ahren's cheek. I felt bad for girls who didn't have brothers. "See you tomorrow."

He grinned. "Get some sleep."

I left his room with every intention of going back to mine. But as I walked, I realized I was hungry. Now that I'd been to the kitchens, I kind of liked it down there. I remembered seeing some fruit, and there was cheese in the refrigerator. Certainly it was late enough that it couldn't bother anyone, so I trotted down the back stairs.

I was wrong in assuming that it would be completely empty. There were a handful of young men and women rolling out dough and chopping vegetables. I took it all in for a moment, entranced by how efficient and driven they were. I loved that, in spite of the hour, they all seemed alert and happy, chatting with one another as they went about their work.

They were so interesting that it took several moments for me to notice the head of floppy blond curls in the back corner of the room. Henri had hung his shirt on a hook, and his blue undershirt was covered in flour. I moved quietly, but as the staff recognized me, they curtsied and bowed as I passed, alerting Henri to my presence.

When he saw me he tried to brush the mess off himself, failing completely. He pushed back his hair and turned to me, smiling as always.

"No Erik?"

"He sleep."

"Why aren't you asleep?"

He squinted, trying to piece together the words. "Umm. Sorry. I cook?"

I nodded. "Can I cook, too?"

He pointed to the pile of apples and dough on the table. "You want? You cook?"

"Yes."

He beamed and nodded. Then, giving me a once-over, he paused before grabbing his dress shirt and wrapping it around me, tying the sleeves together in the back. An apron. He wanted me to have an apron.

I smiled to myself. It was only a nightgown after all, but there weren't enough words between the two of us to argue over it.

He picked up an apple and took the peel off in one long strip. When he was done, he set it on the counter and picked up a different knife. "*Pidäveitsi näin*," he said, pointing to the way his fingers held the handle. "*Pidäomena huolellisesti*." He turned his other hand into a claw, tucking his fingers away as he held the apple. Then he started cutting.

Even with my inexperienced eyes, I could see how he was using the minimum amount of force to do his work and how his simple stance protected his hands.

"You," he said, passing me the knife.

"Okay. Like this?" I curled my hand up like he had.

"Good, good."

I wasn't nearly as fast as he was, and my slices weren't half as uniform, but by the way he grinned, you'd have thought I made an entire feast by myself.

He worked with the dough and mixed cinnamon and sugar and prepped one of the fryers along the wall.

I wondered if he was in charge of desserts at home or if they were simply his favorite.

I helped toss the apples and stuff the dough, and though I was terrified of the hot oil, I did sink one of the baskets. I squealed when the oil came alive, popping and dancing all over the place. Henri only laughed at me a little, which was kind.

When he finally placed the tray in front of me, I was dying of hunger and nearly too excited to wait. But I did, and he gestured that I should try, so I plucked up one of the fritter-doughnut-pastry things and bit in.

It was heaven, even better than the rolls he'd made the other day. "Oh, yum!" I exclaimed as I chewed. He broke into a laugh and picked one up himself. He seemed pretty satisfied, but I could see in his eyes he was evaluating what he'd made.

I thought they were perfect.

"What are these called?"

"Hmm?"

"Umm, name?" I pointed to the food.

"Oh, *omenalörtsy.*"

"*Ohmenalortsee?*"

"Good!"

"Yeah?"

"Good."

I smiled to myself. I'd have to tell Kaden I was seriously mastering the names of several Swendish desserts.

I ate two, feeling a little sick once I was done, and then I watched as Henri passed the plate around to the cooks, who all praised his skills. In the deepest core of myself, I hated that he didn't understand the words they were using.

Delectable. Flawless. Perfection.

I got the sense that if he had understood, he'd have said they were being too generous. It was hard to be sure though. That was just my assumption about who he was. I really didn't know.

And, I reminded myself, *you don't want to.*

There were times when it was getting harder and harder to remember that.

When Henri finished his rounds and the plate came back with hardly a crumb left, I gave him a shy smile.

"I should sleep."

"You sleep?"

"Yes."

"Good, good."

"Um. Tonight? The *Report*?" I asked, trying to keep things simple.

He nodded. "*Report*, yes."

I placed my hand on his chest. "You were so sweet."

"Sweet? Umm, the sugar?"

I laughed. "Yes. Like sugar."

He brought his hand up to cover mine as it was still pressed against his heart. His smile dwindled as he looked at me and swallowed. He shrugged as he held me there, seeming only to want to make the moment last. He held my hand for the longest time, and I could see he was sorting through words in his head, trying so, so hard to find one that he knew I might understand. . . .

But there was nothing.

I wanted Henri to know that I saw what he felt. I could tell in every smile and every gesture that he really cared about me. And, despite my best efforts, I cared about him, too. I worried about how much I would regret it, but there was only one way to express that feeling.

I closed the distance between us and placed a hand on his cheek. He stared into my eyes as if he'd discovered something truly valuable, something rare that he might never see again. I nodded slowly, and he lowered his lips to mine.

Henri was scared. I could feel it. He was afraid to touch me, afraid to hold me, afraid to move. I didn't know if it was because I was a princess or because he'd never done this before, but that kiss was so vulnerable.

That made me love it even more.

I pressed my lips into his, trying to tell him without words that this was okay, that I wanted him to hold me. And finally, after a moment of hesitation, he responded. Henri held me like I was delicate, like if his grip was too tight, I'd crumble. And his kisses were the same way, only now, instead of being driven by fear, they were motivated by what felt like reverence. It was an affection almost too beautiful to endure.

I pulled away, slightly dizzy from the kiss, noting that his eyes looked pained, but he wore the tiniest smile.

"I should go," I said again.

He nodded.

"Goodnight."

"Goodnight."

I moved slowly until I was out of his sight, then I ran. My head was swimming with thoughts that I didn't understand. Why did it bother me so much when Gavril picked at Henri? Why did I have to keep Fox when he should have left? Why did Kile—for goodness' sake, Kile!—keep popping into my mind?

And why was it so terrifying even to ask those questions?

When I got to my room, I flung myself into bed, feeling disoriented. As angry as I was at Gavril for bringing it up, it did bother me that I couldn't speak to Henri, that I couldn't communicate anything intimate to him because of how uncomfortable it would be to go through Erik. As unnerved as the thought made me, if I was going to tell anyone something personal, it would probably be Henri. I felt safe around him, and I knew he was smart, and I admired his passion. Henri was good.

But I didn't speak Finnish. And that was bad.

I rolled over onto my back in frustration, yelping when something dug into my spine. Reaching around, I felt that it was a knot. I was still wearing Henri's shirt.

I untied it and, despite how absurd it was, pulled it up to my nose. Of course. Of course he smelled like cinnamon and honey and vanilla. Of course he smelled like dessert.

Stupid Swendish baker with his stupid spices.

This was making me asinine!

This was why love was a terrible idea: it made you weak.

And there was no one in the world as powerful as me.

CHAPTER 28

AT BREAKFAST I WAS STRUCK by a number of things. First was Henri trying to catch Erik up on everything that had happened the night before. Erik's eyes kept darting over to mine and then back to Henri, and he looked like he was trying to calm him down. I thought for sure Henri would be elated today as the second person in the Selection to get a kiss. Instead, he seemed frantic.

Across from Henri, Kile's confused gaze flipped back and forth between him and Erik, as he clearly didn't know enough words to follow even a fraction of the conversation. He slowly spooned food into his mouth without trying to interject.

I also noticed that Baden was trying to get my attention. He gave me a small wave and nodded toward the door. I mouthed "Later" and did my best not to be irritated by him neglecting protocol again.

But the worst by far were Mom and Dad surreptitiously peeking over at me, obviously wondering how much I knew about the uprising.

I cleared my throat. "So, did I do okay last night?"

Dad's face finally broke into a smile. "I was impressed, Eadlyn. After such a trying week, you were incredibly poised. When Henri got up there and you were so generous with him, it was a wonderful thing to watch. And I'm happy to see that maybe some of them are . . . appealing to you. Gives me hope."

"We'll see where that goes," I hedged, "but I did promise you three months, and I think it will take me at least that long to figure any of this out."

"I know exactly what you mean," he said, looking as if a thousand memories were flooding his head. "Thank you."

"You're welcome." I watched his sweet, wistful smile, and I could see how much this whole thing meant to him. "Will you be disappointed? If I get to the end and there's no engagement?"

"No, dear. *I* won't be disappointed." He only barely accented the word, but it sent me into a sudden tailspin of worry.

What would it mean for me when I got to the end and was still single? If we weren't just dealing with post-caste confusion anymore and trying to quell an outright rebellion, three months wasn't enough to fix this. In fact, two weeks had already disappeared in a rush.

This wasn't going to be enough.

And then I understood why they might want to keep any hint of unrest from me: If I thought this was completely pointless, would I quit? If I quit, then there really was nothing.

"Don't worry, Daddy," I said. "It's all going to be fine."

He put his hand over mine and gave it a squeeze. "I'm sure you're right, dear." Then, taking a deep breath, he went back to his coffee. "I meant to tell you; the background checks are done. If we had made a few calls before the Selection, we would have known that Burke had anger issues and that a girl at Jack's school reported him for inappropriate behavior once. It also turns out Ean spends almost all his time alone. I don't think that's anything worth sending him home for, but we should watch him."

"Ean's actually been pretty generous."

"Oh?"

"Yeah. But I have noticed he's a bit of a loner. Not sure why though; he's a good conversationalist."

Dad sipped his coffee and stared at Ean. "That's strange."

"Anyone else I need to worry about?" I asked, not wanting him to linger on Ean. Isolated didn't mean troublemaker.

"There was one who had some bad grades, but nothing to kick up a fuss about."

"All right then. The worst has passed." I tried to look encouraging.

"I certainly hope so. I'm going to have a special team continue to look into this. I wasn't as diligent as I should have been, and I'm sorry for that," he confessed.

"But on the plus side, I could have actual dates to talk about next Friday."

He chuckled to himself. "True. So maybe give someone you haven't talked to yet a chance. I promise, it is actually possible to meet with all of them."

I surveyed the mass of boys. "I might not be in the office this week."

He shook his head. "Not a problem. Get to know them. I'm still pulling for you to find someone, even if part of you thinks it's pointless."

"I might remind you, that wasn't your goal when you proposed this."

"All the same."

"There are just so many. Anyone you don't like?"

He squinted. "As a matter of fact . . ." Dad gazed over each of their faces, trying to find one in particular. "That one. Green shirt."

"Black hair?"

"Yes."

"That's Julian. What's wrong with him?"

"This might sound trivial, but when you were complimenting the others last night, he didn't smile or clap for any of them. Not a good attitude to have. If he can't stand being in their shadows temporarily, how would he handle being in yours for the rest of his life?"

For all the mental time I spent debating how much he honestly believed in me as a leader, that statement made it all a waste. Of course he saw me as a leader.

"And this might also sound trivial, but I don't think you'd make attractive children."

"Daddy!" I yelled, causing a bit of a stir. I buried my head in my hand as Dad doubled over in laughter.

"I'm just saying!"

"All right. I'm leaving. Thanks for the insight."

I practically bolted from the hall, though I made sure my pace was only slightly faster than what might be considered ladylike. Once I was alone it turned into an all-out sprint. In my room, I filed through the remaining applications, looking for anything that might make one person more exciting than another. I paused on Julian's picture. Dad was right. No matter how I combined his nose and my eyes or my mouth and his cheeks, every variation looked awful in my head.

Not that it mattered.

I'd send him home soon enough, but probably only once a few dates went bad and he had company. The solo eliminations had all been rather awful. For now I had to make a plan. Ten dates. That was the goal before I had to face another *Report*. And I'd need to get at least three of them in the papers. How could I make them look magnificent?

Mom was in the Women's Room with Miss Lucy, meeting with a mayor. There weren't very many ladies holding down those positions, so I knew them by heart. This was Milla Warren from Calgary gracing our home today. I hadn't planned on making this an official visit, but now I had no choice.

I curtsied, greeting Mom and her guest.

"Your Highness!" Ms. Warren sang, standing to give me a deep curtsy. "It's a pleasure to see you, and during such an exciting time!"

"We're very happy to have you as well, ma'am. Please sit."

"How are you, Eadlyn?" Mom asked.

"Good. I have some questions for you later," I added quietly.

"No doubt a little boy talk, eh?" Ms. Warren asked with a wink. Mom and Miss Lucy indulged her with a laugh, but while I smiled, I thought she should know the truth.

"I don't think the Selection is quite what you imagine."

She raised her eyebrows. "Please, give me thirty-five men fighting over me any day!"

"Honestly, it's more work than anything," I promised. "We make it look exciting, but it's challenging."

"I can back that up," Mom said. "No matter what side of the situation you're on, it's hard. There are long hours of nothing happening followed by bursts of events." She shook her head. "Even now, just thinking back on it, I feel tired."

Mom rested her head on her hand and flicked her eyes toward me. There was something in her expression, that motherly, accepting look, that made me feel understood and comforted.

But there was the same worry there, the hint of stress that Dad was wearing this morning. She brushed off the moment and focused on Ms. Warren. "So, Milla, the last I heard, things were going well in Calgary."

"Oh, yes, well, we're a quiet bunch."

She'd stopped by on little more than a social call, and I sat there holding my perfect posture until she decided to leave. Which only happened because I slipped a note to the maid asking that she come in and tell Mom she was needed urgently.

The second Ms. Warren was out the door, Mom straightened her dress. "Let me go see what this is all about."

"Relax, it's just me." I studied my nails. They needed some work.

Mom and Miss Lucy stared.

"I wanted to talk to you and she wouldn't stop, so I made an appointment. Sort of." I flashed a cheeky smile.

Mom shook her head. "Eadlyn, sometimes you can be a little manipulative." She sighed. "And sometimes it's a gift. Ugh, I didn't think I could take much more."

I giggled conspiratorially with her and Miss Lucy, glad I wasn't alone.

"I feel bad for her," Mom said guiltily. "She doesn't get out much, and it's hard to do her job alone. But I didn't appreciate how she spoke to you."

I made a face. "I've had worse."

"True." She swallowed. "What did you need?"

I glanced at Miss Lucy. "Of course," she answered to my unspoken request. "I'm around all day if you need me." She curtsied to Mom, kissed me on my head, and left. It was such a tender gesture.

"She's so good to me," I said. "The boys, too. Sometimes I feel like I ended up with several mothers."

I smiled at Mom, and she nodded. "I kept the people I

love close, and they have fawned over you since the moment they knew you were coming."

"I really wish she had children," I said sadly.

"Me, too." Mom swallowed. "I guess by now it's common knowledge that she's faced a long struggle with no success. I'd do nearly anything to be able to help her."

"Have you tried?" I felt like there was little the Schreaves couldn't accomplish.

Mom blinked a few times, trying not to cry. "I shouldn't tell you this; it's private. But, yes, I've done everything I could. I even went so far as to offer to be a surrogate and carry a baby for her." She pressed her lips together. "It was the one time I regretted being queen. It appears my body isn't always mine, and there are certain things I'm not allowed to do."

"Says who?" I demanded.

"Everyone, Eadlyn. It's not exactly a traditional thing to do, and our advisers thought the people would be upset by it. Some even argued that any baby I carried would have to be in line for the throne. It was ridiculous, so I had to let it go."

I was quiet for a minute, watching my mother recover from a heartbreak years old, and one that wasn't even her own in a way.

"How do you do that?"

"What?"

"It's like you're always giving pieces of yourself away. How do you have anything left for you? I feel exhausted watching you sometimes."

She smiled. "When you know who matters most to you, giving things up, even yourself, doesn't really feel like a sacrifice. There are a handful of people who I'd lay down my life for without a second thought. And then there are the people of Illéa, our subjects, who I lay my life down for in a different way."

She lowered her eyes and touched up her already immaculate dress. "You probably have people you'd sacrifice for and you don't know it. But you will, one day."

For a second I wondered if we were actually related. All the people she was thinking about—Dad, Ahren, Miss Lucy, Aunt May—were important to me, too. But mostly I needed them to help me, not the other way around.

"Anyway," she said, "what was it that you needed?"

"Oh, so Dad has deemed that the remaining boys aren't complete lunatics, so I'm focusing on dates this week," I answered, leaning forward. "I'm looking for ideas that would be easy but look great on camera."

"Ah." She lifted her eyes to the ceiling in thought. "I'm not sure how useful I can be in that department. Nearly all the dates I had with your father during my Selection were walks around the garden."

"Seriously? How did you two even get together? That's so boring!"

She laughed. "Well, it gave us a lot of opportunities to talk. Or to argue, and the majority of our time spent with each other was filled with one or the other."

I squinted. "You guys fought?"

"All. The. Time." For some reason that brought a smile to her face.

"Honestly, the more and more I hear about your Selection,

the less sense it makes. I can't even imagine you and Dad fighting."

"I know. There were a lot of things we needed to work through, and truthfully, we liked having someone who'd be honest with us, even when it was hard to take."

It wasn't that I didn't want someone honest in my life as well—if I ever chose to get married, anyway—but he'd need to find a better way of delivering his words if he wanted a chance of sticking around.

"Okay, dates," she said, sitting back in her chair and thinking. "I was never good at archery, but if there's someone who is skilled at that, it might look nice."

"I think I can do that. Oh, and I've already done horseback riding, so that's out."

"Right. Cooking, too." She smiled to herself as if she couldn't believe I'd allowed that date to happen.

"And it turned out disastrous."

"Well, Kile and Henri did great! And Fox wasn't terrible."

"True," I amended. I found myself thinking about Henri and me cooking alone in the kitchen, the date no one knew about.

"Sweetheart, I think instead of going for something flashy, you might try simpler dates. Have tea, take a walk in the gardens. Meals are always a good standard; you can't eat too many times. It might look better than you riding a horse anyway."

I'd been trying to avoid anything that might be too personal. But those types of dates gave the impression of closeness, which was something I thought the public wanted.

Maybe she was right. If I went in with a list of safe topics and questions, perhaps it wouldn't feel so bad anyway.

"Thanks, Mom. I'll probably give that a go."

"Any time, sweetie. I'm always here for you."

"I know." I fidgeted with my dress. "Sorry if I've been a pain lately."

She reached across to me. "Eadlyn, you're under a lot of stress. We understand. And short of becoming an ax murderer, there's nothing you could do to make me love you less."

I laughed. "An ax murderer? That's your limit?"

"Well . . . maybe even then." She winked at me. "Go on. If you're doing several dates this week, you should make a plan."

I nodded and, for reasons I wasn't entirely sure of, scuttled into her lap for a second.

"*Oof!*" she complained as my weight settled.

"Love you, Mom."

She wrapped her arms around me tightly. "I love you, too. More than you could ever know."

I kissed her cheek and hopped up, thinking of the week ahead and hoping it would somehow appease everyone. But those thoughts were driven from my mind when I stepped into the hallway and found Baden there, waiting for me.

CHAPTER 29

BADEN STOOD AND THEN CROSSED the hall. The midday sun was filtering in through the windows, making the space warm and covering everything with a slight hint of yellow. Even his dark skin looked brighter somehow.

"Stalking me?" I asked, trying to be playful.

The hard set of his eyes told me he wasn't in the mood. "I wasn't sure how else to get ahold of you. You're so hard to find."

I crossed my arms. "Clearly you're upset. Why don't you tell me what it's all about so we can move on?"

He made a face, displeased with my offer. "I want to leave."

I felt like I'd run full speed into a brick wall. "Excuse me?"

"Last night was embarrassing. I asked you out and you shot me down."

I held up a hand. "I never actually said no. You didn't let me get that far."

"Were you going to say yes?" He sounded skeptical.

I raised my arms and let them drop. "I'll never know, because you got an attitude and walked away."

"Are you seriously going to lecture me on having a bad attitude?"

I gasped. How dare he?

I got closer to him, though even at my full height I was dwarfed by his frame. "You know I could have you punished for speaking to me that way, right?"

"So now you're going to bully me? First you reject me, then you use me for a little snippet of entertainment on the *Report*, and now I've had to spend my entire morning tracking you down after you told me you would meet with me during breakfast."

"You're one person out of twenty! I have work to do! How self-centered can you possibly be?"

His eyes widened, and he pointed at his chest. "Me? Self-centered?"

I tried to tuck my heart away, refusing to let him hurt me. "You know, you were one of my favorites. I was going to keep you around for a long time. My family liked you, and I admired your talent."

"I don't need your family's stamp of approval. You were nice to me for all of an hour, then you disappear and it's like nothing happened at all. I have the freedom to leave, and I'm ready to go."

"Then go!"

I started walking away. I didn't have to endure that.

He yelled down the hall, taking one last stab at me. "My friends all told me I was crazy to put my name in! They were so right!"

I kept going.

"You're pushy! You're selfish! What was I thinking?"

I turned a corner, even though it didn't lead to where I was going. I could find my way eventually. I held it in, keeping the brave face I'd always been taught to have. No one could know how much that hurt.

After a trip that took twice as long as it should have, I finally made it to the third floor. I started crying the second I hit the landing, unable to stay composed any longer. Baden's words repeated themselves in my head, and I clutched my stomach, feeling them like literal blows.

Before any of the boys had shown up, I'd had a list of ideas for how to get rid of them. I'd planned on making them so angry they'd say plenty of the things Baden just had . . . but I'd done nothing to provoke him. And he said them anyway. What was so wrong with me that I got rejected simply for being myself?

And his last words did exactly what he wanted them to. It looked like I'd had millions of choices when I drew the names nearly a month ago. How many men hadn't entered because they already objected to me on some level?

Did people think I was pushy? Selfish? Which were the public enjoying more: the sweet moments between me and the boys or the moments when I looked like a failure?

I straightened up to head to my room, only to see that Erik was waiting outside my door for me and had undoubtedly just watched my crying fit.

I swiped at my face, trying to clean it up, but there was no hiding the puffy eyes or red cheeks. Erik seeing me like this was almost as bad as the original issue, but the only way to make it *seem* as if it was nothing was to *act* as if it was nothing.

I walked over to Erik, achingly aware of the sadness in his eyes, and he bowed as I approached.

"I feel like maybe I've come at a bad time," he said, the tiniest hint of sarcasm in his voice.

I smiled. "Ever so slightly," I answered, acknowledging my hurt against my better judgment. "Still, I'm happy to help you if I can."

Erik pressed his lips together, unsure if he should go on. "I wanted to talk to you about Henri. He didn't send me!" he insisted, holding up a hand. "I think he'd come to you himself if he could speak on his own. But he's embarrassed." Erik swallowed. "He, uh . . . he told me about the kiss."

I nodded. "I figured."

"He's afraid he's crossed a line. He said something about holding on to you and that he probably should have let go, but then he didn't and—"

I shook my head. "That makes it sound much worse than it was. He . . . we . . ." I stood there, lost. "We were trying to communicate, and when the words didn't work, well, that did."

For some reason I was upset admitting this to Erik, even though he already knew everything.

"So you're not cross with him?"

I heaved out a breath, almost laughing because the idea was so bizarre. "No. He's one of the kindest people I know. I'm not upset with him in the slightest."

Erik nodded. "Would it be all right if I told him as much?"

"Absolutely." I wiped at my eyes again, pulling off smudged eyeliner in the process. "Ick."

"Are you okay, Your Highness?" His voice was so tender but, mercifully, lacking pity. I almost explained what had happened to him, but it was borderline inappropriate. It was one thing to talk about Henri; it was another to discuss the other suitors at length.

"I am. Or will be. Don't worry about me; just make sure Henri is all right."

His expression changed slightly, and I could see the weight of that role in his eyes. "I do my best."

I studied him. "Henri really wants it, doesn't he?"

Erik shook his head. "There is no 'it.' He wants you."

After Baden's heart-shattering speech, it was hard to imagine this was possible, but Erik confirmed it as he went on.

"He talks of you endlessly. Each day in the Men's Parlor, I'm translating political science books to him or trying to explain the difference between the absolute monarchy you have here and the constitutional monarchy he grew up with in Swendway. He even—" Erik paused to chuckle. "He even studies the way your brothers walk and stand. He wants to be worthy of you in every way."

I swallowed, overcome by this admission. Smirking, trying to dull the feeling, I replied, "But he can't even speak to me."

"I know," he answered solemnly. "Which is why I wonder . . ."

"Wonder what?"

He rubbed his hand over his mouth, trying to decide if he should continue. "It's easiest to learn new languages when you're a child. And it can be taught later in life, but the accent will probably always be bad. Henri simply has a difficult time retaining it. At the rate he's going, it would be *years* before you'd be able to carry on the most basic conversations. And the nuances of languages—slang and colloquialisms— would take years beyond that. Do you understand what that would mean?"

That I wouldn't be able to communicate with him for who knew how long. By the time the Selection should end, we still would hardly know each other.

"I do." Two small words, but they felt massive, like they were filling up the entire hallway, crushing me.

"I just thought you should know that. I wanted you to be aware of what things might look like if you had developed feelings for him, too."

"Thank you," I breathed.

"Do you?" he asked suddenly. "Have feelings for him?"

I'd been so emotional already that the question sent me into a tailspin. "I honestly have no idea how I feel about anything."

"Hey." He reached out a hand before thinking better of it. "I'm sorry. I was being nosy. That's really none of my business, and you're obviously having a rough day. I'm an ass."

I wiped at my nose. "No. You're trying to be a good friend. To him, to me. It's no big deal."

He tucked his hands behind his back. "Well, I am, you know?"

"Huh?"

He sighed, seeming embarrassed. "Your friend. If you need one."

It was such a simple offer, yet generous in a million ways. "I couldn't imagine having a better one."

He beamed but was quiet. It seemed like the times when we were silent were some of the easiest.

Eventually he cleared his throat. "I'm sure you have work to do, but I hate leaving you alone when you feel so bad."

"No. I kind of prefer it."

Erik gave me a halfhearted smile. "If you say so." He bowed. "Hope your day gets better."

"It already has," I promised, walking around him to get into my room, a kind smile on my face.

"Miss?" Neena asked as I came through the doorway. I couldn't imagine how awful I looked.

"Hi, Neena."

"Are you all right?"

"Not exactly, but I'll get there. Can you bring me the Selection forms, please? I have work to do."

Though the confusion on her face was plain, she did as I asked. She also brought a box of tissues.

"Thank you." I thought I was past the worst of it, but I did tear up again as I looked at the pictures, wondering who was maybe here despite having reservations and hating each of them on the off chance it applied to them all.

"Neena, could you get me some paper?"

Once again she obeyed, bringing a cup of tea along with a notebook. She really was too good.

I tried to plot out my week. Apsel's application said he played the piano, so I'd arrange for us to work on duets tomorrow morning; and in the early evening I'd walk outside with Tavish. Monday would be tea with Gunner and a photography walk with Harrison. Dad would probably love that.

I finished my plans and set down my pile of papers beside me. Without a word, Neena started a bath. I sipped the last of my tea and put the cup back on the table next to the pot so she wouldn't have to go hunting for it later.

In the bathroom, steam was filling the air, and I planted myself in front of the mirror, pulling pins out of my hair. Between the soothing water and Neena's calming presence, I was free from most of Baden's harsh words by the time I was ready to dry off.

"Do you want to talk about it?" Neena asked quietly, pulling a brush through my hair.

"There's not much to say. People will throw food at me, people will throw words at me, and I have to be stronger than that if I'm going to survive."

She let out a disapproving sound, and I watched her troubled eyes in the mirror.

"What?"

Neena stopped brushing for a minute, looking at my reflection. "For all my problems, I'd never trade them for yours. I'm so sorry."

I pulled myself up. "Nothing to be sorry for. This was what I was born to do."

"That's not fair though, is it? I thought eliminating the castes meant that no one was born into anything. Does that apply to everyone except you?"

"Apparently."

It didn't matter that Apsel's skills were so good I praised him endlessly. And it didn't matter that the photos of Tavish and me in the garden were positively beautiful. With all the work I put in, neither of those things were headline material Monday morning.

Above the pictures of me and my dates was an entirely different story.

IT'S WORK! screamed the headline above a candid shot of me yawning. An "exclusive source" had shared that I felt the Selection process was "more work than anything" and that "we make it look exciting." All I could think about was how badly I wanted to hurt Milla Warren.

I couldn't blame her completely though. Baden's exposé on how staged the Selection was helped nothing. He described me at length as frigid, two-faced, and distant. He spoke of our one charming moment alone and then my intentional disconnection from him, and said there was no way he could have stayed in the palace, living under such a lie. I knew it was likely that he was paid an exorbitant amount of money for his story and that he was probably worrying about a mountain of debt for his education. But I felt certain he would have said it all for free.

Juxtaposing those stories with the one of my weekend dates cheapened everything about them. It was a waste of effort and worse, it was visibly taking a toll on Dad. Weeks had passed, he still had no idea how to address the caste issues, and pockets of rioters were calling for the end of the monarchy.

I was failing in every possible way.

After breakfast I went to my room, looking at my plans for the day. Were they worthless now? Was there a way to make these dates better?

I heard a knock and turned to see Kile standing at the door. I ran into his arms without a second thought.

"Hey," he said, holding me tight.

"I don't know what to do. Everything's just getting worse and worse."

He pulled back and lowered his eyes to meet mine. "Some of the guys are confused. They don't know if they're being used. Eadlyn," he continued in a whisper, presumably so

Neena wouldn't hear his words, "I know our first kiss was for show. Is it all for show? If it is, you need to come clean."

I stared into his eyes. How had I ever thought he was anything less than smart and funny and handsome and kind? I didn't want to respond in a whisper, so I signaled for Neena to leave, and once she had closed the door behind her, I faced him again.

"It's complicated, Kile."

"I'm a very intelligent person. Explain."

His words were calm, an invitation more than a demand.

"If you had asked me the night before everyone came, I would have said it was all a joke. But it's not anymore, not to me." The words shocked me. I'd fought caring about these boys, and I was still terrified of them getting closer. Even now, Kile was walking the edge of my comfort zone, and I was unsure how I'd manage if he pushed himself over the line.

"You matter to me," I confessed. "A lot of you do. But do I think I'll get married?" I shrugged. "I can't say."

"That doesn't make sense. Either you want this or you don't."

"That's not fair. When your name was called, did you want to participate? Would you say the same thing now?"

I didn't realize how tense he'd become until he let out a breath and closed his eyes. "Okay. I can understand that."

"It's been harder than I thought, with so many disasters along the way. And I'm not as good at showing my emotions as other girls, so it comes across like I don't care, even when

I do. I like to keep things to myself. It looks bad, I know, but it's real."

He'd been around me long enough to know it was true. "You need to address this. You need to say something publicly about that story," he insisted, his eyes focused on mine.

I rubbed my temple. "I'm not sure that's a good idea. What if I somehow make it worse?"

He poked my stomach, something we hadn't done since we were children. "How can the truth make anything worse?"

Well, that confirmed all my anxieties. Admitting how much this meant to me now might also mean owning up to the origins of this particular Selection. With the way things were going, that wouldn't win me any sympathy.

He turned me around and pointed me toward my table and chairs. "Here. Let's sit for a minute."

I sat beside him, piling up some of the dress ideas I had been working on.

"Those are impressive, Eadlyn," he remarked.

I gave him a weak smile. "Thank you, but it's really just a bunch of scribbles."

"Don't do that," he said. "Don't make it seem like it's not important."

I remembered those words, and they soothed me.

Kile pulled over a handful of the pencils and started some sketches of his own.

"What are you drawing?" I asked, looking at the little boxes.

"An idea I've been experimenting with. I've been reading

about some of the poorer provinces. One of their bigger issues is housing right now."

"Because of the manufacturing boom?"

"Yeah." He continued to sketch, making practically perfect straight lines.

Dad did what he could to encourage more industrial growth in some of the primarily agricultural provinces. It was good for everyone if things could be processed where they were grown. But as that took off, more and more people moved to be closer to those areas, meaning not everyone had adequate housing.

"I know a little bit about how much it costs to get supplies, and I figured out that it'd be possible to build these smaller huts, basically like family cubicles, fairly inexpensively. I've been playing with the idea over the last few weeks. If there was someone I could get the design to, they might be able to implement it."

I looked at the little structure, barely as big as my bathroom, abutted against an identical box. They each had a door and a side-facing window. A little tube at the top caught rainwater, and a small bucket collected it by the door. Vents lined the top, and a small tarp jutted out in front, shading the front of the space.

"They look so tiny though."

"But they'd feel like a mansion if you were homeless."

I exhaled, thinking that was probably true. "There can't be space for a bathroom in there."

"No, but most people use facilities inside the plants. That's what I read anyway. This would be strictly for shelter, which means workers would be more rested, have better health . . . and there's just something special about having a place to call your own."

I watched Kile, his eyes focused on the extra little details he was adding to his work. I knew that hit home for him, that he was aching for anything that truly belonged to him. He pushed the paper away gently, adding it to the others.

"Not nearly as exciting as a ball gown, but that's all I know how to draw," he concluded with a laugh.

"And you do it so well."

"Eh. I just wanted to distract you for a minute, but I don't know what else to do."

I reached over and held his hand. "That you came at all is enough. I shouldn't let myself sulk too much anyway. I need to come up with a plan of action."

"Like talking about it?"

I shrugged. "Maybe. I have to speak with my dad first."

I could tell he thought I was being silly, but he didn't know what was going on. Not really. And even as someone in the know, it was hard to understand.

"Thanks for coming, Kile. I owe you one."

"You owe me two. I'm still waiting for that chat with my mom." He winked, not too upset I hadn't delivered yet.

My promise was still in the back of my head, and I'd had more than one opportunity to bring it up with Miss Marlee. But now I was the problem, not her. It was getting harder to imagine the palace without Kile around.

"Of course. I haven't forgotten."

He poked my stomach again, and I giggled. "I know."

"Let me go talk to my parents. I need to figure out what to do."

"Okay." He put an arm around me and walked me out the door, parting with me at the stairs. From there I went straight to the office, nervous about how tired Dad looked when I came in and cleared my throat.

He popped his head up from the papers, shoving the stack of them into a drawer as if I wouldn't see. "Hey, sweetie. I thought you were going to be working on the Selection side of things this week."

"Well, that was the plan, but I'm wondering if that will even be of any help right now."

He was crestfallen. "I don't know how this happened, Eadlyn. I'm sorry."

"I'm the one who should be sorry. Baden exaggerated things, but the barest points of his story were real. And with the mayor, I said those things out loud, it's true. But I was simply venting about the work of it all. Ask Mom; she was there. Everything got twisted around."

"I already spoke to her, honey, and I'm not upset with you. I just can't understand why Milla would do that. It's like everyone is taking aim at us right now. . . ." He kept opening his mouth like he wanted to say more, but he was so confused by the overwhelming unhappiness of the public, he didn't know where to start.

"I'm trying, Dad, but I don't think it's good enough.

Which made me wonder if maybe we wanted to try something different."

He shrugged. "I'm up for most anything at the moment."

"Let's switch the focus. No one trusts me right now. Let's bring Camille in for a visit and let people see how in love Ahren is with her. He always does much better in the spotlight. I can come in and talk about their influence on me, and then we can pick up with the Selection shortly after, try to blend one love story into another."

He stared at his desk, contemplating. "I don't know where you get some of your ideas, but that's inspired, Eadlyn. And I think Ahren will be beside himself. Let me make a call and see if she can even come before we say anything, all right?"

"Absolutely."

"I want you to plan a party for her. You two should know each other better than you do."

As if I didn't have anything else to worry about. "I'll start at once."

He picked up the telephone, and I went back to my room, hoping this would be enough to get things back on the right track.

CHAPTER 30

TWO DAYS LATER I WAS standing on the tarmac next to my giddy brother, who was holding an obnoxiously large bouquet in his hands.

"Why don't you get me flowers like that?"

"Because I'm not trying to impress you."

"You're worse than those boys back at the palace," I said, shaking my head. "She's going to be the queen of France. Girls like us are hard to amaze."

"I know." He looked idiotically happy. "Guess I'm just lucky."

The stairs lowered from the plane, and two guards came down before Camille. She was a willowy thing, blond and petite, with a face that looked eternally well rested and excited. In person and in print, I'd never seen her wearing anything that remotely resembled a frown.

There was protocol to follow, but Ahren and Camille

bypassed it, running into each other's arms. He held her tightly and kissed every corner of her face, ruining half of his flowers in the process. Camille laughed as he peppered her with affection, and I felt a little awkward standing there, waiting for it to end so I could say hello.

"I have missed you so!" she cried, her accent making each word sound like a surprise.

"I have so much to show you. I asked Mom and Dad to make you a permanent suite so you will always have the best room when you come."

"Oh, Ahren! So generous for me!"

He turned, grinning from ear to ear, suddenly recalling my presence. "You remember my sister, of course."

We curtsied to each other, and she rose elegantly. "Your Highness, so nice to see you again. I bring gifts for you."

"For me?"

"Yes. Here is a secret," she said, leaning in. "You can wear all of them."

I perked up. "Wonderful! Maybe I'll have to use some of it at the party I'm throwing for you tonight."

She gasped and placed both hands on her chest. "For me?" She turned her blue eyes on Ahren. "Really?"

"Really."

It was strange to see him with this look in his eyes, like maybe he was in the middle of an act of worship, prepared to sacrifice anything to please Camille.

"Your family is so good to me. Let's go. I'm dying to see your mother."

I tried to keep up with them on the ride back to the palace, but Ahren spoke mostly in French for her benefit, and since I had chosen to master Spanish, I was completely in the dark. Once we got home, Mom, Dad, Kaden, and Osten were all waiting on the front stairs for us. Positioned on the edges of the steps, trying to be inconspicuous, were several photographers.

Ahren exited first, holding out his hand to help Camille. When I scooted over and reached for him, it turned out he'd already run off with Camille, who was rushing into my mother's arms.

Mom, Dad, and Kaden all knew French and were greeting her warmly. I walked over to Osten, who looked like he was itching to climb on something.

"What are you up to today?" I asked.

"I don't know."

"Go find the Selected guys and ask them awkward questions. Report back."

He laughed and went running.

"Where's he off to?" Dad asked quietly.

"Nowhere."

"Let's all go inside," Mom announced. "You should nap before tonight. Eadlyn's been working so hard on this party, it's going to be wonderful."

I'd thought of everything. The music was live—suitable for slow dancing—and there was a mix of foods, both from Illéa and France, as well as some of those delicious apple fritters Henri had made for me. I couldn't wait for him to see.

Mom looked radiant as always, and Dad didn't seem quite so worn-out. Josie was right at home, and I was pleased because for once she hadn't stolen a tiara. Kaden was like a little ambassador, walking around the room and shaking hands.

I was, of course, staying close to the happy couple, which was both captivating and draining. Ahren looked at Camille like she hung the sun in the sky every morning. It was beautiful, the way he watched her, enchanted by every breath that came out of her mouth. But I felt strangely detached from it all because no one had ever done that for me, and I'd never done that for anyone else.

I found myself jealous of Camille. Not for having the unwavering love of my brother—which I knew to be one of the steadiest forces in the world—but because everything about her came so effortlessly.

What had the French queen done to raise her like this? Camille was delicate and sweet, and yet no one would think to try and walk all over her. I kept up with international affairs, and I knew her people cherished her. Last year on her birthday an impromptu party started in the streets in her honor and lasted for three days. Three days!

I thought my education was fair and well-rounded, which meant one thing: my shortcomings had nothing to do with how or what I was taught but with me alone.

The realization forced me to step away from her and Ahren. Standing near her only made me feel worse. Before I could get too far, Ean was in front of me, holding out his arm.

"Long time, no see."

I rolled my eyes. "I see you every day." I laced my arm through his all the same.

"But we don't get to speak. I've been wondering how you're doing."

"Excellent. Can't you tell? I'm running around like a crazy person trying to date while being accused of faking it all, and my brother is in love with a perfect girl, and I know eventually she's going to steal him away."

"Steal him?"

I nodded. "When they finally do get married, which will require her mother's express approval and a lengthy engagement to plan what will surely be the most ostentatious wedding anyone has ever seen, he'll have to live in France with her."

"Hmm," he said, leading me to the dance floor and placing a hand on my waist. "I can't do much about your brother, but, if he does end up leaving, you still have someone you can always depend on."

"Would you happen to be speaking about yourself?" I teased, swaying to the music.

"Of course," he replied. "My offer still stands."

"I haven't forgotten it."

As I took in the room with all its trappings and important guests, it was hard to deny just how well he fit in with the crowd. Ever since Ean had arrived, he'd carried himself with a kind of poise that few people possessed. If I hadn't known better, I would have guessed that he grew up in a palace as well.

"If there's any truth to that article, you don't have to torture yourself with these little boys. I will be everything you could ask for in a husband. I will be faithful, kind, and a true helper. I will never demand love from you. And I will be more than happy simply to live by your side."

I still couldn't understand his motivation. In some ways he could do so much better.

"I thank you again for your offer. But I haven't given up on the Selection yet."

Ean cocked his head to the side, smiling slyly. "Oh, but I think you have."

"And why is that?" I tried to match his know-it-all attitude as best as I could.

"Because I'm still here. And if you were really hoping to find love, I can't see why you would keep me around."

We were both grinning at the audacity of his statement as I stopped dancing, pulling my hands away slowly. "I could send you home right now, you know."

"But you won't," he assumed, that impish grin still plastered to his face. "You know I can give you the one thing you really want, and you're the only one who can give me what I want."

"Which is?"

"Comfort. Comfort in exchange for freedom." He shrugged. "I think that's a pretty good deal." He bowed. "See you tomorrow, Your Highness."

I couldn't stand that he was probably the only person here more calculating than I was. He knew exactly what

I wanted and how far I was willing to go to get it, which was irritating.

I was close to the side door of the Great Room and slipped into the hallway for a moment to be by myself. I rubbed my cheeks, so tired of smiling. It was cooler out here and much easier to think.

"Your Highness?"

Erik came down the hall in the smartest suit I'd seen him in to date. His hair was neater than usual, slightly slicked back. He looked taller, prouder. My jaw fell open at the change. He looked positively gorgeous.

"You clean up nice," I said, trying to get my expression somewhere close to normal again.

"Oh." He looked down. "I was aiming for appropriate."

"You did much better than that." I pushed myself off the wall to face him.

"You think? Hale told me I should consider thinner ties."

I giggled. "Well, Hale is pretty gifted when it comes to style, but you look very good."

He stood there, clearly ill at ease with the praise. "So, are you enjoying the party?"

I peeked back into the room. "It's a success, don't you think? Good food, excellent music, a wide range of company . . . it might be the best party I've ever thrown."

"So diplomatic," he said.

I turned back to Erik and smiled. "I feel like I'm the one competing tonight."

"With who?" he asked, shocked.

"Camille, of course." I looked back into the room, trying to hide behind the door as I watched. Erik came beside me, and we both followed her as she danced with Ahren across the floor.

"That's ridiculous."

"That's kind of you, but I know better. She's everything I try to be." I'd thought this to myself before, but I'd never admitted it to anyone. I wasn't sure how Erik managed to make me want to confide this in him.

"But why would you try to be her when Eadlyn is more than enough?"

I whipped my head back to him, as if the concept was unimaginable. I was in a constant state of striving; I was never enough.

Erik's words nearly brought tears to my eyes, and I reached down to take his hand as I'd done in my bedroom not that long ago.

"I'm so glad I got to meet you. However this whole thing ends, I think I've been enlightened just by crossing paths with some of you."

He smiled. "And I'll never be able to express what a privilege it's been to know you."

I think I meant to shake his hand, but we ended up standing there, connected in silence for a while.

"Did you put your name in?" I asked suddenly. "For the Selection, I mean?"

He smiled and shook his head. "No."

"Why not?"

He shrugged, searching for an answer. "Because . . . who am I?"

"You're Eikko."

He stood there, slightly dazed at the sound of his given name. Finally, he smiled again.

"Yes, I'm Eikko. But you barely know me."

"I know Eikko as well as he knows Eadlyn. And I can tell you, you are enough as well."

He rubbed his thumb against the back of my hand, the tiniest movement. And I could sense we were both wondering what would have happened if his name had been in one of those baskets. Maybe he'd be one of the contenders, maybe he wouldn't have been picked at all . . . it was hard to say if the risk would have been worth it in the end.

"I should get back in there." I pointed over my shoulder to the party.

"Of course. See you."

I focused on my posture and stood as tall as I could, which was much more impressive in these heels Camille brought me. I walked into the room, graciously greeting everyone with a bow of my head. I could have stopped a dozen times, but I pushed on until I found Henri.

"Hello," he greeted.

I meant to go see him a dozen times this week. But between dating at top speed, doing damage control, and planning for Camille, I hadn't gotten to speak to Henri at all. I could see that he was anxious, and though I was sure Erik conveyed everything I'd said, I think we both knew we needed to actually speak, just the two of us.

"Okay?" I asked.

He nodded. "And you okay?"

I nodded.

With that he let out a massive sigh, and the bright face I'd come to expect was back again. I tried to think of all the disagreements and misunderstandings I'd had in my life. There was no way any of them was ended with less than five words. But that was genuinely all I needed from Henri to know his regret at possibly offending me without wishing at all that he could take back that kiss.

Maybe Erik had nothing to worry about. Maybe Henri and I could communicate just fine.

"Dance?" I asked, pointing to the floor.

"Please!"

I was nearly as tall as him in these shoes, and he wasn't much of a dancer, but what he lacked in grace he made up for with enthusiasm. He spun me several times and even dipped me twice. When I came up the second time, laughing, I spotted Erik over his shoulder.

I could have been wrong, but his shy smile looked a little sad.

CHAPTER 31

Camille looked flawless on the front of every paper and a few of the gossip magazines that tended to equate our family with movie stars and singers. She brightened the mood in the Women's Room simply by sitting there, and Aunt May came to visit for a few days solely to see her.

I knew why I had problems with Josie. She was bratty and juvenile and tried so hard to be me that I felt like I had to be overly guarded when she was near. But it was more complicated with Camille. Even her perfection was a quiet thing, as if she hardly noticed it at all. So though I really, really wanted to hate her, I knew that would look much worse for me than for the sweet, unassuming French girl.

"How is your mother?" Mom asked Camille, and something about her tone made it seem like she felt obligated to inquire about Queen Daphne. It was the one subject that seemed to take any effort between them.

Mom handed her a cup of tea, and Camille happily took it, pausing as she thought through her answer.

"Very well. She wanted me to send you her love."

"I've been seeing pictures of her lately, and she looks the most content I've ever seen her." Mom placed her hands in her lap, smiling kindly. This comment felt more genuine.

"She is," Camille agreed. "I don't know what's come over her, but she has never been more joyful. And her happiness only makes me happier." Her eyes grew soft at the thought of her mother, and again I was forced to wonder exactly what was going on in the French palace.

"So," Josie said, crossing her legs quite dramatically and taking over the conversation. "Any chance we'll be hearing wedding bells in your future?"

Camille bashfully looked away, and everyone laughed.

"Perhaps," she hedged. "I know Ahren is the one, but we both want to find the proper time."

Miss Marlee sighed. "So I suppose in the middle of the Selection is not at the top of the list."

"Never!" Camille laid a hand on my lap. "I wouldn't take this moment from such a dear friend!"

Miss Marlee and Miss Lucy clutched their hands together at the thought.

"Which reminds me." Camille straightened up. "Eadlyn, you have told me nothing. What are these boys like?"

I chuckled. "More trouble than they're worth."

"Oh, stop," Mom teased.

"Please don't tell me anything about Kile! Ick!" Josie protested. Her mother swatted her leg.

"I need an update, too!" Aunt May insisted. "I missed a lot. I saw there was a fight!"

"There was." I rolled my eyes, remembering. "The truth is, I'm still getting to know most of them," I admitted. "There are a few standouts, but things change from day to day, so it's hard to measure who might be better than anyone else."

"Measure?" Camille sounded sad. "There is no measure. Isn't there one person who fills your heart and takes up all your thoughts?"

As she said it, a name popped into my head. And I was so surprised that anyone came to mind at all that I didn't have time to absorb exactly who it was.

I forced myself to concentrate on the conversation. "I guess I'm just not as romantically inclined as some people."

"Obviously," Josie muttered under her breath.

Either Camille didn't hear her or she dismissed it. "I believe you will find a wonderful husband. I cannot wait to see!"

The conversation drifted away, and I listened quietly. I wasn't sure if I needed to stay in the room all day or if I was supposed to go work with Dad. It seemed like I'd been doing everything wrong lately, and I didn't want to add to my running list of mistakes.

And I liked girl talk, but I needed a little break. I excused myself and made my way into the hall, not sure of where I would go. Fifteen minutes. I promised myself after that I'd go back and be vibrant and engaging.

By pure luck I caught Hale on his way out to the gardens, holding a tray with carafes of water on it. He saw me and broke into a giant smile.

"Where are you off to?" he asked.

"Nowhere really. Taking a break from the Women's Room."

"Some of the guys are playing baseball outside, if you want to come."

I went over to the window and, sure enough, maybe eight of the boys were out there tossing a ball.

"Where did they even get that stuff?"

"Osten."

Of course. Osten had everything. I watched the boys roll up their pant legs and slide off their dress shoes, pushing one another jovially.

"I've never played baseball," I admitted.

"All the more reason to join us."

"Can you play?"

"I'm more of a pitcher than a hitter, but I do all right. And I'll teach you." Hale's face was so genuine, I really believed he'd take care of me out there.

"Okay. But I'll probably be rotten."

"Since when are you rotten at anything?" he said, leading us out the doorway.

Kile was there, as were Apsel, Tavish, and Harrison. Alex was there, too, and I hated to admit that I'd been very tempted to send him back to Calgary ever since Milla blabbed to the papers. I was still considering it.

Henri was stretching next to Linde, so I instinctively looked for Erik. He was there, sitting on one of the stone benches.

"Your Highness!" Edwin called, getting my attention. "Are you here to watch?"

"No, sir. I'm here to play."

Several of the boys clapped or cheered, though I seriously doubted any of them considered me a positive addition.

"Okay, okay," I said loudly, raising my arms. "Just keep in mind that I need to be back inside in a few minutes, and I've never played before. At all. But I thought I'd give it a quick go before I get to work again."

"You've got this!" Tavish assured me. "Here, give me your shoes. I'll put them by mine."

I slipped off my heels and placed them in his hands.

"Ugh, these are heavy. How do you lift your feet?"

"Strong calves?"

He laughed and carried my shoes to the side.

"All right, Eadlyn's up first then," Kile insisted.

I had a general understanding of how the game worked. Three outs, four bases. What I was lost on were the mechanics.

Hale was standing out in the middle of the diamond, practicing his pitches with Apsel. Raoul, who was going to be catching, came up behind me.

"Here's what you need to do," he said. He had a thick

Hispanic accent, but his instructions were nice and clear. "You grab the bat here and here." He demonstrated, clutching the bat firmly toward the bottom. "Legs apart, and keep your back foot dug into the grass, okay?"

"Okay."

"Just watch the ball."

"Watch the ball . . . all right."

Raoul passed me the bat, which weighed much more than I expected. "Good luck."

"Thanks."

I stood at the makeshift base, trying to do everything Raoul had told me to. I supposed if Hale was pitching, then he and I were on different teams. All the same, he was grinning when he saw me in my stance.

"It'll come in slow, okay?"

I nodded.

He threw the ball, and I swung well above it. The same thing happened the second time. I wasn't sure what happened with the third, but I ended up spinning around.

Hale laughed and so did Raoul, and while I typically would have felt embarrassed, this didn't seem too bad.

"Eadlyn! Eadlyn!"

I recognized my mother's voice instantly, and I faced the open windows of the Women's Room. Everyone was there, and I waited for her to order me back inside.

"Get them!" she yelled. "Hit it!"

Aunt May raised her arms in the air. "Go, Eady!"

The rest of the girls joined in, shouting and clapping.

I laughed and turned back to Hale. He gave me a nod. I returned it, gripping the bat.

I finally connected with the ball, sending it low and to the left. I shrieked, dropped the bat so I could pick up my dress, and bolted to the first base.

"Go, Eady, go!" Kile screamed.

I saw Henri chasing the ball, so I headed to the second base, watching him the whole time. I wasn't going to make it. Impulsively I lunged, falling into the base.

I beat him!

Everyone erupted. It wasn't even still my turn, and it wasn't like I'd won, but it felt huge. Suddenly, Edwin lifted me up off the ground and hugged me, swinging me around.

Moments later, Mom and Josie and all the other ladies were outside, slipping off their shoes and demanding a turn.

Someone alerted Dad and my brothers to the game, and Kaden showed everyone what a superior athlete he was. Mom and Dad stood off to the side, arms around each other. The Selected boys patted one another on the back, and Ahren snuck away with Camille, kissing her every step of the way.

"Go, Henri!" I yelled when he came up to bat. Erik sneaked up beside me and joined in.

We were both a little too dignified to jump around, but we pumped our fists in the air.

"Isn't this great?" I said. "I love that he can just play without worrying about words."

"Me, too," Erik agreed. "And I can't believe you hit that ball!"

I laughed. "I know! It was completely worth getting my dress dirty for."

"Agreed. Is there anything you can't do?" he teased.

"Plenty," I said, soberly thinking over my many faults.

"Like what?"

"Umm . . . speak Finnish?"

He laughed. "Okay. So one thing. That's forgivable."

"What about you?"

Erik looked around. "I couldn't run a country."

I waved my hand. "Trust me, if I can learn to do it, anybody could."

Mom rushed up, embracing me. "This was a great idea."

"The boys did it," I explained. "I happened to be in the right place to get an invitation."

I looked past her, watching Dad walk up to the plate.

"Go, Daddy, go!"

He lifted his arm, pointing into the distance, and Mom shook her head. "Not gonna happen," she mumbled.

As she guessed, he completely struck out. We clapped for him anyway, celebrating as the game continued on, with no one keeping score.

For just one moment we were happy. My family and friends swarmed around me, laughing and clapping and enjoying the sun. Mom wrapped me up in another hug, kissing my head and telling me how proud she was of my hit—though I didn't even try again the whole time. Osten ran in circles, disrupting things and making everyone laugh. Josie had stolen one of the boys' dress shirts and was wearing it open over her dress, looking silly and completely delighted.

It was a bubble of pure joy.

There were no cameras around to capture it, no reporters to tell the world about it. And for some reason, that made it so much better.

CHAPTER 32

I WANTED TO LIVE IN that place, to forget about all the worries hanging over my family, threatening to drop at any moment. But the peace was gone by dinner. Some of the Selected boys who missed out on the game were complaining that they should have been told about it. The ones who were present, they claimed, had gotten an unfair amount of additional face time with me, and they were asking for some sort of group date for them.

They elected Winslow to tell me this, and he stood in front of me with puppy dog eyes relaying the collective dejection of the group. We were outside the dining hall, where he caught me as I was heading back to my room.

"We're simply asking for another group date to keep things fair."

I rubbed my temple. "It wasn't exactly a date. There was

no planning involved, and my family was with me for most of it, including my younger brothers."

"We understand that, and we're willing to do any planning if you'll agree to come."

I sighed, frustrated. "How many people would it be exactly?"

"Only eight. Ean asked not to be included."

I smirked to myself. Of course Ean wanted nothing to do with a bunch of boys grumbling about more time. It made me wonder if I should go grab him right now for a date simply to make a point. I suspected he'd hoped for just that.

"You organize the date, and I'll do my best to make time for it."

Winslow beamed. "Thank you, Your Highness."

"But," I added quickly, "please pass along to the others that griping like this does not elevate my opinion of you. If anything, this is a bit childish. So you'd better make this the date of your lives."

Winslow's face fell as I walked past him and up the stairs.

Two more months. I could do this. Admittedly, there were as many lows as there were highs, but I sensed the worst had passed. I was feeling less intimidated by the boys after the game, and I felt sure I could give Dad the time he needed.

I still wasn't quite certain what to do with my heart.

I rounded the stairs to the third floor, catching Ahren leaving his room. He'd changed out of his suit coat and into a vest, and I felt sure he was heading to Camille's new suite.

"Do you ever stop smiling?" I asked, unable to believe his

face could hold that pose for so many days straight.

"Not when she's here." He straightened his vest. "Do I look okay?"

"As always. I'm sure she doesn't care one way or another. She's as head over heels for you as you are for her."

He sighed. "I think so, too. I hope so."

It was like he was already gone. In his mind, he was in Paris, showering Camille with kisses and debating what to name their children. I felt him leaving me. . . . I wasn't ready.

I swallowed, daring to say what I'd been deliberating over for a very long time. "Look, Ahren, she's a great girl. There's no denying it. But maybe she's not the one."

His smile finally faltered. "What do you mean?"

"Just that you might want to consider other options. There are so many eligible girls in Illéa that you've completely bypassed. Don't rush into something that you can't undo. If you and Camille broke up, it would be nothing. If you got divorced, we could lose our alliance with France."

Ahren stared at me. "Eadlyn, I know you're hesitant to fall in love, but I know how I feel about her. Just because you're scared—"

"I'm not scared!" I insisted. "I'm trying to help you. I love you maybe more than anyone. I'd do nearly anything for you, and I thought you'd do the same for me."

Every ounce of happiness left his face. "I would. You know I would."

"Then, please, think about it. That's all I'm asking."

He nodded, running his fingers over his mouth and

cheeks, looking concerned . . . almost lost.

Ahren brought his eyes to mine, gave me a tiny smile, and opened his arms for a hug. He held me tightly, like he'd never needed a hug so badly in his life.

"I love you, Eady."

"And I love you."

He kissed my hair and let me go, continuing on to Camille's room.

Neena was waiting for me with my nightgown ready. "Any plans for the evening? Or do you want to dress for bed?"

"Bed," I assured her. "But wait until you hear what these boys are doing now." I told her about the demanded group date, adding that Ean had excused himself from it.

"Smart move on his part," she agreed.

"I know. I keep wondering if that warrants a special date, just for him."

"A real date or a spite date?"

I laughed. "I hardly know. Ugh, what am I supposed to do with all these boys?"

"Weed 'em out. Ha! I found a piece of grass we missed earlier." She pulled the blade around for me to see before tossing it in the trash.

"That was so much fun," I said. "I'll never forget Mom's face, hanging out of the window telling me to go for it. I was sure I was in trouble!"

"I wish I could have seen that."

"You really don't need to hide in my room all day. It's

always clean, and it doesn't take too long for me to get dressed in the morning. You should come with me places, see more of the palace than this room and yours."

She shrugged. "Perhaps."

But I could hear in her voice that she was excited about the possibility. I wondered if I should train Neena for travel. It would be nice to have her with me next time I went abroad. But if she really was planning on leaving within the next year or so, it might not be worth it. I knew I couldn't keep one maid forever, but I dreaded the thought of someone replacing her.

I went down for breakfast the next day and noticed that Ahren didn't come. I worried he was upset with me. We never stayed cross with each other for long, but I hated when that happened at all. Ahren felt like a piece of me sometimes.

I didn't notice until a bit later that Camille didn't make it either. I assumed one of two things had happened: Ahren had come to his senses and told her that he needed to consider other options, and they were both in the process of avoiding each other . . . or they'd spent the night together and were maybe still in bed.

I wondered what Dad would think about that.

Then I realized that a few of the boys were missing as well. Maybe Camille and Ahren weren't wrapped in each other's arms after all. It was possible there was a bug going around. That was far more likely . . . and much less exciting.

I left the dining hall to find Leeland and Ivan waiting for

me. They both bowed deeply.

"Your Highness," Ivan greeted. "Your presence is requested in the Great Room for the greatest date of your life."

I smirked. "Oh, really?"

Leeland chuckled. "We were up all night working. Please say you're free right now."

I checked the clock on the wall. "I have maybe an hour."

Ivan perked up. "That's plenty of time. Come with us." They both offered their elbows, and I grabbed on to them, allowing myself to be escorted into the Great Room.

Along the back wall, a small stage had been set up and covered with what appeared to be tablecloths from our Christmas supplies. Spotlights that we sometimes brought out for parties were aimed at the center of the stage, and as we approached, the boys all shushed one another as they stood in a line.

I was brought to the lone chair right in front of the stage, and I took my seat, simultaneously curious and confused.

Winslow spread his arms wide. "Welcome to the first ever Selection Variety Show, starring a bunch of losers competing for your attention."

I laughed. At least they owned it.

Calvin jumped off to the side and sat at the piano, playing music that had a ragtime feel, and everyone left the stage except for Winslow.

He bowed very solemnly. But when he stood back up, he smiled hugely, bringing three beanbags in front of him. Then he started juggling. It was so silly, I had to laugh. Winslow turned to the side, and from offstage someone threw a fourth beanbag. Then a fifth and sixth. He managed to keep them going for a couple of tosses before they all fell to the ground, with one slapping him on the head.

Everyone lamented but applauded his efforts, even me.

Lodge got out a bow and arrow and a target covered with balloons, then managed to shoot and pierce each one. As they burst, glitter flew out of them, slowly settling on the floor. All the while, Calvin played on, switching up tunes for each act.

Fox, who I was surprised would rope himself into another group date, got onstage and drew. Horribly. I was sure Osten had made better stick figures as a child, but since this show seemed to either be highlighting their strengths in a ludicrous way or shrugging off their weaknesses as comedy, it ended up being quite charming. I was trying to think of a way to inconspicuously pilfer the picture he drew of me, which was little more than a balloon-shaped head and some brown waves of hair coming off it. I'd been drawn and painted countless times . . . but they never came out that sweet.

Leeland sang, Julian hula hooped, Ivan bounced a soccer ball for an incredibly long time, and Gunner read a poem.

"Our lovely Princess Eadlyn,
It's hard to rhyme your name.
And though we really ticked you off,
We love you all the same."

I giggled the whole way through it, as did most of the boys.

The grand finale was the eight of them cluttered onstage dancing. Well, trying to dance. There was a lot of grinding and hip shaking, to the point that I blushed a few times. In the end I really was impressed. They'd organized the whole thing overnight, both trying to entertain me and apologize at the same time.

There was something really sweet about it.

I applauded them as they had their final bow, giving them a standing ovation.

"All right, I should go to work . . . but what if I get some drinks in here for us instead and we talk for a bit?"

They all answered affirmatively over one another, so I sent for tea and water and some cold drinks as well. We didn't bother with rolling out tables and instead sat on the floor. Sometimes these pain-in-the-neck boys could be so nice.

Ahren didn't come to dinner either. I watched as the Selected boys filed in, and all our guests, then Mom who was running a little late . . . but no Ahren.

Dad leaned over to me. "Where is your brother?"

I shrugged, cutting my chicken. "I don't know. I haven't seen him today."

"That's not like him."

I glanced around the room, looking at the remaining nineteen candidates. Kile gave me a wink, and Henri waved. Every time I looked at Gunner, all I could think about was his silly poem. Fox nodded his head at me as our eyes met, and when Raoul stretched, I remembered the care he took teaching me to grip a bat.

Oh, no.

It had happened. Even with the boys I hadn't spent much time with, I knew that each of them had a hold on me in some way. I already knew that some of them claimed a spot in my ever-terrified heart, but how had it come to pass that they *all* mattered?

I felt a heaviness settle in my chest. I was going to miss these loud, strange boys. Because even if I miraculously found one to stay with me in the end, there was no way to keep them all.

I was thinking about how worried I used to be about losing my quiet house when Gavril walked in, one of the news staff we kept around for the *Report* trailing him.

He bowed in front of the head table, looking at Dad. "I'm so sorry to bother you, Your Majesty."

"Not at all. What's wrong?"

Gavril glanced at all the watching eyes. "May I approach you?"

Daddy nodded, and Gavril whispered something in his ear.

Dad squinted in disbelief. "Married?" he asked only loud enough that probably Mom and I could hear. He pulled back to look into Gavril's eyes.

"Her mother approved. It's been done, all legal. He's gone."

My body turned cold, and I ran from the room.

"No, no, no," I mumbled, rushing up the stairs. I went to Ahren's room first. Nothing. Everything looked pristine, no sign of packing or an urgent exit. But, more important, no sign of my brother.

I tore from the room, heading to Camille's suite. I'd peeked in the day before and had seen her trunks spilling open with so many outfit choices, they probably could have filled my closet. The trunks were still there, all but the smallest. And no Camille.

I fell into the wall, in far too much shock to process this. Ahren was gone. He'd eloped and left me here alone.

I stood there in a daze, not sure what to do. Could I get him back? Gavril said something about legal. What did that mean? Was there any way to undo this?

My world felt dimmer, slightly misaligned and wrong. How was I supposed to do anything without Ahren?

I ended up in my room without realizing I'd even walked there. Neena held out an envelope to me.

"Ahren's butler delivered this for you about half an hour ago."

I snatched the paper from her hands.

Eadlyn,
On the off chance that the news has not reached you by the time this letter does, let me tell you what I've done. I've gone to France with Camille, and, pending her parents' approval, I intend to marry her immediately. I'm sorry to have run off without you and to have excluded

you and Mom and Dad from what I always knew would be the happiest day of my life, but I felt I had no choice.

After speaking with you last night, the last few years made perfect sense to me. I always assumed your dislike for Camille stemmed from you both being in the same situation. You're young, beautiful women who will inherit a throne. And you and she handle this position in vastly different ways. She is open to everything, while you keep people at a distance. She deals out her power with humility, while you wield yours like a sword. I hate to be so blunt, though I'm sure you already know this about yourself. Still, it brings me no joy to say it.

But your positions are not the reason you dislike her so. You don't like Camille because she's the only person who could ever separate you and me.

Your words hit me so hard, Eadlyn. Because I wanted to believe you. I wanted to hear you out and consider your suggestions. I knew that if I did, one day you'd convince me to give up everything for you. Maybe even put your crown on my head. And, heaven knows, I would have done it. I would do anything for you.

So before you could ask for my life, I gave it to Camille.

I wish you could find love, Eadlyn. The reckless, relentless kind that consumes you. If you could, then maybe you'd understand. I hope someday you will.

My happiness with Camille is tarnished by one thing: that I may be estranged from you if you choose not to forgive me. That sadness will be great, but far more bearable than my separation from my soul mate.

Even as I write this I miss you. I cannot imagine us being so far apart. Please find a way to forgive me and know that I love you. Maybe not as deeply as you'd like, but still.

As a testimony to my desire to always be there for you, I want to give you one last piece of information, something that may help you in the coming months.

More provinces are protesting the monarchy than you could guess. Not all of them, but plenty. And while it pains me to tell you this, the problem people have with the monarchy stems from one person: you.

I don't know why—perhaps because of your youth, perhaps because of your gender, perhaps for reasons none of us could believe—but they worry. Dad's aging beyond his years. The stress of the amount of things he's accomplished in his reign is bigger than his predecessors', and the general population thinks you will ascend soon, and they are not prepared.

I hate saying those words to you, but you've already kind of guessed at this. I didn't want to let you dwell on those thoughts, hoping you could move past it. And I only tell you this because I think you can change their minds. Stop holding everyone at bay Eadlyn. You can be brave and still be feminine. You can lead and still love flowers. Most important, you can be queen and still be a bride.

I think those who cannot know you the way I do would finally have a glimpse of this side of you if you consider finding a mate. I could be wrong, but just in case this is the last time you ever want to speak to me, I must give you the only piece of advice I can.

I hope you can forgive me.

Your brother, your twin, your other piece,

Ahren

CHAPTER 33

I STARED AT THE LETTER for the longest time. He left me.
He left me for her. When the finality of it hit me, I was
consumed by a wild rush of rage. I picked up the closest
breakable thing and flung it across the room with every
ounce of strength I had.

I heard Neena gasp as the glass shattered against the wall,
and that brought me back. I'd completely forgotten she was
there.

Through heavy breaths I shook my head. "I'm sorry."

"I'll fix it."

"I didn't mean to frighten you. It's . . . he's gone. Ahren's
gone."

"What?"

"He eloped with Camille." I ran my fingers through my
hair, feeling slightly unhinged. "I can't imagine why the

queen would have authorized something like this, but she unquestionably did. Gavril said it was legal downstairs."

"So what does that mean?"

I swallowed. "With Camille in line for her throne and Ahren as her prince consort, his primary duty is to France now. Illéa is nothing more than the country he was born in."

"Do your parents know?"

I nodded. "But I'm not sure if he sent them letters as well. I should go to them."

Neena came over and smoothed out my dress and my hair. She took a tissue to my face, blotting away any imperfections.

"There now. That's how my future queen should look."

I threw my arms around her. "You're too good to me, Neena."

"Hush. Go to your parents. They need you."

I stepped back and swiped at the tears that were so, so close to falling. I went down the hall, knocking on the door to Dad's room, which they generally shared.

No one answered, so I risked a quick peek inside.

"Dad?" I stepped into the huge space. I hadn't been here in so long—maybe since I was a child—and I couldn't remember if it had always been this way. The room looked more like something Mom would have decorated than him. Warm colors on the walls, books everywhere. If this was his retreat, why didn't it feel like him at all?

Without Mom and Dad joining me, I felt like I was intruding and turned to go.

But I was stopped in my tracks by the sight behind me. Several large, framed pictures covered the wall. There was one of Mom and Dad when they were my age, with him in his full suit and sash next to Mom in a cream-colored dress. I saw them on their wedding day, their faces covered in cake. Then there was Mom, her hair slicked back with sweat, holding two babies in her arms as Dad kissed her forehead, a tear falling down his cheek. Several candid shots, like a kiss or a smile, had been blown up and changed to black-and-white, making them seem more classic than casual.

Two things became instantly clear. First, the reason Dad's room didn't feel like it was completely his was because it wasn't. He had all but turned it into a shrine to Mom. Or rather, a shrine to the two of them and how deeply they loved each other.

I saw it every day, but it was different seeing the images they both looked at before falling asleep each night. They were meant to be, even after dozens of obstacles, and they liked to be reminded of it constantly.

Second, I could see why Ahren would give me up—give all of us up—for a chance at this. If he even got a scrap of the love Mom and Dad had, it would be justified.

In that moment I knew I needed to tell them what Ahren's letter said. They would understand—perhaps better than anyone on the planet—why he had to go. They'd certainly understand better than I could.

They weren't in the dining hall, or Dad's office, or Mom's room. In fact, the hallways were abnormally empty. There wasn't a single guard in sight.

"Hello?" I called into the dimly lit air. "HELLO?"

Finally, a pair of guards came running around the corner.

"Thank God," one said. "Go to the king and tell him we've found her."

The second guard raced away while the first faced me and took a deep breath. "You need to come with me to the hospital wing, Your Highness. Your mother has had a heart attack."

As quiet as it was, it sounded like he was screaming. I couldn't think of what to say or do, but I knew I had to get to her. Even in heels, I outpaced the guard, running as fast as I could.

The only thoughts passing through my head were how wrong I'd been about so many things, how snippy I'd been with her when I'd wanted my way. And I was sure that she knew I loved her, but I needed to tell her one more time.

In front of the hospital wing, Aunt May sat next to Miss Marlee, who appeared to be deep in prayer. Osten, mercifully, wasn't present, but Kaden was there trying so hard to look brave. Lady Brice was there as well, pacing on the outskirts of the scene, but the true fear of the moment was summed up in Dad.

He clung to General Leger, holding on to him for dear life, his fingers digging into the back of his uniform. He was unabashedly crying, and I'd never heard such a painful sound. I hoped I never would again.

"I can't lose her. I don't know. . . . I don't . . ."

General Leger grabbed him by the shoulders. "Don't think about that now. We need to believe she'll be fine. And you need to think about your children."

Dad nodded, but I could tell he didn't quite believe he was capable.

"Daddy?" I called, my voice breaking.

He turned to me and opened his arms. I bolted right to him, squeezing him. I let myself cry, not concerned with pride at the moment.

"What happened?"

"I don't know, honey. I think the shock of Ahren leaving was too much. Heart problems run in her family, and she's been so anxious lately." His voice changed, and I knew he wasn't really talking to me anymore. "I should have made her rest more. I should have asked her for less. She did everything for me."

General Leger grabbed his arm. "You know how stubborn she is," he said kindly. "Do you think for one second she'd have let you make her slow down?"

They both shared a sad smile.

Dad nodded. "Okay, so now we wait."

General Leger let him go. "I need to go home and tell Lucy and get fresh clothes. I'll call her mother if you haven't already."

Dad sighed to himself. "I didn't even think about it."

"I got it. And I'll be back within an hour. Whatever you need, I'm here."

Dad let me go and embraced General Leger once more. "Thank you."

I walked away, going to stand by the door. I wondered if she could sense I was near. I felt so angry. At everyone, at me. If the people hadn't asked for so much or if I had done more . . . I wasn't ready to lose my mother.

I kept thinking that I couldn't live my life for other people, that love was nothing but chains. And maybe it was, but so help me, I needed these chains. I let myself feel the weight of Ahren leaving, the weight of my father's worry, and, most important, the weight of my mother's life hanging in the balance. These things didn't make me weaker; they held my soul to the earth. I wasn't going to run from them anymore.

I turned at the sound of the footsteps, aware that a mass of people was approaching. I was humbled, moved beyond words, to see each of the Selected come around the corner.

Kile looked at me. "We've come to pray."

Tears filled my eyes, and I nodded. The gentlemen scattered, some leaning in a corner and others perching on benches. They bowed their heads or lifted them, all for my mother. They'd caused such an upheaval in my life . . . and I was so glad they did.

Hale kept his fist to his mouth, rocking on his feet nervously. Ean, as I expected, was very steady, arms crossed in concentration. Henri leaned forward on his bench, his curls flopping over his eyes; and I was happy to see that, even though he didn't need to come, Erik stood beside him.

Kile found his mother, and they held each other. Kile was actually moved to tears for Mom, and, strangely, that tenderness made me feel stronger.

My eyes moved from him to the other remaining boys,

and I thought again of how each of them had grown on me in his own way . . . and I looked over at Dad. His face was red from crying, his suit was all rumpled, and I could see the distress in every molecule of his body, horrified at the thought of his wife dying.

It wasn't all that long ago that he'd stood where I did, that my mom's face was one of many in his world. And yet, despite all the impediments and all the time that had passed, they were still deeply in love.

It was obvious in everything, from their shared room to the way they fretted over each other to the way they seemed to be incapable of not flirting with each other even after being married so long.

If anyone had told me I might consider that a possibility for myself a month ago, I'd have rolled my eyes and walked away. Now? Well, it didn't seem so far-fetched. I didn't expect to find what my parents had or even what Ahren had found with Camille. But . . . maybe I could find *something*. Maybe there would be one person who'd still want to kiss me when I had a runny nose or would rub my shoulders after a long day of meetings. Maybe I could find someone who didn't seem so scary, who made letting him past the wall seem natural. But all that still could be asking for too much.

Either way, I couldn't slow now. I knew that for my sake—for my family's sake—I had to finish my Selection.

And, when I did, I'd have a ring on my finger.

ACKNOWLEDGMENTS

SPECIAL THANKS TO:

You, for being a generally cool person, but mostly for picking up a fourth book when you thought there'd only be three.

Callaway, for everything, but mostly for doing dishes and math, so I don't have to.

Guyden and Zuzu, for being the cutest kids ever, but mostly for giving me snuggles when I'm having a rough day.

Mom, Dad, Jody, for all your encouragement, but mostly for being as weird as I am.

Mimi, Papa, Chris, for being so supportive, but mostly for watching the kids over Christmas break so I could sleep.

Elana, for being a really incredible agent, but mostly for making me feel certain that if anyone tried to pie me in the face, you'd tackle them for me.

Erica, for being a very talented editor, but mostly for letting me call you about eighteen times a week without complaining.

Olivia, Christina, Kara, Stephanie, Erin, Alison, Jon, and

a gazillion other people at HarperTeen, for being generally awesome people, but mostly for making my life much easier even though we, like, never see one another.

God, for being God, but mostly for making a world where things like kittens wearing bowties are a reality.

And to anyone else I forgot—which is undoubtedly a lot of people—because I'm generally forgetful, but mostly because I'm so tired now, I'm typing this with my eyes closed.

Love you all!

The end of the journey is here–
and Princess Eadlyn must make her choice

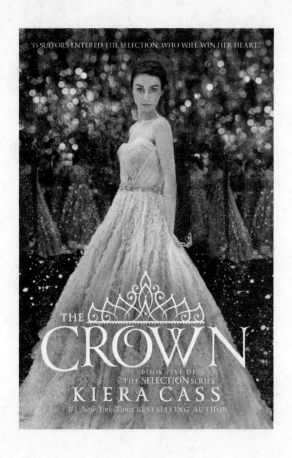

Keep reading for a sneak peek
at the final book in
THE SELECTION SERIES

CHAPTER 1

"I'm sorry," I said, bracing myself for the inevitable backlash. When my Selection started, I'd pictured it ending this way—with dozens of my suitors leaving at a time, many of them unprepared for their moment in the spotlight to be over. But after the last few weeks, after learning how kind, how smart, how generous so many of them were, I found the mass elimination almost heartbreaking.

They'd been fair with me, and now I had to be very unfair to them.

"I know it's abrupt, but given my mother's precarious condition, my father has asked me to take on more responsibilities, and I feel the only way to manage that is to scale down this competition."

"How is the queen?" Ivan asked, swallowing hard.

I sighed. "She looks . . . she looks pretty bad."

Dad had been hesitant to let me visit her, but I had finally worn him down. I understood his reluctance the instant I saw her, asleep, the metronome of her heartbeat keeping time on the monitor. She'd just come out of surgery, where the doctors had to harvest a vein from her leg to replace the one in her chest that had been worked to death.

One of the doctors said they had lost her for a minute but managed to get her back. I sat beside her, holding her hand. Silly as it sounded, I had slouched in my chair, certain that would make her come to and correct my posture. It didn't.

"She's alive though. And my father . . . he's . . ."

Raoul placed a comforting hand on my shoulder. "It's okay, Your Highness. We all understand."

I let my eyes flit across the space, my gaze settling on each of my suitors for a breath as I committed their faces to memory.

"For the record, I was terrified of you," I confessed. There were a few chuckles around the room. "Thank you so much for taking this chance, and for being so gracious with me."

A guard entered, clearing his throat to announce his presence. "I'm sorry, my lady. It's nearly time for the broadcast. The crew wanted to check, um"—he made a fumbling gesture with his hand—"hair and stuff."

I nodded. "Thank you. I'll be ready in a moment."

After he left, I turned my attention back to the boys. "I hope you'll forgive me for this group good-bye. I wish you all the best of luck in the future."

There was a chorus of murmured good-byes as I left.

Once I was outside the doors of the Men's Parlor, I took a deep breath and prepared myself for what was coming. *You are Eadlyn Schreave and no one—literally, no one—is as powerful as you.*

The palace was eerily quiet without Mom and her ladies scuttling around and Ahren's laughter filling the halls. Nothing makes you quite so aware of a person's presence as the loss of it.

I held myself tall as I made my way down to the studio.

"Your Highness," several people greeted me as I came through the doorway, curtseying and moving out of my way, all the while avoiding looking directly in my eyes. I couldn't tell if it was out of sympathy or if they already knew.

"Oh," I said, glancing in the mirror. "I am a bit shiny. Could you—?"

"Of course, Your Highness." A girl expertly dabbed at my skin, covering me in powder.

I straightened the high lace collar of my dress. When I'd gotten dressed this morning, black seemed appropriate, considering the overall mood in the palace, but I was second-guessing myself.

"I look too serious," I worried aloud. "Not respectable serious, but worried serious. This is all wrong."

"You look beautiful, my lady." The makeup girl swept a fresh splash of color across my lips. "Like your mother."

"No, I don't," I lamented. "Not a stitch of her hair or skin or eyes."

"That's not what I mean." The girl, warm and round, with

3

wisps of curls falling across her forehead, stood beside me and gazed at my reflection. "See there," she said, pointing to my eyes. "Not the same color, but the same determination. And your lips, they have the same hopeful smile. I know you have your grandmother's coloring, but you're your mother's daughter, through and through."

I stared at myself. I could almost see what she meant. At this most isolating moment, I felt a little less alone.

"Thank you. That means a great deal to me."

"We're all praying for her, my lady. She's a tough one."

I giggled in spite of my mood. "That she is."

"Two minutes!" the floor director called. I walked onto the carpeted set, smoothing out my gown and touching my hair. The studio was colder than usual, even under the lights, and goose bumps prickled at my skin as I took my place behind the lone podium.

Gavril, slightly dressed down but still very polished, gave me a sympathetic smile as he approached. "Are you sure you want to do this? I'm happy to deliver the news for you."

"Thank you, but I think I have to do it on my own."

"All right then. How's she holding up?"

"Okay as of an hour ago. The doctors are keeping her asleep so she can heal, but she looks so battered." I closed my eyes for a moment, calming myself. "Sorry. This has me a bit on edge. But at least I'm managing better than Dad."

He shook his head. "I can't imagine anyone taking this worse than him. His whole world has hung on her since they met."

I thought back to last night, to the wall of photos in their room, and I thumbed through all the details they'd only recently divulged about how they got together. I still couldn't see any rhyme or reason to fighting through countless obstacles for love only to have it leave you so powerless in the end.

"You were there, Gavril. You saw their Selection." I swallowed, still unsure. "Does it really work? How?"

He shrugged. "Yours is the third I've seen, and I can't tell you how it works, how a lottery can bring in a soul mate. Let me say this: Your grandfather was not exactly a man I admired, but he treated his queen as if she was the most important person to walk the planet. Where he was harsh with others, he was generous with her. She got the best of him, which is more than I can say for . . . Well, he found the right woman."

I squinted, curious about what he was omitting. I knew Grandpa had been a strict ruler, but come to think of it, that was the only way I knew him. Dad didn't talk about him much as a husband or father, and I'd always been much more interested in hearing about Grandma.

"And your dad? I don't think he had a clue what he was looking for. Honestly, I don't think your mother did either. But she was his match in every way. Everyone around them could see it long before they did."

"Really?" I asked. "They didn't know?"

He made a face. "Truthfully, it was more that she didn't know." He gave me a pointed look. "A family trait, it seems."

"Gavril, you're one of the few people I can confess this to. It's not that I don't know what I'm looking for. It's that I wasn't ready to look."

"Ah. I wondered."

"But now I'm here."

"And on your own, I'm afraid. If you choose to go through with this—and after yesterday, no one would blame you if you didn't—only you can make such an important choice."

I nodded. "I know. Which is why this is so scary."

"Ten seconds," the floor director called.

Gavril patted my shoulder. "I'm here in whatever way I can be, Your Highness."

"Thank you."

I squared my shoulders in front of the camera, trying to look calm as the light began glowing red.

"Good morning, people of Illéa. I, Princess Eadlyn Schreave, am here to address some recent events that have taken place in the royal family. I shall deliver the good news first." I tried to smile, really I did, but all I could think of was how abandoned I felt.

"My beloved brother, Prince Ahren Schreave, has married Princess Camille de Sauveterre of France. Though the timing of their wedding was a bit of a surprise, it in no way lessens our joy for the happy couple. I hope you will join me in wishing them both the happiest of marriages."

I paused. *You can do this, Eadlyn.*

"In sadder news, last night, my mother, America Schreave, queen of Illéa, suffered a very serious heart attack."

I paused. The words felt like they had created a dam in my throat, making it harder and harder to speak.

"She is in critical condition and is under constant medical supervision. Please pr—"

I brought my hand to my mouth. I was going to cry. I was going to lose it on national television, and on top of everything Ahren had said about how people felt about me, appearing weak was the last thing I needed.

I looked down. Mom needed me. Dad needed me. Maybe, in a small way, even the country needed me. I couldn't disappoint them. Dabbing away the tears, I went on.

"Please pray for her speedy recovery, as we all adore her and still depend on her guidance."

I breathed. It was the only way to get from any moment to the next. Breathe in, breathe out.

"My mother held such great respect for the Selection, which, as you all know, led to my parents' long and happy marriage. As such, I've decided to honor what I know would be her deepest wish and continue with my own Selection.

"Due to the stress placed on our household in the last twenty-four hours, I think it wise to cut my suitors down to the Elite. My father narrowed his field to six instead of ten because of extenuating circumstances, and I have done the same. The following six gentlemen have been invited to stay on in the Selection: Sir Gunner Croft, Sir Kile Woodwork, Sir Ean Cabel, Sir Hale Garner, Sir Fox Wesley, and Sir Henri Jaakoppi."

These names were a strangely comforting thing, like I

knew how proud they were of this moment and I could feel the glow of it, even from a distance.

It was almost done. They knew Ahren was gone, that my mother might die, and that the Selection would carry on. Now came the news I was terrified to deliver. Thanks to Ahren's letter, I understood exactly what my people thought of me. What kind of response would I receive?

"With my mother in such a delicate state, my father, King Maxon Schreave, has chosen to remain by her side." *Here goes.* "As such, he has named me regent until he feels fit to reclaim his title. I will make all decisions of state until further notice. It is with a heavy heart that I assume this role, but it gives me great joy to bring any peace to my parents.

"We will have more updates on all these matters as they become available. Thank you for your time, and good day."

The cameras stopped rolling, and I moved just off the stage, sitting in one of the chairs that were usually reserved for my family. I felt queasy and would have sat there for hours trying to regain my composure if I thought I could get away with it, but there was too much to do. The first thing on the list was to check on Mom and Dad again, then off to work. At some point today I would have to meet with the Elite as well.

I stopped short as I exited the studio, because my path was blocked by a row of gentlemen. The first face I saw was Hale's. His expression lit up as he held out a flower. "For you."

I looked down the line and saw they all had flowers in

their hands, some with roots still noticeably attached. All I could assume was that they had heard their names on the announcement, rushed to the garden, and come down here.

"You idiots," I sighed. "Thank you."

I took Hale's flower and hugged him. "I know I said something every day," he whispered, "but let me know if you need me to up it to two, okay?"

I held him a little tighter. "Thanks."

Ean was next, and though we'd only ever touched during those staged photos of our date, I found myself unable to refrain from embracing him.

"I get the feeling you were coerced into this," I murmured.

"I took mine from a vase in the hallway. Don't tell the staff on me."

I patted his back, and he did the same to me.

"She'll be okay," he promised. "You all will."

Kile had pricked his finger on a thorn and held his bleeding hand awkwardly away from my clothes as we hugged, which made me laugh and was perfect.

"For smiles," Henri said as I added his flower to my messy bouquet.

"Good, good," I replied, and he laughed at me.

Even Erik had gotten me a flower. I smirked a bit as I took it.

"This is a dandelion," I told him.

He shrugged. "I know. Some see a weed; some see a flower. Perspective."

I wrapped my arms around him, and I could feel him looking at the others as I held him, seeming uncomfortable to be getting the same treatment as they had.

Gunner swallowed, not able to say much, but held me gently before I moved on.

Fox had three flowers in his hand. "I couldn't pick."

I smiled. "They're all beautiful. Thanks."

Fox's embrace was tight, like he needed the support more than the others did. I held on to him as I looked back at my Elite.

No, this whole process made no sense, but I could see how it happened, how your heart could get swept up in the endeavor. And that was my hope now: that somehow duty and love would overlap, and I'd find myself happy in the middle of it all.

CHAPTER 2

MOM'S HANDS FELT SO SOFT, almost papery in a way. The feeling made me think of how water smoothed out the edges of a stone. I smiled, thinking she must have been a very rough stone once upon a time.

"Did you ever used to get it wrong?" I asked. "Say the wrong words, do the wrong things?"

I waited for an answer, receiving nothing but the hum of equipment and the beat of the monitor.

"Well, you and Dad used to fight, so you must have been wrong sometimes."

I held her hand tighter, trying to warm it in mine.

"I made all the announcements. Now everyone knows about Ahren getting married and that you're a little . . . indisposed at the moment. I cut the boys down to six. I know that's a big cut, but Dad said it was okay and that he did that when it was his turn, so no one can get upset." I sighed. "Regardless, I have a feeling people will still find a way to get upset with me."

I blinked back tears, worried she'd sense how scared I was. The doctors believed that the shock of Ahren's departure was the catalyst for her current condition, though I couldn't help but wonder if I'd contributed to her stress daily, like drops of poison so small someone didn't realize they'd ingested something dangerous until it had overtaken them.

"Anyway, I'm off to run my first advisory board meeting as soon as Dad gets back. He says it shouldn't be too difficult. Honestly, I feel like General Leger had the toughest job of anyone today, trying to get Dad to go eat, because he fought so hard to stay here with you. The general was insistent, though, and Dad finally caved. I'm glad he's here. General Leger, I mean. It's kind of like having a backup parent."

I held her hand a little tighter and leaned in, whispering. "Please don't make me need a backup parent, though, okay? I still need you. The boys still need you. And Dad . . . he looks like he might fall apart if you leave. So when it's time to wake up, you've gotta come back, all right?"

I waited for her mouth to twitch or her fingers to move, anything to show that she could hear me. Nothing.

Just then Dad tore through the door with General Leger on his heels. I wiped at my cheeks, hoping no one would notice.

"See," General Leger said. "She's stable. The doctors would come running if anything changed."

"All the same, I prefer to be here," Dad said firmly.

"Dad, you were hardly gone ten minutes. Did you even eat?"

"I ate. Tell her, Aspen."

General Leger sighed. "We'll call it eating."

Dad shot him a look that would have been threatening to some but only made the general smile. "I'll see if I can sneak some food in so you won't have to leave."

Dad nodded. "Look out for my girl."

"Of course." General Leger winked at me, and I stood up and followed him from the room, looking back at Mom just to check.

Still asleep.

In the hallway, he held out an arm for me. "You ready, my not-quite queen?"

I took it and smiled. "No. Let's go."

As we made our way to the boardroom, I nearly asked General Leger if he would take me for another lap around the floor. The day felt so overwhelming already that I wasn't sure I could do this.

Nonsense, I told myself. *You've sat in on these meetings dozens of times. You've almost always thought the same things Dad has said. Yes, this is your first time leading it, but this was always waiting for you. And no one is going to be hard on you today, for goodness' sake; your mother just had a heart attack.*

I pulled the door open with purpose, General Leger trailing behind me. I made sure to nod at the gentlemen as I passed. Sir Andrews, Sir Coddly, Mr. Rasmus, and a handful of other men I'd known for years sat arranging their pens and paper. Lady Brice looked proud as she watched me sweep around to my father's spot, as did the general when he settled into the place beside her.

"Good morning." I took my seat at the head of the table, gazing down at the thin folder in front of me. Thank goodness the agenda looked light today.

"How is your mother?" Lady Brice asked solemnly.

I should have written this answer on a sign so I could stop repeating it. "She's asleep still. I'm not sure how serious her condition is at the moment, but Dad is staying by her side, and we'll be sure to update everyone if there's any change."

Lady Brice smiled sadly. "I'm sure she'll be fine. She always was a tough one."

I tried to hide my surprise, but I didn't realize Lady Brice knew my mother that well. In truth, I didn't know that much about Lady Brice myself, but her tone was so sincere, I was happy to have her beside me at the moment.

I nodded. "Let's get through this so I can tell her my first day on the job was at least slightly productive."

There were gentle chuckles around the room at that, but my smile quickly faded as I read the first page presented to me.

"I hope this is a joke," I said dryly.

"No, Your Highness."

I turned my eyes to Sir Coddly.

"We feel this was a deliberate move to debilitate Illéa, and seeing as neither the king nor queen gave their consent,

France has essentially stolen your brother. This marriage is treasonous, so we have no choice but to go to war."

"Sir, I assure you, this was not treasonous. Camille is a sensible girl." I rolled my eyes, hating to admit it. "It's Ahren who's the romantic one, and I feel certain he urged her into this, not the other way around."

I balled up the declaration of war, unwilling to consider it for another moment.

"My lady, you cannot do that," Sir Andrew insisted. "The relations between Illéa and France have been tense for years."

"That is more on a personal level than a political one," Lady Brice offered.

Sir Coddly waved his hand in the air. "Which makes this all much worse. Queen Daphne is brandishing more emotional suffering on the royal family under the assumption that we will not respond. This time we must. Tell her, general!"

Lady Brice shook her head in frustration as General Leger spoke. "All I will say, Your Highness, is that we can have troops in the sky and on the ground within twenty-four hours if you command it. Though I certainly wouldn't *advise* you to make that command."

Andrews huffed. "Leger, tell her the dangers she's facing."

He shrugged. "I see no danger here. Her brother got married."

"If anything," I questioned, "shouldn't a wedding bring our two countries closer? Isn't that why princesses were married off for years?"

"But those were planned," Coddly stated in a tone that implied I was a little too naive for the conversation at hand.

"As was this," I countered. "We all knew Ahren and Camille would wed one day. It simply happened sooner than expected."

"She doesn't get it," he muttered to Andrews.

Sir Andrews shook his head at me. "Your Highness, this is treason."

"Sir, this is love."

Coddly slammed a fist on the table. "No one will take you seriously if you do not act decisively."

There was a beat of silence after his voice stopped echoing around the room, and the entire table sat motionless.

"Fine," I responded calmly. "You're fired."

Coddly laughed, looking at the other gentlemen at the table. "You can't fire me, Your Highness."

I tilted my head, staring at him. "I assure you, I can. There's no one here who outranks me at the moment, and you are easily replaceable."

Though she tried to be discreet, I saw Lady Brice purse her lips together, clearly determined not to laugh. Yes, I definitely had an ally in her.

"You need to fight!" he insisted.

"No," I answered firmly. "A war would add unnecessary strain to an already stressful moment and would cause an upheaval between us and the country we are now bound to by marriage. We will not fight."

Coddly lowered his chin and squinted. "Don't you think you're being too emotional about this?"

I stood, my chair screeching behind me as I moved. "I'm going to assume that you aren't implying by that statement that I'm actually being too *female* about this. Because, yes, I am emotional."

I strode around the opposite side of the table, my eyes trained on Coddly. "My mother is in a bed with tubes down her throat, my twin is now on a different continent, and my father is holding himself together by a thread."

Stopping across from him I continued. "I have two younger brothers to keep calm in the wake of all this, a country to run, and six boys downstairs waiting for me to offer one of them my hand." Coddly swallowed, and I felt only the tiniest bit of guilt for the satisfaction it brought me. "So, yes, I am emotional right now. Anyone in my position with a soul would be. And you, sir, are an idiot. How dare you try to force my hand on something so monumental on the grounds of something so small? For all intents and purposes, I am queen, and you will not coerce me into anything."

I walked back to the head of the table. "Officer Leger?"

"Yes, Your Highness?"

"Is there anything on this agenda that can't wait until tomorrow?"

"No, Your Highness."

"Good. You're all dismissed. And I suggest you all remember who's in charge here before we meet again."

As soon as I finished speaking, everyone other than Lady Brice and General Leger rose and bowed—rather deeply, I noted.

"You were wonderful, Your Highness," Lady Brice insisted once the three of us were alone.

"I was? Look at my hand." I held it up.

"You're trembling."

I pulled my fingers into a fist, determined to stop shaking. "Everything I said was true, right? They can't force me to sign a declaration of war, can they?"

"No," General Leger assured me. "As you know, there have always been a few members of the board who have thought we should colonize in Europe. I think they saw this as an opportunity to take advantage of your limited experience, but you did everything right."

"Dad wouldn't want to go to war. The banner of his reign has been peace."

"Exactly." General Leger smiled. "He'd be proud of how you stood your ground. In fact, I think I might just go tell him."

"Should I go, too?" I asked, suddenly desperate to hear the little monitor announcing that Mom's heart was still there, still trying.

"You have a country to run. I'll bring you an update as soon as I can."

"Thank you," I called as he exited the room.

Lady Brice crossed her arms on the table. "Feeling better?"

I shook my head. "I knew this role would be a lot of work. I've done my share of it and watched my dad do ten times more. But I was supposed to have more time to get ready. To start the job now, because my mom might die, is too much. And within five minutes of being responsible, I have to make a decision about war? I'm not prepared for this."

"Okay, first things first. You don't have to be perfect yet. This is temporary. Your mom will get better, your dad will come back to work, and you will go back to learning with this great experience under your belt. Think of this time as an opportunity."

I let out a long breath. Temporary. Opportunity. Okay.

"Besides, it's not all completely up to you. This is what your advisers are for. Granted, they weren't much help today, but we're here so you aren't navigating without a map."

I bit my lip, thinking. "Okay. So, what do I do now?"

"First, follow through and fire Coddly. It will show the others you mean what you say. I do feel somewhat bad for him, but I think your father only kept him around to play devil's advocate and help him see all sides of an issue. Trust me, he won't be sorely missed," she confessed dryly. "Second, consider this time a period of hands-on training for your reign. Start surrounding yourself with people you know you can trust."

I sighed. "I feel like they've all just left me."

She shook her head. "Look closer. You probably have friends in places you never expected."

Again, I found myself seeing her in a new light. She'd

stayed in her role longer than anyone; she knew what Dad would decide in most situations; and she was, at the very least, another woman in the room.

Lady Brice stared into my eyes, forcing me to focus. "Who do you know will always be honest with you? Who will be by your side, not because you're royal, but because you're you?"

I smiled, absolutely positive of where I was going once I left this room.

35 SUITORS. 1 PRINCESS.
A NEW SELECTION HAS BEGUN.

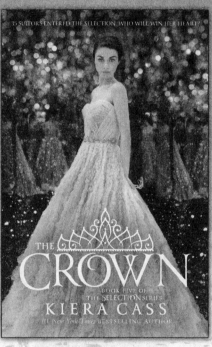

Princess Eadlyn has always found her parents' story romantic, but she never wanted a Selection of her own. Will she be able to find her fairy-tale ending?

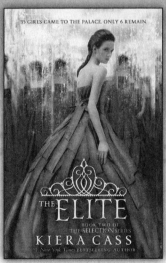

 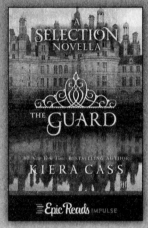

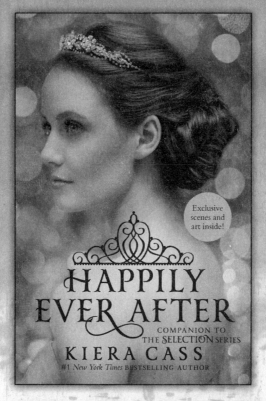

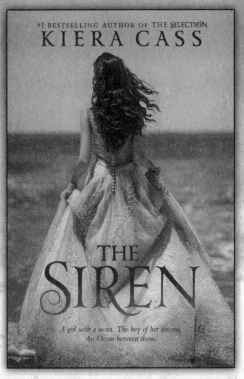

JOIN THE

Epic Reads

COMMUNITY

I PLACED ONE HAND IN his and put my cheek on his chest. He rested his chin on my head as we spun to the music of the rain. In that moment I felt sure we could make it. If we could do this, we'd somehow always find our way back to each other.

ALSO BY KIERA CASS

The Selection
The Elite
The Heir
The Selection Stories: The Prince & The Guard
The Queen (available as an ebook only)

THE ONE

KIERA CASS

HARPER TEEN

An Imprint of HarperCollinsPublishers

HarperTeen is an imprint of HarperCollins Publishers.

The One
Copyright © 2014 by Kiera Cass
All rights reserved. Printed in the United States of America.
No part of this book may be used or reproduced in any manner
whatsoever without written permission except in the case of brief
quotations embodied in critical articles and reviews. For information
address HarperCollins Children's Books, a division of HarperCollins
Publishers, 195 Broadway, New York, NY 10007.
www.epicreads.com

Library of Congress Cataloging-in-Publication Data
Cass, Kiera.
The one / Kiera Cass. — First edition.
    pages cm
Summary: "As her Selection approaches its finish, America must
decide where her heart truly lies—and Prince Maxon must pick one
winner to wear the crown"— Provided by publisher.
ISBN 978-0-06-206000-6
    [1. Marriage—Fiction. 2. Contests—Fiction. 3. Social classes—Fiction.
4. Princes—Fiction. 5. Love—Fiction. 6. Revolutionaries—Fiction.]
I. Title.
PZ7.C2685133One 2014   2013021356
[Fic]—dc23   CIP
                                              AC

Typography by Sarah Hoy
16 17 18 19 20 CG/RRDH   15 14 13 12 11

First paperback edition, 2015

For Callaway,
the boy who climbed into the tree house in my heart
and let me be the crown on his.

CHAPTER 1

THIS TIME WE WERE IN the Great Room enduring another etiquette lesson when bricks came flying through the window. Elise immediately hit the ground and started crawling for the side door, whimpering as she went. Celeste let out a high-pitched scream and bolted toward the back of the room, barely escaping a shower of glass. Kriss grabbed my arm, pulling me, and I broke into a run alongside her as we made our way to the exit.

"Hurry, ladies!" Silvia cried.

Within seconds, the guards had lined up at the windows and were firing, and the bursts of sound echoed in my ears as we fled. Whether they came with guns or stones, anyone showing the smallest level of aggression within sight of the palace would die. There was no more patience left for these attacks.

"I hate running in these shoes," Kriss muttered, a heap of dress draped over her arm, eyes focused on the end of the hall.

"One of us is going to have to get used to it," Celeste said, her breath labored.

I rolled my eyes. "If it's me, I'll wear sneakers every day. I'm already over this."

"Less talking, more moving!" Silvia yelled.

"How do we get downstairs from here?" Elise asked.

"What about Maxon?" Kriss huffed.

Silvia didn't answer. We followed her through a maze of hallways, looking for a path to the basement, watching as guard after guard ran in the opposite direction. I found myself admiring them, wondering at the courage it took to run *toward* danger for the sake of other people.

The guards passing us were completely indistinguishable from one another until a set of green eyes locked with mine. Aspen didn't look afraid or even startled. There was a problem, and he was on his way to fix it. That was simply who he was.

Our gaze was brief, but it was enough. It was like that with Aspen. In a split second, without a word, I could tell him *Be careful and stay safe.* And saying nothing, he'd answer *I know, just take care of yourself.*

While I could easily be at peace with the things we didn't need to say, I had no such luck with the things we'd said out loud. Our last conversation wasn't exactly a happy one. I had been about to leave the palace and had asked him to give me some space to get over the Selection. And then I'd ended up staying and had given him no explanation as to why.

Maybe his patience with me was falling short, his ability to see only the best in me running dry. Somehow I would have to fix that. I couldn't see a life for me that didn't include Aspen. Even now, as I hoped Maxon would choose me, a world without Aspen felt unimaginable.

"Here it is!" Silvia called, pushing a mysterious panel in a wall.

We started down the stairs, Elise and Silvia heading the charge.

"Damn it, Elise, pick up the pace!" Celeste yelled. I wanted to be irritated that she said it, but I knew we were all thinking the same thing.

As we descended into the darkness, I tried to reconcile myself to the hours that would be wasted, hiding like mice. We continued on, the sound of our escape covering the shouts until one man's voice rang out right on top of us.

"Stop!" he yelled.

Kriss and I turned together, watching as the uniform became clear. "Wait," she called to the girls below. "It's a guard."

We stood on the steps, breathing heavily. He finally reached us, gasping himself.

"Sorry, ladies. The rebels ran as soon as the shots were fired. Weren't in the mood for a fight today, I guess."

Silvia, running her hands over her clothes to smooth them, spoke for us. "Has the king deemed it safe? If not, you're putting these girls in a very dangerous position."

"The head of the guard cleared it. I'm sure His Majesty—"

"You don't speak for the king. Come on, ladies, keep moving."

"Are you serious?" I asked. "We're going down there for nothing."

She fixed me with a stare that might have stopped a rebel in his tracks, and I shut my mouth. Silvia and I had built a friendship of sorts as she unknowingly helped me distract myself from Maxon and Aspen with her extra lessons. After my little stunt on the *Report* a few days ago, it seemed that had dissolved into nothing. Turning to the guard, she continued. "Get an official order from the king, and we'll return. Keep walking, ladies."

The guard and I shared an exasperated look and parted ways.

Silvia showed absolutely no remorse when, twenty minutes later, a different guard came, telling us we were free to go upstairs.

I was so irritated by the whole situation, I didn't wait for Silvia or the other girls. I climbed the stairs, exiting somewhere on the first floor, and continued to my room with my shoes still hooked on my fingers. My maids were missing, but a small silver platter holding an envelope was waiting on the bed.

I recognized May's handwriting instantly and tore open the envelope, devouring her words.

> *Ames,*
>
> *We're aunts! Astra is perfect. I wish you were here to meet her in person, but we all understand you need to be at the palace right now. Do you think we'll be together for Christmas? Not that far away! I've got to get back to helping Kenna and James. I can't believe how pretty she is! Here's a picture for you. We love you!*
>
> *May*

I slipped the glossy photo from behind the note. Everyone was there except for Kota and me. James, Kenna's husband, was beaming, standing over his wife and daughter with puffy eyes. Kenna sat upright in the bed, holding a tiny pink bundle, looking equal parts thrilled and exhausted. Mom and Dad were glowing with pride, while May's and Gerad's enthusiasm jumped from the image. Of course Kota wouldn't have gone; there was nothing for him to gain from being present. But I should have been there.

I wasn't though.

I was here. And sometimes I didn't understand why. Maxon was still spending time with Kriss, even after all he'd done to get me to stay. The rebels unrelentingly attacked our safety from the outside, and inside, the king's icy words did just as much damage to my confidence. All the while, Aspen orbited me, a secret I had to keep. And the cameras came and went, stealing pieces of our lives to entertain the people. I was being pushed into a corner from every angle, and I was missing out on all the things that had always mattered to me.

I choked back angry tears. I was so tired of crying.

Instead I went into planning mode. The only way to set things right was to end the Selection.

Though I still occasionally questioned my desire to be the princess, there was no doubt in my mind that I wanted to be Maxon's. If that was going to happen, I couldn't sit back and wait for it. Remembering my last conversation with the king, I paced as I waited for my maids.

I could hardly breathe, so I knew eating would be a waste. But it would be worth the sacrifice. I needed to make some progress, and I needed to do it fast. According to the king, the other girls were making advances toward Maxon—physical advances—and he'd said I was far too plain to have a chance of matching them in that department.

As if my relationship with Maxon wasn't complicated enough, there was a whole new issue of rebuilding trust. And I wasn't sure if that meant I wasn't supposed to ask questions or not. While I felt pretty sure he hadn't gone that far physically with the other girls, I couldn't help but wonder. I'd never tried to be seductive before—pretty much every intimate moment I'd had with Maxon came about without intention—but I had to hope that if I was deliberate, I could make it clear that I was just as interested in him as the others.

I took a deep breath, raised my chin, and walked into the dining hall. I was purposely a minute or two late, hoping everyone would already be seated. I was right on that count. But the reaction was better than I'd hoped.

I curtsied, swinging my leg around so the slit in the dress fell open, leading nearly all the way up my thigh. The dress was a deep red, strapless and practically backless, and I was almost positive my maids had used magic to make it stay up at all. I rose, locking eyes with Maxon, who I noticed had stopped chewing. Someone dropped a fork.

Lowering my gaze, I walked to my seat, settling in next to Kriss.

"Seriously, America?" she whispered.

I tilted my head in her direction. "I'm sorry?" I replied, feigning confusion.

She put her silverware down, and we stared at each other. "You look trashy."

"Well, you look jealous."

I'd hit pretty close to the mark, because she flushed a bit before returning to her food. I took limited bites of my own, already miserably constricted. As dessert was being set in front of me, I chose to stop ignoring Maxon, and as I had hoped, his eyes were on me. He reached up and grabbed his ear immediately, and I demurely did the same. My gaze flickered quickly toward King Clarkson, and I tried not to smile. He was irritated, another trick I'd managed to get away with.

I excused myself first, giving Maxon a chance to admire the back of the dress, and scurried to my room. I closed the door to my room behind me and unzipped the gown immediately, desperate for a breath.

"How'd it go?" Mary asked, rushing over.

"He seemed stunned. They all did."

Lucy squealed, and Anne came to help Mary. "We'll hold it up. Just walk," she ordered. I did as I was told. "Is he coming tonight?"

"Yes. I'm not sure when, but he'll definitely be here." I perched on the edge of my bed, arms folded around my stomach to keep the open dress from falling down.

Anne gave me a sad face. "I'm sorry you'll have to be uncomfortable for a few more hours. I'm sure it'll be worth it though."

I smiled, trying to look like I was fine dealing with the pain. I'd told my maids I wanted to get Maxon's attention. I'd left out my hope that, with any luck, this dress would be on the floor pretty soon.

"Do you want us to stay until he arrives?" Lucy asked, her enthusiasm bubbling over.

"No, just help me zip this thing back up. I need to think some things through," I answered, standing so they could help me.

Mary took hold of the zipper. "Suck it in, miss." I obeyed, and as the dress cinched me in again, I thought of a soldier going to war. Different armor but the same idea.

Tonight I was taking down a man.

CHAPTER 2

I OPENED THE BALCONY DOORS, letting the air sweeten my room. Even though it was December, the breeze was light and tickled my skin. We weren't allowed to go outside at all anymore, not without guards by our sides, so this would have to do.

I scurried around the room, lighting candles, trying to make the space inviting. The knock came at the door, and I blew out the match, bolted over to the bed, picked up a book, and fanned out my dress. *Why yes, Maxon, this is how I always look when I read.*

"Come in," I offered, barely loud enough to be heard.

Maxon entered, and I lifted my head delicately, catching the wonder in his eyes as he surveyed my dimly lit room. Finally he focused on me, his gaze traveling up my exposed leg.

"There you are," I said, closing the book and standing to greet him.

He shut the door and came in, his eyes locked on my curves. "I wanted to tell you that you look fantastic tonight."

I flicked my hair over my shoulder. "Oh, this thing? It was just sitting in the back of the closet."

"I'm glad you pulled it out."

I laced my fingers through his. "Come sit with me. I haven't seen you much lately."

He sighed and followed. "I'm sorry about that. Things have been a bit tense since we lost so many people in that rebel attack, and you know how my father is. We sent several guards to protect your families, and our forces are stretched thin, so he's worse than usual. And he's pressuring me to end the Selection, but I'm holding my ground. I want to have some time to think this through."

We sat on the edge of the bed, and I settled close to him. "Of course. You should be in charge of this."

He nodded. "Exactly. I know I've said it a thousand times, but when people push me, it makes me crazy."

I gave him a little pout. "I know."

He paused, and I couldn't read his face. I was trying to figure out how to move this forward without being pushy, but I wasn't sure how to manufacture a romantic moment.

"I know this is silly, but my maids put this new perfume on me today. Is it too strong?" I asked, tilting my neck so he could lean in and breathe.

He came near, his nose hitting a soft patch of skin. "No,

dear, it's lovely," he said into the curve that led to my shoulder. Then he kissed me there. I swallowed, trying to focus. I needed to have some level of control.

"I'm glad you like it. I've really missed you."

I felt his hand snake around my back, and I brought my face down. There he was, eyes looking into mine, our lips millimeters apart.

"How much have you missed me?" he breathed.

His stare, combined with his voice being so low, was doing funny things to my heartbeat. "So much," I whispered back. "So, so much."

I leaned forward, aching to be kissed. Maxon was confident, pulling me closer with one hand and stringing the other through my hair. My body wanted to melt into the kiss, but the dress stopped me. Then, suddenly nervous again, I remembered my plan.

Sliding my hands down Maxon's arms, I guided his fingers to the zipper on the back of my dress, hoping that would be enough.

His hands lingered there for a moment, and I was seconds away from just asking him to unzip it when he burst out laughing.

The sound sobered me up pretty quickly.

"What's so funny?" I asked, horrified, trying to think of an inconspicuous way to check my breath.

"Of everything you've done, this is by far the most entertaining!" Maxon bent over, hitting his knee as he laughed.

"Excuse me?"

He kissed me hard on my forehead. "I always wondered what it would be like to see you try." He started laughing again. "I'm sorry; I have to go." Even the way he stood held a sense of amusement. "I'll see you in the morning."

And then he left. He just left!

I sat there, completely mortified. Why in the world did I think I could pull that off? Maxon may not know everything about me, but at the very least he knew my character—and this? It wasn't me.

I looked down at the ridiculous dress. It was way too much. Even Celeste wouldn't have gone this far. My hair was too perfect, my makeup too heavy. He knew what I was trying to do from the second he walked through the doorway. Sighing, I went around the room, blowing out candles and wondering how I was supposed to face him tomorrow.

CHAPTER 3

I DEBATED CLAIMING THE STOMACH flu. Or an incapacitating
headache. Panic attack. Really, anything to get out of going
to breakfast.

Then I thought of Maxon and how he always talked about
putting on a brave face. That wasn't a particular strength of
mine. But if I went downstairs at least, if I could just be present, maybe he'd give me some credit.

In hopes that I could erase some of what I'd done, I asked
my maids to put me in the most demure dress I had. Based
on that request alone, they knew not to ask about the night
before. The neckline was a bit higher than the ones we typically wore in the warm Angeles weather, and it had sleeves
that went nearly to my elbows. It was flowery and cheerful,
the opposite of last night's getup.

I could barely look at Maxon when I entered the dining

hall, but I walked tall at least.

When I finally peeked at him, he was watching me, grinning. As he chewed his food, he winked at me; and I ducked my head again, pretending to be very interested in my quiche.

"Glad to see you in actual clothes today," Kriss spat.

"Glad to see you in such a good mood."

"What in the world has gotten into you?" she hissed.

Dejected, I gave up. "I'm not up for this today, Kriss. Just leave me alone."

For a moment, she looked as if she might fight back, but I guessed I wasn't worth it. She sat up a little straighter and continued eating. If I'd had any level of success last night, then I could justify my actions; as it was, I couldn't even fake being proud.

I risked another glance at Maxon, and even though he wasn't watching me, he was still suppressing a smug expression as he cut his food. That was it. I wasn't going to suffer through a day like this. I was about to swoon or clutch my stomach or do anything to get me out of the room when a butler came in. He carried an envelope on a silver platter, and he bowed before placing it in front of King Clarkson.

The king took the letter and read it quickly. "Damn French," he muttered. "Sorry, Amberly, it looks like I'll be leaving within the hour."

"Another problem with the trade agreement?" she asked quietly.

"Yes. I thought we'd settled all this months ago. We need

to be firm on this one." He stood, throwing his napkin on his plate, and made his way to the door.

"Father," Maxon called, standing. "Don't you want me to come?"

It had struck me as odd that the king didn't bark out a command for his son to follow when he exited, seeing as that was his usual method of instructing. Instead he turned to Maxon, his eyes cold and his voice sharp.

"When you're ready to behave the way a king should, you'll get to experience what a king does." Without saying anything more, he left us.

Maxon stood for a moment, shocked and embarrassed by his father's choice to call him out in front of everyone. As he sat down, he turned to his mother. "Wasn't really looking forward to that flight, if I'm being honest," he said, joking away the tension. The queen smiled, as of course she must, and the rest of us ignored it.

The other girls finished their breakfasts and excused themselves to the Women's Room. When it was just Maxon, Elise, and me remaining at our tables, I looked up at him. We both tugged our ears at the same time, then smiled. Elise finally left, and we met in the middle of the room, not bothered by the maids and butlers cleaning up around us.

"It's my fault he's not taking you," I lamented.

"Perhaps," he teased. "Trust me, this isn't the first time he's tried to put me in my place, and he has a million reasons in his head why he thinks he should. It wouldn't surprise me if his only motive this time was spite. He doesn't want to lose control, and the closer I am to picking a wife, the more of a likelihood that is for him. Though we both know he'll never truly let go."

"You might as well just send me home. He's never going to let you pick me." I still hadn't told Maxon about how his father had cornered me, threatening me in the middle of the hall after Maxon talked him into letting me stay. King Clarkson had made it clear I was to keep my mouth shut about our conversation, and I didn't want to cross him. At the same time, I hated keeping it from Maxon.

"Besides," I added, crossing my arms, "after last night, I can't imagine you're that keen on keeping me anyway."

He bit his lips. "I'm sorry I laughed, but really, what else could I do?"

"I had plenty of ideas," I muttered, still embarrassed at my attempt to seduce him. "I feel so stupid." I buried my head in my hands.

"Stop," he said gently, pulling me in for an embrace. "Trust me when I say, it was very tempting. But you're not that girl."

"But shouldn't I be? Shouldn't that be part of what we are?" I whined into his chest.

"Don't you remember the night in the safe room?" he said, his voice low.

"Yes, but that was basically us saying good-bye."

"It would have been a fantastic good-bye."

I stepped away and swatted at him. He laughed, happy to have broken through the uneasiness.

"Let's forget about it," I proposed.

"Very well," he agreed. "Besides, we have a project to work on, you and I."

"We do?"

"Yes, and since my father is gone, this will be a convenient time to start brainstorming."

"All right," I said, excited to be a part of something that was just between the two of us.

He sighed, making me nervous about what he was planning. "You're right. Father doesn't approve of you. But he might be forced to bend if we can manage one thing."

"Which is?"

"We have to make you the people's favorite."

I rolled my eyes. "*That* is what we're working on? Maxon, that's never going to happen. I saw a poll in one of Celeste's magazines after I tried to save Marlee. People can hardly stand me."

"Opinions change. Don't let that one moment bring you down too much."

I still felt hopeless, but what could I say? If this was my only option, I had to at least try.

"Fine," I said. "But I'm telling you, this won't work."

With an impish grin on his face, he came very close and gave me a long, slow kiss. "And I'm telling you it will."

CHAPTER 4

I walked into the Women's Room, thoughts focused on Maxon's new plan. The queen hadn't shown up yet, and the girls were all laughing in a clump by the windows.

"America, come here!" Kriss said urgently. Even Celeste turned back smiling, waving me over.

I was a little uneasy about what could be waiting for me, but I walked to the huddle anyway.

"Oh, my goodness!" I squealed.

"I know," Celeste sighed.

There, running laps in the garden without their shirts on, were half of the guards in the palace. Aspen had told me that all guards got injections to help keep them strong, but apparently they also did a lot of work to keep their bodies in peak condition.

While we were all devoted to Maxon, the sight of cute

boys was something we couldn't ignore.

"The guy with blond hair," Kriss said. "Well, I think he's a blond. Their hair is so short!"

"I like this one," Elise said quietly as another guard ran past our window.

Kriss giggled. "I can't believe we're doing this!"

"Oh, oh! That guy, right there with the green eyes," Celeste said, pointing to Aspen.

Kriss sighed. "I danced with him at Halloween, and he's as funny as he is good-looking."

"I danced with him, too," Celeste bragged. "Easily the most gorgeous guard in the palace."

I had to laugh a little. I wondered how she would feel if she knew he used to be a Six.

I watched him run and thought about the hundreds of times those arms had embraced me. The distance growing between Aspen and me felt unavoidable, but even now I had to wonder if there was a way to keep some piece of what we had. What if I needed him?

"What about you, America?" Kriss asked.

The only one who really caught my eye was Aspen, and after feeling that ache for him, this felt kind of stupid. I dodged the question.

"I don't know. They're all kind of nice."

"Kind of nice?" Celeste echoed. "You have to be kidding! These are some of the best-looking guys I've ever seen."

"It's only a bunch of boys without their shirts on," I countered.

"Yeah, why don't you enjoy it for a minute before it's just the three of us you have to look at," she said snippily.

"Whatever. Maxon looks just as good without his shirt on as any of those guys."

"What?" Kriss shrieked.

A second after the words slipped out of my mouth, I realized what I'd said. Three sets of eyes focused in on me.

"When were you and Maxon topless, exactly?" Celeste demanded.

"I wasn't!"

"But he was?" Kriss asked. "Was that what that god-awful dress was about yesterday?"

Celeste gasped. "You slut!"

"Excuse me!" I yelled.

"Well, what else would you expect?" she snapped, crossing her arms. "Unless you want to tell us all what happened and why we're so wrong."

But there was no way to explain this. Undressing Maxon hadn't exactly been a romantic moment, but I couldn't tell them I'd been tending to wounds on his back specifically delivered by his father. He'd spent his life guarding that secret. If I betrayed him now, it would be the end of us.

"Celeste was half-naked up against him in a hallway!" I accused, pointing a finger at her.

Her mouth popped open. "How did you know?"

"Has everyone been getting naked with Maxon?" Elise asked, horrified.

"We weren't naked!" I shouted.

"Okay," Kriss said, putting out her arms. "We need to clear this up. Who has done what with Maxon?"

Everyone was quiet for a moment, not wanting to speak up first.

"I've kissed him," Elise said. "Three times, but that's it."

"I haven't kissed him at all," Kriss confessed. "But that's by my own choosing. He would kiss me if I'd let him."

"Really? Not once?" Celeste asked, shocked.

"Not once."

"Well, I've kissed him plenty." Celeste flipped her hair, deciding to be proud instead of embarrassed. "The best was in the hallway one night." She eyed me. "We kept whispering about how exciting it was that we might get caught."

Finally all eyes were on me. I thought of the king's words, suggesting that maybe the other girls were being much more promiscuous than I was prepared to be. But now I knew it was one more weapon in his arsenal, a way to make me feel insignificant. I came clean.

"I was Maxon's first kiss, not Olivia. I didn't want anyone to know. And we've had a few . . . more intimate moments, and one of those times Maxon's shirt came off."

"Came off? Like it magically flew over his head?" Celeste pressed.

"He took it off," I admitted.

Not satisfied, Celeste pushed on. "He took it off or *you* took it off?"

"I guess we both did."

After a charged moment, Kriss started again. "Okay, so

now we all know where we stand."

"And where is that?" Elise asked.

No one answered.

"I just want to say . . . ," I started. "All of those moments were really important to me, and I care about Maxon."

"Are you implying that we don't?" Celeste barked.

"I know that *you* don't."

"How dare you?"

"Celeste, it's no secret that you want someone with power. I'm willing to bet you like Maxon well enough, but you're not in love with him. You're shooting for the crown."

Without denying it, she turned on Elise. "What about this one? I've never seen a speck of emotion out of you!"

"I'm reserved. You should try it sometime," Elise fired back quickly. Seeing a spark of anger in Elise made me like her more. "In my family, all the marriages are arranged. I knew what was coming for me, and that's all this is. I may not be head over heels for Maxon, but I respect him. Love can come later."

Sympathetically, Kriss spoke. "That actually sounds kind of sad, Elise."

"It's not. There are bigger things than love."

We stared at Elise, her words echoing. I fought for my family out of love, and for Aspen, too. And now, though it scared me to think it, I was sure that all my actions where Maxon was concerned—even when they were hopelessly stupid—were driven by that feeling. Still, what if there was something more important here than that?

"Well, I'll say it: I love him," Kriss blurted. "I love him, and I want him to marry me."

Snapped back into the discussion at hand, I ached to melt into the carpet. What had I started?

"All right, America, fess up," Celeste demanded.

I froze, breathing shallowly. It took me a moment to find the right words.

"Maxon knows how I feel, and that's all that matters."

She rolled her eyes at my answer but didn't press any further. No doubt she was worried I would do the same to her if she did.

We stood there, looking at one another. The Selection had been going on for months, and now we could finally see the real lines of competition. We'd all gotten a peek into everyone else's relationship with Maxon—at least one aspect of it—and could look at them side by side.

Moments later the queen walked in, wishing us a good morning. After curtsying to her, we all retreated. Into corners, into ourselves. Maybe it was always supposed to come to this. There were four girls and one prince, and three of us would be leaving soon with little more than an interesting story of how we spent our fall.

CHAPTER 5

I WAS WRINGING MY HANDS as I paced the downstairs library, trying to put the words together in my head. I knew I needed to explain what had just happened to Maxon before he heard about it from the other girls, but that didn't mean I was looking forward to the conversation.

"Knock, knock," he said, coming in. He took in my worried expression. "What's wrong?"

"Don't get mad," I warned as he approached.

His pace slowed, and the concerned look on his face became guarded instead. "I'll try."

"The girls know I saw you without your shirt on." I saw the question coming to his lips. "I didn't say anything about your back," I vowed. "I wanted to, because now they just think we were in the middle of some big make-out fest."

He smiled. "It did end up that way."

"Don't joke, Maxon! They hate me right now."

The light didn't leave his eyes as he hugged me. "If it's any consolation, I'm not mad. So long as you kept my secret, I don't mind. Though I am a little shocked you told them. How did it even come up?"

I buried my head in his chest. "I don't think I can tell you."

"Hmm." His thumb rubbed up and down my back. "I thought we were supposed to be working on our trust."

"We are. I'm asking you to trust that this will only get worse if I tell you." Maybe I was wrong, but I was pretty sure confessing to Maxon that we were checking out half-dressed, sweaty guards would get us all into some kind of trouble.

"Okay," he finally said. "The girls know you've seen me partly undressed. Anything else?"

I hesitated. "They know I was your first kiss. And I know everything you have and haven't done with them."

He pulled back. "What?"

"After I let the whole shirtless thing slip, there was a lot of finger-pointing, and everyone came clean. I know you've spent plenty of time kissing Celeste and that you would have kissed Kriss long before now if she would have let you. It all came out."

He wiped his hand over his face, taking a few paces as he processed this. "So I have absolutely no privacy anymore? None? Because the four of you had to check scores with each other?" His frustration was clear.

"You know, for someone concerned with honesty, you ought to be grateful."

He stopped and stared. "I beg your pardon?"

"Everything is out in the open now. We all have a pretty good idea of where we stand, and I, for one, am thankful."

He rolled his eyes. "Thankful?"

"If you had told me that Celeste and I were at about the same point with you physically, I would never have tried to come on to you like I did last night. Do you know how humiliated I was?"

He scoffed and started pacing again. "Please, America, you've said and done so many foolish things, I'm surprised you can even be embarrassed anymore."

Maybe it was because I had been raised with less of an articulate education, but it took a second for the full impact of his words to hit me. Maxon had always liked me, or so he'd said. I knew it was against the better judgment of other people. Was it also against his?

"I'll go then," I said quietly, unable to look him in the eye. "Sorry I let the whole shirt thing out." I started walking away, feeling so small I wondered if he even noticed.

"Come on, America. I didn't mean it like—"

"No, it's fine," I mumbled. "I'll watch my words better."

I made my way upstairs, unsure of whether I wanted Maxon to come after me or not. He didn't.

When I got to my room, Anne, Mary, and Lucy were in

there, changing my sheets and dusting the shelves.

"Hello, my lady," Anne greeted. "Would you like some tea?"

"No, I'm just going to sit on the balcony for a moment. If any visitors come, tell them I'm resting."

Anne frowned a bit but nodded. "Of course."

I spent some time taking in the fresh air, then went over the assigned reading Silvia had prepared for us. I took a short nap and played my violin for a little while. So long as I could avoid the other girls and Maxon, I really didn't care what I was doing.

With the king away, we were allowed to take our meals in our rooms, so I did. Halfway through my lemon-and-pepper chicken, a knock came at the door. Maybe I was being paranoid, but I was sure it was Maxon. There was no way I could see him right now. I grabbed Mary and Anne and headed to the bathroom.

"Lucy," I whispered. "Tell him I'm taking a bath."

"Him? A bath?"

"Yes. Don't let him in," I instructed.

"What's this all about?" Anne asked as I closed the door, pressing my ear up against it.

"Can you hear anything?" I asked.

They both put their ears to the door, too, waiting to see if something intelligible came through.

I heard Lucy's muffled voice, but then I put my ear to the crack of the door and the following conversation was much clearer.

"She's in the bath, Your Majesty," Lucy answered calmly. It *was* Maxon.

"Oh. I was hoping she'd be eating still. I thought maybe I could have my dinner with her."

"She decided to take a bath before she ate." There was a tiny waver in her voice, uncomfortable with being dishonest.

Come on, Lucy. Hold it together.

"I see. Well, maybe you could have her send for me when she's done. I'd like to speak with her."

"Umm . . . it might be a very long bath, Your Majesty."

Maxon paused. "Oh. Very well. Then could you please let her know I came by and tell her to send for me if she'd like to talk. Tell her not to worry about the hour; I'll come."

"Yes, sir."

It was quiet for a long time, and I was starting to think he had left.

"Um, thank you," he said finally. "Good night."

"Good night, Your Majesty."

I hid for a few seconds longer to make sure he was gone. When I came out, Lucy was still standing by the door. I looked at all my maids, seeing the questions in their eyes.

"I just want to be alone tonight," I said vaguely. "In fact, I think I'm ready to wind down. If you could take my dinner tray, I'm going to get ready for bed."

"Do you want one of us to stay?" Mary asked. "In case you decide to send for the prince?"

I could see the hope in their eyes, but I had to let them down.

"No, I just need some rest. I'll see Maxon in the morning."

It was strange tucking myself into bed, knowing something was hanging between Maxon and me, but I didn't know how to talk to him right now. It didn't make sense. We'd already been through so many ups and downs together, so many attempts to make this relationship real; but it was clear that if that was going to happen, we still had a very long way to go.

I was gruffly awoken before dawn. The light from the hallway flooded my room, and I rubbed my eyes as a guard entered.

"Lady America, wake up, please," he said.

"What's wrong?" I asked, yawning.

"There's an emergency. We need you downstairs."

At once my blood turned cold. My family was dead; I knew it. We'd sent guards; we'd warned those at home this was possible, but the rebels were too much. The same thing had happened to Natalie. She left the Selection an only child after the rebels killed her little sister. None of our families was safe anymore.

I threw off the covers and grabbed my robe and slippers. I ran down the hall and stairs as quickly as I could, nearly slipping twice on the steps.

When I got to the first floor, Maxon was there, talking intently to a guard. I ran up to him, forgetting about everything from the last two days.

"Are they all right?" I asked, trying not to cry. "How bad is it?"

"What?" he asked, taking me in for an unexpected hug.

"My parents, my brothers and sisters. Are they okay?"

Quickly Maxon held me at arm's length and looked me in the eye. "They're fine, America. I'm sorry; I should have realized that's what you would have thought of first."

I nearly started weeping I was so relieved.

Maxon seemed a bit confused as he continued. "There are rebels in the palace."

"What?" I shrieked. "Why aren't we hiding?"

"They're not here to attack."

"Then why *are* they here?"

He sighed. "It's only two rebels from the Northern camp. They're unarmed, and they're specifically asking to speak to me . . . and to you."

"Why me?"

"I'm not sure; but I'm going to talk to them, so I thought I would give you the chance to speak to them as well."

I looked down at myself and ran my hand over my hair. "I'm in my nightgown."

He smiled. "I know, but this is very informal. It's fine."

"Do *you* want me to talk to them?"

"That is truly up to you, but I'm curious as to why they want to speak with you in particular. I'm not sure they'll tell me if you're not there."

I nodded, weighing this in my head. I wasn't sure I wanted to talk to rebels. Unarmed or not, they were probably far deadlier than I could ever be. But if Maxon thought I could do it, maybe I should. . . .

"Okay," I said, pulling myself up. "Okay."

"You won't get hurt, America. I promise." His hand was still on mine, and he gave my fingers a tiny squeeze. He turned to the guard. "Lead the way. Keep your holster unlocked, just in case."

"Of course, Your Majesty," he answered, and escorted us around the corner into the Great Room, where two people were standing, surrounded by more guards.

It took me seconds to find Aspen in the crowd.

"Could you call off your dogs?" one of the rebels asked. He was tall and slim and blond. His boots were covered in mud, and his outfit looked like something a Seven might wear: a pair of heavy pants taken in to fit him closely and a patched-up shirt beneath a beaten leather jacket. A rusting compass on a long chain swung around his neck, moving as he shifted. He looked rugged without being terrifying, which wasn't what I'd expected.

Even more unexpected was that his companion was a girl. She, too, wore boots; but as if she was trying to be resource-ful and fashionable at the same time, she had on leggings and a skirt constructed from the same material as the male's pants. Her hip jutted out confidently to the side despite her being surrounded by guards. Even if I hadn't recognized her face, I would have remembered her jacket. Denim and cropped, covered with what looked like dozens of embroi-dered flowers.

Making sure I remembered who she was, she gave me a little curtsy. I made a sound that was somewhere between a laugh and a gasp.

"What's wrong?" Maxon asked.

"Later," I whispered.

Confused but calm, he gave me a comforting squeeze and focused again on our guests.

"We've come to speak to you in peace," the man said. "We are unarmed, and your guards have searched us. I know asking for privacy would be inappropriate, but we have things to discuss with you that no one else should hear."

"What about America?" Maxon asked.

"We want to speak with her as well."

"To what end?"

"Again," the young man said, almost cockily, "we need to be out of earshot of these guys." He playfully gestured around the room.

"If you think you can harm her—"

"I know you're skeptical of us, and for good reason, but we have no cause to hurt either of you. We want to talk."

Maxon deliberated for a minute. "You," he said, looking toward one of the guards, "pull down one of the tables and four chairs. Then all of you, please stay back to give our guests some room."

The guards obeyed, and we were all silent for a few uncomfortable minutes. When the table was finally down from the stack and in the corner with two chairs on either side, Maxon gestured that the pair should join us over there.

As we walked, the guards stepped back, wordlessly forming a perimeter around the room and focusing their eyes on the two rebels as if they were prepared to fire at a second's notice.

As we reached the table, the male stuck out his hand. "Don't you think introductions are in order?"

Maxon eyed him warily but then relented. "Maxon Schreave, your sovereign."

The young man chuckled. "Honored, sir."

"And you are?"

"Mr. August Illéa, at your service."

CHAPTER 6

MAXON AND I LOOKED AT each other, then back to the rebels.

"You heard me right. I'm an Illéa. And by birth, too. This one will be by marriage sooner or later," August said, nodding to the girl.

"Georgia Whitaker," she said. "And of course, we know all about you, America."

She gave me another smile, and I returned it. I wasn't sure I trusted her, but I certainly didn't hate her.

"So Father was right." Maxon sighed. I looked over to him, confused. Maxon knew there were direct descendants of Gregory Illéa walking around? "He said you'd come for the crown one day."

"I don't want your crown," August assured us.

"Good, because I intend to lead this country," Maxon shot back. "I've been raised for it, and if you think you can come in here claiming to be Gregory's great-great-grandson—"

"I don't want your crown, Maxon! Destroying the monarchy is more up the Southern rebels' alley. We have other goals." August sat at the table, leaning back in his seat. Then as if it was his home we'd stepped into, he swept his arm across the chairs, inviting us to sit.

Maxon and I eyed each other again and joined him, Georgia following quickly. August looked at us awhile, either studying us or trying to decide where to start.

Maxon, perhaps reminding us who was in charge, broke the tension. "Would you like some tea or coffee?"

Georgia lit up. "Coffee?"

In spite of himself, Maxon smiled at her enthusiasm and turned behind him to get a guard's attention. "Could you have one of the maids bring some coffee, please? For goodness' sake, make sure it's strong." Then he focused again on August.

"I can't begin to imagine what you want from me. It seems you made a point to come while the palace was asleep, and I'm guessing you'd like to keep this visit as secretive as possible. Say what you must. I can't promise to give you what you want, but I will listen."

August nodded and leaned forward. "We've been looking for Gregory's diaries for decades. We knew they existed long ago and had a recent confirmation from a source I cannot reveal." August looked at me. "It wasn't your presentation on the *Report* that gave it away, just so you know."

I sighed in relief. The second he mentioned the diaries,

I began silently cursing myself and bracing for later when Maxon would add this to the list of stupid things I'd done.

"We have never desired to take down the monarchy," he said to Maxon. "Even though it came about in a very corrupt way, we have no problem with having a sovereign leader, particularly if that leader is you."

Maxon was still, but I could sense his pride. "Thank you."

"What we would like are other things, specific freedoms. We want nominated officials, and we want to end the castes." August said all this as if it was easy. If he'd seen my presentation get cut off on the *Report*, he ought to know better.

"You act like I'm already the king," Maxon answered in frustration. "Even if it was possible, I can't simply give you what you're asking for."

"But you're open to the idea?"

Maxon raised his hands and dropped them to the table. "What I'm open to is irrelevant at the moment. I am not king."

August sighed, looking over to Georgia. They seemed to communicate wordlessly, and I was impressed at their easy intimacy. Here they were, in a very tense situation—one they'd entered maybe suspecting they wouldn't be able to get out of—and their feelings for each other were so close to the surface.

"Speaking of kings," Maxon added, "why don't you explain to America who you are. I'm sure you'd do a better job than I would."

I knew this was a way for Maxon to stall, to think of a

37

way to get control of this situation, but I didn't mind. I was dying to understand.

August smiled humorlessly. "That *is* an interesting story," he promised, the vibrancy in his voice hinting at how exciting his tale would be. "As you know, Gregory had three children: Katherine, Spencer, and Damon. Katherine was married off to a prince, Spencer died, and Damon was the one who inherited the throne. Then when Damon's son, Justin, died, his cousin Porter Schreave became prince, marrying Justin's young widow, who had won the Selection barely three years earlier. And now the Schreaves are the royal family. No more Illéas ought to exist. But we do."

"We?" Maxon asked, his tone calculated, like he was hoping for numbers.

August only nodded. The click of heels announced that the maid was coming. Maxon put a finger to his lips, like August would dare to say more with her in hearing distance. The maid set down the tray and poured coffee for all of us. Georgia's hands were on her cup immediately, waiting for it to be filled. I didn't really care for coffee—it was too bitter for my tastes—but I knew it would help me wake up, so I braced myself to take a drink.

Before I could even sip, Maxon slid the bowl of sugar in front of me. Like he knew.

"You were saying?" Maxon prompted, taking his coffee black.

"Spencer didn't die," August said flatly. "He knew what his father had done to take over the country, he knew his older

38

sister had basically been sold into marriage, and he knew the same was expected of him. He couldn't do it, so he ran."

"Where did he go?" I asked, speaking for the first time.

"He hid with relatives and friends, eventually making a camp with some like-minded people in the north. It's colder up there, wetter, and so hard to navigate that no one tries. We live there quietly most of the time."

Georgia nudged him, her face a little shocked.

August came to his senses. "I suppose I've now given you directions to invade us yourself. I want to remind you that we've never killed any of your officers or staff, and we avoid injuring them at all costs. All we ever wanted was to put an end to the castes. To do that we needed proof that Gregory was the man we'd always been told he was. We have that now, and America hinted at it enough that we feel we could exploit that if we wanted to. We really don't though. Not if we don't have to."

Maxon took a deep swig and set down his cup. "I'm honestly not sure what I'm supposed to do with this information. You're a direct descendant of Gregory Illéa, but you don't want the crown. You've come looking for things only the king could provide, but you asked for an audience with me and one of the Elite. My father isn't even here."

"We know," August said. "This was deliberate timing."

Maxon huffed. "If you don't want the crown and only want things I can't give you, why are you here?"

August and Georgia looked at each other, perhaps preparing themselves for their biggest request yet.

"We came to ask you for these things because we know you're a reasonable man. We've watched you all your life, and we can see it in your eyes. I can see it now."

I tried to be inconspicuous as I studied Maxon's reaction to these words.

"You don't like the castes either. You don't like the way your father holds the country under his thumb. You don't want to fight wars you know are nothing more than a distraction. More than anything, you want peace during your lifetime.

"We're guessing that once you're king, things could really change. And we've been waiting a long time for that. We're prepared to wait longer. The Northern rebels are willing to give you our word never to attack the palace again and to do our best to stop or slow the Southern rebels. We see so much that you can't from behind these walls. We would swear our allegiance to you, without question, if you would be willing to give us a sign of your readiness to work with us toward a future that would finally give the people of Illéa a chance to live their own lives."

Maxon didn't seem to know what to say, so I spoke up.

"What do the Southern rebels want anyway? Just to kill us all?"

August moved his head in a motion that was neither a shake nor a nod. "That's part of it, sure, but only so they'll have no one to combat them. Too much of the population is oppressed, and this growing cell has bought in to the idea that they could rule the country themselves. America, you're a Five; I know you've seen your share of people who hate the monarchy."

Maxon discreetly moved his eyes my way. I gave a brief nod.

"Of course you have. Because when you're on the bottom, your only choice is to blame the top. In this case, they've got good reason—after all, it was a One who sentenced them to their lives with no real hope for bettering them. Those in charge of the Southern rebels have convinced their disciples that the way to get back what they think is theirs is to take it from the monarchy. But I've had people defect from the Southerner rebel leadership and end up with me. I know for a fact that once the Southerners get control, they have no intention of sharing the wealth. When in history has that ever happened?

"Their plan is to obliterate what Illéa has, take over, make a bunch of promises, and leave everyone in the same place they are now. For most people, I'm sure it'll get worse. The Sixes and Sevens won't move up, except for a select few the rebels will manipulate for the sake of the show. Twos and Threes will have everything stripped from them. It'll make a bunch of people feel vindicated, but it won't fix anything.

"If there are no pop stars churning out those mind-numbing songs, then there are no musicians in the booths backing them up, no clerks running back and forth with tapes, no shop owners selling the music. Taking out one person at the top destroys thousands at the bottom."

August paused for a moment, looking consumed with

worry. "It'll be Gregory all over again, only worse. The Southerners are prepared to be far more cutthroat than you could ever be, and the chances of the country bouncing back are slim. It'll be the same old oppression under a brand-new name . . . and your people will suffer like never before." He looked into Maxon's eyes. They seemed to have some understanding between them, something that maybe came from being born to lead.

"All we need is a sign, and we'll do everything we can to help you change things, peacefully and fairly. Your people deserve a chance."

Maxon looked at the table. I couldn't imagine the debate in his head. "What kind of sign?" he asked hesitantly. "Money?"

"No," August said, nearly laughing. "We have more funds than you might guess."

"How is that possible?"

"Donations," he replied simply.

Maxon nodded, but I was surprised. Donations meant there were people—who knew how many—supporting them. How big was the Northern rebel force when those supporters were taken into account? How much of the country was asking for exactly what these two had come here requesting?

"If not money," Maxon said finally, "what do you want?"

August flicked his head toward me. "Pick her."

I buried my face in my hands, knowing how Maxon would take this.

There was a long moment of silence before he lost his temper. "I will not have anyone else telling me who I can and cannot marry! This is my life you're playing games with!"

I looked up in time to see August stand across the table. "And the palace has been playing with other people's lives for years. Grow up, Maxon. You're the prince. You want your damn crown, then keep it. But responsibilities come with that privilege."

Guards were cautiously walking our way, alerted by Maxon's tone and August's aggressive stance. Certainly they could hear everything by now.

Maxon stood to counter him. "You don't get to choose my wife. End of story."

August, completely undeterred, stepped back and crossed his arms. "Fine! We have another option if this one doesn't work."

"Who?"

August rolled his eyes. "As if I would tell you, given how calmly you reacted the first time."

"Come off it."

"This one or that one doesn't really matter. We just need to know you'll have a partner who'll be on the same page for this plan."

"My name is America," I said fiercely, standing and looking him straight in the eye, "not *This One*. I'm not some toy in your little revolution. You keep talking about everyone in Illéa having a chance at the life they want. What about me? What about my future? Do I not count in that plan?"

I searched their faces, waiting for an answer. They were silent. I noticed the guards, surrounding us, on edge.

I lowered my voice. "I'm all for killing off the castes, but I'm not something to be played with. If you're looking for a pawn, there's one girl upstairs so in love with him, she'd do anything you asked if it meant a proposal at the end of the day. And the other two . . . between duty and prestige, they'd be game, too. Go get one of them."

Without waiting to be excused, I turned to leave, storming away as best I could in a robe and slippers.

"America! Wait!" Georgia called. I got out the door before she caught up with me. "Stop for a minute."

"What?"

"We're sorry. We thought you two were in love. We didn't realize we were asking for something he'd be opposed to. We were sure he'd be on board."

"You don't understand. He's so tired of being bullied and bossed around. You have no idea what he's been through." I felt the tears rising, and I blinked them away, focusing on the designs on Georgia's jacket.

"I know more than you think," she said. "Maybe not everything, but a lot. We've been watching the Selection very closely, and it looks like you two get along so well. He seems so happy around you. And then . . . we know about how you rescued your maids."

It took me a second to realize what that meant. Who was watching us on their behalf?

"And we saw what you did for Marlee. We saw you fight.

And then your presentation a few days ago." She stopped to laugh. "That took some guts. We could use a girl with guts."

I shook my head. "I wasn't trying to be a hero. Most of the time, I don't feel anything close to brave."

"So? It doesn't really matter how you feel about your character; it just matters what you do with it. You, more than the others, act on what's right before thinking about what it will mean for yourself. Maxon has some great candidates up there, but they won't get their hands dirty to make things better. Not like you."

"A lot of that was selfish. Marlee was important to me, and so are my maids."

She stepped closer. "But didn't those actions come with consequences?"

"Yes."

"And you probably knew they would. But you acted for those who couldn't speak up for themselves. That's special, America."

This was different praise from what I was used to. I could handle my dad telling me I was a beautiful singer or Aspen saying I was the prettiest thing he'd ever seen . . . but this? It was almost overwhelming.

"Honestly, with some of the stuff you've done, I can't believe the king let you stay. The whole thing on the *Report* . . ." She let out a whistle.

I laughed. "He was so angry."

"I was shocked you made it out alive!"

"It was by the skin of my teeth, let me tell you. And most

days I feel like I'm only seconds away from being kicked out."

"But Maxon likes you, right? The way he guards you . . ."

I shrugged. "There are days when I feel so sure and then others where I have no idea. Today isn't a good day. Neither was yesterday. Or the day before, if I'm honest."

She nodded. "Well, we're pulling for you, all the same."

"Me and someone else," I corrected.

"True."

Again she gave no clue as to her other favorite.

"What was the deal with that curtsy in the woods? Just messing with me?" I asked.

She smiled. "I know it might not seem like it by the way we act sometimes, but we really do care about the royal family. If we lose them, the Southern rebels will win. If they get true control . . . well, you heard August." She shook her head. "Anyway, I'd felt certain I was looking at my future queen, so I figured the least you deserved was a curtsy."

Her reasoning was so silly, it made me laugh again. "I can't tell you how nice it is to talk to a girl I'm not competing with."

"Getting a bit old?" she asked with a sympathetic expression.

"As it's gotten smaller, it's gotten worse. I mean, I knew it would, but . . . it feels like it's moving away from trying to be the girl that Maxon would pick to making sure the *other* girls won't be the one he picks. I don't know if that makes sense."

She nodded. "It does. But, hey, this is what you signed up for."

I chuckled. "Actually, I didn't. I was sort of . . . encouraged to put my name in. I didn't want to be a princess."

"Really?"

"Really."

She smiled. "Not wanting the crown means you're probably the best person to have it."

I stared at her, convinced by her wide eyes that she believed that without a doubt. I hoped to ask more, but Maxon and August came out of the Great Room, looking surprisingly calm. A single guard followed at a distance. August was looking at Georgia like it had hurt him to be away from her even for a few minutes. Maybe that was the only reason she was here today.

"Are you okay, America?" Maxon asked.

"Yes." My ability to look him in the eye had disappeared again.

"You should go get ready for the day," he commented. "The guards have been sworn to secrecy, and I'd appreciate the same from you."

"Of course."

He seemed displeased with my coolness, but how else was I supposed to act right now?

"Mr. Illéa, it was a pleasure. We'll talk again soon." Maxon held out his hand. August took it easily.

"If there's anything you need, don't hesitate to ask. We

truly are on your side, Your Majesty."

"Thank you."

"Georgia, let's go. Some of these guards look a little too trigger-happy."

She chuckled. "See you around, America."

I nodded, sure I'd never see her again and sad because of it. She walked past Maxon and slid her hand into August's. With a guard in tow, they walked out the gaping doors of the palace, leaving Maxon and me alone in the foyer.

His eyes rose to mine. I mumbled something and pointed upstairs, moving as I did so. His quick objection to choosing me only drove home the pain of his words yesterday in the library. I thought after the safe room there was some kind of understanding between us. But it seemed as if everything had gotten even more muddled than it had been when I was still trying to decide how much I liked Maxon in the first place.

I didn't know what this meant for us. Or if there was still an *us* worth worrying about.

CHAPTER 7

FOR AS FAST AS I was at getting to my room, Aspen was faster. I shouldn't have been surprised. Aspen knew the palace so well, this was probably nothing to him now.

"Hey," I started, a little unsure of what to say.

Quickly, he wrapped his arms around me, then pulled away. "That's my girl."

I smiled. "Yeah?"

"You put 'em in their place, Mer." Risking his life, Aspen ran a thumb down my cheek. "You do deserve to be happy. We all do."

"Thank you."

Smiling, he dropped his hand to move the bracelet Maxon had brought me from New Asia and reached underneath to touch the one I'd made of a button he'd given me. His eyes looked sad as he stared at our little memento.

"We'll talk soon. Really talk. There's a lot we need to work out."

With that, Aspen moved down the hall. I sighed and put my head in my hands. Did he assume my rejection meant that I was pushing Maxon away for good? Did he think I wanted to rekindle things with him?

Then again, *hadn't* I just pushed Maxon away?

Hadn't I thought yesterday that Aspen needed to stay in my life?

So then why did everything feel awful?

The mood in the Women's Room was dark. Queen Amberly sat writing her letters, and from time to time, I'd notice her peek up to take in the four of us. After yesterday, we were avoiding doing anything that might require us to interact with one another. Celeste had a pile of magazines and was stretched out on the couch. In a very wise move, Kriss had taken her journal and settled in to write, once again positioning herself near the queen. Why hadn't I thought of that? Elise had gotten out a collection of drawing pencils and was working on something by the window. I was in a wide chair near the door, reading a book.

As it was, we didn't even have to make eye contact.

I tried to concentrate on the words in front of me, but mostly I wondered who the Northern rebels wanted as princess if they couldn't have me. Celeste was very popular, and it would be easy to get people to follow her. I wondered if they were aware of how manipulative she could be. If they knew things about me, maybe they did. Was there more to Celeste than I'd guessed?

Kriss was sweet, and according to that poll a while back, she was one of the people's favorites. Her family didn't have much sway, but she was more of a princess than the rest of us. She had that air about her. Maybe that was her big draw; she wasn't perfect, but she was so lovable. There were days when even I wanted to follow Kriss.

The one I suspected the least was Elise. She'd admitted she didn't love Maxon and that she was here because of duty. I genuinely thought that when she spoke of duty she meant to her family or to her New Asian roots, not to the Northern rebels. Besides that, she was so stoic and calm. There was nothing close to rebellious about her.

And that was why I was suddenly positive she was their favorite. She seemed to be trying the least to compete and had openly admitted her coolness toward Maxon. Maybe she didn't *have* to try because, at the end of the day, she had a quiet army of supporters to put her under the crown anyway.

"That's it," the queen said suddenly. "All of you, come here." She pushed her little table away and stood as we all walked over nervously.

"Something's wrong. What is it?" she demanded.

We looked at one another, none of us wanting to explain. Finally too-perfect Kriss piped up.

"Your Majesty, we've just suddenly realized how intense this competition is. We're a bit more aware of where we each stand with the prince, and it's difficult to let it sink in and still want to chat right now."

The queen nodded in understanding. "How often do you all think of Natalie?" she asked. Natalie had been gone barely a week. I thought of her nearly every day. I also thought of Marlee all the time, and some of the other girls would pop into my head at random as well.

"Always," Elise said quietly. "She was so lighthearted."

A smile came to her lips as she said this. I had always assumed that Natalie got on Elise's nerves since she was so reserved and Natalie was so spacey. But maybe it was one of those opposites-attract kinds of friendships.

"Sometimes she would laugh over the littlest thing," Kriss added. "It was contagious."

"Exactly," the queen said. "I've been where you are, and I know how difficult it is. You second guess the things you do; you second guess everything he does. You wonder over every conversation, trying to read into the breaths between sentences. It's exhausting."

It was as though I could see a weight lifting from everyone. Someone got us.

"But know this: as much tension as you feel with one another now, you will ache every time one of you leaves. No one will ever understand this experience like the other girls who have been through it, the Elite especially. You may fight, but that's what sisters do. These girls," she said, pointing to each of us, "will be the ones you call nearly every day for the first year, terrified of making a mistake and needing their support. When you have parties, these are the names you'll put at the top of your guest lists, just under the names of your family members. Because that's what you are now. You'll never lose these relationships."

We looked at one another. If I was the princess and something was happening where I needed a rational perspective, I'd call Elise first. If I was fighting with Maxon, Kriss would remind me of every good thing about him. And Celeste . . . well, I wasn't so sure, but if anyone was ever going to tell me to toughen up about something, it would be her.

"So take your time," she advised. "Adjust to where you are. And let it go. You don't choose him; he chooses you. There's no point in hating the others for that."

"Do you know who he wants the most?" Celeste asked. And for the first time, I heard worry in her voice.

"I don't," Queen Amberly confessed. "Sometimes I think I could guess, but I don't pretend to understand everything Maxon feels. I know who the king would choose, but that's about it."

"Who would you choose?" I asked, then cursed myself for being so blunt.

She smiled kindly. "I honestly haven't let myself think about it. It would break my heart to start loving one of you like a daughter and then lose you. I couldn't bear it."

I lowered my eyes, not sure if those words were meant to be a comfort or not.

"I will say I'd be happy to have any of you in my family." I looked up and watched as she took the time to meet each set of eyes. "For now, there's work to do."

We stood there silently, soaking in her wisdom. I'd never taken the time to look at the competitors in the last Selection, to find their pictures or anything. I knew a handful of names, mostly because older women would drop them into conversations when I sang at parties. It was never that important to me; we already had a queen, and even as a girl, the possibility of becoming a princess never crossed my mind. But now I wondered how many of the women who showed up to visit the queen or came for Halloween were her former competition, now her closest friends.

Celeste walked away first, heading back to the comfort of the couch. It didn't seem as if Queen Amberly's words meant much to her. For some reason that was the tipping point for me. Everything from the last few days crashed back onto my heart, and I could feel it was seconds away from cracking.

I curtsied. "Excuse me, please," I mumbled, before moving swiftly to the door. I didn't have a plan. Maybe I could go sit in the bathroom for a minute or tuck myself away in one of the numerous parlors downstairs. Maybe I would just go to my room and cry my eyes out.

Unfortunately, it looked like the universe was plotting against me. Just outside the Women's Room, Maxon was pacing back and forth, looking as if he was trying to solve a riddle. Before I could hide somewhere, he saw me.

Of everything I wanted to do right now, this was the last thing on my list.

"I was debating asking you to come out," he said.

"What do you need?" I answered shortly.

Maxon stood there, still working up the nerve to say something that was obviously driving him crazy. "So there's one girl who loves me beyond reason?"

I crossed my arms. After the last few days, I should have seen his change of heart coming. "Yes."

"Not two?"

I looked up at him, almost irritated that he needed me to explain. *Don't you already know how I feel?* I wanted to scream. *Don't you remember the safe room?*

But, honestly, I needed some confirmation right now, too. What had happened to make me so unsure so quickly?

The king. His insinuations about what the other girls had done, his praise of their merits made me feel small. And it was compounded by all my missteps with Maxon this week. The only way we would have ever been brought together was because of the Selection; but it seemed that as long as it went on, there was no way for anything to feel certain.

"You told me you didn't trust me," I accused. "The other day you made a point of humiliating me, and yesterday you basically said I was an embarrassment. And not a few hours ago, the suggestion of marrying me sent you into a rage. Forgive me for not feeling so secure in our relationship right now."

"You forget that I've never done this, America," he said passionately, but without any anger. "You have someone to compare me to. I don't even know how to have a typical relationship, and I only get one chance. You've had at least two. I'm going to make mistakes."

"I don't mind mistakes," I shot back. "I mind the uncertainty. Most of the time I can't tell what's going on."

He was quiet for a moment, and I realized that we'd come to a very serious crossroad. We'd implied so many things, but we couldn't go on like this for much longer. Even if we ended up together, these moments of insecurity would haunt us.

"We keep doing this," I breathed, exhausted with this game. "We get close and then something happens and it falls apart, and you never seem to be able to make a decision. If you want me as much as you've always claimed to, why isn't this over?"

Even though I'd accused him of not caring about me at all, his frustration melted into sadness. "Because half the time I've been sure you loved someone else and the other half I've doubted you could love me at all," he answered, making me feel positively awful.

"Like I haven't had my own reasons to doubt? You treat Kriss like she's heaven on earth, and then I catch you with Celeste—"

"I explained that."

"Yes, but it still hurt to see."

"Well, it hurts me to see how quickly you shut down. Where does that even come from?"

"I don't know, but maybe you should stop thinking about me for a while."

The silence was abrupt.

"What does that mean?"

I shrugged. "There are three other girls here. If you're so worried about your one shot, you might want to make sure you're not wasting it on me."

I walked away, angry with Maxon for making me feel this way . . . and angry with myself for making things so much worse.

CHAPTER 8

I WATCHED AS THE PALACE was transformed. Almost overnight, lush Christmas trees lined the hallways of the first
floor, garlands were strung down the stairways, and all the
floral arrangements were changed to include holly or mis-
tletoe. The strange thing was, if I opened my window, it
still felt like the edge of summer outside. I wondered if the
palace could somehow manufacture snow. Maybe if I asked
Maxon, he'd look into it.

Then again, maybe not.

Days passed. I tried not to be upset that Maxon was doing
exactly what I'd asked, but as the space between us grew icy,
I regretted my pride. I wondered if this was always bound
to happen. Was I destined to say the wrong thing, make the
wrong choice? Even if Maxon was what I wanted, I was

never going to get myself together long enough for it to be real.

The whole thing just felt tired; it was the same problem I'd been facing since Aspen walked through the doorway of the palace. And I ached from it, from feeling so torn, so confused.

I'd taken to walking around the palace during the afternoons. With the gardens off-limits, the Women's Room day after day was too confining.

It was while I was walking that I felt the shift. As if some unseen trigger had set off everyone in the palace. The guards stood a bit stiller, and the maids walked a bit faster. Even I felt strange, like I wasn't quite so welcome here as I was only moments ago. Before I knew what it was I was feeling, the king rounded the corner, a small entourage behind him.

Then it all made perfect sense. His absence made the palace warmer, and now that he was home, we were all subject to his whims again. No wonder the Northern rebels were excited about Maxon.

I curtsied as the king approached. While he walked, he put up a hand, and the men behind him paused as he came close, leaving us with a small bubble of space in which to speak.

"Lady America. I see you're still here," he said, his smile and his words at odds with each other.

"Yes, Your Majesty."

"And how have you been in my absence?"

I smiled. "Silent."

"That's a good girl." He started to walk away but then remembered something and came back. "It was brought to my attention that of the girls left, you're the only one still receiving money for your participation. Elise gave hers up voluntarily almost immediately after the payments were stopped for the Twos and Threes."

That didn't surprise me. Elise was a Four, but her family owned high-end hotels. They weren't hurting for money the way the shopkeepers back in Carolina were.

"I think that should end," he announced, snapping me back into the moment.

My face fell.

"Unless, of course, you're here for a payout and not because you love my son." His eyes burned into me, daring me to challenge his decision.

"You're right," I said, hating the way the words felt in my mouth. "It's only fair."

I could see he was disappointed not to get more of a fight. "I'll see to it immediately."

He walked away, and I stood there, trying not to feel sorry for myself. Really, it was fair. How did it look that I was the only one getting checks? It would all end eventually anyway. Sighing, I headed toward my room. The least I could do was write home and warn them that the money wouldn't be coming anymore.

I opened my door, and, for the first time, I was completely ignored by my maids. Anne, Mary, and Lucy were in the back corner, hovering over a dress that they appeared to be working on, bickering about their progress.

"Lucy, you said you were going to finish this hem last night," Anne said. "You left early to do it."

"I know, I know. I got sidetracked. I can do it now." Her eyes were pleading. Lucy was already a bit sensitive, and I knew Anne's rigid manner sometimes got to her.

"You've been getting sidetracked an awful lot these last few days," Anne commented.

Mary held out her hands. "Calm down. Give me the dress before you mess it up."

"I'm sorry," Lucy said. "Just let me take it now, and I'll get it done."

"What's going on with you?" Anne demanded. "You've been acting so funny."

Lucy looked up at her, eyes frozen. Whatever her secret was, she looked terrified to share it.

I cleared my throat.

They whipped their heads in my direction, all curtsying in turn.

"I don't know what's going on," I said as I walked toward them, "but I highly doubt the queen's maids argue like that. Besides, we're wasting time if there's work to be done."

Anne, still angry, pointed her finger at Lucy. "But she—"

I silenced her with a small gesture of my hand, a bit surprised that it worked so easily.

"No arguing. Lucy, why don't you take that down to the workroom to finish, and we can all get some room to think."

Lucy happily scooped up the fabric, so grateful for the means to escape that she practically ran from the room. Anne watched her go, a full pout on her face. Mary looked worried but dutifully went to work without another word.

It took all of two minutes for me to realize that the mood in my room was too dreary for me to focus. I grabbed some paper and a pen and headed back downstairs. I wondered if I'd done the right thing, sparing Lucy. Maybe they'd all be fine if I'd let them air out whatever was happening. Perhaps my meddling would shake their resolve in helping me. I'd never really bossed them around like that before.

I paused outside the Women's Room. That didn't feel like the right place either. I moved down the main hallway, finding a little nook with a bench. That seemed nice. I ran into the library and picked up a book to lean on and went back to the nook, finding myself practically hidden by the large plant beside the bench. The wide window looked into the garden, and, for a minute, the palace didn't seem so small. I watched birds fly outside the window and tried to form the kindest way to tell my parents there wouldn't be any more checks.

"Maxon, can't we go on a real date? Somewhere outside the palace?" I recognized Kriss's voice immediately. Hmm. The Women's Room might not have been so full after all.

I could hear the smile in his voice as he answered. "I wish we could, sweetheart, but even if things were calm, that would be difficult."

"I want to see you somewhere where you're not the prince," she whined lovingly.

"Ah, but I'm the prince everywhere."

"You know what I mean."

"I do. I'm sorry I can't give that to you, really. I think it would be nice to see you somewhere where you weren't an Elite. But this is the life I live."

His voice grew a little sad.

"Would you regret it?" he asked. "For the rest of your life, it would be like this. Beautiful walls, but walls all the same. My mother scarcely leaves the palace more than once or twice a year." Through the thick leaves of the planted shrub, I watched as they passed me, completely unaware. "And if you think the public is intrusive now, it would be much worse when you're the only girl they're watching. I know your feelings for me run deep. I feel it every day. But what about the life that comes along with me? Do you want that?"

It seemed as if they'd stopped somewhere in the hallway, as Maxon's voice wasn't fading.

"Maxon Schreave," Kriss started, "you make it sound like it's a sacrifice for me to be here. Each day I'm *thankful* for being chosen. Sometimes I try to imagine what it would have been like if we'd never met. . . . I'd rather lose you now than have gone a lifetime without this."

Her voice was getting thick. I didn't think she was crying, but she was close.

"I need you to know I'd want you without the beautiful clothes and the gorgeous rooms. I'd want you without the crown, Maxon. I just want you."

Maxon was momentarily speechless, and I could imagine him holding her close or wiping away the tears that might have come by now.

"I can't tell you what it means to me to hear that. I've been dying for someone to tell me that I was what mattered," he confessed quietly.

"You are, Maxon."

There was another quiet moment between them.

"Maxon?"

"Yes?"

"I . . . I don't think I want to wait anymore."

Even though I knew I'd regret it, at those words I silently put down my paper and pen, slipped off my shoes, and scurried to the end of the hall. I peeked around and saw the back of Maxon's head as Kriss's hand slid just barely into the neck of his suit. Her hair fell to the side as they kissed, and, for her first, it seemed like it was going really well. Better than Maxon's, that was for sure.

I ducked back around the corner and heard her giggle a second later. Maxon let out a sigh that was half triumph and half relief. I walked to my seat quickly, angling myself toward the window again, just in case.

"When can we do that again?" she asked quietly.

"Hmm. How about in as much time as it takes to get from here to your room?"

Kriss's laugh faded as they moved down the hallway. I sat there for a minute, then I picked up my pen and paper, finding the words easily now.

Mom and Dad,
There's so much to do these days, I have to keep this short. In an effort to show my devotion to Maxon and not to the luxuries of being in the Elite, I've given up receiving payments for my participation. I realize this is short notice, but I'm sure with everything we've been given by now, there's not much more we could want for.
I hope you won't be too disappointed by this news. I miss you and hope we'll get to see each other again soon.
I love you all.
America

CHAPTER 9

THE *REPORT* WAS LACKING MATERIAL following what the public would see as a rather uneventful week. After the brief updates from the king on his visit to France, the floor was turned over to Gavril, who was now interviewing the remaining Elite in a casual manner about things that didn't seem to matter at this point in the competition.

Then again, the last time they'd asked us about something that *did* matter, I suggested dissolving the castes and nearly got thrown out of the competition.

"Lady Celeste, have you seen the princess's suite?" Gavril asked jovially.

I grinned to myself, grateful he didn't ask me the same question. Celeste's perfect smile managed to widen, and she flipped her hair over her shoulder playfully before answering.

"Well, Gavril, not yet. But I'm certainly hoping to earn the privilege. Of course, King Clarkson has provided us with the most beautiful accommodations, I can't imagine anything better than what we already have. The, um . . . the beds are so . . ."

Celeste stammered just a bit as her eyes caught two guards rushing into the studio. Our seats were arranged in such a way that I could see them as they ran to the king, but Kriss and Elise had their backs to the action. They both tried to turn their heads discreetly, but it did them no good.

"Luxurious. And it would be more than I could dream of to . . ." Celeste continued, not totally focused on her answer.

But it appeared she didn't need to be. The king stood and came over, cutting her off.

"Ladies and gentlemen, I apologize for the interruption, but this is very urgent." He clutched a piece of paper in one hand as he smoothed his tie with the other. He was composed as he spoke. "Since our country's birth, the rebel forces have been the bane of our society. Over the years, their means of attacking the palace, not to mention the common man, have become far more aggressive.

"It appears they have sunk to new lows. As you may well know, the four remaining young ladies of the Selection represent a wide range of castes. We have a Two, a Three, a Four, and a Five. We're honored to have such a varied group, but this has given a strange incentive to the rebels."

The king looked over his shoulder at us before continuing.

"We are prepared for attacks on the palace, and when the rebels attack the public, we intercede as best we can. And I would not worry you if I thought that I, as your king, could protect you, but . . .

"The rebels are attacking by caste."

The words hung in the air. In an almost friendly gesture, Celeste and I shared a confused glance.

"They have wanted to end the monarchy for a long time. Recent attacks on the families of these young girls have shown the lengths that they're prepared to go to, and we've sent guards from the palace to protect the Elite's loved ones. But now that is not enough. If you are a Two, Three, Four, or Five—that is, in the same caste as any of these ladies—you may be subject to an attack from the rebels based on that fact alone."

I covered my mouth and heard Celeste suck in a breath.

"Beginning today, the rebels intend to attack Twos and work their way down the castes," the king added solemnly.

It was sinister. If they couldn't get us to abandon the Selection for our families, they would get a very large portion of the country to want us out. The longer we held on, the more the people would hate *us* for risking *their* lives.

"That is sad news, indeed, my king," Gavril said, breaking the silence.

The king nodded. "We will seek a solution, of course. But we have reports of eight attacks today in five different provinces, all of them against Twos and all of them resulting in at least one death."

The hand that had been frozen over my mouth dropped to my heart. People had died today at our expense.

"For now," King Clarkson continued, "we encourage you to stay close to home and to take any security measures possible."

"Excellent advice, my king," Gavril said. He turned to us. "Ladies, anything you'd like to add?"

Elise merely shook her head.

Kriss took a deep breath. "I know that Twos and Threes are being targeted, but your homes are safer than most of the ones for lower castes. If you can take in a family of Fours or Fives that you know well, I think that would be a good idea."

Celeste nodded. "Stay safe. Do what the king says."

She turned to me, and I realized I needed to say something. When I was on the *Report* and feeling a bit lost, I tended to look to Maxon, as if he could silently give me advice. Falling into that habit, I searched for his eyes. But all I saw was his blond hair as he stared into his lap, his dejected frown the only thing visible.

Of course he was worried about his people. But this was about more than protecting his citizens. He knew we might leave.

And shouldn't we? How many Fives could lose their lives because I sat on my stool in the bright lights of the palace studio?

But how could I—or any of the girls—shoulder that burden? We weren't the ones taking their lives. I remembered everything August and Georgia said to us, and I knew there was only one thing we could do.

"Fight," I said to no one in particular. Then remembering where I was, I turned to the camera. "Fight. The rebels are bullies. They're trying to scare you into doing what they want. And what if you do? What kind of future do you think they'll offer you? These people, these tyrants, aren't going to suddenly stop being violent. If you give them power, they're going to be a thousand times worse. So fight. However you can, fight."

I felt blood and adrenaline pulsing through me, like I was ready to attack the rebels myself. I'd had enough. They'd kept us all in terror, victimized our families. If one of those Southern rebels was in front of me right now, I wouldn't run.

Gavril started speaking again, but I was so angry, all I could hear was my heart beating in my ears. Before I knew it, the cameras were off and the lights were powering down.

Maxon went over to his father and whispered something to which the king shook his head.

The girls stood and started to leave.

"Go straight to your rooms," Maxon said gently. "Dinner will be brought up, and I'll be visiting you all soon."

As I walked past them, the king put a single finger on my arm, and in that small gesture, I knew he meant for me to stop.

"That wasn't very smart," he said.

I shrugged. "What we're doing isn't working. Keep this up and you won't have anyone left to rule over."

He flicked his hand, dismissing me, fed up with me again.

Maxon quietly knocked on my door, letting himself in. I was already in my nightgown, reading in my bed. I'd begun to wonder if he was going to come at all.

"It's so late," I whispered, though there was no one to disturb.

"I know. I had to speak with all the others, and it's been extremely taxing. Elise was very shaken. She's feeling particularly guilty. I wouldn't be surprised if she left in the next day or two."

Even though he'd expressed his lackluster feelings for Elise more than once, I could see just how much this hurt him. I curled my legs to my chest so he could sit.

"What about Kriss and Celeste?"

"Kriss is almost too optimistic. She's sure that people will be careful and protect themselves. I don't see how that's possible if there's no way to tell when or where the rebels will attack next. They're all over the country. But she's hopeful. You know how she is."

"Yeah."

He sighed. "Celeste is fine. She's concerned, of course; but as Kriss pointed out, the Twos are most likely to be the safest during all this. And she's always so determined." He laughed to himself, staring at the floor. "Mostly she seemed concerned that I would be upset with her if she stayed. As if I could hold it against her for choosing this over going home."

I sighed. "It's a good point. Do you want a wife who isn't worried about her subjects being threatened?"

Maxon looked at me. "You're worried. You're just too smart to be worried the way everyone else is." He shook his head and smiled. "I can't believe you told them to fight."

I shrugged. "It seems like we do a whole lot of cowering."

"You're absolutely right. And I don't know if that will scare the rebels off or make them more determined, but there's no doubt you changed the game."

I cocked my head. "I don't think I'd call a group of people trying to kill the population at random a game."

"No, no!" he said quickly. "I can't think of a word bad enough to call that. I meant the Selection." I stared at him. "For better or worse, the public got a real glimpse into your character tonight. They can see the girl who drags her maids to safety, who stands up to kings if she thinks she's right. I'll bet everyone will look at you running after Marlee in an entirely different light now. Before this, you were just the girl who yelled at me when we met. Tonight, you became the girl who's not afraid of the rebels. They'll think of you differently now."

I shook my head. "That's not what I was trying to do."

"I know. For all the planning I was doing to get you to show the people who you are, it turns out you just do it on an impulse. It's so you." There was a look of astonishment in his eyes, as if he should have been expecting this all along.

"Anyway, I think it was the right thing to say. It's about time we did more than hide."

I looked down at my bedspread, tracing the seams with my finger. I was glad he approved, but the way he spoke—as if it was one more of my little quirks—felt too intimate at the moment.

"I'm tired of fighting with you, America," he said quietly. I looked up and saw the sincerity in Maxon's eyes as he continued. "I like that we disagree—it's one of my favorite things about you, actually—but I don't want to argue anymore. Sometimes I have a bit of my father's temper. I fight it, but it's there. And you!" he said with a laugh. "When you're upset, you're a force!"

He shook his head, probably remembering a dozen things at the same time I did. A knee to the groin, the whole thing with the castes, Celeste's busted lip when she talked about Marlee. I'd never thought of myself as temperamental, but apparently I was. He smiled, and I did, too. It was kind of funny when I thought about all my actions piled up like that.

"I'm looking at the others, and I'm being fair. It makes me nervous to feel some of the things I do. But I want you to know, I'm still looking at you, too. I think you know by now I can't help it." He shrugged, seeming so boyish at that moment.

I wanted to say the right thing, to let him know that I still wanted him to look at me. But nothing felt right, so I slid my hand into his. We sat there quietly, looking at our hands. He toyed with my two bracelets, seeming very concerned with them, and spent a little while rubbing the back of my hand with his thumb. It was nice to have a still moment, just the two of us.

"Why don't we spend the day together tomorrow?" he asked.

I smiled. "I'd like that."

CHAPTER 10

"So, long story short: more guards?"

"Yeah, Dad. Lots more." I laughed into the phone, though the situation was hardly a funny one. But Dad had a way of making the toughest things light. "We're all staying. For now anyway. And even though they say they're starting with Twos, don't let anyone be careless. Warn the Turners and the Canvasses to stay safe."

"Aw, kitten, everyone knows to be careful. After what you said on the *Report*, I think people will be braver than you'd guess."

"I hope so." I looked down at my shoes and had a funny flashback. Right now my feet were covered with jeweled heels. Five months ago they were wearing dingy flats.

"You made me proud, America. Sometimes I'm surprised

at the things you say, but I don't know why. You were always stronger than you knew."

Something about his voice then was so genuine that I was humbled. No one's opinion of me mattered as much as his.

"Thanks, Dad."

"I'm serious, now. Not every princess would say something like that."

I rolled my eyes. "Uh, Dad, I'm not a princess."

"Matter of time," he shot back playfully. "Speaking of which, how is Maxon?"

"Good," I said, fidgeting with my dress. The silence grew. "I really like him, Dad."

"Yeah?"

"Yeah."

"Why exactly?"

I thought for a minute. "I'm not really sure. But part of it is that he makes me feel like me, I think."

"Did you ever feel like not you?" Dad joked.

"No, it's like . . . I've always been aware of my number. Even when I came to the palace, I obsessed about it for a while. Was I a Five or a Three? Did I want to be a One? But now I'm not conscious of it at all. And I think it's because of him.

"He screws up a lot, don't get me wrong." Dad chuckled. "But when I'm with him I feel like I'm America. I'm not a caste or a project. I don't even think of him as elevated, really. He's just him, and I'm just me."

Dad was quiet for a moment. "That sounds really nice, kitten."

Boy talk with my dad was a little awkward, but he was the only one back home who I thought saw Maxon more like a person than a celebrity; no one else would get it like he would.

"Yeah. It's not perfect though," I added as Silvia poked her head in the doorway. "I feel like there's always something going wrong."

She gave me a pointed look and mouthed *Breakfast*. I nodded.

"Well, that's okay, too. Mistakes mean it's real."

"I'll try to remember that. Listen, Dad, I've got to go. I'm late."

"Can't have that. Take care, kitten, and write your sister soon."

"I will. Love you, Daddy."

"Love you."

As the girls exited after breakfast, Maxon and I lingered in the dining room. The queen passed, winking in my direction, and I felt my cheeks redden. But the king came along soon after, and the look in his eyes took away any lingering blush.

Once we were alone, Maxon walked over to me and laced his fingers through mine. "I'd ask what you want to do today, but our options are pretty limited. No archery, no hunting, no riding, no anything outside."

I sighed. "Not even if we took a slew of guards?"

"I'm sorry, America." He gave me a sad smile. "But what about a movie? We can watch something with spectacular scenery."

"It's not the same." I pulled on his arm. "Come on. Let's go make the best of it."

"That's the spirit," he said. Something about that actually made me feel better, like we were in this together. It had been a while since it really felt that way.

We went into the hallway and were headed toward the stairway to the theater when I heard the musical clinks on the window.

I turned my head to the sound and gasped in wonder. "It's raining."

I let go of Maxon's arm and pressed my hand against the glass. In the months I'd been at the palace, it had yet to rain, and I'd wondered if it ever would. Now that I could see it, I realized I missed it. I missed the ebb and flow of seasons, the way things changed.

"It's so beautiful," I whispered.

Maxon stood behind me, wrapping an arm around my waist. "Leave it to you to find beauty in something others would say ruins a day."

"I wish I could touch it."

He sighed. "I know you do, but it's just not—"

I turned to Maxon, trying to see why he cut himself off. He looked up and down the hall, and I did the same. Besides a couple of guards, we were alone.

"Come on," he said, grabbing my hand. "Let's hope we're not seen."

I smiled, ready for whatever adventure he had in mind. I loved when Maxon was like this. We wound our way up the stairs, heading for the fourth floor. For a moment, I got nervous, worried he'd show me something similar to the hidden library. That hadn't turned out so well for me.

We walked down to the middle of the floor, passing one guard on his rounds but no one else. Maxon pulled me into a large parlor and steered me to the wall next to a wide, dormant fireplace. He reached inside the lip of the fireplace and, sure enough, found a hidden latch. He pushed open a panel in the wall, and it led to yet another secret stairwell.

"Hold my hand," he said, stretching his out to me. I did so, following him up the dimly lit steps until we came to a door. Maxon undid the simple lock, pulled open the door . . . and there was a wall of rain.

"The roof?" I asked over the sound.

He nodded. There were walls surrounding the entrance, leaving an open space about as large as my bedroom to walk on. It didn't matter that all I could see were walls and sky. At least I was outside.

Positively beside myself, I stepped forward, reaching into the water. The drops were fat and warm as they collected on my arm and ran down to my dress. I heard Maxon laugh once before shoving me out into the downpour.

I gasped, soaked in seconds. Turning around, I grabbed

his arm, and he smiled as he pretended to fight. His hair fell in strands around his eyes as we were both quickly drenched, and he was still grinning as he pulled me over to the edge of the wall.

"Look," he said into my ear.

I turned, noticing our view for the first time. I stared in awe as the city spread out in front of me. The web of streets, the geometry of buildings, the array of colors—even dimmed in the gray hue of rain, it was breathtaking.

I found myself feeling attached to it all, as if it belonged to me somehow.

"I don't want the rebels to take it, America," he said over the rain, as if he was reading my mind. "I don't know how bad the death toll is, but I can tell that my father is keeping it a secret from me. He's afraid I'll call off the Selection."

"Is there a way to find out the truth?"

He debated. "I feel like, if I could get in touch with August, he'd know. I could get a letter to him, but I'm afraid of putting too much in writing. And I don't know if I could get him into the palace."

I considered that. "What if we could get to him?"

Maxon laughed. "How do you suggest we do that?"

I shrugged playfully. "I'll work on it."

He stared at me, quiet for a minute. "It's nice to say things out loud. I'm always watching what I say. I feel like no one can hear me up here, I guess. Just you."

"Then go ahead and say anything."

He smirked. "Only if you will."

"Fine," I answered, happy to play along.

"Well, what do you want to know?"

I wiped the wet hair from my forehead, starting with something important but impersonal. "Did you really not know about the diaries?"

"No. But I'm up to speed now. Father made me read them all. If August had come two weeks ago, I would have thought he was lying about everything, but not anymore. It's shocking, America. You only scratched the surface with what you read. I want to tell you about it, but I can't yet."

"I understand."

He stared me down, determined. "How did the girls find out about you taking off my shirt?"

I looked at the ground, hesitating. "We were watching the guards work out. I said you looked as good as any of them without your shirt on. It slipped out."

Maxon threw back his head and laughed. "I can't be mad about that."

I smiled. "Have you ever brought anyone else up here?"

He looked sad. "Olivia. One time, and that's it."

I actually remembered that, come to think of it. He'd kissed her up here, and she'd told us all about it.

"I kissed Kriss," he blurted out, not looking at me. "Recently. For the first time. It seems only right that you should know."

He peeked down, and I gave him a small nod. If I hadn't

seen them kiss myself, if this had been how I found out, I might have broken down. And even though I already knew, it hurt to hear him say it.

"I hate dating you this way." I fidgeted, my dress getting heavy with water.

"I know. It's just how it is."

"Doesn't make it fair."

He laughed. "When has anything in either of our lives ever been fair?"

I gave him that. "I'm not supposed to tell you—and if you let on that you know, he'll get worse, I'm sure—but . . . your father's been saying things to me. He also took away the payments for my family. None of the other girls has them anymore, so I guess it looked bad anyway."

"I'm sorry," he said. He looked out over the city. I was temporarily distracted by the way his shirt was sticking to his chest. "I don't think there's a way to undo that one, America."

"You don't have to. I just wanted you to know it was happening. And I can handle it."

"You're too tough for him. He doesn't understand you." He reached down for my hand, and I gave it to him freely.

I tried to think of anything else I might want to know, but it mostly pertained to the other girls, and I didn't want to bother with that. I was sure at this point I could guess close enough to the truth, and if I was wrong, I didn't think I wanted that to ruin this.

Maxon looked down at my wrist. "Do you . . ." He looked

up at me, seeming to rethink his question. "Do you want to dance?"

I nodded. "But I'm awful."

"We'll go slow."

Maxon pulled me close, placing a hand on my waist. I put one hand in his and used the other to pick up my soaking dress. We swayed, barely moving. I settled my cheek on Maxon's chest, he rested his chin on my head, and we spun to the music of the rain.

As he made his grip on me a little bit tighter, it felt like all the bad had been erased and Maxon and I were stripped to the core of our relationship. We were friends who realized they didn't want to be without each other. We were the other's opposite in many ways but also so very similar. I couldn't call our relationship fate, but it did seem bigger than anything I'd known before.

I raised my face to Maxon's, placing a hand on his cheek, pulling him down for a kiss. His lips, wet, met mine with a brush of heat. I felt both his hands wrap around my back, holding me to him as if he'd fall apart otherwise. While the rain pummeled the roof, the whole world went silent. It felt like there wasn't enough of him, not enough skin or space or time.

After all these months of trying to reconcile what I wanted and hoped for, I realized then—in this moment Maxon created just for us—that it would never make sense. All I could do was move forward and hope that whenever we drifted, we would somehow find a way back to each other.

And we had to. Because . . . because . . .

For as long as it took to get to this moment, when it came it was fast.

I loved Maxon. For the first time, I could feel it solidly. I wasn't keeping the feeling at a distance, holding on to Aspen and all the what-ifs that went along with him. I wasn't walking into Maxon's affections while keeping one foot out the door in case he let me down. I simply let it come.

I loved him.

I couldn't pinpoint what made me so certain, but I knew it then, as surely as I knew my name or the color of the sky or any fact written in a book.

Could he feel it, too?

Maxon broke the kiss and looked at me. "You're so pretty when you're a mess."

I laughed nervously. "Thank you. For that and for the rain and for not giving up."

He ran his fingers along my cheek and nose and chin. "You're worth it. I don't think you get that. You're worth it to me."

I felt as if my heart was on the edge of bursting, and I just wanted everything to end today. My world had settled onto a new axis, and it felt like the only way to handle how dizzy it made me was for us to finally be real. I felt certain now that it would come. It would have to. Soon.

Maxon kissed the tip of my nose. "Let's go get dry and watch a movie."

"Sounds good."

I carefully tucked my love for Maxon away in my heart, a little afraid of this feeling. Eventually, it would have to be shared, but for now it was my secret.

I tried to wring out my dress in the little canopy where the door was, but it was hopeless. I was going to leave a little trail of water back to my room.

"I vote for a comedy," I said as we went down the stairs, Maxon leading the way.

"I vote for action."

"Well, you just said I was worth it, so I think I'm going to win this one."

Maxon laughed. "Nicely done."

He chuckled again as he pushed on the panel that led us back into the parlor only to stop dead in his tracks a second later.

I peeked over his shoulder to see King Clarkson standing there, looking as irritated as ever.

"I'm assuming this was your idea," he said to Maxon.

"Yes."

"Do you have any idea how much danger you put yourself in?" he demanded.

"Father, there are no rebels waiting on the roof," Maxon countered, trying to sound rational but looking a bit ridiculous in his dripping clothes.

"One well-aimed bullet is all it would take, Max" let the words hang in the air. "You know ~ tight, sending guards to watch the girls ens of those who've been sent have gon<

vulnerable." He glared past his son at me. "And why is it that when anything happens these days, she's got her hands all over it?"

We stood there, silent, knowing there was nothing we could say anyway.

"Get cleaned up," the king ordered. "You have work to do."

"But I—"

A single look from his father told Maxon that any plans he'd had for the day were done.

"Very well," he said, caving.

King Clarkson took Maxon's arm and pushed him away, leaving me behind. Over his shoulder, Maxon mouthed the word *Sorry,* and I gave him a little smile.

I wasn't afraid of the king. Or the rebels. I knew how much Maxon meant to me, and I was sure that it was all going to work, somehow.

CHAPTER 11

AFTER ENDURING MARY'S SILENT SMIRK as she made me back up, I went to the Women's Room, happy the rain was still coming down. It would always mean something special to me now.

But while Maxon and I could escape for a little while, once we were out of our bubble, the tension of the ultimatum the rebels had placed on the Elite was thick. All the girls were distracted and anxious.

Celeste wordlessly painted her nails at a nearby table, and I could see the slight tremor in her hand from time to time. I watched as she cleaned up her mistakes and tried to carry on. Elise held a book in her hands, but her eyes were trained on the window, lost in the downpour. None of us could quite manage to finish even the smallest task.

"How do you think it's going out there?" Kriss asked me,

her hand paused over the needlepoint pillow she was working on.

"I don't know," I answered quietly. "It doesn't seem like they'd threaten something huge and then do nothing." I was penciling out a melody I'd had in my head on some sheet music. I hadn't written anything original in nearly six months. There wasn't much point to it. At parties, people preferred the classics.

"Do you think they're hiding the number of deaths from us?" she wondered.

"It's possible. If we leave, they win."

Kriss did another stitch. "I'm going to stay no matter what." Something about the way she said it seemed to be directed specifically at me. Like I needed to know she wasn't giving up on Maxon.

"Same here," I promised.

The next day was much of the same, though I'd never been disappointed to see the sun shine before. The worry was so heavy that it was all we could do to stay put. I ached to run, to put some of the energy into *something*.

After lunch, our return to the Women's Room was staggered. Elise was reading as I sat with my sheet music, but Kriss and Celeste were missing. Maybe ten minutes later, Kriss walked in with full arms. She sat down with drawing paper and a collection of colored pencils.

"What are you working on?" I asked.

She shrugged. "Whatever keeps me busy."

She sat for a long time with a red pencil in her hand, hovering over the paper.

"I don't know what I'm doing," she finally said. "I know that people are in danger, but I love him. I don't want to leave."

"The king won't let anyone die," Elise offered comfortingly.

"But people already have died." Kriss wasn't argumentative, only worried. "I just need to think about something else."

"I bet Silvia would have work for us," I offered.

Kriss gave a single chuckle. "I'm not that desperate." She put the tip of the pencil down, making a smooth curve across the page. It was a start. "Everything will be fine. I'm sure of it."

I rubbed my eyes, looking at my music. I needed to switch things up.

"I'm going to hop over to one of the libraries. I'll be right back."

Elise and Kriss each gave me a cursory nod as they attempted to focus on their tasks, and I stood to leave.

I wandered down the hall to one of the rooms on the far end of the floor. There were a few books on those shelves I'd been wanting to read. The door of the parlor swung open quietly, and I realized I wasn't alone. Someone was crying.

I searched for the source and found Celeste, hugging her knees to her chest, sitting on the wide perch of a windowsill. I felt immediately awkward. Celeste *did not* cry. Up until this moment, I hadn't even been sure she was capable.

The only thing to do was leave, but as she wiped her eyes, she caught sight of me.

"Ugh!" she whined. "What do you want?"

"Nothing. Sorry. I was looking for a book."

"Well, get it and go. You get everything you want anyway."

I stood there blankly for a moment, confused by her words. She heaved a sigh and pushed herself up from her seat. Snatching one of her many magazines, she flung the glossy pages at me, and I caught it clumsily.

"See for yourself. Your little speech on the *Report* pushed you over the top. They love you." Her voice was angry, accusing. As if I'd planned this all along.

I turned the magazine right side up, finding half of the page full of pictures of the four remaining girls with a graph beside our photos. Above the image, an elegant headline asked *Who do YOU want as Queen?* Next to my face, a wide line shot out, showing thirty-nine percent of the people were pulling for me. It wasn't as high as I thought it should be for whoever won, but it was much higher than the others!

Quotes from those polled edged the graph, saying that Celeste was positively regal, though she was in third. Elise was so poised, it said, but she also only had eight percent of the population pulling for her. By my picture were opinions that made me want to cry.

"Lady America is just like the queen. She's a fighter. It's more than wanting her; we need her!"

I stared at the words. "Is . . . is this real?"

Celeste snatched back the magazine. "Of course it's real. So go ahead, marry him or whatever. Be princess. Everyone will love it. The sad little Five gets a crown."

She started walking away, her sour mood ruining the most incredible news I'd gotten during the entirety of the Selection.

"You know, I don't even see why this matters so much to you. Some very happy Two is going to marry you anyway. And you're still going to be famous when this is over," I accused.

"As a has-been, America."

"You're a model, for goodness' sake!" I yelled. "You've got everything."

"But for how long?" she shot back. Then quieter. "How long?"

"What do you mean?" I said, my voice becoming softer. "Celeste, you're beautiful. You're a Two for the rest of your life."

She was shaking her head before I was even done speaking. "You think you're the only one who's ever felt trapped by your caste? Yes, I'm a model. I can't sing. I can't act. So when my face isn't good enough anymore, they're going to forget all about me. I've got maybe five years left, ten if I'm lucky."

She stared at me. "You've spent your whole life in the background. I can see you miss it sometimes. Well, I've spent mine in the spotlight. Maybe it's a stupid fear to you, but it's real for me: I don't want to lose it."

"That makes sense, actually."

"Yeah?" she dabbed under her eyes, gazing out the window.

I walked over and stood beside her. "Yeah. But, Celeste, did you ever even like him?"

She tilted her head to the side, thinking. "He's cute. And a great kisser," she added with a smile.

I grinned back. "I know."

"I know you do. That was a serious blow to my plan, when I found out how far you two had gone. I thought I had him in the palm of my hand, making him dream about the possibility of more."

"That's no way to get to someone's heart."

"I didn't need his heart," she confessed. "I just needed him to want me enough to keep me. Fine, it's not love. I need the fame more than I need the love."

For the first time, she wasn't my enemy. I understood that now. Yes, she was conniving when it came to the competition, but that was her being desperate. She simply felt she had to intimidate us out of something that most of us *wanted* but that she felt she *needed*.

"First of all, you do need the love. Everyone does. And it's okay to want that right along with the fame."

She rolled her eyes but didn't interrupt.

"Second of all, the Celeste Newsome I know doesn't need a man to get fame."

She laughed out loud at that. "I have been a bit vicious,"

she said, more playful than ashamed.

"You ripped my dress!"

"Well, at the time I needed it!"

And suddenly all of it was funny. All the arguing, the wicked faces, the little tricks—they felt like a really long joke. We stood there for a minute, laughing over the past few months, and I found myself wanting to look after her the way I did Marlee.

Surprisingly, her laughter faded away quickly, and she averted her eyes as she spoke.

"I've done so many things, America. Horrible, shameful things. Part of it was not reacting well to the stress of this, but mostly it was because I was ready to do anything to get that crown, to get to Maxon."

I was a little shocked as I watched my hand rise up to pat her on the shoulder.

"Honestly," I started, "I don't think you need Maxon to get anything you want out of life. You've got the drive, the talent; and probably, most importantly, you've got the ability. Half of the country would give anything to have what you have."

"I know," she said. "It's not that I'm completely unaware of how lucky I am. It's just hard to accept the possibility of . . . I don't know, being less."

"Then don't accept it."

She shook her head. "I didn't stand a chance, did I? It's been you the whole time."

"Not only me," I admitted. "Kriss. She's at the top, too."

"Do you need me to break her leg? I could make it happen." She chuckled to herself. "I'm kidding."

"You want to come back with me? It's hard to sit through the days right now, and you do add a little something to the mix."

"Not right now. I don't want the others to know I was crying." She gave me a pleading look.

"Not a word, I promise."

"Thanks."

There was a tense pause, as if one of us ought to say more. It felt significant, this moment of finally, truly seeing Celeste. I wasn't sure if I could let go of everything she'd done to me, but at least I understood now. There was nothing to add, so I gave her a little wave and left.

Only once I closed the door did I realize that I'd forgotten to grab a book. And then I thought of the glossy chart with my smiling face and the huge number beside it. I'd have to tug my ear at dinner. Maxon needed to know about this. I hoped that maybe if he knew how the people felt about me, it would raise his feelings a little closer to the surface.

As I reached the corner to turn toward the Women's Room, a familiar face reminded me that I had even bigger plans to think about right now. I'd told Maxon that I'd find us a way to get to August, and I felt certain our only shot was coming my way.

Aspen walked down the hall, seeming even bigger and taller than the last time I'd seen him.

I looked around, seeing if we were alone. There were a

few guards down the hall just past him, but they were out of earshot.

"Hey," I said, beckoning him over. I bit my lip, hoping that Aspen would be as able as I thought he was. "I need your help."

Without batting an eye, he responded. "Anything."

CHAPTER 12

I WAS RIGHT. ASPEN HAD every corner of the palace memorized, and he knew exactly how to get us out of it.

"Are you quite sure about this?" Maxon asked as we got dressed in my room the following evening.

"We need to know what's going on. I have no doubt we'll be safe," I assured him.

We spoke through the cracked-open bathroom door as he dropped the pieces of his suit to the floor and climbed into the denim and cotton a Six would wear. Aspen's clothes were going to be a bit big on Maxon, but they would do. Thankfully, Aspen had found a smaller guard to borrow clothes from for me, but even then I had to roll up the hem of the pants several times to find my feet.

"You seem to trust this guard a lot," Maxon commented,

and I couldn't figure out the tone he was using. Perhaps he was anxious.

"My maids say he's one of the best you have. And he got me to the safe room that time the Southerners came, when everyone was running late. He always looks ready to go, even when things are quiet. I have a good feeling about him. Trust me."

I heard the rustling of clothes as he continued. "How did you know he could get us out of the palace?"

"I didn't. I just asked."

"And he simply told you?" Maxon replied, astonished.

"Well, I told him it was for you, of course."

He made a sound, something like a sigh. "I still don't think you should come."

"I'm going, Maxon. Are you done yet?"

"Yes. I need to get my shoes on."

I opened the door, and after a quick once-over, Maxon started laughing. "I'm sorry. I'm used to seeing you in gowns."

"You look a bit different when you're not in a suit yourself." And he did, but not in any way that was close to comical. Even though Aspen's clothes were too big, Maxon looked good in plain old denim. The shirt had short sleeves, and I got a peek at those strong arms I'd only ever seen the one time in the safe room.

"These pants are far too heavy. Why are you so partial to jeans?" he asked, remembering my request from my very first day in the palace.

I shrugged. "I just like them."

He smiled at me, shaking his head a bit. He walked over to my closet, not asking if it was all right to open it. "We need something to hold your pants up or it's going to be a very scandalous evening. Well, more so than it already is."

Maxon pulled out a dark-red sash and returned to me with it, lacing it through my belt loops.

I couldn't say why, but this felt meaningful. My heart pounded, and for a minute I wondered if he could hear it shouting how much I loved him. If so, he ignored it in favor of the business at hand.

"Listen," he said, making a little knot in the sash, "what we're doing is very dangerous. If something happens, I want you to run. Don't even try to get back to the palace. Find a family who will hide you through the night."

Maxon stepped back and looked into my worried eyes. I tilted my head. "Right now, asking a family to hide me is almost as dangerous as facing the rebels. People might be upset that we girls aren't leaving the competition."

"If the article Celeste showed you is right, then people might be proud of you."

I wanted to tell Maxon I disagreed, but a knock at the door interrupted us. He went over to answer it, and quickly Aspen and a second guard walked into my dimly lit room.

"Your Majesty," Aspen said with a small bow. "Lady America has informed me that you need to get outside the palace walls."

Maxon sighed deeply. "Yes. And I hear you're the man to

help me. Officer . . ." He looked for Aspen's badge. "Leger."

Aspen nodded. "It's not very difficult, actually. The secrecy might be more of an issue than getting out in the first place."

"How so?"

"Well, I have to assume there's a reason for you to be doing this at night, without the king's knowledge. If we're specifically asked," Aspen said, glancing over to the other guard, "I don't think we could lie to him."

"And I wouldn't ask you to. I'm hoping to be able to reveal this to my father soon enough, but, for tonight, discretion is imperative."

"It shouldn't be a problem." Aspen hesitated. "I don't think the lady should go."

As if he'd won the argument, Maxon looked at me with a face that said *See!*

I stood as tall as I could manage. "I'm not just going to sit here. I've been chased by rebels once already, and I'm fine."

"But those weren't Southerners," Maxon countered.

"I'm going," I said. "And we're wasting time."

"To be clear, no one agrees with you."

"To be clear, I don't care."

Sighing, Maxon pulled the knit hat over his hair. "So what do we need to do?"

"The plan is pretty simple," Aspen said decisively. "Twice a week, a truck is sent out for groceries. Sometimes the kitchen staff simply falls short of the needs for the week, so the truck goes out again to pick up whatever's lacking. Usually people from the kitchen go, along with a few guards."

"And no one will suspect?" I asked.

Aspen shook his head. "These runs are often done at night. If the cook says we need more eggs for breakfast, well, we'd better go before sunup."

Maxon ran over to his suit pants, rummaging through his pocket. "I did manage to get a note out to August. He said we should meet him at this address." Maxon handed the paper to Aspen, who shared the note with the other guard.

"You know where this is?" Aspen asked.

The guard—a dark-skinned young man whose name tag I finally noticed said AVERY—nodded. "Not the best part of town, but close enough to the food storage area that we shouldn't raise any alarm."

"All right," Aspen said. He looked at me. "Tuck your hair beneath your hat."

I grabbed my hair and twisted it up, hoping it would all fit beneath the knit hat Aspen had provided. I pushed up the last strands and looked to Maxon. "Well?"

He choked on a laugh. "Great."

I gave him a playful punch in the arm before turning to follow Aspen's next instructions.

I saw the hurt in his eyes to see me so casual with Maxon. And maybe it went beyond that. We'd hid in a tree house for two years, but here I was wandering into the streets, past curfew, with the man the Southern rebels wanted to see dead more than anyone.

This moment was a slap in the face of everything we were.

And even though I wasn't in love with Aspen, he still mattered to me, and I didn't want to cause him pain.

Before Maxon probably even noticed, Aspen straightened his face. "Follow us."

Slipping into the hallway, Aspen and Officer Avery took us down the stairway that led to the massive safe room reserved for the royal family. Instead of heading toward the great steel doors, we moved quickly across the length of the palace, where we ascended another spiral staircase. I had assumed we would be heading to the first floor, but we exited into the kitchen.

Immediately, I was hit with billowing warmth and the sweet smell of bread rising. For a split second, it felt like home. I expected something clinical, professional, like the big bakeries we had in Carolina on the nice end of town. But there were huge wooden tables with vegetables laid out, ready to be prepped. Notes were left in places, reminding whoever was on duty next of what had to be done. All in all, the kitchen seemed cozy, even for as big as it was.

"Keep your heads down," Officer Avery whispered to Maxon and me.

We studied the floor as Aspen called out. "Delilah?"

"Hold on, honey!" someone shouted back. Her voice was rich and had the slight drawl of a southern accent that I'd heard sometimes back in Carolina. Heavy footsteps came around the corner, but I avoided looking up to see the woman's face. "Leger, you cutie, how've you been?"

"Been good. Just heard there was a delivery to pick up,

and I was wondering if you had a list for me."

"Delivery? Not that I know of."

"That's funny. I was sure."

"Might as well drive out," she said, no hint of worry or suspicion in her voice. "Don't want to miss something."

"Good point. Shouldn't be too long," Aspen answered. I heard the swift sound of him catching a set of keys. "See you later, Delilah. If you're asleep, I'll put the keys on the hook."

"Okay, honey. You come see me soon. It's been too long."

"Will do."

Aspen was already walking, and we followed him word-lessly. I smiled to myself. The woman, Delilah, had a deeper voice, mature sounding. But even she was sweet on Aspen.

We walked around a corner and up a wide incline to a set of broad doors. Aspen undid the lock and pushed the doors open. Waiting in the dark was a large black truck.

"There's nothing to hold on to, but I think you two should get in the back," Avery said. I looked at the large cargo space. At least we wouldn't be recognized.

I went around to the back, where Aspen was already opening the doors. "My lady," he said, offering me his hand, which I took. "Your Majesty," he added as Maxon passed, refusing assistance.

There were a couple of crates inside and a shelving unit along one wall, but otherwise it was an empty metal box. Maxon passed me, surveying the area.

"Come here, America," he said, pointing to the corner. "We'll wedge ourselves against the shelf."

"We'll try to drive smoothly," Aspen called.

Maxon nodded. Aspen gave us both a solemn look before shutting the doors.

In the pitch-dark, I pushed myself against Maxon.

"Are you scared?" he asked.

"No."

"Me neither."

But I was pretty sure we were both lying.

CHAPTER 13

I COULDN'T TELL HOW LONG we'd been traveling, but I was very aware of every move the giant truck made. Maxon, in an effort to keep us stable, had pushed his back against the shelf and braced a leg across me on the wall, caging me in. But even with that, we both slid a bit against the metal floor at every turn.

"I don't like not knowing where I am," Maxon said, trying to secure us again.

"Have you ever been out in Angeles before?"

"Only in a car," he confessed.

"Is it strange that I feel better going into a den of rebels than I did when I had to entertain the women of the Italian royal family?"

Maxon laughed. "Only you."

It was hard talking over the rumble of the engine and the squeal of the wheels, so we were quiet for a while. In the dark, the sounds felt bigger. I inhaled deeply, trying to focus myself, and noticed a hint of coffee in the air. I couldn't tell if it was some lingering scent in the truck or if we were passing a shop on the road. After what felt like a very long time, Maxon put his lips to my ear.

"I wish you were safe at home, but I'm really glad you're here." I laughed quietly. I doubted he could hear it, but he probably felt it, we were so close. "Promise me that you'll run though."

I decided that I'd be of no help to Maxon if something really bad happened anyway. I searched and put my mouth by his ear. "I promise."

We went over a pretty jarring bump, and he grabbed me. I felt our noses brush in the dark, and the urge to kiss him came unexpectedly fast. Though our kiss on the roof had only been three days ago, it felt like an eternity. He held me close, and I could feel his breath on my skin. It was coming; I was sure of it.

Maxon used his nose, nudging at my cheek, bringing our lips closer together. The same way I could smell coffee and hear every tiny squeak in the dark, the lack of light made me focus on the clean scent that hung around Maxon, feel the pressure of his fingers moving up my neck to the wisps of hair peeking out from under my cap.

In the second before our lips touched, the truck came

to an abrupt stop, flinging us forward. I knocked my head against the wall, and I was pretty sure I felt Maxon's teeth against my ear.

"Ow!" he exclaimed, and I felt him adjusting his position in the dark. "Are you hurt?"

"No. My hair and the hat took most of it." If I hadn't wanted that kiss so badly, I would have laughed.

As soon as we'd stopped, we started moving slowly in reverse. After a few seconds, the truck halted again and the engine cut off. Maxon switched positions, and it felt as if he was ducking low in a crouch, facing the door. I got into a similar position as one of Maxon's hands come back to protect me, just in case.

The light of the streetlamp coming into the cabin was shocking, and I squinted against it as someone climbed into the back of the truck.

"We're here," said Officer Avery. "Follow me closely."

Maxon stood and extended a hand to me. He let go to hop out of the truck, then reached up to help me down and immediately slid his hand back into mine. The thing I noticed right away was the large brick wall cornering us in the alley, followed by the stinging smell of something rotting. Aspen was standing in front of us, looking around intently, a gun held low in his hand.

He and Avery started moving toward the back entrance of the building, and we kept close to them. The walls surrounding us were high and reminded me of the apartment buildings back home with their fire escapes snaking down the sides, though this didn't seem like an area where people lived. Aspen knocked on the grime-covered door and waited. It cracked open, a small chain there to protect whoever was inside. But I saw August's eyes before the door was quickly shut again. The next time, it opened wide, and August ushered in all of us.

"Hurry," he said quietly.

In the shadowy room was a younger boy and Georgia. I could see she was just as anxious as we were, and I couldn't stop myself from bolting across the room to embrace her. She held me back, and I was happy to find I'd acquired an unexpected friend.

"Were you followed?" she asked.

Aspen shook his head. "No. But you should be quick."

Georgia pulled me over to a small table, and Maxon sat next to me, with August and the younger boy beside him.

"How bad is it?" Maxon asked. "I have a feeling my father is keeping the truth from me."

August gave a surprised shrug. "As best we can tell, the numbers are low. The Southerners are doing their typical destruction, but as far as the attacks on Twos specifically, it looks like it's less than three hundred people."

I gasped. Three hundred people? How could that be deemed low?

"America, it's not that bad, all things considered," Maxon comforted me, taking my hand again.

"He's right," Georgia said, her face warm. "It could have been so much worse."

"It's what I would expect from them: starting at the top and working their way down. We're guessing they'll pick it up before too long," August interjected. "It looks like the attacks are still isolated on the Twos, but we're watching and will alert you if or when that changes. We've got allies in every province, and they're all trying to keep watch. But there's only so much they can do without exposing themselves, and we all know what would happen if they did."

Maxon nodded soberly. They'd die, of course.

"Should we cave?" Maxon suggested. I looked over at him, surprised.

"Trust us," Georgia said. "They're not going to get any better if you give in."

"But there must be something more we can do," Maxon insisted.

"You've already done something pretty empowering. Well, she did," August said, dipping his head in my direction. "From what we're able to tell, farmers are keeping their axes with them if they leave their fields, seamstresses walk the street with scissors clutched in their hands, and you'll see Twos parading around with disarming spray. No matter the caste, everyone seems to have found some way to arm themselves, just in case. Your people don't want to live in fear, and they're not. They're fighting back."

I wanted to cry. For maybe the first time in all of the Selection, I'd done something right.

Maxon squeezed my hand, proud. "That's a comfort," he said. "Still, it doesn't feel like enough."

I nodded. I was so happy the public wasn't rolling over, but there had to be a way to stop this once and for all.

August sighed. "We've wondered if there was a way for us to attack them. They're not fighting with any sort of training—they just go after people. Our supporters are nervous about being identified, but they're everywhere. And they might be the best source for a surprise assault.

"In many ways, we're already an army of sorts, but we're essentially unarmed. We can't possibly beat the Southerners when the majority of our forces fight with bricks or rakes."

"You want weapons?"

"Wouldn't hurt."

Maxon considered this. "There are things you can do that we simply can't from the palace. But I don't like the idea of sending any of my people on a mission to take out these savages. Certainly they would die."

"That's possible," August confessed.

"There's also the small issue of me not being able to guarantee you won't use any weapons I give you against me eventually."

August snorted. "I don't know how to make you believe that we're on your side, but it's true. All we've ever wanted was to see an end to the castes, and we're prepared to support you to that end. I have no intentions of ever harming you, Maxon, and I think you know that." He and Maxon shared a very long look. "If you didn't, you wouldn't be here now."

"Your Majesty," Aspen said. "I'm sorry to interrupt, but there are some of us who would like to see the Southern

rebels gone as much as you would. I would personally volunteer to train anyone in something more along the lines of
hand-to-hand combat."

My chest swelled with pride. That was my Aspen, always
trying to fix things.

Maxon nodded at him before turning back to August.
"That's something I'll need time to think about. I might be
able to provide training, but I couldn't arm you. Even if I
was sure of your intentions, if there's any link between us, I
can't imagine what my father would do."

Without thinking, Maxon flexed the muscles across his
back. It seemed to me that maybe he'd done that a lot in the
time I'd known him, only I hadn't understood its meaning.
Even now he was hyperaware of his secret.

"True. In fact, you should probably already be leaving. I'll
get word to you as soon as we have more information, but
for now it looks good. Well, as good as we could hope for."
August passed Maxon a note. "We have one landline. You
can call if there's something urgent. Micah here, he's on top
of those things."

August motioned to the boy who hadn't made a sound the
whole time. He pulled his lips into his mouth like he might
be biting them and gave us a small nod. Something about his
stance suggested he was both shy and eager at once.

"Very good. I'll use it with discretion." Maxon placed the
paper in his pocket. "I'll be in touch soon." He stood and I
followed suit, looking over at Georgia as I did so.

She came around the table to me. "Be safe getting back.

And that number is for you, too, you know."

"Thank you." I gave her a quick hug and headed out with Maxon, Aspen, and Officer Avery. I took one last glance at our strange friends before the door closed and was bolted behind us.

"Get away from the truck," Aspen said. I turned to see what he meant, as we weren't even close yet.

Then I saw that Aspen wasn't talking to me. A handful of men were circling the vehicle. One had a wrench in his hands, looking as if he was about to try and steal the tires. Another two were at the back, trying to open the metal doors.

"Just give us the food, and we'll go," one said. He looked younger than most of the others, maybe Aspen's age. His voice was cold and desperate.

I hadn't noticed back at the palace that the truck we were jumping into had a massive Illéa emblem on the side. As I stood there looking at the small crowd of haggard men, this seemed like an incredibly stupid oversight. And while Maxon and I weren't dressed like ourselves, that wouldn't help very much if anyone got too close. Even though I wouldn't have known the first thing to do with one, I wished I had a weapon.

"There is no food," Aspen said calmly. "And if there was, it wouldn't be yours to take."

"How well they train their puppets," another man remarked. As he gave us an amused smile, I could see that a few of his teeth were missing. "What were you before they turned you into this?"

"Step away from the truck," Aspen ordered.

"You couldn't have been a Two or a Three; you'd have bought your way out. So come on, little man, what were you?" the toothless man taunted, stepping closer.

"Back. Away." Aspen put one hand in front of himself, reaching down toward his hip with the other.

The man stopped, shaking his head. "You don't know who you're messing with, boy."

"Wait!" someone said. "That's her. That's one of the girls."

I turned my head to the voice, giving myself away.

"Get her!" the young one said.

Before I could even think, Maxon jerked me back. I saw a blur of Aspen and Officer Avery pulling out their guns as my head got whipped around by the force of Maxon's strong arms. I was moving sideways, stumbling to keep up while Aspen and Avery held the men at bay. Quickly, Maxon and I were against the brick wall, trapped.

"I don't want to kill you," Aspen said. "Leave. Now!"

The toothless man chuckled darkly, his hands raised in front of him as if he meant no harm. In a move so fast I nearly missed it, he reached down and drew a gun of his own. Aspen fired, and shots came in return.

"Come on, America," Maxon said urgently.

Come where? I thought, my heart pounding in terror.

I looked at him and saw that he had laced his fingers together, making a cradle for my foot. Suddenly understanding, I put my shoe in his hands, and he pushed me up as I grappled at the wall for some stability. I reached the top, and

I felt something funny in my arm as I crawled over.

I ignored it as I pulled my body across the ledge, lowering myself as much as I could before dropping to the concrete. I fell to the side, positive I'd messed up my hip or leg; but Maxon had instructed me to run if I was in danger, so I did.

I didn't know why I assumed he would be right behind me, but when I reached the end of the street and he wasn't there, I realized no one would be free to give him a boost. In that moment, I noticed that funny feeling in my arm was starting to burn. I looked down, and in the faint glow of a streetlight, I saw something wet coming from a rip in my sleeve.

I'd been shot.

I'd been shot?

There were guns and I was there, but it didn't seem real. Still, there was no denying the searing pain that was growing bigger every second. I cupped my hand over the wound, but that made it worse.

I looked around. The city was still.

Of course it was. We were out well after curfew. I'd gotten so used to the palace that I'd forgotten that the world outside stopped after eleven.

If an officer came by, I'd be thrown in jail. How was I supposed to explain that to the king? *How are you going to talk away a bullet wound, America?*

I started moving, staying to the shadows. I had no idea where to go. I didn't know if trying to get back to the palace was a good idea. Even if it was, I didn't know how to get there.

God, the burning. It was hard to think. I made my way past a narrow backstreet between two apartment buildings. That alone told me I wasn't in the best part of town. Generally, only Sixes and Sevens had to squeeze into apartments.

There was nowhere for me to go, so I walked down the poorly lit alley, tucking myself behind a tight pack of trash cans. The night was cool, but it had been a typical hot Angeles day, and the stink was rising from the metal bins. Between the smell and the pain, I felt myself on the edge of vomiting.

I peeled off my right sleeve, trying not to irritate the wound any more than necessary. My hands were trembling, either from fear or adrenaline, and just bending my arm made me want to scream. I bit my lips together to keep the sound in, but even with that my muffled whimpers escaped into the night.

"What happened?" a tiny voice asked.

I jerked my head up, looking for the source. There were two glittering eyes in the darker depths of the alley.

"Who's there?" I asked, voice trembling.

"I won't hurt you," she said, crawling out. "I'm having a bad night, too."

The girl, maybe fifteen if I had to guess, crept out of the shadows and came to look at my arm. She sucked in a breath at the sight.

"That looks really painful," she said sympathetically.

"I got shot," I blurted, ready to cry. It burned so badly.

"Shot?"

I nodded.

She looked at me hesitantly, like maybe she should run away. "I don't know what you did or who you are, but you don't mess with rebels, okay?"

"Huh?"

"I haven't been out here long, but I know that the only people who can get guns are rebels. Whatever you did to them, don't do it again."

In all the times they'd attacked us, I'd never considered that. No one was supposed to have a gun unless they were an officer. Only a rebel would be able to get around that. Even August had just said the Northerners were *essentially unarmed*. I wondered if he'd been carrying tonight.

"What's your name?" she asked. "I know you're a girl under there."

"Mer," I said.

"I'm Paige. Looks like you're new to being an Eight yourself. Your clothes are pretty clean." She was turning my arm gently, looking at the oozing wound as if she could do something even though we both knew better.

"Something like that," I hedged.

"You can starve out here if you're alone. You got anywhere to go?"

I shuddered with a roll of pain. "Not exactly."

She nodded. "It was just my dad and me. I was a Four. We had a restaurant, but my grandma had made some rule that he was supposed to leave it to my aunt when he died, not to me. I think she was worried my aunt wouldn't have anything or something like that. Well, my aunt hates me, always has. She got the restaurant, but she got me, too. Didn't like that.

"Two weeks after Dad died, she started hitting me. I had to sneak food because she said I was getting fat and wouldn't give me anything to eat. I thought about going to a friend's house, but my aunt would just be able to come and get me, so I left. I took some money, but not enough. Even if it was, I got robbed my second night out here."

I looked Paige over as she talked. I could see it, under the growing layer of grime. There was a girl in there who used to be very well taken care of. She was trying to be tough now. She had to be. What else was there for her?

"Just this week I found a group of girls. We work together and share all the profits. If you can forget what you're doing, it's not so bad. I have to cry afterward. That's why I was hiding back there. If the other girls see you cry, they make my aunt look like a saint. J.J. says they're just trying to toughen me up and that I better get that way fast, but it still hurts.

"Anyway, you're pretty. I know they'd be glad to have you."

My stomach rolled, processing her offer. In what seemed like a few weeks, she'd lost her family, her home, and herself.

And still she was sitting in front of me—a girl who'd been chased by a pack of rebels, a girl who could be nothing but danger—and she was kind.

"We can't get you a doctor, but there would be something

to ease the pain. And they could get you some stitches from this guy they know. You'd have to work it off though."

I focused on my breathing. Even though she was distracting, the conversation couldn't stop the pain.

"You don't talk much, do you?" Paige asked.

"Not when I've been shot."

She laughed, and the ease of it made me laugh a little, too. Paige sat down beside me for a little while, and I was glad I wasn't alone.

"If you don't want to come with me, I get it. It's dangerous and kind of sad."

"I . . . can we just be quiet for a minute?" I asked.

"Yes. Do you want me to stay with you?"

"Please."

And she did. Without question, she sat beside me, as silent as a mouse. It felt like an eternity was passing, though it couldn't have even been twenty minutes. The pain was becoming more severe, and I was getting desperate. Maybe I could get to a doctor. Of course, I'd have to find one. The palace would pay for it, but I had no clue how to get ahold of Maxon.

Was Maxon even okay? Was Aspen?

They were outnumbered, but they were armed. If the rebels recognized me so quickly, did they recognize Maxon, too? If so, what would they do to him?

I sat still, trying to talk myself out of the worry. It was all I could do to focus on myself. But what was I going to do if Aspen died? Or if Maxon——

"Shh!" I ordered, though Paige still hadn't made a sound. "Do you hear that?"

We both tuned our ears to the street.

". . . Max," someone yelled. "Come out, Mer; it's Max."

That would have been Aspen's idea, no doubt, using those names.

I scrambled to my feet and went to the edge of the alley, with Paige right behind me. I saw the truck coming down the street at a snail's pace, heads poking out of the windows, searching.

I turned around. "Paige, would you want to come with me?"

"Where?"

"I promise you, you'll have a real job and food, and no one will hit you."

Her heavy eyes filled with tears. "Then I don't care where it is. I'll go."

I took her with my good hand, my coat sleeve still hanging off the wounded arm. We made our way down the road, sticking close to the buildings.

"Max!" I called as we got closer. "Max!"

The massive truck skidded to a stop, and Maxon, Aspen, and Officer Avery came running out.

I dropped Paige's hand, seeing Maxon's open arms. He embraced me, hitting my wound, and I yelled.

"What's wrong?" he asked.

"I was shot."

Aspen parted us, grabbing my arm to see for himself.

"That could have been a lot worse. We need to get you back and find a way to treat you. I'm assuming we'll want to leave the doctor out of this?" He looked to Maxon.

"I don't want her to suffer," he insisted.

"Your Majesty," Paige said, dropping to her knees. Her shoulders started shaking like she might be crying.

"This is Paige," I said, offering nothing else. "Let's get in the back."

Aspen lowered a hand to Paige. "You're safe," he assured her.

Maxon put an arm around me, escorting me to the back of the truck.

"I was sure it would take all night to find you," he worried aloud.

"Me, too. But I was in too much pain to get very far. Paige helped."

"Then she'll be taken care of, I promise."

Maxon, Paige, and I crawled into the back of the truck, and the metal floor was strangely comforting as we sped back to the palace.

CHAPTER 14

IT WAS ASPEN WHO LIFTED me from the back of the truck and hurriedly carried me to a tiny room. The space was smaller than my bathroom and held two slim beds and a dresser. There were little notes and photos on the wall, which gave it some personality; but it was otherwise barren, not to mention incredibly cramped with Aspen, me, Officer Avery, Maxon, and Paige filling every spare inch.

Aspen laid me on a bed as gently as possible, but my arm continued to throb.

"We ought to get the doctor," he said. But I could tell he doubted his own words. Getting Dr. Ashlar would mean either telling the absolute truth or making up an outrageous lie, and neither of those options was something we wanted.

"Don't," I urged weakly. "I won't die from this. It'll just be a bad scar. We have to clean it up." I grimaced.

"You'll need something for the pain," Maxon added.

"She might get infected. That alley was really dirty, and I touched her," Paige said guiltily.

A sliver of fire burned across the wound, and I hissed. "Anne. Get Anne."

"Who?" Maxon asked.

"Her head maid," Aspen explained. "Avery, get Anne and a medical kit. We'll have to make do. And we need to do something with her," he added, nodding his head at Paige.

I watched Maxon's worried eyes finally move from my bloody arm to Paige's troubled face.

"Are you a criminal? A runaway?" he asked her.

"Not that kind of criminal. And I did run away, but there's no one looking for me."

Maxon considered her words. "Welcome aboard. Follow Avery down to the kitchens and tell a Mallory you'll be working with her on the prince's command. Instruct her to come to the officers' wing immediately."

"Mallory. Yes, Your Majesty." Paige gave him a deep curtsy and followed Officer Avery from the room, leaving me alone with Maxon and Aspen. I'd been with both of them all night, but this was the first time it was just the three of us. I could feel the weight of our secrets filling up the already restricting room.

"How'd you make it out?" I asked.

"August, Georgia, and Micah heard the gunshots and came running," Maxon said. "He wasn't kidding when he said they'd never hurt us." He paused, his eyes quickly distant and sad. "Micah didn't make it."

I turned my head away. I didn't know a thing about him, but he died tonight for us. I felt as guilty as if I'd taken his life myself.

I went to wipe a tear away, forgetting to use my left arm, and cried out.

"Calm down, America," Aspen said, forgetting to be formal.

"Everything's going to work out," Maxon promised.

I nodded, pursing my lips together to avoid crying anymore. What a waste.

We were quiet for what felt like a long time, but maybe it was the pain stretching out the minutes.

"It's wonderful to have such devotion," Maxon said suddenly.

At first I thought he was talking about Micah again. But Aspen and I looked over and saw him gazing at a space on the wall behind me.

I turned my head, happy to focus on anything that wasn't the searing pain in my arm. There, beside several pictures drawn by one of his younger siblings, was a note.

I'll always love you. I'll wait for you forever. I'm with you, no matter what.

My handwriting was a little sloppier a year ago when I'd left that note by my window for Aspen to find, and it was surrounded by silly little hearts that I would never put in a love letter now, but I could still feel the importance of those words. It was the first time I'd put them in writing, afraid of how much more I felt those things once they were on paper. I also remembered the fear of my mother finding that note surpassing any other worry about the enormity of knowing, without a doubt, that I loved Aspen.

Right now I feared Maxon recognizing my handwriting.

"It must be nice to have someone to write to. I've never had the luxury of love letters," Maxon said, a sad smile on his face. "Has she kept her word?"

Aspen was moving pillows from the other bed to prop under my head, avoiding eye contact with either Maxon or myself.

"Writing is difficult," he said. "But I do know she's with me, no matter what. I don't doubt it."

I looked at Aspen's short, dark hair—the only part of him I could really see—and I felt a new pain. In a way he was right. We would never truly leave each other. But . . . the words on that paper? That encompassing love that used to overwhelm me? It wasn't here anymore.

Was Aspen still counting on it?

My eyes flickered to Maxon, and the sadness on his face read a bit like jealousy. I wasn't surprised. I remembered telling Maxon that I'd been in love before; he'd looked as if he'd been cheated out of something, so unsure at that point if he would ever fall in love.

If he knew that the love I'd spoken about and the love

Aspen just shared were the same one, I was sure it would crush him.

"Write her soon," Maxon advised. "Don't let her forget."

"What's taking them so long?" Aspen muttered, and left the room, not bothering to acknowledge Maxon's words.

Maxon watched him go and turned back to face me. "I'm so useless. I have no idea how to help you, so I thought I'd at least try to help him. He saved both our lives tonight." Maxon shook his head. "Seems I only upset him."

"Everyone's just worried. You're doing fine," I assured him.

He gave an exasperated laugh, coming to kneel by the bed. "You're lying there with a seeping gash on your arm, and you're trying to comfort me. You're absurd."

"If you ever decide to write me a love letter, I'd lead with that," I joked.

He smiled. "Can't I do anything for you?"

"Hold my hand? Not too hard though."

Maxon placed his fingers in the loose grip of my palm, and even though it didn't change anything, it was nice to feel him there.

"I probably won't. Write you a love letter, that is. I try to stave off embarrassment as often as possible."

"You can't plan wars, don't know how to cook, and refuse to write love letters," I teased.

"That's correct. My list of faults is ever growing." He wiggled his fingers in my hand, and I was so grateful for the distraction.

"That's fine. I'll continue to guess at your feelings since you refuse to write me a note. With a purple pen. All the *i*'s dotted with hearts."

"Which is exactly how I would do it," he said in mock seriousness. I giggled but stopped quickly when the movement reignited the burning. "I don't think you have to guess at my feelings though."

"Well," I started, finding it harder and harder to breathe, "it's not like you've ever said it out loud."

Maxon opened his mouth to object and silenced himself. His eyes gazed toward the ceiling as he thought through our history, trying to pinpoint the moment when he'd told me he loved me.

In the safe room, it was suggested in every way. He'd let the feeling slip into a dozen romantic gestures or indicated it was there by dancing around the words . . . but the actual statement had never come. Not between us. I would have remembered, and I would have made them my reason never to question him, my reason to confess what I was feeling, too.

"My lady?" Anne said, her voice making its way through the door a moment before her worried face.

Maxon stepped back, letting go of my hand as he made space for her.

Anne's focused eyes took in the wound, and she touched it gingerly as she inspected how bad it was.

"You'll need stitches. I'm not sure we have anything that will completely numb you," she assessed.

"It's okay. Just do your best," I said. I felt calmer with her there.

She nodded. "Someone get some boiling water. We should have antiseptic in the kit, but I want water, too."

"I'll get it." By the door, Marlee was standing, her face lined with worry.

"Marlee," I whimpered, losing control. I put the Mallory thing together. Of course she and Carter couldn't go by their real names while they were hiding right under the king's nose.

"I'll be right back, America. Hold tight." She scurried away, but I felt a great relief knowing she would be with me.

Anne absorbed the shock of Marlee's presence in stride, and I watched as she pulled out a needle and thread from the medical kit. I took comfort in the fact that she sewed almost all my clothes. My arm shouldn't be a problem.

With incredible speed, Marlee was back with a pitcher of steaming water, an armful of towels, and a bottle of amber liquid. She set the pitcher and towels on top of the dresser, unscrewing the bottle as she came over.

"For the pain." She lifted my head so I could drink, and I obeyed.

The stuff in the bottle was a new kind of burning, and I coughed my way through swallowing it. She urged me to take another sip, and I did, hating it the whole time.

"I'm so glad you're here," I whispered.

"I'm always here for you, America. You know that." She smiled; and for the first time in our friendship, she seemed older than me, so calm and sure. "What in the world were you doing?"

I made a face. "It seemed like a good idea."

Her eyes became sympathetic. "America, you are full of nothing but bad ideas. Great intentions but awful ideas."

She was right, of course, and I should have known better by now. But having her here, even to tell me how dumb I'd been, made the whole thing less awful.

"How soundproof are these walls?" Anne asked.

"Pretty good," Aspen said. "Don't hear too much this deep in the palace."

"Good," she said. "Okay, I need everyone in the hall. Miss Marlee, I'm going to need some space, but you can stay."

Marlee nodded. "I'll keep out of your way, Anne."

Avery left first, with Aspen trailing close behind him, and Maxon was last. The look in his eyes reminded me of the day I'd told him I'd gone hungry before: sad to know about it and devastated that he couldn't undo it.

The door clicked shut, and Anne started working quickly. She'd already set up everything she needed and held out her hand to Marlee for the bottle.

"Gulp it," she ordered, lifting my head.

I braced myself. I had to come off the lip of the bottle and go back to it several times because of the coughing, but I managed to get a good amount of it down. Or at least it was good enough for Anne.

"Hold this," she said, passing me a small towel. "Bite down on it when things hurt."

I nodded.

"The stitches won't hurt like the cleaning will. I can see dirt from here, so I'm going to have to be thorough." She sighed, looking again at the wound. "You'll have a scar, but I'm going to make it as small as I can. We'll put loose sleeves on your dresses for a few weeks to cover it while you heal. No one will know. And seeing as you were with the prince, I won't ask questions. Whatever you did, I'll trust it was something important."

"I think so," I said, not really sure anymore.

She got a towel wet and held it inches away from the gash. "Ready?"

I nodded.

I bit into the towel, hoping it would muffle the screams. I was sure that everyone in the hall could hear, but no one else probably would. It felt as if Anne was poking every nerve in my arm, and Marlee crawled on top of me to keep me from writhing.

"It'll be over soon, America," she promised. "Think of something happy. Think about your family."

I tried. I fought to put May's laugh or my dad's knowing smile in the front of my thoughts, but they wouldn't stay. I could only catch them long enough to feel them slip away under a new wave of pain.

How in the world did Marlee make it through her caning alive?

Once my wound was clean, Anne started sewing me up. She was right: the stitches didn't hurt as much. I couldn't tell if it was because it was actually less painful or if the liquor they'd given me was finally kicking in. It did seem like the edges of the room weren't quite as sharp anymore.

Then people were back, talking about things, about me. Who should stay, who should go, what we would say in the morning . . . so many details that I couldn't contribute to.

In the end, it was Maxon who scooped me up to return me to my room. It took some effort to hold my head upright, but it made it easier to hear him.

"How are you feeling?"

"Your eyes look like chocolate," I mumbled.

He smiled. "And yours look like the morning sky."

"Can I have water?"

"Yes. Lots," he promised. "Let's get her upstairs," he said to someone else. And I fell asleep to the rocking of his steps.

CHAPTER 15

I WOKE WITH A HEADACHE. I moaned as I rubbed my temple, then yelped when the action sent a sharp pain across my arm.

"Here," Mary said, coming to sit on the edge of my bed. She held out two pills and a glass of water.

I slowly pushed myself up to take her offering, my head throbbing through all of it. "What time is it?"

"Nearly eleven," Mary said. "We sent word that you weren't feeling well and wouldn't be at breakfast. If we hurry, we could probably get you ready for lunch with the other Elite."

The thought of rushing or even eating didn't sound appealing, but I thought it was wisest to get back into a normal routine. It was becoming clear just how much we'd risked last night, and I didn't want to give anyone a reason to suspect anything at all had happened.

I gave Mary a nod, and we both stood. My legs weren't quite as reliable as I'd have liked, but I moved toward the bathroom anyway. Anne was just outside the door, cleaning, as Lucy sat in a wide chair sewing sleeves onto a dress that had probably been designed for simple straps.

She looked up from her handiwork. "Are you all right, miss? You gave us quite a scare."

"I'm sorry. I think I'm as good as I can be."

She smiled at me. "We're ready to do what we can to help you, miss. You only need to ask."

I wasn't completely sure what she was offering, but I would take her up on any help that might get me through the next few days.

"Oh, Officer Leger stopped by, as well as the prince. They both hoped you would let them know how you were feeling once you were up to it."

I nodded. "After lunch, I'll take care of that."

With no warning, my arm was in someone's hands. Anne was looking closely at the wound, gingerly peeking under the bandages to check my progress.

"It doesn't look infected. As long as we keep it clean, I think it will heal nicely. I wish I could have done something better. I know it'll leave a mark," she lamented.

"Don't worry. The best people all have some kind of scar." I thought of Marlee's hands and Maxon's back. They both held permanent marks of their bravery. I was honored to join them.

"Lady America, your bath is ready," Mary said from around the bathroom door.

I took in her face, then Lucy's, then Anne's. I'd always been close to my maids, had always trusted them. But something changed last night. It was the first time those bonds were tested; and in the light of day, they were still there, strong and holding.

I wasn't sure there was a way to prove that I was as loyal to them as they were to me. But I hoped an opportunity would show itself.

If I focused, I could lift my fork to my mouth without grimacing. It took an extraordinary amount of effort, to the point where I started sweating in the middle of the meal. I decided to stick to nibbling on bread. I didn't need my right arm to hold that.

Kriss asked how my headache was—which I guessed was the story circulating—and I told her I was fine now, though my head and arm were impossible to ignore. That was the extent of the questioning, and it looked as if no one had guessed that anything was out of the ordinary.

As I chewed a bite of bread, I debated how well the other girls would have done if they had gone in my place last night. I decided the only person who would have fared better was Celeste. Without a doubt, she'd have found a way to fight back, and I was a little jealous for a minute that I wasn't more like her.

Once our trays were carted out of the Women's Room, Silvia came in and asked for our attention.

"It's time for you ladies to shine again. In a week, we'll be

having a small tea party, and you all, of course, are invited!"
I sighed to myself, worried about who we were meant to
entertain this time. "You won't be in charge of any preparations for this particular party, but you must be on your best
behavior, because this will be filmed for the public."

I perked up a bit. I could handle that.

"You will each invite two people to be your personal
guests at this tea party, and that will be your only responsibility. Choose wisely, and let me know your two contacts
by Friday."

She walked away, leaving us all mentally scrambling. This
was a test, and we knew it. Who in the room had the most
impressive connections, the most valuable ones?

Maybe I was being paranoid, but it felt as if this task specifically targeted me. The king must be searching for ways
to remind everyone I was useless.

"Who are you picking, Celeste?" Kriss asked.

She shrugged. "Not sure yet. But I promise they'll be
spectacular."

If I had Celeste's list of friends at my disposal, I wouldn't
be nervous either. Who was I going to invite? My mom?

Celeste turned to me, her voice warm. "Who do you
think you'll bring, America?"

I tried to hide my shock. Even though we'd had a little
breakthrough in the library, this was the first time she'd
addressed me the same way she would a friend. I cleared my
throat. "I have no idea. I'm not sure I know anyone who
would be appropriate to invite. It might be better if I bring

no one." I probably shouldn't have been so open about how disadvantaged I was, but it wasn't as if the others weren't aware.

"Well, if you really can't find anyone, let me know," Celeste said. "I'm positive I have more than two friends who would like to visit the palace, and I could make sure you at least have an idea of who they are. If you want to, that is."

I stared at her, tempted to ask her what the catch was; but, looking into her eyes, I didn't think there was one. Then I was sure of it when she winked at me with the eye that Elise and Kriss couldn't see. Celeste, the consummate fighter, was pulling for me.

"Thank you," I said, feeling truly humbled.

She shrugged. "No problem. If we're going to have a party, might as well make it a good one." She leaned back in her chair, smiling to herself, and I was sure she was picturing this event as her last hurrah. Part of me wanted to tell her not to give up, but I couldn't. Only one of us could have Maxon in the end.

By the afternoon, I had the rough outline of a plan, but it was dependent upon one big thing: I'd have to get Maxon's help.

I was sure we would find each other before the end of the day, so I didn't let myself worry about it too much. For the time being, I needed to rest again, so I headed back up to my room.

Anne was there, waiting with more pills and water. I

couldn't believe how calm she was about it all.

"I owe you one," I said, downing the medicine.

"No," Anne protested.

"Yes! Things would have been a lot different last night if you hadn't been there."

She gently took the glass from me. "I'm just glad you're okay."

She started walking to the bathroom to dispose of the water, and I followed her. "Isn't there anything I could do for you? Anything at all?"

She stood there at the counter, something clearly on her mind.

"Really, Anne. It would make me so happy."

She sighed. "Well, there's one thing. . . ."

"Please tell me."

Anne raised her eyes from the sink. "But you couldn't let it slip to anyone. Mary and Lucy would never let me live it down."

I creased my forehead. "What do you mean?"

"It's . . . it's very personal." She started fidgeting with her hands, something she never did, and I knew this was important to her.

"Okay, come talk to me about it," I encouraged, wrapping my good arm around her shoulder and ushering her to the table to sit with me.

She crossed her ankles and put her hands in her lap. "See, it's just that you get along with him so well. He seems to think so highly of you."

"You mean Maxon?"

"No," she whispered, a wild blush filling her cheeks.

"I don't understand."

She took a deep breath. "Officer Leger."

"Ooooh," I said, more shocked than I could express.

"You think it's hopeless, don't you?"

"Not hopeless," I insisted. I just didn't know how to tell the person who'd promised he'd always fight for me that he should pursue her instead.

"He's always speaking so kindly of you. I know if you maybe mentioned me to him, or could even find out if he's got a girlfriend at home . . ."

I sighed. "I can try, but I can't promise anything."

"Oh, I know. Don't worry. I've been telling myself it won't happen, but I can't stop thinking about him."

I tilted my head. "I know how that is."

She put a hand in front of her. "And it's not because he's a Two. If he was an Eight, I'd want someone like him."

"Lots of people would," I said. And that was true. Celeste noticed him, Kriss said he was funny, and even that Delilah woman sounded like she had a crush on him. That wasn't even taking into account all the girls back home who'd chased him. Hearing things like that didn't bother me so much anymore, not even from someone as close to me as Anne.

It was one more thing that made me sure that my feelings for Aspen were gone. If I was happy to suggest that someone else should take my place, then I really didn't belong with him.

Still, I wasn't sure how to broach the subject.

I reached over the polished wood and put my hand on hers. "I'll try, Anne. I swear."

She smiled but bit her lip anxiously. "Just please don't tell the others."

I held her hand tighter. "You've always kept my secrets. I'll always keep yours."

CHAPTER 16

IT WAS ONLY A FEW hours later when Aspen knocked on my door. My maids merely curtsied and exited, knowing without instruction that whatever we would say needed to be private.

"How are you feeling?"

"Not too bad," I said. "My arm throbs a bit and I have a headache, but otherwise I'm fine."

He shook his head. "I shouldn't have let you go."

I patted the space beside me on the bed. "Come sit."

He hesitated a bit. In my mind now, he was past suspicion. Maxon and my maids knew we communicated, and he'd led us out of the palace last night. Where was the risk? He must have thought the same thing, because he finally sat, choosing to keep a respectable distance just in case.

"I'm a part of this, Aspen. I couldn't have stayed behind.

And there's nothing wrong with me. I honestly owe that to you. You saved me last night."

"If I hadn't been fast enough, or if Maxon hadn't gotten you over that wall, you'd be a prisoner somewhere right now. I almost let you die. I almost let *Maxon* die." He shook his head at the floor. "Do you know what would have happened to Avery and me if you two hadn't made it back? Do you know what—" He paused, seeming to hold back tears. "Do you know what would have happened to me if we hadn't found you?"

Aspen looked at me, into me. The pain in his eyes was clear.

"But you did. You found me, you protected me, and you got me help. You were amazing." I put my hand on Aspen's back, running it up and down, trying to comfort him.

"I'm just realizing, Mer, that no matter what happens . . . there will always be a string tying you to me. I'll never not worry about you. I'll never not care about what you do. You'll always be something to me."

I took my hand and laced it through his arm, resting my head on his shoulder. "I know what you mean."

We stayed like that for a while, and I guessed that maybe Aspen was doing the same thing I was: replaying everything in his head. The way we avoided each other as children, the way we couldn't stop looking at each other when we were older, a thousand stolen moments in the tree house—all the things that made us who we were.

"America, I need to say something." I lifted my head, and Aspen turned to face me, holding me gently by my arms.

"When I told you that I would always love you, I meant it. And I . . . I . . ."

He couldn't manage to get the words out, and to be honest, I was grateful. Yes, I was tied to him, but we weren't that couple in the tree house anymore.

He gave a weak laugh. "I guess I need some sleep. I can't think straight."

"You and me both. And there's so much to think about."

He nodded. "Look, Mer, we can't do that again. Don't tell Maxon I'll help him with something so risky, and don't expect me to sneak you anywhere."

"I'm not sure it was worth it anyway. I can't imagine Maxon would want to go again."

"Good." He stood, then picked up my hand and kissed it. "My lady," he said, his voice teasing.

I smiled and squeezed his hand a little. And he did the same back. As we held hands, my grip tightening more every second, I realized that soon I'd need to let go. I'd need to really let go.

I looked into Aspen's eyes, and I could feel the tears threatening to come. *How do I say good-bye to you?*

He ran his thumb over the back of my hand and placed it on my lap. He bent and kissed my hair. "Take it easy. I'll come check on you tomorrow."

After a quick tug of my ear at dinner, Maxon knew I would be waiting for him tonight. I sat in front of my mirror, wishing the minutes would move faster. Mary brushed the length of my hair, calmly humming to herself. I vaguely recognized the tune as something I once played at someone's wedding. When I'd gotten chosen for the Selection, I'd wanted so badly to find my way back to that life. I wanted a world full of the music I'd always loved.

But, truly, that was never something I could have held on to. No matter which path I took in life now, music might only be something I pulled out at parties to entertain a guest or a way I relaxed on a weekend.

I looked at myself in the mirror and realized I wasn't bitter about that, not like I thought I'd be. I'd miss it, but it was just a piece of who I was now, not *everything* I was. There were possibilities in front of me no matter how the Selection unfolded.

I really was more than my caste.

Maxon's light knock pulled me from my thoughts, and Mary answered the door.

"Good evening," Maxon said to Mary as he entered, and she curtsied in response.

His eyes met mine briefly, and I wondered again if he could see how I felt about him, if it was as real to him as it was to me.

"Your Majesty," Mary greeted quietly. She was about to leave the room when Maxon held up a hand.

"Forgive me, but could you tell me your name?"

She stared at him for a moment, looked to me, and then

focused on Maxon again. "I'm Mary, Your Majesty."

"Mary. And Anne, we met last night." He gave her a small bow of his head. "And you?"

"Lucy." Her voice was small, but I could sense her joy in being acknowledged.

"Excellent. Anne, Mary, and Lucy. Lovely to properly meet you. I'm sure Anne has filled you both in on last night so you can serve Lady America the best way possible. I want to thank you for your dedication and discretion."

His eyes fell on each of them in turn. "I realize I've put you in a compromising position, and if anyone ever raises questions about what happened, feel free to send them directly to me. It was my decision, and you shouldn't be held responsible for any consequences that follow because of that."

"Thank you, Your Majesty," Lucy said.

I'd always sensed that my maids had a deep devotion to Maxon, but tonight I felt like it went beyond the typical obligation. It seemed to me in the past as if the highest level of loyalty was to the king, but now I wondered if that was true. More and more, I saw little things that made me think people preferred his son.

Maybe I wasn't the only one who saw King Clarkson's methods as barbaric, his way of thinking cruel. Maybe the rebels weren't the only ones ready for Maxon. Perhaps there were others out there who were looking for more.

My maids curtsied and left, leaving Maxon standing beside me.

"What was that about? Learning their names, I mean?"

He sighed. "Last night when Officer Leger said Anne's name and I didn't know who he meant . . . it was embarrassing. Shouldn't I know the people who tend to you better than some random guard?"

He's not that random. "To be fair, the maids all gossip about the guards. It wouldn't surprise me if the guards did the same."

"Still. They're with you every day. I should have known their names months ago."

I smiled at his reasoning and went to stand, though he looked uneasy about me moving at all.

"I'm fine, Maxon," I insisted, taking his outstretched hand.

"You were shot last night, if I remember correctly. You can't blame me for worrying."

"It wasn't like a real bullet wound. It only cut me."

"All the same, I won't quickly forget the sound of your muffled screams as Anne sewed you back together. Come, you should be resting."

Maxon ushered me to the bed, and I crawled in. He tucked me under the covers before lying down on top of them himself, facing me. I waited for him to talk about everything that had happened or to warn me of the coming fallout. But he didn't say anything. He lay there, brushing my hair back with his fingers, sometimes letting the tips linger on my cheek.

It felt as if we were the whole world just then.

"If something had happened—"

"But it didn't."

Maxon rolled his eyes, his voice getting serious. "It most certainly did! You came home bleeding. We nearly lost you in the streets."

"Look, I'm not upset with the choice I made," I said, trying to calm him. "I wanted to go, to hear for myself. Besides, it's not as if I could have let you go without me."

"I can't believe how unprepared we were, going out in a palace truck without more guards. And there are rebels just walking the streets. Since when are they not hiding? Where are they getting these guns? I feel clueless, helpless. I'm losing the country I love a little every day. I nearly lost you, and I—"

Maxon stopped himself, his frustration fading into something new. He moved his hand back to my cheek. "Last night, you said something . . . about love."

I looked down. "I remember." I tried to contain my blush.

"It's funny how you can think you've said something when you never really did."

I giggled, feeling that the words were coming in his very next breath.

"It's also funny how you can think you've heard something when you didn't either," he said instead.

All the humor vanished from the moment. "I know what you mean." I swallowed and watched as his hand moved from my cheek to lace his fingers through mine, knowing that he and I were both watching them. "Maybe, for some people, it would be hard to confess that. Like, if they worried they might not make it to the end."

He sighed. "Or it would be hard to say if you worried that someone might not *want* to make it to the end . . . maybe never quite gave up on someone else."

I shook my head. "That's not . . ."

"Okay."

For everything we'd said in the safe room, for everything we'd confessed to each other, for everything that had firmly settled in my heart, these small words were the most frightening things to pass between us. Because once they were out there, we could never take them back.

I didn't completely understand his reasons for hesitating, but I knew mine. If he ended up with Kriss after I'd put my heart out there, I would be upset with him, but I would *hate* myself. It was a risk I was too frightened to take.

The silence was making me uneasy, and when it became too much, I spoke.

"Maybe we could talk about this again when I'm feeling better?"

He sighed. "Of course. Completely thoughtless of me."

"No, no. There's just something else I wanted to ask you about." There were bigger things than us to consider right now.

"Go ahead."

"I had a thought about my guests for the upcoming tea party, but I would need your approval."

He looked at me, confused.

"And I want you to know everything I would intend to discuss with them. We might be breaking several laws, so I won't do it if you say not to."

Intrigued, Maxon propped himself up on one arm to listen. "Tell me everything."

CHAPTER 17

THE BACKDROP FOR OUR PHOTOS was plain and light blue. My maids put together a lovely dress for me, with little off-the-shoulder cuffs that just covered my scar. For now, my days of strapless gowns were gone.

Though I looked pretty good, I was completely overshadowed by Nicoletta, and even Georgia was dazzling in her gown.

"Lady America," the woman next to the camera called. "We remember Princess Nicoletta from when the women of the Italian royal family came to visit the palace, but who is your other guest?"

"This is Georgia, a dear friend of mine," I replied sweetly. "One of the things that I've learned from the Selection so far is that moving forward means joining your life before coming to the palace with the future that lies in front of you. I'm hoping to make another step in joining those two worlds today."

Some of those standing around let out satisfied noises as the cameras continued to capture the three of us.

"Excellent, ladies," the photographer said. "You can go enjoy the party. We'll be taking some candid shots later."

"Sounds fun," I answered, motioning for my guests to come with me.

Maxon had made it clear that of all days, today was one when I really needed to be on. I hoped to be the lead example of what an Elite should be, but it was hard for me to try and be so perfect.

"Tone it down, America, or rainbows are going to shoot out of your eyes." I loved that even though our friendship was brief, Georgia could see right through my act.

I laughed, and Nicoletta joined in. "She's right. You do seem a bit perky."

I sighed with a smile. "Sorry. Today is a high-stakes kind of day."

Georgia put an arm on my shoulder as we walked deeper into the room. "After everything you and Maxon have been through, I highly doubt he'll send you home over a tea party."

"That's not exactly what I mean. But we'll have to talk about it later." I turned to face them. "Right now, it would be a huge help to me if we could mingle. Once things settle down, we need to have a pretty serious discussion."

Nicoletta looked over at Georgia, then back to me. "What

kind of friend are you introducing me to here?"

"A valuable one. I swear. I'll explain later."

For their part, Georgia and Nicoletta made me shine. As a princess, Nicoletta was quite possibly the best guest in the room, and I saw in Kriss's eyes that she wished she had thought of that. Of course, she didn't have a direct line to Italian royalty like I did. Nicoletta herself had given me a phone number to contact her if I ever needed to.

No one knew who Georgia was, but when they'd heard my line—the one Maxon had specifically fed to me—about joining my past and my future, they thought that was a spectacular idea as well.

Elise's choices were predictable. Powerful but predictable. Two very distant cousins from New Asia representing her ties to the leaders of the nation paraded next to her in their traditional dresses. Kriss had chosen a professor from the college her father worked at and her mother. I was dreading my family hearing about that. When Mom or May realized they had a chance to be here, I was sure to get a very disappointed letter from them.

Celeste, true to her word, brought full-fledged celebrities. Tessa Tamble—who had allegedly given a show at Celeste's last birthday party—was there in a very short but glamorous dress. Celeste's other guest was Kirstie Summer, another musician who was mostly known for her outlandish concerts, and her outfit was more like a costume. My guess was that it was either something she usually performed in or an experiment in painted leather. Either way, I was surprised she got through the door, both because of the way she was dressed and the fact that if you passed within a foot of her, you could smell the alcohol radiating off her.

"Nicoletta," Queen Amberly said, approaching us. "How wonderful to see you again."

They exchanged kisses on both cheeks before Nicoletta spoke. "The joy is all mine. I was elated when I received America's invitation. We all had such a wonderful time on our last visit."

"I'm glad to hear that," the queen commented. "I'm afraid it's going to be a bit calmer today."

"I don't know," Nicoletta countered, pointing over to where Kirstie and Tessa were standing in a corner and talking loudly. "I'm betting those two will send me home with at least one story."

We all laughed, though I could see a little anxiety in the queen's eyes. "I suppose I should go introduce myself."

"Always the picture of bravery," I joked.

She smiled. "Please, relax and enjoy yourselves. I hope you get to meet some new acquaintances but, honestly, just take some time together with your friends."

I nodded, and Queen Amberly left to meet Celeste's guests. Tessa was looking fine, but Kirstie appeared to be picking up and smelling every finger sandwich on a nearby table. I made a mental note not to eat anything near where she'd been standing.

I surveyed the room. Everyone seemed busy eating or talking, so I decided now was as good a time as any.

"Follow me," I said, heading to a small table in the back. We sat, and a maid brought us tea. Once we were alone, I dived in, hoping this would go smoothly.

"Georgia, first, I haven't had a chance to apologize about Micah."

She was shaking her head even as I spoke. "He always wanted to be a hero. We all accept that things might . . . end like that. But I think he was proud."

"I'm still really sorry. Is there anything we can do?"

"No. Everything's taken care of. Trust me, he wouldn't have chosen a different end," she insisted.

I thought of the mouselike boy in the corner of the room that night. He willingly ran out into the fray for me, for all of us. Bravery hides in amazing places.

I turned back to the matter at hand. "Well, Georgia, as you can see, Nicoletta is the princess of Italy. She visited with us a few weeks ago." I looked between them. "At that time she made it clear that Italy would like to be an ally to Illéa if certain things changed."

"America!" Nicoletta hissed.

I held up a hand. "Trust me. Georgia here is a friend, but I don't know her from Carolina. She's one of the leaders of the Northern rebels."

Nicoletta sat up in her seat. Georgia gave her a timid nod, confirming what I'd said.

"She came to our aid recently. And lost someone close to her in the process," I explained.

Nicoletta placed her hand on Georgia's. "I'm sorry." Then

she turned to me, curious as to how all this tied together.

"What we say needs to stay among us, but I thought we might be able to talk about some things that would benefit everyone here," I explained.

"Are you trying to overthrow the king?" Nicoletta asked.

"No," Georgia assured her. "We're hoping to align ourselves with Maxon's reign, and work toward eliminating the castes. Maybe within his lifetime. He seems to have more compassion for his people."

"He does," I added.

"Then why do you attack the palace? And all those people?" Nicoletta accused sharply.

I shook my head. "They're not like the Southern rebels. They don't kill people. They sometimes deliver justice that they see as fit—"

"We've gotten unwed mothers out of jail, things like that," Georgia interjected.

"They *have* broken into the palace, but never with the intent to kill," I added.

Nicoletta sighed. "I'm not so bothered by that, but I'm not sure why you need me to know them."

"Neither am I," Georgia confessed.

I took a breath. "The Southern rebels are getting more and more aggressive. In the last few months alone, their attacks have increased, not just at the palace but across the country. They're merciless. I worry, as does Maxon, that they're very close to making a move we won't be able to recover from. Their idea of killing their way down the Elite's castes is pretty drastic, and we're all afraid those attacks are going to escalate."

"They already have," Georgia said, more to me than to Nicoletta. "When you invited me here, I was happy if only to be able to give you more news. The Southern rebels have moved to the Threes."

I placed a hand over my mouth, shocked that they were progressing so quickly. "Are you sure?"

"Positive," Georgia confirmed. "The numbers shifted yesterday."

After a moment of quiet worry, Nicoletta spoke. "Why are they doing this?"

Georgia turned to her. "To scare the Elite into leaving, to scare the royal family in general. It seems like they think that if they can stop the Selection from finishing and isolate Maxon, they'll only have to get rid of him in order to take over."

"And that's the real worry. If they come to power, there's nothing for Maxon to offer you as king. The Southern rebels would only oppress people further."

"So what do you propose?" Nicoletta asked.

I tried to walk lightly into the criminal territory in front of me. "Georgia and the other Northerners have a better opportunity to stop the Southern rebels than any of us in the palace. They can see their moves more easily and have had chances to confront them . . . but they're untrained and unarmed."

They both waited, not seeing what I was implying.

I lowered my voice. "Maxon can't siphon money from the palace to help them buy weapons."

"I see," Nicoletta finally said.

"It would be under the full understanding that these weapons would only be used to stop the Southerners. Never against an officer of any government-issued position," I said, looking at Georgia.

"That wouldn't be a problem." I saw in her eyes how much she meant that, and I already knew it in my own heart. If she'd wanted to, she could have taken me out when she found me in the woods or chosen not to come running into the alley after us. But that was never her goal.

Nicoletta was strumming her fingers across her lips, thinking. I knew we were asking a lot, but I wasn't sure how to move forward otherwise.

"If anyone found out . . . ," she said.

"I know. I've thought about that." If the king ever knew, a caning wouldn't be enough where I was concerned.

"If we could make sure there isn't a trail." Nicoletta kept fidgeting her fingers near her mouth.

"It would need to be cash, at least. That makes it harder," Georgia offered.

Nicoletta nodded and dropped her hand to the table. "I said if I could do anything for you, I would. We could use a strong friend, and if your country is lost, I fear we would only gain another enemy."

I gave her a sad smile.

She turned to Georgia. "I can get the cash today, but it

would need to be converted."

Georgia smiled. "We have means."

Over her shoulder I saw a photographer approaching. I picked up my teacup and whispered, "Camera."

"And I've always thought America was a lady. I think sometimes we miss those traits because we see Fives as performers and Sixes as housekeepers. But look at Queen Amberly. She's so much more than a Four," Georgia said kindly. Nicoletta and I both nodded.

"She's an incredible woman. It's been a privilege to live with her," I shared.

"Maybe you'll get to stay with her!" Nicoletta said with a wink.

"Smile, ladies!" the photographer instructed, and we all showed our brightest faces, hoping to cover our dangerous secret.

CHAPTER 18

THE DAY AFTER NICOLETTA AND Georgia left, I caught myself looking over my shoulder a lot. I was sure someone knew what I'd said, what I'd handed over to the rebels in a brief afternoon. I kept reminding myself that if anyone had overheard, I certainly would have been arrested by now. Seeing as I was still enjoying a wonderful breakfast with the other Elite and the royal family, I had to believe that everything was fine. Besides, Maxon would defend me if he had to.

After breakfast, I went back to my room to touch up my makeup. While I was in the bathroom, sweeping on another layer of lipstick, a knock sounded at the door. It was just Lucy and me, and she went to see who it was while I finished up. A minute later she popped her head around the corner.

"It's Prince Maxon," she whispered.

I whipped my head around. "He's here?"

She nodded, beaming. "He remembered my name."

"Of course he did," I replied with a smile. I put everything down and ran my fingers through my hair. "Lead me out, then leave quietly."

"As you wish, miss."

Maxon was standing tentatively by the door, uncharacteristically waiting for an invitation to enter. He held a small, thin box, and he drummed his fingers against it, fidgeting. "Sorry to interrupt. I was wondering if I could have a moment."

"Of course," I said, walking over. "Please come in." Maxon and I perched on the edge of my bed.

"I wanted to see you first," he said, getting situated. "I wanted to explain before the others came in bragging."

Explain? For some reason his words put me on edge. If the others were bragging, I was about to be excluded from something.

"What do you mean?" I realized I was biting my freshly glossed lip.

Maxon passed the box over to me. "I'll clarify, I promise. But first, this is for you."

I took the box and unhooked a small button in the front so I could open it. I think I inhaled every millimeter of air in the room.

Resting inside the box were a breathtaking set of earrings and matching bracelet. They coordinated beautifully, with blue and green gems woven into a subtle floral design.

"Maxon, I love it, but I can't possibly take this. It's too . . . too . . ."

"On the contrary, you must take them. It's a gift, and it's tradition that you wear them in the Convicting."

"The what?"

He shook his head. "Silvia will explain all that; but the point is, it's tradition for the prince to present the Elite with jewelry and for them to wear the pieces to the ceremony. There will be quite a few officials there, and you need to look your best. And unlike the things you've been presented with so far, these are all real and yours to keep."

I smiled. Of course we wouldn't have been given real jewelry to wear until now. I wondered how many girls had taken things home, thinking that if they hadn't gotten Maxon, at least they got a few thousand in jewelry.

"They're wonderful, Maxon. Just my taste. Thank you."

Maxon raised a finger. "You're welcome, and that's part of what I wanted to discuss. I chose the gifts for each of you personally and intended that they should all be equal. However, you prefer to wear the necklace from your father, and I'm sure it would be a comfort to you in the middle of something as big as the Convicting. So, while the others got necklaces, you have a bracelet."

He reached over to my hand and lifted it. "And I see you're attached to your little button, and I'm glad you still like the bracelet I brought back from New Asia, but they really aren't appropriate. Try this on so we can see how it rests."

I took off Maxon's bracelet and set it on the edge of my

nightstand. But I took Aspen's button and set it in my jar with its single penny. It seemed like it should be there for now.

I turned back and caught Maxon staring at the jar, something hard in his eyes. It disappeared swiftly enough, and he went to removing the bracelet from the box. His fingers tickled my skin, and when he moved away, I nearly gasped again at how beautiful his gift was.

"It really is perfect, Maxon."

"I hoped you'd think so. But that is precisely why I needed to talk to you. I set out to spend the same amount on all of you. I wanted to be fair."

I nodded. That sounded reasonable.

"The problem with that being, your tastes are much simpler than the others. And you have a bracelet as opposed to a necklace. I ended up spending half as much on you as the rest, and I wanted you to know that before you saw what I gave them. And I wanted you to know that it came from wanting to give you what I felt you would like the best, not because of your place or anything like that." Maxon's face was so sincere.

"Thank you, Maxon. I wouldn't have had it any other way," I said, placing a hand on his arm.

As always, he seemed so happy to be touched. "I suspected as much. Though thank you for saying so. I was afraid I might hurt you."

"Not at all."

Maxon's smile grew. "Of course, I still wanted to be fair,

so I had a thought." He reached into his pocket and pulled out a thin envelope. "Perhaps you would like to send the difference to your family."

I stared at the envelope. "Are you serious?"

"Of course. I want to be impartial, and I thought this would be the best way to handle the discrepancy. And I hoped it would make you happy." He placed the envelope in my hands, and I took it, still shocked.

"You didn't have to do that."

"I know. But sometimes it's about what you want to do, not what you have to."

Our eyes met, and I realized that he did a lot for me out of simply wanting to. Giving me pants when I wasn't allowed to wear them, bringing me a bracelet from the other side of the world . . .

Surely he loved me. Right? Why wouldn't he just say it?

We're alone, Maxon. If you say it, I'll say it back.

Nothing.

"I don't know how to thank you for this, Maxon."

He smiled. "Hearing you say it is nice." He cleared his throat. "I'm always interested in hearing how you feel."

Oh, no. Nope. I was not putting it out there first.

"Well, I'm very grateful. As always."

Maxon sighed. "I'm happy you like it." Unsatisfied, he took to watching the carpet. "I need to go. I still have to deliver the gifts to the others."

We stood together, and I escorted him to the door. As he left, he turned and kissed my hand. With a friendly nod of his head, he disappeared around the corner to visit the others.

I walked back to the bed and looked again at my gifts. I couldn't believe that something this beautiful was mine to keep, forever. I vowed to myself that, even if I went home and all the money ran out and my family was absolutely destitute, I would never sell these or give them away, or the bracelet he'd gotten me in New Asia. I would hold on to them no matter what.

"The Convicting is simple enough," Silvia said to us the next afternoon as we followed her to the Great Room. "It's one of those things that sounds much more challenging than it is, but above all it's symbolic.

"It will be a grand event. There will be several magistrates here, not to mention the extended members of the royal family, and enough cameras to make your heads spin," Silvia barked over her shoulder.

So far this was sounding anything but simple. We rounded the corner, and Silvia flung open the doors to the Great Room. In the middle of the space was Queen Amberly herself, giving instructions to men setting up rows of stadium seats. In another corner, someone was debating which carpet to roll out, and two florists were discussing which blossoms would be most appropriate. They apparently didn't think the Christmas decorations should stay. So much was happening, I almost forgot Christmas was coming at all.

Toward the back of the room a stage was set up with stairs

across the front of it, and three massive thrones were centered on the platform. To our right were four small stages with lone seats on them, looking beautiful but also very isolating. Those alone were enough to decorate the room, and I couldn't imagine how it would look once everything was in place.

"Your Majesty," Silvia said with a curtsy, and we all followed suit. The queen walked over to us, her face lit up with a smile.

"Hello, ladies," she said. "Silvia, how far have you gotten?"

"Not far at all, Majesty."

"Excellent. Ladies, let me enlighten you about your next task in the Selection process." She motioned for us to follow her inside the Great Room. "The Convicting is meant to be a symbol of your submission to the law. One of you will become the new princess, and someday queen. The law is how we live, and it will be your duty not only to live by it but to uphold it. And so," she said, stopping and facing us, "you will start with the Convicting.

"A man who has committed a crime, most likely a theft, will be brought in. These are cases that are worthy of a whipping, but these men will spend time in jail instead. And you will send them there."

The queen smiled at our bewildered expressions. "I know it sounds harsh, but it's not. These men have each committed a crime, and instead of facing the difficulties of a physical punishment, they'll be paying their debts with time.

You've seen firsthand how painful a caning can be. Being whipped isn't much better. You're doing them a favor," she said encouragingly.

I still didn't feel good about it.

Those who stole were penniless. Twos and Threes who broke laws paid their way out of punishment with money. The poor paid their way in flesh or time. I remembered Jemmy, Aspen's younger brother, leaning over a block while men took a handful of food out of his back in lashes. While I hated that, it was better than locking him away. The Legers needed him to work, young as he was, and it seemed that once you got above a Five, people forgot that.

Silvia and Queen Amberly walked us through the ceremony over and over until our lines were perfect. I tried to deliver mine with the grace that Elise or Kriss had, but they came out sounding flat every time.

I did not want to put a man in jail.

When we were dismissed, the other girls headed to the door together, but I went to the queen. She was finishing a conversation with Silvia. I should have used that time to come up with something more eloquent. Instead, when Silvia walked away and the queen addressed me, I just blurted it out.

"Please don't make me do this," I pleaded.

"I beg your pardon?"

"I can submit to the law, I swear. It's not that I'm trying to be difficult, but I can't put a man in jail. He didn't do anything to me."

Her expression was kind as she reached to touch my face. "But he did, dear girl. If you became the princess, you'd be the embodiment of the law. When someone breaks the smallest rule, they stab you. The only way to keep from bleeding out is to take a stand against those who have already harmed you so that others will not be so brazen."

"But I'm not the princess!" I implored. "No one's hurting me."

She smiled and lowered her head to mine, whispering, "You're not the princess today, but it wouldn't surprise me if that was a temporary issue."

Queen Amberly stepped back and winked.

I sighed, getting desperate. "Bring me someone else. Not some petty thief who probably only stole because they were hungry." Her face stiffened. "I'm not suggesting it's okay to steal. I know it's not. But bring me someone who did something really bad. Bring me the person who killed the guard that got Maxon and me into a safe room the last time the rebels came. That person should be locked up forever. And I'll say that happily. But I can't do this to some hungry Seven. I can't."

I could see she wanted to be gentle with me, but I could also see she wouldn't budge on this. "Allow me to be very blunt with you, Lady America. Of all the girls, you need to do this the most. People have seen you run to stop a caning, suggest undoing the castes on national television, and encourage people to fight when their lives are in serious danger." Her kind face was serious. "I'm not saying those were bad things, but they have given most people the impression that you run wild."

I fidgeted with my hands, knowing this was going to end with me doing the Convicting no matter what I said.

"If you want to stay, if you care about Maxon"—she paused, giving me a moment to consider—"then you need to do this. You need to show you have the ability to be obedient."

"I do. I just don't want to put someone in jail. That's not a princess's job. Magistrates do that."

Queen Amberly patted my shoulder. "You can do it. And you will. If you want Maxon at all, you need to be perfect. I'm sure you understand that there's opposition where you're concerned."

I nodded.

"Then do it."

She walked away, leaving me alone in the Great Room. I went up to my seat, practically a throne itself, and mumbled the lines again. I tried to tell myself that it wasn't a big deal. People broke laws and went to jail all the time. It was one person out of thousands. And I needed to be perfect.

Perfect was my only option.

CHAPTER 19

THE DAY OF THE CONVICTING I was a bundle of nerves. I was afraid I'd trip, or forget what to say. Even worse, I was afraid I'd fail. The one thing I didn't have to worry about was my clothes. My maids had to confer with the head dresser to make something suitable for me, though I wouldn't use a word as plain as *suitable* to describe it.

Following again on tradition, the dresses were all white and gold. Mine had a high waist and no strap on the left but did have a small, off-the-shoulder strap on the right, covering my scar and looking really lovely at the same time. The top was snug, but the skirt was billowing, kissing the floor with scallops of golden lace. It came together with pleats in the back that fell behind me in a short train. When I looked at myself in the mirror, it was the first time I actually thought I looked like a princess.

Anne grabbed the olive branch I was meant to carry and situated it in my arm. We were supposed to place the branches at the foot of the king as a sign of peace toward our leader and our willingness to yield to the law.

"You look beautiful, miss," Lucy said. I couldn't help but notice how calm and confident she seemed lately. I smiled.

"Thank you. I wish you were all going to be there," I said.

"Me, too." Mary sighed.

Ever proper, Anne turned the focus back in my direction. "Don't you worry, miss; you'll do perfectly. And we'll be watching with the other maids."

"You will?" That was encouraging, even though they wouldn't be downstairs.

"We wouldn't miss it," Lucy assured me.

A sharp knocking snapped us from our conversation. Mary opened the door, and I was happy to see it was Aspen.

"I'm here to escort you to the Convicting, Lady America," he said.

Lucy piped up. "What do you think of our handiwork, Officer Leger?"

He smiled slyly. "You've outdone yourselves."

Lucy giggled, and Anne quietly shushed her as she made final adjustments to my hair. Now that I knew about Anne's feelings for Aspen, it was obvious how perfect she tried to be in front of him.

I took a deep breath, remembering the masses waiting for me downstairs.

"Ready?" he asked.

I nodded, readjusted my branch, and went to the door, peeking back just once to see my maids' happy faces. I looped my arm through Aspen's and headed with him down the hall.

"How have you been?" I asked casually.

"I can't believe you're going through with this," he shot back.

I swallowed, immediately nervous again. "I don't have a choice."

"You always have a choice, Mer."

"Aspen, you know I don't like this. But in the end, it's only one person. And he's guilty."

"Just like the rebel sympathizers that the king demoted a caste. Just like Marlee and Carter." I didn't have to look up to see how disgusted he was.

"That was different," I mumbled, not sounding convincing at all.

Aspen stopped dead in his tracks and forced me to look at him. "It's never different with him."

His tone was so serious. Aspen knew more than most people did, because he'd stood guard during meetings or delivered orders himself. He was holding a secret right now.

"Are they thieves at all?" I asked quietly as we continued to move.

"Yes, but nothing deserving the years of jail they'll receive today. And it's going to be a pretty loud message to their friends."

"What do you mean?"

"They're people who've gotten in his way, Mer. Rebel sympathizers, men a bit too outspoken about what a tyrant he is. This is being broadcast everywhere. The people they've tried to sway will see this, will warn others about what happens to those who attempt to go against the king. This is deliberate."

I whipped my arm from his, hissing my words at him. "You've been here almost as long as I have. In all that time, did you ever not deliver one of the sentences you were ordered to?"

He considered. "No, but—"

"Then don't judge me. If he's not above putting his enemies in prison without real cause, what do you think he'll do to me? He hates me!"

Aspen's eyes were pleading. "Mer, I know it's scary, but you've—"

I put up my hand. "Do your job. Take me downstairs."

He swallowed once, turned forward, and put his arm out for me. I gripped it, and we walked on in silence.

Halfway down the stairs, as the buzz of conversation started to reach us, he spoke up again.

"I always wondered if they'd change you."

I didn't respond. What could I say anyway?

In the grand foyer, the other girls were staring into the distance, quietly moving their lips as they recited their lines. I detached myself from Aspen and moved to join them.

Elise had talked about her dress so much, I felt as if I'd already seen it. Gold and cream were woven together in a slim, sleeveless design, and her golden gloves looked dramatic. Her gifts from Maxon were deep, dark gems, and they made her slick hair and dark eyes pop.

Kriss once again managed to be the embodiment of all things royal, and it was like she wasn't even trying. Her dress was fitted through the waist and burst out like a flower blossoming toward the ground. And Maxon's necklace and earrings for her were iridescent, gently rounded, and perfect. It did, for a moment, make me sad that mine were so simple.

Celeste's dress . . . well, it would certainly be unforgettable. Her neckline was plunging, and it seemed a little inappropriate for the occasion. She caught me staring, and pushed her lips together and shook her shoulders at me.

I laughed once and put my hand to my forehead, feeling a little sick. I inhaled deeply, trying to calm myself.

Celeste met me halfway, swinging her branch with each step. "What's wrong?"

"Nothing. Just not feeling well, I guess."

"Do. Not. Puke," she ordered. "Especially not on me."

"I won't throw up," I assured her.

"Who threw up?" Kriss asked, joining the conversation; and Elise followed behind her.

"No one," I said. "I'm just tired or something."

"It won't last too long," Kriss reassured me.

It'll last forever, I thought. I looked at each of their faces. They'd come to my side just now. Wouldn't I have done the same for them? Maybe . . .

"Do any of you actually feel *good* about doing this?" I asked.

They all looked at one another or the floor, but no one answered.

"Then let's not do it," I urged.

"Not do it?" Kriss questioned. "America, it's tradition. We have to."

"No we don't. Not if we all decide not to."

"What would we do? Refuse to walk in there?" Celeste asked.

"That's one option," I offered.

"You want us to sit in there and do nothing?" Elise sounded appalled.

"I hadn't thought it through. I just know I don't think this is a good idea."

I could see that Kriss was genuinely considering it.

"It's a trick!" Elise accused.

"What?" How could she come to that conclusion?

"She's going last. If we all do nothing and then she follows through, she looks obedient while the rest of us look like idiots." Elise shook her branch at me as she spoke.

"America?" Kriss looked at me, disappointment filling her eyes.

"No, I swear; that's not what I was going to do!"

"Ladies!" We all turned toward Silvia's correcting tone. "I understand that you're nervous, but that's no reason to shout."

Her gaze hit each of us, and we all exchanged looks as

they decided whether to go in on this with me.

"All right," Silvia began. "Elise, you'll be first, just as we practiced. Celeste and Kriss, you will follow; and America, you'll be last. One at a time, carry your branch up the red carpet and place it at the feet of the king. Then come back and take your seat. The king will say a few words, and the ceremony will start."

She stepped over to what looked like a small box on a stand and turned it around to show a television monitor with a view of everything happening inside the Great Room. It was magnificent. Red carpeting divided the room into the seats for the press and guests, and the four seats delegated for us. In the back of the space, the thrones sat, waiting for the royal family.

As we watched, the side door to the Great Room opened, and the king, the queen, and Maxon came in to applause and trumpeting fanfare. Once they were seated, a slower, more dignified melody started playing.

"There it is. Now, head high," Silvia instructed. Elise gave me a pointed look and strode around the corner.

The music was dotted by the sound of hundreds of cameras taking her picture. It made for a strange rhythm section. She did great, though, as we could all see on the monitor Silvia was watching. Celeste followed, straightening her hair before she left. Kriss's smile looked absolutely genuine and natural as she paraded down the aisle.

"America," Silvia whispered. "Your turn."

I tried to wipe the worry off my face and focus on positive

things, but I realized there weren't any. I was about to kill a part of myself by punishing someone beyond what I thought was deserved and give the king something he wanted in a neat, short stroke.

The cameras clicked, the bulbs flashed, and people whispered their praises to one another as I walked quietly toward the royal family. I made eye contact with Maxon, who was the picture of calm. Was that his years of discipline or true happiness coming through? His face was reassuring, but I was certain he could see the anxiety in my gaze. I saw my open spot for the olive branch and curtsied before placing my offering at the king's feet, deliberately looking at anything in the room other than him.

As soon as I was in my place, the music came to a perfectly calculated stop. King Clarkson walked forward, standing on the edge of his stage, the circle of branches at his feet.

"Ladies and gentlemen of Illéa, today the final four beautiful young women of the Selection come before us all to present themselves to the law. Our great laws are what hold our nation together, the foundation for the peace we've so long enjoyed."

Peace? I thought. *Are you kidding?*

"One of these young ladies will stand before you soon, no longer a commoner, but a princess. And as a member of the royal family, it will be her job to hold on to what is right, not for her own benefit, but for yours."

. . . and how am I doing that now?

"Please join me in applauding their humility in their

submission to the law and their bravery in upholding it."

The king started clapping, and the room joined him. The applause continued as he stepped away, and I glanced down the row of girls. The only face I could really see was Kriss's. She shrugged and gave me a half smile before facing forward again and raising herself to her full height.

A guard by the door trumpeted into the room. "We call into the presence of His Majesty King Clarkson, Her Majesty Queen Amberly, and His Royal Highness Prince Maxon the criminal Jacob Digger."

Slowly, no doubt embarrassed by the spectacle, Jacob walked into the Great Room. His wrists were in handcuffs, and he flinched at the cameras' lights and went skittishly to bow in front of Elise. I couldn't see her very well without leaning too far forward, so I turned slightly and listened as she spoke the lines we all would in turn.

"Jacob, what is your crime?" she asked. She projected her voice really well, much better than usual.

"Theft, my lady," he answered meekly.

"And how long is your sentence?"

"Twelve years, my lady."

Slowly, not drawing attention to herself, Kriss looked my way. With hardly a change in her expression, she questioned what was happening. I nodded.

Small crimes of theft, we'd been told. If that was true, then this man would have been beaten in his town square, or, if he had been put in prison, it would have been for two or three years at the most. In two words, Jacob confirmed all my fears.

Subtly, I turned my eyes toward the king. There was no mistaking his pleasure. Whoever this man was, he wasn't just some thief. The king was delighting in his downfall.

Elise stood and walked down to Jacob, placing her hand on his shoulder. He hadn't truly looked her in the eye until that moment.

"Go, faithful subject, and pay your debt to the king." Her voice rang out in the quiet of the room.

Jacob nodded his head. He looked at the king, and I could see he wanted to do something. He wanted to fight or make an accusation, but he didn't. No doubt someone else would pay for any mistakes he made today. Jacob stood and exited the room as the audience applauded.

The next man had difficulty moving. As he turned to make his way down the carpet toward Celeste, he doubled over and fell. A collective gasp came from the room, but before he could garner too much sympathy, two guards came and walked him to Celeste. To her credit, her voice wasn't as sure as it usually was as she ordered the man to pay his debt.

Kriss looked as steady as ever until her criminal got closer. He was younger, probably around our age, and his steps were steady, almost determined. When he turned up the carpet to Kriss, I saw a tattoo on his neck. It looked like a cross, though it seemed as if whoever had done it messed up a bit.

Kriss delivered her lines well. Anyone who didn't know

her wouldn't be able to read the hint of regret in her voice. The room applauded, and she sat back down, her smile only slightly less bright than it usually was.

The guard yelled out the name Adam Carver, and I realized it was my turn. Adam, Adam, Adam. I needed to remember his name. Because I had to do this now, right? The other girls had. Maxon might forgive me if I failed, and the king would never like me either way; but I would certainly lose the queen, and that backed me into a corner. If I wanted a chance at all, I needed to deliver.

Adam was older, maybe my dad's age, and there was something wrong with his leg. He didn't fall, but it took him so long to reach me that it made the whole thing that much worse. I just wanted it to be done.

As Adam knelt in front of me, I focused on the few lines I needed to deliver.

"Adam, what is your crime?" I asked.

"Theft, my lady."

"And how long is your sentence?"

Adam cleared his throat. "Life," he squeaked out.

Around the room, murmurs began as people were sure they hadn't heard that right.

Though I hated to deviate from my lines, I too needed confirmation. "How long did you say?"

"Life, my lady." It was apparent in Adam's voice that he was on the verge of tears.

I peeked over at Maxon. He looked uncomfortable.

Wordlessly, I pleaded for help. His eyes conveyed how sorry he was that he couldn't guide me.

As I was about to focus again on Adam, my eyes flickered to the king, who had quickly shifted his weight. I watched him run his hand across his mouth in an effort to hide his smile.

He'd set me up.

Perhaps he suspected I would hate this part of the Selection and planned to do what he could to make me look disobedient. But even if I went through with it, what kind of person was I to put a man in prison forever? No one would love me now.

"Adam," I said softly. He looked up at me, tears threatening to fall at any moment. I noticed quickly that every whisper in the room ceased. "How much did you steal?"

People were trying to hear, but it was impossible.

He swallowed and darted his eyes toward the king. "Some clothes for my girls."

I spoke quickly. "But this isn't about that, is it?"

In a gesture so minute I almost missed it, Adam shook his head once.

So I couldn't do it. I *couldn't* do it. But I had to do something.

The idea hit me so quickly, and I was positive it was our only way out. I wasn't sure if it would gain Adam his freedom, and I tried not to think of how sad it would make me. It was simply right, and I had to do it.

I stood and made my way to Adam, touching him on his shoulder. He winced, waiting for me to tell him he was going to prison.

"Stand up," I said.

Adam looked at me, confusion in his eyes.

"Please," I said, and took one of his cuffed hands to pull him along.

Adam walked with me up the aisle, to the raised area where the royal family sat. When we got to the stairs, I turned to him and sighed.

I took off one of the beautiful earrings that Maxon had given me, then the other. I placed both in Adam's hands; and he stood there, dumbstruck, as my beautiful bracelet followed. And then—because, if I was truly going to do this, I wanted to give everything—I reached behind my neck and unclasped my songbird necklace, the one my dad had given me. I hoped he was watching and not hating me for giving his gift away. Once I dropped it into Adam's hand, I curled his fingers around the treasures, then stepped to the side so that he was standing directly in front of King Clarkson.

I pointed toward the thrones. "Go, faithful subject, and pay your debt to the king."

There were gasps and murmurs around the room, but I ignored them. All I could see was the sour expression on the king's face. If he wanted to play a game with my character, then I was prepared to answer in turn.

Adam slowly climbed the steps, and I could see both the joy and fear in his eyes. As he approached the king, he fell to his knees and held out his hands, full of jewels.

King Clarkson shot me a glance, letting me know this wouldn't be the end of it, but then reached out and took the jewelry out of Adam's hands.

The crowd erupted, but when I looked back, the other girls had mixed reactions on their faces. Adam backed away from the king quickly, perhaps afraid he'd change his mind. My hope was that, with so many cameras going and so many people writing articles about this, someone would follow up and make sure he made it home. When Adam got back to my level, he tried to hug me, even with the handcuffs on. He cried and blessed me, and went from the room looking like the happiest soul on earth.

CHAPTER 20

THE ROYAL FAMILY EXITED OUT the side door, and the other Elite and I left the way we'd come as the cameras and guests filmed and applauded.

Silvia's eyes when we came out the doorway were positively deadly. It looked like it was taking every last bit of strength she had to keep from throttling me. She led us around the corner to a small parlor.

"In," she ordered, as if anything more would push her past the brink. She shut the doors, not bothering to join us.

"Do you always have to be the center of attention?" Elise snapped.

"I didn't do anything except what I tried to ask you to do. You were the one who didn't believe me!"

"You act like such a saint. They were criminals. We weren't doing anything a magistrate wouldn't do; we just did it in pretty dresses."

"Elise, did you see those men? Some of them were sick. And the sentences for their crimes were way too long," I implored.

"She's right," Kriss said. "Life for theft? Unless he carted the palace away, what could he have possibly taken to deserve that?"

"Nothing," I vowed. "He took clothes for his family. Look, you guys are lucky. You were born into better castes. If you're in the lower ones, and you lose your main provider . . . things don't go well. I couldn't send him to jail for life and at the same time sentence his family to becoming Eights. I couldn't."

"Where is your pride, America?" Elise begged. "Where is your sense of duty or honor? You're just a girl; you aren't even the princess. And if you were, you wouldn't be allowed to make decisions like that. You are here to follow the king's rules, and you have never done that! Not even from the first night!"

"Maybe the rules are wrong!" I screamed, at perhaps the worst time possible.

The doors were flung open, and King Clarkson stormed in while Queen Amberly and Maxon stood in the hall. He grabbed my arm, hard—thankfully not my injured one—and dragged me out of the room.

"Where are you taking me?" I asked, fear making my breath come out in short bursts.

He didn't answer.

I looked over my shoulder at the girls as the king pulled me down the hall. Celeste wrapped her arms around herself, and Elise reached for Kriss's hand. For as upset as she was, Elise didn't seem happy to see me go.

"Clarkson, don't act in haste," the queen urged quietly.

We rounded a corner, and I was forced into a room. The queen and Maxon filed in behind us as the king shoved me toward a small couch.

"Sit," he commanded unnecessarily. He paced the floor, a lion in a cage. When he stopped, he faced Maxon.

"You swore!" he bellowed. "You said she was under control. First the outburst on the *Report*, then you nearly get yourself killed on the roof, and now this? It ends today, Maxon."

"Father, did you hear the cheers? People appreciate her sympathy. She's your greatest asset right now."

"I beg your pardon?" His voice was an iceberg, slow and deadly.

Maxon paused a moment at the chill but continued. "When she suggested that people defend themselves, the public responded positively. I daresay the reason more people aren't dead is because of her. And this? Father, I couldn't put a man in jail for life over what was supposed to be a petty crime. How can you expect that from someone who's probably seen more than her fair share of friends beaten for less? She's refreshing. The majority of the population is in the lower castes, and they relate to her."

The king shook his head and started walking again. "I let

her stay because she kept you alive. *You* are my most valuable asset, not her. If we lose you, we lose everything. And I don't just mean through death. If you aren't committed to this life, if you lose your focus, this will all fall apart." He waved his arms at the wide room, letting the silence hang.

"You're being brainwashed," the king accused. "You change a little every day. These girls, this one more than the others, are all useless."

"Clarkson, perhaps—" He silenced the queen with a look, and whatever her opinion was fell away.

The king turned back to Maxon. "I have a proposition for you."

"I'm not interested," he shot back.

King Clarkson raised his arms in front of him, gesturing that he meant no harm. "Hear me out."

Maxon sighed.

"These girls have been disastrous. Even the Asian's connections have done nothing for me. The Two is too concerned with fame; and the other, well, she's not entirely hopeless but not good enough, if you ask me. This one," he said, pointing at me, "whatever value she's had has been completely overshadowed by her inability to contain herself.

"This has all gone terribly wrong. And I know you. I know you're afraid of missing something, so this is my thought."

I watched the king walk around Maxon. "Let's call this off. Let's get rid of all the girls."

Maxon opened his mouth to protest, but the king held up a hand. "I'm not suggesting you stay single. I'm simply saying that we still have the entries of all the eligible girls in the country sitting around somewhere. Wouldn't it be nice if you got to handpick a few girls to come to the palace? Maybe find one who looks like the French king's daughter; remember how fond you were of her?"

I lowered my eyes. Maxon had never mentioned a French girl.

It genuinely felt as if someone took a chisel and chipped a crack in my heart.

"Father, I couldn't."

"Oh, but you could. You're the prince. And I think we've had enough outbursts that we could deem this lot unfit. You could have a real choice this time."

I looked up again. Maxon's eyes were focused on the floor. I could see he was struggling.

"This might even appease the rebels temporarily. Think of that!" the king added. "If we send these girls home, wait a few months like we're calling off the Selection, and then bring in a new group of lovely, educated, pleasant women . . . that could change a lot of things."

Maxon tried to say something but only closed his mouth again.

"Either way, you should ask yourself if that," he said, pointing to me again, "is someone you could really spend your life with. Dramatic, selfish, money hungry, and, to be quite honest, very plain. Look at her, son."

Maxon's eyes darted down to mine, holding them for a second before I had to turn away from humiliation.

"I'll give you a few days. For now there's the press to deal with. Amberly."

The queen scurried over, placing her arm through the king's, leaving us alone and speechless.

After a short pause, Maxon came to help me stand up.

"Thanks."

Maxon only nodded. "I should probably go with them. No doubt they'll have questions for me as well."

"That's a pretty nice offer," I commented.

"Maybe the most generous one he's ever made."

I didn't want to know if he was seriously considering this. There was nothing else to say, so I made my way past him, taking the back route to my room, hoping to outrun everything I was feeling.

My maids informed me that dinner would be on our own tonight, and when I couldn't be bothered to communicate with them, they graciously excused themselves. I lay on my bed, lost in my thoughts.

I'd done the right thing today, hadn't I? I believed in justice, but the Convicting wasn't justice. Still, I kept wondering if I'd actually accomplished anything. If that man was an enemy to the king somehow, which I had to believe he was, then surely he would be punished in some other way. Was it all for nothing?

And as frivolous as it was when I considered everything else going on, I couldn't stop thinking about this French girl. Why hadn't Maxon mentioned her? Was she here a lot? Why would he keep her a secret?

I heard the knock and assumed it was my food, even though it seemed a little early.

"Come in," I called, not wanting to get out of bed.

The door opened, and Celeste's dark hair swished into view.

"In the mood for some company?" she asked. Kriss peeked in behind her, and I saw the edge of Elise's arm hiding in the back.

I sat up. "Sure."

They ambled in, leaving the door open. Celeste, still shocking me every time she smiled so genuinely, climbed into my bed without even asking. Not that I minded. Kriss followed, sitting closer to my feet, and Elise balanced on the edge, ever the lady.

Kriss quietly asked what I was sure they were all wondering. "Did he hurt you?"

"No." Then I realized that wasn't entirely true. "He didn't hit me or anything; he just pulled me away a little too roughly."

"What did he say?" Elise fiddled with a piece of her dress as she spoke.

"He's not happy with my outburst. If it was the king choosing, I'd be long gone by now."

Celeste touched my arm. "But he's not. Maxon's fond of you, and so are the people."

"I don't know if that's enough." *For any of us,* I added in my head.

"Sorry I yelled at you," Elise said quietly. "It's frustrating. I try so hard to keep cool and confident, but I feel like nothing I do matters. You all outshine me."

"That's not true," Kriss argued. "At this point, we all mean something to Maxon. We wouldn't be here otherwise."

"He's afraid to get to the final three," Elise countered. "He's supposed to choose within, what, four days when it's down to three? He's holding on to me to keep from making that decision."

"Who's to say he's not holding on to me?" Celeste suggested.

"Listen," I said, "after today I'll probably be going home next. It was bound to happen sooner or later. I'm just not cut out for this."

Kriss giggled. "None of us is an Amberly, are we?"

"I like shocking people too much," Celeste said with a smile.

"And I'd rather hide than do half the things she has to." Elise ducked her head.

"I'm too wild." I shrugged my shoulders, embracing my faults.

"I'll never have her confidence," Kriss mourned.

"So there. We're all messed up. But Maxon has to pick one of us, so there's no point worrying anymore." Celeste toyed with the blanket. "But I think we can all agree that any of you would be a better choice than me."

After a heavy silence, Kriss spoke up. "What do you mean?"

Celeste looked across at her. "You know. Everyone does." She took a deep breath and continued. "I've kind of already had this discussion with America, and I broke down to my maids the other day, but I've never actually apologized to you two."

Kriss and Elise looked at each other briefly before focusing again on Celeste.

"Kriss, I ruined your birthday party," she blurted. "You were the only one who's been able to celebrate in the palace, and I took that moment from you. I'm so sorry."

Kriss shrugged. "It turned out okay in the end. Maxon and I had a great talk because of you. I forgave you a long time ago."

Celeste actually looked like she might cry, but she pushed her lips together into a tight smile. "That's generous considering I'm having a hard time forgiving myself." Celeste dabbed at her lashes. "I just didn't know how to hold his attention, so I stole it from you."

Kriss took a deep breath. "It felt awful at the time, but it really is all right. I'm fine. At least it wasn't like with Anna."

Celeste rolled her eyes shamefully. "Don't even get me started. Sometimes I wonder how far she would have made it if I hadn't . . ." She shook her head before moving her gaze to Elise. "I don't know how you could ever excuse all the things I've done to you. Even the ones you don't know were me."

Elise, ever poised, didn't explode like I might have in her place. "You mean the glass in my shoes, the ruined gowns hanging in my closet, the bleach in my shampoo?"

"Bleach!" I gasped, finding confirmation in Celeste's tired face.

Elise nodded. "I missed a morning in the Women's Room so my maids could dye it back." She turned from me to Celeste. "I knew it was you," she confessed calmly.

Celeste hung her head, absolutely mortified. "You didn't speak, you barely did anything. In my eyes, you were the easiest target, and I was shocked you never broke."

"I would never dishonor my family by quitting," Elise said. I loved her conviction, even if I didn't completely understand it.

"They should be proud of everything you've endured. If my parents had any idea how low I've sunk . . . I don't know what they'd say. If Maxon's parents knew, I'm sure they'd have kicked me out by now. I'm not fit for this." She breathed out, struggling to confess.

I leaned forward, putting my hands on hers. "I think this change of heart would prove otherwise, Celeste."

She tilted her head and gave me a sad smile. "All the same, I don't think he wants me. Even if he did," she added, pulling her hands from mine to tidy up her eye makeup, "someone recently reminded me that I don't need a man to get what I want out of life."

We shared a grin before she turned back to Elise.

"I can never begin to apologize for everything I've done to you, but I need you to know how sincerely I regret it. I'm sorry, Elise."

Elise didn't waver, staring Celeste down. I braced myself for her vicious words now that Celeste was finally at her mercy.

"I could tell him. America and Kriss would be my witnesses, and Maxon would have to send you home."

Celeste swallowed. How humiliating it would be to leave like that!

"I won't though," Elise said, finally. "I would never force Maxon's hand, and win or lose, I want to do it with integrity. So let's move forward."

It wasn't an actual statement of forgiveness, but it was above and beyond what Celeste was expecting. It was all she could do to keep herself together as she nodded and whispered her thanks to Elise.

"Wow," Kriss said, attempting to change the subject, "I mean, I didn't want to tell on you either, Celeste, but . . . I didn't think about honor being behind that choice." Kriss turned to Elise, thinking over the words.

"It's always on my mind," Elise confessed. "I have to hold on to it however I can, especially since I'll be an embarrassment to my family if I don't win."

"How is it your fault if he's the one doing the choosing?" Kriss asked, shifting her weight and settling back in. "How would that make you an embarrassment?"

Elise turned in more, moving from one worry to another. "Because of the arranged-marriage thing. The best girls get the best men and vice versa. Maxon is the height of perfection. If I lose, it means that I wasn't good enough. My family won't think about the feelings behind his choice, which is what I'm sure he'll judge by. They'll look at it logically. My breeding, my talents—I was raised to be worthy of the best, so if I'm not, then who will have me when I leave?"

I'd thought about how my life would change if I won or lost a million times, but I'd never considered what it would mean for the others. After everything with Celeste, I really should have.

Kriss put a hand on Elise's. "Almost all the girls who went home are already engaged to wonderful men. To be a part of the Selection at all makes you a prize. And you made it to the top four of the Elite at the very least. Trust me, Elise, guys will be lined up around the block for you."

Elise smiled. "I don't need a line. I just need one."

"Well, I need a line," Celeste said, making us all chuckle, even Elise.

"I'd like a handful," Kriss said. "A line does sound overwhelming."

They looked at me. "One."

"You're nuts," Celeste decided.

We talked for a while about Maxon, about home, about our hopes. We'd never really spoken like this, without any kind of wall between us. Kriss and I had been working on it, trying to be honest and upfront about the competition; but now that we could just talk about life, I could tell that our relationships would survive the palace. Elise was a surprise, but the fact that her perspective came from such a different place than mine made me think on a deeper level, opening me up.

And the bombshell: Celeste. If someone had told me that the brunette in the heels who walked over so menacingly that first day in the airport would be the girl I was happiest to have settled next to me at this very moment, I would have laughed in their face. The thought was almost as unbelievable as the fact that I was still here, one of the last girls and very heartbroken about how close I was to losing Maxon.

As we spoke, I could see her being accepted by the others as fully as she was now by me. She even looked different with the weight of her secrets cast off from her. Celeste had been raised to be a specific kind of pretty. That beauty depended on covering things up, shifting the light, and seeking to be perfect at all times. But there is a different kind of beauty that comes with humility and honesty, and she was glowing with it now.

Maxon must have walked up very quietly, because I had no idea how long he had been standing at the door, watching us. It was Elise who saw his figure on the edge of my room and stiffened first.

"Your Majesty," she said, bowing her head.

We all looked over, sure we'd misheard her.

"Ladies." He nodded his head back at us. "I didn't mean to interrupt. I think I just ruined something here."

We looked at one another, and I felt sure I wasn't the only one thinking, *No, you made something really amazing.*

"Everything's fine," I said.

"Again, I'm sorry to intrude, but I need to speak to America. Alone."

Celeste sighed and started moving, looking back to wink at me before she stood. Elise rose quickly, and Kriss followed, giving my leg a little squeeze as she hopped off the bed. Elise gave Maxon a curtsy as she left, while Kriss paused to straighten his lapel. Celeste walked up, as strong as I'd ever seen her, and whispered something into Maxon's ear.

When she was done, he smiled. "I don't think that will be necessary."

"Good." She left, closing the door behind her, and I stood to take whatever was coming.

"What was that about?" I asked, nodding toward the door.

"Oh, Celeste was making it clear that if I hurt you, she'd make me cry," he said with a smile.

I laughed. "I've been on the receiving end of those nails, so be careful there."

"Yes, ma'am."

I took in a breath, letting my smile fade. "So?"

"So?"

"Are you going to do it?"

Maxon grinned and shook his head. "No. It was an intriguing thought for a moment, but I don't want to start over. I like my imperfect girls." He shrugged, his face content. "Besides, Father doesn't know about August, or what the Northern rebels' goals are, or any of that. His solutions are shortsighted. Jumping ship now would be just that."

I sighed in relief. I'd hoped that Maxon cared about me enough not to let me go, but after sitting with the girls, I didn't want to see that happen to them either.

"Besides," he added, seeming pleased, "you should have seen the press."

"Why? What happened?" I begged, moving closer.

"They were impressed with you once again. I don't think even I quite understand the mood of the country right now. It's as if . . . it's as if they know things could be different. The way he governs the country is the same way he governs me. He feels no one is capable of making the right decisions but him, so he forces his opinions on people. And, after reading Gregory's diaries, it sounds like it's been that way for a while.

"But no one wants that anymore. People want a choice." Maxon shook his head. "You're terrifying to him, but he can't expel you. They *adore* you, America."

I swallowed. "Adore?"

He nodded. "And . . . I feel similarly. So, no matter what he says or does, don't lose faith. This isn't over."

I placed my fingers on my lips, shocked by the news. The Selection would continue, the girls and I still had our chance, and, based on Maxon's report, the people were approving of me more and more.

But for all the good news, one thing was still pressing on me.

I looked down at the blanket, almost afraid to ask. "I know this will sound stupid . . . but who's the French king's daughter?"

Maxon was silent for a moment before he sat down on the bed. "Her name is Daphne. Before the Selection, she was the only girl I really knew."

"And?"

He huffed out a soundless laugh. "And a little late in the game I discovered her feelings for me went a little bit deeper than friendship. But I didn't return those feelings. I couldn't."

"Was there something wrong with her or—"

"America, no." Maxon reached for my hand, forcing me to look at him. "Daphne is my friend. That's all she ever could be. I spent my life waiting for you, for all of you. This was my chance to find a wife, and I've known that for as long as I can remember. Romantically, my interactions with Daphne were nonexistent. I'd never have thought to mention her name to you, and I'm certain the only reason Father did was to give you yet another opportunity to doubt yourself."

I bit my lip. The king knew my weaknesses too well.

"I watch you do it, America. You compare yourself to my mother, to the other Elite, to a version of yourself you think you ought to be, and now you're about to do the same thing with a person you didn't know existed until a few hours ago."

It was true. I was already wondering if she was prettier than me, smarter than me, and if she said Maxon's name with a ridiculously flirtatious accent.

"America," he said, cupping my face in his hand. "If she had mattered, I would have told you. The same way you would with me."

My stomach turned. I hadn't been completely honest with Maxon. But with his eyes right there, staring so deeply into mine, it was easy to dismiss all that. I could forget about everything surrounding us when he looked at me like that. And so I did.

I fell into Maxon's arms, holding him tightly. There was no place in the world I wanted to be more.

CHAPTER 21

CELESTE HAD BECOME THE CHAMPION of our newfound sisterhood. It was her idea to drag all our maids and a bunch of big mirrors down to the Women's Room and essentially spend the day making one another over. There wasn't much point, seeing as there was no way any of us could do a better job than the palace staff, but it was fun all the same.

Kriss held the ends of my hair across my forehead. "Have you ever considered getting bangs?"

"A couple of times," I admitted, fluffing the fringe hanging just above my eyes. "But my sister usually ends up annoyed with hers, so I change my mind."

"I think you'd look cute," Kriss said enthusiastically. "I cut some for my cousin once. I could do yours if you want."

"Yeah," Celeste chimed in. "Let her near your face with scissors, America. Great idea."

We all burst into laughter. I even noticed a tiny giggle from the other end of the room. I glanced over to see the queen pursing her lips together tightly as she attempted to read the file in front of her. I was worried she'd find all this a bit improper, but, honestly, I wasn't sure I'd ever seen her so happy.

"We should take pictures!" Elise said.

"Anyone got a camera?" Celeste asked. "I'm a pro at this."

"Maxon does!" Kriss shouted. "Come here for a minute," she said to a maid, waving her over encouragingly.

"Hold on," I said, grabbing some paper. "Okay, okay. 'Your Highest of Highnesses, the ladies of the Elite require, immediately, the least fancy of your cameras for . . .'"

Kriss giggled, and Celeste shook her head.

"Oh! A study in feminine diplomacy," Elise added.

"Is that a real thing?" Kriss asked.

Celeste tossed her hair. "Who cares?"

Maybe twenty minutes later, Maxon knocked on the door and pushed it open an inch. "Can I come in?"

Kriss ran over. "No. We just want the camera." And she snatched it from his hand and closed the door in his face.

Celeste fell on the floor, laughing.

"What are you doing in there?" he called. But we were all too busy doubling over to answer.

There were lots of poses behind the shrubs and a thousand kisses blown, and Celeste showed us all how to "find the light."

As Kriss and Elise lay down on the couch and Celeste

climbed above them to snap more photos, I looked over and saw the satisfied smile on the queen's face. It felt wrong that she wasn't a part of this. I snatched up one of the brushes and walked over to her.

"Hello, Lady America," she greeted.

"Could I brush your hair?"

Several emotions played across her face, but she only nodded and spoke quietly. "Of course."

I walked behind her and picked up a handful of her absolutely gorgeous hair. I raked the brush down again and again, watching the other girls as I did so.

"It does my heart good to see you all getting along," she commented.

"Me, too. I like them." I was quiet for a while. "I'm sorry about the Convicting. I know I shouldn't have done that. I just . . ."

"I know, dear. You explained it all beforehand. It's a difficult task. And you did seem to have a sickly bunch."

I realized then how out of the loop she was. Or maybe she simply chose to believe the best about her husband at all costs.

As if she could read my thoughts, she spoke. "I know you think Clarkson's harsh, but he's a good man. You have no idea how stressful it is to be in his shoes. We all deal with it in our own ways. He has a temper sometimes; I need lots of rest; Maxon jokes it off."

"He does, doesn't he?" I said, laughing.

"The question is, how would you handle it?" She turned

her head. "I think your passion is one of your best features. If you could learn to control it, you could be a wonderful princess."

I nodded. "I'm sorry I let you down."

"No, no, dear," she said, turning forward. "I see potential in you. I worked in a factory when I was your age. I was dirty and hungry, and sometimes I was angry. But I had an undying crush on the prince of Illéa, and when I got the chance to make him my own, I learned to check those feelings. There's a lot to be done from here, but it might not happen the way you want it to. You need to learn to accept that, okay?"

"Yes, Mom," I joked.

She looked back at me, her face like stone.

"I mean, ma'am. Ma'am."

Her eyes started glistening, and she blinked a few times, turning forward again. "If it ends as I suspect it will, Mom will be just fine."

And then it was my turn to blink back the tears. It wasn't like I was ever going to replace my mother; but it felt special to be accepted, with all my flaws, by the mother of the person I might marry.

Celeste turned and saw us, and she ran over. "You're so cute! Smile."

I leaned down, wrapping my arms around Queen Amberly, and she reached up to touch my hands. After that, we all took turns crowding around her, getting her to finally make one silly face for the camera. The maids helped take pictures so we could all be in some together; and, by the end of it, I could easily say that was my best day in the palace. I didn't know if that would hold though. Christmas was right around the corner.

My maids were fixing my hair after Elise's last terrible attempt at an up-do when there was a knock on the door.

Mary rushed to answer it, and a guard whose name I didn't know came into the room. I'd seen him around a lot, almost exclusively at the king's side.

My maids curtsied as he walked closer, and I was more than a little anxious when he stopped in front of me.

"Lady America, the king requires your presence at once," he said coolly.

"Is anything wrong?" I asked, stalling.

"The king will answer your questions."

I swallowed. Every awful thing ran through my head. My family was in danger. The king had found a way to punish me quietly for all the ways I'd wronged him. He'd discovered we'd sneaked out of the palace. Or, perhaps worst of all, someone had figured out my connection to Aspen, and we were both about to pay for it.

I tried to shake the fear out of my system. I didn't want any of it to show in front of King Clarkson.

"I'll follow you then." I stood and started walking behind the guard, giving one last glance to the girls as I left. When I saw the worry on their faces, I wished I hadn't.

We went down the hall and started up the stairs to the

third floor. I didn't quite know what to do with my hands, and I kept touching my hair or my dress or lacing my fingers together.

When we were about halfway down the hall, I saw Maxon, and that helped. He paused just outside a room, waiting for me. There was no concern in his eyes, but he was better at hiding his fear than I was.

"What's this about?" I whispered.

"Your guess is as good as mine."

The guard took his place outside the door as Maxon escorted me inside. In the wide room, there were shelves of books along one wall. On easels, several maps were set up. There were at least three separate ones of Illéa, with markers in different colors. At a wide desk, the king sat with a piece of paper in his hand.

As he noticed Maxon and me enter the room, the king straightened.

"What exactly have you done with the Italian princess?" King Clarkson demanded, staring at me.

I froze. The money. I'd forgotten all about that. Conspiring to sell weapons to people he viewed as enemies was worse than any of the other scenarios for which I'd been preparing.

"I'm not sure what you mean," I lied, looking to Maxon. Even though he knew everything, he remained calm.

"We have been trying to make an alliance with the Italians for decades, and all of a sudden the royal family is quite interested in having us visit. However"—the king picked up the letter, searching for a specific section—"ah, here. 'While it would be more than an honor to have Your Majesty and your family grace us with your company, we hope that Lady America will also be able to visit with you. After meeting all the Elite, we can't imagine anyone following in the queen's footsteps quite like her.'"

The king raised his eyes back to me. "What have you done?"

Realizing I'd dodged something huge, I relaxed marginally. "All I've done was try to be polite toward the princess and her mother when they've visited. I didn't know she liked me so much."

King Clarkson rolled his eyes. "You're subversive. I've been watching you, and you're here for something; and it sure as hell isn't him."

Maxon turned to me at those words. I wished I hadn't seen the flicker of doubt in his eyes. I shook my head. "That's not true!"

"Then how did a girl of no means, no connections, and no power manage to get this country within the reach of something it's been trying to achieve for years? How?"

In my heart, I knew that there were factors here that he was oblivious to. But it was Nicoletta who had offered assistance to me, who had asked if she could do anything for a cause she wanted to support. If he'd accused me of something that was actually my fault, his rising voice would have been frightening. As it was, he came across like a child.

In response, I spoke quietly. "You were the ones who

assigned us to entertain your foreign guests. I never would have met any of those women otherwise. And she's the one who wrote, inviting me to come. I didn't beg for a trip to Italy. Maybe if you were simply more welcoming, you'd have had your alliance with Italy years ago."

He stood forcefully. "Watch. Your. Mouth."

Maxon put an arm around me. "Perhaps it's best you left, America."

I happily started moving, keen to be anywhere the king wasn't. But that was not what King Clarkson had in mind.

"Stop. I have more," he insisted. "This changes things. We can't reset the Selection and risk upsetting the Italians. They have a lot of influence. If we can get them, they'll open a lot of doors for us."

Maxon nodded, not upset at all. He had already made the choice to keep us here, but we had to play along and let the king think he was in control.

"We'll simply have to draw out the Selection," he concluded. My heart plummeted. "We have to give the Italians time to accept the other options as viable without offending them. Perhaps we should schedule a trip over there soon, give everyone an opportunity to shine."

He looked so pleased with himself, so proud of his solution. I wondered how far he would go. Prep Celeste, maybe. Or arrange for some private time with Kriss and Nicoletta. I wouldn't put it past him to make me look bad deliberately, the way he had tried to in the Convicting. If he went to all the lengths he could without openly incriminating himself,

I wasn't sure I had much of a chance.

And forget the political side of it. More time meant more opportunities to embarrass myself.

"Father, I'm not sure that would help," Maxon interjected. "The Italian ladies have already met all the candidates. If they're showing a preference for America, it must have come from something they like in her that wasn't visible in the others. You can't simply make that exist."

The king looked at Maxon, venom in his eyes. "Are you declaring your choice right now then? Is the Selection over?"

My pulse stopped altogether.

"No," Maxon answered, as if the very thought was ridiculous. "I'm just not sure what you're suggesting is the right course."

King Clarkson propped his chin on his hand, looking back and forth between Maxon and me, staring at us like some equation he couldn't solve.

"She has yet to prove herself trustworthy. Until that time, you cannot choose her." The king's face was unyielding.

"And how do you suggest she does that?" Maxon countered. "What exactly do you need in order to be satisfied?"

The king raised his eyebrows, seeming amused at his son's questions. After a moment of consideration, he pulled a small file out of his drawer.

"Even excluding your recent stunt on the *Report*, there seems to be a bit of unrest these days between the castes. I've been wanting to find a way to . . . aid in soothing the opinions of the moment; but it occurred to me that someone as fresh and young and, dare I say, popular as you are might do better at this than I would."

Pushing the file across the desk, he continued. "It seems the people follow your tunes. Perhaps you would sing one of mine for them."

I opened the folder and read the papers. "What is this?"

"Just some service announcements we'll be making soon. We know, of course, the caste makeup of each province and all the communities within them, so we'll be sending specific ones to certain areas. Encouraging them."

"What is it, America?" Maxon asked, confused by his father's words.

"They're like . . . commercials," I answered. "Advertisements to be happy with your own caste, not to associate closely with those outside it."

"Father, what's this about?"

The king leaned back in his chair, relaxing. "It's nothing serious. I'm merely trying to quell the unrest. If I don't do it, you'll have an uprising on your hands by the time I pass down the crown."

"How so?"

"The lower castes tend to get unruly from time to time—it's natural. But we have to subdue the anger and squash the ideas of usurping power quickly, before they unite and undo our great nation."

Maxon stared at his father, still not fully comprehending his words. If Aspen hadn't clued me in to sympathizers, I might have been the same way. The king was planning to divide and conquer: make the castes absurdly grateful for what they had—even if they were being treated like they didn't matter—and tell them not to associate with those outside of their castes, for they certainly wouldn't understand the plight of anyone outside their own.

"This is propaganda," I spat, remembering the word from Dad's tattered history book.

The king tried to soothe me. "No, no. It's a suggestion. It's reinforcement. It's a way of looking at the world that will keep our country happy."

"Happy? So you want me to tell some Seven that . . ."—I hunted for the words on the sheet—"'your task is possibly the greatest of our nation. You toil with your body and build the very roads and buildings that make our land.'" I searched for more. "'No Two or Three could equal your talent, so turn your eyes away from them on the street. No need to speak with those who may rank higher than you by caste but are beneath you in your contribution.'"

Maxon turned from me to his father. "Surely, that will alienate our people."

"On the contrary. It will help settle them into their places and make them feel that the palace has their best interests at heart."

"Do you?" I shot.

"Of course I do!" the king yelled.

His outburst made me take a few steps back.

"People need to be led by the bit, with blinders on like horses. If you do not guide their steps, they run astray, straight into what's worst for them. You may not like these little speeches, but they'll do more, *save* more, than you know."

My heart was still slowing as he finished speaking, and I stood silently with the papers in my hands.

I knew he was worried. Every time he got a report of something happening beyond his control, he crushed it. He lumped all change together, calling it treason before inspecting it. His answer this time was to have me do what Gregory did and isolate his people.

"I can't say it," I whispered.

He responded calmly. "Then you cannot marry my son."

"Father!"

King Clarkson held up a hand. "We're at that point, Maxon. I've let you have your way, and now we must negotiate. If you want this girl to stay, then she must be obedient. If she cannot follow through with the simplest of tasks, my only conclusion is that she doesn't love you. If that's the case, I can't see why you would want her in the first place."

I locked eyes with the king, hating him for putting the thought in Maxon's head.

"Do you? Do you love him at all?"

This wasn't how I was going to say it. Not at the end of an ultimatum, not for business.

The king tilted his head. "How sad, Maxon. She needs to think about it."

Do not cry. Do not *cry.*

"I'll give you some time to find out where you stand. If you won't do this, then rules be damned, *I'll* be kicking you out by Christmas Day. What a special gift that will be for your parents."

Three days.

He smiled. I set the folder on his desk and left, trying not to break into a run. All I needed was another excuse for him to say I was flawed.

"America!" Maxon yelled. "Stop!"

I kept walking until he grabbed me by the wrist, forcing me to pause.

"What the hell was that?" he demanded.

"He's insane!" I was on the verge of tears, but I held them in. If the king came out and saw me that way, I'd never live it down.

Maxon shook his head. "Not him. You. Why didn't you agree to do it?"

I looked at him, gob-smacked. "It's a trick, Maxon. Everything he's doing is a trick."

"If you had said yes, I would have ended this now."

Incredulous, I fired back. "Two seconds before, you had the chance to end it and didn't. How is this my fault?"

"Because," he answered, his whole demeanor urgent, "you are denying me your love. It's the only thing I've wanted in this entire competition, and you still hold back. I keep waiting for you to say it, and you won't. If you couldn't say it out loud in front of him, fine. But if you had simply agreed, that would have been good enough for me."

"And why would I when, for as far as we've come, he could still push me out? While I'm humiliated over and over again, and you stand by? That's not love, Maxon. You don't even know what love is."

"The hell I don't! Do you have any idea what I've been through—"

"Maxon, you were the one who said you wanted to stop arguing. So stop giving me reasons to argue with you!"

I stormed away. What was I still doing here? I kept torturing myself for someone who had no idea what it meant to be faithful to one person. And he never would, because his whole concept of romance revolved around the Selection. He wouldn't ever understand.

As I was about to hit the stairwell, I was whipped back again. Maxon held me tightly, both of his hands gripping my arms. Surely he could see how furious I still was, but in the seconds that had passed, his demeanor had shifted completely.

"I'm not him," he said.

"What?" I demanded, trying to free myself.

"America, stop." I huffed and quit struggling. Without any other options, I looked into Maxon's eyes. "I'm not him, all right?"

"I don't know what you mean."

He sighed. "I know that you spent years pouring yourself into another person who you thought was going to love you forever; and when he was faced with the realities of the world, he abandoned you." I froze, taking in his words. "I'm not him, America. I have no intentions of giving up on you."

I shook my head. "You can't see it, Maxon. He might

have let me down, but at least I knew him. After all this time, I still feel like there's a gap between us. The Selection has forced you to hand over your affection in slices. I'll never really have all of you. None of us will."

When I shrugged myself free this time, he didn't fight me.

CHAPTER 22

I DIDN'T REMEMBER MUCH OF the *Report*. I sat on my pedestal, thinking as every second passed that I was that much closer to being sent home. Then it dawned on me that staying wasn't much better. If I caved and read those horrible messages, the king would win. Maybe Maxon did love me, but if he wasn't man enough to say it out loud, then how could he ever protect me from the most frightening thing in my life: his father.

I would always be bending to King Clarkson's will; and for all the support Maxon had from the Northern rebels, behind these walls, he would be alone.

I was angry at Maxon, and I was angry at his father, and I was angry at the Selection and everything that came with it. All the frustration knotted itself around my heart to the point where it made no sense, and I wished more than anything that I could talk to the girls about what was going on.

That wasn't possible though. It wouldn't make anything better for me, and it would only make things worse for them. Sooner or later, I'd have to face my concerns by myself.

I peeked to my left, looking down the row of the Elite. I realized that whoever stayed would have to face this without the rest of us. The pressures the public would set on us, demanding to be a part of our lives, as well as the commands of the king, ever seeking to use anyone within reach as a tool in his plans—all on the shoulders of one girl.

I tentatively reached out for Celeste's hand, fingers brushing against hers. The second she felt them, she took hold, looking into my eyes with concern.

What's wrong? she mouthed.

I shrugged.

And so she just held my hand.

After a minute, she seemed to get a little sad, too. While the men in suits prattled on, she stretched out, reaching for Kriss's hand. Kriss didn't question it, and it took her only seconds to extend her hand for Elise's.

And there we were, in the background of it all, holding on to one another. The Perfectionist, the Sweetheart, the Diva . . . and me.

I spent the next morning in the Women's Room, being as obedient as I could. Several of the extended family members were in town, ready to spend Christmas Day in style. Tonight there was supposed to be a magnificent dinner and carol singing. Typically Christmas Eve was one of my favorite times of the year, but I felt too unsettled to even get excited.

There was a fantastic meal that I didn't taste and beautiful gifts from the public that I barely saw. I was crushed.

As the relatives started getting tipsy on eggnog, I slipped away, not up to pretending to be jolly. By the end of the night, I'd either have to agree to do King Clarkson's ridiculous commercials or let him send me home. I needed to think.

Back in my room, I sent my maids away and sat at my table, considering. I didn't want to do this. I didn't want to tell the people to be satisfied with what they had, even if it was nothing. I didn't want to discourage people from helping one another. I didn't want to eliminate the possibility of more, to be the face and voice of a campaign that said, "Be still. Let the king run your life. That's the best you can hope for."

But . . . didn't I love Maxon?

A second later, a knock came at the door. I reluctantly went to answer it, dreading King Clarkson's cold eyes as he followed through on his ultimatum.

I opened the door to Maxon. He stood there wordlessly.

And all my anger made sense. I wanted everything *from* him and everything *for* him, because I wanted every *piece of* him. It was infuriating that everyone had to have their hands on this—the girls, his parents, even Aspen. So many conditions and opinions and obligations surrounded us, and

I hated Maxon because they came with him.

And I loved him even so.

I was about to agree to do those awful announcements when he quietly held out his hand.

"Come with me?"

"Okay."

I closed the door behind me and followed Maxon down the hall.

"You have a point," he started. "I am afraid to show all of you every piece of me. You get some, Kriss gets others, and so on. And I've based that on what feels appropriate for each of you. With you, I always like coming to you, to your room. It's as if I'm stepping into a bit of your world, and if I do that enough, I can get all of you. Does that make sense?"

"Kind of," I said as we turned up the stairs.

"But that's not really fair, or even accurate. You explained to me once that these are our rooms, not yours. Anyway, I thought it was time I show you another piece of my world, maybe the last one where you're concerned."

"Oh?"

He nodded as we stopped in front of a door. "My room."

"Really?"

"Only Kriss has seen it, and that was a bit of an impulse. I'm not unhappy I showed her, but I feel as if it pushed things forward quickly. You know how private I can be."

"I do."

He wrapped his fingers around the handle. "I've wanted to share this with you, and I think it's well past the time.

It's not exactly something special, but it's mine. So, I don't know, I just want you to see it."

"Okay." I could tell he was feeling bashful, like maybe he'd built it up to be a bigger deal than it was, or maybe he'd regret showing me at all.

He took a deep breath and opened the door, letting me walk in first.

It was huge. The paneling was dark, some wood I wasn't familiar with lining the whole space. On the far wall, a wide fireplace stood, waiting to be used. The whole thing must have been for show since it never seemed to get cold enough here to justify a fire.

His bathroom door was cracked open, and I could see a porcelain tub on the elaborately tiled floor. He had his own collection of books and a table near the fireplace that looked like it was intended for dining rather than work. I wondered how many lonely meals he'd had here. Near the doors that opened to his private balcony, a glass case full of guns sat, perfectly lined up. I'd forgotten his love of hunting.

His bed, also made from a dark wood, was massive. I wanted to go and touch it, to see if it felt as good as it looked.

"Maxon, you could fit a football team in there," I teased.

"Tried it once. Not as comfortable as you'd think."

I turned to swat at him, glad to see him in a playful mood. It was then, looking past his smiling face, that I saw the pictures. I inhaled sharply, taking in the beautiful display behind him.

On the wall by Maxon's door was a vast collage, wide

enough to be wallpaper for my room back home. There didn't appear to be any sort of order to it, just image upon image piled up for him to enjoy.

I could see photos that surely had to have been taken by him, because they were of the palace, which was where he was almost all the time. Close-ups of tapestries, shots of the ceiling he must have lain flat on the carpet to get, and so many pictures of the gardens. There were others, maybe of places he hoped to see or had at least visited. I saw an ocean so blue it didn't seem possible. There were a few bridges, and one of a wall-like structure that looked like it went on for miles.

But above all this, I saw my face a dozen times over. There was the picture of me that was taken for my Selection application, and the one of Maxon and me taken for the magazine when I wore that sash. We seemed happy there, as if it was all a game. I'd never seen that photo, or the one from the article on Halloween. I remembered Maxon standing behind me while we looked at designs for my costume. While I'm staring at the sketch, Maxon's eyes are slightly turned toward me.

Then there were the photos he took. One of me shocked when the king and queen of Swendway visited and he'd quickly yelled out "Smile." One of me sitting on the set for the *Report*, laughing at Marlee. He must have been hiding behind the blinding lights, stealing little images of us when we were all just being ourselves. And there was another one of me in the night, standing on my balcony and looking at the moon.

The other girls were in them, too, the remaining ones

more than the others; but every once in a while I'd see Anna's eyes peek out from under a landscape or Marlee's smile hiding in a corner. And though they were just taken, pictures of Kriss and Celeste posing in the Women's Room were up there, too, next to Elise pretending to faint on a couch and me with my arms wrapped around his mother.

"Maxon," I breathed. "It's beautiful."

"You like it?"

"I'm in awe of it. How many of these did you take?"

"Nearly all of them, but ones like this," he said, pointing to one of the pictures used in the magazines, "I asked for." He pointed again. "I took this one in the very southern part of Honduragua. I used to think it was interesting, but now it makes me sad."

The image was of some pipes spilling smoke into the sky. "I used to look at the air, but now I remember how much I hated the smell of it. And people live in that all the time. I was so self-absorbed."

"Where is this?" I asked, pointing to the long brick wall.

"New Asia. It used to be to the north of what was the Chinese border. They called it the Great Wall. I hear it was once quite spectacular, but now it's mostly gone. It runs less than halfway through the middle of New Asia. That's how much they've expanded."

"Wow."

Maxon put his hands behind his back. "I was really hoping you would like it."

"I do. So much. I want you to make me one."

"You do?"

"Yes. Or teach me to. I can't even tell you how often I wished I could catch snippets of my life and hold on to them like this. I have a few torn pictures of my family and the new one with my sister's baby, but that's all. I've never even thought of keeping a journal or writing things down. . . . I feel like you make so much more sense now."

This was the center of who he was. I could feel the things that were permanent, such as his constant confinement in the palace and the brief bits of traveling. But there were also elements that shifted. The girls and I were on the wall so much because we'd taken over his world. Even as we left, we weren't really gone.

I stepped over and laced an arm behind his back. He did the same to me, and we stood there quietly for a minute, taking it all in. And then something that should have been obvious the whole time suddenly came to me.

"Maxon?"

"Yes?"

"If things were different and you weren't the prince, and you could pick what you did for a living, would this be it?" I pointed to the collage.

"Taking pictures, you mean?"

"Yes."

He barely needed a second to think. "Absolutely. For art or even just family portraits. I'd do advertising, pretty much whatever I could. I'm very passionate about it. I think you can see that though."

"I can." I smiled, happy with this knowledge.

"Why do you ask?"

"It's just . . ." I moved to look at him. "You'd be a Five."

Maxon slowly took in my words, and he smiled quietly. "That makes me happy."

"Me, too."

Suddenly, decisively, Maxon faced me, taking my hands in his.

"Say it, America. Please. Tell me you love me, that you want to be mine alone."

"I can't be yours alone with all the other girls here."

"And I can't send them home until I'm sure of your feelings."

"And I can't give you what you want while I know that tomorrow you could be doing this with Kriss."

"Doing what with Kriss? She's already seen my room, I told you."

"Not that. Just pulling her away, making her feel like . . ."

He waited. "How?" he whispered.

"Like she's the only one who matters. She's crazy about you. She's told me so. And I don't think it's one-sided."

He sighed, searching for the words. "I can't tell you she means nothing. I can tell you that you mean more."

"How am I supposed to be sure of that if you can't send her home?"

A devilish smirk came to his face. He moved his lips to my ear. "I can think of a few other ways to show you how you make me feel," he whispered.

I swallowed, both frightened and hopeful he'd say more. His body was now up against mine, his hand low on my back, holding me to him. The other hand pushed my hair off my neck. I trembled as he ran his open lips over a tiny patch of skin, his breath so very tempting.

It was as if I forgot how to use my limbs. I couldn't hold on to him or think of how to move. But Maxon took care of that, backing me up a few steps so I was pressed against his collection of pictures.

"I want you, America," he murmured into my ear. "I want you to be mine alone. And I want to give you every-thing." His lips kissed their way across my cheek, stopping at the corner of my mouth. "I want to give you things you didn't know you wanted. I want"—he breathed into me—"so desperately to—"

A loud knock came at the door.

I was so lost in Maxon's touch and words and scent that the sound was jarring. We both turned toward the door, but Maxon quickly put his lips back on mine.

"Don't move. I fully intend to finish this conversation." He kissed me slowly, then pulled away.

I stood there gasping for air. I told myself this was prob-ably a bad idea, to let him kiss me into a confession. But, I reasoned, if there was ever a way to cave, this was it.

He opened the door, shielding me from the visitor. I ran my hands through my hair, trying to pull myself together.

"Sorry, Your Majesty," someone said. "We're looking for Lady America, and her maids said she would be with you."

I wondered how my maids had guessed, but I was pleased they seemed so in tune with me. Maxon's brow furrowed as he looked toward me and opened the door all the way to allow the guard to walk through. He came in, and his eyes had the air of inspecting me, like he was double-checking. Once he was satisfied, he leaned over Maxon's shoulder and whispered something.

Maxon's shoulders slumped, and he brought his hand to his eyes as if he was unable to deal with the news.

"Are you all right?" I asked, not wanting him to suffer alone.

He turned toward me, sympathy in his face. "I'm so sorry, America. I hate to be the one to tell you this. Your father has died."

I didn't quite understand the words for a minute. But no matter how I arranged them in my head, they all led to the same unthinkable conclusion.

And then the room tilted, and Maxon's expression became urgent. The last thing I felt was Maxon's arms keeping me from hitting the floor.

CHAPTER 23

"—UNDERSTAND. SHE'LL WANT TO VISIT her family."

"If she does, it can only be for a day at the most. I don't approve of her, but the people are fond of her, not to mention the Italians. It would be very inconvenient if she died."

I opened my eyes. I was on my bed, but not under my covers. I saw out of the corner of my eye that Mary was in the room with me.

The shouting voices were muted, and I realized that was because they were just outside my door.

"That won't be enough. She loved her father dearly; she'll want time," Maxon argued.

I heard something like a fist hitting a wall, and Mary and I both jumped at the sound. "Fine," the king huffed. "Four days. That's it."

"What if she decides not to come back? Even though this wasn't rebel caused, she might want to stay."

"If she's dumb enough to want that, then good riddance. She was supposed to give me an answer about those announcements anyway, and if she's not willing, then she can stay home."

"She said she would. She told me earlier tonight," Maxon lied. But he knew, didn't he?

"About time. As soon as she returns, we'll get her in the studio. I want this done by the New Year." His tone was irritated, even as he got what he wanted.

There was a pause before Maxon dared to speak. "I want to go with her."

"Like hell you will!" King Clarkson yelled.

"We're down to four, Father. That girl might be my wife. Am I supposed to send her alone?"

"Yes! If she dies, it's one thing. If you die, it's a whole other issue. You're staying here!"

I thought the fist hitting the wall this time was Maxon's. "I am not a commodity! And neither are they! I wish for once you would look at me and see a person."

The door opened quickly, and Maxon came in. "I'm so sorry," he said, walking over and sitting on the bed. "I didn't mean to wake you."

"Is it real?"

"Yes, darling. He's gone." He gently took my hand, looking pained. "There was a problem with his heart."

I sat up and threw myself into Maxon's arms. He held me tightly, letting me weep into his shoulder.

"Daddy," I cried. "Daddy."

"Hush, darling. It'll be all right," Maxon soothed. "You'll fly out tomorrow morning to go pay your respects."

"I didn't get to say good-bye. I didn't . . ."

"America, listen to me. Your father loved you. He was proud you'd done so well. He wouldn't hold this against you."

I nodded, knowing he was right. Practically everything my dad had told me since I'd come here was about how proud he was.

"This is what you need to do, okay?" he instructed, wiping tears off my cheeks. "You need to sleep as best as you can. You'll fly out tomorrow and stay at home for four days with your family. I wanted to get you more time, but Father is quite insistent."

"It's okay."

"Your maids are making an appropriate dress for the funeral, and they'll pack everything you need. You're going to have to take one of them with you, and a few guards. Speaking of which," he said, standing to acknowledge the figure standing in the open door. "Officer Leger, thank you for coming."

"Not at all, Your Majesty. I apologize for being out of uniform, sir."

Maxon reached out and shook Aspen's hand. "Least of my

concerns right now. I'm sure you know why you're here."

"I do." Aspen turned to me. "I'm very sorry for your loss, miss."

"Thank you," I mumbled.

"With the elevated rebel activity, we're all concerned about Lady America's safety," Maxon started. "We've already had some local officers dispatched to her home and to the sites being used over the next few days, and there are still palace-trained guards there, of course. But with her actually in the house, I think we should send more."

"Absolutely, Your Majesty."

"And you're familiar with the area?"

"Very, sir."

"Good. You'll be heading up the team going with her. Pick whomever you like, between six and eight guards."

Aspen raised his eyebrows.

"I know," Maxon conceded. "We're stretched tight right now, but at least three of the palace guards we've sent to her house have already abandoned their posts. And I want her to be as safe as, if not safer than, she is here."

"I'll take care of it, sir."

"Excellent. There will also be a maid going with her; watch her as well." He turned to me. "Do you know who you want to go?"

I shrugged, unable to think straight.

Aspen spoke on my behalf. "If I may, I know Anne is your head maid, but I remember Lucy getting along well with your sister and mother. Maybe it would be good for them to see a friendly face right now."

I nodded. "Lucy."

"Very good," Maxon said. "Officer, you don't have much time. You'll be leaving after breakfast."

"I'll get to work, sir. See you in the morning, miss," Aspen said. I could tell he was having a hard time keeping his distance, and, in that moment, I wanted nothing more than for him to comfort me. Aspen really knew my dad, and I wanted someone who understood him like I did to miss him with me.

Once Aspen left, Maxon came to sit with me again.

"One more thing before I go." He reached for my hands, holding them tenderly. "Sometimes when you're upset, you tend to be impulsive." He looked at me, and I actually smiled a little at the accusing look in his eyes. "Try to be sensible while you're away. I need you to take care of yourself."

I rubbed the back of his hands with my thumbs. "I will. I promise."

"Thank you." A sense of peace encircled us, the way it did sometimes. Even though my world would never be the same now, for that moment, with Maxon holding me, the loss didn't ache so much.

He leaned his head toward mine until our foreheads touched. I heard him draw in a breath as if he might say something and then change his mind. After a few seconds, he did it again. Finally, Maxon leaned back and shook his head and kissed my cheek. "Stay safe."

Then he left me alone in my sadness.

It was cold in Carolina, the humidity from the ocean coming inland and making the chill in the air damp. Secretly, I'd hoped for snow, but it didn't happen. I felt guilty for wanting anything at all.

Christmas Day. I'd spent the last few weeks imagining it several different ways. I thought maybe I'd be here, eliminated and home. We'd all be around our tree, dejected that I wasn't a princess but blissfully happy to be together. I'd also considered opening gifts under the massive tree at the palace, eating myself sick, and laughing with the other girls and Maxon, for one day every corner of the competition suspended to celebrate.

Never could I have imagined I'd be bracing myself for the task of putting my father in the ground.

As the car pulled up to my street, I started to see the masses. Though people ought to be home with their families, they instead crowded outside in the cold. I realized they were hoping to catch a glimpse of me, and I felt a little sick. People pointed as we passed, and some local news crews took footage.

The car stopped in front of my house, and the people waiting started cheering. I didn't understand. Didn't they know why I was here? I walked up the cracked sidewalk with Lucy by my side and six guards surrounding us. No chance was being taken.

"Lady America!" people called.

"Can I have your autograph?" someone screamed, and others joined in.

I kept moving, looking ahead. For once, I felt I could excuse myself from being theirs. I lifted my head to the lights hanging off the roof. Dad did that. Who was going to take them down?

Aspen, at the head of my entourage, knocked on the front door and waited. Another guard came to answer and he and Aspen spoke quickly before we were allowed inside. It was hard to get all of us down the hall, but once the space opened into the living room, I immediately felt something . . . wrong.

This wasn't home anymore.

I told myself I was crazy. Of course this was home. It was just the unfamiliarity of how this was unfolding. Everyone was here, even Kota. But Dad was gone, so it was only natural that it wouldn't seem quite right. And Kenna was holding a baby who I'd never seen in real life before. I'd have to get used to that.

And while Mom was in an apron and Gerad was in his pajamas, I was dressed for dinner at the palace: hair up, sapphires on my ears, and layers of luxurious fabrics draping to my heeled shoes. It felt as if I wasn't welcome for a moment.

But May hopped to her feet and ran to hug me, crying

into my shoulder. I held her back. I remembered that this might be a strange adjustment, but this was the only place I could be right now. I had to be with my family.

"America," Kenna said, standing with her child in her arms. "You look so beautiful."

"Thanks," I muttered, embarrassed.

She gave me a one-armed hug, and I peeked into the blankets at my sleeping niece. Astra's little face was serene as she slept, and every few seconds she'd unclench her tiny fist or fidget just a bit. She was breathtaking.

Aspen cleared his throat. "Mrs. Singer, I'm very sorry for your loss."

Mom gave him a tired smile. "Thank you."

"I'm sorry we're not here under better circumstances, but with Lady America home, we're going to have to be quite diligent about security," he said, a ring of authority in his voice. "We're going to have to ask everyone to stay in this house. I know it'll be tight, but it's only for a few days. And the guards have been provided an apartment nearby so we can rotate easily. We're going to try to be as out of the way as possible.

"James, Kenna, Kota, we're prepared to leave for your homes to pick up your necessities whenever you're ready to go. If you need some time to make a list, that's fine. We're on your schedule."

I smiled a little, happy to see Aspen this way. He'd grown so much.

"I can't stay away from my studio," Kota said. "I have

deadlines. There are pieces due."

Aspen, still professional, answered him. "Any materials you need can come to the studio here." He pointed toward our converted garage. "We'll make as many trips as necessary."

Kota crossed his arms and mumbled. "That place is a dump."

"Fine," Aspen said firmly. "The choice is yours. You can either work in the dump, or you can risk your life at your apartment."

The tension in the air was awkward, and very unnecessary at the moment. I decided to break it. "May, you can sleep with me. Kenna and James can have your room."

They nodded.

"Lucy," I whispered. "I want you near us. You might have to sleep on the floor, but I want you close by."

She stood a bit taller. "I wouldn't be anywhere else, miss."

"Where am I supposed to sleep?" Kota demanded.

"With me," Gerad offered, though he didn't seem excited about it.

"Absolutely not!" Kota scoffed. "I'm not sleeping on a bunk bed with a child."

"Kota!" I said, stepping away from my sisters and Lucy. "You can sleep on the couch or in the garage or in the tree house for all I care; but if you don't check your attitude, I'll send you back to your apartment right now! Have some gratitude for the security you've been offered. Need I remind you that tomorrow we're burying our father? Either stop the bickering or go home." I turned on my heel and headed down the hall. Without checking, I knew Lucy was right behind me, suitcase in hand.

I opened the door to my room, waiting for her to come in with me. Once her skirts swished past the frame, I slammed it shut, heaving a sigh.

"Was that too much?" I asked.

"It was perfect!" she replied with delight. "You might as well be the princess already, miss. You're ready for it."

CHAPTER 24

THE NEXT DAY PASSED IN a blur of black dresses and hugs. Lots of people I'd never even seen before came to Dad's funeral. I wondered if I just didn't know all his friends or if they were here because I was.

A local pastor gave the service, but for security reasons, the family was asked not to stand and speak. There was a reception, far more elaborate than anything we could have ever hoped for. Though no one told me so, I was sure Silvia or some other palace employee had a hand in making this as easy for us and as beautiful as possible. For safety, it was short, but that was fine with me. I wanted to let him go as painlessly as I could.

Aspen stayed near me at all times, and I was grateful for his presence. I couldn't have trusted anyone with my life as I could him.

"I haven't cried since I left the palace," I said. "I thought I'd be a wreck."

"It hits at funny times," he replied. "I fell apart for a few days after my father died, before I realized I had to get it together for everyone else's sake. But sometimes when something would happen and I'd want to tell my dad about it, the whole thing would hit me in the chest again, and I'd break down."

"So . . . I'm normal?"

He smiled. "You're normal."

"I don't know a lot of these people."

"They're all local. We checked identification. It's probably a bit higher of a number because of who you are, but I think your dad made a painting for the Hampshires, and I saw him speaking to Mr. Clippings and Albert Hammers in the market area more than once. It's hard to know everything about people close to you, even the people you love the most."

I sensed there was something more in that sentence, something I was supposed to respond to. I just couldn't right now.

"We need to get used to this," he said.

"To what? Everything feeling awful?"

"No," he answered, shaking his head. "Nothing is the same anymore. Everything that ever made sense is shifting."

I laughed humorlessly. "It is, isn't it?"

"We've got to stop being afraid of the change." He looked at me, eyes pleading. I couldn't help but wonder what change he meant.

"I'll confront the change. But not today." I walked away, embracing more strangers, trying to comprehend that I couldn't talk to my dad anymore about how confused I was feeling.

After the funeral, we tried to keep the spirits up. There were presents left over from Christmas to open since no one had been in the mood for a big gift-giving spree. Gerad was given special permission to play ball in the house, and Mom spent most of the afternoon next to Kenna, holding Astra. Kota was beyond pleasing, so we let him go off into the studio without bothering to check up on him. It was May I worried about the most. She kept saying her hands wanted to work, but she didn't want to go into the studio and not see Dad there.

In an inspired moment, I pulled her and Lucy into my room for some playtime. Lucy was a willing subject as May brushed out her hair, giggling as the makeup brushes tickled her cheeks.

"You do this to me every day!" I complained lightly.

May really had a talent for arranging hair, her artist's eyes ready to work with any medium. While May wore one of the maid uniforms even though it was too big for her, we put dress after dress on Lucy. We settled on a blue one, long and delicate, pinning it in the back so it fit.

"Shoes!" May cried, running to find a matching pair.

"My feet are too wide," Lucy complained.

"Nonsense," May insisted, and Lucy obediently sat on the bed while May tried the most bizarre forms of shoe application on the planet.

Lucy's feet really were too big, but with every attempt she laughed herself into a stupor at May's antics, and I was doubled over watching it all. We were so loud, it was only a matter of time until someone came to see what was going on.

After three quick knocks, I heard Aspen's voice through the door. "Is everything all right in there, miss?"

I ran over and opened the door wide. "Officer Leger, look at our masterpiece." I gave a wide sweep of my arm toward Lucy, and May pulled her up, her poor bare feet hidden under the dress.

Aspen looked at May in her baggy uniform and laughed and then took in Lucy, looking like a princess. "An amazing transformation," he said, grinning from ear to ear.

"Okay, I think we should put your hair all the way up now," May insisted.

Lucy rolled her eyes jokingly toward Aspen and me and let May drag her back to the mirror.

"Was this your idea?" he asked quietly.

"Yes. May looked so lost. I had to distract her."

"She looks better. And Lucy looks happy, too."

"It does as much for me as it does for them. It feels like, if we can do things that are silly or even just typical, I'll be okay."

"You will be. It'll take time, but you'll be okay."

I nodded. But then I started thinking about Dad again, and I didn't want to cry now. I took a deep breath and moved on.

"It seems wrong that I'm the lowest caste left in the Selection," I whispered back to him. "Look at Lucy. She's as pretty and sweet and smart as half of the girls who were in that pool of thirty-five, but this is the best she'll ever have. A few hours in a borrowed dress. It's not right."

Aspen shook his head. "I've gotten to know all your maids pretty well over the last few months, and she's a really special girl."

Suddenly a promise I'd made came back to me.

"Speaking of my maids, I need to talk to you about something," I said, dropping my voice.

Aspen stiffened. "Oh?"

"I know this is awkward, but I need to say it all the same."

He swallowed. "Okay."

I bashfully looked him in the eye. "Would you ever consider Anne?"

His expression was strange, as if he was simultaneously relieved and amused. "Anne?" he whispered incredulously. "Why her?"

"I think she likes you. And she's a really sweet girl," I said, trying to hide the depth of Anne's feelings but build her up at the same time.

He shook his head. "I know you want me to think about the possibility of other people, but she's not at all the kind of girl I'd want to be with. She's so . . . rigid."

I shrugged. "I thought Maxon was like that until I got to know him. Besides, I think she's had it rough."

"So? Lucy's had it rough, and look at her," he said, nodding his head toward her laughing reflection.

I took a guess. "Did she tell you how she ended up at the palace?"

He nodded. "I've always hated the castes, Mer; you know that. But I'd never heard of them being manipulated that way, to acquire slaves."

I sighed, looking over at May and Lucy, this stolen moment of joy in the middle of sorrow.

"Prepare yourself for words you thought you'd never hear," Aspen warned, and I looked up at him, waiting. "I'm actually really glad Maxon met you."

I coughed out something close to a laugh.

"I know, I know," he said, rolling his eyes but smiling. "But I don't think he would have ever stopped to wonder about the lower castes if it wasn't for you. I think just you being there has changed things."

We looked at each other for a moment. I remembered our conversation in the tree house, when he urged me to sign up for the Selection, hoping I'd have a chance for something better. I didn't know yet if I'd gotten something better for myself—it was still hard to tell—but the thought of maybe giving something better to everyone else in Illéa . . . that possibility meant more to me than I could say.

"I'm proud of you, America," Aspen said, looking from me to the girls by the mirror. "Really proud." He moved into the hallway, back to his rounds. "Your father would be, too."

CHAPTER 25

THE NEXT DAY WAS ANOTHER sentence of house arrest. From time to time, I'd hear the floor creak, and I'd turn my head, thinking that Dad would walk out of the garage, paint in his hair like always. But knowing that wasn't going to happen didn't feel as bad when I could hear May's voice or smell Astra's baby powder. The house felt full, and that was enough for now—its own kind of comfort.

I'd decided Lucy shouldn't wear her uniform while she was here, and after a little protesting, I wiggled her into some of my old clothes that were too small for me but too big for May. Since Mom was busy distracting herself by cooking and serving everyone and I'd decided to tone down my look to sit around the house, Lucy's main job was to play with May and Gerad, a task she took on happily.

We were all gathered in the living room, busying ourselves in our own ways. I had a book in hand, and Kota was hogging the television, reminding me of Celeste. I smiled, betting she was doing exactly that now.

Lucy, May, and Gerad were playing a card game on the floor, each one laughing when they won a round. Kenna was propped up against James on the couch, and baby Astra was finishing a bottle in his arms. It was easy to see the exhaustion in his face, but also the absolute pride in his beautiful wife and daughter.

It was almost as if nothing had changed. Then I'd see Aspen out of the corner of my eye in his uniform, standing watch over us, and remember that, in reality, nothing would ever be the same.

I heard Mom sniffling before I saw her coming down the hall. I turned my head and watched her walk toward us, holding a handful of envelopes.

"How are you feeling, Mom?" I asked.

"I'm fine. I just can't believe he's gone." She swallowed, forcing herself not to cry again.

It was strange. There had been so many times when I had doubted Mom's devotion to Dad. I'd never caught the glimpses of affection between them that I'd seen in other couples. Even Aspen, when everything was on the verge of being real but still very much a secret, showed me he loved me more than Mom did Dad.

But I could tell that this was more than the worry of

raising May and Gerad alone getting to her, or stress over money. Her husband was gone, and nothing would ever make that right.

"Kota, could you turn off the TV for a minute? And Lucy, honey, could you take May and Gerad into America's room? I have some things to discuss with the others," she said quietly.

"Of course, ma'am," Lucy replied, and turned to May and Gerad. "Let's go then."

May didn't look happy about being excluded from whatever was going on, but she chose not to put up a fight. I wasn't sure if it was because of Mom's heavy demeanor or her love for Lucy, but either way I was glad.

Once they were gone, Mom turned to the rest of us. "You know your father's condition was something that ran in the family. I think he could tell he only had a little time left, because about three years ago, he sat down and started writing these letters to you, to all of you." She looked down to the envelopes in her hands.

"He made me promise that if anything ever happened, I'd give them to you. I have ones for May and Gerad, but I'm not sure they're old enough. I haven't read them or anything. They were meant for you, so . . . I thought this would be a nice time to read them. This is Kenna's," she said, handing over a letter. "Kota." He sat up straighter and took his. Mom walked over to me. "And America."

I took my letter, unsure whether I wanted to open it or not. These were my last words from my father, the goodbye I thought I'd lost. I ran my hand over my name on the envelope, thinking of my father dashing the pen across it. He dotted the *i* in my name with some kind of squiggle. I smiled to myself, trying to guess what made him decide to do that and not caring at the same time. Maybe he knew I'd need to smile.

But then I looked at it closer. That little mark had been added later. The ink on my name had mostly faded, but that scribble was darker, fresher than the rest.

I flipped over the envelope. The seal had been broken and taped back together.

I glanced over to Kenna and Kota, who were both diving into the words. They seemed engrossed, so they hadn't known that these existed before this moment. That meant either Mom was lying and had read mine or Dad had opened this again.

That was all it took for me to decide I had to know what he'd left for me. I carefully picked at the retaped seal and pulled open the envelope.

There was a letter on faded paper and then a short, quick note on bright white paper. I wanted to read the short note, but I was afraid I wouldn't understand it without reading the long one first. I pulled out the letter and took in Dad's words in the sunlight by the window.

AMERICA,

My SWEET GIRL. I'M HAVING A HARD TIME EVEN STARTING THIS LETTER BECAUSE I FEEL LIKE THERE'S SO MUCH TO TELL YOU. THOUGH I LOVE ALL MY CHILDREN EQUALLY, YOU HAVE A SPECIAL

PLACE IN MY HEART. KENNA AND MAY BOTH LEAN ON YOUR MOTHER, KOTA IS SO INDEPENDENT THAT GERAD IS DRAWN TO HIM, BUT YOU HAVE ALWAYS COME TO ME. WHEN YOU SCRAPED YOUR KNEES OR WERE PICKED ON BY THE UPPER KIDS, MY ARMS WERE ALWAYS THE ONES YOU WANTED. IT MEANS THE WORLD TO ME TO KNOW THAT, AT LEAST FOR ONE OF MY CHILDREN, I WAS THEIR ROCK.

BUT EVEN IF YOU DIDN'T LOVE ME THE WAY THAT YOU DO, WITHOUT ANY SORT OF WORRY OR RESTRAINT, I'D STILL BE INCREDIBLY PROUD OF YOU. YOU'RE COMING INTO YOUR OWN AS A MUSICIAN, AND THE SOUNDS OF YOU PLAYING YOUR VIOLIN OR JUST SINGING AROUND THE HOUSE ARE THE LOVELIEST, MOST SOOTHING SOUNDS IN ALL THE WORLD. I WISH I COULD GIVE YOU A BETTER STAGE, AMERICA. YOU DESERVE SO MUCH MORE THAN STANDING IN THE SHADOWS AT STUFFY PARTIES. I KEEP HOPING YOU'LL BE ONE OF THE LUCKY ONES, THE BREAKOUTS. I THINK KOTA HAS A CHANCE AT IT, TOO. HE'S GIFTED AT WHAT HE DOES. BUT I FEEL LIKE KOTA WOULD FIGHT FOR IT, AND I'M NOT SURE YOU HAVE THAT INSTINCT IN YOU. YOU WERE NEVER A CUTTHROAT KIND OF GIRL, THE WAY SOME OF THE OTHER LOWERS CAN BE. AND THAT'S PART OF WHY I LOVE YOU, TOO.

YOU'RE GOOD, AMERICA. YOU'D BE SURPRISED AT HOW RARE THAT IS IN THIS WORLD. I'M NOT SAYING YOU'RE PERFECT; HAVING DEALT WITH SOME OF YOUR TEMPER TANTRUMS, I KNOW THAT'S FAR FROM THE TRUTH! BUT YOU'RE KIND, AND YOU ACHE FOR THINGS TO BE FAIR. YOU'RE GOOD, AND I SUSPECT YOU SEE THINGS IN THIS WORLD THAT NO ONE ELSE SEES, NOT EVEN ME.

AND I WISH I COULD TELL YOU HOW MUCH I SEE.

AS I'VE BEEN WRITING THESE LETTERS TO YOUR BROTHERS AND SISTERS, I'VE FELT THE NEED TO PASS ON WISDOM. I SEE IN THEM,

EVEN IN LITTLE GERAD, THE THINGS IN THEIR PERSONALITIES THAT COULD MAKE EVERY YEAR MORE DIFFICULT IF THEY DON'T MAKE THE EFFORT TO FIGHT AGAINST THE HARDNESS IN LIFE. I DON'T QUITE FEEL THAT URGE WITH YOU.

I SENSE THAT YOU WON'T LET THE WORLD PUSH YOU INTO A LIFE YOU DON'T WANT. MAYBE I'M WRONG, SO LET ME AT LEAST SAY THIS: FIGHT, AMERICA. YOU MIGHT NOT WANT TO FIGHT FOR THE THINGS THAT MOST OTHERS WOULD FIGHT FOR, LIKE MONEY OR NOTORIETY, BUT FIGHT ALL THE SAME. WHATEVER IT IS THAT YOU WANT, AMERICA, GO AFTER IT WITH ALL THAT YOU HAVE IN YOU.

IF YOU CAN DO THAT, IF YOU CAN KEEP FROM LETTING FEAR MAKE YOU SETTLE FOR SECOND BEST, THEN I CAN'T ASK FOR ANYTHING MORE FROM YOU AS A PARENT. LIVE YOUR LIFE. BE AS HAPPY AS YOU CAN BE, LET GO OF THE THINGS THAT DON'T MATTER, AND FIGHT.

I LOVE YOU, KITTEN. SO MUCH THAT I CAN'T FIND THE WORDS TO SAY IT. I COULD PAINT IT MAYBE, BUT I CAN'T FIT A CANVAS IN THIS ENVELOPE. EVEN THEN IT WOULD NEVER DO YOU JUSTICE. I LOVE YOU BEYOND PAINT, BEYOND MELODIES, BEYOND WORDS. AND I HOPE YOU WILL ALWAYS FEEL THAT, EVEN WHEN I'M NOT AROUND TO TELL YOU SO.

LOVE, DAD

I wasn't sure at what point I had started crying, but it was hard to make out the last of the letter. I wished so badly I'd had a chance to tell him I loved him the same way. And for a minute there, I could feel it, that warmth of absolute acceptance.

I looked up and saw that Kenna was crying, too, still trying to make her way through the letter. Kota looked confused as he flipped past the pages, seeming to go over them again.

Turning away, I pulled out the little note, hoping it wasn't nearly as touching as his letter. I wasn't sure I could take any more of that today.

AMERICA,

I'M SORRY. WHEN WE VISITED, I WENT TO YOUR ROOM AND FOUND ILLÉA'S DIARY. YOU DIDN'T TELL ME IT WAS THERE; I JUST FIGURED IT OUT. IF THERE'S ANY TROUBLE FROM THIS, THE BLAME IS MINE. AND I'M SURE THERE WILL BE REPERCUSSIONS BECAUSE OF WHO I AM AND BECAUSE OF WHO I TOLD. I HATE TO BETRAY YOU THAT WAY, BUT TRUST THAT I DID IT HOPING THAT YOUR FUTURE AND EVERYONE ELSE'S COULD BE BETTER.

LOOK UNTO THE NORTH STAR,

YOUR EVERLASTING GUIDE.

LET TRUTH, HONOR, ALL THAT'S RIGHT,

BE ALWAYS BY YOUR SIDE.

LOVE YOU,

SHALOM

I stood there for several minutes, trying to riddle this out. Repercussions? Who he was and who he had told? And what was with that poem?

Slowly, August's words came back to me, that my display on the *Report* wasn't how they knew the diaries existed and how they knew more of what was inside than I'd exposed. . . .

Who I am . . . who I told . . . look unto the North Star . . .

I stared at Dad's signature and remembered the way he signed the letters he'd sent me at the palace. I always thought the way he wrote his *o*'s looked funny. They were eight-point stars: North Stars.

The scribble over the *i* in my name. Did he want it to mean something to me, too? Did it already mean something because we'd talked to August and Georgia?

August and Georgia! His compass: eight points. The designs on her jacket weren't flowers at all. Both different but absolutely stars. The boy Kriss got at the Convicting. That wasn't a cross on his neck.

This was how they identified their own.

My father was a Northern rebel.

I felt as if I'd seen the star in other places. Maybe walking in the market or even in the palace. Had this been staring me in the face for years?

Stricken, I looked up; Aspen was waiting there, his eyes holding questions he couldn't ask aloud.

My dad was a rebel. A half-destroyed history book hidden in his room, friends at his funeral I knew nothing about . . . a daughter named America. If I'd paid attention at all, I would have seen it years ago.

"That's it?" Kota asked, sounding offended. "What the hell am I supposed to do with that?"

I turned away from Aspen, focusing on Kota.

"What's wrong?" Mom asked, coming back into the room with some tea.

"Dad's letter. He left me this house. What am I supposed to do with this dump?" He stood up, gripping the pages in his hand.

"Kota, Dad wrote that before you moved out," Kenna explained, still emotional. "He was trying to provide for you."

"Well, he failed then, didn't he? When have we ever not been hungry? This house sure as hell wouldn't have changed things. I did that for myself." Kota threw the papers across the room, and they flitted to the floor haphazardly.

Running his fingers through his hair, he huffed out a sigh. "Do we have any liquor in this place? Aspen, go get me a drink," he demanded, not even looking in Aspen's direction.

I turned and saw Aspen's face as a thousand emotions flickered across it: irritation, sympathy, pride, acceptance. He started toward the kitchen.

"Stop!" I commanded. Aspen paused.

Kota looked up, frustrated. "That's what he does, America."

"No, he doesn't," I spat. "You might have forgotten, but Aspen's a Two now. It would do you better to get *him* something to drink. Not just for his status, but for everything he's been doing for all of us."

A sly smirk fell across Kota's face. "Huh. Does Maxon know? Does he know this is still going on?" he asked, waving a lazy finger between the two of us.

My heart stopped beating.

"What would he do, you think? The caning thing's been done, and lots of people say that girl didn't get it bad enough for what she did." Kota placed his satisfied hands on his hips, staring us down.

I couldn't speak. Aspen didn't either, and I wondered if our silence was helping us or condemning us.

Finally Mom broke the silence. "Is it true?"

I needed to think; I needed to find the right way to explain this. Or a way to fight it, because really, it wasn't true . . . not anymore.

"Aspen, go check on Lucy," I said. He started walking until Kota protested.

"No, he stays!"

I lost it. "I say he goes! Now sit!"

The tone in my voice, unlike anything I had ever heard before, startled everyone. Mom plopped down immediately, shocked. Aspen made his way down the hall, and Kota slowly, begrudgingly sat as well.

I tried to focus.

"Yes, before the Selection, I was dating Aspen. We were planning on telling everyone once we saved up the money to get married. Before I left, we broke it off, and then I met Maxon. I care about Maxon, and even though Aspen is with me a lot, nothing is happening there." *Anymore,* I amended in my head.

Then I turned to Kota. "If you think, even for a second, you can twist my past into something and try to blackmail me with it, think again. You once asked if I told Maxon about you, and I did. He knows exactly what a spineless, ungrateful jackass you are."

Kota pressed his lips together, ready to boil over. I spoke quickly.

"And you should know that he adores me," I said grandly. "If you think he'd take your word over mine, you might be surprised by how quickly my suggestion of putting a cane to your hands would happen if I chose to make it so. You want to test me?"

He clenched his fists, clearly debating. If I was right and his hands got injured, that would be the end of his career.

"Good," I said. "And if I hear you say another unkind word about Dad, I might do it anyway. You were damn lucky to have a father who loved you so much. He left you the house, and he could have taken it away after you left, but he didn't. He still had hope for you, which is more than I can say."

I stormed off, heading into my room and slamming the door. I'd forgotten that Gerad, May, Lucy, and Aspen would be waiting for me there.

"You were dating Aspen?" May asked.

I gasped.

"You were a little loud," Aspen said.

I looked to Lucy. There were tears in her eyes. I didn't want to make her keep another secret, and clearly it pained her to think about it. She was so honest and loyal, how could I ask her to choose between me and the family she was sworn to serve?

"I'll tell Maxon when we go back," I said to Aspen. "I thought I was protecting you, I thought I was protecting myself, but all I've been doing is lying. And if Kota knows, then maybe other people do. I want to be the one to tell him."

CHAPTER 26

I SPENT THE REST OF the day hiding in my room. I didn't want to see Kota's accusing face or deal with Mom's questions. The worst was Lucy. She looked so sad to find out that I'd kept this secret from her. I didn't even want her serving me, and it seemed she was mostly fine with helping Mom however she could or playing with May.

I had too much to think about to have her around anyway. I kept rehearsing my speech to Maxon. I was trying to figure out the best way to confess this news. Should I leave out anything Aspen and I had done at the palace? If I did and he asked about it, would that be worse than me admitting to it in the first place?

And then I would get distracted thinking about Dad, wondering just what he'd said and done over the years. Were all those people I didn't know at his funeral really other rebels?

Could there possibly be that many?

Should I tell Maxon about that? Would he want me if he knew my family had rebel ties? It seemed as if some of the other Elite were there because of who they were linked to. What if my link undid me? It seemed unlikely now that we were so close to August, but still.

I wondered what Maxon was doing now. Working, maybe. Or finding a way to avoid it. I wasn't there for him to take walks with or sit with. I wondered if Kriss was taking my place.

I covered my eyes, trying to think. How was I supposed to get through all this?

There was a knock on my door. I didn't know if what was coming would make things better or worse, but I told the visitor to come in anyway.

Kenna walked in, and, for the first time since I'd come home, Astra was nowhere in sight.

"You okay?"

I shook my head, and the tears came. She walked in and sat beside me on the bed, wrapping an arm around me.

"I miss Dad. His letter was so . . ."

"I know," she said. "He hardly even spoke when he was here. But he left us with all these words. Part of me is glad. I don't know if I would remember it all if he hadn't written it down."

"Yeah." In that I had the answer to a question I was afraid to ask. No one else knew Dad had been a rebel.

"So . . . you and Aspen?"

"It's over, I swear."

"I believe you. When you're on TV, you should see the way you look at Maxon. Even that other girl, Celeste?" She rolled her eyes.

I smiled to myself.

"She tries to look like she's in love with him, but you can see it's not real. Or at least not as real as she wishes it was."

I snorted. "You have no idea how right you are on that one."

"I was wondering how long that had been happening. With Aspen, I mean."

"Two years. It started after you got married and Kota moved out. We'd been meeting in the tree house about once a week. We were saving up to get married."

"You were in love then?"

Shouldn't I have been able to answer right away? Shouldn't I have been able to tell her that I knew without a doubt that I'd loved Aspen? But now it didn't really seem that way. Maybe it was, but time and distance made it look different.

"I think so. But it doesn't feel . . ."

"It doesn't feel like things with Maxon?" she guessed.

I shook my head. "It just seems so strange now. For the longest time, Aspen was the only person I could imagine being with. I was ready to be a Six. And now?"

"And now you're five minutes away from being the next princess?" Her deadpan voice made the whole thing funny, and I laughed with her at the drastic change in my life.

"Thanks for that."

"That's what sisters are for."

I looked into her eyes and sensed that this hurt her somehow. "Sorry I didn't tell you sooner."

"You're telling me now."

"It wasn't because I didn't trust you. It was part of what made it special, I think. Keeping him a secret." Saying it out loud, I realized that it was true. Yes, I had feelings for him, but there were other things that surrounded us that made having Aspen that much sweeter: the secrecy, the rush of being touched, the thought of having something worth working toward.

"I understand, America, I really do. I just hope you never felt like you *had* to keep it a secret. Because I'm here for you."

I exhaled, and so many of my worries seemed to leave with that breath. At least for a moment. I propped my head on Kenna's shoulder, and it was nice to be able to think.

"So, is anything going on between you and Aspen anymore? How does he feel about you?"

I sighed, sitting up. "He keeps trying to tell me something, something about how he's always loved me. And I know I should tell him that it doesn't matter and that I love Maxon, but . . ."

"But?"

"What if Maxon picks someone else? I can't walk away from this with nothing. At least if Aspen still thinks there's a chance, maybe we could try again when everything's over."

She stared at me. "You're using Aspen as a safety net?"

I buried my head in my hands. "I know, I know. It's awful, isn't it?"

"America, you're better than that. And if you've ever cared about him at all, you need to tell him the truth just as badly as you need to tell Maxon the truth."

A knock came at the door. "Come in."

I blushed a little as Aspen walked in the doorway, a dejected Lucy close behind.

"You need to get dressed and packed," he said.

"Is something wrong?" I stood up, suddenly tense.

"All I know is that Maxon wants you back at the palace immediately."

I sighed, confused. I was supposed to have one more day. Kenna wrapped her arm around me again and gave me a tiny squeeze before heading back to the living room. Aspen left, and Lucy merely grabbed her uniform and went to the bathroom to change, closing the door behind her.

Alone again, I thought over everything. Kenna was right. I already knew how I felt about Maxon, and it was time to do what Dad had told me to do, what I'd meant to be doing this whole time: I was going to fight.

And because it felt like the bigger task, I would talk to Maxon first. Once that was settled, no matter the outcome, then I would figure out what to say to Aspen.

It had happened so slowly that it took me a while to realize how much we'd changed. But I'd known for weeks and had still kept my feelings to myself. I had to do the right thing and tell him so. I had to let go of Aspen.

I reached into my suitcase, hunting for the bundle at the bottom. Once I found the ball of fabric, I unrolled it, taking out my jar. The penny wasn't so lonely in there now with the bracelet, but that didn't matter.

I took the jar and placed it on my windowsill, leaving it where it should have stayed a long time ago.

I spent the majority of the plane ride going over my confession to Maxon. I was dreading this, but we could only move forward if he knew the truth.

I looked up from my comfy seat near the rear of the plane. Aspen and Lucy were sitting toward the front on opposite sides of the aisle, deep in conversation. Lucy looked upset still, and she seemed to be giving Aspen some sort of instructions. He was quiet as he took in her words, nodding at her suggestions. She retreated into her seat, and Aspen stood. I ducked back, hoping he didn't notice me spying.

I tried to look very interested in my book until he approached.

"The pilot says another half hour or so," he informed me.

"All right. Good."

He hesitated. "I'm sorry about everything with Kota."

"You don't have anything to be sorry for. He's just mean."

"No, I do. Years ago he teased me for having a crush on you, and I brushed it off; but I think he saw through it. He must have been paying attention since then. I should have been more careful or something. I should have—"

"Aspen."

257

"Yes?"

"It'll be fine. I'm going to tell Maxon the truth, and I'm going to take responsibility for this. You've got people at home depending on you. If something happens to you—"

"Mer, you tried to keep me from this, and I was too stubborn to listen. It's my fault."

"No, it's not."

He took a deep breath. "Listen . . . I need to tell you something. I know it's going to be difficult, but you need to know. When I told you I'd always love you, I meant it. And I—"

"Stop," I pleaded. I knew I had to tell him the truth, but I could only deal with one confession at a time. "I can't handle this right now. I just had my world turned upside down, and I'm about to do something I'm terrified to do. I need you to give me some room right now."

Aspen didn't look happy with this decision, but he let me make it all the same.

"As you wish, my lady." He walked away, and I felt even worse than I had before.

CHAPTER 27

Walking back into the palace felt impossibly right. A maid I'd never seen before was there to take my coat, and Aspen was next to a guard, explaining quietly that he'd give a full report on the trip in the morning. I started up the stairs, but another maid stopped me.

"Don't you want to go to the reception, miss?"

"Excuse me?" Was I supposed to have some fantastic homecoming or something?

"In the Women's Room, my lady. I'm sure they're waiting for you."

That was less of an explanation than I was hoping for, but I climbed back down the stairs and headed around the corner to the Women's Room. Strolling down the familiar halls was more comforting than I could have imagined. Of course I still missed my dad, but it was nice not to see things that made me think of him everywhere I turned. The only thing that would have made this homecoming better was Maxon walking here with me.

I was toying with the possibility of sending for him when I heard the wild noise coming from the Women's Room. I was confused by the sound. By the volume, half of Illéa was waiting in there.

Tentatively, I opened the door. The second Tiny—what was she doing here?—caught a glimpse of my hair, she called out to the room.

"She's here! America's back!"

The room exploded with cheers, and I was so confused. Emmica, Ashley, Bariel . . . everyone was here. I hunted, but I knew it was pointless. Marlee wouldn't be invited to this.

I was rushed by Celeste, who embraced me tightly. "Ahh, you bitch, I *knew* you'd make it!"

"What?" I asked.

She didn't get her words out fast enough. A split second later, Kriss was hugging me and half screaming in my ear. The smell on her breath said she'd been drinking quite a bit, and the glass in her hand confirmed she wasn't planning on stopping.

"It's us!" she yelled. "Maxon's announcing his engagement tomorrow! It's one of us!"

"Are you sure?"

"Elise and I got the boot last night, but he sent for all the girls to come back and celebrate, so we stayed," Celeste confirmed. "Elise isn't taking it well; you know how it is with her family. She thinks she failed."

"What about you?" I asked nervously.

She shrugged and smiled. "Eh."

I laughed at that, and a moment later a drink was shoved in my hand.

"To Kriss and America, the last girls standing!" someone yelled.

I was dizzy with the news. He'd decided to end it, to send everyone home. And he did it while I was away. Did that mean he missed me? Did that mean he realized he was fine without me?

"Drink!" Celeste insisted, tipping the glass back for me. I downed the champagne and came up coughing. Between the jet lag, the emotional stress of the last few days, and the sudden intake of alcohol, I was immediately giddy.

I watched as girls danced on the couches, celebrating even though they had lost. Celeste was in a corner with Anna; it looked as if she was apologizing repeatedly for her actions. Elise crept in quietly and came to offer me a hug before retreating again. It was a blur of excitement, and I found myself happy even though I wasn't totally certain of the outcome in front of me.

I turned around, and Kriss was suddenly there, embracing me.

"Okay," she said. "Let's promise that tomorrow, no matter what, we'll be happy for each other."

"I think that's a good plan," I shouted over the din. I laughed and lowered my eyes. In that quick second, a serious realization flooded me. That flash of silver on her neck suddenly meant so much more than it had a few days ago.

I sucked in a breath, and she looked at me with an expression that asked what was wrong. Even though it was rude and abrupt, I pulled her out of the room and down the hall.

"Where are we going?" she asked. "America, what's wrong?"

I dragged her around the corner and into the ladies' bathroom, double-checking to make sure we were alone before speaking.

"You're a rebel," I accused.

"What?" she said, a little too rehearsed. "You're crazy." But her hand fluttered to her neck, giving her away.

"I know what that star means, Kriss, so don't lie to me," I said calmly.

After a calculated pause she sighed. "I haven't done anything illegal. I'm not mounting protests anywhere; I just support the cause."

"Fine," I spat. "But how much of your part in the Selection is you wanting Maxon and how much is your group wanting one of their own on the throne?"

She was quiet for a moment, choosing her words. Clenching her jaw, she walked over to the door and locked it. "If you must know, yes, I was . . . *presented* to the king as an option. I'm sure you've guessed by now that the lottery was a joke."

I nodded.

"The king was—and still is—unaware of how many Northerners were promoted while the choice was being made. I was the only one of all the hopefuls to make it through, and, at first, I was completely dedicated to my cause. I didn't understand Maxon, and it didn't seem like he wanted me at all. But then I got to know him, and I was really sad about him not taking an interest in me. After Marlee left and you lost your hold on him, I saw him in a totally new light.

"You might think that my motives for coming here were wrong, and maybe you're right. But my reasons for being here *now* are completely different. I love Maxon, and I'm still fighting for him. And we can do great things together. So if you're thinking about trying to blackmail me or sell me out, forget it. I'm not backing down. Do you understand me?"

Kriss had never spoken so forcefully, and I didn't know if the reason was her absolute faith in her words or the heavy amount of champagne. She looked so fierce at the moment, I wasn't sure what to say.

I wanted to tell her that Maxon and I could do great things, too, that we'd probably already done more than she could guess. But now wasn't the time to brag. Besides, she and I had a lot in common. I came here for my family; she came here for a family of sorts. That got us through the doorway and into Maxon's heart. What good would it do us to tear each other apart now?

She took my silence as an agreement to behave, and she relaxed her stance.

"Good. Now, if you'll excuse me, I'm going back to the party."

Giving me a cold stare, she swept out of the room, leaving me torn. Should I keep my mouth shut? Should I at least let someone know? Was this even a bad thing?

I sighed and left the bathroom. I wasn't in the mood to celebrate anymore, so I took the back stairway up to my room.

Even though I wanted to see Anne and Mary, I was glad no one was there. I flopped onto the bed and tried to think. So Kriss was a rebel. Nothing dangerous, according to her, but I still wondered what that meant exactly. She must be who August and Georgia were talking about. What had ever made me think it was Elise?

Had Kriss helped them get into the palace? Had she pointed them in the direction of things they had been looking for? I had my secrets in the palace, but I'd never stopped to think about what the other girls could be hiding. I should have though.

Because what could I say now? If there was something real between Maxon and Kriss, any attempt to expose her would look like a desperate last effort to win. And even if that worked, that wasn't how I wanted to get Maxon.

I wanted him to know I loved him.

A knock came at the door, and I considered not answering it. If it was Kriss coming to explain more or one of the girls trying to drag me downstairs, that wasn't anything I wanted to deal with. Eventually, I heaved myself upright and went to the door.

Maxon stood there with a stuffed envelope and a small, gift-wrapped package.

In the second it took us to register that we were in the same place again, it felt as if the whole space charged with a magical kind of electricity, making me acutely aware of just how much I missed him.

"Hi," he said. He seemed a little stunned, as if he couldn't think of anything more to say.

"Hi."

We stared.

"Do you want to come in?" I offered.

"Oh. Um, yes, I do." Something was off. He was different, nervous maybe.

I stood aside, making room for him to enter. He looked around the space as if it had changed somehow since the last time he saw it.

He turned to gaze at me. "How are you feeling?"

I realized he probably meant about my dad, and I reminded myself that the end of the Selection wasn't the only shift in my world right now. "Okay. It doesn't really feel like he's gone, especially now that I'm here. I feel like I could write him a letter, and he'd still get it."

He gave me a sympathetic smile. "How's your family?"

I sighed. "Mom is holding it together, and Kenna is a rock. It's mostly May and Gerad I'm worried about. Kota couldn't have been any meaner about the whole thing. It's like he didn't love him at all, and I don't understand that," I confessed. "You met my dad. He was so sweet."

"He was," Maxon agreed. "I'm glad I at least got to meet him. I can see bits of him in you, you know."

"Really?"

"Absolutely!" He put his parcels in one hand, holding me with his free one. He walked me over to the bed, sitting next to me. "Your sense of humor, for one. And your tenacity. When he and I spoke during his visit, he grilled me. It was nerve-racking, but kind of funny at the same time. You've never just let me off the hook either.

"Of course, you have his eyes and I think his nose, too. And I can see your optimism beaming out sometimes. He gave me that impression as well."

I soaked up the words, holding on to all the parts of me that were like him. And here I thought Maxon didn't know him.

"All I'm saying is, it's okay to be sad about this, but you can be sure the best of him is still around," he concluded.

I threw my arms around him, and he held me with his free hand. "Thank you."

"I mean it."

"I know you do. Thanks." I moved back beside him and decided to change the subject before I got too emotional. "What's this all about?" I asked, nodding toward his full hand.

"Oh." Maxon fumbled with his thoughts a moment.

"These are for you. A late Christmas present."

He held up the envelope, thick with folded papers. "I can't believe I'm actually giving this to you, and you have to wait to look at them until I'm not here, but . . . it's for you to keep."

"Okay," I said questioningly as he set the envelope on my bedside table.

"This is a little less embarrassing," he added playfully, handing me the gift. "Sorry the wrapping is so bad."

"It's fine," I lied, trying not laugh at the crooked seams and tearing at the paper on the back.

Inside, the gift was a frame holding a picture of a house. Not just any house, but a beautiful one. It was a warm yellow color with plush grass that I wanted to put my feet in just from looking at the print. The windows were tall and wide on both stories, with trees offering shade to a section of the lawn. One tree even had a swing hanging from it.

I tried not to look at the house but at the photo itself. I was sure that this little piece of art was something Maxon made himself, though I couldn't guess when he'd gotten out of the palace to find its subject.

"It's beautiful," I admitted. "Did you take it yourself?"

"Oh, no." He laughed, shaking his head. "The picture isn't the gift; the house is."

I tried to let that sink in. "What?"

"I thought you'd want your family close by. It's a short drive away, with plenty of room. Your sister and her little family would even be comfortable there, I think."

"Wha . . . I . . ." I stared at him, searching for clarification.

Patient as ever, Maxon gave me the explanation he thought I already understood. "You told me to send everyone home. I did. I had to keep one other girl—those are the rules—but . . . you said that if I could prove I loved you . . ."

". . . It's me?"

"Of course it's you."

I was speechless. I laughed in shock and started giving him kisses and giggling between each one. Maxon, so pleased with the affection, took every kiss and laughed along with me.

"We're getting married?" I yelled, kissing him again.

"Yes, we're getting married." He chuckled and let me attack him in my excitement. I realized then that I was in his lap. I didn't remember getting there.

I kissed him on and on . . . and somewhere in there the laughing stopped. After a while, the smiling dwindled. The kisses turned from playful to something much deeper. When I pulled away and looked into his eyes, they were intense, focused.

Maxon held me close, and I could feel his heart racing against my chest. Guided by a deep hunger for him, I pushed his suit coat down his back, and he helped me as best as he could while holding on to me. I let my shoes fall to the floor, thudding a little song on their way down. I felt Maxon's legs shift underneath me as he slipped his off as well.

Without breaking our kiss, he lifted me, crawling deeper onto the bed and laying me down gently somewhere near the middle. His lips traveled down my neck as I loosened his tie, throwing it somewhere near our shoes.

"You're breaking a lot of rules, Miss Singer."

"You're the prince. You can just pardon me."

He chuckled darkly, his lips at my throat, my ear, my cheek. I untucked his shirt, fumbling with the buttons. He helped with the last few, sitting up to toss it aside. The last time I'd seen Maxon without his shirt on, I didn't get to really appreciate it because of the circumstance. But now . . .

I ran my fingers lightly down his stomach, admiring how strong he was. When my hand got to his belt, I gripped it and pulled him back down. He came willingly, dragging a hand up my leg, resting it comfortably on my thigh underneath the layers of my dress.

I was going crazy, wanting so much more of him, aching to know if he'd let me have it. Without even thinking, I reached around and dug my fingers into his back.

Immediately, he stopped kissing me, pulling back to look at me.

"What?" I whispered, terrified to break this moment.

"Does it . . . does it repulse you?" he asked nervously.

"What do you mean?"

"My back."

I ran a hand down his cheek, staring directly into his eyes, wanting to leave him with no doubt about how I felt.

"Maxon, some of those marks are on your back so they wouldn't be on mine, and I love you for them."

He stopped breathing for a second. "What did you say?"

I smiled. "I love you."

"One more time, please? I just—"

I took his face in both of my hands. "Maxon Schreave, I love you. I love you."

"And I love you, America Singer. With all that I am, I love you."

He kissed me again, and I let my hands move to his back, and this time he didn't pause. He moved his hands beneath me, and I felt his fingers playing with the back of my dress.

"How many damn buttons does this thing have?" he complained.

"I know! It's—"

Maxon sat up, placing his hands along the bust line of my dress. With one firm pull, he ripped my dress down the front, exposing the slip underneath.

There was a charged silence as Maxon took that in. Slowly, his eyes returned to mine. Without breaking that contact, I sat up, sliding the sleeves of my dress down my back. It took a little bit of work to get it all off; and, by the end of it, Maxon and I were kneeling on my bed, my hardly covered chest pressed to his, kissing slowly.

I wanted to stay up all night with him, to explore this new feeling we'd discovered. It felt as if everything else in the world was gone . . . until we heard a crash in the hall. Maxon stared at the door, seeming to expect it to burst open at any second. He was tense, more frightened than I'd ever seen him.

"It's not him," I whispered. "It's probably one of the girls stumbling to her room, or a maid cleaning something. It's okay."

He finally released a breath I didn't see he was holding and fell back onto the bed. He draped an arm over his eyes, frustrated or exhausted or maybe both.

"I can't, America. Not like this."

"But it's okay, Maxon. We're safe here." I lay down beside him, cuddling onto his free shoulder.

He shook his head. "I want to let all the walls down with you. You deserve that. And I can't now." He looked over to me. "I'm sorry."

"It's okay." But I couldn't hide my disappointment.

"Don't be sad. I want to take you on a proper honeymoon. Someplace warm and private. No duties, no cameras, no guards." He wrapped his arms around me. "It will be so much better that way. And I can really spoil you."

It didn't sound so bad to wait when he put it that way, but as always, I pushed back. "You can't spoil me, Maxon. I don't want anything."

We were nose to nose by then. "Oh, I know. I don't intend on giving you things. Well," he amended, "I do intend on giving you things, but that's not what I mean. I'm going to love you more than any man has ever loved a woman, more than you ever dreamed you could be loved. I promise you that."

The kisses that followed were sweet and hopeful, like our first ones. I could feel it, the promise he'd just made, starting now. And I was afraid and excited by the possibility of being loved so much.

"Maxon?"

"Yes?"

"Would you stay with me tonight?" I asked. Maxon raised an eyebrow, and I giggled. "I'll behave, I promise. Just . . . would you sleep here?"

He looked to the ceiling, debating. Finally he caved. "I will. But I'll need to leave early."

"Okay."

"Okay."

Maxon took off his pants and socks, neatly stacking his clothes so they wouldn't be too wrinkled in the morning. He crawled back into the bed, snuggling up with his stomach against my back. One of his arms he laced under my neck and the other he gently wrapped around me.

I loved my bed at the palace. The pillows were like clouds, and the mattress cradled me into it. I was never too warm or too cold under my covers, and the feeling of my nightgown against my skin was almost as if I was wearing air.

But I'd never felt so settled as I did with Maxon's arms around me.

He placed a gentle kiss behind my ear. "Sleep well, my America."

"I love you," I said quietly.

He held me a little tighter. "I love you."

I lay there, letting the happiness of the moment sink into me. It seemed only seconds later that Maxon's breathing was slow and steady. He was already asleep.

Maxon never slept.

I must have made him feel safer than I'd imagined. And, after all my worries about how his father acted toward me, he made me feel safe, too.

I sighed, promising myself that we'd talk about Aspen tomorrow. It would need to happen before the ceremony, and I felt sure I knew how to explain things in the best way. For now, I would enjoy this tiny bubble of peace and rest securely in the arms of the man I loved.

CHAPTER 28

I WOKE TO THE FEELING of Maxon sliding an arm around me. Somewhere in the night, I ended up with my head on his chest, and the slow sound of his heartbeat was echoing in my ear.

Without a word, he kissed my hair and went to hold me closer. I couldn't believe this was happening. I was here with Maxon, together, waking up in my bed. This morning he would be giving me a ring. . . .

"We could wake up like this every day," he mumbled.

I giggled. "You're reading my mind."

He sighed contentedly. "How are you feeling, my dear?"

"I feel like punching you for calling me 'my dear' mostly." I poked his bare stomach.

Smiling, he crawled to sit over me. "Fine then. My darling? My pet? My love?"

"Any of those would work, so long as you've reserved it solely for me," I said, my hands mindlessly wandering his chest, his arms. "What am I supposed to call you?"

"Your Royal Husbandness. It's required by law, I'm afraid." His own hands glided over my skin, finding a delicate spot on my neck.

"Don't!" I said, shying away.

His responding smile was triumphant. "You're ticklish!"

Despite my protests, he started running his fingers all over me, making me shriek at the playful touching.

Nearly as quickly as I began squealing, I stopped. A guard rushed through the door, gun drawn.

This time I screamed, pulling up the sheet to cover myself. I was so frightened that it took me a moment to realize the determined eyes of the guard belonged to Aspen. It felt as if my face caught on fire, I was so humiliated.

Aspen looked stricken. He couldn't even put a sentence together as his eyes flashed back and forth between Maxon in his underwear and me draped in a sheet to cover mine.

My shock was finally broken by a deep laugh.

For as terrified as I was, Maxon was the picture of ease. In fact, he seemed pleased at being caught. His voice was a little smug as he spoke. "I assure you, Leger, she's perfectly safe."

Aspen cleared his throat, unable to look either of us in the eye. "Of course, Your Majesty." He bowed and left, closing the door behind him.

I fell over, moaning into my pillow. I would never live that down. I should have told Aspen how I felt on the plane when I had the chance.

Maxon came to hug me. "Don't be so embarrassed. It's not as if we were naked. And it's bound to happen in the future."

"It's so humiliating," I wailed.

"To be caught in bed with me?" The pain in his voice was clear. I sat up and faced him.

"No! It's not you. It's just, I don't know, this was supposed to be private." I ducked my head and played with a piece of the blanket.

Tenderly, Maxon stroked my cheek. "I'm sorry." I looked up at him, his voice too sincere to ignore. "I know it's going to be hard for you, but people will always be looking at our lives now. For the first few years, there will probably be a lot of interference. All the kings and queens have had only children. Some by choice, I'm sure; but after the difficulty my mother had, they'll want to make sure we can even have a family."

He stopped talking, his eyes having moved from my face to a spot on the bed.

"Hey," I said, cupping his cheek. "I'm one of five, remember? I have really good genes in that department. It'll be all right."

He gave me a weak smile. "I really hope so. Partly because, yes, we're duty bound to produce heirs. But also . . . I want everything with you, America. I want the holidays and the birthdays, the busy seasons and lazy weekends. I want peanut butter fingerprints on my desk. I want inside jokes and fights and everything. I want a life with you."

Suddenly the last few minutes were erased from my mind. The growing warmth in my chest was pushing everything else away.

"I want that, too," I assured him.

He smiled. "How about we make it official in a few hours?"

I shrugged. "I guess I don't have any other plans today."

Maxon tackled me on the bed, covering me with kisses. I would have let him kiss me like that for hours, but Aspen seeing us together was enough. There was no way I'd be able to stop my maids from gushing if they saw this.

He got dressed, and I pulled on my robe. It should have felt funny, maybe, this little moment in the afterward. All I could think about, though, as I watched Maxon cover his scars with his shirt, was how incredible this was. This thing I'd never wanted to happen was making me so happy.

Maxon gave me one last kiss before opening the door and heading on his way. It was harder to part with him than I thought it would be. I told myself it was only for a few hours and that the wait would be so worth it.

Before I closed the door, I heard Maxon whisper, "The lady would appreciate your discretion, officer."

There was no response, but I could imagine Aspen's solemn nod. I stood behind the closed door, debating what to say, wondering if I should even say anything. Minutes passed, but I knew I had to face Aspen. I couldn't move forward with everything that was going to happen today without talking to him first. I drew in a breath and nervously opened the door. He tilted his head toward the hallway listening for voices. Finally Aspen turned his accusing eyes my way, and the weight of his stare broke me.

"I'm so sorry," I breathed.

He shook his head. "It's not as if I didn't know it was coming. It was just a shock."

"I should have told you," I said, stepping into the hall.

"It doesn't matter. I just can't believe you slept with him."

I put my hands on his chest. "I didn't, Aspen. I swear."

And then, at the last possible moment, everything was ruined.

Maxon stepped around the corner, holding Kriss by the hand. His eyes locked on to me, body pressed into Aspen with the intensity of my defense. I backed away, but not quickly enough. Aspen turned to face Maxon, prepared to give an excuse but still too stunned to speak.

Kriss's mouth dropped open, and she quickly covered it with a hand. Looking into Maxon's shocked eyes, I shook my head, trying to explain without words that this was all a misunderstanding.

It was only a second before Maxon regained his cool demeanor. "I found Kriss in the hall and was coming to explain my choice to you both before the cameras showed up, but it seems we have other things to discuss."

I looked at Kriss and was at least consoled by the fact that there was no triumph in her eyes. On the contrary, she looked sad for me.

"Kriss, would you please return to your room? Quietly?" Maxon instructed.

She curtsied and disappeared down the hall, eager to get away from the situation. Maxon took a deep breath before looking at us again.

"I knew it," he said. "I told myself I was crazy, because surely you would have told me if I was right. You were supposed to be honest with me." He rolled his eyes. "I cannot believe I didn't trust myself. From that first meeting, I knew it. The way you looked at him, how distracted you were. That damn bracelet you wore, the note on the wall, all those times when I thought I had you and then suddenly lost you again . . . it was you," he said, turning to Aspen.

"Your Majesty, this is my fault," Aspen lied. "I pursued her. She made it perfectly clear that she had no intentions of being in a relationship with anyone but you, but I went after her anyway."

Without responding to Aspen's excuses, he walked right up to him, looking him in the eye. "What's your name? Your first name?"

He swallowed. "Aspen."

"Aspen Leger," he said, testing the words. "Get out of my sight before I send you to New Asia to die."

Aspen's breath caught. "Your Majesty, I—"

"GO!"

Aspen looked at me once, then turned and walked away.

I stood there, silent and still, afraid to risk a peek into Maxon's eyes. When I finally did, he nudged his chin toward my room, and I went in, with him following me. I turned to see him close the door and run his hand through his hair one time. He moved to face me, and I saw his eyes catch on the unmade bed. He laughed humorlessly to himself.

"How long?" he asked quietly, still in control.

"Do you remember that fight—" I started.

Maxon erupted. "We've been fighting since the day we met, America! You'll have to be more specific!"

I shook where I stood. "After Kriss's party."

His eyes widened. "So basically since he got here," he said, something like sarcasm in his voice.

"Maxon, I'm so sorry. At first I was protecting him, and then I was protecting myself. And after Marlee was caned, I was afraid to tell you the truth. I couldn't lose you," I pleaded.

"Lose me? Lose *me*?" he asked, astonished. "You're going home with a small fortune, a new caste, and a man who is still pursuing you! I'm the one losing here today, America!"

The words took my breath away. "I'm going home?"

He looked at me as if I was an idiot for asking. "How many times am I supposed to let you break my heart, America? Do you think I'd honestly marry you, make you my princess, when you've been lying to me for most of our relationship? I refuse to torture myself for the rest of my life. You might have noticed, I get plenty of that already."

I erupted into sobs. "Maxon, please. I'm sorry; it's not what it looked like. I s-swear. I love you!"

He sauntered up to me, his eyes dead. "Of all the lies

you've told me, that's the one I resent the most."

"It's not—" The look in his eyes silenced me.

"Have your maids do their best. You should go out in style."

He walked past me, out the doorway and out of the future I'd held in my hands only a few minutes before. I turned back to the room, holding my stomach as if the core of my body was about to crack from the pain. I went over to the bed, rolling onto my side, no longer able to stand.

I cried, hoping to get the ache out of my body before the ceremony. How was I supposed to face that? I looked to the clock to see how much time I had . . . and saw the thick envelope Maxon had given me last night.

I decided this was the last piece of him I would ever have, so I opened the seal, desperate.

CHAPTER 29

December 25, 4:30 p.m.

Dear America,

It's been seven hours since you left. Twice now I've started to go to your room to ask how you liked your presents and then remembered you weren't here. I've gotten so used to you, it's strange that you aren't around, drifting down the halls. I've nearly called a few times, but I don't want to seem possessive. I don't want you to feel like I'm a cage to you. I remember how you said the palace was just that the first night you came here. I think, over time, you've felt freer, and I'd hate to ruin that freedom. I'm going to have to distract myself until you come back.

I decided to sit and write to you, hoping maybe it would feel like I was talking to you. It sort of does. I can imagine you sitting here, smiling at my idea, maybe shaking your head at me as if to say I'm being silly. You do that sometimes, did you know? I like that expression on you. You're the only person who wears it in a way that doesn't come across like you think I'm completely hopeless. You smile at my idiosyncrasies, accept that they exist, and continue to be my friend. And, in seven short hours, I've started to miss that.

I wonder what you've done in that time. I'm betting by now you've flown across the country, made it to your home, and are safe. I hope you are safe. I can't imagine what a comfort you must be to your family right now. The lovely daughter has finally returned!

I keep trying to picture your home. I remember you telling me it was small, that you had a tree house, and that your garage was where your father and sister did all their work. Beyond that I've had to resort to my imagination. I imagine you curled up in a hug with your sister or kicking around a ball with your little brother. I remember that, you know? That you said he liked to play ball.

I tried to imagine walking into your house with you. I would have liked that, to see you where you grew up. I would love to see your brother run around or be embraced by your mother. I think it would be comforting to sense the presence of people near you, floorboards creaking and doors shutting. I would have liked to sit in one part of the house and still probably be able to smell the kitchen. I've always imagined that real homes are full of the aromas of whatever's being cooked. I wouldn't do a scrap of work. Nothing having to do with armies or budgets or negotiations. I'd sit with you, maybe try to work on my photography while you played the piano. We'd be Fives together, like you said. I could join your family for dinner, talking over one another in a collection of conversations instead of whispering and waiting our turns. And maybe I'd sleep in a spare bed or on the couch. I'd sleep on the floor beside you if you'd let me.

I think about that sometimes. Falling asleep next to you, I mean, like we did in the safe room. It was nice to hear your breaths as they came and went, something quiet and close, keeping me from feeling so alone.

This letter has gotten foolish, and I think you know how I detest looking like a fool. But still I do. For you.

Maxon

December 25, 10:35 p.m.
Dear America,

It's nearly bedtime, and I'm trying to relax, but I can't. All I can think about is you. I'm terrified you're going to get hurt. I know someone would tell me if you weren't all right, and that has led to its own kind of paranoia. If anyone comes up to me to deliver a message, my heart stops for a moment, fearing the worst: You are gone. You're not coming back.

I wish you were here. I wish I could just see you.

You are never getting these letters. It's too humiliating.

I want you home. I keep thinking of your smile and worrying that I'll never see it again.

I hope you come back to me, America.

Merry Christmas.

Maxon

December 26, 10:00 a.m.

Dear America,

Miracle of miracles, I've made it through the night. When I finally woke up, I convinced myself I was worried for nothing. I vowed that I would focus on work today and not fret so much about you.

I got through breakfast and most of a meeting before thoughts of you consumed me. I told everyone I was sick and am now hiding in my room, writing to you, hoping this will make me feel like you're home again.

I'm so selfish. Today you will bury your father, and all I can think of is bringing you here. Having written that out, seeing it in ink, I feel like an absolute ass. You are exactly where you need to be. I think I already said this, but I'm sure you're such a comfort to your family.

You know, I haven't told this to you and I ought to have, but you've gotten so much stronger since I met you. I'm not arrogant enough to believe that has anything to do with me, but I think this experience has changed you. I know it's changed me. From the very beginning you had your own brand of fearlessness, and that has been polished into something strong. Where I used to imagine you as a girl with a bag full of stones, ready to throw them at any foe who crossed her path, you have become the stone itself. You are

steady and able. And I bet your family sees that in you. I should
have told you that. I hope you come home soon so I can.

    Maxon

December 26, 7:40 p.m.

Dear America,

    I've been thinking of our first kiss. I suppose I should say first
kisses, but what I mean is the second, the one I was actually invited
to give you. Did I ever tell you how I felt that night? It wasn't
just getting my first kiss ever; it was getting to have that first kiss
with you. I've seen so much, America, had access to the corners of
our planet. But never have I come across anything so painfully
beautiful as that kiss. I wish it was something I could catch with
a net or place in a book. I wish it was something I could save and
share with the world so I could tell the universe: this is what it's
like; this is how it feels when you fall.

    These letters are so embarrassing. I'll have to burn them before
you get home.

    Maxon

December 27, noon

America,

    I might as well tell you this since your maid will tell you
anyway. I've been thinking of the little things you do. Sometimes
you hum or sing when you walk around the palace. Sometimes
when I come up to your room, I hear the melodies you've saved
up in your heart spilling out the doorway. The palace seems empty
without them.

I also miss your smell. I miss your perfume drifting off your hair when you turn to laugh at me or your scent radiating on your skin when we walk through the garden. It's intoxicating.

So I went to your room to spray your perfume on my handkerchief, another silly trick to make me feel like you were here. And as I was leaving your room, Mary caught me. I'm not sure what she was looking after since you're not here; but she saw me, shrieked, and a guard came running in to see what was wrong. He had his staff gripped, and his eyes flashed threateningly. I was nearly attacked. All because I missed your smell.

December 27, 11:00 p.m.
My Dear America,

I've never written a love letter, so forgive me if I fail now. . . .

The simple thing would be to say that I love you. But, in truth, it's so much more than that. I want you, America. I need you.

I've held back so much from you out of fear. I'm afraid that if I show you everything at once, it will overwhelm you, and you'll run away. I'm afraid that somewhere in the back of your heart is a love for someone else that will never die. I'm afraid that I will make a mistake again, something so huge that you retreat into that silent world of yours. No scolding from a tutor, no lashing from my father, no isolation in my youth has ever hurt me so much as you separating yourself from me.

I keep thinking that it's there, waiting to come back and strike me. So I've held on to all my options, fearing that the moment I wipe them away, you will be standing there with your arms closed, happy to be my friend but unable to be my equal, my queen, my wife.

And for you to be my wife is all I want in the world. I love you. I was afraid to admit it for a long time, but I know it now.

I would never rejoice in the loss of your father, the sadness you've felt since he passed, or the emptiness I've experienced since you left. But I'm so grateful that you had to go. I'm not sure how long it would have taken for me to figure this out if I hadn't had to start trying to imagine a life without you. I know now, with absolute certainty, that is nothing I want.

I wish I was as true an artist as you so that I could find a way to tell you what you've become to me. America, my love, you are sunlight falling through trees. You are laughter that breaks through sadness. You are the breeze on a too-warm day. You are clarity in the midst of confusion.

You are not the world, but you are everything that makes the world good. Without you, my life would still exist, but that's all it would manage to do.

You said that to get things right one of us would have to take a leap of faith. I think I've discovered the canyon that must be leaped, and I hope to find you waiting for me on the other side.

I love you, America.

Yours forever,

Maxon

CHAPTER 30

THE GREAT ROOM WAS PACKED. For once, instead of the king and queen being the focal point of the room, it was Maxon. On a slightly raised platform, Maxon, Kriss, and I sat at an ornate table. I felt as if our positioning was deceitful. I was on Maxon's right. I always thought being on someone's right was a good thing, an honored position. But so far he'd spent the entire time speaking to Kriss. As if I didn't already know what was coming.

I tried to seem happy as I looked around the room. It was packed. Gavril, of course, was in a corner, speaking into a camera, narrating the events as they happened.

Ashley smiled and waved, and beside her Anna winked at me. I gave them a nod, still too nervous to speak. Toward the back of the room, in deceptively clean clothes, August, Georgia, and some of the other Northern rebels sat at a table by themselves. Of course Maxon would want them here to meet his new wife. Little did he know she was one of their own.

They surveyed the room tensely, as if they feared any second a guard would recognize them and attack. The guards didn't seem to be paying attention though. In fact, this was the first time I'd ever seen them look so poorly focused, eyes meandering around the room, several of them on edge. I'd even noticed that one or two hadn't shaved and looked a little rough. It was a big event though. Maybe they were just rushed.

My eyes flitted over to Queen Amberly, speaking with her sister Adele and her gaggle of children. She looked radiant. She'd been waiting for this day for so long. She would love Kriss like her own. For a moment, I was so jealous of that fact.

I turned and scanned the faces of the Selected again, and this time my eyes landed on Celeste. I could see the clear question in her eyes: What are you so worried about? I gave her a minuscule shake of my head, letting her know that I'd lost. She sent me a thin smile and mouthed the words *It'll be okay.* I nodded, and I tried to believe her. She turned away, laughing at something someone said; and I finally looked to my right, taking in the face of the guard stationed closest to our table.

Aspen was distracted though. He was looking around the room like so many of the other men in uniform, but he seemed to be trying to think of something. It was as if he was doing a puzzle in his head. I wished he would look my way, maybe try to explain wordlessly what he was worried about, but he didn't.

"Trying to arrange a time to meet later?" Maxon asked, and I whipped my head back.

"No, of course not."

"It's not like it matters. Kriss's family will be here this afternoon for a small celebration, and yours will be here to take you home. They don't like for the last loser to be alone. She tends to get dramatic."

He was so cold, so distant. It was as if it wasn't even Maxon at all.

"You can keep that house if you want. It's been paid for. I'd like my letters back though."

"I read them," I whispered. "I loved them."

He huffed as if it was a joke. "Don't know what I was thinking."

"Please don't do this. Please. I love you." My face was crumpling.

"Don't. You. Dare," Maxon ordered through gritted teeth. "You put on a smile, and you wear it to the last second."

I blinked away the tears and gave a weak smile.

"That'll do. Don't let that slip until you leave the room, do you understand?" I nodded. He looked into my eyes. "I'll be glad when you're gone."

After he spat out those last words, his smile returned and

he faced Kriss again. I stared into my lap a minute, slowing my breathing and putting on a brave face.

When I brought my eyes up again, I didn't dare to look directly at anyone. I didn't think I could honor Maxon's last wish if I did. Instead, I focused on the walls of the room. It was because of that I noticed when most of the guards stepped away from them at some signal I didn't see. Pieces of red fabric were pulled out of their pockets and tied across their foreheads.

I watched in confusion as a red-marked guard walked up behind Celeste and put a bullet squarely through the back of her head.

The screaming and gunfire exploded at once. Guttural shouts of pain filled the room, adding to the cacophony of chairs screeching, bodies hitting walls, and the stampede of people trying to escape as fast as they could in their heels and suits. The men shouted as they fired, making the whole thing far more terrifying. I watched, stunned, seeing death more times in a handful of seconds than ought to be possible. I looked for the king and queen, but they were gone. I was gripped with fear, unsure if they'd escaped or been captured. I looked for Adele, for her children. I couldn't see them anywhere, and that was even worse than losing sight of the king and queen.

Beside me, Maxon was trying to calm Kriss. "Get on the floor," he told her. "We're going to be fine."

I looked to my right for Aspen and was in awe for a

moment. He was on one knee, taking aim, firing deliberately into the crowd. He must have been very sure of his target to do that.

Out of the corner of my eye, I saw a flicker of red. Suddenly a rebel guard was standing in front of us. As I thought the words *rebel guard*, it all clicked into place. Anne had told me this had happened once before, when the rebels had gotten the guards' uniforms and had sneaked into the palace. But how?

As Kriss let out another cry, I realized that the guards who were sent to our houses hadn't abandoned their posts at all. They were dead and buried, their clothes stolen and standing in front of us.

Not that this information did me any good now.

I knew that I should run, that Maxon and Kriss should run if they were going to make it. But I was frozen as the menacing figure raised his gun and directed it at Maxon. I looked up at Maxon, and he looked to me. I wished I had time to speak. I turned away, back to the man.

A look of amusement crossed his face. As if he suspected this would be much more entertaining for himself and much more painful for Maxon, he slid his gun ever so slightly to his left and aimed it at me.

I didn't even think to scream. I couldn't move at all, but I saw the blur of Maxon's suit coat as he leaped toward me.

I fell to the ground, but not in the direction I thought I would. Maxon missed me, flying across in front of me. When

I hit the floor, I looked up to see Aspen. He'd sprinted to the table and pushed over my chair, crashing on top of me.

"I got him!" someone shouted. "Find the king!"

I heard several shouts of delight, pleased with the declaration. And screaming. So much screaming. As I came out of my stupor, the sounds crashed into my ears again. Other chairs and bodies clamored to the floor. Guards yelled out orders. Shots were fired, and the sickening pops pierced my ears. It was pure pandemonium.

"Are you hurt?" Aspen demanded over the commotion.

I think I shook my head.

"Don't move."

I watched as he stood, widened his stance, and aimed. He fired several times, eyes focused and body at ease. By the angle of his shots, it looked like more rebels were trying to get close to us. Thanks to Aspen, they failed.

After a quick survey, he popped down again. "I'm going to get her out of here before she really loses it."

He crawled over me and grabbed Kriss, who was covering her ears and crying in earnest. Aspen pulled her face up and slapped her. She was stunned into silence long enough to listen to his orders and follow him from the room, shielding her head as she went.

It was getting quieter. People must be leaving now. Or dying.

And then I noticed a very still leg hanging out from under the tablecloth. Oh, God! Maxon!

I scurried under the table to find Maxon breathing with great labor, a large red stain growing across his shirt. There was a wound below his left shoulder, and it looked very serious.

"Oh, Maxon," I cried. Unsure of what else to do, I balled up the hem of my dress in my hands and pressed it to the bullet wound. He winced a bit. "I'm so sorry."

He reached up his hand and covered mine. "No, I'm sorry," he said. "I was about to ruin both our lives."

"Don't talk right now. Just focus, okay?"

"Look at me, America."

I blinked a few times and pulled my gaze up to his eyes. Through the pain, he smiled at me.

"Break my heart. Break it a thousand times if you like. It was only ever yours to break anyway."

"Shhh," I urged.

"I'll love you until my very last breath. Every beat of my heart is yours. I don't want to die without you knowing that."

"Please don't," I choked.

He took his hand off mine and laced it through my hair. The pressure was light, but it was enough for me to know what he wanted. I bent to kiss him. It was every kiss we'd ever had, all the uncertainty, all the hope.

"Don't give up, Maxon. I love you; please don't give up."

He took an unsteady breath.

Aspen ducked under the table then, and I squealed in fear before I realized who it was.

"Kriss is in a safe room, Your Majesty," Aspen said, all business. "Your turn. Can you stand?"

He shook his head. "A waste of time. Take her."

"But, Your Majesty—"

"That's an order," he said as forcefully as he could manage.

Maxon and Aspen stared at each other for a long second.

"Yes, sir."

"No! I won't go!" I insisted.

"You'll go," Maxon said, sounding tired.

"Come on, Mer. We'll have to hurry."

"I'm not leaving!"

Quickly, as if he might suddenly be fine, Maxon reached up to Aspen's uniform and clutched it in his hands. "She lives. Do you understand me? Whatever it takes, she lives."

Aspen nodded and grabbed my arm harder than I thought possible.

"No!" I cried. "Maxon, please!"

"Be happy," he breathed, squeezing my hand one last time as Aspen dragged me away, screaming.

As we got to the door, Aspen pushed me up against the wall. "Shut up! They'll hear you. The sooner I get you to a safe room, the sooner I can come back for him. You have to do whatever I say, got it?"

I nodded.

"Okay, stay low and quiet," he said, pulling out his gun again and dragging me into the hall.

We looked up and down, and saw someone running away

from us at the far end of the corridor. Once he was gone we moved. Around the corner we stumbled upon a guard on the ground. Aspen checked his pulse and shook his head. He reached over and grabbed the guard's gun, and handed it to me.

"What am I supposed to do with this?" I whispered, terrified.

"Fire it. But make sure you know if it's a friend or a foe before you do. This is mayhem."

It was a tense few minutes of ducking into corners and checking safe rooms that were already taken and locked. It seemed that most of the action had moved upstairs or outside, because the pops of gunshots and faceless screams were muffled by walls. Still, each time we heard a whisper of a sound, we paused before moving.

Aspen peeked around a corner. "This is a dead end, so keep a lookout."

I nodded. We moved quickly to the end of the short hallway, and the first thing I noticed was the bright sun coming in through the window. Didn't the sky know the world was falling apart? How could the sun shine today?

"Please, please, please," Aspen whispered, reaching for the lock. Mercifully, it opened. "Yes!" He sighed, pulling back the door, blocking half the hall from view.

"Aspen, I don't want to do this."

"You have to. You have to be safe, for so many people. And . . . I need you to do something for me."

"What?"

He fidgeted. "If something happens to me . . . I need you to tell—"

Over his shoulder, a hint of red came from behind the corner at the end of the hall. I jerked the gun up and pointed it past Aspen, firing at the figure. Not a second later, Aspen pushed me into the safe room and slammed the door, leaving me alone in the dark.

CHAPTER 31

I DON'T KNOW HOW LONG I sat there. I kept listening for something outside the door, even though I knew it was useless. When Maxon and I had been locked in a safe room a few weeks ago, we couldn't hear a single sound from the outside world. And there had been so much destruction then.

Still, I hoped. Maybe Aspen was okay and would open the door at any second. He couldn't be dead. No. Aspen was a fighter; he'd always been a fighter. When hunger and poverty threatened him, he pushed back. When the world took away his dad, he made sure his family survived. When the Selection took me, when the draft took him, he didn't let it stop him from hoping. Compared to all that, a bullet was tiny, insignificant. No bullet was taking down Aspen Leger.

I pressed my ear up to the door, praying for a word, a breath, anything. I focused, listening for something that sounded like Maxon's labored breathing as he lay dying underneath the table.

I pinched my eyes together, begging God to keep him alive. Certainly, everyone in the palace would be looking for Maxon and his parents. They would be the first ones helped. They wouldn't let him die; they couldn't.

But was it past hope?

He'd looked so pale. Even the last squeeze of my hand was weak.

Be happy.

He loved me. He really loved me. And I loved him. In spite of everything that should have kept us apart—our castes, our mistakes, the world around us—we were supposed to be together.

I should be with him. Especially now, while he lay dying. I shouldn't be hiding.

I stood up and started feeling around the walls for the light switch. I slapped the steel until I found it. I surveyed the space. It was smaller than the other room I'd been in. It had a sink but no toilet, just a bucket in one corner. A bench was pressed up against the wall by the door, and a shelf with some packets of food and blankets lined the back. And then finally, on the floor, the gun sat cold and waiting.

I didn't even know if this would work, but I had to try. I pulled the bench over to the middle of the room and tipped it on its side with the wide seat propped up toward the door. I crouched below it, checking the height, and realized that wasn't going to be much cover. It would have to do though.

As I stood, I tripped over my stupid dress. Huffing, I hunted on the shelves. The thin knife was probably for opening and dividing food, but it worked on the material just fine. Once my dress was cut into an uneven hem around my knees, I took some of the fabric and made a makeshift belt and tucked the knife in it for good measure.

I pulled the blankets over myself, expecting there to be some sort of shrapnel. Looking one more time around the room, I tried to see if there was anything I should take with me, something I could repurpose. No. This was it.

Ducking behind the bench, I aimed the gun at the lock, took a steadying breath, and fired.

The sound echoed in the tiny space, scaring me even though I'd been expecting it. Once I was sure that the bullet wasn't ricocheting around the room, I went up to check the door. Above the lock, a small crater sat, exposing rough layers of metal. I was upset that I'd missed, but at least I knew this might work. If I hit the lock enough times, maybe I could get out of here.

I hid behind the bench and tried again. Shot after shot hit the door, but never in the same place. After a while, I got frustrated and stood up straight, hoping it would help. All I managed to do was get my arms cut by pieces of the door flying back at me.

It wasn't until I heard the hollow click that I realized I'd used all the bullets and was stuck. I threw down the gun and ran over to the door. I hit it with all the force of my body.

"Move!" I rammed into it again. "MOVE!"

I hit the door with my fists, accomplishing nothing. "No! No, no, no! I have to get out!"

The door stood there, silent and severe, mocking my heartbreak with its stillness.

I slid down to the floor, crying now that I knew there was nothing I could do. Aspen might be a lifeless body only feet away from me, and Maxon . . . surely by now he was gone.

I curled my legs to my chest and rested my head against the door.

"If you live," I whispered, "I'll let you call me your dear. I won't complain, I promise."

And then I was left to wait.

Every so often I'd try to guess at the time, though I had no way of knowing if I was right. Each sluggish minute was maddening. I'd never felt so powerless, and the worry was killing me.

After an eternity, I heard the click of the lock. Someone was coming for me. I didn't know if it was a friend or not, so I pointed the empty gun at the door. It would at least look intimidating. The door creaked open, and the light from the window glared in. Did that mean it was still the same day? Or was it the next? I held my aim though I had to squint to do so.

"Don't shoot, Lady America!" a guard pleaded. "You're safe!"

"How do I know that? How do I know you're not one of them?"

The guard looked down the hall, acknowledging an approaching figure. August stepped into the light, followed closely by Gavril. Though his suit was practically destroyed, his pin—which I now realized looked an awful lot like a North Star—still hung proudly on his bloody lapel.

No wonder the Northern rebels knew so much.

"It's over, America. We got them," August confirmed.

I sighed, overwhelmed with relief, and dropped the gun.

"Where's Maxon? Is he alive? Did Kriss make it?" I asked Gavril before focusing again on August. "There was an officer; he brought me here. His name is Officer Leger; have you seen him?" The words tumbled out almost too quickly to be understood.

I was feeling funny, light-headed.

"I think she's in shock. Take her to the hospital wing, quickly," Gavril ordered, and the guard scooped me up easily.

"Maxon?" I asked. No one answered. Or maybe I was gone by then. I couldn't remember.

When I woke up, I was on a cot. I could feel the stings of my many cuts now, but as I picked up my arm to inspect it, the cuts were all clean, and the larger ones were bandaged. I was safe.

I sat up and looked around, and realized I was in a tiny office. I inspected the desk and the diplomas on the wall and discovered it was Dr. Ashlar's. I couldn't stay here. I needed answers.

When I opened the door, I discovered why I'd been tucked away. The hospital wing was packed. Some of the less injured were placed two to a bed, and others were on the floor between them. It was easy to tell that the worst were in beds toward the back of the room. Despite the number of people, the space was remarkably quiet.

I scanned the area, looking for familiar faces. Was it good not to find them here? What did that mean?

Tuesday was in a bed, holding on to Emmica as they cried quietly. I recognized a few of the maids, but only vaguely. They nodded their heads at me as I passed, as if I somehow deserved it.

I started losing hope as the crowd started to thin. Maxon wasn't here. If he was, he'd have a swarm of people around him, jumping to meet his every need. But I'd been placed in a side room. Maybe he had, too?

I saw a guard, and his face was scarred from what I couldn't guess. "Is the prince down here somewhere?" I asked quietly.

Solemnly, he shook his head.

"Oh."

A bullet wound and a broken heart would seem like two different injuries. But I could feel myself bleeding out just as surely as Maxon had. No amount of pressure or stitching would ever fix this; nothing would ever stop the ache.

I didn't break into a scream, though it felt as if something similar was happening inside. I just let the tears fall. They didn't wash anything away, but they felt like a promise.

Nothing will ever replace you, Maxon. And I sealed our love away.

"Mer?"

I turned and saw a bandaged figure in one of the last beds in the wing. Aspen.

My breathing hitched as I took unsteady steps toward him. His head was bandaged, and there was blood staining its way through. His chest was bare and bruised in several places, but the worst part was his leg. A thick cast was wrapped around the bottom, and several bandages were sloppily placed over gashes on his thigh. Wearing nothing but some shorts and a bit of a sheet over his other leg, it was easy to see how badly he'd been wounded.

"What happened?" I whispered.

"I'd rather not relive the details. I made it for a long time, and I took out maybe six or seven of them before one got my leg. The doctor says I'll probably be able to walk on it, but I'll need a cane. At least I'm alive."

A tear continued silently down my cheek. I was so grateful and scared and hopeless, I couldn't help it.

"You saved my life, Mer."

My eyes flew from his leg to his face.

"The shot you took spooked that rebel and gave me just enough time to fire. If you hadn't done it, he would have shot me in the back, and that would have been it. Thank you."

I wiped my eyes. "It was you who saved my life. You always have. It's about time I started paying you back."

He smiled. "I do have a tendency for heroics, don't I?"

"You always wanted to be someone's knight in shining armor." I shook my head, thinking over everything he'd ever done for anyone he loved.

"Mer, listen to me. When I said that I'd always love you, I meant it. And I think if we had stayed in Carolina, we would have gotten married, and we would have been happy. Poor, but happy." He smiled sadly. "But we didn't stay in Carolina. And you've changed. I have, too. You were right when you said that I'd never given anyone else a chance, and why would I have ever bothered except for all this happening?

"It's my instinct to fight for you, Mer. It took me a long time to see that you didn't want me to do that anymore. But once I did, I realized I didn't want to fight for you either."

I stared at him, stunned.

"You'll always have a piece of my heart, Mer, but I'm not in love with you anymore. I think sometimes that you still need me or want me, but I don't know if that's right. You deserve better than me being with you because I feel obligated."

I sighed. "And you deserve better than being someone I settle for."

He held out his hand to me and I took it. "I don't want you to be mad at me."

"I'm not. It's good to know you're not mad at me. Even if he is dead, I still love him."

Aspen's forehead creased. "Who's dead?"

"Maxon," I breathed, ready to cry again.

There was a pause. "Maxon's not dead."

"What! But that guard said he wasn't here and—"

"Of course he's not here. He's the king. He's recovering in his room."

I lunged to hug him, and he grunted at the impact of my embrace; but I was too happy to be cautious. Then the happy and sad news mixed together.

I stepped back slowly. "The king died?"

Aspen nodded. "The queen, too."

"No!" I shuddered, blinking again. *She said I could call her Mom.* What was Maxon going to do without her?

"Actually, if it hadn't been for the Northern rebels, Maxon might not have made it either. They were really the tipping point."

"They were?"

I could see the wonder and appreciation in his eyes. "We should have had rebels training us. They fight differently. They knew what to do. I recognized August and Georgia in the Great Room. They had backup outside the palace walls. Once they realized something was wrong, well, they already have a talent for getting into the palace quickly. I don't know where they got the artillery from, but we'd all be gone with-out them."

I could hardly take in all this. I was still putting the pieces together when the opening door disturbed the quiet mur-murs in the wing. A worried face surveyed the room, and though her dress was torn and her hair was tumbling down around her face, I recognized her immediately.

Before I could call out to her, Aspen did. "Lucy!" he cried, sitting up. I knew the motion had to hurt him, but there was no sign of pain in his face.

"Aspen!" She gasped and ran across the wing, hopping over people as necessary. She fell into his arms, kissing his face over and over. While he'd grunted in pain when I'd hugged him, it was clear that in this moment, Aspen wasn't feeling anything but pure happiness.

"Where were you?" he demanded.

"Fourth floor. They're only now reaching the rooms up there. I came as fast as I could. What happened?" Though she was usually so panicked after rebel attacks, Lucy seemed focused now, seeing only Aspen.

"I'm fine. What about you? Do you need to see the doc-tor?" Aspen looked around, trying to find someone to help.

"No, I don't even have a scratch," she promised. "I was just worried about you."

Aspen stared into Lucy's eyes with absolute devotion. "Now that you're here, everything's right."

She stroked his face, careful not to disturb his bandages.

He put a hand behind her neck and gently pulled her to him, kissing her deeply.

No one needed a knight more than Lucy, and no one could protect her better than Aspen.

They were so lost in each other; they didn't notice me walk away, heading off to find the one person I really wanted to see.

CHAPTER 32

LEAVING THE HOSPITAL WING, I got my first look at the palace. It was hard to process the destruction. So much broken glass strewn across the floor, glittering hopefully in the sunlight. Ruined paintings, parts of the wall blown out, and menacing red stains on the carpets reminded me of how close we'd all been to death.

I started up the stairs, trying to avoid eye contact with anyone. As I passed from the second floor to the third, I noticed an earring on the floor. I couldn't help but wonder if its owner was still alive.

I made my way to the landing and saw a number of guards as I walked toward Maxon's room. I supposed it was unavoidable. If I had to, maybe I'd call out to him. Maybe he'd tell them to let me pass . . . just like the night we met.

The door to Maxon's room was open, and people buzzed

in and out, bringing in papers or taking away platters. Six guards lined the wall leading up to the door, and I braced myself for the brush-off. But as I got closer, one of the guards noticed me. He squinted, as if double-checking that I was who he thought I was. Beside him, another guard recognized me, and one by one they bowed, deeply and reverently.

One of the guards by the door extended an arm. "He's been waiting for you, my lady."

I tried to be someone deserving of the honor they were giving me. I stood taller as I walked, though my scratched arms and cut-off dress did nothing to help. "Thank you," I said with a gentle nod.

A maid rushed past as I went in. Maxon was on his bed, the left side of his chest padded with gauze under his plain cotton shirt. His left arm was in a sling, and he used his right to hold up the paper some adviser was explaining to him.

He looked so normal there, dressed down, hair a mess. But at the same time, he looked like so much more than he had been before. Was he sitting a little taller? Had his face somehow become more serious?

He was so clearly the king.

"Your Majesty," I breathed, falling into a low curtsy. Standing, I saw the quiet smile in his eyes.

"Set the papers here, Stavros. Would everyone please leave the room? I need to speak with the lady."

Everyone circling around him bowed and headed toward the hall. Stavros quietly placed the papers on Maxon's bedside table, and as he passed, he winked at me. I waited until the door closed before I moved.

I wanted to run to him, to fall into his embrace and stay there forever. But I moved slowly, worried that maybe he regretted his last words to me.

"I'm so sorry about your parents."

"It doesn't seem real yet," he said, motioning that I should sit on the bed. "I keep thinking that Father is in his study, and Mom's downstairs, and any minute one of them will come in here with something for me to do."

"I know exactly what you mean."

He gave me a sympathetic smile. "I know you do." He reached out and put his hand on mine. I took that as a good sign and held his hand back. "She tried to save him. A guard told me a rebel had my father in his sights, but she ran behind him. She went down first, but they got Father immediately after."

He shook his head. "She was always selfless. To her very last breath."

"You shouldn't be so surprised. You're a lot like her."

He made a face. "I'll never be quite as good as her. I'm going to miss her so much."

I rubbed his hand. She wasn't my mother, but I would miss her as well.

"At least you're safe," he said, not looking into my eyes. "At least there's that."

There was a long stretch of silence, and I didn't know what to say. Should I bring up what he said? Should I ask about Kriss? Would he even want to think about any of this now?

"There's something I want to show you," he suddenly announced. "Mind you, it's a bit rough, but I think you'll still like it. Open the drawer here," he instructed. "It should be on the top."

I pulled out the drawer in his bedside table, noticing a pile of typed papers right away. I gave Maxon a questioning look, but he just nodded toward the writing.

I started reading the document, trying to process what it said. I got to the end of the first paragraph and then reread it, sure I was mistaken.

"Are you . . . you're going to dissolve the castes?" I asked, looking up to Maxon.

"That's the plan," he answered, smiling. "I don't want you to get too excited. This will take a long time to do, but I think it will work. You see," he said, turning the pages of the vast file and pointing to a paragraph. "I want to start from the bottom. I'm planning on eliminating the Eight label first. There's a lot of construction we need to do; and I feel like, with a little bit of work, the Eights could be absorbed into the Sevens. After that, it gets tricky. There's got to be a way to get rid of the stigmas that come along with the numbers, but that's my goal."

I was awestruck. I'd only ever known a world in which I wore my caste like a piece of clothing. And here I was, holding something saying that those invisible lines we'd drawn between people could finally be erased.

Maxon's hand touched mine. "I want you to know that this is all your doing. Since the day you called me into the hallway and told me about being hungry, I've been working on this. It was one of the reasons I got so upset after you did your presentation; I had a quieter way of reaching the exact same goal. But of all the things I wanted to do for my country, this would have never crossed my mind if I hadn't known you."

I took in a breath and gazed at the pages again. I thought over the years of my life, so short and fast. I'd never expected to do more than sing in the background of people's house parties and maybe get married one day. I thought about what this would mean for the people of Illéa, and I was beside myself. I felt both humbled and proud.

"There's something else," Maxon said hesitantly as I continued to take in the words in front of me. Then suddenly, on top of the papers, Maxon slid over an open box with a ring resting in it, shining in the light cascading through his windows.

"I've been sleeping with that darn thing under my pillow," he said, sounding playfully irritated. I looked up to him, not saying anything, as I was still too stunned to speak. I was sure he could read the questions in my eyes, but he had his own to address. "Do you like it?"

A web of thin gold vines crawled up, forming the circle of the ring, holding at the top two gems—one green, one purple—that kissed at the crown of it. I knew the purple one was my birthstone, so the green one must be his. There we were, two little spots of light growing together, inseparable.

I meant to speak and opened my mouth several times to try. All I could manage to do was smile, blink back my tears, and nod.

Maxon cleared his throat. "Twice now I've tried to do this on a grand scale and failed spectacularly. As it is, I can't even get on one knee. I hope you won't mind if I just speak to you plainly."

I nodded. I still couldn't find a word in my entire body.

He swallowed and shrugged his uninjured shoulder. "I love you," he said simply. "I should have told you a long time ago. Maybe we could have avoided so many stupid mistakes if I had. Then again," he added, beginning to smile, "sometimes I think it was all those obstacles that made me love you so deeply."

Tears pooled in the corners of my eyes, balancing on my lashes.

"What I said was true. My heart is yours to break. As you already know, I'd rather die than see you in pain. In the moment I was hit, when I fell to the floor sure my life was ending, all I could think about was you."

Maxon had to stop. He swallowed, and I could see he was as close to tears as I was. After a moment, he continued.

"In those seconds, I was mourning everything I'd lost. How I'd never get to see you walk down an aisle toward me, how I'd never get to see your face in our children, how I'd never get to see streaks of silver in your hair. But, at the same time, I couldn't be bothered. If me dying meant you living"—he did his one-shoulder shrug again—"how could that be anything but good?"

At that, I lost my control, and the tears came in earnest. How had I ever thought that I knew what it meant to be loved before this very second? Nothing had come close to this feeling radiating in my heart, filling every inch of me with absolute warmth.

"America," Maxon said sweetly, forcing me to wipe my eyes and face him. "I know you see a king here, but let me be clear; this isn't a command. This is a request, a plea. I beg you; make me the happiest man alive. Please do me the honor of becoming my wife."

I couldn't get out how much I wanted this. But where my voice failed, my body succeeded. I crawled into Maxon's arms, holding on to him tightly, certain that nothing could ever pull us apart. When he kissed me, I felt my life settle into place. I had found everything I'd ever wanted—things I didn't even know I was looking for—here in Maxon's arms. And if I had him to guide me, to hold me, then I could take on the world.

It seemed too soon our kiss slowed, and Maxon pulled back to look into my eyes. I saw it in his face. I was home. And I finally found my voice.

"Yes."

EPILOGUE

I TRY NOT TO SHAKE, but it does no good. Any girl would do the same. The day is big, the dress is heavy, and the eyes watching are uncountable. Brave as I ought to be, I tremble.

I know that once the doors open, I will see Maxon waiting for me, so while all the last-second details are settled around me, I hold on to that promise and try to relax.

"Oh! This is our cue," Mom says, noting the change in the music. Silvia waves my family over. James and Kenna are ready to go. Gerad is running around, already wrinkling his suit, and May keeps trying desperately to get him to stand in one place for two seconds back-to-back. Even if he is a bit rumpled, they all look surprisingly regal today.

As happy as I am that everyone who loves me is with me, I can't help but feel an ache that Dad isn't here. I feel him, though, whispering how much he loves me, how proud he is, how lovely I look. I knew him so well that I feel like I can pick out the exact words he would say to me today; and I hope it stays like that always, that he'll never really be gone.

I'm so lost in my daydreams that May sneaks up on me. "You look beautiful, Ames," she says, reaching up to touch the intricate high collar of my dress.

"Mary outdid herself, didn't she?" I answer, touching parts of the dress myself. Mary is the only one of my original maids still with me. When the dust settled, we found out so many more lives were lost than we'd guessed at first. While Lucy made it through the attack and chose to retire, Anne was simply gone.

Another empty place today that ought to be filled.

"My gosh, Ames, you're shaking." May grabs my hands and tries to still them, laughing at my nerves.

"I know. I can't help it."

"Marlee," May calls. "Come help me calm America down."

My one and only bridesmaid walks over, her eyes as bright as ever; and with the two of them surrounding me, I do start to feel less tense.

"Don't worry, America; I'm sure he'll show up," she teases. May laughs, and I swat at them both.

"I'm not worried he'll change his mind! I'm afraid I'll trip or mispronounce his name or something. I have a talent for messing things up," I lament.

Marlee puts her forehead on mine. "Nothing could mess up today."

"May!" Mom hisses.

"Okay, Mom's losing it. See you up there." She gives me a ghost kiss on my cheek, making sure not to leave a lipstick smudge, and goes on her way. The music plays, and they walk together around the corner and down the aisle that's waiting for me.

Marlee steps back. "Am I next?"

"Yes. I love this color on you, by the way."

She juts out her hip, posing in the gown. "You have great taste, Your Majesty."

I suck in a breath. "No one's called me that yet. Oh, goodness, that's going to be my name to pretty much everyone." I try to adjust to the words quickly. The coronation is part of the wedding. First the vows to Maxon, then the ones to Illéa. Rings, then crowns.

"Don't start getting nervous again!" she insists.

"I'm trying! I mean, I knew it was coming; it's just a lot for one day."

"Ha!" she exclaims as the music shifts. "Wait until tonight."

"Marlee!"

Before I can scold her, she scampers away, winking as she goes, and I'm forced to giggle. I'm so glad to have her back in my life. I officially made her one of my attendants, and Maxon did the same for Carter. It was a clear sign to the public of what was coming with Maxon's reign, and I was happy to see how many people welcomed the change.

I listen, waiting. I know the notes are coming soon, so I

take one last chance to straighten my dress.

It's truly magnificent. The white gown is fitted through my hips, flitting out in waves to the floor. The lace sleeves are short and lead to a high collar that genuinely makes me look like a princess. Over the dress, a sleeveless capelike coat flows out behind me, making a train. I'll take it off for the reception, where I intend to dance with my husband until I can't stand anymore.

"Ready, Mer?"

I turn to Aspen. "Yes. I'm ready."

He holds an arm out for me, and I put mine through his. "You look incredible."

"You clean up pretty nice yourself," I comment. And though I smile, I know he sees my nervousness.

"There's nothing to worry about," he assures me, that confident smile making me believe that whatever he says is true, same as always.

I take in a deep breath and nod. "Right. Just don't let me fall, okay?"

"Don't worry. If you look unsteady, I'll hand you this." He holds up the deep-blue cane, specially made to match his dress uniform, and the idea makes me laugh.

"There we go," he says, happy to see me genuinely smile.

"Your Majesty?" Silvia asks. "It's time." Her tone is slightly awed.

I give her a nod, and Aspen and I make our way to the doors.

"Knock 'em dead," he says just before the music rises and

we're revealed to the guests.

All the fear rushes back. Though we tried to keep the guest list small, hundreds of people line the aisle that will take me to Maxon. And as they all rise to greet me, I can't see him.

I just need to see his face. If I can find those steady eyes, I'll know I can do this.

I smile, trying to stay calm, graciously nodding at our guests, thanking them for their presence here today. But Aspen knows.

"It's okay, Mer."

I look to him, and the encouragement in his expression helps.

I keep moving.

It's not the most graceful parade down the aisle. It's also not the fastest. With Aspen's leg so injured, we have to hobble our way slowly to the front. But who else could I have asked? Who else *would* I have asked? Aspen had shifted to fill a desperate place in my life. Not my boyfriend, not my friend, but my *family*.

I had expected him to say no, afraid it was somehow an insult. But he'd said he was honored and embraced me when I'd asked.

Devoted and true, even to the very end. That's my Aspen.

Finally I see a familiar face in the crowd. Lucy is there, sitting with her father. She beams with pride for me, though really she can hardly tear her eyes off Aspen. He stands a little taller as we pass her. I know that soon it will be her turn, and I'm looking forward to it. Aspen couldn't have made a better choice.

Beside her, filling up the closest rows, are the other Selected girls. It was brave of them to come back for me, considering not everyone who should be here is. Still, they smile, even Kriss, though I can see the sadness in her eyes. I'm shocked by how much I wish Celeste was here. I can imagine her rolling her eyes and then winking, or something like that. Making some wisecrack that was almost snotty but not quite. I really, really miss her.

I miss Queen Amberly, too. I can only imagine how happy she would have been today, finally getting a daughter. I feel as if marrying Maxon makes it okay for me to love her that way, like a mother. I'm certain I always will.

And then there's my mom and May holding on to each other so tightly they look as if they're supporting each other. Around them are so many smiles. It's almost overwhelming how loved I feel.

I'm so distracted by their faces that I forget how close I am to the end of the aisle. As I turn forward . . . he's there.

And then it seems as if no one else is here at all.

No cameras filming, no bulbs flashing. It's just us. It's just Maxon and me.

He's wearing his crown, and the suit with the blue sash and the medals. What did I say the first time he wore it? Something about hanging him up with the chandeliers, I think. I smile, remembering the long journey that got us here, standing at the altar.

Aspen's last few steps are slow but steady. When we reach our destination, I turn to him. Aspen gives me one last smile, and I reach over to kiss his cheek, saying good-bye to so many things. We share a look for a moment, and he takes my hand and puts it in Maxon's, giving me away.

They nod to each other, nothing but respect in their faces. I don't think I could ever understand all that's passed between them, but it feels peaceful in that moment. Aspen steps back, and I step forward, arriving at the one place I never thought I'd be.

Maxon and I move close to each other as the ceremony starts.

"Hello, my dear," he whispers.

"Don't start," I warn in return, and we're both left smiling.

He holds my hands as if they're the only things pinning him to the earth, and I focus on that as I prepare myself for the words coming, the promises I'll never break. It's magical, really, the power this day has.

But even now I know this isn't a fairy tale. I know that we'll have hard times, confusing times. I know that things won't always happen the way we want them to and that we'll have to work to remember that we chose this. It won't be perfect, not all the time.

This isn't happily ever after.

It's so much more than that.

ACKNOWLEDGMENTS

CAN YOU JUST PUT YOUR hand on the page and pretend I'm giving you a high five? Seriously. How else do I thank you for reading my books? I hope you've had as much fun with America's story as I have, and I'll never be able to express how happy I am that you took the time to go through it with me. You're keen. Thank you so much!

First of all, a huge thank-you to Callaway. It still makes my day when I see your "Husband of the #1 *New York Times* bestselling author Kiera Cass" email signature, and I'm so glad you're proud of me. Thanks for being my biggest supporter through this whole journey. Love you!

Thank you, Guyden and Zuzu, for being such great kids and letting mommy run off to her office to work. You're wonderful little people, and I love you bunches.

To Mimoo, Poopa, and Uncle Jody, thanks for all your encouragement, and the same goes for Mimi, Papa, and Uncle Chris. Lots of little things couldn't have happened without your help, so thank you for being there, not just for me, but for our whole little family.

To the best agent ever, Elana Roth Parker. I wanted you to want me so bad! Thanks for your faith and hard work and for just plain old being cool. If I was ever in a street fight, I'd want you right there beside me. I mean that in the best way possible. *HUGS*

To Erica Sussman, my fantastic editor. So much of this story worked because of you. Thank you so much for taking me on. I'm crazy about you and your purple pens and your smiley faces! I feel bad for any author who has to work with an editor that isn't you. Absolutely the best!

To everyone at HarperTeen, for being so brilliant and for working so hard. You were the place I longed to call home, and I can't believe how good you are to me! Thank you so much!

To Kathleen, who takes care of all the foreign rights. Thanks for getting my books (and me!) all over the world! It's still unbelievable.

To Samantha Clark, for running the Kiera Cass fan page on Facebook without ever being asked to do it or complaining about any work it brings her way. So, so cool of you! Thank you!

To everyone who runs a Selection-based Twitter, Tumblr, or Facebook account. Half of the time I can't read the language you're posting in, and that alone is insane to me! Thanks for being diligent and creative and for talking to me. For realsies, you guys are the best!

To Georgia Whitaker, for making a really rad video and earning her name a spot in the book. Thanks for letting me borrow it!

Who am I forgetting? Like a thousand people, I just know it . . .

To Northstar church (which I *swear* I started going to years after *The Selection* was born), thanks for being home to the Cass family and for your constant encouragement.

To FTW . . . I don't even know what to say. You guys are ridiculous, and I love you.

To The Fray, One Direction, Jack's Mannequin, Paramore, Elbow, and a slew of other musicians, thanks for keeping me inspired over the years. You were fuel for these stories.

As well as Coke Zero and low-fat Wheat Thins. Sometimes also Milk Duds. Very important to my survival over the years, so thanks.

Lastly, and most important, to God. Years ago, writing saved me from a very dark time in my life. It wasn't on my radar at all, but it became my lifeline. I believe it was grace that brought this into my life, and even on the most stressful days, my job makes me happy. I feel blessed a thousand times over and even though I write for a living, I still can't find the words to express my gratitude. Thank you.

Twenty years ago, her mother won the crown.
Now Eadlyn will enter a Selection of her own. . . .

Turn the page for a sneak peek
at the fourth book in
THE SELECTION SERIES

I COULD NOT HOLD MY breath for seven minutes. I couldn't even make it to one. I once tried to run a mile in seven minutes after hearing some athletes could do it in four but failed spectacularly when a side stitch crippled me about halfway in.

However, there was one thing I managed to do in seven minutes that most would say is quite impressive: I became queen.

By seven tiny minutes I beat my brother, Ahren, into the world, so the throne that ought to have been his was mine. Had I been born a generation earlier, it wouldn't have mattered. Ahren was the male, so Ahren would have been the heir.

Alas, Mom and Dad couldn't stand to watch their firstborn be stripped of a title by an unfortunate but rather lovely set of breasts. So they changed the law, and the people rejoiced, and I was trained day by day to become the next ruler of Illéa.

What they didn't understand was that their attempts to make my life fair seemed rather *unfair* to me.

I tried not to complain. After all, I knew how fortunate I was. But there were days, or sometimes months, when it felt like far too much was piled on me, too much for any one person, really.

I flipped through the newspaper and saw that there had been yet another riot, this time in Zuni. Twenty years ago, Dad's first act as king was to dissolve the castes, and the old system had been phased out slowly over my lifetime. I still thought it was completely bizarre that once upon a time people lived with these limiting but arbitrary labels on their backs. Mom was a Five; Dad was a One. It made no sense, especially since there was no outward sign of the divisions. How was I supposed to know if I was walking next to a Six or a Three? And why did that even matter?

When Dad had first decreed that the castes were no more, people all over the country had been delighted. Dad had expected the changes he was making in Illéa to be comfortably in place over the course of a generation, meaning any day now everything should click.

That wasn't happening—and this new riot was just the most recent in a string of unrest.

"Coffee, Your Highness," Neena said, setting the drink on my table.

"Thank you. You can take the plates."

I scanned the article. This time a restaurant was burned to the ground because its owner refused to promote a waiter to a position as a chef. The waiter claimed that a promotion had been promised but was never delivered, and he was sure it was because of his family's past.

Looking at the charred remains of the building, I honestly didn't know whose side I was on. The owner had the right to promote or fire anyone he wanted, and the waiter had the right not to be seen as something that, technically, didn't exist anymore.

I pushed the paper away and picked up my drink. Dad was going to be upset. I was sure he was already running the scenario over and over in his head, trying to figure out how to set it right. The problem was, even if we could fix one issue, we couldn't stop every instance of post-caste discrimination. It was too hard to monitor and happening far too often.

I set down my coffee and headed to my closet. It was time to start the day.

"Neena," I called. "Do you know where that plum-colored dress is? The one with the sash?"

She squinted in concentration as she came over to help.

In the grand scheme of things, Neena was new to the palace. She'd only been working with me for six months, after my last maid fell ill for two weeks. Neena was acutely attuned to my needs and much more agreeable to be around, so I kept her on. I also admired her eye for fashion.

Neena stared into the massive space. "Maybe we should reorganize."

"You can if you have the time. That's not a project I'm interested in."

"Not when I can hunt down your clothes for you," she teased.

"Exactly!"

She took my humor in stride, laughing as she quickly sorted through gowns and pants.

"I like your hair today," I commented.

"Thank you." All the maids wore caps, but Neena was still creative with her hairdos. Sometimes a few thick, black curls would frame her face, and other times she twisted back strands until they were all tucked away. At the moment there were wide braids encircling her head, with the rest of her hair under her cap. I really enjoyed that she found ways to work with her uniform, to make it her own each day.

"Ah! It's back here." Neena pulled down the knee-length dress, fanning it out across the dark skin of her arm.

"Perfect! And do you know where my gray blazer is? The one with the three-quarter sleeves?"

She stared at me, her face deadpan. "I'm definitely rearranging."

I giggled. "You search; I'll dress."

I pulled on my outfit and brushed out my hair, preparing for another day as the future face of the monarchy. The outfit was feminine enough to soften me but strong enough that I'd be taken seriously. It was a fine line to walk, but I did it every day.

Staring into the mirror, I talked to my reflection.

"You are Eadlyn Schreave. You are the next person in line to run this country, and you will be the first girl to do it on your own. No one," I said, "is as powerful as you."

Dad was already in his office, brow furrowed as he took in the news. Other than my eyes, I didn't look much like him. Or Mom, for that matter.

With my dark hair, oval-shaped face, and a hint of a tan that lingered year round, I looked more like my grandmother than anyone else. A painting of her on her coronation day hung in the fourth-floor hallway, and I used to study it when I was younger, trying to guess at how I would look as I grew. Her age in the portrait was near to mine now, and though we weren't identical, I sometimes felt like her echo.

I walked across the room and kissed Dad's cheek. "Morning."

"Morning. Did you see the papers?" he asked.

"Yes. At least no one died this time."

"Thank goodness for that." Those were the worst, the ones where people were left dead in the street or went missing. It was terrible, reading the names of young men who'd been beaten simply for moving their families into a nicer neighborhood or women who were attacked for trying to get a job that in the past would not have been open to them.

Sometimes it took no time at all to find the motive and the person behind these crimes, but more often than not we were faced with a lot of finger-pointing and no real answers. It was exhausting for me to watch, and I knew it was worse for Dad.

"I don't understand it." He took off his reading glasses and rubbed his eyes. "They didn't want the castes anymore. We took our time, eliminated them slowly so everyone could adjust. Now they're burning down buildings."

"Is there a way to regulate this? Could we create a board to oversee grievances?" I looked at the photo again. In the corner, the young son of the restaurant owner wept over losing everything. In my heart I knew complaints would come in faster than anyone could address them, but I also knew Dad couldn't bear doing nothing.

Dad looked at me. "Is that what you would do?"

I smiled. "No, I'd ask my father what he would do."

He sighed. "That won't always be an option for you, Eadlyn. You need to be strong, decisive. How would you fix this one particular incident?"

I considered. "I don't think we can. There's no way to prove the old castes were why the waiter was denied the promotion. The only thing we can do is launch an investigation into who set the fire. That family lost their livelihood today, and someone needs to be held responsible. Arson is not how you exact justice."

He shook his head at the paper. "I think you're right. I'd like to be able to help them. But, more than that, we need to figure out how to prevent this from happening again. It's become rampant, Eadlyn, and it's frightening."

Dad tossed the paper into the trash, then stood and walked to the window. I could read the stress in his posture. Sometimes his role brought him so much joy, like visiting the schools he'd worked tirelessly to improve or seeing communities flourish in the war-free era he'd ushered in. But those instances were becoming few and far between. Most days he was anxious about the state of the country, and he had to fake his smiles when reporters came by, hoping that his sense of calm would somehow spread to everyone else. Mom helped shoulder the burden, but at the end of the day the fate of the country was placed squarely on his back. One day it would be on mine.

Vain as it was, I worried I would go gray prematurely.

"Make a note for me, Eadlyn. Remind me to write Governor Harpen in Zuni. Oh, and put to write it to Joshua Harpen, not his father. I keep forgetting he was the one who ran in the last election."

I wrote his instructions in my elegant cursive, thinking how pleased Dad would be when he looked at it later. He used to give me the worst time over my penmanship.

I was grinning to myself when I looked back at him, but my face fell almost immediately when I saw him rubbing his forehead, trying so desperately to think of a solution to these problems.

"Dad?"

He turned and instinctively squared his shoulders, like he needed to act strong even in front of me.

"Why do you think this is happening? It wasn't always like this."

He raised his eyebrows. "It certainly wasn't," he said, almost to himself. "At first everyone seemed pleased. Every time we removed a new caste, people held parties. It's only been in the last few years, since all the labels have officially been erased, that it's gone downhill."

He stared back out the window. "The only thing I can think is that those who grew up with the castes are aware of how much better this is. Comparatively, it's easier to marry or work. A family's finances aren't capped by a single profession. There are more choices when it comes to education. But those who are growing up without the castes and are still running into opposition . . . I guess they don't know what else to do."

He looked at me and shrugged. "I need time," he muttered. "I need a way to put things on pause, set them right, and press play again."

I noted the deep furrow in his brow. "Dad, I don't think that's possible."

He chuckled. "We've done it before. I can remember. . . ."

The focus in his eyes changed. He watched me for a moment, seeming to ask me a question without words.

"Dad?"

"Yes."

"Are you all right?"

He blinked a few times. "Yes, dear, quite all right. Why don't you get to work on those budget cuts. We can go over your ideas this afternoon. I need to speak with your mother."

"Sure." Math wasn't a skill that came to me naturally,

so I had to work twice as long on any proposals for budget cuts or financial plans. But I absolutely refused to have one of Dad's advisers come behind me with a calculator to clean up my mess. Even if I had to stay up all night, I always made sure my work was accurate.

Of course, Ahren was naturally good at math, but he was never forced to sit through meetings about budgets or rezoning or health care. He got off scot-free by seven stupid minutes.

Dad patted me on the shoulder before dashing out of the room. It took me longer than usual to focus on the numbers. I couldn't help but be distracted by the look on his face and the unmistakable certainty that it was tied to me.

CHAPTER 2

AFTER WORKING ON THE BUDGET report for a few hours, I decided I needed a break and retreated to my room to get a hand massage from Neena. I loved those little bits of luxury in my day. Dresses made to my exact measurements, exotic desserts flown in simply because it was Thursday, and an endless supply of beautiful things were all perks; and they were easily my favorite parts of the job.

My room overlooked the gardens. As the day shifted, the light changed to a warm, honey color, brightening the high walls. I focused on the heat and Neena's deliberate fingers.

"Anyway, his face got all funny. It was kind of like he disappeared for a minute."

I was trying to explain Dad's out-of-character departure this morning, but it was hard to get it across. I didn't even know if he found Mom or not, as he never came back to the office.

"Do you think he's sick? He does seem tired these days." Neena's hands worked her magic as she spoke.

"Does he?" I asked, thinking that Dad didn't seem tired exactly. "He's probably just stressed. How could he not be with all the decisions he has to make?"

"And someday that will be you," she commented, her tone a mix of genuine worry and playful amusement.

"Which means you will be giving me twice as many massages."

"I don't know," she said. "I think in a few years I might like to try something new."

I scrunched my face. "What else would you do? There aren't many positions better than working in the palace."

There was a knock on the door, and she didn't have a chance to answer the question.

I stood, throwing my blazer back on to look presentable, and gave a nod to Neena to let my guests in.

Mom came around the door, smiling, with Dad contentedly trailing her steps. I couldn't help but notice it was always this way. At state events or important dinners, Mom was beside Dad or situated right behind him. But when they were just husband and wife—not king and queen—he followed her everywhere.

"Hi, Mom." I walked over to hug her.

Mom tucked my hair behind my ear, smiling at me. "I like this look."

I stood back proudly and smoothed out my dress with my

hands. "The bracelets really set it off, don't you think?"

She giggled. "Excellent attention to detail." Every once in a while Mom let me pick out jewelry or shoes for her, but it was rare. Mom didn't find it as much fun as I did, and she didn't rely on the extras for beauty. In her case, she really didn't need it. I liked that she was classic.

Mom turned and touched Neena's shoulder. "You're excused," she said quietly.

Neena instantly curtsied and left us alone.

"Is something wrong?" I asked.

"No, sweetheart. We simply want to speak in private." Dad held out a hand and ushered us all to the table. "We have an opportunity to talk to you about."

"Opportunity? Are we traveling?" I adored traveling. "Please tell me we're finally going on a beach trip. Could it just be the six of us?"

"Not exactly. We wouldn't be going somewhere so much as having visitors," Mom explained.

"Oh! Company! Who's coming?"

They exchanged glances, then Mom continued talking. "You know that things are precarious right now. The people are restless and unhappy, and we cannot figure out how to ease the tension."

I sighed. "I know."

"We're seeking a way to boost morale," Dad added.

I perked up. Morale boosting typically involved a celebration. And I was always up for a party.

"What did you have in mind?" I started designing a new

dress in my head and dismissed it almost as quickly. That wasn't what needed my attention at the moment.

"Well," Dad started, "the public responds best to something positive with our family. When your mother and I were married, it was one of the best seasons in our country. And do you remember how people threw parties in the street when they found out Osten was coming?"

I smiled. I was eight when Osten was born, and I'd never forget how excited everyone got just over the announcement. I heard music playing from my bedroom practically until dawn.

"That was marvelous."

"It was. And now the people look to you. It won't be long before you're queen." Dad paused. "We thought that perhaps you'd be willing to do something publicly, something that would be exciting for the people but also might be very beneficial to you."

I narrowed my eyes, not sure where this was going. "I'm listening."

Mom cleared her throat. "You know that in the past, princesses were married off to princes from other countries to solidify our international relations."

"I did hear you use the past tense there, correct?"

She laughed, but I wasn't amused. "Yes."

"Good. Because Prince Nathaniel looks like a zombie, Prince Hector dances like a zombie, and if the prince from the German Federation doesn't learn to embrace personal hygiene by the Christmas party, he shouldn't be invited."

Mom rubbed the side of her head in frustration. "Eadlyn, you've always been so picky."

Dad shrugged. "Maybe that's not a bad thing," he said, earning a glare from Mom.

I frowned. "What in the world are you talking about?"

"You know how your mother and I met," Dad began.

I rolled my eyes. "Everyone does. You two are practically a fairy tale."

At those words their eyes went soft, and smiles washed over their faces. Their bodies seemed to tilt slightly toward each other, and Dad bit his lip looking at Mom.

"Excuse me. Firstborn in the room, do you mind?"

Mom blushed as Dad cleared his throat and continued. "The Selection process was very successful for us. And though my parents had their problems, it worked well for them, too. So . . . we were hoping. . . ." He hesitated and met my eyes.

I was slow to pick up on their hints. I knew what the Selection was, but never, not even once, had it been suggested as an option for any of us, let alone me.

"No."

Mom put up her hands, cautioning me. "Just listen—"

"A Selection?" I burst out. "That's insane!"

"Eadlyn, you're being irrational."

I glared at her. "You promised—*you promised*—you'd never force me into marrying someone for an alliance. How is this any better?"

"Hear us out," she urged.

"No!" I shouted. "I won't do it."

"Calm down, love."

"Don't talk to me like that. I'm not a child!"

Mom sighed. "You're certainly acting like one."

"You're ruining my life!" I ran my fingers through my hair and took several deep breaths, hoping it would help me think. This couldn't happen. Not to me.

"It's a huge opportunity," Dad insisted.

"You're trying to shackle me to a stranger!"

"I told you she'd be stubborn," Mom muttered to Dad.

"Wonder where she gets that from," he shot back with a smile.

"Don't talk about me like I'm not in the room!"

"I'm sorry," Dad said. "We just need you to consider this."

"What about Ahren? Can't he do it?"

"Ahren isn't going to be the future king. Besides, he has Camille."

Princess Camille was the heir to the French throne, and a few years ago she'd managed to bat her lashes all the way into Ahren's heart.

"Then make them get married!" I pleaded.

"Camille will be queen when her time comes, and she, like you, will have to ask her partner to marry her. If it was Ahren's choice, we'd consider it; but it's not."

"What about Kaden? Can't you have him do it?"

Mom laughed humorlessly. "He's fourteen! We don't have that kind of time. The people need something to be excited about now." She narrowed her eyes at me. "And, honestly, isn't it time you look for someone to rule beside you?"

Dad nodded. "It's true. It's not a role that should be shouldered alone."

"But I don't want to get married," I pleaded. "Please don't make me do this. I'm only eighteen."

"Which is how old I was when I married your father," Mom stated.

"I'm not ready," I urged. "I don't want a husband. Please don't do this to me."

Mom reached across the table and put her hand on mine. "No one would be doing anything to you. You would be doing something for your people. You'd be giving them a gift."

"You mean faking a smile when I'd rather cry?"

She gave me a fleeting frown. "That has always been part of our job."

I stared at her, silently demanding a better answer.

"Eadlyn, why don't you take some time to think this over?" Dad said calmly. "I know this is a big thing we're asking of you."

"Does that mean I have a choice?"

Dad inhaled deeply, considering. "Well, love, you'll really have thirty-five choices."

I leaped up from my chair, pointing toward the door.

"Get out!" I demanded. "Get! Out!"

Without another word they left my room.

Didn't they know who I was, what they'd trained me

for? I was Eadlyn Schreave. No one was more powerful than me.

So if they thought I was going down without a fight, they were sadly mistaken.

CHAPTER 3

I DECIDED TO TAKE DINNER in my room. I didn't feel like seeing my family at the moment. I was irate with all of them. At my parents for being happy, at Ahren for not picking up the pace eighteen years ago, at Kaden and Osten for being so young.

Neena circled me, filling my cup as she spoke. "Do you think you'll go through with it, miss?" she asked.

"I'm still trying to figure a way out."

"What if you said you were already in love with somebody?"

I shook my head as I poked at my food. "I insulted my three most likely candidates right in front of them."

She set a small plate of chocolates in the middle of the table, guessing correctly that I'd probably want those more than the caviar-garnished salmon.

"Perhaps a guard then? Happens to the maids often enough," she suggested with a giggle.

I scoffed. "That's fine for them, but I'm not that desperate."

Her laughter faded.

I saw immediately that I had offended her, but that was the truth. I couldn't settle for any old person, let alone a guard. Even considering it was a waste of time. I needed a way out of this whole situation.

"I don't mean it like that, Neena. It's just that people expect certain things from me."

"Of course."

"I'm done. You can go for the night; I'll leave the cart in the hallway."

She nodded and left without another word.

I grazed on the chocolates before completely giving up on the food and slipped into my nightgown. I couldn't reason with Mom and Dad right now, and Neena didn't understand. I needed to talk to the only person who might see my side, the person who sometimes felt like he was half of me. I needed Ahren.

"Are you busy?" I asked, cracking open his door.

Ahren was sitting at his desk, writing. His blond hair was end-of-the-day messy, but his eyes were far from tired, and he looked so much like the pictures of Dad when he was younger it was eerie. He was still dressed from dinner but had taken off his coat and tie, settling in for the evening. "Knock, for goodness' sake."

"I know, I know; but it's an emergency."

"Then get a guard," he snapped back, returning to his papers.

"That's already been suggested," I muttered to myself. "I'm serious, Ahren; I need your help."

Ahren peeked over his shoulder at me, and I could see he was already planning to give in. He used his foot to push out the seat next to him casually. "Step into my office."

Sitting, I sighed. "What are you writing?"

He quickly piled papers on top of the one he'd been working on. "A letter to Camille."

"You know you could simply phone her."

He grinned. "Oh, I will. But then I'll send her this, too."

"That makes no sense. What could you possibly have to talk about that would fill an entire phone call and a letter?"

He tilted his head. "For your information, they serve different purposes. The calls are for updates and to see how her day went. The letters are for the things I can't always say out loud."

"Oh, really?" I leaned over, reaching for the paper.

Before I could even get close, Ahren's hand gripped my wrist. "I will murder you," he vowed.

"Good," I shot. "Then you can be the heir, and you can go through a Selection and kiss your precious Camille good-bye."

He scrunched his forehead. "What?"

I slumped back into my chair. "Mom and Dad need to

boost morale. They've decided that, for the sake of Illéa," I said in mock patriotism, "I need to go through a Selection."

I was expecting abject horror. Perhaps a sympathetic hand on my shoulder. But Ahren threw back his head and laughed.

"Ahren!"

He continued to howl, pitching himself forward and hitting his knee.

"You're going to wrinkle your suit," I warned, which only made him laugh harder. "For goodness' sake, stop it! What am I supposed to do?"

"As if I know! I can't believe they think this would even work," he added, his smile still not fading.

"What's that supposed to mean?"

He shrugged. "I don't know. I guess I thought, if you ever did get married, it'd be down the line. I think everyone assumed that."

"And what is *that* supposed to mean?"

The warm touch I'd been hoping for finally came as he reached for my hand. "Come on, Eady. You've always been independent. It's the queen in you. You like to be in charge, do things on your own. I didn't think you'd partner up with anyone until you at least got to reign for a while."

"Not like I really had a choice in the first place," I mumbled, tilting my head to the floor but still looking to my brother.

He gave me a little pout. "Poor little princess. Don't want to rule the world?"

I swatted his hand away. "Seven minutes. It should have

been you. I'd much rather sit alone and scribble away instead of do all that stupid paperwork. And this ridiculous Selection nonsense! Can't you see how dreadful this is?"

"How did you get roped into this anyway? I thought they'd done away with it."

I rolled my eyes again. "It has absolutely nothing to do with me. That's the worst part. Dad's facing public opposition, so he's trying to distract them." I shook my head. "It's getting really bad, Ahren. People are destroying homes and businesses. Some have died. Dad isn't completely sure where it's coming from, but he thinks it's people our age, the generation that grew up without castes, causing most of it."

He made a face. "That doesn't make sense. How could growing up without those restrictions make you upset?"

I paused, thinking. How could I explain what we could only really guess at? "Well, I grew up being told I was going to be queen one day. That was it. No choice. You grew up knowing you had options. You could go into the military, you could become an ambassador, you could do plenty of things. But what if that wasn't really happening? What if you didn't have all the opportunities you thought you would?"

"Huh," he said, following. "So they're being denied jobs?"

"Jobs, education, money. I've heard of people refusing to let their kids get married because of old castes. Nothing is happening the way Dad thought it would, and it's nearly impossible to control. Can we force people to be fair?"

"And that's what Dad's trying to figure out now?" he asked, skeptical.

"Yes, and I'm the smoke-and-mirror act diverting their attention while he comes up with a plan."

He chuckled. "That makes much more sense than you suddenly being romantically inclined."

I cocked my head. "Let it go, Ahren. So I'm not interested in marriage. Why does that matter? Other women can stay single."

"But other women aren't expected to produce an heir."

I hit him again. "Help me! What do I do?"

His eyes searched mine, and I knew, as easily as I could read any emotion in him, that he saw I was terrified. Not irritated or angry. Not outraged or repulsed.

I was scared.

It was one thing to be expected to rule, to hold the weight of millions of people in my hands. That was a job, a task. I could check things off lists, delegate. But this was much more personal, one more piece of my life that ought to be mine but wasn't.

His playful smile disappeared, and he pulled his chair closer to mine. "If they're looking to distract people, maybe you could suggest other . . . opportunities. A possible marriage isn't the only choice. That said, if Mom and Dad came to this conclusion, they might have already exhausted every other option."

I buried my head in my hands. I didn't want to tell him I tried to offer up him as an alternative or that I thought Kaden might even be acceptable. I sensed he was right, that the Selection was their last hope.

"Here's the thing, Eady. You'll be the first girl to hold the throne fully in her own right. And people expect a lot from you."

"Like I don't already know that."

"But," he continued, "that also gives you a lot of bargaining power."

I raised my head marginally. "What do you mean?"

"If they really need you to do this, then negotiate."

I sat up straight, my mind running around in circles, trying to think of what I could ask for. There might be a way to get through this quickly, without it even ending in a proposal.

Without a proposal!

If I spoke fast enough, I could probably get Dad to agree to practically anything so long as he got his Selection out of it.

"Negotiate!" I whispered.

"Exactly."

I stood up, grabbed Ahren by his ears, and planted a kiss on his forehead. "You are my absolute hero!"

He smiled. "Anything for you, my queen."

I giggled, shoving him. "Thanks, Ahren."

"Get to work." He waved me toward the door, and I suspected he was actually more eager to get back to his letter than he was for me to come up with a plan.

I dashed from the room, heading to my own to fetch some paper. I needed to think.

As I rounded the corner, I ran smack into someone, falling backward onto the carpet.

"Ow!" I complained, looking up to see Kile Woodwork, Miss Marlee's son.

Kile and the rest of the Woodworks had rooms on the same floor as our family, a singularly huge honor. Or irritation, depending on how one felt about the Woodworks.

"Do you mind?" I snapped.

"I wasn't the one running," he answered, picking up the books he'd dropped. "You ought to be looking where you're going."

"A gentleman would offer his hand right now," I reminded him.

Kile's hair flopped across his eyes as he looked over at me. He was in desperate need of a cut and a shave, and his shirt was too big for him. I didn't know who I was more embarrassed for: him for looking so sloppy or my family for having to be seen with such a disaster.

What was especially irritating was that he wasn't always so scruffy, and he didn't have to be now. How hard would it be to run a brush through his hair?

"Eadlyn, you've never thought I was a gentleman."

"True." I pulled myself up without help and brushed off my robe.

For the last six months I had been spared Kile's less-than-thrilling company. He'd gone to Fennley to enroll in some accelerated course, and his mother had been lamenting his absence ever since the day he left. I didn't know what he was studying, and I didn't particularly care. But he was back now, and his presence was another stressor on an ever-growing list.

"And what would make such a lady run like that in the first place?"

"Matters you are far too dim to comprehend."

He laughed. "Right, because I'm such a simpleton. It's a miracle I manage to bathe myself."

I was about to ask if he did bathe, because he looked like he'd been running away from anything that resembled a bar of soap.

"I hope one of those books is a primer on etiquette. You seriously need a refresher."

"You're not queen yet, Eadlyn. Take it down a notch." He walked away, and I was furious with myself for not getting the last word.

I pressed on. There were bigger problems in my life right now than the state of Kile's manners. I couldn't waste my time quibbling with people or being distracted by anything that couldn't put the Selection to death.

JOIN THE
Epic Reads
COMMUNITY

THE ULTIMATE YA DESTINATION

◀ **DISCOVER** ▶
your next favorite read

◀ **FIND** ▶
new authors to love

◀ **WIN** ▶
free books

◀ **SHARE** ▶
infographics, playlists, quizzes, and more

◀ **WATCH** ▶
the latest videos

◀ **TUNE IN** ▶
to Tea Time with Team Epic Reads

Find us at **www.epicreads.com**
and **@epicreads**

※·※

"IT TURNS OUT I'M ABSOLUTELY terrible at staying away from you. It's a very serious problem."

I smiled. "Have you really tried?"

He pretended to think about it. "Well, no. And don't expect me to start."

We laughed quietly, holding on to each other. In these moments, it was so easy to picture this being the rest of my life.

※·※

ALSO BY KIERA CASS

The Selection
The One
The Selection Stories: The Prince and the Guard

THE ELITE

KIERA CASS

HARPER TEEN

An Imprint of HarperCollinsPublishers

HarperTeen is an imprint of HarperCollins Publishers.

The Elite

Copyright © 2013 by Kiera Cass

All rights reserved. Printed in the United States of America.
No part of this book may be used or reproduced in any manner
whatsoever without written permission except in the case of brief
quotations embodied in critical articles and reviews. For information
address HarperCollins Children's Books, a division of HarperCollins
Publishers, 195 Broadway, New York, NY 10007.

www.epicreads.com

Library of Congress Cataloging-in-Publication Data
Cass, Kiera.
   The Elite / Kiera Cass. — 1st ed.
      p. cm.
   Summary: "Sixteen-year-old America Singer is one of only six girls
still competing in the Selection—but before she can fight to win
Prince Maxon and the Illean crown, she must decide where her own
heart truly lies"— Provided by publisher.
   ISBN 978-0-06-205997-0
   [1. Marriage—Fiction. 2. Contests—Fiction. 3. Social classes—
Fiction. 4. Princes—Fiction. 5. Love—Fiction.
6. Revolutionaries—Fiction.] I. Title.
PZ7.C2685133Eli 2013   2012038124
[Fic]—dc23   CIP
                                                                 AC

Typography by Sarah Hoy
16 17 18 19 20   CG/RRDH   23 22 21 20 19

First paperback edition, 2014

Call out the servants! The queen is awake!

(For Mom)

CHAPTER 1

THE ANGELES AIR WAS QUIET, and for a while I lay still, listening to the sound of Maxon's breathing. It was getting harder and harder to catch him in a truly calm and happy moment, and I soaked up the time, grateful that he seemed to be at his best when he and I were alone.

Ever since the Selection had been narrowed down to six girls, he'd been more anxious than he was when the thirty-five of us arrived in the first place. I guessed he thought he'd have more time to make his choices. And though it made me feel guilty to admit it, I knew I was the reason why he wished he did.

Prince Maxon, heir to the Illéa throne, liked me. He'd told me a week ago that if I could simply say that I cared for him the way he did for me, without anything holding me back, this whole competition would be over. And sometimes

I played with the idea, wondering how it would feel to be Maxon's alone.

But the thing was, Maxon wasn't really mine to begin with. There were five other girls here—girls he took on dates and whispered things to—and I didn't know what to make of that. And then there was the fact that if I accepted Maxon, it meant I had to accept a crown, a thought I tended to ignore if only because I wasn't sure what it would mean for me.

And, of course, there was Aspen.

He wasn't technically my boyfriend anymore—he'd broken up with me before my name was even drawn for the Selection—but when he showed up at the palace as one of the guards, all the feelings I'd been trying to let go of flooded my heart. Aspen was my first love; when I looked at him . . . I was his.

Maxon didn't know that Aspen was in the palace, but he did know that there was someone at home that I was trying to get over, and he was graciously giving me time to move on while attempting to find someone else he'd be happy with in the event I couldn't ever love him.

As he moved his head, inhaling just above my hairline, I considered it. What would it be like to simply love Maxon?

"Do you know when the last time was that I really looked at the stars?" he asked.

I settled closer to him on our blanket, trying to keep warm in the cool Angeles night. "No idea."

"A tutor had me studying astronomy a few years ago. If

you look closely, you can tell that the stars are actually different colors."

"Wait, the last time you looked at the stars was to *study* them? What about for fun?"

He chuckled. "Fun. I'll have to pencil in some between the budget consultations and infrastructure committee meetings. Oh, and war strategizing, which, by the way, I am terrible at."

"What else are you terrible at?" I asked, running my hand across his starched shirt. Encouraged by the touch, Maxon drew circles on my shoulder with the hand he had wrapped behind my back.

"Why would you want to know that?" he asked in mock irritation.

"Because I still know so little about you. And you seem perfect all the time. It's nice to have proof you're not."

He propped himself up on an elbow, focusing on my face. "You *know* I'm not."

"Pretty close," I countered. Little flickers of touch ran between us. Knees, arms, fingers.

He shook his head, a small smile on his face. "Okay, then. I can't plan wars. I'm rotten at it. And I'm guessing I'd be a terrible cook. I've never tried, so—"

"Never?"

"You might have noticed the teams of people keeping you up to your neck in pastries? They happen to feed me as well."

I giggled. I helped cook practically every meal at home. "More," I demanded. "What else are you bad at?"

He held me close, his brown eyes bright with a secret. "Recently I've discovered this one thing. . . ."

"Tell."

"It turns out I'm absolutely terrible at staying away from you. It's a very serious problem."

I smiled. "Have you really tried?"

He pretended to think about it. "Well, no. And don't expect me to start."

We laughed quietly, holding on to each other. In these moments, it was so easy to picture this being the rest of my life.

The rustle of leaves and grass announced that someone was coming. Even though our date was completely acceptable, I felt a little embarrassed and sat up quickly. Maxon followed suit as a guard made his way around the hedge to us.

"Your Majesty," he said with a bow. "Sorry to intrude, sir, but it's really unwise to stay out this late for so long. The rebels could—"

"Understood," Maxon said with a sigh. "We'll be right in."

The guard left us alone, and Maxon turned back to me. "Another fault of mine: I'm losing patience with the rebels. I'm tired of dealing with them."

He stood and offered me his hand. I took it, watching the sad frustration in his eyes. We'd been attacked twice by the rebels since the start of the Selection—once by the simply disruptive Northerners and once by the deadly Southerners—and even with my brief experience, I could understand his exhaustion.

Maxon was picking up the blanket and shaking it out, clearly not happy that our night had been cut short.

"Hey," I said, urging him to face me. "I had fun."

He nodded.

"No, really," I said, walking over to him. He moved the blanket to one hand to wrap his free arm around me. "We should do it again sometime. You can tell me which stars are which colors, because I seriously can't tell."

Maxon gave me a sad smile. "I wish things were easier sometimes, normal."

I moved so I could wrap my arms around him, and as I did so, Maxon dropped the blanket to return the gesture. "I hate to break it to you, Your Majesty, but even without the guards, you're far from normal."

His expression lightened a bit but was still serious. "You'd like me more if I was."

"I know you find it hard to believe, but I really do like you the way you are. I just need more—"

"Time. I know. And I'm prepared to give you that. I only wish I knew that you'd actually want to be with me when that time was over."

I looked away. That wasn't something I could promise. I weighed Maxon and Aspen in my heart over and over, and neither of them ever had a true edge. Except, maybe, when I was alone with one of them. Because, at that moment, I was tempted to promise Maxon that I would be there for him in the end.

But I couldn't.

"Maxon," I whispered, seeing how dejected he looked at my lack of an answer. "I can't tell you that. But what I can tell you is that I *want* to be here. I *want* to know if there's a possibility for . . . for . . ." I stammered, not sure how to put it.

"Us?" Maxon guessed.

I smiled, happy at how easily he understood me. "Yes. I want to know if there's a possibility for us to be an us."

He moved a lock of hair behind my shoulder. "I think the odds are very high," he said matter-of-factly.

"I think so, too. Just . . . time, okay?"

He nodded, looking happier. This was how I wanted to end our night, with hope. Well, and maybe one more thing. I bit my lip and leaned into Maxon, asking with my eyes.

Without a second of hesitation, he bent to kiss me. It was warm and gentle, and it left me feeling adored and somehow aching for more. I could have stayed there for hours, just to see if I could get enough of that feeling; but too soon, Maxon backed away.

"Let's go," he said in a playful tone, pulling me toward the palace. "Better get inside before the guards come for us on horseback with spears drawn."

As Maxon left me at the stairs, the tiredness hit me like a wall. I was practically dragging myself up to the second floor and around the corner to my room when, suddenly, I was quite awake again.

"Oh!" Aspen said, surprised to see me, too. "I think it makes me the worst guard ever that I assumed you were in your room this whole time."

I giggled. The Elite were supposed to sleep with at least one of their maids on watch in the night. I really didn't like that, so Maxon insisted on stationing a guard by my room in case there was an emergency. The thing was, most of the time that guard was Aspen. It was a strange mix of exhilaration and terror knowing that nearly every night he was right outside my door.

The lightness of the moment faded quickly as Aspen grasped what it meant that I hadn't been safely tucked in my bed. He cleared his throat uncomfortably.

"Did you have a good time?"

"Aspen," I whispered, looking to make sure no one was around. "Don't be upset. I'm part of the Selection, and this is just how it is."

"How am I supposed to stand a chance, Mer? How can I compete when you only ever talk to one of us?" He made a good point, but what could I do?

"Please don't be mad at me, Aspen. I'm trying to figure all this out."

"No, Mer," he said, gentleness returning to his voice. "I'm not mad at you. I *miss* you." He didn't dare say the words aloud, but he mouthed them. *I love you.*

I melted.

"I know," I said, placing a hand on his chest, letting myself forget for a moment all that we were risking. "But that doesn't change where we are or that I'm an Elite now. I need time, Aspen."

He reached up to hold my hand in his and nodded. "I can give you that. Just . . . try to find some time for me, too."

I didn't want to bring up how complicated that would be, so I gave him a tiny smile before gently pulling my hand away. "I need to go."

He watched me as I walked into my room and shut the door behind me.

Time. I was asking for a lot of it these days. I hoped that if I had enough, everything would somehow fall into place.

CHAPTER 2

"No, no," Queen Amberly answered with a laugh. "I only had three bridesmaids, though Clarkson's mother suggested I have more. I just wanted my sisters and my best friend, who, coincidentally, I'd met during my Selection."

I peeked over at Marlee and was happy to find she was looking at me, too. Before I arrived at the palace, I had assumed that with this being such a high-stakes competition, there'd be no way any of the girls would be friendly. Marlee had embraced me the first time we met, and we'd been there for each other from that moment on. With a single almost-exception, we'd never even had an argument.

A few weeks ago, Marlee had mentioned that she didn't think she wanted to be with Maxon. When I'd pushed her to explain, she clammed up. She wasn't mad at me, I knew that, but those days of silence before we'd let it go were lonely.

"I want seven bridesmaids," Kriss said. "I mean, if Maxon chooses me and I get to have a big wedding."

"Well, I won't have bridesmaids," Celeste said, countering Kriss. "They're just distracting. And since it would be televised, I want all eyes on me."

I fumed. It was rare that we all got to sit and talk with Queen Amberly, and here Celeste was, being a brat and ruining it.

"I'd want to incorporate some of my culture's traditions into my wedding," Elise added quietly. "Girls back in New Asia use a lot of red in their ceremonies, and the groom has to bring gifts to the bride's friends to reward them for letting her marry him."

Kriss piped up. "Remind me to be in your wedding party. I love presents!"

"Me, too!" Marlee exclaimed.

"Lady America, you've been awfully quiet," Queen Amberly said. "What do you want at your wedding?"

I blushed because I was completely unprepared to comment.

There was only one wedding I'd ever imagined, and it was going to take place at the Province of Carolina Services Office after an exhausting amount of paperwork.

"Well, the one thing I've thought about is having my dad give me away. You know when he takes your hand and puts it in the hand of the person you marry? That's the only part

I've ever really wanted." Embarrassingly enough, it was true.

"But everyone does that," Celeste complained. "That's not even original."

I should have been mad that she called me out, but I merely shrugged. "I want to know that my dad completely approves of my choice on the day it really matters."

"That's nice," Natalie said, sipping her tea and looking out the window.

Queen Amberly laughed lightly. "I certainly hope he approves. No matter who it is." She added the last words quickly, catching herself in the middle of implying that Maxon would be my choice.

I wondered if she thought that, if Maxon had told her about us.

Shortly after, the wedding talk died down, and the queen left to go work in her room. Celeste parked herself in front of the large television embedded in the wall, and the others started a card game.

"That was fun," Marlee said as we settled in at a table together. "I'm not sure I've ever heard the queen talk so much."

"She's getting excited, I think." I hadn't mentioned to anyone what Maxon's aunt had told me about how Queen Amberly tried many times for another child and failed. Adele had predicted that her sister would warm up to us once the group was smaller, and she was right.

"Okay, you have to tell me: Do you honestly not have any other plans for your wedding or did you just not want to share?"

"I really don't," I promised. "I have a hard time picturing a big wedding, you know? I'm a Five."

Marlee shook her head. "You *were* a Five. You're a Three now."

"Right," I said, remembering my new label.

I was born into a family of Fives—artists and musicians who were generally poorly paid—and though I hated the caste system in general, I liked what I did for a living. It was strange to think of myself as a Three, to consider embracing teaching or writing as a profession.

"Stop stressing," Marlee said, reading my face. "You don't have anything to worry about yet."

I was about to protest but was interrupted by a cry from Celeste.

"Come on!" she yelled, slamming the remote against the couch before pointing it at the television again. "Ugh!"

"Is it just me or is she getting worse?" I whispered to Marlee. We watched as Celeste hit the remote over and over before giving up and going to change the channel manually. I guessed if I had grown up as a Two, that would be something worth getting worked up over.

"It's the stress, I think," Marlee commented. "Have you noticed that Natalie's getting, I don't know . . . more aloof?"

I nodded, and we both looked over to the trio of girls playing their card game. Kriss was smiling as she shuffled, but Natalie was examining the ends of her hair, occasionally pulling out a strand she didn't seem to like. Her expression was distracted.

"I think we're all starting to feel it," I confessed. "It's harder to sit back and enjoy the palace now that the group is so small."

Celeste grunted, and we peeked over at her but quickly averted our eyes when she caught us looking.

"Excuse me for a moment," Marlee said, shifting in her seat. "I think I'm going to go to the bathroom."

"I was just thinking the same thing. Do you want to go together?" I offered.

Smiling, she shook her head. "You go ahead. I'll finish my tea first."

"Okay. I'll be back."

I left the Women's Room, taking my time walking down the gorgeous hallway. I wasn't sure I would ever get over how spectacular it was here. I was so distracted that I ran smack into a guard as I turned the corner.

"Oh!" I said.

"Pardon me, miss. Hope I didn't startle you." He held me by my elbows, helping me regain my footing.

"No," I said, giggling. "It's fine. I should have been watching where I was going. Thanks for catching me. Officer . . ."

"Woodwork," he answered, giving me a quick bow.

"I'm America."

"I know."

I smiled and rolled my eyes. Of course he knew.

"Well, I hope the next time I run into you, it won't be quite so literal," I joked.

He chuckled. "Agreed. Have a nice day, miss."

"You, too."

I told Marlee about my embarrassing run-in with Officer Woodwork when I got back and warned her to watch her step. She laughed at me and shook her head.

We spent the rest of the afternoon sitting by the windows, chatting about home and the other girls as we drank in the sunshine.

It was sad to think about the future just then. Eventually the Selection would be over, and while I knew Marlee and I would still be close, I would miss talking to her every day. She was the first real friend I'd ever made, and I wished I could keep her beside me all the time.

As I tried to stay in the moment, Marlee gazed dreamily out the window. I wondered what she was thinking about; but everything was so peaceful, I didn't ask.

CHAPTER 3

THE WIDE DOORS OF MY balcony were open, as well as the one to the hallway, and my room was filled with the warm, sweet air blowing in from the gardens. I had hoped the soft breezes would be a consolation for the fact that I had so much work to do. Instead they distracted me, making me ache to be anywhere but stuck at my desk.

I sighed and reclined in my seat, letting my head drape over the back of the chair. "Anne," I called.

"Yes, miss?" my head maid answered from the corner where she was sewing. Without looking, I knew that Mary and Lucy, my other two maids, had perked up, waiting to see if they could serve me as well.

"I command you to figure out what this report means," I said, pointing a lazy arm at the detailed account on military statistics that sat in front of me. It was a task that all the Elite would be tested on, but I couldn't bring myself to focus on it.

My three maids laughed, probably from both the ridiculousness of my demand and the fact that I'd issued one at all. I wouldn't have called leadership one of my strong suits.

"I'm sorry, my lady, but I think that might be overstepping my boundaries," Anne answered. Even though my request was a joke and her answer was, too, I could hear the genuine apology in her voice for not being able to help me.

"Fine." I moaned, heaving myself into an upright position. "I'll simply have to do it myself. The whole lot of you are worthless. I'm getting new maids tomorrow. This time I mean it."

They all chuckled again, and I focused on the numbers one more time. I was getting the impression that this was a bad report, but I couldn't be sure. I reread paragraphs and charts, furrowing my brow and biting the back of my pen as I tried to concentrate.

I heard Lucy laugh quietly, and I looked up to see what she was so amused by, following her eyes to the door. There, leaning against the frame, was Maxon.

"You gave me away!" he complained to Lucy, who continued to snicker.

I pushed back my chair in a rush and ran into his arms. "You read my mind!"

"Did I?"

"Please tell me we can go outside. Just for a little while?"

He smiled. "I have twenty minutes before I have to be back."

I pulled him down the hall, the excited chatter of my maids fading behind us.

There was no denying the gardens had become *our* place. Almost every chance we got to be alone, we came out here. It was such a stark contrast to how I used to spend my time with Aspen: holed up in the tiny tree house in my backyard, the only place we could be together safely.

Suddenly I wondered if Aspen was around somewhere, indistinguishable from the numerous guards in the palace, watching as Maxon held my hand.

"What are these?" Maxon asked, brushing across the tips of my fingers as we walked.

"Calluses. They're from pressing down on violin strings four hours a day."

"I've never noticed them before."

"Do they bother you?" I was the lowest caste of the six girls left, and I doubted any of them had hands like mine.

Maxon stopped moving and lifted my fingers to his lips, kissing the tiny, worn tips.

"On the contrary. I find them rather beautiful." I felt myself blush. "I've seen the world—admittedly mostly through bulletproof glass or from the tower of some ancient castle—but I've seen it. And I have access to the answers of a thousand questions at my disposal. But this small hand here?" He looked deeply into my eyes. "This hand makes sounds incomparable to anything I've ever heard. Sometimes I think I only dreamed that I heard you play the violin, it was so beautiful. These calluses are proof that it was real."

At times the way he spoke to me was overwhelming, too romantic to believe. But though I cherished the words in my heart, I was never completely sure I could trust them. How did I know he wasn't saying such sweet things to the other girls? I had to change the subject.

"Do you really have the answers to a thousand questions?"

"Absolutely. Ask me anything; and if I don't know the answer, I know where we can find it."

"Anything?"

"Anything."

It was tough to come up with a question on the spot, much less one that would stump him, which was what I wanted. I took a moment to think of the things I'd been most curious about when I was growing up. How planes flew. What the United States used to be like. How the tiny music players that the upper castes had worked.

And then it hit me.

"What's Halloween?" I asked.

"Halloween?" Clearly, he'd never heard of it. I wasn't surprised. I'd only seen the word once myself in an old history book my parents had. Some parts of that book were tattered beyond recognition, with pages missing or mostly destroyed. Still, I was always fascinated by the mention of a holiday we knew nothing about.

"Not so certain now, Your Royal Smartness?" I teased.

He made a face at me though it was clear he was only playing at being annoyed. He checked his watch and sucked in a breath.

"Come with me. We have to hurry," he said, grabbing my hand and launching himself into a run.

I stumbled a bit in my little heels, but I kept up pretty well as he led me back to the palace with a huge grin on his face. I loved when Maxon's carefree side came through; too often he was so serious.

"Gentlemen," he said as we raced past the guards by the door.

I made it halfway down the hall before my shoes got the better of me. "Maxon, stop!" I gasped. "I can't keep up!"

"Come on, come on, you're going to love this," he complained, tugging my arm as I slowed. He finally eased back to my pace but was obviously itching to move faster.

We headed toward the north corridor, near the area where the *Reports* were filmed, but ducked into a stairwell before we got that far. We went up and up, and I couldn't contain my curiosity.

"Where are we going exactly?"

He turned and faced me, immediately serious. "You have to swear never to reveal this little chamber. Only a few members of the family and a handful of the guards even know it exists."

I was beyond intrigued. "Absolutely."

We reached the top of the stairs, and Maxon held open the door for me. He took my hand again and pulled me down the hallway, finally stopping in front of a wall that was mostly covered by a magnificent painting. Maxon looked behind us to make sure no one was there, then reached behind the frame on the far side. I heard a faint click, and the painting swung toward us.

I gasped. Maxon grinned.

Behind the painting was a door that didn't go all the way to the ground and had a small keypad on it, like the kind on a telephone. Maxon punched in a few numbers and then a tiny beep sounded. He turned the handle as he looked back to me.

"Let me help you. It's quite a high step." He gave me his hand and gestured for me to walk in first.

I was shocked.

The windowless room was covered with shelves full of what appeared to be ancient books. Two of the shelves contained books that had curious red slashes on the bindings, and I saw a massive atlas against one wall, opened to a page that held the shape of some country I couldn't name. In the middle was a table with a handful of books on it, looking as if they'd been handled recently and left out for quick recovery. And finally, embedded in one wall was a wide screen that looked like a TV.

"What do the red slashes mean?" I asked in wonder.

"Those are banned books. As far as we know, they may be the only copies that still exist in all of Illéa."

I turned to him, asking with my eyes what I didn't dare say out loud.

"Yes, you can look at them," he said in a manner that implied I was putting him out but with an expression that said he had been hoping I'd ask.

I lifted one of the books carefully, terrified that I might accidentally destroy a one-of-a-kind treasure. I flipped through the pages but ended up setting it back down almost immediately. I was simply too awestruck.

I turned around to find Maxon typing on something that looked like a flat typewriter attached to the TV screen.

"What's that?" I asked.

"A computer. Have you never seen one?" I shook my head, and Maxon didn't seem too surprised. "Not many people have them anymore. This one is specifically for the information held in this room. If anything about your Halloween exists, this will tell us where it is."

I wasn't fully sure of what he was saying, but I didn't ask him to clarify. In a few seconds his hunt produced a three-bullet list on the screen.

"Oh, excellent!" he exclaimed. "Wait right there."

I stood by the table as Maxon found the three books that would reveal what Halloween was. I hoped it wasn't something stupid and that I hadn't made him go through all this effort for nothing.

The first book defined Halloween as a Celtic festival that marked the end of summer. Not wanting to slow us, I didn't bother mentioning I had no idea what a Celtic was. It said they believed that spirits passed in and out of the world on Halloween, and people would put on masks to ward off the evil ones. Later, it evolved into a secular holiday, mainly for children. They dressed up in costumes and went around their towns singing songs and were rewarded with candy, creating the saying "trick or treat," as they did a trick to get a treat.

The second book defined it as something similar, only it mentioned pumpkins and Christianity.

"This will be the interesting one," Maxon claimed, flipping through a book that was much thinner than the others and handwritten.

"How so?" I asked, coming around to get a better look.

"This, Lady America, is one of the volumes of Gregory Illéa's personal diaries."

"What?" I exclaimed. "Can I touch it?"

"Let me find the page we're searching for first. Look, it even has a picture!"

And there, like an apparition, an image from an unknown past showed Gregory Illéa with a tight expression on his face, his suit crisp and his stance tall. It was bizarre how much of the king and Maxon I could see in the way he stood. Beside him, a woman was giving the camera a halfhearted smile. There was something to her face that hinted she was once very lovely, but the luster had gone out of her eyes. She seemed tired.

Surrounding the couple were three figures. The first was a teenage girl, beautiful and vibrant, grinning widely and wearing a crown and a frilly gown. How funny! She was dressed as a princess. And then there were two boys, one slightly taller than the other and both dressed as characters I didn't recognize. They looked like they were on the verge of mischief. Below the image was an entry, amazingly enough, in Gregory Illéa's own hand.

THE CHILDREN CELEBRATED HALLOWEEN THIS YEAR WITH A PARTY. I SUPPOSE IT'S ONE WAY TO FORGET WHAT'S GOING ON AROUND THEM, BUT TO ME IT FEELS FRIVOLOUS. WE'RE ONE OF THE FEW FAMILIES REMAINING WHO HAVE ENOUGH MONEY TO DO SOMETHING FESTIVE, BUT THIS CHILD'S PLAY SEEMS WASTEFUL.

"Do you think that's why we don't celebrate anymore? Because it's wasteful?" I asked.

"Could be. If the date's any indication, this was right after the American State of China started fighting back, just before the Fourth World War. At that point, most people had nothing—picture an entire nation of Sevens with a handful of Twos."

"Wow." I tried to imagine the landscape of our country like that, blown apart by war, then fighting to pull itself back together. It was amazing.

"How many of these diaries are there?" I asked.

Maxon pointed to a shelf with a row of journals similar to the one we held. "About a dozen or so."

I couldn't believe it! All this history right in one room.

"Thank you," I said. "This is something I would never even have dreamed of seeing. I can't believe all this exists."

He was beaming. "Would you like to read the rest of

23

it?" He motioned to the diary.

"Yes, of course!" I practically shouted before my duties came back to me. "But I can't stay; I have to finish studying that terrible report. And you have to get back to work."

"True. Well, how about this? You can take the book and keep it for a few days."

"Am I allowed to do that?" I asked in awe.

"No." He smiled.

I hesitated, afraid of what I held. What if I lost it? What if I ruined it? Surely he had to be thinking the same thing. But I would never have an opportunity like this again. I could be careful enough for the sake of this gift.

"Okay. Just a night or two and then I'll give it straight back."

"Hide it well."

And I did. This was more than a book; it was Maxon's trust. I tucked it inside my piano stool under a pile of sheet music—a place my maids never cleaned. The only hands that would touch it would be mine.

CHAPTER 4

"I'M HOPELESS!" MARLEE COMPLAINED.

"No, no, you're doing great," I lied.

I'd been giving Marlee piano lessons nearly every day for more than a week, and it genuinely sounded like she was getting worse. For goodness' sake, we were still working on scales. She hit another sour note, and I couldn't help but wince.

"Oh, look at your face!" she exclaimed. "I'm terrible. I might as well be playing with my elbows."

"We should try that. Maybe your elbows are more accurate."

She sighed. "I give up. Sorry, America, you've been so patient, but I hate hearing myself play. It sounds like the piano is sick."

"More like it's dying, actually."

Marlee collapsed into laughter, and I joined her. Little did I know that when she'd asked for piano lessons, my ears would be in for such painful—but hilarious—torture.

"Maybe you'd be better at the violin? Violins make very beautiful music," I offered.

"I don't think so. With my luck, I'd destroy it." Marlee rose and went over to my little table, where the papers we were supposed to be reading were pushed to one side and my sweet maids had left tea and cookies for us.

"Oh, well, that's fine. The one here belongs to the palace anyway. You could throw it at Celeste's head if you wanted."

"Don't tempt me," she said, pouring us both some tea. "I'm so going to miss you, America. I don't know what I'll do when we don't get to see each other every day."

"Well, Maxon's very indecisive, so you don't have to worry about that just yet."

"I don't know," she said, turning serious. "He hasn't come right out and said it, but I know that I'm here because the public likes me. With the majority of the girls gone, it won't be long before their opinions change and they have a new favorite, and then he'll let me go."

I was careful with my words, hoping she'd explain the reason for the distance she'd put between the two of them but not wanting her to shut down on me again. "Are you okay with that? With not getting Maxon, I mean?"

She gave a small shrug. "He's just not the one. I'm fine with being out of the competition, but I really don't want to leave," she clarified. "Besides, I wouldn't want to end up with a man who's in love with someone else."

I sat bolt upright. "Who is he—"

The look in Marlee's eyes was triumphant, and the smile hiding behind her cup of tea said *Gotcha!*

She had.

In a split second, I realized that the thought of Maxon being in love with someone else made me so jealous I couldn't stand it. And the moment after that—the understanding that she meant me—was infinitely reassuring.

I'd put up wall after wall, making jokes at Maxon's expense and talking up the merits of the other girls; but in a single sentence, she found her way behind all that.

"Why haven't you ended this, America?" she asked sweetly. "You know he loves you."

"He never said that," I promised, and that was true.

"Of course he hasn't," she said, as if this would be obvious. "He's trying so hard to catch you, and every time he gets close you push him away. Why do you do that?"

Could I tell her? Could I confess that while my feelings for Maxon went deep—deeper than I knew, apparently— there was someone else I couldn't let go of?

"I'm just . . . not sure, I guess." I trusted Marlee; I really did. But it was safer for us both if she didn't know.

She nodded. It looked like she could tell there was more to it than that, but she didn't press me. It was almost comforting, this mutual acceptance of our secrets.

"Find a way to be sure. Soon. Just because he's not the one

for me doesn't mean Maxon's not a great guy. I'd hate for you to lose him because you were afraid."

She was right again. I was afraid. Afraid that Maxon's feelings weren't as genuine as they seemed, afraid of what being a princess might mean for me, afraid of losing Aspen.

"On a lighter note," she said, setting down her cup of tea, "all that talk about weddings yesterday made me think of something."

"Yes?"

"Would you want to, you know, be my maid of honor? If I get married someday?"

"Oh, Marlee, of course I would! Would you be mine?" I reached to grab her hands, and she took them happily.

"But you have sisters; won't they mind?"

"They'll understand. Please?"

"Absolutely! I wouldn't miss *your* wedding for the world." Her tone implied that my wedding would be the event of the century.

"Promise me that even if I get married to a nobody Eight in an alley somewhere, you'll be there."

She gave me a disbelieving look, positive that no such thing could ever happen. "Even if that's the case. I promise."

She didn't ask me to make a similar vow for her, which made me wonder as I had in the past if there was another Four back home who she had her heart set on. I wouldn't press her though. It was clear we both had secrets; but Marlee was my best friend, and I would do anything for her.

★ ★ ★

That night I was hoping to spend some time with Maxon. Marlee had me questioning a lot of my actions. And thoughts. And feelings.

After dinner, as we all stood to leave the Dining Room, I caught Maxon's eye and tugged my ear. It was our secret sign to ask for time together, and it was rare to pass up an invitation. But tonight Maxon's expression was disappointed as he mouthed the word "work" to me. I gave him a mock pout and a tiny wave before leaving for the night.

Perhaps it was for the best anyway. I really needed to think on some things where Maxon was concerned.

When I rounded the corner to my room, Aspen was there again, standing guard. He looked me up and down, taking in the snug green dress that did amazing things for the few curves I had. Without a word, I walked past him. Before I could turn the handle on my door, he gently grazed the skin on my arm.

It was slow but brief, and in those few seconds I felt that need, that sense of longing, that Aspen tended to inspire in me. One look at his emerald eyes, hungry and deep, and I felt my knees start to go shaky.

I moved into my room as quickly as I could, tortured by our connection. Thank goodness I barely had time to think about what Aspen made me feel, because the moment the door shut, my maids swarmed around me, preparing me for bed. As they chatted away and brushed my hair, I tried to let myself forget about everything for a moment.

It was impossible. I had to choose. Aspen or Maxon.

But how was I supposed to decide between two good possibilities? How could I make a choice that would leave some part of me devastated either way? I comforted myself with the thought that I still had time. I still had time.

CHAPTER 5

"So, Lady Celeste, you're saying that the quantities aren't sufficient, and you feel the number of men taken in the next draft should be raised?" Gavril Fadaye, the moderator of discussions on the *Illéa Capital Report* and the only person who ever interviewed the royals, asked.

Our debates on the *Report* were tests, and we knew it. Even though Maxon didn't have a timeline, the public was aching for the field to narrow; and I sensed the king, queen, and their advisers were, too. If we wanted to stay, we had to perform, whenever and wherever they said. I was glad I'd made it through that awful report about the soldiers. I remembered some of the statistics, so I stood a decent chance of making a good impression tonight.

"Exactly, Gavril. The war in New Asia has been going on

for years. I think one or two rounds of inflated drafts would give us the numbers we need to end it."

I really couldn't stand Celeste. She'd gotten one girl kicked out, ruined Kriss's birthday party last month, and literally tried to rip a dress off my back. Her status as a Two made her consider herself a cut above the rest of us. To be honest, I didn't have an opinion about the number of soldiers Illéa had, but now that I knew Celeste's, I was unwaveringly opposed.

"I disagree," I said in as ladylike a tone as I could manage. Celeste turned my way, her dark hair whipping over her shoulder in the process. With her back to the camera, she felt perfectly comfortable blatantly glaring at me.

"Ah, Lady America, you think increasing the numbers is a bad idea?" Gavril asked.

I felt the heat of a blush on my cheeks. "Twos can afford to pay their way out of the draft, so I'm sure Lady Celeste has never seen what it does when families lose their only sons. Taking more would be devastating, particularly for the lowest castes, who tend to have larger families and need every member to work in order to survive."

Marlee, beside me, gave me a friendly nudge.

Celeste took over. "Well, then what should we do? Certainly you aren't suggesting that we sit back and let these wars drag on?"

"No, no. Of course I want Illéa to be done with the war." I paused to gather my thoughts and looked across at Maxon for some sort of support. Next to him, the king looked peeved.

I needed to switch directions, so I blurted out the first thing that came to mind. "What if it was voluntary?"

"Voluntary?" Gavril asked.

Celeste and Natalie chuckled, which made it worse. But then I thought about it. Was it such a terrible idea?

"Yes. I'm sure there would need to be certain requirements, but perhaps we'd get more out of an army of men who wanted to be soldiers as opposed to boys who were only doing what it took to stay alive and get back to the life they left behind."

A hush of consideration fell on the studio. Apparently, I'd made a point.

"That's a good idea," Elise chimed in. "Then we'd also be sending out new soldiers every month or two as people sign up. It might be invigorating to the men who've been serving awhile."

"I agree," Marlee added, which was usually the extent of her comments. She clearly wasn't comfortable in debate situations.

"Well, I know this might sound a little modern, but what if it was open to women?" Kriss commented.

Celeste laughed aloud. "Who do you think would sign up? Would you be heading into the battlefield?" Her voice dripped with an insulting disbelief.

Kriss kept her head together. "No, I'm not soldier material.

But," she continued, to Gavril, "if there's one thing I've learned from being in the Selection, it's that some girls have a frightening killer instinct. Don't let the ball gowns fool you," she finished with a smile.

Back in my room, I allowed my maids to stay a little later than usual to help me get the pile of pins out of my hair.

"I liked your idea of the army being voluntary," Mary said, her nimble fingers hard at work.

"Me, too," Lucy added. "I remember watching my neighbors struggle when their oldest sons were taken. It was almost unbearable when so many didn't come home." I could see a dozen memories flash before her eyes. I had some of my own.

Miriam Carrier was widowed young; but she and her son, Aiden, managed all right, just the two of them. When the soldiers had shown up at her door with a letter and a flag and their meaningless condolences, she'd caved in on herself. She couldn't make it on her own. Even if she had the ability, she didn't have the heart.

Sometimes I saw her begging as an Eight in the same square where I had said my good-byes to Carolina. But it wasn't as if I had anything to give her.

"I know," I said to Lucy's reflection.

"I thought Kriss went a bit too far," Anne commented. "Women in battle sounds like a terrible idea."

I smiled at her prim face as she focused intently on my

hair. "According to my dad, women used to—"

A short burst of knocks came at the door, startling all of us.

"I had a thought," Maxon announced, walking in without waiting for an answer. It appeared we had a standing date Friday nights after the *Report*.

"Your Majesty," they said together, Mary dropping pins as she sank into her curtsy.

"Let me help you," Maxon offered, coming to Mary's aid.

"It's all right," she insisted, blushing fiercely and backing out of the room. Far less subtly than I'm sure she intended, she made wide eyes at Lucy and Anne, begging them to leave with her.

"Oh, um, goodnight, miss," Lucy said, tugging on the hem of Anne's uniform to get her to follow.

Once they were gone, Maxon and I both broke down into laughter. I turned to the mirror and continued to work the pins out of my hair.

"They're a funny lot," Maxon commented.

"It's just that they admire you so much."

Modestly, he waved the compliment away. "Sorry I interrupted," he said to my reflection.

"It's fine," I answered, tugging out the last pin. I ran my fingers through my hair and draped it over my shoulder. "Do I look okay?"

Maxon nodded, staring a little longer than necessary. He came to his senses and spoke. "Anyway, this idea . . ."

"Do tell."

"You remember that Halloween thing?"

"Yes. Oh, I still haven't read the diary. It's well hidden though," I promised.

"It's fine. No one's looking for it. Anyway, I was thinking. All those books said it fell in October, right?"

"Yes."

"It's October now. Why don't we have a Halloween party?"

I spun around. "Really? Oh, Maxon, could we?"

"Would you like that?"

"I would love it!"

"I figure all the Selected girls could have costumes made. The off-duty guards could be spare dance partners since there's only one of me and it would be unfair to make everyone stand around waiting for a turn. And we could do dancing lessons over the next week or two. You did say there wasn't much to do during the days sometimes. And candy! We'll have the best candies made and imported. You, my dear, will be stuffed by the end of the night. We'll have to roll you off the floor."

I was mesmerized.

"And we'll make an announcement, tell the entire country to celebrate. Let the children dress up and go door-to-door doing tricks, like they used to. Your sister will love that, yes?"

"Of course she will! *Everyone* will!"

He deliberated a moment, pursing his lips. "How do you think she would like celebrating here, at the palace?"

I was stunned. "What?"

"At some point in the competition, I'm supposed to meet the parents of the Elite. Might as well have siblings come and do this around a festive time as opposed to waiting—"

His words were cut off by me barreling into his arms. I was so elated by the possibility of seeing May and my parents, I couldn't contain my enthusiasm. He wrapped his arms around my waist and stared into my eyes, his own glittering with delight. How did this person—someone I'd imagined would be my polar opposite—always seem to find the things that would make me the happiest?

"Do you mean it? Can they really come?"

"Of course," he answered. "I've been longing to meet them, and it's part of the competition. Anyway, I think it would do all of you good to see your families."

Once I was sure I wouldn't cry, I whispered back, "Thank you."

"You're quite welcome. . . . I know you love them."

"I do."

He chuckled. "And it's clear you'd do practically anything for them. After all, you stayed in the Selection for them."

I jerked back, putting space between us so I could see his eyes. There was no judgment there, only shock at my abrupt movement. I couldn't let this pass though. I had to be absolutely clear.

"Maxon, they were part of the reason I stayed in the beginning, but they're not why I'm here now. You know that, right? I'm here because . . ."

"Because?"

I looked at Maxon, his adoring face so hopeful. *Say it, America. Just tell him.*

"Because?" he asked again, this time with an impish smile coming to his lips, which made me soften even more.

I thought about my conversation with Marlee and the way I'd felt the other day when we talked about the Selection. It was hard to think of Maxon as my boyfriend when there were other girls dating him, but he wasn't just my friend. That hopeful feeling hit me again, the wonder that we might be something special. Maxon was more to me than I'd let myself believe.

I gave him a flirtatious smile and started walking toward the door.

"America Singer, you get back here." He ran in front of me, wrapping an arm around my waist as we stood, chest to chest. "Tell me," he whispered.

I pinched my lips together.

"Fine, then I shall have to rely on other means of communication."

Without any warning, he kissed me. I felt myself dip backward a bit, completely supported by his arms. I placed my hands on his neck, wanting to hold him to me . . . and something shifted in my head.

Usually when we were alone together, I could block out the other girls. But tonight I thought about the possibility of someone else in my place. Just imagining it: someone else in Maxon's arms, making him laugh, *marrying* him . . . It broke my heart. I couldn't help it; I started to cry.

"Darling, what's wrong?"

Darling? The word, so tender and personal, enveloped me. In that moment, any desire I had to fight my feelings for Maxon disappeared. I wanted to be his dear, his darling. I wanted to be Maxon's alone.

It might mean welcoming a future I never thought I would and saying good-bye to things I never intended to, but the thought of leaving him now wasn't something I could handle.

It was true that I wasn't the best candidate for the crown, but I didn't deserve to be in the running at all if I couldn't at least be brave enough to confess how I felt.

I sighed, trying to keep my voice steady. "I don't want to leave all this."

"If I remember correctly, the first time we met, you said it was like a cage." He smiled. "It does grow on you, though, doesn't it?"

I gave my head a small shake. "Sometimes you can be so stupid." A weak laugh pushed through my choked-up throat.

Maxon let me pull away just enough so I could look into his brown eyes.

"Not the palace, Maxon. I could care less about the clothes or my bed or, believe it or not, the food."

Maxon laughed. It was no secret how excited I had been about the extravagant meals here.

"It's you," I said. "I don't want to leave you."

"Me?"

I nodded.

"You want me?"

I giggled at his bewildered expression. "That's what I'm saying."

He paused a moment. "How— But— What did I do?"

"I don't know," I said with a shrug. "I just think that we'd be a good us."

He smiled slowly. "We'd be a wonderful us."

Maxon pulled me in, roughly by his standards, and kissed me again.

"Are you sure?" he asked, holding me at arm's length, staring intently at me. "Are you absolutely positive?"

"If you're sure, I'm sure."

For a flicker of a second, something changed in his expression. But it passed so quickly, I wondered if it—whatever it was—was even real.

In the very next moment, he led me over to the bed, and we perched on the edge together, holding hands as my head rested on his shoulder. I was expecting him to say something. After all, wasn't this what he had been waiting for? But there were no words. Every once in a while he'd let out a long sigh, and in that sound alone I could hear how happy he was. That helped me not to feel so anxious.

After a while—perhaps because neither of us knew what to say—Maxon sat up straighter. "I should probably go. If we're going to add all the families to the celebration, I need to make extra plans."

I pulled back and smiled, still giddy that I was going to get to hug my mom, dad, and May soon. "Thank you again."

We stood together, walking toward the door. I held on to his hand tightly. For some reason, I dreaded letting it go. It felt like this whole moment was fragile somehow, and if it shifted too much it might break.

"I'll see you tomorrow," he promised in a whisper, his nose millimeters away from mine. He looked upon me with such adoration that I felt silly for worrying. "You're astonishing."

Once he was gone, I closed my eyes and pulled in everything from our short time together: the way he stared at me, the playful smiles, the sweet kisses. I thought about them over and over as I got ready for bed, wondering if Maxon was doing the same thing.

CHAPTER 6

"LOVELY, MISS. KEEP POINTING AT the sketches, and the rest of you, try not to look at me," the photographer asked.

It was Saturday, and all the Elite had been excused from our obligatory day of sitting in the Women's Room. At breakfast, Maxon made his announcement about the Halloween party; and by the afternoon, our maids had started working on costume designs, and photographers had shown up to document the whole process.

Now I was attempting to look natural as I went over Anne's drawings while my maids stood behind the table with pieces of fabric, containers of sequins, and an absurd amount of feathers.

The camera snapped and flashed as we tried to give several options. Just as I was about to pose with some gold fabric held up to my face, we had a visitor.

"Good morning, ladies," Maxon said, strolling through the open doorway.

I couldn't help but stand a little straighter, and it felt like my smile was taking over my face. The photographer caught that moment before addressing Maxon.

"Your Majesty, always an honor. Would you mind posing with the young lady?"

"It would be my pleasure."

My maids stepped back, and Maxon picked up a few sketches and stood right behind me, the papers in front of us in one hand and his other settled low on my waist. That touch conveyed so much to me. *See,* it said, *soon I'll get to touch you like this in front of the world. You don't have to worry about anything.*

A few pictures were taken, and the photographer left for the next girl on his list. I realized my maids had inconspicuously dismissed themselves at some point as well.

"Your maids are quite talented," Maxon said. "These are wonderful concepts."

I tried to act like I always did with Maxon, but things felt different now, better and worse at the same time. "I know. I couldn't be in better hands."

"Have you settled on one yet?" he asked, fanning out the papers on my desk.

"We're all fond of the bird idea. I think it's meant to be a reference to my necklace," I said, touching the thin string of silver. My songbird necklace was a gift from my dad, and I preferred it over the heavy jewelry the palace provided for us.

"I hate to say this, but I think Celeste has picked something avian as well. She seemed awfully determined," he said.

"That's all right," I replied with a shrug. "I'm not crazy about feathers anyway." My smile faltered. "Wait. You were with Celeste?"

He nodded. "Just a quick visit to chat. I'm afraid I can't stay long here, either. Father's not thrilled about all this, but with the Selection still going on, he understood that it would be nice to have some more festivities. And he agreed it would be a much better way to meet the families, all things considered."

"Like what?"

"He's eager for an elimination, and I'm supposed to do one after I meet with everyone's parents. The sooner they come, the better in his eyes."

I hadn't realized sending someone home was part of the Halloween plan. I thought it was just a big party. It made me nervous, though I told myself there was no reason I should be. Not after our conversation last night. Of all the moments I'd shared with Maxon, nothing seemed quite so real as that one.

Still scanning the designs, he spoke absentmindedly. "I suppose I ought to finish my rounds."

"You're leaving already?"

"Not to worry, darling. I'll see you at dinner."

Yes, I thought, *but you'll see all of us at dinner.*

"Is everything all right?" I asked.

"Of course," he answered, offering me a quick kiss. On the cheek. "I have to run. We'll talk again soon."

And, just as suddenly as he appeared, he was gone.

As of Sunday, the Halloween party was eight days away, which meant the palace was a hurricane of activity.

On Monday the Elite spent the morning with Queen Amberly taste testing and approving a menu for the party. It was easily the best task we'd been given so far. That afternoon, however, Celeste was missing from the Women's Room for a few hours. When she returned around four, she announced to us all, "Maxon sends his love."

Tuesday afternoon we greeted extended members of the royal family who were coming to town for the festivities. But that morning we all watched out the window as Maxon gave Kriss an archery lesson in the gardens.

Meals were full of guests who had come to stay early, but Maxon was often missing, as well as Marlee and Natalie.

I felt more and more embarrassed. I'd made a mistake by confessing my feelings to Maxon. For all his talk, he couldn't really be interested in me if his first instinct was to spend time with everyone else.

I'd all but lost hope by Friday when I found myself sitting at the piano in my room after the *Report*, wishing that Maxon would come.

He didn't.

I tried to put it out of my mind on Saturday, as the Elite were obligated to entertain the influx of ladies at the palace in the Women's Room in the morning and have yet another dance rehearsal in the afternoon.

Thank goodness our family chose to focus on music and art as Fives, because I was a terrible dancer. The only person in the room worse than me was Natalie. Obnoxiously enough, Celeste was the epitome of gracefulness. More than once the instructors asked her to help others in the room, the result of which was Natalie nearly twisting her ankle because of Celeste's intentionally poor guidance.

Smooth as a snake, Celeste faulted Natalie's two left feet for her problems. The teachers believed her, and Natalie laughed it all off. I admired Natalie for not letting Celeste get to her.

Aspen had been there for all the lessons. The first few times I avoided him, not really sure I wanted to interact with him. I heard rumors that the guards were switching schedules so fast it was dizzying. Some wanted to go to the party desperately while others had girls back home and would be in huge trouble if they were seen dancing with someone else, especially since five of us would be eligible again soon and in very high demand.

But seeing as this was our last formal rehearsal, when Aspen was near enough to offer me a dance, I didn't turn him down.

"Are you all right?" he asked. "You've seemed down the last few times I've seen you."

"Just tired," I lied. I couldn't talk with him about boy problems.

"Really?" he asked doubtfully. "I was sure that it meant bad news was coming."

"What do you mean?" Did he know something I didn't?

He sighed. "If you're preparing to tell me that I need to stop fighting for you, that's not a conversation I want to have."

In truth, I hadn't even thought about Aspen in the last week or so. I was so consumed by my mistimed words and mistaken guesses, I couldn't consider anything else. And here, while I'd been worried about Maxon letting me go, Aspen had been worrying about me doing the same to him.

"That's not what it is," I answered vaguely, feeling guilty.

He nodded, satisfied with that response for now. "Ouch!"

"Oops!" I said. I genuinely hadn't meant to step on him. I worked to focus a little more on the dancing.

"I'm sorry, Mer, but you're terrible." He was chuckling even though the heel of my shoe had to have hurt him.

"I know, I know," I said breathlessly. "I'm trying, I swear!"

I pranced around the room like a blind moose, but what I lacked in grace I made up for in effort. Aspen, kindly, did his best to make me look good, attempting to be a little less on the beat to be in time with me. That was so typical of him, always trying to be my hero.

By the end of that last lesson, I at least knew all the steps. I couldn't promise I wouldn't accidentally take out a visiting diplomat with an energetic kick of my leg, but I'd do my best. As I considered that image, I realized it was no wonder Maxon was having second thoughts. I'd be an embarrassment to take to another country let alone receive anyone here. I just didn't have that princess air about me.

I sighed and went to get a cup of water. Aspen followed me while the rest of the girls left.

"So," he started. I did a sweep of the room to make sure no one was watching. "I have to assume that if you're not worried about me, you're worried about him."

I lowered my eyes and blushed. How well he knew me.

"Not that I'm cheering for him or anything, but if he can't see how amazing you are, he's an idiot."

I smiled, continuing to study the floor.

"And if you don't get to be princess then, so what? That doesn't make you any less incredible. And you know . . . you know . . ." He couldn't get out what he wanted to say, and I risked looking at his face.

In Aspen's eyes I saw a thousand different endings to that sentence, all of them connecting him to me. That he was still waiting for me. That he knew me better than anyone. That we were the same. That a few months at the palace couldn't erase two years. No matter what, Aspen would always be there for me.

"I know, Aspen. I do."

CHAPTER 7

I STOOD IN LINE WITH the other girls in the massive foyer of the palace, bouncing on the balls of my feet.

"Lady America," Silvia whispered, and that was all it took to know I was behaving in an unacceptable way. As our main tutor for the Selection, she took our actions quite personally.

I tried to still myself. I envied Silvia and the staff and the handful of guards who were moving around the space if only for the fact that they were allowed to walk. If I could do the same, I knew I'd feel much calmer.

Maybe if Maxon was here already it wouldn't be so bad. Then again, maybe it would make me more anxious. I still couldn't figure out why, after everything, he hadn't made any time for me lately.

"They're here!" I heard through the palace doors. I wasn't the only one who made sounds of delight.

"All right, ladies!" Silvia called. "Best behavior! Butlers and maids against the wall, please."

We tried to be the lovely, regal young women Silvia wanted us to, but the second Kriss's and Marlee's parents made it through the doorway, it all fell apart. I knew that both girls were only children, and it was obvious their parents missed them too much to bother with decorum. They ran in screaming, and Marlee dashed out of the line without so much as a pause.

Celeste's parents were more put together, though they clearly were thrilled to see their daughter. She broke rank as well, but in a much more civilized way than Marlee. I didn't even register Natalie's or Elise's parents, because a short figure with wild red hair blazed around the open door, her eyes searching.

"May!"

She heard my call and saw my waving arm and rushed to me, Mom and Dad following her lead. I knelt on the floor, embracing her.

"Ames! I can't believe it!" she crooned, admiration and jealousy in her voice. "You look so, so beautiful!"

I couldn't speak. I could barely even see her, I was crying so much.

A moment later, I felt the steady arms of my father taking us both in. Then Mom, abandoning her usual propriety, joined us, and we all held one another in a heap on the palace floor.

I heard a sigh that I knew was Silvia's, but I really didn't care at the moment.

Once I could breathe again, I spoke. "I'm so happy you guys are here."

"We are, too, kitten," Dad said. "Can't even tell you how much we missed you." I felt his kiss on the back of my head.

I twisted so I could hug him better. I didn't know until this very moment how badly I had needed to see them.

I reached for Mom last. I was shocked that she was so quiet. I couldn't believe she hadn't already demanded a detailed report of my progress with Maxon. But when I pulled back, I noticed the tears in her eyes.

"You're so beautiful, sweetheart. You look like a princess."

I smiled. It was nice not to have her question or instruct me for once. She was just happy in the moment, and that meant the world to me. Because I was, too.

I noticed May's eyes focus on something over my shoulder.

"That's him," she breathed.

"Hmm?" I asked, looking down at her. I turned to see Maxon watching us from behind the grand stairwell. His smile was amused as he made his way to where we were huddled on the floor. My father stood immediately.

"Your Highness," he said, his voice full of admiration.

Maxon walked up to him, hand outstretched. "Mr. Singer, it's an honor. I've heard so much about you. And you, too,

Mrs. Singer." He moved to my mother, who had also risen and straightened her hair.

"Your Majesty," she squeaked, a little starstruck. "Sorry about all that." She motioned to the floor as May and I stood, still holding each other tightly.

Maxon chuckled. "Not at all. I'd expect no less enthusiasm from anyone related to Lady America." I was sure Mom would want an explanation for that later. "And you must be May."

May blushed as she extended her hand, expecting a shake but getting a kiss. "I never did get to thank you for not crying."

"What?" she asked, blushing even more in her confusion.

"No one told you?" Maxon said brightly. "You won me my first date with your lovely sister here. I'll be forever in your debt."

May giggled back. "Well, you're welcome, I guess."

Maxon put his hands behind his back, his education coming back to him. "I'm afraid I must meet the others, but please stay here for a moment. I'll be making a short announcement to the group. And I'm hoping to get to speak with you more very soon. So glad you could come."

"He's even cuter in person!" May whispered loudly, and I could tell by the slight shake of his head that Maxon had heard.

He went off to Elise's family, who were easily the most refined of the group. Her older brothers looked as rigid as the guards, and her parents bowed to Maxon as he approached. I wondered if Elise had told them to do that or if that was just who they were. They all looked so polished, with matching heads of jet-black hair topping their small, smartly dressed frames.

Beside them, Natalie and her very pretty younger sister were whispering to Kriss as their parents shook hands. The whole space was full of warm energy.

"What does he mean, he expected enthusiasm from us?" Mom demanded in a low whisper. "Is this because you yelled at him when you met? You haven't been doing that again, have you?"

I sighed. "Actually, Mom, we argue pretty regularly."

"What?" She gaped at me. "Well, stop it!"

"Oh, and I kneed him in the groin once."

There was a split second of silence before May barked a laugh. She covered her mouth and tried to stop, but it kept coming out in awkward, squeaky sounds. Dad's lips were pressed together, but I could tell he was on the verge of losing it himself.

Mom was paler than snow.

"America, tell me you're joking. Tell me you didn't assault the prince."

I didn't know why, but the word *assault* pushed us all over the edge; and May, Dad, and I bent over laughing as Mom stared at us.

"Sorry, Mom," I managed.

"Oh, good lord." She suddenly seemed very excited to meet Marlee's parents, and I didn't stop her from going.

"So he enjoys a girl who stands up to him," Dad said once we all calmed down. "I like him more already."

Dad looked around the room, taking in the palace, and I stood there trying to absorb his words. How many times in the years Aspen and I had been dating in secret had he and my father been in the same room? A dozen at least. Maybe more. And I'd never really worried about him approving of Aspen. I knew getting him to consent to me marrying down a caste would be hard, but I had always assumed I'd get his permission in the end.

For some reason, this felt a thousand times more stressful. Even with Maxon being a One, with him being able to provide for the lot of us, I was suddenly aware that there was a chance my dad might not like him.

Dad wasn't a rebel, out burning houses or anything. But I knew he was unhappy with the way things were run. What if his issues with the government extended to Maxon? What if he said I shouldn't be with him?

Before I could go too far down that path of thought, Maxon bounded up a few of the steps so he could see all of us.

"I want to thank you again for coming. We're so pleased to have you at the palace, not only to celebrate the first Halloween in Illéa in decades, but so that we can get to know all of you. I'm sorry my parents weren't able to greet you as well. You will meet them very soon.

"The mothers, sisters, and Elite are invited to have tea with my mother this afternoon in the Women's Room. Your daughters will be able to escort you there. And the gentlemen will be having cigars with my father and myself. We'll have a butler come for you, so no worries about getting lost.

"Your maids will escort you to the rooms you'll use for the duration of your stay, and they will get you properly suited for your visit, as well as for the celebration tomorrow night."

He gave us all a quick wave and went on his way. Almost immediately, a maid was at our side.

"Mr. and Mrs. Singer? I'm here to escort you and your daughter to your quarters."

"But I want to stay with America!" May protested.

"Sweetie, I'm sure the king gave us a room every bit as nice as America's. Don't you want to see it?" my mother encouraged.

May turned to me. "I want to live exactly how you live. Just for a little while. Can't I stay with you?"

I sighed. So I'd have to forgo some privacy for a few days, so what? There was no way I could say no to that face.

"Fine. Maybe with two of us, my maids will actually have something to do."

She hugged me so tightly, it was instantly worth it.

"What else have you learned?" Dad asked. I looped my arm through his, still getting used to him in a suit. If I hadn't seen Dad a thousand times in his dirty paint clothes, I could have sworn he was born to be a One. He looked so young and smart in the formal outfit. He even seemed taller.

"I think I told you everything we were taught about our history, how President Wallis was the last leader of what was the United States, and then he led the American State of China. I didn't know about him at all, did you?"

Dad nodded. "Your grandpa told me about him. I heard he was a decent guy, but there wasn't much he could do when things got as bad as they did."

I'd only learned the solid truth of the history of Illéa since I'd been at the palace. For some reason, the story of our country's origin was mostly passed on orally. I'd heard several different things, and none of them was as complete as the education I'd received in the last few months.

The United States was invaded at the beginning of the Third World War after they couldn't repay their crippling debt to China. Instead of getting money, which the United States didn't have, the Chinese set up a government here, creating the American State of China and using the Americans as labor. Eventually the United States rebelled—not only against China, but also against the Russians, who were trying to steal the labor force set up by the Chinese—joining with Canada, Mexico, and several other Latin countries to form one country. That was the Fourth World War, and— while we survived it, became a new country because of it—it was pretty economically devastating.

"Maxon told me that right before the Fourth World War people hardly had anything."

"He's right. It's part of why the caste system is so unfair. No one had much to offer in the way of help in the first place, which is why so many people ended up in the lower castes."

I didn't really want to go down this path with Dad, because I knew he could get really worked up. He wasn't wrong—the castes weren't fair—but this was a happy visit, and I didn't want to waste it talking about things we couldn't change.

"Besides the little history, it's mostly etiquette lessons. We're getting a bit more into diplomacy now. I think we might have to do something with that soon, they're pushing it so hard. The girls who stay will have to anyway."

"Who stay?"

"It turns out one girl will be going home with her family. Maxon's supposed to make an elimination after meeting you all."

"You sound unhappy. Do you think he'll send you home?"

I shrugged.

"Come on now. You must know if he likes you or not by this point. If he does, you have nothing to worry about. If he doesn't, why would you even want to stay?"

"I guess you're right."

He stopped walking. "So which is it?"

This was kind of embarrassing to talk about with my dad, but I wouldn't have talked about it with Mom either. And May would be worse at interpreting Maxon than I was.

"I think he likes me. He says he does."

Dad laughed. "Then I'm sure you're doing fine."

"But he's been a little . . . distant this last week."

"America, honey, he's the prince. He's probably been busy passing legislation or something like that."

I didn't know how to explain that Maxon seemed to be making time for everyone else. It was too humiliating. "I guess."

"Speaking of legislation, have you all learned anything about that yet? About how to write up proposals?"

I wasn't any more excited about this topic, but at least it was boy-free. "Not yet. We've been reading a lot of them though. They're hard to understand sometimes; but Silvia, the woman from downstairs, she's sort of a guide or tutor or whatever. She tries to explain things. And Maxon is helpful if I ask him questions."

"Is he?" Dad seemed happy about this.

"Oh, yes. I think it's important to him that we all feel like we could be successful, you know? So he's really great about explaining things. He even . . ." I deliberated. I wasn't supposed to mention the book room. But this was my dad. "Listen, you have to promise not to say anything about this."

He chuckled. "The only person I ever talk to is your mother, and we all know she can't be trusted with a secret, so I promise I won't tell her."

I giggled. Trying to imagine Mom keeping anything to herself was impossible.

"You can trust me, kitten," he said, giving me a little side hug.

"There's a room, a secret room, and it's full of books,

Dad!" I confessed quietly, double-checking to make sure no one was around. "There are books that are banned and these maps of the world, old ones with all the countries like they used to look. Dad, I didn't know there used to be that many! And there's a computer in there. Have you ever seen one in real life?"

He shook his head, stunned.

"It's amazing. You type what you're looking for, and it searches through all the books in the room and finds it."

"How?"

"I don't know, but that's how Maxon found out what Halloween was. He even . . ." I looked up and down the hall again. I decided there was no way Dad would tell about the library, but if I told him I had one of those secret books in my room, it might be too much.

"He even?"

"He let me borrow one once, just to see."

"Oh, that's very interesting! What did you read? Can you tell me?"

I bit my lip. "It was one of Gregory Illéa's personal diaries."

Dad's mouth dropped open before he composed himself. "America, that's incredible. What did it say?"

"Oh, I haven't finished. Mostly, it was to figure out what Halloween was."

He considered my words for a moment and shook his head. "Why are you worried, America? Clearly, Maxon trusts you."

I sighed, feeling foolish. "I guess you're right."

"Amazing," he breathed. "So there's a hidden room around here somewhere?" He looked at the walls in a whole new way.

"Dad, this place is crazy. There are doors and panels everywhere. For all I know, if I tipped this vase, we might fall through a trapdoor."

"Hmm," he said, amused. "I'll be very careful making my way back to my room then."

"Which you should probably do soon. I need to get May ready for tea with the queen."

"Ah, yes, you and your teas with the queen," he joked. "All right, kitten. I'll see you tonight for dinner. Now . . . how best not to fall into a secret hatch?" he wondered aloud, spreading his arms out like a protective shield as he walked.

Once he got to the stairwell, he tentatively put his hand on the rail. "Just so you know, this is safe."

"Thanks, Dad." I shook my head and made my way back to my room.

It was difficult not to skip down the halls. I was so happy my family was here, I could hardly stand it. If Maxon didn't send me home, it was going to be harder than ever to be separated from them.

I rounded the corner to my room and saw that the door was open.

"What did he look like?" I heard May ask as I approached.

"Handsome. To me anyway. His hair was kind of wavy, and it never stayed down." May giggled, and so did Lucy as she spoke. "A few times, I actually got to run my fingers through it. I think of that sometimes. Not as much as I used to."

I tiptoed closer, not wanting to disturb them.

"Do you still miss him?" May asked, curious about boys as always.

"Less and less," Lucy admitted, a tiny lilt of hope in her voice. "When I got here, I thought I would die from the ache. I kept dreaming up ways to escape the palace and get back to him, but that would never really happen. I couldn't leave my dad, and even if I got outside the walls, there's no way I could have found my way back."

I knew a little about Lucy's past, how her family gave themselves as servants to a family of Threes in exchange for the money to pay for an operation for Lucy's mother. Lucy's mom eventually died, and when the mother found out her son was in love with Lucy, she sold Lucy and her father to the palace.

I peeked through the door to find May and Lucy on the bed. The balcony doors were open, and the delicious Angeles air wafted in. May fell into the palace look so naturally, her day dress hanging perfectly on her frame as she sat braiding parts of Lucy's hair back and letting the rest fall free. I'd never seen Lucy without her hair pulled up tight into a bun. She looked lovely like this, young and carefree.

"What's it like to be in love?" May asked.

Part of me ached. Why hadn't she ever asked me? Then I remembered, as far as May knew, I'd never been in love.

Lucy's smile was sad. "It's the most wonderful and terrible

thing that can ever happen to you," she said simply. "You know that you've found something amazing, and you want to hold on to it forever; and every second after you have it, you fear the moment you might lose it."

I sighed softly. She was absolutely right.

Love is beautiful fear.

I didn't want to let myself think too much about losing things, so I walked inside.

"Lucy! Look at you!"

"Do you like it?" She reached back, touching the delicate braids.

"It's wonderful. May used to braid my hair all the time, too. She's very talented."

May shrugged. "What else was I supposed to do? We couldn't afford to have dolls, so I used Ames instead."

"Well," Lucy said, turning to face her, "while you're here, you will be our little doll. Anne, Mary, and I are going to make you look as pretty as the queen."

May tilted her head. "No one's as pretty as her." Then she quickly turned to me. "Don't tell Mom I said that."

I chuckled. "I won't. For now, though, we have to get ready. It's almost time for tea."

May clapped her hands together excitedly and went to settle in front of the mirror. Lucy pulled her hair up, managing to keep the braids together as she made her bun, putting her cap on to cover most of it. I couldn't blame her for wanting it to stay as it was a little bit longer.

"Oh, a letter came for you, miss," Lucy said, handing an

envelope to me with great care.

"Thank you," I replied, unable to keep the shock out of my voice. Most of the people I expected to hear from were currently with me. I tore it open and read the brief note, its deliberate scratch completely familiar.

America,

I have found out belatedly that the families of the Elite were recently invited to the palace, and that Father, Mother, and May have left to visit you. I know that Kenna is far too pregnant to travel, and Gerad is much too young. I'm trying to understand why this invitation wasn't extended to me. I'm your brother, America.

My only guess is that Father chose to exclude me. I certainly hope it wasn't you. We are on the edge of great things, you and I. Our positions can be very helpful to each other. If any other special privileges are ever offered to your family, you ought to remember me, America. We can help each other.

Did you happen to mention me to the prince? Just curious.

Write soon.

Kota

I debated crumpling it up and tossing it in the trash. I had hoped Kota might be getting over his caste climbing and learn to be content with the success he had. No such luck, it seemed. I threw the letter in the back of a drawer, choosing to forget about it entirely. His jealousy wasn't going to spoil this visit.

Lucy rang for Anne and Mary, and we all had a wonderful time getting ready. May's effervescent attitude kept us all in good spirits, and I found myself singing while we dressed. Not long after, Mom came by, asking all of us to double-check that she looked all right.

She did, of course. She was shorter and curvier than the queen, but she was every bit as regal in her dress. As we walked downstairs, May clutched my arm, looking sad.

"What's wrong? You're excited to meet the queen, aren't you?" I asked.

"I am. It's just . . ."

"What?"

She sighed. "How am I supposed to go back to khakis after all this?"

The girls were animated, and everyone was sparkling with energy. Natalie's sister, Lacey, was about May's age, and they sat in a corner, talking. I could see how Lacey resembled her sister. Physically, they were thin, blond, and lovely. But where May and I were opposites personality-wise, Natalie and Lacey were so similar. I would have described Lacey as a bit less whimsical, however. Not quite as clueless as her sister.

The queen made her rounds, speaking to all the mothers, asking questions in her sweet way. I was in a small group listening to Elise's mother talk about her family back in New

Asia when May tugged on my dress, pulling me away.

"May!" I hissed. "What are you doing? You can't act like that, especially when the queen's present!"

"You have to see!" she insisted.

Thank goodness Silvia wasn't here. I wouldn't put it past her to admonish May for something like this, even though May didn't know any better.

We made our way to the window, and May pointed outside. "Look!"

I peered past the shrubs and fountains and saw two figures. The first was my father, speaking with his hands as he either explained or asked something. The second was Maxon, pausing to think before responding. They walked slowly, and sometimes my dad would put his hands in his pockets or Maxon would tuck his behind his back. Whatever this conversation was, it seemed intense.

I glanced around. The women were all still engrossed with the experience, with the queen herself, and no one seemed to notice us.

Maxon stopped, stood in front of my father, and spoke deliberately. There was no aggression or anger, but he looked determined. After a pause, Dad held out his hand. Maxon smiled and shook it eagerly. A moment later, they both seemed lighter, and Dad slapped Maxon on the back. Maxon seemed to stiffen a bit at that. He wasn't used to being touched. But then Dad put his arm around Maxon's shoulder, the way he did with me and Kota, the way he did with all his kids. And Maxon seemed to like that very much.

"What was that about?" I asked aloud.

May shrugged. "It looked important though."

"It did."

We waited to see if Maxon had a conversation with anyone else's father; but if he did, they didn't go to the gardens.

CHAPTER 8

THE HALLOWEEN PARTY WAS AS amazing as Maxon had promised. When I walked into the Great Room with May by my side, I was stunned by the sheer beauty before me. Everything was golden. Ornaments on the walls, glittering jewels in the chandeliers, cups, plates, even the food—everything had hints of gold in it. It was nothing short of magnificent.

Popular music was playing through a sound system, but in the corner a small band waited to play the songs for the traditional dances we'd learned. Cameras—both for photography and video—dotted the room. No doubt this would be the highlight of Illéa programming tomorrow. There couldn't be a celebration equal to this one. I briefly wondered what it would be like if I was still here at Christmastime.

Everyone's costumes were gorgeous. Marlee was dressed

as an angel and dancing with that guard I ran into, Officer Woodwork. She even had wings that looked like they'd been made out of iridescent paper floating behind her. Celeste's dress was short and made of feathers, with a large plume behind her head announcing she was a peacock.

Kriss was standing with Natalie, and they seemed to have coordinated. Natalie's dress had flowers blossoming on the bodice, and her full skirt was fluttery blue tulle. Kriss's dress was as golden as the room and covered with cascading leaves. Guessing, I'd say they were spring and fall. It was a cute idea.

Elise's Asian heritage was being taken full advantage of. Her silken dress was an exaggeration of the demure ones she tended to favor. The draping sleeves were incredibly dramatic, and I was in awe of her ability to walk with the ornate headdress she was wearing. Elise didn't typically stand out, but tonight she looked lovely, almost regal.

Around the room, all the family and friends were in costume, too, and the guards were equally dashing. I saw a baseball player, a cowboy, someone in a suit with a name tag that said GAVRIL FADAYE, and one guard so bold as to put on a lady's dress. A few girls were near him, laughing up a storm. But many of the guards were in the dress version of their uniforms, which was simply pressed white pants and their blue jackets. They had on gloves but no hats, and these features helped distinguish them from the guards who were actually on duty, surrounding the perimeter of the room.

"So, what do you think?" I asked May, but when I turned, I saw she had disappeared into the crowd, already exploring.

I laughed to myself as I surveyed the room, trying to find her puffy little dress. When she said she wanted to go to the party as a bride—"the kind we see on TV"—I had thought it was a joke. She looked absolutely adorable in her veil though.

"Hello, Lady America," someone whispered in my ear.

I started and turned to see Aspen in his dress uniform beside me.

"You scared me!" I put my hand over my heart as if that would slow it. Aspen only chuckled.

"I like your costume," he said jovially.

"Thank you. I do, too." Anne had made me into a butterfly. My dress was tapered from front to back in a fluttering material edged in black that floated around me. A tiny mask that looked like wings covered my eyes, making me feel mysterious.

"Why didn't you dress up?" I asked. "Couldn't you think of anything?"

He shrugged. "I prefer the uniform."

"Oh." It seemed sad to waste a perfectly good reason to be extravagant. Aspen had even fewer opportunities than I did in that department. Why not live it up?

"I just wanted to say hello, see how you were."

"Good," I said quickly. I felt so awkward.

"Oh." He sounded unsatisfied. "All right then."

Maybe after his little speech the other day, he expected more of an answer, but I wasn't ready to say anything yet. He gave me a bow and went off to see another guard who embraced him like a brother. I wondered if being a guard gave him a sense of family the way the Selection had done for me.

Marlee and Elise found me moments later and dragged me onto the dance floor. As I swayed, trying not to hit anyone, I caught Aspen standing on the edge of the floor, talking with Mom and May. Mom ran her hand over Aspen's sleeve, like she was straightening it out, and May was beaming. I could imagine them telling him how handsome he looked in his uniform, how proud his mother must be. He smiled back, and I could see how pleased he was, too. Aspen and I were rarities, a Five and Six pulled out of our monotonous lives and placed in the palace. The Selection had been so life changing that I sometimes forgot to appreciate the experience.

I danced in a circle with some of the other girls and guards until the music quieted and the DJ spoke.

"Ladies of the Selection, gentlemen of the guard, and friends and relatives of the royal family, please welcome King Clarkson, Queen Amberly, and Prince Maxon Schreave!"

The band swelled with music, and we all curtsied and bowed as they came in together. The king was apparently dressed as a king, simply that of another country. I didn't catch the reference. The queen's dress was a blue so deep it almost appeared black, with glittering jewels across it. She looked like the night sky. And Maxon, comically, was a pirate. His pants were torn in places, and he wore a loose shirt with a vest and a bandanna over his hair. To add to the effect, he hadn't shaved in a day or two, and a shadow of dark blond fuzz covered the bottom half of his face like a smile.

The DJ asked us to clear the floor, and the king and queen had a first dance together. Maxon stood to one side beside Kriss and Natalie, whispering things to each in turn and making them laugh. Finally I saw that he was doing a sweep of the room. I didn't know if he was looking for me or not, but I didn't want to be caught staring at him. I fluffed out my dress and stared at his parents instead. They looked very happy.

I thought about the Selection and how crazy it seemed, but I couldn't argue with the outcome. King Clarkson and Queen Amberly were suited for each other. He seemed forceful, and she combated that with a calming nature. She was a quiet listener, and he always seemed to have something to say. Though the whole thing should be archaic and wrong, it worked.

Did they ever grow apart during their Selection the way I felt Maxon might be growing apart from me? Why had he not made a single attempt to see me in the midst of dating the rest of the girls? Maybe that was why he was speaking with Dad, to explain to him why he'd have to let me go. Maxon was a polite person, so that seemed like something he would do.

I surveyed the crowd, looking for Aspen. In the process, I saw that Dad had finally arrived and was standing arm in arm with Mom on the opposite side of the room. May had found her way to Marlee and was tucked right in front of her. Marlee held her arms across May's chest in a sisterly gesture, and their white dresses shone in the lights. It didn't surprise me at all that they got so close in less than a day. I sighed. Where was Aspen?

In a last effort, I peeked behind me. There he was, just over my shoulder, waiting by me as always. When our eyes met, he gave me a quick wink, and it lifted my entire mood.

After the king and queen finished, we all crowded onto the dance floor. Guards shuffled around, pairing up with girls easily. Maxon was still standing on the side of the room with Kriss and Natalie. I hoped maybe he'd come ask me to dance. I certainly didn't want to ask him.

Gathering my nerve, I smoothed my dress and walked in his direction. I decided that I would at least present him with an opportunity to ask me. I made my way across the floor, planning to jump into their conversation. When I got close enough to do that, Maxon turned to Natalie.

"Would you like to dance?" he asked.

She laughed and tilted her blond head to the side like it was the most obvious thing in the world, and I breezed past them, my eyes trained on a table of chocolates, as if that was my goal the entire time. I kept my back to the room as I ate the delicious treats, hoping no one could see how deeply I was blushing.

Perhaps a half-dozen songs in, Officer Woodwork appeared next to me. Like Aspen, he had opted to stay in his uniform.

"Lady America," he said with a bow. "May I have this dance?"

His voice was bright and warm, and his enthusiasm washed over me. I took his hand easily.

"Absolutely, sir," I replied. "I should warn you, though, I'm not very good."

"That's fine. We'll take it slow." His smile was so inviting that I couldn't be worried about my poor dancing skills, and I happily followed him to the floor.

The dance was an upbeat one, which suited his mood. He spoke through the entire thing, and it was hard to keep up. So much for taking it slow.

"It seems you've fully recovered from me nearly running you over," he joked.

"It's a shame you didn't do any damage," I shot back. "If I was in a splint, I wouldn't have to dance at least."

He laughed. "I'm glad you're as funny as everyone says you are. I hear you're a favorite of the prince, too." He made it sound as if it was common knowledge.

"I don't know about that." Part of me was sick of people saying that. Another part yearned for it still to be true.

Over Officer Woodwork's shoulder, I saw Aspen dancing with Celeste. Something knotted in my chest at the sight.

"Sounds like you get along well with most everyone. Someone even said that during the last attack you took your maids with you to the hiding place for the royal family. Is that true?" He sounded amazed. At the time, it seemed like

73

a completely normal thing to protect the girls I loved, but to everyone else it came across as daring or strange.

"I couldn't leave them behind," I explained.

He shook his head in awe. "You're a true lady, miss."

I blushed. "Thank you."

I was left gasping for breath after the song, so I took a seat at one of the many tables sprinkled around the room. I drank orange punch and fanned myself with a napkin, watching others dancing on the floor. I found Maxon with Elise. They looked happy as they spun around in circles. He'd danced with Elise twice now and still hadn't sought me out.

It took awhile to find Aspen on the floor since so many men were in uniform, but I finally spotted him in a corner, talking with Celeste. I watched as she winked at him, her lips turned up in a flirtatious smile.

Who does she think she is? I stood to go and tell her to stop but realized what that would mean for both Aspen and myself before I took a step forward. I sat back down and continued to sip my punch. By the time the song ended, though, I was on the move and had situated myself close enough to Aspen for it to be appropriate for him to ask me to dance.

And he did, which was good, because I didn't think I could have been patient.

"What in the world was that?" I asked quietly but with obvious outrage in my voice.

"What was what?"

"Celeste was running her hands all over you!"

"Somebody's jealous," he sang into my ear.

"Oh, stop it! She's not supposed to be acting like that; it's against the rules!" I looked around to make sure no one could see how intimately we were talking, particularly my parents. I noticed Mom sitting and talking with Natalie's mother. Dad had disappeared.

"This from you," he said, rolling his eyes playfully. "If we aren't together, you can't tell me who I'm not allowed to talk to."

I made a face. "You know it's not like that."

"So what is it like?" he whispered. "I don't know if I'm supposed to be holding on or letting go." He shook his head. "I don't want to give up, but if there's nothing for me to hope for, then tell me."

I could see the effort behind him keeping his face so calm, the lingering sadness in his voice. And I hurt, too. Thinking about letting this end brought a stabbing pain to my chest.

I sighed and confessed. "He's been avoiding me. He'll say hello, but he's been very devoted to dating the other girls recently. I think I must have imagined that he actually liked me."

He stopped dancing for a moment, shocked at what I was saying. He quickly picked back up, studying my face for a moment.

"I didn't realize that was what was going on," he said softly. "I mean, you know I want us to be together, but I didn't want you to get hurt."

"Thanks." I shrugged. "I feel stupid more than anything."

Aspen pulled me in a little closer, still keeping a respectful distance though I knew he didn't want to. "Trust me, Mer, any man who passes up the chance to be with you is the stupid one."

"You tried to pass me up," I reminded him.

"That's how I know," he replied with a smile. I was glad we could joke about that now.

I looked over Aspen's shoulder and found Maxon dancing with Kriss. Again. Wasn't he even going to ask me once?

Aspen leaned in. "You know what this dance reminds me of?"

"Tell me."

"Fern Tally's sixteenth birthday party."

I gave him a look like he was crazy. I remembered Fern's sixteenth birthday. Fern was a Six, and sometimes we got help from her when Aspen's mom was too busy to fit us in. Her sixteenth birthday party came about seven months after Aspen and I had started dating. We were both invited, and it wasn't much of a party. A cake and water, the radio turned on because she didn't own any music discs, and the lights dimmed in her unfinished basement. The big thing was that it was the first party I'd been to that wasn't a "family" party. It was just the local kids alone in a room, and that was exciting. However, it in no way compared to the splendor of what was happening around us now.

"How in the world is this party like that one?" I asked disbelievingly.

Aspen swallowed once and spoke. "We danced. Remember? I was so proud to have you there, in my arms, in front of other people. Even if you did look like you were having a seizure." He winked at me.

The words stirred my heart. I did remember that. I lived off that moment for weeks.

In an instant a thousand secrets that Aspen and I had built and saved flooded my mind: the names we'd picked out for our imaginary children, our tree house, his ticklish spot on the back of his neck, the notes we'd written and hidden away, my failed efforts in making homemade soap, games of tic-tac-toe played with our fingers on his stomach . . . games where we couldn't remember our invisible moves . . . games he always let me win.

"Tell me you'll wait for me. If you'll wait for me, Mer, I can handle anything else," he breathed into my ear.

The music switched to a traditional song, and a nearby officer asked for a dance. I was swept away, leaving both Aspen and myself without any answers.

The night went on, and I found myself peeking over at Aspen more than once. Though I tried to seem casual about it, I bet anyone really paying attention might have noticed, particularly my dad, if he had been in the room. But he seemed more interested in touring the palace than in dancing.

I tried to distract myself with the party and must have danced with everyone in the room except for Maxon. I was sitting down resting my tired feet when I heard his voice beside me.

"My lady?" I turned to see him. "May I have this dance?"

That feeling, that indefinable something, coursed through me. As dejected as I'd felt, as embarrassed as I'd been, when he offered me that moment, I had to take it.

"Of course." He took my hand and walked me out to the floor, where the band was starting a slow song. I felt a rush of happiness. He didn't seem upset or uncomfortable. On the contrary, Maxon held me so close I could smell his cologne and feel his stubble against my cheek.

"I was wondering if I was going to get a dance at all," I commented, trying to sound playful.

Maxon managed to pull me even closer. "I was saving this one. I've put in time with all the other girls, so my obligations are over. Now I can enjoy the rest of the evening with you."

I blushed the way I always did when he said things like that to me. Sometimes his words were like single lines of poetry. After the last week, I didn't think I'd ever hear him speak to me that way again. It made my pulse race.

"You look lovely, America. Much too beautiful to be on the arm of a scraggly pirate."

I giggled. "How could you have possibly dressed to match? Come as a tree?"

"At the very least, some kind of shrubbery."

I laughed again. "I would pay money to see you dressed as a shrubbery!"

"Next year," he promised.

I looked at him. *Next year?*

"Would you like that? For us to have another Halloween

party next October?" he asked.

"Will I even be here next October?"

Maxon stopped dancing. "Why wouldn't you?"

I shrugged. "You've been avoiding me all week, dating the other girls. And . . . I saw you talking to my dad. I thought you might be telling him why you had to kick out his daughter." I swallowed the lump in my throat. I was *not* going to cry here.

"America."

"I get it. Someone has to go, and I'm a Five, and Marlee's the people's favorite—"

"America, stop," he said gently. "I'm such an idiot. I had no idea you'd see it that way. I thought you felt secure in your standing."

I was missing something here.

Maxon sighed. "Honestly? I was trying to give the other girls a sporting chance. From the beginning, I've really only looked at you, wanted you." I ducked my head for a moment, overcome by his deep stare. "When you told me how you felt, I was so relieved that a part of me didn't believe it. I still have a hard time accepting that it was real. You'd be surprised how infrequently I get something I truly want." Maxon's eyes were hiding something, some sadness he wasn't prepared to share. But he shook it away and continued explaining, starting to sway to the music again.

"I was afraid I was wrong, that you would change your mind any second. I've been looking for a suitable alternative, but the truth is . . ."—Maxon looked me in the eyes again, unwavering—"there's only you. Maybe I'm not really look-ing, maybe they aren't right for me. It doesn't matter. I just know I want you. And that terrifies me. I've been waiting for you to take back the words, to beg to leave."

It took me a moment to find my breath. Suddenly all that time away looked different. I could understand that feeling—that it was too good to be true, too good to trust. I felt like that every day with him.

"Maxon, that's not going to happen," I whispered into his neck. "If anything, you're going to realize I'm not good enough."

His lips were at my ear. "Darling, you're perfect."

My arm on his back drew him toward me, and he did the same, until we were closer to each other physically than we'd ever been. In the back of my mind, I realized we were in a crowded room, that somewhere my mother was prob-ably fainting at the sight, but I didn't care. For that moment, it felt like we were the only two people in the world.

I pulled back to look at Maxon, noticing that I needed to get the moisture out of my eyes to do so. But I liked these tears.

Maxon explained everything. "I want us to take our time. After I announce the dismissal tomorrow, that will appease the public and my father, but I don't want to rush you at all. I want you to see the princess's suite. It adjoins mine, actu-ally," he said quietly. Something about being that close to him all the time made my bones feel weak.

"I think you should start deciding what you want in there. I want you to feel completely at home. You'll have to pick a few more maids, too, and figure out if you want your family in the palace or just nearby. I'll help you with everything." A tiny beat of my heart whispered, *What about Aspen?* But I was so taken in by Maxon that I barely even heard it.

"Soon, when it's proper for me to end the Selection, when I propose to you, I want it to be as easy as breathing for you to say yes. I promise to do everything in my power between now and that moment to make it that way. Anything you need, anything you want, say the words. I will do everything I can for you."

I was overwhelmed. He understood me so well, how nervous I was about making this commitment, how frightening it was for me to become a princess. He was going to give me every last second he could and, in the meantime, lavish me with everything possible. I had another one of those moments when I couldn't believe this was all happening.

"That's not fair, Maxon," I mumbled. "What in the world am I supposed to be able to give you?"

He smiled. "All I want is your promise to stay with me, to be mine. Sometimes it feels like you can't possibly be real. Promise me you'll stay."

"Of course. I promise."

With that I rested my head on his shoulder, and we slow danced through song after song. Once May caught my eye, and she looked like she was about to die with happiness watching us together. Mom and Dad stood looking on, and Dad shook his head as if to say *And you thought he was sending you home.*

Something occurred to me.

"Maxon?" I asked, turning my face toward him.

"Yes, darling?"

I smiled at the name. "Why were you talking with my dad?"

Maxon smiled. "He is aware of my intentions. And you should know that he approves wholeheartedly, so long as you're happy. That seemed to be his only stipulation. I assured him that I'd do everything I could to see that you were, and I told him you seemed happy here already."

"I am."

I felt Maxon's chest rise. "Then he and I both have everything we need."

Maxon's hand moved slightly and settled low on my back, encouraging me to stay close. In that touch I knew so many things. I knew that this was real, that it was happening, and that I could let myself believe it. I knew I'd let go of the friendships I'd made here if I had to, though I was sure Marlee wouldn't mind losing in the slightest. And I knew I'd let the torch I held for Aspen burn out. It would be slow, and I would have to tell Maxon, but I would do it.

Because now I was his. I knew it. I'd never been so sure.

For the first time I could see it. I saw the aisle, the guests waiting, and Maxon standing at the end of it all. With that touch, it all made perfect sense.

The party went on late into the night, when Maxon dragged the six of us to the balcony at the front of the palace for the best view of the fireworks. Celeste was stumbling up the marble steps, and Natalie had acquired some poor guard's hat. Champagne was being passed around, and Maxon was celebrating our engagement prematurely with a bottle he'd kept all to himself.

As the fireworks lit up the sky in the background, Maxon raised his bottle in the air.

"A toast!" he exclaimed.

We all raised our glasses and waited expectantly. I noticed Elise's glass was smeared with the dark lipstick she'd been wearing, and even Marlee held a glass quietly, choosing to sip rather than gulp.

"To all you beautiful ladies. And to my future wife!" Maxon called.

The girls hooted, thinking this toast might be especially for each of them, but I knew better. As everyone tipped their glasses back, I watched Maxon—my almost fiancé—who gave me a tiny wink before taking another swig of champagne. The glow and excitement of the entire evening was overwhelming, like a fire of happiness was swallowing me whole.

I couldn't imagine anything strong enough to take that happiness away.

CHAPTER 9

I BARELY SLEPT. BETWEEN GETTING in so late and the excitement over what was coming, it was impossible. I curled closer to May, comforted by her warmth. I'd miss her so much once she left, but at least I had the prospect of her living here with me to look forward to.

I wondered who would be leaving today. It didn't seem polite to ask, so I didn't; but if pressed, I would guess it was Natalie. Marlee and Kriss were popular with the public—more popular than I was—and Celeste and Elise had connections. I had Maxon's heart, and that left Natalie without much to hold on to.

I felt bad because I really didn't have anything against Natalie. If anything, I wished Celeste would go. Maybe Maxon would send her home since he knew how much I disliked her, and he did say he wanted me to be comfortable here.

I sighed, thinking of everything he'd said last night. I'd never imagined this was possible. How did I, America Singer—a Five, a nobody—fall for Maxon Schreave—a One, *the* One? How did this happen when I'd spent the last two years bracing myself for life as a Six?

A tiny part of my heart throbbed. How would I explain this to Aspen? How would I tell him that Maxon had chosen me and that I wanted to be with him? Would he hate me? The thought made me want to cry. No matter what, I didn't want to lose Aspen's friendship. I couldn't.

My maids didn't knock when they came in, which was typical. They always tried to let me rest as long as I could, and after the party, I certainly needed it. But instead of going to prep things, Mary went around to May and gently rubbed her shoulder to wake her.

I rolled over to see Anne and Lucy with a garment bag. A new dress?

"Miss May," Mary whispered, "it's time to get up."

May slowly roused. "Can't I sleep?"

"No," Mary said sadly. "There's some important business this morning. You need to go to your parents right away."

"Important business?" I asked. "What's going on?"

Mary looked to Anne, and I followed her eyes. Anne shook her head, and that seemed to be the end of it.

Confused but hopeful, I got out of bed, encouraging May to do the same. I gave her a big hug before she went to Mom and Dad's room.

Once she left, I turned back to my maids. "Can you

explain now that she's gone?" I asked Anne. She shook her head. Frustrated, I huffed. "Would it help if I commanded you to tell?"

She looked at me, a clear solemnity in her eyes. "Our orders come from much higher. You'll have to wait."

I stood at the door to my bathroom and watched them move. Lucy's hands were shaking as she pulled out fistfuls of rose petals for my bath, and Mary's eyebrows were knit together as she lined up my makeup and the pins for my hair. Lucy sometimes trembled for no reason at all, and Mary tended to do that with her face when she was concentrating. It was Anne's look that made me scared.

She was always put together, even in the most frightening and taxing of situations, but today she looked as if her body was full of sand, her whole frame low with worry. She kept stopping and rubbing her forehead as if she could smooth away the anxiety in her face.

I looked on as she pulled my dress out of the garment bag. It was understated, simple . . . and jet-black. I looked at that dress and knew it could only mean one thing. I started crying before I even knew who I was mourning.

"Miss?" Mary came to help me.

"Who died?" I asked. "Who died?"

Anne, steady as ever, pulled me upright and wiped the tears from under my eyes.

"No one has died," she said. But her voice wasn't comforting; it was commanding. "Be grateful for that when this is all over. No one died today."

She gave me no further explanation and sent me straight to my bath. Lucy tried to keep herself under control; but when she finally broke into tears, Anne asked her to go get me something light to eat, and she jumped on the command obediently. She didn't even curtsy as she left.

Lucy eventually returned with some croissants and apple slices. I wanted to sit and eat slowly, stretching out my time, but one bite was all it took for me to know that food was not my friend today.

Finally Anne placed my name pin on my chest, the silver shining beautifully against the black of my dress. There was nothing left for me to do but face this unimaginable fate.

I opened my door but found myself frozen. Turning back to my maids, I breathed out my fear. "I'm scared."

Anne put her hands on my shoulders and spoke. "You are a lady now, miss. You must handle this like a lady."

I gave a small nod as she released me, unclenched my hands from the door, and walked away. I wish I could have said my head was high; but honestly, lady or not, I was terrified.

To my immense surprise, when I reached the foyer, the rest of the girls were waiting, all wearing dresses and expressions similar to my own. A wave of relief hit me. I wasn't in trouble. If anything, we all were, so at least I wouldn't be going through whatever this was alone.

"There's the fifth," a guard said to his counterpart. "Follow us, ladies."

Fifth? No, that wasn't right. It was six. As we walked down the stairs, I quickly scanned the girls. The guard *was* right. Only five. Marlee wasn't here.

My first thought was that Maxon had sent Marlee home, but wouldn't she have come by my room to say good-bye? I tried to think of a relationship between all this secrecy and Marlee's absence, and nothing I came up with made sense.

At the bottom of the stairs, an assembly of guards waited, along with our families. Mom, Dad, and May seemed anxious. Everyone did. I looked at them, hoping for some sort of clarity, but Mom shook her head while Dad gave me a shrug. I scanned the uniformed men for Aspen. He wasn't there.

I saw a pair of guards escorting Marlee's parents to the back of our line. Her mother was hunched with worry, and she leaned into her husband, his face heavy, as if he had aged years in a single night.

Wait. If Marlee was gone, why were they here?

I turned as a burst of light flooded the foyer. For the first time since I'd been at the palace, the front doors were both opened wide, and we were paraded outside. We crossed the short circular driveway and headed past the massive walls that fenced us into the grounds. As the gates creaked open, the deafening sound of a massive crowd greeted us.

A large platform had been set up in the street. Hundreds, maybe thousands of people were crowded together, children sitting on the shoulders of their parents. Cameras were positioned around the platform, and production people were running in front of the crowds, capturing the scene. We were led to a small section of stadium seats, and the crowd cheered for us as we walked out. I could see the shoulders of every girl in front of me relax as the people in the streets called out our names and threw flowers at our feet.

I lifted my hand in a wave as people called my name. I felt so silly for worrying. If the people were this happy, then nothing bad could be happening. The staff at the palace really needed to rethink the way they handled the Elite. All that anxiety for nothing.

May giggled, happy to be a part of the excitement, and I was relieved to see her back to herself. I tried to keep up with all the well-wishers, but I was distracted by the two odd structures waiting on the platform. The first was a ladder-like contraption in the shape of an *A*; the second was a large wooden block with loops on either end. With a guard at my side, I climbed into my seat in the middle of the front row and tried to figure out what was going on.

The crowd erupted again as the king, queen, and Maxon emerged. They too were dressed in dark clothes and wore sober expressions. I was close to Maxon, so I turned his way. Whatever was happening, if he looked at me and smiled, I knew it would be fine. I kept willing him to glance at me, to give me some sort of acknowledgment. But Maxon's face was hard.

A moment later the crowd's cheers turned into cries of disdain, and I turned to see what made them so unhappy.

My stomach twisted as I watched my world shatter.

Officer Woodwork was being dragged out in chains. His lip was bleeding, and his clothes were so dirty he looked like he'd spent the night rolling in mud. Behind him,

Marlee—her beautiful angel costume lacking its wings and covered in grime—was also in chains. A suit coat covered her hunched shoulders, and she squinted into the light. She took in the massive crowd, finding my eyes for a split second before she was pulled forward again. She searched once more, and I knew who she was seeking out. To my left, I saw Marlee's parents watching, gripping each other tightly. They were visibly crushed, gone from this place, as if their very hearts had abandoned them.

I looked back to Marlee and Officer Woodwork. The anxiety in their faces was obvious, yet they walked with a certain pride. Only once, when Marlee tripped over the hem of her dress, did that veneer crack. Beneath it, terror awaited.

No. No, no, no, no, no.

As they were led up onto the platform, a man in a mask began speaking. The crowd hushed for him. Apparently, this—whatever it was—had happened before, and the people here knew how to respond. But I didn't; my body lurched forward, and my stomach heaved. Thank goodness I hadn't eaten.

"Marlee Tames," the man called, "one of the Selected, a Daughter of Illéa, was found last night in an intimate moment with this man, Carter Woodwork, a trusted member of the Royal Guard."

The crier's voice was full of an inappropriate amount of self-importance, as if he was reciting the cure for some deadly disease. The crowd booed again at his accusations.

"Miss Tames has broken her vow of loyalty to our prince

Maxon! And Mr. Woodwork has essentially stolen property of the royal family through his relations with Miss Tames! These offenses are treason to the royal family!" He was shrieking out his statements, willing the crowd to agree. And they did.

But how could they? Didn't they know this was Marlee? Sweet, beautiful, trusting, giving Marlee? She made a mistake, maybe, but nothing deserving of this much hatred.

Carter was being strapped up to the A-shaped frame by another masked man, his legs spread wide and his arms pulled into a position that mimicked the structure. Padded belts were wrapped around his waist and legs, tightened to a point that looked uncomfortable even from here. Marlee was forced to kneel in front of the large wooden block as a man ripped the coat from her back. Her wrists were bound down to the loops on either side, palms up.

She was crying.

"This is a crime punishable by death! But, in his mercy, Prince Maxon is going to spare these two traitors their lives. Long live Prince Maxon!"

The crowd chanted after the man. If I had been in my right mind, I would have known I was supposed to call out, too, or at least applaud. The girls around me did, and so did our parents, even if they were in shock. But I wasn't paying attention. All I saw were Marlee's and Carter's faces.

We had been given front-row seats for a reason—to show us what would happen if we made such a stupid mistake—but from here, not more than twenty feet from the platform,

I could see and hear everything that really mattered.

Marlee was staring at Carter, and he was looking right back at her, craning his neck to do so. The fear was unmistakable, but there was also this look on her face, as if she was trying to reassure him that he was worth all this.

"I love you, Marlee," he called to her. It was barely audible over the crowd, but it was there. "We're going to be okay. It'll be okay, I promise."

Marlee couldn't speak in her fear, but she nodded back at him. In that moment, all I could think of was how beautiful she looked. Her golden hair was messy and her dress a disaster, and she'd lost her shoes at some point; but, my God, she looked radiant.

"Marlee Tames and Carter Woodwork, you are both hereby stripped of your castes. You are the lowest of the low. You are Eights!"

The crowd cheered, which seemed wrong. Weren't there any Eights standing here who hated being referred to that way?

"And to inflict upon you the shame and pain you have brought on His Majesty, you will be publicly caned with fifteen strikes. May your scars remind you of your many sins!"

Caned? What did that even mean?

My answer came a second later. The two masked men who had bound Carter and Marlee pulled long rods out of a bucket of water. They swiped them in the air a few times, testing them out, and I could hear the sticks whistling as they cut at the air. The crowd applauded this warm-up with the same frenzy and adoration they had just given the Selected.

In a few seconds, Carter's backside would be humiliatingly struck, and Marlee's precious hands . . .

"No!" I cried. "No!"

"I think I'm going to be sick," Natalie whispered as Elise made a weak moan into her guard's shoulder. But nothing stopped.

I stood up and lunged toward Maxon's seat, falling over my father's lap.

"Maxon! Maxon, stop this!"

"You have to sit down, miss," my guard said, trying to wrangle me back into my chair.

"Maxon, I beg you, please!"

"It's not safe, miss!"

"Get off me!" I yelled at my guard, kicking him as hard as I could. Try as I may, he held on tight.

"America, please sit down!" my mother urged.

"One!" cried the man on the stage, and I saw the cane fall on Marlee's hands.

She let out the most pathetic whimper, like a dog that had been kicked. Carter made no sound.

"Maxon! Maxon!" I yelled. "Stop it! Stop it, please!"

He heard me; I knew he did. I saw him slowly close his eyes and swallow one time, as if he could push the sound out of his head.

"Two!"

Marlee's cry was pure anguish. I couldn't imagine her pain—and there were still thirteen more strikes to go.

"America, sit!" Mom insisted. May was between her and Dad, her face averted, her cries almost as pained as Marlee's.

"Three!"

I looked at Marlee's parents. Her mother buried her head in her hands, her father's arms wrapped around her, as if he could protect her from everything they were losing in that moment.

"Let me go!" I yelled at my guard to no avail. "MAXON!" I screamed. My tears were blurring my vision, but I could see him enough to know he'd heard me.

I looked at the other girls. Shouldn't we do something? Some appeared to be crying, too. Elise was bent over, a palm pressed to her forehead, looking as if she might pass out. No one seemed angry though. Shouldn't they be?

"Five!"

The sound of Marlee's shrieks would haunt me for the rest of my life. I'd never heard anything like it. Or the sickening echo of the crowd cheering it on, as if this was merely entertainment. Or Maxon's silence, allowing this to happen. Or the crying of the girls around me, accepting it.

The only thing that gave me any sort of hope was Carter. Even though he was sweating from the trauma and shaking with pain, he managed to pant out comforting words to Marlee.

"It'll be . . . over soon," he managed.

"Six!"

"Love . . . you," he stammered.

I couldn't handle this. I tried to claw at my guard, but his thick sleeves protected him. I shrieked as he gripped me tighter.

"Get your hands off my daughter!" Dad yelled, pulling the guard's arms. With that space, I wiggled myself until I was facing him and thrust my knee up as hard as I could.

He let out a muffled cry and fell back, my dad catching him on the way down.

I hopped over the railing, clumsy in my dress and heeled shoes. "Marlee! Marlee!" I screamed, running as quickly as I could. I almost got to the steps; but two guards caught up with me, and that was a fight I couldn't win.

From the angle behind the stage, I saw that they'd exposed Carter's backside, and his skin was already torn, pieces hanging sickeningly. Blood was trickling down, ruining what used to be his dress pants. I couldn't imagine the state of Marlee's hands.

The thought sent me into an even deeper hysteria. I screamed and kicked at the guards, but all that accomplished was the loss of one of my shoes.

I was dragged inside as the man cried out for the next strike, and I didn't know whether to be grateful or ashamed. On the one hand, I didn't have to see it all; on the other, I felt like I'd abandoned Marlee in the worst possible moment of her life.

If I had been a true friend, wouldn't I have done better than that?

"Marlee!" I screamed. "Marlee, I'm sorry!" But the crowd was so frenzied, and she was crying so much, I didn't think she heard me.

CHAPTER 10

I THRASHED AND SHRIEKED ALL the way back. The guards had to hold me so tightly that I knew I'd be covered in bruises later, but I didn't care. I had to fight.

"Where's her room?" I heard one ask, and twisted to see a maid walking down the hall. I didn't recognize her, but she clearly knew me. She escorted the guards to my door. I heard my maids shouting in protest at the way I was being handled.

"Calm down, miss; that's no way to behave," a guard said with a grunt as they threw me onto my bed.

"Get the hell out of my room!" I screamed.

My maids, all of them in tears, rushed over to me. Mary started trying to get the dirt from my fall off my dress, but I slapped her hands away. They knew. They knew, and they didn't warn me.

"You, too!" I yelled at them. "I want all of you out! NOW!"

They recoiled at my words, and the tremors running down Lucy's little body almost made me regret saying them. But I had to be alone.

"We're sorry, miss," Anne said, pulling the other two back. They knew how close I was to Marlee.

Marlee . . .

"Just go," I whispered, turning to bury my face in my pillow.

Once the door clicked shut, I slipped off my remaining shoe and climbed deeper into bed, finally making sense of a hundred tiny details. So this was the secret she had been too afraid to share. She didn't want to stay because she wasn't in love with Maxon, but she didn't want to leave and be separated from Carter.

A dozen moments suddenly made sense: why she chose to stand in certain places or stared toward doors. It was Carter; he was there. The time the king and queen of Swendway came and she refused to get out of the sun . . . Carter. It was Marlee he was waiting for when I ran into him outside the bathroom. It was always him, standing silently by, perhaps sneaking a kiss here and there, waiting for a time when they could truly be together.

How much must she have loved him to be so careless, to risk so much?

How could this even be real? It didn't seem possible. I knew that there would be a punishment for something like this, but that it happened to Marlee, that she was gone. . . . I couldn't understand it.

My stomach writhed. It so easily could have been me. If Aspen and I hadn't been so careful, if someone had overheard our conversation on the dance floor last night, that could have been us.

Would I ever see Marlee again? Where would she be sent? Would her parents have anything to do with her? I didn't know what Carter was before the draft made him a Two, though my guess was he was a Seven. Seven was low, but it was better than Eight by a long shot.

I couldn't believe she was an Eight. This *could not* be real.

Would Marlee ever be able to use her hands again? How long did such wounds take to heal? And what about Carter? Would he even be able to walk after that?

That could have been Aspen.

That could have been me.

I felt so sick. I had a cruel sense of relief that it *wasn't* me, and the guilt of that relief was so heavy it was hard to breathe. I was a terrible person, a terrible friend. I was ashamed.

There was nothing left to do but cry.

I spent the morning and most of the afternoon curled in a ball on my bed. My maids brought me lunch, but I couldn't touch it. Mercifully, they didn't insist on staying and let me be alone in my sadness.

I couldn't pull myself together. The more I thought over

what had happened, the sicker I felt. I couldn't get the sound of Marlee screaming out of my head. I wondered if a time would come when I'd forget.

A hesitant knock came at the door. My maids weren't here to open it, and I didn't feel like moving, so I didn't. After a brief pause the visitor came in anyway.

"America?" Maxon said quietly.

I didn't answer.

He shut the door and walked across the room to stand by my bed.

"I'm sorry," he said. "I didn't have a choice."

I stayed still, unable to speak.

"It was that or kill them. The cameras found them last night and circulated the footage without us knowing," he insisted.

He didn't talk for a while, maybe thinking that if he stood there long enough, I'd find something I wanted to say to him.

Finally he knelt beside me. "America? Look at me, darling?"

The endearment made my stomach turn. I did look at him though.

"I had to. I *had* to."

"How could you just stand there?" My voice sounded funny. "How could you not do anything?"

"I told you once before that part of this job is looking calm, even when you aren't. It's something I've had to master. You will, too."

My brow folded together. He couldn't still think I wanted that now? Apparently, he did. As he slowly took in my expression, his fell into absolute shock.

"America, I know you're upset, but please? I told you; you're the only one. Please don't do this."

"Maxon," I said slowly, "I'm sorry, but I don't think I can do this. I could never stand by and watch someone get hurt like that, knowing it was my judgment that sent them there. I can't be a princess."

He drew in a staggered breath, probably the closest thing to a truly sad emotion I'd ever seen from him.

"America, you're basing the rest of your life on five minutes of someone else's. Things like that rarely happen. You wouldn't have to do that."

I sat up, hoping it would help me see matters more clearly. "I just . . . I can't even think right now."

"Then don't," he urged. "Don't let this make a decision for the both of us when you're so upset."

Somehow those words sounded like a trick.

"Please," he whispered intensely, clutching my hands. The desperation in his voice made me look at him. "You promised you'd stay with me. Don't give up, not like this. Please."

I let out a breath and nodded.

His relief was palpable. "Thank you."

Maxon sat there, holding on to my hand like a lifeline. It didn't feel like it did yesterday.

"I know . . . ," he started. "I know that you're hesitant

about the job. I always knew that would be hard for you to embrace. And I'm sure this makes it harder. But . . . what about me? Do you still feel sure about me?"

I fidgeted, uncertain of what to say. "I told you I couldn't think."

"Oh. Right." His absolute dejection was clear. "I'll let you be for now. We'll talk soon though."

He leaned forward like he might kiss me. I looked down, and he cleared his throat. "Good-bye, America."

Then he was gone.

And I broke down all over again.

Maybe minutes or hours later, my maids came in and found me bawling. I rolled over, and there was no way they could miss the pleading in my eyes.

"Oh, my lady," Mary cried, coming to embrace me. "Let's get you ready for bed."

Lucy and Anne began working on the buttons of my dress while Mary cleaned my face and smoothed my hair.

My maids sat around me, comforting me as I cried. I wanted to explain that it was more than Marlee, that it was this sick ache over Maxon, too; but it was embarrassing to admit how deeply I cared, how wrong I'd been.

Then my heartbreak doubled when I asked for my parents, and Anne told me that all the families had been escorted away quickly. I didn't even get to say good-bye.

Anne stroked my hair, gently shushing me. Mary was at my feet, rubbing my legs comfortingly. Lucy simply held her hands to her heart, as if she felt it all with me.

"Thank you," I whispered between sniffles. "I'm sorry about earlier."

They exchanged glances. "There's nothing to apologize for, miss," Anne insisted.

I wanted to correct her, because I'd certainly crossed the line with how I treated them, but another knock came at the door. I tried to think of how to politely say I didn't want to see Maxon right now, but when Lucy hopped up to answer it, Aspen's face was on the other side.

"I'm sorry to disturb you, ladies, but I heard the crying and wanted to make sure you were all right," he said.

He crossed the floor toward my bed, a bold move considering the day we'd all had.

"Lady America, I'm very sorry about your friend. I heard she was something special. If you need anything, I'm here." The look in Aspen's eyes communicated so much: that he was willing to sacrifice any number of things to make this better if he could, that he wanted to take it all away if only for my sake.

What an idiot I'd been. I'd almost given up the one person in the world who really knew me, really loved me. Aspen and I had been building a life together, and the Selection nearly destroyed it.

Aspen was home. Aspen was safe.

"Thank you," I replied quietly. "Your kindness means a great deal to me."

Aspen gave me an almost imperceptible smile. I could tell he wanted to stay, and I wanted that as well; but with my maids bustling around, it couldn't happen. I remembered thinking the other day that I would always have Aspen, and I was happy to find that it was absolutely true.

CHAPTER 11

HEY KITTEN,

I'M SO SORRY WE DIDN'T GET TO SAY GOOD-BYE. THE KING
SEEMED TO THINK IT WOULD BE SAFEST FOR THE FAMILIES TO LEAVE
AS SOON AS POSSIBLE. I TRIED TO GET TO YOU, I PROMISE. IT JUST
DIDN'T HAPPEN.

I WANTED TO LET YOU KNOW WE GOT HOME SAFELY. THE KING
LET US KEEP OUR CLOTHES, AND MAY IS SPENDING EVERY SPARE
MOMENT IN THOSE DRESSES. I SUSPECT SHE'S SECRETLY HOPING SHE
NEVER GROWS ANOTHER INCH SO SHE CAN USE HER BALL GOWN
AT HER WEDDING. IT REALLY LIFTS HER SPIRITS. I'M NOT SURE
I'LL EVER FORGIVE THE ROYAL FAMILY FOR MAKING TWO OF MY
CHILDREN WATCH THAT FIRSTHAND, BUT YOU KNOW HOW RESILIENT
MAY IS. IT'S YOU I'M WORRIED ABOUT. WRITE US SOON.

MAYBE THIS ISN'T THE RIGHT THING TO SAY, BUT I WANT YOU
TO KNOW: WHEN YOU RAN FOR THE STAGE, I'VE NEVER BEEN SO
PROUD OF YOU IN ALL MY LIFE. YOU'VE ALWAYS BEEN BEAUTIFUL;
YOU'VE ALWAYS BEEN TALENTED. AND NOW I KNOW THAT YOUR

MORAL COMPASS IS PERFECTLY ALIGNED, THAT YOU SEE CLEARLY
WHEN THINGS ARE WRONG, AND YOU DO EVERYTHING YOU CAN TO
STOP IT. AS A FATHER, I CAN'T ASK FOR MORE.

I LOVE YOU, AMERICA. AND I'M SO, SO PROUD.

DAD

How was it that Dad always knew what to say? I kind of wanted someone to rearrange the stars so they spelled out his words. I needed them big and bright, and somewhere I could see them when things felt dark. *I love you. And I'm so, so proud.*

The Elite were given the option of breakfast in their rooms, and I took it. I wasn't ready to see Maxon yet. By the afternoon I was a bit more put together and decided to go down to the Women's Room for a while. If nothing else, there was at least a television, and I could stand to be distracted.

The girls seemed surprised when I walked in, which I guessed was to be expected. I did tend to hide from time to time, and if there was ever a moment to do that, it was now. Celeste was lounging on a couch, flipping through a magazine. Illéa didn't have newspapers like I'd heard other countries did. We had the *Report*. Magazines were the closest things we had to printed news, and people like me could never afford them. Celeste always seemed to have one on hand, and, for some reason, that irritated me today.

Kriss and Elise were at a table drinking tea and talking as

Natalie stood in the back, looking out a window.

"Oh, look," Celeste said to no one in particular. "Here's another one of my ads."

Celeste was a model. The idea of her flipping through pictures of herself drove my irritation deeper.

"Lady America?" someone called. I turned and saw the queen and some of her attendants in the corner. She looked like she was doing needlework.

I curtsied, and she waved me over. My stomach did a flip as I considered my behavior yesterday. I'd never intended to offend her and was suddenly afraid I'd done just that. I felt the eyes of the other girls on me. The queen usually spoke to us as a group, rarely one-on-one.

I gave another curtsy as I approached. "Majesty."

"Please sit, Lady America," she said kindly, motioning to an empty chair across from her.

I obliged, still very nervous.

"You put up quite a fight yesterday," she commented.

I swallowed. "Yes, Your Majesty."

"You were very close to her?"

I choked back my sadness. "Yes, Your Majesty."

She sighed. "A lady ought not to behave in such a way. The cameras were so focused on the action at hand that they missed your conduct. Still, it doesn't behoove you to lash out like that."

It wasn't the order of a queen. It was the reprimand of a mother. That made it a thousand times worse. It was like she felt responsible for me, and I'd let her down.

I bowed my head. For the first time, I truly felt bad about how I reacted.

She reached over and rested her hand on my knee. I looked up to her face, shocked by the casual touch.

"All the same," she whispered, "I'm glad you did it." And she smiled at me.

"She was my best friend."

"That doesn't stop because she's gone, sweetheart." Queen Amberly patted my leg kindly.

It was exactly what I needed: motherly affection.

Tears bit at the corners of my eyes. "I don't know what to do," I whispered. I nearly let everything spill out right there about how I was feeling, but I was conscious of the eyes of the other girls on me.

"I told myself I wouldn't get involved," she stated, and sighed. "Even if I wanted to, I'm not sure there's much to say."

She was right. What words could undo all that had happened?

The queen leaned in to me and spoke sweetly. "Still, go easy on him."

I knew she meant well, but I really didn't want to discuss her son. I nodded and rose. She smiled at me kindly and gestured that I was free to go. I wandered over to sit with Elise and Kriss.

"How are you doing?" Elise asked sympathetically.

"I'm fine. It's Marlee I'm worried about."

"At least they're together. They'll make it as long as they have each other," Kriss commented.

"How do you know Marlee and Carter are together?"

"Maxon told me," she replied, as if it was common knowledge.

"Oh," I said, disappointed.

"I can't believe he didn't tell you, of all people. You and Marlee were so close. Besides, you're his favorite, right?" she said.

I glanced at Kriss, then at Elise. They both carried a look of concern in their eyes but also maybe a sense of relief.

Celeste laughed. "She's obviously not anymore," she muttered, not bothering to look up from her magazine. Clearly, my fall was to be expected.

I changed the subject back to Marlee. "I still can't believe Maxon put them through that. It was disturbing how calm he was about it."

"But what she did was wrong," Natalie remarked. There wasn't anything judgmental about her tone, only a quiet acceptance, like she was following instructions.

Elise spoke up. "He could have had them killed. The law is on his side in that one. He showed them mercy."

"Mercy?" I scoffed. "You call having your skin torn apart in public merciful?"

"Yes, all things considered," she continued. "I bet if we could ask Marlee, she'd choose caning over *dying*."

"Elise is right," Kriss said. "I agree that it was absolutely terrible, but I would rather have that than death."

"Please," I sneered, my anger coming to the surface. "You're a Three. Everyone knows your dad's a famous professor, and you've lived your whole life in libraries, completely comfortable. You'd never survive the beating, let alone a life as an Eight afterward. You'd be begging to die."

Kriss glared at me. "Don't pretend that you know anything about what I can and cannot tolerate. Just because you're a Five, you think you're the only one who's ever suffered?"

"No, but I'm sure I've experienced far worse than you," I said, my voice rising in anger, "and I couldn't take what Marlee went through. I'm saying I doubt you'd fare any better."

"I'm braver than you think, America. You have no idea the things I've sacrificed over the years. And if I make a mistake, I own up to the consequences."

"Why should there be any consequences at all?" I posed. "Maxon keeps saying how difficult the Selection is for him, how hard it is to make the choice, and then one of us falls for someone else. Shouldn't he be thanking her for making his decision easier?"

Natalie, seeming distressed, tried to interject. "I heard the funniest thing yesterday!"

"But the law—" Kriss called over her.

"America has a point," Elise countered quickly, and the ordered conversation crumbled.

We were speaking over one another, trying to make our opinions heard, justifying why we thought what happened was wrong or right. This was a first, but something I'd been expecting from the start. With this many girls together, competing against one another, there was no way we wouldn't fight eventually.

Then, in a disconnected voice, Celeste mumbled to her magazine as we continued to argue, "Got what she deserved. Whore."

The following silence was as charged as our quarrel.

Celeste looked over her shoulder just in time to see me lunge at her. She screamed as I landed on her, knocking us both into a coffee table. I heard something, probably a cup of tea, smash onto the floor.

I'd closed my eyes midjump, and when I opened them, Celeste was underneath me, trying to grab at my wrists. I pulled back my right arm and slapped her as hard as I could across her face. The burning sensation in my hand was nearly overwhelming, but it was worth it to hear the satisfying smack that erupted when it made contact.

Celeste immediately let out a shriek and started clawing at me. For the first time I regretted not keeping my nails long like the other girls did. She made a few cuts on my arm, which only angered me more, and I struck her again. This time I cut her lip. In response to the pain, she reached for something—the saucer from her cup of tea—and slammed it against the side of my head.

Thrown off, I tried to grab at her again, but people were pulling us apart. I was so consumed, I hadn't noticed someone calling for the guards. I took a swing at one of them, too. I was tired of being manhandled.

"Did you see what she did to me?" Celeste cried.

"You keep your mouth shut!" I screamed. "Don't you ever talk about Marlee again!"

"She's crazy! Don't you hear her? Did you see what she did?"

"Let me go!" I said, struggling against the guard.

"You're psychotic! I'm going to tell Maxon right now. You can kiss the palace good-bye!" she threatened.

"No one's seeing Maxon right now," the queen said sternly. She looked into Celeste's eyes and then into mine. Her disappointment was clear. I hung my head. "You're both going to the hospital wing."

The hospital wing was a long, pristine corridor with beds against the walls. Pinned by the head of each bed was a curtain to wrap around for privacy. Cabinets of medical supplies were scattered throughout.

Wisely, Celeste and I were placed at opposite ends of the wing, with Celeste being closer to the entrance and me near a window in the back. She'd pulled her curtain partially around her bed almost immediately so she wouldn't have to see me. I couldn't blame her. I did have a rather smug look on my face. Even while the nurse tended to the sore spot behind my hairline where Celeste had hit me, I couldn't bring myself to grimace.

"Now, hold this ice here, and that will help keep the swelling down," she offered.

"Thanks," I replied.

The nurse looked up and down the wing quickly, seeming to check that no one could hear us. "Good for you," she whispered. "Most everyone's been waiting for something like this to happen."

"Really?" I asked, my voice as low as hers. I probably shouldn't have been smiling this much.

"I can't begin to count the horror stories I've heard about that one," she said, nodding her head toward Celeste's curtained bed.

"Horror stories?"

"Well, she provoked that one girl who hit her."

"Anna? How do you know?"

"Maxon's a good man," she said simply. "He made sure she was checked out here before she went home. She told us what Celeste said about her parents. It was so filthy, I can't repeat it." The look on her face conveyed her disgust.

"Poor Anna. I knew it had to be something like that."

"One girl came in with her feet bleeding after someone slipped glass in her shoes in the night. We can't prove it was Celeste, but who else would do something so mean?"

"I never heard about that." I gasped.

"She looked terrified that she might get worse. I suppose she chose to keep her mouth shut. And Celeste hits her maids. Not with anything more than her hands, but they come in for ice from time to time."

"No!" All the maids I'd encountered were sweet girls. I couldn't imagine any of them doing something that would provoke getting hit at all, let alone regularly.

"Suffice to say, your antics are making the rounds already. You're a hero around here," the nurse said with a wink.

I didn't feel like a hero.

"Wait," I said suddenly. "You said Maxon had Anna checked out before he sent her home?"

"Yes, miss. He's very concerned that you're all taken care of."

"What about Marlee? Did she come here? How was she when she left?"

Before the nurse could answer, I heard Celeste's pouty voice pierce the room.

"Maxon, sweetheart!" she called as he marched through the doorway.

We shared a brief moment of eye contact before he approached Celeste's bed. The nurse walked away, leaving me alone and aching to know if she'd actually seen Marlee.

The sound of Celeste's whiny voice was almost too irritating to bear. I heard Maxon murmur his condolences, comforting the poor thing before extricating himself. He made his way around her curtain and focused his eyes on me, seeming exhausted as he walked down the wing.

"You're lucky my father had the cameras barred from the palace, otherwise there'd be hell to pay for your actions." He ran his hand through his hair, exasperated. "How am I supposed to defend this, America?"

"Are you going to kick me out, then?" I played with a piece of my dress while I waited for his answer.

"Of course not."

"What about her?" I asked, nodding my head toward Celeste's bed.

"No. You're all stressed after yesterday, and I can't hold that against you. I'm not sure my father will accept that excuse, but that's what I'm going to say."

I paused. "Maybe you should tell him it was my fault. Maybe you should just send me home."

"America, you're overreacting."

"Look at me, Maxon," I urged. I felt the lump rising in my throat and fought to speak past it. "I've known from the beginning I don't have what it takes, and I thought that I could—I don't know—change, or somehow make it work; but I can't stay here. I can't."

Maxon moved to sit on the edge of my bed. "America, you might hate the Selection, and you might be mad about what happened to Marlee; but I know that you care about me enough not to just abandon me in this."

I reached for his hand. "I also care enough about you to tell you you're making a mistake."

I could see the pain in Maxon's face as he held my hand tighter, as if he could hold me there and keep me from disappearing. Hesitantly, he leaned in and whispered, "It's not always so difficult. And I want to show that to you, but you have to give me time. I can prove that there are good things to this, but you have to wait."

I inhaled to contradict him, but he cut me off. "For weeks,

America, you've asked me for time, and I gave it to you without question because I had faith in you. Please, I need you to have a little bit of faith in me, too."

I didn't know what Maxon could possibly show me that might change my mind, but how could I not give him more time when he'd done that for me?

I sighed. "Fine."

"Thank you." The relief in his voice was obvious. "I have to get back, but I'll come see you soon."

I nodded. Maxon stood and left, stopping briefly to tell Celeste good-bye. I watched him go and wondered if trusting him was a bad idea.

CHAPTER 12

BOTH CELESTE'S AND MY INJURIES were minimal, so we were sent back to our rooms within an hour. They staggered our release times so we didn't have to leave together, and thank goodness for that.

As I turned the corner at the top of the stairs, I saw a guard coming toward me. Aspen. Even though he was bigger after being bulked up from training, I knew his walk and his shadow and a thousand other things that were ingrained in my heart.

As he approached, he stopped to give me an unnecessary bow.

"Jar," he whispered, and rose again, continuing on his path.

I stood there for a split second, confused, and then realized what he meant. Fighting the urge to run, I moved down the hall eagerly.

I opened the door and was both surprised and relieved to find that all three of my maids were out.

I went over to the jar on my bedside table and found that the one little penny in there had company. I opened the lid and pulled out the folded sheet of paper. How clever of him. My maids probably wouldn't have noticed it; and if they had, they never would have intruded on my privacy.

I unfolded the note and read a very clear list of instructions. It seemed Aspen and I had a date tonight.

The directions Aspen gave me were complicated. I took a roundabout way to get to the first floor, where I was to look for the door next to the five-foot-high vase. I remembered that vase from walking around the palace before. What flower in the world needed a container that big?

I found the door and looked around to double-check that no one saw me. I'd never managed to find myself so free from the eyes of the guards. Not a one in sight. I opened the door slowly and crept inside. The moon shone through the window, giving the room sparse light and making me feel a little nervous.

"Aspen?" I whispered into the darkness, feeling silly and scared all at once.

"Just like old times, eh?" his voice called, though I couldn't see him.

"Where are you?" I squinted, trying to find his form.

Then the shadow of the heavy drape by the window shifted in the moonlight, and Aspen appeared from behind it.

"You startled me," I complained jokingly.

"Wouldn't be the first time, won't be the last." I heard the smile in his voice.

I walked over to him, knocking into every obstacle along the way it seemed.

"Shhh!" he complained. "The entire palace is going to know we're in here if you keep pushing things over." But I could tell he was playing.

"Sorry," I said, laughing quietly. "Can't we turn on a light?"

"No. If someone sees it shining under the door, we might get caught. This corridor isn't checked a lot, but I want to be smart."

"How did you even know about this room?" I reached out, making contact with Aspen's arms at last. He pulled me in for a hug and then started walking me toward the back corner.

"I'm a guard," he said simply. "And I'm very good at what I do. I know the entire grounds of the palace, inside and out. Every last pathway, all the hiding spots, and even most of the secret rooms. I also happen to know the rotations of the guards, which areas are usually the least checked, and the points in the day when the guards are at their fewest. If you ever want to sneak around the palace, I'm the guy to do it with."

"Unbelievable," I mumbled. We sat behind the broad back of a couch, the floor blanketed in a patch of moonlight.

Finally I could make out Aspen's face.

I questioned him seriously. "Are you sure this is safe?" If he hesitated at all, I was planning to bolt that very second. For both our sakes.

"Trust me, Mer. An extraordinary number of things would have to happen for someone to find us here. We're safe."

I was still worried, but I needed to be comforted so badly, I went along.

He wrapped an arm around me and pulled me in close. "How are you doing?"

I sighed. "Okay, I guess. I've been sad a lot, and angry. Mostly I wish I could undo the last two days and get Marlee back. Carter, too, and I didn't even know him."

"I did." He sighed. "He's a great guy. I heard he was telling Marlee he loved her the whole time and trying to help her get through it."

"He was," I confirmed. "At least in the beginning anyway. I got hauled off before it was over."

Aspen kissed my head. "Yeah, I heard about that, too. I'm proud you went out with a fight. That's my girl."

"My dad was proud, too. The queen said I shouldn't act that way, but she was glad I did. It's been confusing. Like it was almost a good idea but not really, and then it didn't fix anything anyway."

Aspen held me closer. "It was good. It meant a lot to me."

"To you?"

"Yeah," he whispered, seeming reluctant to share. "Every

once in a while I wonder if the Selection has changed you. You've been so taken care of, and everything is so fancy. I keep wondering if you're the same America. That let me know that you are, that they haven't gotten to you."

"Oh, they're getting to me all right, but not like that. Mostly this place reminds me that I wasn't born to do this."

I ducked my head into Aspen's chest, the safe place where I'd always hidden when things were bad.

"Listen, Mer, the thing about Maxon is that he's an actor. He's always putting on this perfect face, like he's so above everything. But he's just a person, and he's as messed up as anyone is. I know you care about him or you wouldn't have stayed here. But you have to know now that it's not real."

I nodded. Maxon with his talk about putting on a calm face. Was that what he was always doing? Was he acting when he was with me? How was I supposed to be able to tell?

Aspen continued. "It's better you know now. What if you got married and then found out it was like this?"

"I know. I've been thinking about that myself." Maxon's words on the dance floor played themselves on repeat in my head. He seemed so sure of our future, prepared to give me so much. I sincerely thought the only thing he wanted was for me to be happy. Couldn't he see how *unhappy* I was now?

"You've got a big heart, Mer. I know you can't just get over things, but it's okay to *want* to. That's all."

"I feel so stupid," I whispered, wanting to cry.

"You're not stupid."

"I am, too."

"Mer, do you think I'm smart?"

"Of course."

"That's because I am. And I'm way too smart to be in love with a stupid girl. So you can drop that right now."

I gave a tiny laugh and let Aspen hold on to me.

"I feel like I've hurt you so much. I don't understand how you can still possibly be in love with me," I confessed.

He shrugged. "It's just the way it is. The sky is blue, the sun is bright, and Aspen endlessly loves America. It's how the world was designed to be. Seriously, Mer, you're the only girl I ever wanted. I couldn't imagine being with anyone else. I've been trying to prepare myself for that, just in case, and . . . I can't."

We sat there, holding each other for a moment. Every little tickle of Aspen's fingers, the warmth of his breath in my hair felt like medicine for my heart.

"We shouldn't stay much longer," he said. "I'm pretty confident in my abilities, but I don't want to push it."

I sighed. It felt like we'd only just gotten here, but he was probably right. I moved to stand, and Aspen jumped up to help me. He pulled me in for one last hug.

"I know it's hard to believe, but I'm really sorry Maxon turned out to be such a bad guy. I wanted you back, but I didn't want you to get hurt. Especially not like that."

"Thanks."

"I mean it."

"I know you do." Aspen had his faults, but he didn't have it in him to be a liar. "It's not over though. Not if I'm still here."

"Yeah, but I know you. You'll ride it out so your family gets money and you can see me, but he'd have to reverse time to fix this."

I let out a long breath. It felt like he might be right. Maxon's hold on me was slipping away, shrugging off my skin like a coat.

"Don't worry, Mer. I'll take care of you."

Aspen didn't have any way to prove that at the moment, but I believed him. He'd do anything for the people he loved, and I knew without question that I was the person he loved the most.

The next morning I let my mind wander to Aspen all through getting ready, breakfast, and my hours in the Women's Room. I was blissfully detached until the slap of a pile of papers on the table in front of me jarred me back to the real world.

I looked up to see Celeste, still sporting a puffy lip. She pointed to one of her gossip magazines opened to a two-page spread. It didn't even take a full second for me to recognize Marlee's face, even though it was twisted with pain from the caning. .

"Thought you should see this," Celeste said before she walked away.

I wasn't exactly sure what she meant, but I was so eager to know anything about Marlee, I dived in.

Of all our country's great traditions, perhaps none is looked upon with such excitement as the Selection. Created specifically to bring joy to a saddened nation, it seems everyone still gets a little giddy watching the great love story of a prince and his future princess unfold. When Gregory Illéa took the throne more than eighty years ago and his elder son, Spencer, died suddenly, the entire country mourned the loss of such an enigmatic and promising young man. When his younger son, Damon, was set to inherit the throne, many wondered if he was ready even to train for the task at nineteen. But Damon knew he was prepared to step into adulthood and set out to prove it via the greatest commitment in life: marriage. Within months the Selection was born, and the spirits of the country were lifted by the possibility of an average girl becoming the first princess of Illéa.

However, since then we have been forced to wonder at the effectiveness of the competition. While a romantic idea at heart, some say it's unfair to force princes to marry women beneath them, though no one can deny the absolute poise and beauty of our current queen, Amberly Station Schreave. Some of us still remember the rumors of Abby Tamblin Illéa, who allegedly poisoned her husband, Prince Justin Illéa, only a few years into their marriage before agreeing to marry his cousin, Porter Schreave, thus keeping the royal line intact.

While that rumor has never been confirmed, what we can say for sure is that the behavior of the women in the palace this time around is nothing short of scandalous. Marlee Tames, now an Eight, was caught with a guard undressing her in a closet Monday night after the Halloween Ball that was billed to be the highlight of the Selection programming. Its splendor was completely overshadowed by Miss Tames's reckless behavior, sending the palace into a frenzy the very next morning.

But beyond Miss Tames's inexcusable actions, the girls remaining at the palace might not be crown-worthy either. An unnamed source tells us that some of the Elite are constantly bickering, rarely making the effort to perform the duties they're required to. Everyone remembers Anna Farmer's dismissal in early September after deliberately attacking the lovely Celeste Newsome, a model from Clermont. And our source confirms that that isn't the only physical interaction to take place at the palace between the Elite, forcing this reporter to question the pool of girls chosen for Prince Maxon.

When asked for a comment on these rumors, King Clarkson only said, "Some of the girls come from less-refined castes and aren't used to the proper behavior expected at the palace. Clearly Miss Tames wasn't prepared for life as a One. My wife has a particular indefinable quality about her and is one of the rare exceptions to the rule of lower castes. She has always sought to raise herself to a level befitting a queen, and it would be quite a challenge to find someone more suited for the throne than she. But for some of the lower castes remaining in the current Selection, it would be difficult to say we weren't expecting this from them."

While Natalie Luca and Elise Whisks are both Fours, they have always been the height of refinement when presented to the public, particularly Lady Elise, who is quite sophisticated. We are forced to assume our king is referring to America Singer, the only Five who made it past day one of the Selection. Miss Singer has had an average run at the Selection. She's pretty enough, but not quite what Illéa was expecting for its new princess. From time to time her interviews on the *Capital Report* are entertaining, but we need a new leader, not a comedienne.

In further disturbing news, we have heard reports that Miss Singer attempted to release Miss Tames during her caning, which in this reporter's eyes makes her an accessory to the treacherous activities in which Miss Tames was partaking by being unfaithful to our prince.

With all of these reports (and with Miss Tames no longer in the top spot) one question remains: Who should be the new princess?

A quick poll of readers has confirmed what we've suspected all along.

We congratulate Miss Celeste Newsome and Miss Kriss Ambers for their neck-and-neck places on the top of our public poll. Elise Whisks takes the third spot, with Natalie Luca not too far behind. In a wide gap between fourth and fifth places, America Singer comes (unsurprisingly) in last.

I think I speak for all of Illéa when I encourage Prince Maxon to take his time finding us a good princess. We narrowly avoided disaster by Miss Tames exposing her true nature before a crown was placed on her head. Whoever you love, Prince Maxon, make sure she's worthy. We want to love her, too!

CHAPTER 13

I RAN FROM THE ROOM. Of course Celeste wasn't doing me a favor. She was showing me my place. Why was I even bothering with this? The king was expecting me to fail, the public didn't want me, and I was sure I couldn't be a princess.

I made my way upstairs quickly and quietly, trying not to draw attention to myself. There was no telling who that magazine's unnamed source was.

"My lady," Anne said when I walked through the doorway. "I thought you'd be downstairs until lunch for sure."

"Could you leave, please?"

"I'm sorry?"

I huffed, trying not to lose my patience. "I need to be alone. Please?"

Without a word, they curtsied and left me. I went to the piano. I would distract myself until I couldn't think about this anymore. I played a handful of songs that I knew by heart, but that was too easy. I needed to really focus.

I stood up and dug through the bench for something more challenging. I burrowed past pages of sheet music until the edge of a book peeked out at me. Illéa's diary! I'd completely forgotten it was down here. This would be a great distraction. I carried the book over to the bed and opened it, taking in the ancient pages as they flipped through my hands.

The diary opened to the page with the Halloween picture, the stiff photo acting as a natural bookmark, and I reread the entry.

THE CHILDREN CELEBRATED HALLOWEEN THIS YEAR WITH A PARTY. I SUPPOSE IT'S ONE WAY TO FORGET WHAT'S GOING ON AROUND THEM, BUT TO ME IT ALL FEELS FRIVOLOUS. WE'RE ONE OF THE FEW FAMILIES REMAINING WHO HAS ENOUGH MONEY TO DO SOMETHING FESTIVE, BUT THIS CHILD'S PLAY SEEMS WASTEFUL.

I looked at the picture again, wondering about the girl in particular. How old was she? What was her job? Did she like being Gregory Illéa's daughter? Did it make her very popular?

I turned the page and realized that it wasn't a new entry but a continuation of the Halloween post.

I GUESS I THOUGHT THAT AFTER CHINA INVADED WE'D SEE THE ERROR OF OUR WAYS. IT'S BEEN OBVIOUS TO ME,

PARTICULARLY RECENTLY, JUST HOW LAZY WE'VE BECOME.
REALLY, IT'S NO WONDER CHINA CAME IN SO EASILY,
AND IT'S NO WONDER IT TOOK SO LONG FOR US TO GET
IN A POSITION TO FIGHT BACK. WE'VE LOST THAT SPIRIT
THAT DROVE PEOPLE ACROSS OCEANS AND THROUGH
DEVASTATING WINTERS AND CIVIL WAR. WE GOT LAZY.
AND WHILE WE WERE SITTING BACK, CHINA TOOK THE
REINS.

IN THE LAST FEW MONTHS IN PARTICULAR, I'VE
FELT DRIVEN TO GIVE MORE THAN MONEY TO THE WAR
EFFORTS. I WANT TO LEAD. I HAVE IDEAS, AND PERHAPS
SINCE I'VE DONATED SO GENEROUSLY, NOW IS THE TIME
TO OFFER THEM UP. WHAT WE NEED IS CHANGE. I CAN'T
HELP BUT WONDER IF I MIGHT BE THE ONLY PERSON WHO
CAN PROVIDE IT.

I got chills. I couldn't help but compare Maxon to his
predecessor. Gregory seemed inspired. He was trying to take
something broken and make it whole. I wondered what he'd
say about the monarchy if he was here today.

When Aspen slid my door open that night, I was nearly
bursting at the seams to tell him what I'd read. But I
remembered that I'd already mentioned to my dad that the
diary existed, and even that was going past what I'd sworn
to do.

"How have you been?" he asked, kneeling by my bed.

"All right, I suppose. Celeste showed me this article

today." I shook my head. "I'm not sure I want to get into it. I'm so tired of her."

"I guess with Marlee gone, he won't be sending anyone home for a while, huh?"

I shrugged. I knew the public had been looking forward to an elimination, and what happened with Marlee was more dramatic than anything anyone expected.

"Hey," he said, risking a touch in the light of the wide-open door. "It's going to be all right."

"I know. I just miss her. And I'm confused."

"Confused about what?"

"Everything. What I'm doing here, who I am. I thought I knew. . . . I don't even know how to explain it right." That seemed to be the problem lately. Every thought that passed through my head was sloppy. I couldn't line up anything.

"You know who you are, Mer. Don't let them try to change you." His voice was so sincere, and for a minute I did feel sure. Not because I had any answers, but because I had Aspen. If I ever lost sight of who I really was, I knew he'd be there to guide me back.

"Aspen, can I ask you something?" He nodded. "This is kind of strange, but if being the princess didn't mean I had to marry someone, if it was just a job someone could pick me for, do you think I could do it?"

Aspen's green eyes grew wide for a second, taking in the enormity of that question. To his credit, I could see him considering the possibility.

"Sorry, Mer. I don't. You don't have it in you to be as

calculating as they are." There was an apology in his expression, but I wasn't offended that he thought I couldn't do it. I was a bit surprised at his reasoning though.

"Calculating? How so?"

He sighed. "I'm everywhere, Mer. I hear things. There's a lot of turmoil down South, in the areas with a heavy concentration of lower castes. From what the older guards say, those people never particularly agreed with Gregory Illéa's methods, and there's been unrest down there for a long time. Rumor has it, that was part of why the queen was so attractive to the king. She came from the South, and it appeased them for a while. Not so much anymore it seems."

I thought again about bringing up the diary, but I didn't. "That doesn't explain what you meant by calculating."

He hesitated. "I was in one of the offices the other day, before all the Halloween stuff. They were mentioning rebel sympathizers in the South. I was told to see these letters to the postal wing safely. It was over three hundred letters, America. Three hundred families who were getting knocked down a caste for not reporting things or for helping someone the palace saw as a threat."

I sucked in a breath.

"I know. Can you imagine? What if it was you, and all you knew how to do was play the piano? Suddenly you're supposed to know how to do clerical work, how to find those jobs even? It's a pretty clear message."

I nodded. "Do you . . . Does Maxon know?"

"I think he has to. He's not that far off from running the country himself."

In my heart, I didn't want to believe that he'd *agreed* with this, but it seemed likely he was aware of what was going on. He was expected to fall in line.

Could *I* do that?

"Don't tell anyone, okay? A slip like that could cost me my job," Aspen warned.

"Of course. It's already forgotten."

Aspen smiled at me. "I miss being with you, away from all this. I miss our old problems."

I laughed. "I know what you mean. Sneaking out of my window was so much better than sneaking around a palace."

"And scrounging to find a penny for you was better than having nothing to give you at all." He tapped on the glass jar by my bed, the one that used to hold hundreds of pennies that he'd given me for singing to him in the tree house back home, payment that he thought I deserved. "I had no idea you'd saved them all until the day before you left."

"Of course I did! When you were away, they were all I had to hold on to. Sometimes I used to pour them over my hand on the bed, just to scoop them up again. It was nice to have something you touched." Our eyes met, and everything else felt distant for the moment. It was comforting finding myself in that bubble again, the place that Aspen and I had created for ourselves years ago. "What did you do with all of them?"

I had been so mad at him when I left, I'd given them back. All except for the one that stuck to the bottom of the jar.

He smiled. "They're at home, waiting."

"For what?"

His eyes glittered. "That, I cannot say."

I sighed through my smile. "Fine, keep your secrets. And don't worry about not giving me anything. I'm just happy you're here, that you and I can at least fix things, even if it's not what it used to be."

But clearly, for Aspen, that wasn't enough. He reached down to the bottom of his sleeve and tore off one of his golden buttons. "I literally have nothing else to give you, but you can hold on to this—something I've touched—and think of me anytime. And you can know that I'm thinking of you, too."

As silly as it seemed, I wanted to cry. It was unavoidable, the natural instinct to compare Aspen to Maxon. Even now, when thinking of choosing one or the other felt like something very distant, I measured them side by side.

It seemed very easy for Maxon to give me things—to resurrect a holiday for my sake, to make sure I had the best of everything—because he had the entire world at his disposal. Here Aspen was, giving me precious stolen moments and the tiniest trinket to connect us to each other, and it felt like he'd given me so much more.

I remembered suddenly that Aspen had always been this way. He sacrificed sleep for me, he risked getting caught out after curfew for me, he scrounged together pennies for me. Aspen's generosity was harder to see because it wasn't as grand as Maxon's, but the heart behind what he gave was so much bigger.

I sniffed back the lingering urge to cry. "I don't know how to do this right now. I feel like I don't know how to do anything. I . . . I haven't forgotten you, okay? It's still here."

I put my hand to my chest, partly to show Aspen what I meant and partly to soothe the strange longing there. He understood.

"That's enough for me."

CHAPTER 14

I SURREPTITIOUSLY WATCHED MAXON THE next morning at breakfast. I wondered how much he knew about the people losing their castes in the South. Only once did he glance my way, but he didn't seem to be looking at me so much as at something near me.

Anytime I felt uncomfortable, I'd reach down and touch Aspen's button, which I'd laced on a tiny ribbon and made into a bracelet. He would get me through my time here.

Toward the end of the meal, the king stood and we all turned to him. "As there are so few of you now, I thought it would be nice for us to have tea tomorrow night before the *Report*. Since one of you will be our new daughter-in-law, the queen and I would like to make more opportunities to speak with you, learn your interests and such."

I felt a little nervous. Relating to the queen was one thing, but I wasn't sure how I felt about the king. While the other girls watched him eagerly, I sipped my juice.

"Please come an hour before the *Report* to the lounge on the first floor. If you're not familiar, don't worry. The doors will be open, and there will be some music playing. You'll hear us before you see us," he said with a chuckle. The others giggled lightly in return.

Soon after, girls started making their way to the Women's Room. I sighed. Sometimes that room, huge as it was, made me feel claustrophobic. I usually tried to interact with people or use the time to read. This would be a Celeste day. I was going to park myself in front of the television and zone out.

It was easier said than done. The girls seemed particularly chatty today.

"I wonder what the king wants to know about us," Kriss gabbed.

"We just have to remember everything Silvia taught us about poise," Elise commented.

"I hope my maids have a good dress for tomorrow night. I don't want to have to go through what I did for Halloween. They're so scatterbrained sometimes." Celeste sounded put out.

"I wish the king would grow a beard," Natalie said wistfully. I peeked over my shoulder to see her stroking an imaginary beard on her own chin. "I think he'd look good."

"Yes, I can see that," Kriss said graciously before moving on.

I shook my head and tried to focus on the ridiculous show

in front of me, but no matter how I tried, I couldn't tune out the words of the other girls.

By lunch I was a ball of nerves. What would he want to say to me—the girl from the lowest caste left in the competition? What would he want to discuss with the girl he expected so little from?

King Clarkson was right. I heard the floating melody from the piano long before I found the lounge. The musician was good. Better than me, that was for sure.

I hesitated before walking in. I decided to pause before I spoke, really think about my words. I realized I wanted to prove him wrong. I wanted to prove that reporter wrong, too. Even if I lost, I didn't want to go home a loser. I was surprised by how much this suddenly meant to me.

I stepped through the doorway, and the first thing I saw was Maxon standing along the back wall of the room talking to Gavril Fadaye. Gavril was sipping wine as opposed to tea, and he'd suddenly lost Maxon's attention. I saw Maxon's eyes rake over me, and I could have sworn his lips made the shape of a *Wow*.

I turned my head and blushed, walking away. I took the risk of glancing at him again and saw that he was watching me move. It was hard to think rationally when he looked at me that way.

King Clarkson was talking to Natalie in one corner, and Queen Amberly was with Celeste in another. Elise was sipping her tea, and Kriss was walking around the room. I watched as she passed Maxon and Gavril, giving Gavril a warm smile. She said something, which they both chuckled at, and kept walking, peeking over her shoulder at Maxon once as she did so.

After that she made her way to me. "You're late," she jokingly scolded.

"I was feeling a little nervous."

"Oh, it's nothing to worry about. It was actually kind of fun."

"You're already done?" If the king was finished speaking with at least two girls, I'd have less time to compose myself than I thought.

"Yes. Sit with me. We can have some tea while you wait."

Kriss pulled me over to a table, and a maid approached us immediately, setting tea, milk, and sugar in front of us.

"What did he ask you?" I pressed.

"Actually, it was very conversational. I don't think he's trying to get any information exactly, more like he's trying to get a feeling for our personalities. I made him laugh once!" she gushed. "It went really well. And you're naturally funny, so if you just talk like you would to anyone else, you'll be fine."

I nodded before picking up my tea. She made it sound all right. Maybe the king had to compartmentalize himself. When it came to dealing with threats to the country, he had to be decisive, cold. He had to act quickly and deliberately. This was just tea with a bunch of girls. There was no need for him to be that way with us.

The queen had moved away from Celeste and was now speaking softly to Natalie. The look on Natalie's face was adoring. For a while I'd been irritated by her dreamy disposition; but she was simple, and it was refreshing.

I sipped my tea again. King Clarkson drifted over to Celeste, and she gave him a seductive smile. It was a little disturbing. Where were her boundaries?

Kriss leaned over to touch my dress. "That fabric is amazing. With your hair, you look like a sunset."

"Thank you," I said, blinking my eyes. The light had caught on her necklace, an explosion of silver on her throat, and it blinded me for a moment. "My maids are very talented."

"Absolutely. I like mine, but if I become princess, I'm stealing yours!"

She laughed, maybe meaning her words as a joke, maybe not. Either way, something about my maids hemming her clothes bothered me. I forced a smile though.

"What's so funny?" Maxon asked, walking over.

"Just girl talk," Kriss said flirtatiously. She was really on tonight. "I was trying to calm America. She's nervous about speaking to your father."

Thank you for that, Kriss.

"You don't have a thing to worry about. Be natural. You already look fantastic." Maxon gave me an easy smile. He was clearly trying to open up our lines of communication again.

"That's what I said!" Kriss exclaimed. They shared a quick

look, and there was this feeling of them being on a team. It was strange.

"Well, I'll leave you to your girl talk. Good-bye for now." Maxon gave us both a short bow and went over to join his mother.

Kriss sighed and watched Maxon go. "He's really something." She gave me a quick smile and went to talk to Gavril.

I watched the elaborate dance of the room, couples coming together to speak, separating to find new partners. I was even happy to have Elise join me in my corner, though she didn't say much.

"Oh, ladies, the time has gotten away from us," the king called. "We need to make our way downstairs."

I looked up at the clock, and he was right. We had about ten minutes to get down to the set and prepare ourselves.

It didn't seem to matter how I felt about being a princess, or how I felt about Maxon, or how I felt about anything. The king clearly thought I was so unlikely a candidate that he didn't even want to bother speaking with me. I was excluded, perhaps on purpose, and no one even noticed.

I held it together through the *Report*. I even made it through dismissing my maids. But once I was alone, I broke down.

I wasn't sure how I'd explain myself when Maxon came knocking, but that ended up not mattering. He never showed. And I couldn't help but wonder whose company he was enjoying instead.

CHAPTER 15

MY MAIDS WERE GIFTS. THEY didn't ask about the puffy eyes or the tear-stained pillows. They merely helped me pull myself together. I allowed myself to be pampered, grateful for the attention. They were wonderful to me. Would they be this nice to Kriss if she managed to win and took them away?

I watched them as I debated, and I was surprised to notice a tension among them. Mary seemed mostly fine, maybe a little worried. But Anne and Lucy looked like they were deliberately avoiding eye contact with each other and not speaking unless they absolutely had to.

I couldn't begin to guess at what was happening, and I didn't know if it was my place to ask. They never intruded on my sadness or anger. I supposed it was only right that I do the same for them.

I tried not to let the silence bother me as they did my hair and dressed me for a long day in the Women's Room. I ached to put on one of the luxurious pants that Maxon had given me for Saturday use, but this seemed like a bad time for that. If I was heading down, I wanted to be a lady about it. Points to me for effort.

As I settled in for another day of tea and books, the others chatted about the night before. Well, all of them except for Celeste, who had more gossip magazines waiting to be read. I wondered if the one in her hands said anything about me.

I was debating trying to take it when Silvia came in with a thick pile of paper in her arms. Great. More work.

"Good morning, ladies!" Silvia crooned. "I know you usually wait for guests on Saturdays, but today the queen and I have a special assignment for you."

"Yes," the queen said, walking over to us. "I know this is short notice, but we have visitors coming next week. They will be touring the country and stopping by the palace to meet all of you."

"As you know, the queen is usually in charge of receiving such important guests. You all saw how she graciously hosted our friends from Swendway." Silvia gestured over to Queen Amberly, who smiled demurely.

"However, the visitors we have coming from the German Federation and Italy are even more important than the Swendish royal family. And we thought this visit would be an excellent exercise for you all, especially since we've been so focused on diplomacy lately. You will work in teams to prepare a reception for your respective guests, including a meal, entertainment, and gifts," Silvia explained.

I gulped as she continued.

"It is very important for us to maintain the relationships we have as well as to forge new ones with other countries. We have outlines of proper etiquette for interacting with these guests, as well as guides for what's typically frowned on when hosting events for them. However, the actual execution is in your hands."

"We wanted to make it as fair as possible," the queen said. "I think we've done a good job of putting you all on the same field. Celeste, Natalie, and Elise, you will be organizing one reception. Kriss and America, you will take care of the other. And since you have one less person, you will have one more day. Our visitors from the German Federation will be coming on Wednesday, and we'll be receiving guests from Italy on Thursday."

There was a short moment of silence as we took that in.

"You mean we have four days?" Celeste screeched.

"Yes," Silvia said. "But a queen has to do this work alone and sometimes on far less notice."

The panic was palpable.

"Can we have our papers, please?" Kriss asked, holding out her hand. Instinctively, I put mine out as well. Within seconds we were devouring the pages.

"This is going to be tough," Kriss said. "Even with the extra day."

"Don't worry," I assured her. "We're going to win."

She laughed nervously. "How can you be so sure?"

"Because," I said decisively, "there's no way I'm letting Celeste do better than me."

It took two hours to read through the packet and one more to digest everything it said. There were so many different things to consider, so many details to plan. Silvia claimed she would be at our disposal, but I had a feeling asking for help would make her think we couldn't do a good enough job on our own, so that was out.

The setup was going to be challenging. We weren't allowed to use red flowers because they were associated with secrecy. We weren't allowed to use yellow flowers because they were associated with jealousy. And we weren't allowed to use purple *anything* because that color was associated with bad luck.

The wine, food, everything had to be opulent. Luxury wasn't seen as showing off; it was meant to make a statement about the palace. If it wasn't good enough, our guests might leave unimpressed and completely unwilling to meet with us again. On top of all that, the regular things we were supposed to have learned—speaking clearly, proper table manners, and the like—had to be adapted to a culture of which neither Kriss nor I had any knowledge besides what was printed in our packets.

It was incredibly intimidating.

Kriss and I spent the day taking notes and brainstorming while the others did the same thing at a nearby table. As the afternoon wore on, our groups started complaining back and forth about who had the worse situation, and after a while it was actually kind of funny.

"You two at least get another day to work," Elise said.

"But Illéa and the German Federation are already allies. The Italians might hate everything we do!" Kriss worried.

"Do you know we're supposed to wear dark colors for ours?" Celeste complained. "It's going to be a very . . . rigid event."

"We probably don't want it to be floppy anyway," Natalie said, doing a little shimmy. She laughed at her own joke, and I smiled before moving on.

"Well, ours is supposed to be superfestive. And you all have to wear your best jewelry," I instructed. "You need to make a great first impression, and appearances are very important."

"Thank goodness I'll get to look good at one of these stupid things." Celeste sighed, shaking her head.

In the end, it was clear we were all struggling. After everything that had happened with Marlee and then being somewhat dismissed by the king, I felt strangely comforted to know we were miserable together. But it would be a lie to say that paranoia didn't take over before the end of the day. I was convinced that one of the other girls—Celeste in particular—might try to sabotage our reception.

"How loyal are your maids?" I asked Kriss at dinner.

"Very. Why?"

"I wonder whether we should store some things in our

rooms instead of in the parlor. You know, so the other girls don't try to take our ideas." It was only a tiny lie.

She nodded. "That's a good idea. Especially since we go second, and it would look like we copied them."

"Exactly."

"You're so smart, America. It's no wonder Maxon liked you so much." And she went back to eating.

I didn't miss her casual use of the past tense. Maybe while I'd been worrying about being good enough to be a princess and feeling completely unsure I wanted to be one at the same time, Maxon was forgetting all about me.

I convinced myself that she was just trying to make herself feel more confident about her standing with Maxon. Besides, it had only been a few days since Marlee was caned. How much could she possibly know?

The piercing scream of a siren jerked me from my sleep. The sound was so foreign, I couldn't even begin to process what it was. All I knew was that my heart was pounding in my chest from the sudden rush of adrenaline.

Before a second had passed, the door to my room flew open and a guard ran in.

"Damn it, damn it, damn it," he repeated.

"Huh?" I said groggily as he raced over to me.

"Get up, Mer!" he urged, and I did as he said. "Where are your damn shoes?"

Shoes. So I was going somewhere. Only then did the sound make sense to me. Maxon had told me once before that there was an alarm for when the rebels came, but it had been thoroughly dismantled in a recent attack. It finally must have been repaired.

"Here," I said, finding and slipping my feet into them. "I need my robe." I pointed to the end of the bed, and Aspen grabbed it, trying to open it for me. "Don't bother, I'll carry it."

"You need to hurry," he said. "I don't know how close they are."

I nodded, heading for the door, Aspen's hand on my back. Before I hit the hallway, he jerked me toward him. I found myself in a deep, rough kiss. Aspen's hand was behind my head, holding my lips to his for one long moment. Then, as if he forgot the danger, his other hand pulled my waist to his, and the kiss deepened. It had been a long time since he'd kissed me this way—between my fickle heart and the fear of being caught, there was no reason to. But I could feel an urgency tonight. Something might go wrong, and this could be our last kiss.

He wanted to make it count.

We stepped apart, barely taking a second to look at each other one more time. He put his hand around my arm and pushed me out the door. "Go. Now."

I dashed for the secret passage hidden at the end of the hall. Before I pushed the wall, I looked behind me and caught sight of Aspen's back as he ran around the corner.

There was nothing I could do but run myself, so I did. As quickly as I could manage, I made my way down the steep, dark stairs to the safe room reserved for the royal family.

Maxon had told me once that there were two kinds of rebels: Northern and Southern. The Northern ones were pesky, but the Southern ones were deadly. I hoped whatever I was running from was more interested in disturbing us than in killing.

As I descended the stairs, the cold set in. I wanted to throw on my robe, but I worried I might trip. I felt steadier as the light of the safe room came into view. I leaped from the last step, and I could see a figure standing out among the shapes of the guards. Maxon. Though it was late, he was still in his suit pants and his shirt, slightly rumpled but presentable.

"Am I the last?" I asked, pulling on my robe as I approached.

"No," he answered. "Kriss is still out there. So is Elise."

I looked behind me at the darkened corridor that seemed to go on forever. In either direction, I could make out the skeletons of three or four stairways stemming from their secret origins in the palace above. They were empty.

If anything Maxon had told me was true, his feelings for Kriss and Elise were limited. But there was no mistaking the concern for them in his eyes. He rubbed his temple and craned his neck, as if that would really help in the dark. We looked past each other, watching the stairs as guards milled around the door, clearly anxious to close it.

Suddenly he sighed and put his hands on his hips. Then, with no warning at all, he embraced me. I couldn't help but clutch him to my chest.

"I know you're still probably upset, and that's fine. But I'm happy you're safe."

Maxon hadn't touched me since Halloween. It hadn't even been a week, but for some reason, it felt like an eternity. Maybe because so much had happened that night, and even more had happened since.

"I'm glad you're safe, too."

He held me tighter. Suddenly he gasped. "Elise."

I turned to see her thin figure coming down the stairs. Where was Kriss?

"You should go inside," Maxon gently urged. "Silvia is waiting."

"We'll talk soon."

He gave me a small, hopeful smile and nodded. I headed into the room, with Elise following right behind. As she walked in, I saw she was crying. I put an arm around her shoulder, and she did the same to me, happy to have the company.

"Where were you?" I asked.

"I think my maid is sick. She was a little slow to help me. And then I was so frightened by the alarm, I got confused for a moment and couldn't remember where to go. I pushed on four different walls before I found the right one." Elise shook her head at her forgetfulness.

"Don't worry," I said, hugging her. "You're safe now."

She nodded her head to herself, trying to slow her breathing. Of the five of us, she was easily the most delicate.

As we went deeper, I saw the king and queen sitting close together, both of them in robes and slippers. The king had a small stack of papers on his lap, as if he was going to use the time down here to work. The queen had a maid massaging one of her hands, and they both wore serious expressions.

"What, no company this time?" Silvia joked, drawing our attention to her.

"They weren't with me," I said, suddenly worried about the safety of my maids.

She smiled gently. "I'm sure they're fine. This way."

We followed her to a row of cots set up against an uneven wall. The last time I was in this place, it was clear that the people who maintained the room weren't prepared for the chaos of all the Selected girls down here. They'd made progress since then, but it wasn't completely up-to-date. There were six beds.

Celeste was curled up on the one closest to the king and queen, though we were still quite a ways from them. Natalie had settled in next to her and was braiding thin pieces of her own hair.

"I expect you to sleep. You all have a serious week ahead of you, and I can't have you planning if you're deliriously tired." Silvia went away, probably to look for Kriss.

Elise and I both sighed. I couldn't believe they were going to make us go through with the whole reception thing. Wasn't this stressful enough? We let go of each other and made our way to neighboring cots. Elise was quick to tuck herself into the blankets, obviously worn out.

"Elise?" I said quietly. She peeked up at me. "If you need anything, let me know, okay?"

She smiled. "Thank you."

"Sure thing."

She rolled back over, and it looked like she was asleep within seconds. I knew it was true when she didn't turn over at the bustle of noise coming from the door. I glanced back and saw Maxon carrying Kriss into the safe room, with Silvia close by. Immediately after she was through, the door was sealed shut.

"I tripped," she explained to Silvia, who was fretting over her. "I don't think I broke my ankle, but it really hurts."

"There are bandages in the back. We can at least wrap it," Maxon instructed. Silvia walked away quickly, passing us as she went hunting for bandages.

"Sleep! Now!" she ordered.

I sighed, and I wasn't the only one. Natalie took it in stride, but Celeste seemed very irritated. I checked myself then. If my behavior was anything like hers, it needed to change. Though I didn't want to, I crawled into my cot and faced the wall.

I tried not to think about Aspen fighting upstairs, or my maids maybe not making it to their hiding place fast enough. I tried not to worry about the upcoming week, or the possibility of the rebels being Southern and trying to slaughter people above us as we rested.

But I did think about all of that. And it was so exhausting, I eventually found sleep on my cold, hard cot.

I didn't know what time it was when I woke up, but it must have been hours since we'd come to the safe room. I rolled over, looking at Elise. She was sleeping peacefully. The king was reading his papers, whipping them through his hands so quickly, he appeared to be mad at them. The queen's head rested on the back of her chair. She looked even more beautiful when she slept.

Natalie was still asleep, or at least she looked that way. But Celeste was awake, propped up on one arm and looking across the room. Her eyes held a fire that she usually reserved for me. I followed her gaze over to the opposite wall, where she was watching Kriss and Maxon.

They sat side by side, his arm wrapped around her shoulder. Kriss had her legs curled to her chest, looking as if she was trying to keep warm, even though she was wearing a robe. Her left ankle was wrapped in gauze and didn't appear to be bothering her at the moment. They spoke quietly with smiles on their faces.

I didn't want to watch, so I rolled back over.

By the time Silvia tapped me on my shoulder to wake me, Maxon was already gone. So was Kriss.

CHAPTER 16

As I EMERGED FROM THE stairwell that had ushered me to safety the night before, it was all too apparent that the Southerners had been here. In the short hallway that led to my room, there was a pile of debris that I had to climb over to get to my door.

Typically, the worst of the mess was gone by the time we were released from the safe room. This time, however, it looked like there had been too much for the staff to get to, and we would have been down there all day. Still, I wished they'd tried a little harder. I spied a group of maids working to scrub away giant letters on a far wall.

WE'RE COMING

The line was repeated down the hall, sometimes written in mud, other times in paint; and one appeared to be done in blood. Chills ran through me, and I wondered what that meant.

As I stood there, my maids dashed up to me. "Miss, are you all right?" Anne asked.

I was startled by their sudden appearance. "Um, yes. Fine." I looked back to the words on the wall.

"Come away, miss. We'll get you ready," Mary insisted.

I followed obediently, slightly stunned from everything I saw and too confused to do anything else. They worked deliberately, the way they did when they tried to soothe me with the routine of getting dressed. Something about their steady hands—even Lucy's—was calming.

By the time I was ready, a maid came to escort me outside, where we would apparently be working this morning. The smashed glass and chilling graffiti were easy to forget about in the Angeles sun. Even Maxon and the king were standing at a table with advisers, reviewing piles of documents and making decisions.

Under a tent, the queen read over papers, pointing out details to a nearby maid. Near her, Elise, Celeste, and Natalie sat at a table discussing plans for their reception. They were so engrossed, it looked like they'd completely forgotten the rough night.

Kriss and I sat on the opposite side of the lawn, under a similar tent, but our work was going slowly. I was having a hard time talking to her as I fought to get the image of her sharing a moment with Maxon out of my head. I watched as she underlined sections in the papers Silvia gave us and scribbled notes in the margin.

"I think I might have figured out how to do our flowers," she commented without looking up.

"Oh. Good."

I let my eyes wander over to Maxon. He was trying to look busier than he was. Anyone really watching could see how the king pretended not to hear his comments. I didn't understand that. If the king was worried about Maxon being a good leader, the thing to do was to truly instruct him, not keep him from doing anything because he worried his son would make a mistake.

Maxon shuffled some papers and looked up. He caught my eye and waved. As I went to raise my hand, I saw Kriss enthusiastically wave back from the corner of my eye. I focused on the papers again, fighting a blush.

"Isn't he handsome?" Kriss asked.

"Sure."

"I keep imagining how children would look with his hair and my eyes."

"How's your ankle?"

"Oh," she said with a sigh. "It hurts a little, but Doctor Ashlar says I'll be fine by the reception."

"That's good," I said, finally looking up at her. "Wouldn't want you hobbling around when the Italians come." I was trying to sound friendly, but I could tell she was questioning my tone.

She opened her mouth to speak but then quickly looked

away. I followed her gaze and saw that Maxon was heading over to the refreshment table the butlers had set up for us.

"I'll be right back," she said quickly, and limped toward Maxon faster than I would have thought possible.

I couldn't help but watch. Celeste had walked over, too, and they were all talking quietly as they poured water or grabbed finger sandwiches. Celeste said something, and Maxon laughed. It looked like Kriss was smiling, but she was clearly too bothered by Celeste interrupting her time to be genuinely amused.

I was almost grateful for Celeste at that moment. She might have been a hundred things that irritated me, but she was also impossible to intimidate. I could use some of that.

The king bellowed something to one of his advisers, and my head snapped in his direction. I missed exactly what he'd said, but he sounded irritated. Over his shoulder, I caught a glimpse of Aspen, walking his rounds.

He looked my way briefly, risking a fast wink. I knew that was meant to ease my worries, and it did a little. Still, I couldn't help but wonder what he went through last night that led to the slight limp in his step and the bandaged gash by his eye.

As I was debating whether there was a way to inconspicuously ask him to come see me tonight, a call rang out from just inside the palace doors.

"Rebels!" a guard yelled. "Run!"

"What?" another guard called back, confused.

"Rebels! Inside the palace! They're coming!"

The guard's words made the threat on the walls this morning flash through my mind: WE'RE COMING.

Things started moving very quickly. The maids ushered the queen toward the far side of the palace, some pulling her hands to make her move faster while others dutifully raced behind her, blocking her from an attack.

Celeste's red dress blazed as she followed the queen, rightly assuming that was probably the safest way to go. Maxon scooped up Kriss and her injured foot, turning to place her in the arms of the nearest guard, who happened to be Aspen.

"Run!" he screamed at Aspen. "Run!"

Aspen, faithful to a fault, bolted, carrying Kriss like she weighed nothing at all.

"Maxon, no!" she cried over Aspen's shoulder.

I heard a loud pop from inside the opened doors to the palace and screamed. As several of the guards reached under their dark uniforms and pulled out guns, I understood what that sound was. Two more pops came, and I found myself frozen, watching the flurry of bodies move around me. The guards pushed people to the sides of the palace, urging them to move out of the way as a swarm of people in rugged pants and sturdy jackets raced outside, running with backpacks or satchels packed to the brim. Another shot came.

Finally realizing that I needed to move, I turned and ran without thinking.

With the rebels flooding out of the palace, the logical thing to do seemed to be to run away from them. But that put me heading toward the great forest with a pack of vicious people chasing me. I ran and slipped a few times in the flats I was wearing, and I considered taking them off. In the end, I decided slippery shoes were better than none.

"America," Maxon called. "No! Come back!"

I risked peeking back and saw the king grabbing Maxon by the neck of his suit jacket, pulling him away. I could see the terror in Maxon's eyes as he stared after me. Another shot was fired.

"Stand down!" Maxon shrieked. "You'll hit her! Cease fire!"

There were some more shots, and Maxon continued to scream his orders until I was too far away to make them out. I ran through the open field and realized then that I was alone in this. Maxon was being held back by his father, and Aspen was doing his duty. Any guard coming for me would be behind the rebels. All I could do was run for my life.

Fear made me fast, and I was surprised by how well I avoided the undergrowth once I hit the woods. The ground was dry, parched from months with no rain, and it was solid. I vaguely felt my legs getting scratched, but I didn't slow down to see how bad it was.

I was sweating, and my dress was sticking to my chest as I moved. It was cooler in the woods, and steadily getting darker, but I was hot. At home I sometimes ran for fun, to play with Gerad or just to feel the ache of exertion. But I'd been sitting in the palace for months, eating real food for the first time, and I could feel it now. My lungs burned, and my legs were throbbing. Still, I ran.

After I got far enough in the woods, I looked over my shoulder to check how close the rebels were. I couldn't hear them with the blood pounding in my ears, and when I checked, I couldn't see them either. I decided this was my best chance to hide, before they caught sight of the bright dress in the dim woods.

I didn't stop until I saw a tree that looked wide enough to conceal me. Once I was behind it, I noticed that there was a branch low enough to grab and climb, too. I took off my shoes, tossing them away, hoping they wouldn't lead the rebels right to me. I climbed, though not very high, and turned my back to the tree, making myself as small as I could.

I focused hard on slowing my breath, fearing the sound would give me away. But even after I did that, for a moment it was quiet. I figured I'd lost them. I didn't move, waiting to be sure. Seconds later, I heard a loud rustling.

"We should have come at night," someone—a girl— huffed. I flattened myself against the tree, praying nothing would snap.

"They wouldn't have been outside at night," a man replied.

They were still running, or trying to, and it sounded like they were having a rough go of it.

"Let me carry some," he offered. It sounded like they were getting very close.

"I can do it."

I held my breath and watched as they passed right under my tree. Just when I thought I might be safe, the girl's bag ripped, and a pile of books fell to the forest floor. What was she doing with so many books?

"Damn it," she cursed, getting down on her knees. She was wearing a denim jacket with some kind of flower embroidered on it over and over again. She had to be burning in that.

"Told you to let me help."

"Shut up!" The girl pushed at the boy's legs. In that playful gesture, I could see how much affection there was between them.

In the distance, someone whistled.

"Is that Jeremy?" she asked.

"Sounds like him." He bent and picked up a few books.

"Go get him. I'll be right behind you."

He looked unsure but agreed, kissing her forehead before jogging off.

The girl gathered the rest of her books, using a knife to cut the strap off her bag and bind them together.

I felt a sense of relief as she rose, assuming she would start moving. But she flipped her hair back out of her face, raising her eyes to the sky.

And she saw me.

No amount of quiet or stillness would help me now. If I screamed, would the guards come? Or were the rest of the rebels too close for that to matter?

We stared at each other. I waited for her to call the others, hoping that whatever they had planned for me wasn't too painful.

But she didn't make a sound except to let out a single quiet laugh, amused at our situation.

Another whistle sounded, slightly different from the last, and we both glanced in the direction it came from before looking at each other again.

And then, in the least expected of all possible gestures, she swung one leg behind the other, lowering herself in a graceful curtsy. I looked on, completely stunned. She rose, smiling, and ran off toward the whistle. I watched her back as a hundred tiny sewn flowers disappeared into the brush.

When it felt like more than an hour had passed, I decided I could get down. I stood at the foot of the tree, realizing I didn't know where my shoes were. I walked around the base of the trunk, trying to locate the little white slippers to no avail. Giving up, I decided I should make my way back to the palace.

Looking around, it became clear that that wasn't going to happen. I was lost.

CHAPTER 17

I SAT AT THE BASE of the tree, legs folded up to my chest, waiting. Mom always said that was what we were supposed to do when we were lost. It gave me time to think about what had happened.

How was it possible that rebels had gotten into the palace two days in a row? *Two days in a row!* Had things gotten so much worse on the outside since the Selection had begun? Based on what I'd seen back in Carolina and had experienced at the palace, this was unprecedented.

My legs had a bunch of scratches on them, and now that I wasn't hiding, I could finally feel the sting. There was also a small bruise halfway up my thigh that I wasn't sure how I'd acquired. I was thirsty; and as I settled down, I felt worn-out from the emotional, mental, and physical strain of the day. I let my head rest against the tree, closing my eyes. I didn't intend to fall asleep. But I did.

Sometime later, I heard the distinct sound of footsteps. My eyes flashed open, and the forest was darker than I remembered. How long had I been asleep?

My first instinct was to climb back up the tree, and I ran around to the other side, stepping on the torn remnants of the rebel girl's bag. But then I heard people calling my name.

"Lady America!" someone said. "Where are you?"

"Lady America?" another voice called. Then, after a while, in a loud voice, a command came. "Be sure to look everywhere. If they've killed her, they might have hung her or tried to bury her. Pay attention."

"Yes, sir," men chorused back.

I peeked around the tree, focusing on the sound. I squinted, trying to make out the figures moving through the shadows, unsure they could really be here to save me. But one guard, his slight limp not slowing him at all, made me finally sure that I was safe.

A small patch of fading sunlight fell across Aspen's face, and I ran. "I'm here!" I yelled. "I'm over here!"

I ran straight into Aspen's arms, for once not caring about who saw. "Thank goodness," he breathed into my hair. Then, turning toward the other figures, "I've got her! She's alive!"

Aspen bent down and picked me up, cradling me. "I was terrified we were going to find your body somewhere. Are you hurt?"

"My legs a little."

A second later, several guards were surrounding us, congratulating Aspen on a job well done.

"Lady America," the one in charge said, "are you injured at all?"

I shook my head. "Just some scratches on my legs."

"Did they try to hurt you?"

"No. They never caught up to me."

He looked a bit shocked. "None of the other girls could have outrun them, I don't think."

I smiled, finally at ease. "None of the other girls is a Five."

Several of the guards chuckled, Aspen included.

"Good point. Let's get you back." He went in front of us and called out to the other guards, "Be on the lookout. They could still be lingering in the area."

As we moved, Aspen talked to me quietly. "I know you're fast and smart, but I was terrified."

"I lied to the officer," I whispered.

"What do you mean?"

"They did catch up with me, eventually."

Aspen looked at me in horror.

"They didn't do anything, but this one girl saw me. She curtsied and ran off."

"Curtsied?"

"I was surprised, too. She didn't look angry or threatening at all. In fact, she just looked like a normal girl."

I thought over Maxon's comparison of the two rebel groups and knew this girl must be a Northerner. There was absolutely no aggression in her, only a drive to do her task.

And there was no doubt that the attack last night was from the Southern rebels. Did that mean something, that the attacks weren't only back-to-back, but by different groups? Were the Northerners watching us, waiting for us to be this drained? Thinking about them spying on the palace so intently was a little frightening.

At the same time, the attack was almost funny. Did they simply walk in the front doors? How many hours were they in the palace collecting their treasures? Which reminded me.

"She had books, lots of them," I said.

Aspen nodded. "That seems to happen a lot. No clue what they're doing with them. My guess is kindling. I think it's cold where they stay."

"Hmm," I replied, not really answering. If I needed kindling, I could think of much easier places to get it than the palace. And the way the girl was so desperate to gather up the books made me sure it was something more than that.

It took nearly an hour of slow, steady trekking to get back to the palace. Even though he was injured, Aspen never let his hold on me slip. In fact, he looked to be enjoying the walk despite the extra labor. I liked it, too.

"The next few days might be busy for me, but I'll try to come see you soon," Aspen whispered as we crossed the wide, grassy lawn leading up to the palace.

"Okay," I answered quietly.

He smiled a little as he looked forward, and I joined him, taking in the view. The palace was glittering in the evening sun, with windows lit up on every story. I'd never seen it like this. It was beautiful.

For some reason I thought Maxon would be there, waiting by the back doors for me. He wasn't. No one was. Aspen was instructed to take me to the hospital wing so Dr. Ashlar could tend to my legs while another guard went off to tell the royal family I'd been found alive.

My homecoming was a nonevent. I was alone in a hospital bed with bandaged legs, and that was how I stayed until I fell asleep.

I heard someone sneeze.

I opened my eyes, confused for a second before remembering where I was. I blinked, looking around the room.

"I didn't mean to wake you," Maxon said in hushed tones. "You should go back to sleep." He was propped up in a chair by my bed, so close he could rest his head by my elbow if he wanted to.

"What time is it?" I rubbed my eyes.

"Almost two."

"In the morning?"

Maxon nodded. He watched me carefully, and I was suddenly very worried about how I looked. I had washed my face and pulled my hair up when I came back, but I was pretty sure I had a pillow imprinted on my cheek.

"Don't you ever sleep?" I asked.

"I do. I'm just on edge a lot."

"Occupational hazard?" I sat up a bit more.

He gave me a thin smile. "Something like that."

There was a long pause as we sat there, unsure of what to say next.

"I thought of something today, when I was in the woods," I said casually.

He smiled a bit more at how easily I brushed off the incident. "Oh, really?"

"It was about you."

He inched closer, his brown eyes focused on mine. "Do tell."

"Well," I started, "I was thinking about how you were last night when Elise and Kriss weren't in the hall, how worried you were. And then today I saw you try to run after me when the rebels came."

"I tried. I'm so sorry." He shook his head, ashamed that he hadn't done more.

"I'm not upset," I explained. "That's the thing. When I was out there alone, I thought about how worried you probably were, how worried you are about the others. And I can't pretend to know how you feel about all of us, but I know that you and I aren't exactly a highlight right now."

He chuckled. "We've seen better days."

"But you still ran after me. You handed Kriss off to a guard because she couldn't run. You're trying to keep us all safe. So why would you ever hurt one of us?"

He sat silently, not sure where I was going.

"I understand now. If you're that concerned with our safety, you couldn't have wanted to do that to Marlee. I'm sure you would have stopped it if you could."

He sighed. "In a heartbeat."

"I know."

Tentatively, Maxon reached across the bed for my hand. I let him take it. "Do you remember how I said I had something I wanted to show you?"

"Yes."

"Don't forget, okay? It's coming. This position requires a lot of things, and they aren't always pleasant. But sometimes . . . sometimes you can do great things."

I didn't understand what he meant, but I nodded.

"I suppose it will have to wait until you're done with this project though. You're a bit behind."

"Ugh!" I pulled my hand from Maxon's to cover my eyes. I'd completely forgotten about the reception. I looked back at him. "Are they still going to make us do that? There've been two rebel attacks, and I spent the majority of my day lost in the woods. We're going to mess it up."

Maxon's face was sympathetic. "You'll have to push through."

I let my head flop back on the pillow. "It's going to be a disaster."

He chuckled. "Don't worry. Even if you don't do as well as the others, I don't have it in me to kick you out."

Something in that sounded funny. I sat back up. "Are you saying that if the others do worse, one of *them* could be kicked out?"

Maxon hesitated a moment, clearly unsure how to respond.

"Maxon?"

He sighed. "I have about two weeks before they expect another cut. This is supposed to be a big part of it. You and Kriss have the harder setup. A new relationship, fewer people to do the work; and while the culture is very celebratory, the Italians are easy to offend. Add to that the fact that you've hardly been able to do any work at all . . ."

I wondered if the blood was visibly draining from my face.

"I'm not supposed to help, but if you need something, please say so. I can't send either of you home."

When we'd had our first fight, a stupid spat over Celeste, I thought a piece of me shattered for Maxon. And then when Marlee left so abruptly, I thought it did again. I was sure that every time something blocked my way, bits of my heart were crumbling to nothing. But I was wrong.

There, lying in the hospital wing, my heart broke for the first time over Maxon Schreave. And the ache was unthinkable. Up until then I could convince myself that I'd imagined everything I'd seen between him and Kriss, but now I knew for sure.

He liked her. Maybe as much as he liked me.

I nodded at his offer for help, unable to say anything else.

I told myself to tug my heart back, that he couldn't have it. Maxon and I started all this as friends, and maybe that's all we were meant to be: close friends. But I was crushed.

"I should go," he said. "You need sleep. You had a very long day."

I rolled my eyes. That wasn't the half of it.

Maxon stood and straightened his suit. "I wanted to say so

much more to you. I really thought I'd lost you today."

I shrugged. "I'm fine. Really."

"I can see that now, but there were several hours today when I was forced to brace myself for the worst." He paused, measuring his words. "Usually, of all the girls, you're the easiest to talk to about what we are. But I have a feeling that perhaps that's not the wisest thing to do right now."

Ducking my head, I gave a slight nod. I couldn't try to talk about my feelings for a person who obviously had a crush on someone else.

"Look at me, America," he asked gently.

I did.

"I'm fine with that. I can wait. I just want you to know . . . I'm not able to find words big enough to express how relieved I am that you're here, in one piece. I've never been so grateful for anything."

I was stunned into silence, the way I always was when he touched the shy places of my heart. A corner of myself worried at how easily I trusted his words.

"Goodnight, America."

CHAPTER 18

IT WAS MONDAY NIGHT. OR Tuesday morning. It was so late, it was hard to tell.

Kriss and I had worked all day finding appropriate swaths of fabric, having butlers hang them, choosing our clothes and jewelry, picking china, creating a rough draft of the menu, and listening to a language coach speak lines in Italian to us in the hope that some of it would stick. At least I had the advantage of knowing Spanish, which helped me pick it up faster; they were so similar. Kriss was just doing all she could to keep up.

I ought to have been exhausted, but all I could think about were Maxon's words.

What had happened with Kriss? Why was she all of the sudden so close to him? Should I even care this much?

But this was Maxon.

And try as I might to pull away, I still cared about him. I wasn't ready to give up completely.

There had to be a way to figure this out. As I debated everything that was happening, attempting to separate my issues from one another, it looked like all the pieces fell into one of four categories.

My feelings about Maxon. Maxon's feelings about me. Whatever was going on between Aspen and me. And my feelings about actually becoming a princess.

Of all the things swimming in my head right now, it actually felt like the princess thing might be the easiest to tackle. At least in that area, I had something the other girls didn't. I had Gregory.

I went over to my piano stool, drew out his diary, and hoped with all my heart that he would have some wisdom for me. He hadn't been born into royalty; he must have had to adjust. Based on what he'd said in his Halloween entry, he was already preparing for a big change in his future.

I pulled up the covers, protecting the words from the world, and dove in.

I WANT TO EMBODY THE OLD-FASHIONED AMERICAN IDEAL. I HAVE A BEAUTIFUL FAMILY, AND I'M VERY WEALTHY; AND BOTH OF THOSE THINGS SUIT THIS IMAGE BECAUSE THEY WEREN'T HANDED TO ME. ANYONE WHO SEES ME NOW KNOWS HOW HARD I WORKED FOR WHAT I HAVE.

BUT THE FACT THAT I'VE BEEN ABLE TO USE MY

POSITION, TO GIVE SO MUCH WHERE OTHERS EITHER
HAVE NOT OR COULD NOT, HAS CHANGED ME FROM SOME
FACELESS BILLIONAIRE INTO A PHILANTHROPIST. STILL,
I CANNOT REST ON THIS. I NEED TO DO MORE, TO BE
MORE. WALLIS IS IN CHARGE, NOT ME, AND I NEED TO
FIGURE OUT HOW TO PROPERLY GIVE THE PUBLIC WHAT
THEY NEED WITHOUT BEING SEEN AS A USURPER. A TIME
MAY COME WHEN I WILL LEAD AND CAN DO WHAT I SEE
FIT. FOR NOW I WILL PLAY BY THE RULES AND GO AS
FAR AS I CAN WITH THAT.

I tried to glean some actual wisdom from his words. He said to use your position. He said to play by the rules. He said not to be afraid.

Maybe that should have been enough, but it wasn't. It didn't even feel close to helpful. Since Gregory failed me, there was only one other man I could count on. I went over to my desk, pulled out a pen and paper, and scribbled a brief letter to my father.

CHAPTER 19

THE NEXT DAY FLEW BY, and suddenly Kriss and I were arriving at the other girls' reception in conservative gray dresses.

"What's the plan?" Kriss asked as we walked down the hall.

I considered for a moment. I disliked Celeste and wouldn't mind seeing her fail, but I wasn't sure I wanted her to do it on this grand a scale. "Be polite, but not helpful. Watch Silvia and the queen for cues. Absorb everything we can . . . and work all night to make ours better."

"All right." She sighed. "Let's go."

We were on time, as was crucial to the culture, and the girls were already a mess. It was like Celeste was sabotaging herself. Where Elise and Natalie were in respectable deep blues, Celeste's dress was practically white. Put a veil on her, and this was a wedding. Not to mention how revealing it was, especially when she stood next to any of the German women. Most of them were wearing sleeves to their wrists despite the warm weather.

Natalie had been put in charge of the flowers and missed the detail that lilies were traditionally used at funerals. All the flower arrangements had to be removed hastily.

Elise, though clearly more agitated than she usually was, appeared to be the image of calm. To our guests, she would look like the star.

It was intimidating, trying so hard to communicate with the women from the German Federation—who spoke very broken English—particularly when I had so much Italian in my brain. I tried to be hospitable; and despite their severe appearance, the ladies were actually quite friendly.

It became clear pretty quickly that the true threat of disaster was Silvia and her clipboard. While the queen graciously aided the girls in hosting the German guests, Silvia walked the perimeter of the room, her sharp eyes missing nothing. It seemed she had pages of notes before the event had ended. Kriss and I quickly realized that our only hope was to have Silvia fall in love with our reception.

The next morning, Kriss came to my room with her maids, and we got ready together. We wanted to make an effort to look similar enough so it was clear we were in charge but not so much alike we looked silly. It was kind of fun having so many girls in my room. The maids all knew one another, and they talked animatedly behind us as they worked. It reminded me of how things had felt when May was here.

Hours before our guests were supposed to arrive, Kriss and I made our way to the parlor to double-check everything one last time. Unlike the other reception, we were forgoing place cards and letting our guests sit wherever they liked. The band came to practice in the space, and as a lucky bonus, it seemed our choice of fabrics to cover the bland walls made for great acoustics.

I straightened Kriss's necklace as we quizzed each other on the conversational phrases one last time. She sounded very natural speaking Italian.

"Thank you," she said.

"*Grazie,*" I answered.

"No, no," she replied, facing me. "I mean thank you. You did an amazing job on this, and . . . I don't know. I thought that after Marlee, you might give up. I was afraid that I'd be doing this alone, but you've worked so hard. You've done great."

"Thanks. You have, too. I don't know if I would have survived if I had to work with Celeste. You made it almost easy." Kriss smiled. I meant it, too. She was tireless. "And you're right; it's been hard without Marlee, but I wouldn't quit. This is going to be great."

Kriss bit her lip and considered for a moment. Quickly, as if she might lose her nerve, she spoke. "So you're still competing then? You still want Maxon?"

It wasn't like I didn't know what we were all doing here, but none of the other girls had spoken about it like that. I was caught off guard for a moment, wondering if I should answer her. And, if I did, what would I say?

"Girls!" Silvia trilled, rushing in through the doorway. I'd never been so grateful to see that woman. "It's nearly time. Are you ready?"

Behind her, the queen came in, a soothing calm to balance Silvia's energy. She studied the room, admiring our work. It was a huge relief to see her smile.

"Almost ready," Kriss said. "We just have a few details to take care of. One we specifically need you and the queen for."

"Oh?" Silvia said curiously.

The queen approached us then, her dark eyes warm with pride. "It's beautiful. And you both look stunning."

"Thank you," we chorused. The pale-blue dresses with large gold accents had been my idea. Festive and lovely, but not too over the top.

"Well, you might notice our necklaces," Kriss said. "We thought that if they were similar, it would help people identify us as hosts."

"Excellent idea," Silvia said, scribbling on her clipboard.

Kriss and I smiled at each other. "Since you are both hosts here, too, we thought you should have ones as well," I said as Kriss pulled the boxes off the table.

"You didn't!" The queen gasped.

"For . . . for me?" Silvia asked.

"Of course," Kriss said sweetly, handing over the jewelry.

"You've both been so helpful. This is your project, too," I added.

I could see how touched the queen was by our gesture, but Silvia was completely speechless. I suddenly wondered if anyone at the palace ever gave her any kind of attention. Yes, we'd thought up the idea yesterday as a way to get Silvia on our side, but I was glad we'd done it for more than just that now.

Silvia might be overwhelming, but she did try to do all this instruction for our benefit. I vowed to do a better job of thanking her.

A butler told us our guests were arriving, and Kriss and I stood on either side of the double doors to welcome people as they came. The band started playing softly in the background, maids began circulating with hors d'oeuvres, and we were ready.

Elise, Celeste, and Natalie were walking toward us, surprisingly on time. Once they caught sight of our setup—the billowing fabric covering the drab walls, the sparkling centerpieces towering on our tables, the overflowing flowers—there was a clear ache in the eyes of Elise and Celeste. Natalie, however, was too excited to be bothered.

"It smells like the gardens," she said with a sigh, practically dancing into the room.

"A bit too much like it," Celeste added. "You're going to give people a headache." Leave it to her to find fault with something beautiful.

"Try to sit at different tables," Kriss suggested as they poured past. "The Italians are here to make friends."

Celeste sucked her teeth, acting as if this was putting her

out. I wanted to tell her to pull it together: We had been on our best behavior for her reception. But then I heard the warm buzzing conversation of the Italian women as they came down the hall and forgot all about her.

The best way to describe the Italian ladies was statuesque. They were tall, golden skinned, and absolutely beautiful. As if that wasn't enough, they were all so good-natured. It was like they carried the sun inside their souls and let it shine out on everything around them.

The Italian monarchy was even younger than Illéa's. They had been closed off to our attempts at friendship for decades, according to the packet I'd read, and this was the only time they'd ever reached out to us. This meeting was the first step toward a closer relationship with a growing government. It had been frightening to think about until the moment they walked through the doorway, and their kindness melted my worries. They kissed Kriss and me on both cheeks and yelled *"Salve!"* I happily tried to match their level of enthusiasm.

I botched some of my Italian phrases, but our visitors were gracious, laughing off my mistakes and helping to correct me. Their English was impressive, and we doted on one another's hairstyles and dresses. It seemed we'd made a good first impression appearance-wise, and that helped me relax.

I ended up settling in for most of the party next to Orabella and Noemi, two of the princess's cousins.

"This is delicious!" Orabella cried, raising her glass of wine.

"We're glad you like it," I replied, worrying that I was

coming across as too shy. They were so loud when they talked.

"You must have some!" she insisted. I hadn't had anything to drink since Halloween, and I wasn't very fond of alcohol in the first place. I didn't want to be rude, though, so I took the glass she handed me and sipped.

It was incredible. Champagne was all bubbles; but the deep, red wine had several flavors overlapping, each coming to the forefront in its own time.

"Mmmm." I sighed.

"Now, now," Noemi said, drawing my attention to her. "This Maxon, he is handsome. How can I get into the Selection?"

"A heap of paperwork," I joked.

"That's all? Where's my pen?"

Orabella cut in. "I will take some of this paper, too. I would love to take Maxon home with me."

I laughed. "Trust me, it's a bit of a mess in here."

"You need more wine," Noemi insisted.

"Absolutely!" Orabella seconded, and they called over a butler to refill my glass.

"Have you ever been to Italy?" Noemi asked.

I shook my head. "Before the Selection, I'd never even left my province."

"You must come!" Orabella insisted. "You can stay with me anytime."

"You always hog the company," Noemi complained. "She stays with me."

I felt the wine warming me all over, and their excitement was making me almost too happy.

"So, is he a good kisser?" Noemi asked.

I choked a little on the sip I was taking, pulling the glass away to laugh. I was trying not to give too much away, but they knew.

"How good?" Orabella demanded. When I didn't answer, she waved her hand. "Have some more wine!" she exclaimed.

I pointed an accusing finger at them, realizing what they were doing. "You two are nothing but trouble!"

They threw back their heads laughing, and I couldn't help but join them. Admittedly, girl talk was much more tempting when we weren't all competing for the same boy, but I couldn't get too drawn into this.

I stood to leave before I ended up passed out under the table. "He's very romantic. When he wants to be," I said. They clapped and laughed as I walked away, smiling at how playful they were.

After I got some water and food in me, I played some of the folk songs I'd learned on my violin, and most of the room sang along. Out of the corner of my eye, I spotted Silvia taking notes and tapping her foot to the beat at the same time.

When Kriss got up and proposed a toast to the queen and Silvia for their help, the room applauded them. When I raised my glass to our guests, they shrieked with delight, downing their glasses and then throwing them against the walls. Kriss and I weren't expecting that and shrugged before tossing ours as well.

The poor maids scuttled around to clean the shattered pieces as the band started up again and the whole room began to dance. Perhaps the highlight was Natalie on top of the table, doing some kind of dance that made her look like an octopus.

Queen Amberly sat in a corner, speaking jovially with the Italian queen. I felt a rush of accomplishment at the sight and was so engrossed, I nearly jumped when Elise addressed me.

"Yours is better," she said reluctantly but genuinely. "You two really pulled together an incredible reception."

"Thanks. I was worried for a while—we got off to such a bad start."

"I know. That makes it even more impressive. It looks like you two have been working for weeks." She looked around the room, staring longingly at the bright decor.

I put a hand on her shoulder. "You know, Elise, anyone could see yesterday that you worked the hardest on your team. I'm sure Silvia will make sure Maxon knows that."

"You think?"

"Of course. And I promise, if this is some sort of a competition and you lose, I'll tell Maxon myself what a good job you did."

She squinted her already thin eyes. "You would do that?"

"Sure. Why not?" I said with a smile.

Elise shook her head. "I really admire you for how you

are. Honest, I guess. But you need to realize we're competing, America." My smile disappeared. "I wouldn't lie and say anything bad about you, but I wouldn't go out of my way to tell Maxon you did something good. I can't."

"It doesn't have to be that way," I said quietly.

She shook her head. "Yes, it does. This isn't just some prize. This is a husband, a crown, a future. And you probably have the most to gain or lose by it."

I stood there, completely stunned. I thought we were friends. Except for Celeste, I really trusted these girls. Was I too blind to see how hard they were fighting?

"That doesn't mean I don't like you," she went on. "I like you a lot. But I can't cheer for you to win."

I nodded, still taking in her words. It was obvious I wasn't as mentally in this as she was. One more thing that made me doubt my ability to do this job.

Elise smiled over my shoulder, and I turned to see the Italian princess coming toward us.

"Pardon me. Can I have the hostess, please?" she asked in her lovely accent.

Elise gave her a curtsy before heading back to the dancing. I tried to shake off that conversation and focus on the person I was meant to impress.

"Princess Nicoletta, I'm sorry we haven't gotten to speak much today," I said, giving her a curtsy myself.

"Oh, no! You've been very busy. My cousins, they love you!"

I laughed. "They're very funny."

Nicoletta pulled me into a corner of the room. "We've been hesitant to make bonds with Illéa. Our people are much . . . freer than yours."

"I can see that."

"No, no," she said seriously. "I mean, in *personal* freedoms. They enjoy more than you. You have the castes still, yes?"

Suddenly understanding that this was more than a friendly conversation, I nodded.

"We watch, of course. We see what happens here. The riots, the rebels. It seems people are not happy?"

I wasn't sure what to say. "Your Majesty, I don't know if I'm the best person to talk to about this. I don't really control anything."

Nicoletta took my hands. "But you could."

A shiver ran through me. Was she saying what I thought?

"We saw what happened to the girl. The blonde?" she whispered.

"Marlee." I nodded. "She was my best friend."

She smiled. "And we saw you. There's not much footage, but we saw you run. We saw you fight."

The look in her eyes mirrored the way Queen Amberly had looked at me this morning. There was unmistakable pride there.

"We are very much interested in forming a bond with a powerful nation, if that nation can change. Unofficially, if there is anything we can do to help you acquire the crown, let us know. You have our full support."

She crammed a piece of paper into my hand and walked

away. As she turned her back, she shouted out something in Italian, and the room roared with delight. I didn't have pockets, so I quickly shoved the note in my bra, praying that no one would notice.

Our reception went on much longer than the first, and I suspected it was because our guests were too happy to actually leave. Still, for as lengthy as it was, the whole thing passed in a blur.

Hours later, I headed back to my room completely worn out. I was much too full to even think about dinner, and though it was early in the evening, the idea of going straight to bed was very appealing.

Before I could even look at my bed, however, Anne walked up to me with a surprise. I gasped and took the letter from her hand immediately. I had to give the postal workers at the palace credit; they were very fast.

I tore open the envelope and went to the balcony, soaking up my father's words and the last few rays of sunshine at the same time.

DEAR AMERICA,

YOU'LL NEED TO WRITE A LETTER TO MAY SOON. WHEN SHE SAW THIS WAS INTENDED FOR MY EYES ONLY, SHE WAS VERY DISAPPOINTED. I HAVE TO SAY, I WAS A LITTLE CAUGHT OFF GUARD MYSELF. I DON'T KNOW WHAT I WAS EXPECTING, BUT CERTAINLY NOT WHAT YOU ASKED.

FIRST, IT'S TRUE. WHEN WE CAME TO VISIT, I SPOKE WITH MAXON, AND HE WAS VERY CLEAR ABOUT HIS INTENTIONS TOWARD you. I don't think he has it in him to be less than genuine, and I believed (and still do) that he cares about you very much. I think if the whole process was simpler, he'd have chosen you already. Part of me thinks the slowness is on your side. Am I wrong?

The simple answer is yes. I approve of Maxon, and if you want to be with him, I support that. If you don't, I support that, too. I love you, and I want you to be happy. Maybe that means you live in our scrubby little house instead of a palace. I'm fine with that.

As for your other question, I have to say yes to that, too.

America, I know you don't see much in yourself, but you need to start. We told you for years you were talented, but you didn't believe it until your bookings went up. I remember the day you saw the full week and knew it was because of your voice and the way you play, and you were so proud. It was like you were suddenly aware of everything you could do. And we've said for as long as I can remember that you are beautiful, but I'm not sure you ever truly saw yourself that way until you were picked for the Selection.

You have it in you to lead, America. You have a good head on your shoulders; you are willing to learn; and, perhaps most importantly, you show compassion. That is something people in this country yearn for more than you know.

If you want the crown, America, take it. Take it. Because it should be yours.

AND YET . . . IF YOU DON'T WANT THAT BURDEN, I COULD
NEVER BLAME YOU. I WOULD WELCOME YOU HOME WITH OPEN ARMS.
I LOVE YOU.
DAD

The tears spilled out quietly. He genuinely thought I could do it. He was the only one. Well, he and Nicoletta.

Nicoletta!

I'd forgotten completely about the note. I fished inside my dress and pulled it out. It was a telephone number. She didn't even put her name on it.

I couldn't imagine how much she was risking to make that offer.

I held the tiny piece of paper and the letter from my dad in my hands. I thought of Aspen's certainty that I couldn't be a princess. I remembered the last-place spot in the public poll. I thought of Maxon's cryptic promise earlier this week. . . .

I closed my eyes and tried to search within myself.

Could I really do this? Could I be the next princess of Illéa?

CHAPTER 20

THE DAY AFTER THE ITALIAN reception we gathered in the Women's Room after breakfast. The queen was absent, and none of us knew what that meant.

"I bet she's helping Silvia write up the final report," Elise guessed.

"I don't think she's supposed to have much of a say," Kriss countered.

"Maybe she's hung over," Natalie offered as she pressed her fingers to her temples.

"Just because you are doesn't mean she is," Celeste spat.

"She might not be feeling well," I said. "She tends to get sick a lot."

Kriss nodded. "I wonder why that is."

"Didn't she grow up in the South?" Elise asked. "I hear the air and water aren't very clean down there. Maybe it's because of how she was raised."

"I hear everything is bad below Sumner," Celeste added.

"She's probably just resting," I interjected. "There's a *Report* tonight, and she simply wants to be ready. She's smart. It's barely ten, and I need a nap."

"Yeah, we should all take naps," Natalie said wearily.

A maid entered with a small platter and walked quietly across the room, almost too nimble to be noticed.

"Wait," Kriss said. "You don't think they'll talk about the reception stuff on the *Report*, do you?"

Celeste groaned. "I hated that stupid thing. You and America lucked out."

"You're joking, right? Do you have any . . ."

Kriss's words dropped off as the maid stopped just to my left, revealing a small, folded note on the platter.

I felt everyone's eyes on me as I tentatively picked up the letter and read it.

"Is that from Maxon?" Kriss asked, trying not to seem as interested as she was.

"Yes." I didn't look up.

"What's it say?" she probed.

"That he needs to see me for a moment."

Celeste laughed. "Sounds like you're in trouble."

I sighed and stood to follow the maid from the room. "Guess there's only one way to find out."

"Maybe he's finally kicking her out," Celeste whispered loudly enough for me to hear.

"You think?" Natalie asked a little too excitedly.

A chill went through me. Maybe he *was* kicking me out! If he wanted to talk to me or spend time with me, wouldn't he have said it differently?

Maxon was waiting in the hallway, and I walked up timidly. He didn't look upset, but he did seem tense.

I braced myself. "So?"

He took my arm. "We have fifteen minutes. What I'm about to show you, you can't share with anyone. Do you understand?"

I nodded.

"All right then."

We darted up the stairs, all the way to the third floor. Gently but quickly, Maxon pulled me down the hallway to a set of white double doors. "Fifteen minutes," he reminded.

"Fifteen minutes."

He took a key out of his pocket and unlocked one of the doors, holding it open so I could go in before him. The room was wide and bright, with lots of windows and two doors opening onto a balcony along the wall. There was a bed, a massive armoire, and a table with chairs; but other than that the room was empty. No paintings on the walls, no pieces on the inlaid shelves. Even the paint was a little drab.

"This is the princess's suite," Maxon said quietly.

My eyes widened.

"I know it's not much to look at right now. The princess is supposed to choose the decor, so once my mother moved to the queen's suite, the room was stripped."

Queen Amberly had slept here. Something about the room felt magical.

Maxon came up behind me and started pointing. "Those doors go to the balcony. And over there"—he pointed to the other end of the room—"those doors go to the princess's personal study. Right here"—he noted a door to our right—"this goes to my room. Can't have the princess too far off."

I felt myself blush thinking of sleeping here with Maxon so close.

He stepped toward the armoire. "And this? Behind this piece of furniture is the escape to the safe room. You can get to other places in the palace this way, too, but that's its main purpose." He sighed. "This is a slight misuse, but I thought it would be worth it."

Maxon placed his hand on a hidden latch, and the armoire and the panel of wall behind it swung forward. I saw him smile at the space behind it. "Right on time."

"I wouldn't miss it," another voice said.

I sucked in a breath. There was no way that voice belonged to who I thought it did. I stepped to see around the hulking piece of furniture and Maxon's smiling face. There, dressed in very plain clothes and with her hair pulled into a bun, was Marlee.

"Marlee?" I whispered, sure I had to be dreaming. "What are you doing here?"

"I've missed you so much!" she cried, and ran to me with her arms open. With her hands out, I could see clearly the red, healing welts on her palms. It really was Marlee.

She wrapped me in a hug, and we crumpled to the ground, I was so overcome. I couldn't stop from crying and asking over and over what in the world she was doing here.

When I quieted down long enough, Maxon got my attention. "Ten minutes. I'll be waiting outside. Marlee, you can leave the way you came."

She gave him her word, and Maxon left us alone.

"I don't understand," I said. "You were supposed to go south. You were supposed to be an Eight. Where's Carter?"

She smiled through my misunderstanding. "We've been here the whole time. I just started working in the kitchens; and Carter's still on the mend, but I think he'll be in the stables soon."

"On the mend?" So many questions were racing through my mind, I wasn't sure why that one popped out.

"Yes, he walks and can sit and stand, but it's hard for him to do anything too strenuous. He's helping in the kitchens until he's fully healed. He's going to be fine though. And look at me," she said, holding out both hands. "We've been very well taken care of. They aren't pretty, but at least they don't hurt anymore."

I carefully touched the swollen lines on her palms, sure they couldn't actually be painless. But she didn't flinch, and after a moment I slid my hand into hers. It felt funny, but at the same time completely natural. Marlee was here. And I was holding her hand.

"So Maxon's had you in the palace the whole time?"

She nodded. "After the caning, he was afraid we would be hurt if we were left on our own, so he kept us here. Two other servants, a brother and sister who had family in Panama, were sent instead. We're going by new names, and Carter is growing out his beard, so after a while we'll blend in. Not a lot of people know we're in the palace in the first place, just a few of the cooks I work with, one of the nurses, and Maxon. I don't even think the guards know because they have to answer to the king, and he wouldn't be pleased to find out."

She shook her head before quickly moving on. "Our little apartment is small, basically just enough room for our bed and some shelves; but at least it's clean. I'm trying to sew us a new bedspread, but I'm not—"

"Hold on. *Our* bed? As in, you share one?"

She smiled. "We got married two days ago. I told Maxon the morning we were caned that I loved Carter and that he was the one I wanted to marry, and I apologized for hurting him. He didn't care, of course. He came to me two days ago saying there was some big event happening and that if we wanted to get married, this was the time."

I counted back. Two days ago was when the German Federation had come. The entire palace staff was either helping serve them or preparing for the ladies from Italy.

"Maxon gave me away. I'm not sure I'll ever see my parents again. The more distance they have from me, the better."

I could tell she was pained to say so, but I understood why. If it had been me and I was suddenly an Eight, the kindest thing I could do for my family was disappear. It would take time, but people would forget. Eventually, my parents would recover.

To push away her sad thoughts, she fanned out her left hand, and I noticed the little band across her finger for the first time. It was twine tied in a simple knot, but it was a clear statement: I'm taken.

"I think I'm going to have to get him to give me a new one soon; I'm already fraying this one. I guess if he works in the stables, I'll have to make him a new ring every day." She playfully shrugged. "Not that I mind."

My mind had jumped to another question that I worried might be rude to ask, but I knew I would never be able to have this kind of conversation with my mom or Kenna. "So, have you . . . you know?"

It took her a moment to understand, but then she laughed. "Oh! Yes, we have."

We both giggled. "How is it?"

"Honestly? A little uncomfortable at first. The second time was better."

"Oh." I didn't know what else to say.

"Yeah."

There was a bit of a pause.

"I've been really lonely without you. I miss you." I played with the little piece of twine on her finger.

"I miss you, too. Maybe once you're the princess, I can sneak up here all the time."

I snorted. "I'm not so sure that'll happen."

"What do you mean?" she asked, her face turning serious.

"You're still his favorite, right?"

I shrugged.

"What happened?" The question was laced with concern, and I didn't want to admit that it had started with losing her. It wasn't her fault.

"Just things."

"America, what's going on?"

I sighed. "After you got caned, I was upset with Maxon. It took me a while to realize that he wouldn't have done something like that if he could have stopped it."

Marlee nodded. "He tried so hard, America. And when he couldn't, he did everything he could to make the situation better. So don't be mad at him."

"I'm not anymore, but I'm also not sure I want to be the princess. I don't know if I could do what he did. And then there was this poll in a magazine Celeste showed me. The people don't like me, Marlee. I'm at the bottom.

"I'm not sure I have what it takes. I was never a good choice, and it seems like I'm plummeting. And now . . . now . . . I think Maxon wants Kriss."

"Kriss? When did that happen?"

"I have no idea, and I don't know what to do. Part of me thinks it's a good thing. She'd make a better princess; and if he really likes her, I want him to be happy. And he's supposed to do another elimination really soon. When he called me out today, I thought I might be going home."

Marlee laughed. "You're so ridiculous. If Maxon didn't have feelings for you, he'd have sent you home a long time ago. The reason you're still here is because he refuses to lose hope."

Something between a choke and a laugh came out of my mouth.

"I wish we could talk more, but I should go," she said. "We're taking advantage of guards changing to do this."

"I don't care that it's short. I'm just glad to know you're okay."

She pulled me in for a hug. "Don't give up yet, all right?"

"I won't. Maybe you could send me a letter or something sometime?"

"That might work. We'll see." She let me go, and we stood together. "If they polled me, I would have voted for you. I've always thought it should be you."

I blushed. "Go on, now. Say hello to your husband for me."

She smiled. "I will." Nimbly, she went over to the armoire and found the latch. For some reason, I thought the caning would break her, but she was stronger now. She even carried herself differently. Marlee turned to blow me a kiss and disappeared.

I quickly exited the room and found that Maxon was waiting in the hallway. At the sound of the door, he looked up from his book, smiling, and I went over to sit by him.

"Why didn't you tell me sooner?"

"I had to make sure they were safe first. My father doesn't know I did this; and until I knew it wouldn't endanger them, I had to keep it to myself. I'm hoping to arrange for you to see her more, but that will take time."

I felt my shoulders lighten, as if the bricks of worry I'd been carrying around were falling off all at once. The happiness at seeing Marlee, the assurance that Maxon was as kind as I thought he was, and the general relief that this meeting wasn't about him sending me home were overwhelming.

"Thank you," I whispered.

"Of course."

I wasn't sure what else to say. After a moment Maxon cleared his throat.

"I know that you are averse to doing the difficult parts of this job, but there are a lot of opportunities here. I think you could do great things. I can tell you see the prince in me now, but that had to come eventually if you were ever going to truly be mine."

My eyes held his. "I know."

"I can't read you anymore. I used to be able to see it in the beginning when you didn't really care for me; and when things changed between us, you looked at me differently. Now there are moments when I think it's there and others when it seems like you're already gone."

I nodded.

"I'm not asking you to say you love me. I'm not asking for you to suddenly decide you want to be a princess. I just need to know if you want to be here at all."

That was the question, wasn't it? I still didn't know if I could do the job, but I wasn't sure I wanted to give up on it. And seeing this kindness in Maxon shifted my heart. There was still so much to consider, but I couldn't give up. Not now.

Maxon's hand was resting on his leg, and I slid mine under his. He gave me a welcoming squeeze. "If you'll still have me, I want to stay."

Maxon let out a relieved sigh. "I'd like that very much."

I returned to the Women's Room after a quick stop in the bathroom. No one said anything until I sat down, and it was Kriss who was bold enough to ask.

"What was that all about?"

I looked not just to her, but to all the watching eyes. "I'd rather not say."

With my puffy face, a response like that was enough to make it seem like nothing good could have come from the meeting; but if that was what I had to say to protect Marlee, then I was fine with it.

What really stung was Celeste pressing her lips together to hide her smile, Natalie's raised eyebrows as she pretended to read her borrowed magazine, and the hopeful glance between Kriss and Elise.

The competition was deeper than I had guessed.

CHAPTER 21

WE WERE SPARED THE HUMILIATION of dealing with the aftermath of our receptions on the *Report*. The visits from our foreign friends were mentioned in passing, but the actual events were kept from the public. It wasn't until the next morning that Silvia and the queen came to speak to us about our performances.

"It was a very daunting task we gave you, and it absolutely could have gone horribly wrong. I'm pleased to say, however, that both teams did very well." Silvia looked at each of us appraisingly.

We all sighed, and I reached for Kriss's hand as she did the same. As confused as I was about her and Maxon, I knew there was no way I could have made it through that without her.

"If I'm honest, one event was slightly better than the other, but you should all be proud of your accomplishments. We received thank-you letters from our longtime friends in the German Federation for your gracious hosting," Silvia said, looking at Celeste, Natalie, and Elise. "There were a few minor hiccups, and I don't think any of us truly enjoy such serious affairs, but they certainly did.

"And as for you two," Silvia turned toward Kriss and me. "The ladies from Italy enjoyed themselves immensely. They were quite impressed with your style, and the food; and they made a special point to ask for the wine you served, so, bravo! I wouldn't be surprised if Illéa gained a wonderful new ally based on that welcome. You're to be commended."

Kriss squeaked, and I let out a nervous laugh, happy enough that it was over, let alone that we'd beat the others.

Silvia went on to talk about how she would be writing up an official report to hand over to the king and Maxon but said that none of us had a thing to worry about. As she spoke, a maid scurried into the room and ran over to the queen, whispering in her ear.

"Absolutely, they may," the queen said, suddenly standing and walking forward.

The maid rushed back and opened the door for the king and Maxon. I knew men weren't supposed to come into this room without the queen's permission, but it was comical to see it in action.

As they entered, we stood to curtsy, but they didn't seem to care about formalities.

"Dear ladies, we are sorry to intrude, but we have urgent news," the king informed us.

"I'm afraid we've had a development with the war in New Asia," Maxon said firmly. "The situation is so dire that Father and I are leaving this very moment to see if we can do any good."

"What's wrong?" the queen asked, clutching her chest.

"It's nothing to worry about, my love," the king said confidently. But that couldn't be a completely honest statement if they had to rush out of here so suddenly.

Maxon walked over to his mother. They had a brief, whispered conversation before she kissed his forehead. He hugged her and stepped away. The king then began rattling off a list of instructions to the queen while Maxon came to say good-bye to each of us.

His good-bye to Natalie was so short it almost didn't happen. Natalie didn't seem too bothered, and I didn't know what to make of that. Was she actually not worried by Maxon's lack of affection, or was she so bothered that she was forcing herself to be calm?

Celeste draped herself across Maxon and exploded into the worst display of fake crying that I'd ever seen. It reminded me of May when she was younger, thinking tears would magically bring money for us to have what we wanted. When he went to untangle himself, she planted a kiss on his lips that he promptly—and in as polite a manner as possible—wiped away after his back was turned.

Elise and Kriss were so close that I heard his good-byes to them.

"Call ahead and tell them to go easy on us," he said to Elise. I'd almost forgotten that the main reason she was still here was that she had family ties to leaders in New Asia. I wondered if this war going downhill would cost her her spot.

Then I suddenly realized that I had no clue what Illéa stood to lose if we lost this war.

"If you get me a phone, I will talk to my parents," she promised.

Maxon nodded and kissed Elise's hand, then walked over to Kriss.

She immediately laced her fingers in his.

"Will you be in danger?" she asked quietly, her voice beginning to shake.

"I don't know. During our last trip to New Asia, the situation wasn't nearly so tense. I can't be sure this time." His voice was so tender, I felt they should have been having this conversation in private. Kriss lifted her gaze to the ceiling and sighed, and in that quick second Maxon looked over to me. I averted my eyes.

"Please be careful," she whispered. A tear fell onto her cheek.

"Of course, my dear." Maxon gave her a silly little salute, which made her laugh a bit. He then kissed her cheek and put his lips to her ear. "Please try to keep my mother entertained. She worries."

He pulled back to look into her eyes, and Kriss nodded once and let his hands go. The second they were no longer touching, a tremor went through her body. Maxon's hands twitched for a second, like he was going to embrace her, but then he stepped away and started to walk toward me.

As if Maxon's words of last week weren't enough, here was physical proof of their relationship. By the look of it, they had something very sweet and real. One glimpse of Kriss with her face in her hands was proof of how much she cared for him. Either that, or she was an incredible actress.

I tried to gauge his expression when he looked at me versus the way he had looked at Kriss. Was it the same? Was there less warmth there?

"Try not to get into any trouble while I'm gone, all right?" he said teasingly.

He didn't joke with Kriss. Did *that* mean something?

I raised my right hand. "I promise to be on my best behavior."

He chuckled. "Excellent. One less thing to worry about."

"What about us? Should we worry?"

Maxon shook his head. "We should be able to smooth over whatever's going on. Father can be very diplomatic and—"

"You are such an idiot sometimes," I said as Maxon's brow furrowed. "I mean about you. Should we worry about you?"

His face was very serious then and did nothing to help my fears.

"Flying in and flying out. If we can make it to the

ground . . ." Maxon swallowed once, and I saw how frightened he was.

I wanted to ask something else, but I didn't know what to say.

He cleared his throat. "America, before I go . . ."

I looked up to Maxon's face and felt the tears rising.

"I need you to know that everything—"

"Maxon," the king barked. Maxon lifted his head and waited for his father's instructions. "We need to go."

Maxon nodded. "Good-bye, America," he said quietly, and lifted my hand to his lips. As he did so, he noted the little homemade bracelet I wore. He studied it, seeming confused, then kissed my hand tenderly.

That little feather of a kiss sent me back to a memory that felt years old. He had kissed my hand like that my first night in the palace when I'd yelled at him, when he'd let me stay anyway.

The other girls' eyes were glued to the king and Maxon as they left, but I was watching the queen. Her entire body seemed weak. How many times would her husband and only child be put in danger before she cracked?

The moment the door shut behind her family, Queen Amberly blinked a few times, inhaled deeply, and pulled herself up to her full height.

"Forgive me, ladies, but this sudden news will require a lot of work from me. I think it's best if I go to my room so I can focus." She was fighting so hard. "How about I have lunch delivered here so you can eat at your leisure, and I will join you all for dinner tonight?"

We nodded. "Excellent," she said, and turned to leave. I knew she was strong. She'd grown up in a poor neighborhood in a poor province, working in a factory until she was chosen for the Selection. Then, once she was queen, she suffered miscarriage after miscarriage before she finally had a child. She would make it to her room looking like a lady, as her position demanded. But she would cry once she was alone.

After the queen left, Celeste went, too. Then I decided I didn't have to stay either. I went to my room, wanting to be alone and to think.

I kept wondering about Kriss. How had she and Maxon suddenly connected? Not too long ago, he was making me promises about our future. He couldn't have been that interested in her if he was saying such intimate things to me. It must have happened after that.

The day passed quickly. After dinner, as my maids quietly helped me prepare for bed, a single sentence lifted me from my reflections.

"Do you know who I found in here this morning, miss?" Anne asked as she gently pulled a brush through my hair.

"Who?"

"Officer Leger."

I froze, but only for a fraction of a second. "Oh?" I said. I kept my eyes on my reflection as they continued.

"Yes," Lucy said. "He said he was doing a sweep of your room. Something about security." She looked a little confused.

"It was strange though," Anne said, echoing Lucy's expression. "He was in his plain clothes, not his uniform. He shouldn't be doing security work on his time off."

"He must be very dedicated," I commented in a disconnected tone.

"I think he is," Lucy said with awe. "Whenever I see him around the palace, he's always noticing things. He's a very good soldier."

"True," Mary said matter-of-factly. "Some of the men who come through here really aren't fit for the job."

"And he looks good in his plain clothes. Most of them look terrible once you get them out of their uniforms," Lucy commented.

Mary giggled and blushed, and even Anne cracked a smile. It had been a long time since they'd seemed so relaxed. On another day, in another moment, it might be fun to gossip about the guards. Not today though. All I could think about was that there was a letter in my room from Aspen. I wanted to peek over my shoulder at my jar, but I didn't dare.

It felt like an eternity before they left me alone. I forced myself to be patient and wait a few minutes to make sure they didn't come back. Finally I darted over to my bed and clutched my jar. Sure enough, a tiny slip of paper was waiting for me.

Maxon is gone. This changes everything.

CHAPTER 22

"Hello?" I whispered, following the instructions Aspen had left for me the day before. I cautiously walked into a room lit only by the fading daylight spilling in through the gossamer curtains, but it was enough for me to see the excitement on Aspen's face.

I closed the door behind me, and he immediately ran over and scooped me up.

"I've missed you."

"I missed you, too. I was so busy with that reception, I barely had time to breathe."

"Glad it's over. Did you have a hard time getting here?" he joked.

I giggled. "Seriously, Aspen, you're way too good at your job." It was almost comical how simple his idea was. The queen was a little more relaxed when it came to running the palace. Or maybe she was distracted. Either way, she'd made dinner an option: in your room or downstairs. My maids prepped me for the meal, but instead of heading to the dining room, I walked across the hall to Bariel's old room. It was too easy.

He smiled as he took in my praise and sat me down in the back corner of the room on some pillows he'd already piled there. "Are you comfortable?"

I nodded and expected him to sit too, but he didn't. Instead he pushed over a large couch, which blocked the door from sight, and then pulled in a table that brushed the top of our heads as we sat on the floor. Finally he grabbed a bundle he'd left on top of the table—it smelled like food—and settled next to me.

"Almost like home, huh?" He moved behind me so I was between his legs. The position was so familiar and the space was so small that it did feel a little like our old tree house. It was like he'd taken a piece of something I thought was gone forever and placed it neatly in my hands.

"It's even better." I sighed, leaning into him. After a minute I felt his fingers combing down my hair. It gave me shivers.

For a while we sat there in silence, and I closed my eyes and focused on the sound of Aspen's breathing. Not so long ago, I'd done the same thing with Maxon. But this was different. If I had to, I thought I could pick Aspen's breathing out of a crowd. I knew him so well. And, clearly, he knew me. This tiny bit of peace was everything I'd been aching for, and Aspen made it real.

"What are you thinking about, Mer?"

"Lots of things." I sighed. "Home, you, Maxon, the Selection, everything."

"What are you thinking about all of that?"

"Mostly how confused I get about them. Like how I'll think I understand what's happening to me, and then something shifts, and my feelings change."

Aspen was quiet for a moment, and his voice sounded pained when he asked, "Do your feelings about me change a lot?"

"No!" I said, pushing myself closer to him. "If anything, you're the one constant. I know that if everything turns upside down, you'll still be here, in the exact same place. Everything gets so crazy that my love for you gets pushed to the background, but I know it's always there. Does that make sense?"

"It does. I know I make this whole thing more complicated than it already is. I'm glad to know I'm not completely out of the running though."

Aspen wrapped his arms around me, like he could hold me there forever.

"I haven't forgotten us," I promised.

"Sometimes I feel like Maxon and I are in our own version of the Selection. It's just him and me, and one of us will get you in the end; and I can't decide who's worse off. Maxon doesn't exactly know we're competing, so he might not be able to try as hard. But then, I have to hide, so it's not like I can give you everything he can. It's not really a fair fight either way."

"You shouldn't think about it that way."

"I don't know how else to see it, Mer."

I exhaled. "Let's not talk about that."

"All right. I don't like talking about him anyway. What about all the other stuff you're confused about? What's going on?"

"Do you like being a soldier?" I asked, turning toward him.

He nodded enthusiastically as he reached down and opened the food. "I love it, Mer. I thought I'd hate every minute, but it's fantastic." He popped a chunk of bread into his mouth and kept talking. "I mean, there's the obvious stuff, like I'm always being fed. They want us to be big, so there's plenty of food. And the injections, too," he said, amending his thoughts. "But they're not so bad. And I get an allowance. Even though I have everything I need, I get money."

He stopped for a moment, toying with an orange slice. "I know you know how good it feels to send money home."

I could tell he was thinking about his mom and his six siblings. He had been the father figure at his home; I wondered whether that made him even more homesick than I was.

He cleared his throat and went on. "But there are other things that I wasn't expecting to like, too. I really enjoy the discipline of it and the routine. I like knowing that I'm doing something necessary. I feel so . . . content. I've been restless for years, counting stock or cleaning houses. Now I feel like I'm doing what I was meant to do."

"So that's a big yes? You love it?"

"Completely."

"But you don't like Maxon. And I know you don't like the way Illéa is run. We used to talk about it back home, and then that whole thing with the people in the South losing their castes. I know that bothers you, too."

He nodded. "I think it's cruel."

"Then how are you okay with protecting it? You fight against rebels to keep the king and Maxon safe. They're the ones who make everything happen, and you don't like any of what they do. So how do you love your job?"

He chewed as he thought. "I don't know. I guess it doesn't make sense, but . . . okay, like I said, there's the sense of purpose. And feeling challenged and engaged, the ability to do something more with my life. Maybe Illéa isn't perfect. In fact, it's far from it. But I have . . . I have hope," he said simply.

We were both quiet for a moment while the word washed over us.

"I have this feeling that things have gotten better than they were, though I honestly don't know enough about our history to prove that. And I have this feeling that things will get even better in the future. I think that there are possibilities.

"And maybe this is silly, but it's *my* country. I get that it's broken, but that doesn't mean these anarchists can just come and take it. It's still mine. Does that sound crazy?"

I nibbled my bread and reflected on Aspen's words. They took me back to our tree house and all the times I would ask him questions about things. Even if I disagreed, it helped me understand them better. But I didn't disagree on this point. In fact, it helped me see what was probably hiding in my heart all this time.

"It doesn't sound crazy at all. It sounds completely reasonable."

"Does that help with whatever you've been thinking about?"

"It does."

"Are you going to explain any of it?"

I smiled up at him. "Not yet." Though Aspen was smart, and he might have already guessed. The wistful look in his eyes suggested that he probably had.

He looked away for a moment, running his hand down my arm, finishing by playing with the button bracelet around my wrist. "We're a mess, aren't we?"

"A big one."

"Sometimes I feel like we're a knot, too tangled to be taken apart."

I nodded. "It's true. So much of me is tied up in you. I feel kind of lost without you."

Aspen pulled me close, running a hand over my temple and down my cheek. "We'll just have to stay tangled then."

He kissed me gently, like, if he pushed too hard, the moment might shatter and we'd lose everything. Maybe he was right. Slowly, he lowered me to the mattress of pillows, holding on to me, tracing curves as he kissed me on and on. It was all so familiar, so safe.

I ran my fingers through Aspen's cropped hair, remembering the way it used to fall and tickle my face when he kissed me. I noted his arms around me, so much fuller than they used to be, so much sturdier. Even the way he held me had changed. There was a newfound confidence there, something instilled in him through becoming a Two, becoming a soldier.

Too soon it was time to leave, and Aspen walked me to the door. He gave me a lingering kiss, making me a little light-headed. "I'll try to get another note to you soon," he promised.

"I'll be waiting." I leaned into him, holding on to him for one long moment. Then, to keep us safe, I left.

My maids prepped me for bed, and I went through it in a daze. It used to feel like the Selection was one choice: Maxon or Aspen. And as if that was some decision my heart could make simply, it grew into so many more things. Was I a Five or a Three? When this was over, would I be a Two or a One? Would I live out my days as an officer's wife or a king's? Would I slide quietly into the background in which I'd always been so comfortable or force myself into the spotlight I'd always feared? Could I happily do either? Could I not hate whoever Maxon ended up with if I chose Aspen? Could I not hate whoever Aspen chose if I stayed with Maxon?

As I got into bed and turned out the light, I reminded myself that it was my decision to be here. Aspen may have asked, and my mother may have pushed, but no one forced me to fill out the form for the Selection.

Whatever was coming, I'd just face it. I'd have to.

CHAPTER 23

I CURTSIED TO THE QUEEN as I walked into the dining room, but she didn't notice. I looked over to Elise, who was the only one already there, and she merely shrugged. I sat down as Natalie and Celeste entered and were equally ignored; and finally Kriss arrived, sitting next to me but keeping her eyes on Queen Amberly. The queen seemed to be in her own world, staring at the floor or occasionally glancing at Maxon's and the king's chairs as if something was wrong.

The butlers began serving food, and most of the girls started eating; but Kriss kept watch on the head table.

"Do you know what's going on?" I whispered.

Kriss sighed and turned to me. "Elise called her family to get some insight into what was happening and to have her relatives meet Maxon and the king once they got to New Asia. But Elise's family says they never arrived."

"They never came?"

Kriss nodded. "The weird thing is, the king called when they landed, and he and Maxon both spoke with Queen Amberly. They're fine, and they told her they were in New Asia; but Elise's family kept saying they never showed."

I scrunched my forehead, trying to understand. "What does that all mean?"

"I don't know," she confessed. "They say they're there, so how could they not be? It doesn't make sense."

"Huh," I said, not sure of what else to add. Why would Elise's family not know they were there? What if, maybe, they weren't actually in New Asia? Where could they be?

Kriss leaned closer to me. "There's something else I wanted to talk to you about," she whispered. "Could we go for a walk in the gardens after breakfast?"

"Of course," I answered, eager to hear what she knew.

We both ate quickly. I wasn't sure what she'd found out, but if she wanted to talk outside, there was clearly a need for secrecy. The queen was so distracted, she barely even noticed as we left.

Stepping into the sunlit gardens felt wonderful. "It's been awhile since I've been out here," I said, closing my eyes and lifting my face to the sun.

"You usually come with Maxon, right?"

"Mm-hmm." A second later, I wondered how she knew that. Was it common knowledge?

I cleared my throat. "So, what did you want to talk about?"

She stopped under the shade of a tree and turned to face

me. "I think you and I should talk about Maxon."

"What about him?"

She fidgeted. "Well, I had prepared myself to lose. I think we all had, except for maybe Celeste. It was obvious, America. He wanted you. And then everything with Marlee happened, and it changed."

I wasn't quite sure what to say. "So, are you just telling me you're sorry for moving to the top or something?"

"No!" she said emphatically. "I can see he still cares about you. I'm not blind. I'm only saying, I think you and I might be neck and neck at this point. I like you. I think you're a really great person, and I don't want for things to get ugly, however it turns out."

"So this is . . . ?"

She clasped her hands in front of her, trying to think of the right words. "This is me offering to be completely honest about my relationship with Maxon. And I'm hoping you'll do the same."

I crossed my arms and went for the one question I'd been dying to ask. "When did you two get so close?"

Her eyes got a little dreamy, and she toyed with a piece of her light-brown hair. "I guess right after everything with Marlee. It probably sounds stupid, but I made him a card. That's what I always did back home when my friends were sad. Anyway, he loved it. He said no one had given him a present yet."

What? Oh. Wow. After everything he'd done for me, had I really never done anything for him in return?

"He was so happy, he asked me to sit with him awhile in his room and—"

"You've seen his room?" I asked, shocked.

"Yes, haven't you?"

My silence was all the answer she needed.

"Oh," she said awkwardly. "Well, you're not missing anything. It's dark, and there's a gun rack, and then he has this mess of pictures on the wall. It's nothing special," she promised, waving it away. "Anyway, after that he started visiting me during pretty much every free moment he had." She shook her head. "It happened kind of fast."

I sighed. "He basically told me," I confessed. "He made a little comment about needing us both here."

"So . . ." She bit her lip. "You're pretty sure he still likes you?"

Hadn't she already suspected that? Did she simply need me to confirm it? "Kriss, do you really want to hear all this?"

"Yes! I want to know where I stand. And I'll tell you anything you want to know, too. We aren't running this thing, but that doesn't mean we have to be lost in it."

I walked in a short circle, trying to make sense of everything. I wasn't sure I was brave enough to ask Maxon about Kriss. I could barely talk honestly with him about me. But I kept feeling like I was missing pieces of the truth about where I stood. Maybe this was my only hope of really knowing.

"I'm pretty sure he wants me to stay around for a while. But I think he wants you here, too."

She nodded. "I figured."

"Has he kissed you?" I blurted out.

She smiled bashfully. "No, but I think that he would have if I hadn't asked him not to. In my family, we sort of have this tradition where we don't kiss until we're engaged. Sometimes we have a party when people announce their wedding date, and everyone gets to see the first kiss. I want that for me."

"But he tried to?"

"No, I explained before we got that far. He kisses my hands a lot, though, or sometimes my cheek. I think it's kind of sweet," she gushed.

I nodded, looking at the grass.

"Wait," she said, hesitating. "Did he kiss you?"

Part of me wanted to brag that I was his first kiss ever. That when we kissed, it felt like time stopped.

"Sort of. It's kind of hard to explain," I hedged.

She made a face. "No, it's not. Has he or hasn't he?"

"It's complicated."

"America, if you're not going to be honest, then this is a waste of time. I came here wanting to be open with you. I thought it would benefit us both to be friendly."

I stood there, wringing my hands, trying to think of a way to explain myself. It wasn't that I disliked Kriss. If I went home, I'd want her to win.

"I do want to be friends with you, Kriss. I kind of thought we already were."

"Me, too," she said gently.

"It's just hard for me to share private things. And I appreciate your honesty, but I'm not sure I want to know everything. Even though I asked," I said quickly, seeing the words coming to her lips. "I already knew he had feelings for you. I could see it. I think I need things to be vague for the time being."

She smiled. "I can respect that. Would you do me a favor though?"

"Sure, if I can."

She bit her lip and turned her eyes away for a minute. When she looked back, I could see the hint of tears in her eyes. "If you're certain that he doesn't want me, could you maybe warn me? I don't know how you feel, but I love him. And I'd appreciate being told. If you know for sure anyway."

She loved him. She said it out loud, fearlessly. Kriss loved Maxon.

"If he ever told me for sure, I would tell you."

She nodded. "And maybe we could make another promise? Not to purposely get in each other's way? I don't want to win that way, and I don't think you do either."

"I'm no Celeste," I said with disgust, and she laughed. "I promise to be fair."

"Okay then." She dabbed at her eyes and straightened her dress. I could see it so easily, how elegant she would look with the crown on her head.

"I need to go," I lied. "Thanks for talking to me."

"Thanks for coming. I'm sorry if I was too intrusive."

"It's fine." I stepped away. "I'll see you later."

"Okay."

I turned as quickly as I could without being rude and made my way to the palace. Once inside, I quickened my pace and bolted up the stairs, aching to hide.

I made my way to the second floor and headed toward my room. I noticed a piece of paper on the floor, which was unusual for the typically immaculate palace. It was by the corner leading to my door, so I guessed it might be for me. To be sure, I flipped it over and read.

Another rebel attack this morning, this time in Paloma. Current count is over three hundred dead, at least one hundred more wounded. Again, the main demand appears to be terminating the Selection, calling for an end to the royal line. Please advise on best response.

My body went cold. I scanned both sides of the paper, looking for a date. Another attack this morning? Even if this was a few days old, it was at least the second one. And the demand was *again* ending the Selection. Was this what all the recent attacks had been about? Were they trying to get rid of us? If so, were both the Northern and Southern rebels pursing that end?

I didn't know what to do. I wasn't supposed to have seen this message, so it wasn't like I could talk to anyone. But did the people who were supposed to know already have this information? I decided to put the paper back on the ground. Hopefully, a guard would come around soon and get it to the right place.

For now I would just be optimistic that someone was responding.

CHAPTER 24

I TOOK ALL MY MEALS in my room for the next two days, managing to avoid Kriss until dinner on Wednesday. I thought I wouldn't feel so awkward by then. I was sadly mistaken. We gave each other quiet smiles, but I couldn't bring myself to speak. I almost wished I was across the room sitting between Celeste and Elise. Almost.

Just before dessert was served, Silvia came sprinting in as fast as her heeled shoes could carry her. Her curtsy was particularly brief before she made her way to the queen and whispered something to her.

The queen gasped and ran with Silvia out of the room, leaving us alone.

We'd been taught never to raise our voices, but in the moment we couldn't help ourselves.

"Does anyone know what's going on?" Celeste called, abnormally concerned.

"You don't think they're hurt, do you?" Elise said.

"Oh, no," Kriss breathed, and put her head down on the table.

"It's okay, Kriss. Have some pie," Natalie offered.

I found myself speechless, afraid even to think about what this could mean.

"What if they were captured?" Kriss worried aloud.

"I don't think the New Asians would do that," Elise said, though I could see she was worried. I wasn't sure if her concern was strictly for Maxon's safety or because any aggression on the part of the people she had a connection with would ruin her chances.

"What if their plane went down?" Celeste said quietly.

She looked up, and I was surprised to see genuine fear on her face. It was enough to silence us all.

What if Maxon was dead?

Queen Amberly returned with Silvia in tow, and we all watched her eagerly. To our intense relief, she was beaming.

"Good news, ladies. The king and prince will be home tonight!" she sang.

Natalie clapped as Kriss and I simultaneously fell back into our chairs. I hadn't realized how tense my body was for those few minutes.

Silvia chimed in. "Since they've had such an intense few days, we've decided to forgo any big celebration. Depending on when they leave New Asia, we might not even see them before bedtime."

"Thank you, Silvia," the queen said patiently. Really, who cared? "Forgive me, ladies, but I have some work to do. Please enjoy your desserts and have a lovely night," she said, then turned and flew out the door.

Kriss left seconds later. Maybe she was making a welcome home card.

After that I ate quickly and made my way back upstairs. As I was walking down the hall toward my room, I saw a little flash of blond hair under a white cap and the fluttering black skirt of a maid's uniform running toward the far-side stairs. It was Lucy, and it sounded like she was crying. She seemed so determined to get away unnoticed that I decided not to call out after her. Rounding the corner to my room, I saw that my door was wide-open. Without it to block their voices, Anne and Mary's argument spilled into the hallway, where I overheard everything.

"—why you always have to be so hard on her," Mary complained.

"What was I supposed to tell her? That she can have whatever she wants?" Anne shot back.

"Yes! What would the harm be in simply saying you had faith in her?"

What was going on? Was this why they had all seemed so distant lately?

"She aims too high!" Anne accused. "It would be unkind

of me to give her false hope."

Mary's voice bled with sarcasm. "Oh, and everything you told her was *so* kind. You're just bitter!" she accused.

"What?" Anne lashed back.

"You're bitter. You can't stand that she might be closer to something you want than you are," Mary yelled. "You've always looked down on Lucy because she wasn't raised at the palace as long as you were, and you've been jealous of me because I was born here. Why can't you be happy with who you are instead of stepping on her to make yourself feel better?"

"That's not what I was trying to do!" Anne said, her voice breaking.

The tight sobs were enough to silence Mary. It would have stopped me, too. Anne crying seemed like an impossibility.

"Is it so bad that I want more than this?" she asked, her voice thick with tears. "I understand that my position is an honor, and I'm glad to do my job; but I don't want to do this for the *rest of my life*. I want more. I want a husband. I want . . ." She was finally overcome by her sadness.

My heart broke into a thousand pieces. The only way for Anne to get out of this job was to marry her way out. And it wasn't like a slew of Threes or Fours were going to parade down the palace halls looking for a maid to take as a wife. She really was stuck.

I sighed, steadied myself, and entered the room.

"Lady America," Mary said with a curtsy, and Anne followed. Out of the corner of my eye, I saw her feverishly mopping the tears off her face.

Given her pride, I didn't think acknowledging them was a good thing, so I strode past the both of them to the mirror.

"How are you?" Mary continued.

"Really tired. I think I'll be going to bed right away," I said, focusing on the pins in my hair. "You know what? Why don't you both go relax? I can take care of myself."

"Are you sure, miss?" Anne asked, trying so hard to keep her voice composed.

"Very. I'll see you all tomorrow."

They didn't need any more encouragement than that, and thank goodness. I didn't want them to take care of me right now any more than they probably felt like it. Once I managed to get out of my dress, I lay in bed for a long time thinking of Maxon.

I wasn't even sure exactly what I was thinking about him. It was all slightly vague and unfixed, but I kept flashing back to my overwhelming happiness when I found out he was safe and on his way back. And there was a corner of my mind that wondered if he'd thought about me at all while he was gone.

I tossed for hours, completely unsettled. At about one in the morning, I figured that if I couldn't sleep, I might as well read. I turned on the lamp and pulled out Gregory's diary. I skipped past the fall entries and picked one from February.

SOMETIMES I ALMOST HAVE TO LAUGH AT HOW SIMPLE THIS HAS BEEN. IF THERE WAS EVER A TEXTBOOK WRITTEN ON THE TOPIC OF OVERTHROWING COUNTRIES, I WOULD BE THE STAR OF IT. OR I COULD PROBABLY WRITE IT MYSELF. I'M NOT SURE WHAT I'D SAY STEP ONE WAS, AS YOU CAN'T REALLY FORCE ANOTHER COUNTRY TO TRY AND INVADE OR PUT IDIOTS IN CHARGE OF WHAT ALREADY EXISTS; BUT I CERTAINLY WOULD ENCOURAGE ANY OTHER WOULD-BE LEADERS TO ACQUIRE UNGODLY AMOUNTS OF MONEY BY ANY MEANS NECESSARY.

A FASCINATION WITH MONEY WOULDN'T BE ENOUGH, HOWEVER. YOU MUST POSSESS IT AND BE IN A POSITION TO LORD IT OVER OTHERS. MY LACK OF BACKGROUND IN POLITICS HASN'T BEEN AN ISSUE IN GAINING ALLEGIANCE. IN FACT, I WOULD SAY AVOIDING THAT SECTOR ALTOGETHER MAY BE ONE OF MY GREATEST STRENGTHS. NO ONE TRUSTS POLITICIANS, AND WHY WOULD THEY? WALLIS HAS BEEN MAKING EMPTY PROMISES FOR YEARS IN THE HOPES THAT ONE OF THEM MIGHT COME THROUGH, AND THERE ISN'T A CHANCE IN HELL ANY OF THEM COULD. I, ON THE OTHER HAND, OFFER THE IDEA OF MORE. NO GUARANTEES, MERELY THAT FAINT GLIMMER OF OPTIMISM THAT CHANGE MIGHT COME. IT DOESN'T EVEN MATTER AT THIS POINT WHAT THE

CHANGE MIGHT BE. THEY'RE SO DESPERATE, THEY DON'T CARE. THEY DON'T EVEN THINK TO ASK.

PERHAPS THE KEY IS STAYING CALM WHILE OTHERS PANIC. WALLIS IS SO HATED NOW, HE'S ALL BUT HANDED THE PRESIDENCY OVER TO ME, AND NOT A SOUL IS COMPLAINING. I SAY NOTHING, DO NOTHING, AND WEAR A PLEASANT SMILE AS EVERYONE AROUND ME SINKS INTO HYSTERICS. ONE GLANCE AT THAT COWARD NEXT TO ME, AND THERE'S NO DENYING I LOOK BETTER AT A PODIUM OR SHAKING A PRIME MINISTER'S HAND. AND WALLIS IS SO DESPERATE TO HAVE SOMEONE THE PEOPLE LOVE ON HIS SIDE, I'M PRETTY SURE IT WILL ONLY TAKE TWO OR THREE INCONSPICUOUSLY WORDED DEALS TO HAVE ME RUNNING EVERYTHING.

THIS COUNTRY IS MINE. I FEEL LIKE A BOY WITH A CHESS SET PLAYING A GAME HE KNOWS HE WILL WIN. I'M SMARTER, RICHER, AND FAR MORE QUALIFIED IN THE EYES OF A COUNTRY THAT ADORES ME FOR REASONS NO ONE CAN SEEM TO NAME. BY THE TIME SOMEONE THINKS TO CONSIDER IT, IT WON'T MATTER ANYMORE. I CAN DO WHAT I LIKE, AND THERE'S NO ONE LEFT TO STOP ME. SO WHAT'S NEXT?

I FEEL IT'S TIME TO COLLAPSE THE SYSTEM. THIS PITIFUL REPUBLIC IS ALREADY IN SHAMBLES AND BARELY WORKS. THE REAL QUESTION IS, WHO DO I ALIGN MYSELF WITH? HOW DO I MAKE THIS SOMETHING THE PUBLIC BEGS FOR?

I slammed the book shut, confused and frustrated. Was I missing something? Collapsing what system? Lording over people? Was the structure of our country not a necessity but a convenience?

I considered hunting through the book for what happened to his daughter, but I was already so disoriented, I decided against it. Instead I went to the balcony, hoping some fresh air would help me wrap my mind around the words I'd just read.

I looked to the sky, trying to process all this, but I didn't even know where to start. I sighed, and my eyes wandered the gardens, stopping on a flicker of white. Maxon was walking alone on the grounds. He was finally home. His shirt was untucked, and he wasn't wearing a coat or tie. What was he doing out so late? I saw that he was holding one of his cameras. He must have been having a rough night himself.

I hesitated a moment, but who else could I talk to about this?

"*Pssst!*"

He jerked his head around, looking for the source. I did it again, waving my arms until he saw me. A surprised smile flashed across his face as he waved back. Hoping he'd be able to see it, I pulled on my ear. He did the same. I pointed to him, then to my room. He nodded, holding up a finger to tell me it'd be a minute. I nodded back and went inside as he did the same.

I put on my robe and ran my fingers through my hair, wanting to look half as put together as he did. I wasn't sure exactly how to talk about this, because I was essentially about to ask Maxon if he knew he was sitting on top of something that was much less altruistic than the public had been led to believe. Just as I was starting to wonder what was taking him so long, he knocked on the door.

I rushed over to open it and was greeted by the lens of his camera. It clicked a still of my shocked smile. My expression dissolved into something that expressed how unamused I was by this little stunt, and he captured that, too, laughing.

"You're ridiculous. Get in here," I ordered, grabbing him by the arm.

He followed. "Sorry, I couldn't resist."

"You took your time," I accused, settling on the edge of the bed. He came to sit beside me, far enough away that we could face each other.

"I had to stop by my room." He placed his camera safely on my bedside table, flicking at my jar with the penny in it. He made a sound that was almost a laugh and turned back to me, not explaining his detour.

"Oh. So how was your trip?"

"Odd," he confessed. "We ended up going to the rural part of New Asia. Father said it was some local dispute; but by the time we got there, everything was fine." He shook his head. "Honestly, it made no sense. We spent a few days walking through old cities and trying to speak to the natives. Father is quite disappointed with my grasp of the language and is insisting I study more. As if I'm not doing enough these days," he said with a sigh.

"That is kind of strange."

"I'm guessing it was some sort of test. He's been throwing them at me randomly lately, and I don't always know they're happening. Maybe this was about decision making or dealing with the unexpected. I'm not sure." He shrugged his shoulders. "Either way, I'm sure I failed."

He fidgeted with his hands for a minute. "He also really wanted to talk about the Selection. I think he felt like distance would do me good, give me perspective or something. Honestly, I'm tired of everyone else talking about a decision that *I'm* supposed to make."

I was sure the king's idea of perspective meant getting me out of Maxon's head. I'd seen the way he smiled at the other girls at meals or nodded to them in the hallways. He never did that to me. I felt instantly uncomfortable and didn't know what to say.

It appeared Maxon didn't either.

I decided I couldn't ask him about the diary yet. He seemed so humble about these things—the way he led, the kind of king he wanted to be—that I couldn't demand answers from him that I wasn't anywhere close to sure he had. A tiny corner of my brain couldn't shake the worry that he knew more than he'd ever shared, but I needed to know more myself before I spoke.

Maxon cleared his throat and pulled a little string of beads out of his pocket.

"As I said, we were walking through a bunch of towns, and I saw this in an old woman's street shop. It's blue," he added, pointing out the obvious. "You seem to like blue."

"I love blue," I whispered.

I looked at the little bracelet. A few days ago, Maxon was walking on the other side of the world, and he saw this in a shop . . . and it made him think of me.

"I didn't find anything for anyone else, so maybe you could keep this between us?" I nodded my head in agreement. "You never were the type to brag," he mumbled.

I couldn't stop staring at the bracelet. It was so understated, with polished stones that weren't quite gems. I reached out and ran a finger over one of the oval-shaped beads, and Maxon wiggled the bracelet in his hand, which made me laugh.

"Do you want me to put it on?" he offered.

I nodded and stretched out the wrist that didn't have Aspen's button on it. Maxon placed the cool stones against my skin and tied the little ribbon that held them together.

"Lovely," he said.

And there it was, pushing up through all the worries: hope.

It lifted the heavy parts of my heart and made me miss him. I wanted to erase everything since Halloween, go back to that night, and hold on to those two people on the dance floor. And then, at the same time, it made my heart plummet. If we were back at Halloween, I wouldn't have a reason to doubt this gift.

Even if I let myself be everything my father said I was, everything Aspen said I wasn't . . . I couldn't be Kriss. Kriss was better.

I was so tired and stressed and confused, I started crying.

"America?" he asked hesitantly. "What's wrong?"

"I don't understand."

"What don't you understand?" he asked quietly. I mentally noted that he was doing much better around crying girls these days.

"You," I admitted. "I'm just really confused about you right now." I wiped away a tear on one side of my face, and, so gently, Maxon's hand moved to wipe the tears on the other.

In a way, it was strange to have him touch me like that again. At the same time, it was so familiar that it would have seemed wrong if he hadn't. Once the tears were gone, he left his hand there, cupping my face.

"America," he said earnestly, "if you ever want to know anything about me—what matters to me or who I am—all you need to do is ask."

He looked so sincere that I nearly did ask. I almost begged

him to tell me everything: if he'd always considered Kriss, if he knew about the diaries, what it was about this perfect little bracelet that made him think of me.

But how did I know it would be the truth? And—because I was slowly realizing he was the steadier choice—what about Aspen?

"I don't know if I'm ready to do that yet."

After a moment of thought, Maxon looked at me. "I understand. I think I do anyway. But we should talk about some serious things very soon. And when you're ready, I'm here."

He didn't press me; instead he stood, giving me a small bow before grabbing his camera and making his way to the door. He looked back at me one last time before disappearing into the hall, and I was surprised by how much I ached to see him go.

CHAPTER 25

"PRIVATE LESSONS?" SILVIA ASKED. "As in, several a week?"

"Absolutely," I replied.

For the first time since I arrived, I was truly grateful for Silvia. I knew that there was no way she'd be able to resist having someone willing to hang on her every word; and if she was making me do extra work, it meant I could keep myself busy.

Thinking about Maxon and Aspen and the diary and the girls was too much right now. Protocol was black-and-white. The steps for proposing a law were orderly. These were things I could master.

Silvia looked at me, still slightly stunned, before she broke into a huge smile. Embracing me, she cried out, "Oh, this will be wonderful. Finally one of you understands how important this is!" She held me at arm's length. "When do you want to start?"

"Now?"

She was bursting with delight. "Let me go get some books."

I dove into her studies, so grateful for the words and facts and statistics she crammed into my head. If I wasn't with Silvia, I was reading up on something she'd assigned me as I spent countless hours in the Women's Room, all but tuning out the other girls.

I worked, and I was excited about the next time the five of us had a joint class.

When that time came, Silvia started by asking us what we were passionate about. I scribbled down my family, music, and then, as if the word demanded to be written, justice.

"The reason I ask is because the queen is typically in charge of a committee of some kind, something that benefits the country. Queen Amberly, for example, began a program for training families to take care of their mentally and physically infirmed members. So many get deposited in the streets once the families can no longer deal with them, and the amount of Eights grows to an unmanageable number. The statistics over the last ten years have proven that her program has helped keep the numbers lower, thus keeping the general population safer."

"Are we supposed to come up with a program like that?" Elise asked, sounding nervous.

"Yes, that will be your new project," Silvia said. "On the

Capital Report in two weeks' time, you'll be asked to present your idea and propose how you might start it."

Natalie made a little squeak of a sound, and Celeste rolled her eyes. Kriss looked like she was already dreaming something up. Her instant enthusiasm made me nervous.

I remembered Maxon talking about an upcoming elimination. I felt like Kriss and I were at a slight advantage, but still.

"Is this really helpful?" Celeste asked. "I'd rather learn about something we'll actually use."

I could tell that beneath her concerned tone, she was either bored with this idea already or intimidated by it.

Silvia looked appalled. "You will use this! Whoever becomes the new princess will be in charge of a philanthropy project."

Celeste muttered something under her breath and started fiddling with a pen. I hated that she wanted the position with none of the responsibility.

I'd make a better princess than she would, I thought. And in that moment I realized there was some truth to that. I didn't have her connections or Kriss's poise, but at least I cared. And wasn't that worth something?

For the first time in a while, I felt a true shot of enthusiasm course through me. Here was a project that would allow me to show off the one thing that separated me from the others. I was determined to pour myself into this and hopefully produce something that might genuinely make a difference. Maybe I'd still lose in the long run; maybe I wouldn't even want to win. But I would be as close to a princess as I possibly could, and I would make my peace with the Selection.

It was hopeless. Try as I might, I couldn't come up with a single idea for my philanthropy project. I thought and read and thought some more. I asked my maids, but they had no ideas. I would have sought out Aspen, but I hadn't heard from him in days. I guessed he was being extracautious with Maxon home.

What was worse was that Kriss was clearly deep into her presentation. She skipped hours of time in the Women's Room to go read; and when she was present, she had her nose in a book or was scribbling notes furiously.

Damn.

When Friday came, I felt like dying as I suddenly realized I only had a week left and no prospects on the horizon. During the *Report*, Gavril set up the structure for the next show, explaining that there would be a few brief announcements and then the rest of the evening would be dedicated to our presentations.

A light sweat broke out on my forehead.

I caught Maxon looking at me. He reached up and tugged his ear, and I wasn't sure what to do. I didn't quite want to say yes, but I didn't want to just brush him off. I pulled on my ear, and he looked relieved.

I fidgeted while I waited for him to show up, twiddling the ends of my hair and pacing around my room.

Maxon's knock was brief before he let himself in the way

he used to. I stood, feeling I needed to be a bit more formal than usual. I could tell that I was being ridiculous, but I felt completely unable to stop it at the same time.

"How are you?" he asked, crossing the room.

"Honestly? Nervous."

"It's because I'm so good-looking, isn't it?"

I laughed at the sympathetic face he made. "I should avert my eyes," I said, playing along. "Actually, it's mostly about that philanthropy project."

"Oh," he said, sitting at my table. "You could run your presentation by me if you like. Kriss did."

I felt deflated. Of course she was done. "I don't even have an idea yet," I confessed, sitting across from him.

"Ah. Yes, I can see how that would be stressful."

I gave him a look as if to say he had no idea.

"What's important to you? There has to be something that really touches you that the others might miss." Maxon leaned back in the chair comfortably, one hand on the table.

How was he so at ease? Couldn't he see how on edge I was?

"I've been thinking all week, and nothing's come to mind."

He laughed quietly. "I would have thought that you'd have the easiest time. You've seen more hardships in your life than the other four combined."

"Exactly, but I've never known how to change any of it. That's the problem." I stared at the table, remembering Carolina with perfect clarity. "I can see it all . . . the Sevens who get injured doing their labor-heavy jobs and are suddenly downgraded to Eights because they can't work anymore. The girls who walk the streets on the edge of curfew, wandering into the beds of lonely men for practically anything. The kids who never have enough—enough food, enough heat, enough love—because their parents are working themselves to death. I can remember my worst days like they're nothing. But coming up with a feasible way to do anything about it?" I shook my head. "What could I possibly say?"

I looked at him, hoping there was an answer in his eyes. There wasn't.

"You make an excellent point." Then he was quiet.

I thought over everything I said as well as his response. Did it mean that he knew more about Gregory's plans than I thought? Or did it mean he felt guilty because he had so much when others had so little?

He sighed. "This really wasn't what I was hoping we'd talk about tonight."

"What did you have on your mind?"

Maxon looked up at me as if I must be crazy. "You, of course."

I tucked my hair behind my ear. "What about me exactly?"

He changed positions, angling his chair so we were a bit closer and leaning in as if this was a secret. "I thought that after you saw that Marlee was fine, things would change. I was sure you'd find a way to care about me again. But that hasn't happened. Even tonight, you agreed to see me, but everything about you is standoffish."

So he did notice.

I ran my fingers across the table, not looking him in the eyes. "It's not exactly you I have a problem with. It's the position." I shrugged. "I thought you knew that."

"But after Marlee—"

My head popped up. "After Marlee, things kept happening. I'll have a grasp on what being a princess will mean one minute and lose it the next. I'm not like the other girls. I'm the lowest caste here; and Elise might have been a Four, but her family is way different from most Fours. They own so much, I'm surprised they haven't bought their way up yet. And you were raised in this. It's a serious change for me."

He nodded, his endless patience still there. "I do understand that, America. That's part of why I wanted you to have time. But you need to consider me in this, too."

"I am."

"No, not like that. Not like I'm part of the equation. Consider my predicament. I don't have much time left. This philanthropy project will be the springboard for another elimination. Surely, you've guessed that."

I lowered my head. Of course I had.

"So what am I to do once it's down to four? Give you more time? When it gets to three, I'm supposed to choose. If there are only three of you and you're still debating if you want the responsibility, if you want the workload, if you want *me* . . . what am I supposed to do then?"

I bit my lip. "I don't know."

Maxon shook his head. "That's not acceptable. I need

an answer. Because I can't send someone who really wants this—who wants me—home if you're going to bail out in the end."

My breathing picked up. "So I have to give you an answer now? I don't even know what I'm giving an answer to. Does saying I want to stay mean saying I want to be the one? Because I don't know that." I felt my muscles tensing, like they were preparing to run.

"You don't have to say anything now; but by the *Report* you need to know if you want this or not. I don't like giving you an ultimatum, but you're being a bit careless with my one shot."

He sighed before continuing. "That wasn't where I wanted this conversation to go either. Maybe I should leave." I could hear in his voice that he wanted me to ask him to stay, to tell him this was all going to work itself out.

"I think you should," I whispered.

He shook his head, irritated, and stood. "Fine." He walked across the room in quick, angry strides. "I'll just go see what Kriss is doing."

CHAPTER 26

I WENT DOWN FOR BREAKFAST on the late side. I didn't want to risk running into Maxon or any of the girls alone. Before I made it to the stairs, Aspen came walking up the hall. I made an exasperated sound, and he looked around before approaching me.

"Where have you been?" I quietly demanded.

"Working, Mer. I'm a guard. I can't control when and where they schedule me. I've stopped being placed on the round for your room."

I wanted to ask why, but this wasn't the time. "I need to talk to you."

He thought for a moment. "At two, go to the end of the first-floor hallway, down past the hospital wing. I can be there, but not for long." I nodded. He gave me a quick bow and went on his way before anyone noticed our conversation, and I continued downstairs, not feeling satisfied at all.

I wanted to scream. Saturday being a day-long sentence to the Women's Room was really unfair. When people came to visit, they wanted to see the queen, not us. When one of us was princess, that would probably change, but for now I was stuck watching Kriss pour over her presentation again. The others were reading things, too, notes or reports, and I felt sick to my stomach. I needed an idea and fast. I was sure Aspen would help me figure this out, and I had to start something tonight no matter what.

As if she could read my thoughts, Silvia, who had been visiting with the queen, stopped by to see me.

"How's my star pupil?" she asked, keeping her voice low enough that the others wouldn't notice.

"Great."

"How is your project going? Do you need any help fine-tuning?" she offered.

Fine-tuning? How was I supposed to tweak *nothing*?

"It's going great. You're going to love it, I'm sure," I lied.

She cocked her head to the side. "Being a bit secretive are we?"

"A bit." I smiled.

"That's fine. You've been doing wonderful work lately. I'm sure it'll be fantastic." Silvia patted my shoulder as she headed out of the room.

I was in so much trouble.

The minutes passed so slowly that it was like a special

kind of torture. Just before two I excused myself and went down the hallway. At the very end, there was a burgundy upholstered couch underneath a massive window. I sat to wait. I didn't see a clock, but the minutes passed too slowly for comfort. Finally Aspen came around a corner.

"About time." I sighed.

"What's wrong?" he asked, standing by the couch, looking official.

So much, I thought. *So many things I can't talk to you about.*

"We have this assignment, and I don't know what to do. I can't think of anything, and I'm stressed, and I can't sleep," I said spastically.

He chuckled. "What's the assignment? Tiara designing?"

"No," I said, shooting him a frustrated glare. "We have to come up with a project, something good for the country. Like Queen Amberly's work with the disabled."

"This is what you've been worked up about?" he asked, shaking his head. "How is that stressful? That sounds like fun."

"I thought it would be, too. But I can't come up with anything. What would you do?"

Aspen thought for a moment. "I know! You should do a caste exchange program," he said, his eyes glittering with excitement.

"A what?"

"A caste exchange program. People from the upper castes switch places with people from the lower castes so they can know what it feels like to walk in our shoes."

"I don't think that would work, Aspen, at least not for this project."

"It's a great idea," he insisted. "Can you imagine someone like Celeste breaking her nails stocking shelves? It'd serve them right."

"What's gotten into you? Aren't some of the guards natural Twos? Aren't they your friends now?"

"Nothing's gotten into me," he answered defensively. "I'm the same as ever. You're the one who's forgotten what it was like to live in a house with no heat."

I straightened my back. "I haven't forgotten. I'm trying to come up with a service project to stop things like that. Even if I go home, someone might use my idea, so I need it to be good. I want to help people."

"Don't forget, Mer," Aspen implored me with a quiet passion in his eyes. "This government sat by while you went without food. They let my brother get beaten in the square. All the talk in the world won't undo what we are. They put us in a corner we could never get out of on our own, and they're not in a rush to pull us out. Mer, they just don't get it."

I huffed and stood.

"Where are you going?" he asked.

"Back to the Women's Room," I answered, starting to move.

Aspen followed. "Are we seriously fighting over some stupid project?"

I turned on him. "No. We're fighting because you don't get it either. I'm a Three now. And you're a Two. Instead of being bitter about what we were handed, why can't you see the chance you have? You can change your family's life. You could probably change lots of lives. And all you want to do is settle the score. That's not going to get anyone anywhere."

Aspen didn't say anything, and I left. I tried not to be upset with him for being passionate about what he wanted. If anything, wasn't that an admirable quality? But it made me think so much about the castes and how they couldn't be undone that I started getting angry about the situation.

Nothing was going to change it. So why bother?

I played my violin. I took a bath. I tried to nap. I spent part of the evening sitting in a quiet room. I sat on my balcony.

None of it mattered. It was getting dangerously late in the game, and I still had nothing for my project.

I lay in bed for hours, trying to sleep and not getting far with that either. I kept flashing back to Aspen's angry words, his constant struggle with his lot in life. I thought about Maxon and his ultimatum, his demand for me to commit. And then I wondered if any of this mattered anyway, since I was certainly going home as soon as I showed up Friday night without anything to present.

I sighed and pulled back my blankets. I'd been avoiding looking at Gregory's diary again; I was worried that it would give me more questions than answers. But maybe something in there would give me direction, something I could talk about on the *Report*.

Besides, even if I couldn't help myself, I had to know what happened to his daughter. I was pretty sure her name was Katherine, so I flipped through the book looking for any mention of her, ignoring everything else, until I found a picture of a girl standing next to a man who appeared to be much older. Maybe it was just my imagination, but she looked like she'd been crying.

KATHERINE WAS FINALLY MARRIED TODAY TO EMIL DE MONPEZAT OF SWENDWAY. SHE SOBBED THE WHOLE WAY TO THE CHURCH UNTIL I MADE IT CLEAR THAT IF SHE DIDN'T STRAIGHTEN UP FOR THE CEREMONY, THERE'D BE HELL TO PAY AFTERWARD. HER MOTHER ISN'T HAPPY, AND I SUSPECT SPENCER IS UPSET NOW THAT HE'S AWARE OF HOW LITTLE HIS SISTER WANTED TO GO THROUGH WITH THIS. BUT SPENCER IS BRIGHT. I THINK HE'LL FALL INTO LINE QUICKLY ONCE HE SEES ALL THE POSSIBILITIES I'VE CREATED FOR HIM. AND DAMON IS SO SUPPORTIVE; I WISH I COULD TAKE WHATEVER IT IS IN HIS SYSTEM AND INJECT IT INTO THE REST OF THE POPULATION. THERE'S SOMETHING TO BE SAID FOR THE YOUNG. IT'S SPENCER AND DAMON'S GENERATION THAT HAS BEEN THE MOST HELPFUL IN GETTING ME WHERE I AM. THEIR ENTHUSIASM IS UNSWAYABLE, AND THEY ARE A FAR MORE POPULAR CROWD FOR OTHERS TO LISTEN TO THAN THE FEEBLE ELDERLY WHO INSIST WE'VE GONE DOWN THE WRONG PATH. I KEEP

WONDERING IF THERE'S A WAY TO SILENCE THEM FOR GOOD
THAT WOULDN'T MIRE MY NAME.

EITHER WAY, WE ARE SLATED TO HAVE THE
CORONATION TOMORROW. NOW THAT SWENDWAY HAS
GOTTEN THE POWERFUL ALLY OF THE NORTH AMERICAN
UNION, I CAN HAVE WHAT I WANT: A CROWN. I THINK
THIS IS A FAIR TRADE. WHY SETTLE FOR PRESIDENT
ILLÉA WHEN I CAN BE KING ILLÉA INSTEAD? THROUGH
MY DAUGHTER, I'VE BEEN DEEMED ROYAL.

EVERYTHING IS IN PLACE. AFTER TOMORROW THERE
WILL BE NO TURNING BACK.

He sold her. The pig sold his daughter to a man she hated
so he could have everything he wanted.

My instinct was to close the book again, to shut it all out.
But I forced myself to flip through it, reading passages at random. In one place a rough diagram of the caste system was
laid out, originally dreamed up with six tiers instead of eight.
On another page he plotted to change people's last names to
separate them from their pasts. One line made it clear that he
intended to punish his enemies by placing them lower on the
scale and reward the loyal by placing them higher.

I wondered if my great-grandparents simply had nothing
to offer or if they had resisted this. I hoped it was the latter.

What should my last name have been? Did Dad know?

My whole life I'd been led to believe that Gregory Illéa
was a hero, the person who saved our country when we were
on the edge of oblivion. Clearly, he was nothing more than

a power-hungry monster. What kind of man manipulated people so willingly? What kind of man hawked his daughter for his own convenience?

I looked at the older entries I'd read in a new light. He never said he wanted to *be* a great family man; he just wanted to *look* like one. He would play by Wallis's rules *for now*. He was using his son's peers to gain support. He was playing a game from the very beginning.

I felt nauseated. I stood and paced the floor, trying to wrap my head around it all.

How had an entire history been forgotten? How was it that no one ever spoke of the old countries? Where was all this information? Why didn't anyone know?

I opened my eyes and looked to the sky. It seemed impossible. Surely, someone would have disapproved, would have told their children the truth. But then again, maybe they had. I'd often wondered why Dad never let me talk about the timeworn history book he had hidden in his room, why the history I did know about Illéa was never in print. Maybe it was because, if it was there in writing that Illéa was a hero, people would have rioted. But if it was always a point of speculation, where one person insisted it was a certain way and another denied it, how would anyone ever hold on to the truth?

I wondered if Maxon knew.

Suddenly a memory came to me. Not so long ago, Maxon and I had our first kiss. It was so unexpected that I had pulled away, leaving him embarrassed. Then when I realized that I wanted Maxon to kiss me, I suggested that we simply erase that memory and plant a new one.

America, he'd said, *I don't think you can change history.* To which I replied, *Sure we can. Besides, who'd ever know about it but you and me?*

I'd meant it as a joke. Surely, if he and I end up together, we'd remember what really happened no matter how silly it was. We'd never actually replace it with a more perfect-sounding story simply for the sake of show.

But the whole Selection *was* a show. If Maxon and I were ever asked about our first kiss, would we tell anyone the truth? Or would we keep that little detail a secret between the two of us? When we died, no one would know, and that fraction of a moment that was so important to who we were would be gone.

Could it be that simple? Tell one story to one generation and repeat it until it was accepted as fact? How often had I asked someone older than Mom or Dad what they knew or what their parents had seen? They were old. What did they know? It was so arrogant of me to discount them completely. I felt so stupid.

But the important issue wasn't how this all made me feel. The important issue was what I was going to do with it.

I'd lived my whole life stuck in a hole in our society; and because I loved music, I didn't complain. But I had wanted to be with Aspen, and because he was a Six, it was harder than it had to be. If Gregory Illéa hadn't coldly designed the laws of our country, sitting comfortably at his desk all those years ago, then Aspen and I wouldn't have fought and I never would have cared about Maxon. Maxon wouldn't even be a prince. Marlee's hands would still be intact, and she and Carter wouldn't be living in a room barely big enough for their bed. Gerad, my sweet baby brother, could study all the science he wanted instead of pushing himself into the arts for which he had no passion.

By obtaining a comfy life in a beautiful house, Gregory Illéa had robbed most of the country of its ability to ever attempt to have the very same thing.

Maxon said if I wanted to know who he was, all I had to do was ask. I'd been afraid to face the possibility of him being this person, but I had to know. If I was meant to make a decision about being a part of the Selection or going home, I needed to know exactly what he was made of.

Donning my slippers and robe, I left my room, passing the nameless guard on my way.

"You all right, miss?" he asked.

"Yes. I'll be back soon."

He looked like he wanted to say more, but I left too quickly for him to speak. I headed up the stairs to the third floor. Unlike the other floors, guards stood at the landing, preventing me from simply walking to Maxon's door.

"I need to speak to the prince," I said, trying to sound firm.

"It's very late, miss," the one to the left said.

"Maxon won't mind," I promised.

The one to the right smirked a little. "I don't think he'd

appreciate any company right now, miss."

My forehead creased in thought as I played that sentence in my head again.

He was with another girl.

I had to assume it was Kriss, sitting there in his room, talking, laughing, or maybe giving up on her no-kissing rule.

A maid came around the corner with a tray in her hands, passing me as she descended the stairs. I stepped to the side, trying to decide if I should push the guards to let me through anyway or give up. As I went to open my mouth again, the guard cut me off.

"You need to go back to bed, miss."

I wanted to yell at them or do something because I felt so powerless. It wouldn't help, though, so I left. I heard the one guard—the smirking one—mumble something as I walked away, and that made it worse. Was he making fun of me? Feeling sorry for me? I didn't need his pity. I was feeling bad enough on my own.

When I got back to the second floor, I was surprised to see that the maid who had passed me was there, kneeling as if she was adjusting her shoe but clearly doing nothing of the sort. She raised her head as I approached, picking up her tray and walking toward me.

"He's not in his room," she whispered.

"Who? Maxon?"

She nodded. "Try downstairs."

I smiled, shaking my head in surprise. "Thank you."

She shrugged. "He's not anywhere you couldn't find him

if you looked anyway. Besides," she said, her eyes full of admiration, "we like you."

She moved away, heading down to the first floor very quickly. I wondered exactly who "we" was, but for now, her simple act of kindness was enough. I stood for a moment, leaving some space between the two of us, and headed downstairs.

The Great Room was open but empty, as was the dining room. I checked the Women's Room, thinking that would be a funny place to go on a date, but they weren't there either. I asked the guards by the door, and they assured me that Maxon hadn't gone into the gardens, so I checked a few of the libraries and parlors before guessing that he and Kriss must have either parted ways or gone back to his room.

Giving up, I turned a corner and headed for the back stairwell, which was closer than the main one. I didn't see anything; but as I approached, I heard the distinct hiss of a whisper. I slowed, not wanting to intrude and not completely sure where the sound was coming from.

Another whisper.

A flirtatious giggle.

A warm sigh.

The sounds focused, and I was certain where they were coming from. I took one more step forward, looked to my left, and saw a couple embracing in the shadows. After the image settled and my eyes adjusted to the light, a shock went through me.

Maxon's blond hair was unmistakable, even in the

darkness. How many times had I seen it just so in the dim light of the gardens? But what I'd never seen before, never *imagined* before, was how that hair would look with Celeste's long fingers, nails painted red, digging into it.

Maxon was all but pinned to the wall by Celeste's body. Her free hand was pressed against his chest, and her leg was wrapped around his, the slit of her dress revealing her long leg, tinted slightly blue in the dark of the hall. She pulled back slightly, only to fall back into him slowly, teasing him it seemed.

I kept waiting for him to tell her to get off him, to tell her she wasn't what he wanted. But he didn't. Instead he kissed her. She lavished in it and giggled again at his affection. He whispered something in her ear, and Celeste leaned in and kissed him, deeper, harder than before. The strap of her dress fell off her shoulder, leaving what seemed like miles of exposed skin down her back. Neither of them bothered to fix it.

I was frozen. I wanted to scream or cry, but my throat felt constricted. Why, of everyone, did it have to be her?

Celeste's lips slid off Maxon's and settled onto his neck. She gave another obnoxious giggle and kissed him once more. Maxon closed his eyes and smiled. With Celeste no longer blocking him, I was in Maxon's line of sight.

I meant to run. I meant to disappear, to evaporate. Instead I stood there.

So when Maxon opened his eyes, he saw me.

As Celeste drew pictures in kisses up and down his neck,

Maxon and I merely stared at each other. His smile now gone, Maxon had suddenly turned to stone. The shock in his eyes willed me finally to move. Celeste didn't notice, so I backed away quietly, not even stirring a breath.

Once I was out of earshot, I broke into a run, blazing past all the guards and butlers working late into the night. The tears started coming before I made it up the main stairway.

I pulled myself up and moved quickly to my room. I pushed past the concerned guard and through the doorway, sitting on my bed facing the balcony. In the quiet stillness of my room, I felt my heart ache. *So stupid, America. So stupid.*

I'd go home. I'd forget this ever happened. And I'd marry Aspen.

Aspen was the only person I could count on.

It wasn't long before there was a knock on my door, and Maxon came in without waiting for an answer. He stormed across the room, looking about as angry as I was.

Before he could say a word, I confronted him.

"You lied to me."

"What? When?"

"When haven't you been? How could the same person who talked about proposing to me want to be caught dead in a hallway with someone like her?"

"What I do with her has absolutely nothing to do with how I feel about you."

"You're joking, right? Or because you're the next king, I suppose it's acceptable for you to have half-naked girls draped across you whenever you like?"

Maxon looked stricken. "No. That's not what I think at all."

"Why her?" I asked, looking to the ceiling. "Why, of anyone on the planet, would you want her?"

When I looked to Maxon for an answer, he was shaking his head and looking around the room.

"Maxon, she's an actress, a fake. You have to be able to see that under all that makeup, and the push-up bra is nothing but a girl who wants to manipulate you to get what she wants."

Maxon huffed out a laugh. "Actually, I do."

I was taken aback by his calm. "Then why—"

But I already had my answer.

He knew. Of course he knew. He'd been raised here. Gregory's diaries were probably his bedtime stories. I didn't know why I'd expected otherwise.

How naive had I been? When I kept thinking that there was a better option than me for his princess, I'd been imagining Kriss. She was lovely and patient and a million things that I wasn't. But I'd been seeing her next to a different Maxon. For the man he would have to be to follow in Gregory Illéa's footsteps, the only girl here for him was Celeste. No one else would be so content to keep a country under her thumb.

"That's it," I said, wiping my hands in front of me. "You wanted a decision, and here it is: I am done with this. I'm done with the Selection, I'm done with all the lies, and I am especially done with you. God, I can't believe how stupid I was."

"You're not done, America," he contradicted me quickly, his stance saying as much as his words. "You're done when I say you are. You're upset right now, but you aren't done."

I gripped my hair, feeling like I was seconds away from pulling it all out by the roots. "What is wrong with you? Are you delusional? What makes you think that I will ever be okay with what I just saw? I *hate* that girl. And you were kissing her. I want nothing to do with you."

"Good God, woman, you never let me get a word in edgewise!"

"What could you possibly say that could explain that away? Just send me home. I don't want to be here anymore."

Our conversation had been going back and forth so quickly that his silence was startling.

"No."

I was enraged. Wasn't this exactly what he'd been asking for? "Maxon Schreave, you are nothing but a child who has his hands on a toy that he doesn't want but can't stand for someone else to have."

Quietly, Maxon spoke. "I understand that you're angry, but—"

I shoved him. "I'm beyond angry!"

Maxon remained calm. "America, do not call me a child. And do not push me."

I shoved him again. "What are you going to do about it?"

Maxon grabbed my wrists, pinning my arms behind my back, and I saw the anger in his eyes. I was glad it was there. I wanted him to provoke me. I wanted a reason to hurt him.

I could tear him to bits right now.

But there was no rage in him. Instead I felt the warm buzz of electricity that had been missing for a long time. Maxon's face was inches from mine, his eyes searching my own, perhaps wondering how he'd be received, perhaps not caring at all. Though it was all wrong, I still wanted it. My lips parted before I realized what was happening.

I shook my head to clear it and stepped back, moving toward the balcony. He didn't put up a fight as I pulled away. I took a few steadying breaths before I turned to him.

"Are you going to send me home?" I asked quietly.

Maxon shook his head, either unable or unwilling to speak.

I ripped his bracelet off my wrist and threw it across the room. "Then go," I whispered.

I turned back to look out my balcony and waited a few heavy moments to hear the click of the door. Once he left, I fell to the floor and sobbed.

He and Celeste were so much alike. Everything about them was a show. And I knew that he would spend the rest of his life sweet-talking the public into thinking he was wonderful, all the while keeping them trapped where they were. Just like Gregory.

I sat on my floor, legs crossed under my nightgown. As upset as I was with Maxon, I was even more upset with myself. I should have fought harder. I should have done more. I shouldn't be sitting here so defeated.

I wiped the tears away and assessed the situation. I was

done with Maxon, but I was still here. I was done with the competition, but I still had a presentation due. Aspen might not think I was tough enough to be a princess—and he was right—but he did have faith in me. I knew that. And so did my father. And so did Nicoletta.

I wasn't here to win anymore. So how could I go out with a bang?

CHAPTER 27

WHEN SILVIA ASKED WHAT I would need for my presentation, I told her a small desk for some books and an easel for a poster I was designing. She was particularly excited about my poster. I was the only girl here with any true experience making art.

I spent hours writing my speech onto note cards so I wouldn't miss anything, flagging sections in books to be my resources midpresentation, and rehearsing it in the mirror to get through the parts that particularly worried me. I tried not to think too hard about what I was doing; otherwise my whole body started trembling.

I asked Anne to make me a dress that looked innocent, which made her eyebrows pucker.

"You make it sound like we've been sending you out in lingerie," she said mockingly.

I chuckled. "That's not what I mean at all. You know I love all the dresses you've made me. I just want to seem . . . angelic."

She smiled to herself. "I think we can come up with something."

They must have been working like crazy, because I didn't see Anne, Mary, or Lucy the day of the *Report* until the hour before it started, when they came bustling in with the dress. It was white, gauzy, and light, adorned with one long stream of green and blue tulle running along the right side. The bottom fell in such a way that it looked like a cloud, and its empire waist added a level of virtue and grace to the gown. I felt lovely in that dress. It was by far my favorite of everything they'd designed for me, and I was glad it worked out that way. It would probably be the last dress of theirs I'd ever wear.

It had been hard to keep my plan a secret, but I did. When the girls asked what I was doing, I simply said it was a surprise. I got a few skeptical looks for that, but I didn't care. I asked my maids not to touch the things on my desk, not even to clean, and they obeyed, leaving my notes facedown.

No one knew.

The person I most wanted to tell was Aspen, but I refrained. Part of me feared he would talk me out of it, and I would cave. Another part feared he would be far too gung-ho.

As my maids worked to make me look beautiful, I stared into the mirror and knew I was walking into this alone. And that was for the best. I didn't want anyone—not my maids, not the other girls, and especially not Aspen—to get in trouble for my actions.

All that was left to do was to put things in order.

"Anne, Mary, would you please go get me some tea?"

They looked at each other. "Both of us?" Mary clarified.

"Yes, please."

They looked suspicious but curtsied and left all the same. Once they were gone, I turned to Lucy.

"Sit with me," I invited, pulling her down to the padded bench on which I was sitting. She complied, and I asked her simply, "Are you happy?"

"Miss?"

"You've seemed kind of sad lately. I was wondering if you were all right."

She dropped her head. "Is it that obvious?"

"A little," I admitted, wrapping my arm around her and holding her close. She sighed and placed her head on my shoulder. I was so happy that she forgot the invisible boundaries between us for a moment.

"Have you ever wanted something you couldn't have?"

I snorted. "Lucy, before I came here I was a Five. There were too many things I couldn't have to bother counting."

In a very un-Lucy-like manner, a single tear fell to her cheek. "I don't know what to do. I'm stuck."

I straightened up and made her face me. "Lucy, I want you to know I think you can do anything, be anything. I think you're an amazing girl."

She gave me a weak smile. "Thank you, miss."

I knew we didn't have much time. "Listen, I need you to do something for me. I wasn't sure if I could count on the others, but I'm trusting you."

Though she looked confused, I could tell she meant it when she said, "Anything."

I reached over to one of the drawers and pulled out a letter. "Could you give this to Officer Leger?"

"Officer Leger?"

"I wanted to tell him thank-you for how kind he's been, and I thought it might be inappropriate to give him a letter myself. You know." It was a lame excuse, but it was the only way I could explain to Aspen why I did what I was going to do and to tell him good-bye. I assumed I wouldn't have much time in the palace after tonight.

"I can get this to him within the hour," she said eagerly.

"Thank you." Tears threatened to come, but I pushed them down. I was scared, but there were so many reasons this needed to be done.

We all deserved better. My family, Marlee and Carter, Aspen, even my maids were all stuck because of Gregory's plans. I would think of them.

When I walked into the studio for the *Report*, I was clutching an armful of marked books and a portfolio for my poster. The setup was the same as always—the king's, queen's, and Maxon's seats to the right near the door, the Selected in seats on the left—but in the middle, where there was usually a podium for the king to speak at or a set of chairs for interviews, there was a space for our presentations instead. I saw a desk and my easel, but also a screen that I assumed someone was showing slides on. That was impressive. I wondered who had found the resources to go that far.

I went over to the last open chair—next to Celeste, unfortunately—and placed my portfolio beside me, keeping my books on my lap. Natalie had a few books, too; and Elise was reading through her notes over and over. Kriss was looking toward the sky and appeared to be reciting her presentation mentally. Celeste was checking her makeup.

Silvia was there, which sometimes happened when we had to discuss something she'd briefed us on, and today she was beside herself. This was probably the hardest we'd worked to date, and it would all reflect back on her.

I inhaled sharply. I'd forgotten about Silvia. Too late now.

"You look beautiful, ladies, fantastic!" she said as she approached. "Now that you're all here, I want to explain a few things. First, the king will get up and give a few announcements, and then Gavril will introduce the topic of the evening: your philanthropy presentations."

Silvia, usually a level-headed, palace-hardened machine, was giddy. She was actually bouncing as she spoke. "Now, I know you've been practicing. You have eight minutes; and if anyone has a question for you afterward, Gavril will facilitate that. Remember to stay alert and poised. The country is watching you! If you get lost, take a breath and move on. You're going to be wonderful. Oh, and you'll be going in the order in which you're seated, so Lady Natalie, you're first; and Lady America will be last. Good luck, girls!"

Silvia skipped off to check and double-check things, and I tried to calm myself. Last. I guessed that was a good thing. I supposed Natalie had it worse by being first up. Looking over, I saw her breaking into a sweat. It must be torture for her to try and focus like this. I couldn't help but stare at Celeste. She didn't know I'd seen her and Maxon, and I kept wondering why she never told anyone about it. The fact that she kept it to herself led me to believe it wasn't the first time.

That made it so much worse.

"Nervous?" I asked, watching her pick at something on her nail.

"No. This is a stupid idea, and no one really cares. I'll be glad when it's over. And I'm a model," she said, finally looking at me. "I'm naturally good at being in front of an audience."

"You do seem to have mastered how to pose," I mumbled.

I could see the wheels turning as she tried to weed out the insult in there. She ended up rolling her eyes and looking away.

Just then the king walked in with the queen by his side. They were speaking in whispers, and it looked very important. A moment later, Maxon entered, adjusting his cuff links as he made his way to his seat. He came across so innocent, so clean in his suit; I had to remind myself that I knew better.

He looked over at me. I wasn't going to be intimidated and turn away first, so I stared back. Then, tentatively, Maxon reached up and tugged at his ear. I slowly shook my head with an expression that conveyed we would never speak again if I had anything to do with it.

A cold sweat broke out on my entire body as the presentations started. Natalie's proposal was short. And slightly misinformed.

She claimed that everything the rebels were doing was hateful and wrong, and their presence should be outlawed to keep Illéa's provinces safer. We all stared at her quietly once she was done. How did she not know that everything they did was already considered illegal?

The queen's face in particular seemed incredibly sad as Natalie sat back down.

Elise proposed a program that would involve members of the upper castes getting involved in a pen pal–type of relationship with people in New Asia. She suggested that it would help strengthen the bonds between our countries and aid in ending the war. I wasn't sure that it would do any good, but it was a fresh reminder to Maxon and the public of the reason she was still here. The queen asked if she happened to know anyone in New Asia who would be open to being in the program, and Elise assured her that she did.

Kriss's presentation was spectacular. She wanted to revamp the public school systems, which I already knew was an idea near and dear to both the queen's and Maxon's hearts. As the daughter of a professor, I was sure she'd been thinking about this her whole life. She used the screen to show pictures from her home province's school that her parents had sent to her. It was plain to see the exhaustion on the teachers' faces, and in one picture it showed a room where four children were sitting on the floor since there weren't enough chairs. The queen piped up with dozens of questions, and Kriss was quick to answer. Using copies of old reports about financial issues we'd read, she'd even found a place where we could borrow the money to start the work and had ideas on how to continue the funding.

As she sat down, I saw Maxon give her a smile and a nod. She responded by blushing and studying the lace on her dress. It was really cruel of him to play with her like that, considering how intimate he was with Celeste. But I was done interfering. Let him do what he wanted.

Celeste's presentation was interesting, if slightly manipulative. She suggested that there be a minimum-payment wage for some of the lower castes. It would be a sliding scale, based on certifications. However, to get these certifications, the Fives, Sixes, and Sevens would have to go to school . . . which they would have to pay for . . . which would mostly benefit the Threes, as they were the authorized teachers. Since Celeste was a Two, she had no idea how we had to work around the clock to make ends meets. No one would have the time to get these certifications, meaning their pay would never change. On the surface it sounded nice, but there was no way it would work.

Celeste returned to her seat, and I trembled when I stood. For a brief second I considered pretending to pass out. But I wanted this to happen. I just didn't want to face what would come after.

I placed my poster—a diagram of the castes—on the easel, and set my books in order on the desk. I took a deep breath and gripped my cards, surprised to find that when I started, I didn't even need them.

"Good evening, Illéa. Tonight I come to you not as one of the Elite, not as a Three or a Five, but as a citizen, an equal. Based on your caste, your experience of our country is shaded a very specific way. I can say that for certain myself. But it wasn't until recently that I understood how deep my love for Illéa went.

"Despite growing up sometimes without food or electricity, despite watching people I love forced into the stations we are assigned at birth with little hope for change, despite seeing the gaps between myself and others because of this number even though we aren't very different"—I looked over to the girls—"I find myself in love with our country."

I switched the card automatically, knowing the break. "What I propose wouldn't be simple. It might even be painful, but I genuinely believe it would benefit our entire kingdom." I inhaled. "I think we should eliminate the castes."

I heard more than one gasp. I chose to ignore them.

"I know there was a time, when our country was new, when the assignment of these numbers helped organize something that was on the brink of not existing. But we are no longer that country. We are so much more now. To allow the talentless to have exalted privileges and suppress what could be the greatest minds in the world for the sake of an archaic organization system is cruel, and it only stops us from becoming the best we can be."

I noted a poll from one of Celeste's discarded magazines after we talked about having a volunteer army, and sixty-five percent of the people thought it was a good idea. Why eliminate that career path completely for people? I also cited an old report we had studied about the standardized testing in the public schools. The article was slanted, stating that only three percent of Sixes and Sevens tested to elevated levels of intelligence; and since it was so low, it was clear they were intended to stay where they were. My argument was that we ought to be ashamed that those people are stuck digging ditches when they could be performing heart surgeries.

Finally the daunting task was nearly over. "Perhaps our country is flawed, but we cannot deny its strength. My fear is that, without change, that strength will become stagnate. And I love our country too much to let that happen. I *hope* too much to let that happen."

I swallowed, grateful that at least it was over now. "Thank you for your time," I said, and turned slightly toward the royal family.

It was bad. Maxon's face was stony again, like the way he'd looked when Marlee was caned. The queen averted her eyes, looking disappointed. The king, however, stared me down.

Without so much as a blink, he focused in on me. "And how do you suggest we eliminate the castes?" he challenged. "Just suddenly take them all away?"

"Oh . . . I don't know."

"And you don't think that would cause riots? Complete mayhem? Allow for rebels to take advantage of public confusion?"

I hadn't thought this part through. All I could process was how unfair it all was.

"I think the creation caused a decent amount of confusion, and we managed that. In fact"—I reached to my pile of books—"I have a description here."

I started looking for the right page in Gregory's diary.

"Are we off?" he bellowed.

"Yes, Majesty," someone called.

I looked up and saw that all the lights that usually indicated that the cameras were on had gone dim. In some gesture I'd missed, the king had shut down the *Report*.

The king stood. "Point them to the ground." Each camera was aimed to the floor.

He stormed over to me and ripped the diary from my hands.

"Where did you get this?" he yelled.

"Father, stop!" Maxon jogged up nervously.

"Where did she get this? Answer me!"

Maxon confessed. "From me. We were looking up what Halloween was. He wrote about it in the diaries, and I thought she'd like to read more."

"You idiot," the king spat. "I knew I should have made you read these sooner. You're completely lost. You have no clue of the duty you have!"

Oh, no. Oh, no, no, no.

"She leaves tonight," King Clarkson ordered. "I've had enough of her."

I tried to shrink down, distance myself from the king as much as I could without being obvious. I tried not to even breathe too loudly. I turned my head toward the girls, for some reason focusing on Celeste. I'd expected her to be smiling, but she was nervous. The king had never been like this.

"You can't send her home. That's my choice, and I say she stays," Maxon responded calmly.

"Maxon Calix Schreave, I am the king of Illéa, and I say—"

"Could you stop being the king for five minutes and just be my father?" Maxon yelled. "This is my choice. You got to make yours, and I want to make mine. No one else is leaving without my say so!"

I saw Natalie lean in to Elise. They both looked like they were shaking.

"Amberly, take this back to where it belongs," he said, shoving the book in her hand. She stood there, nodding her head but not moving. "Maxon, I need to see you in my office."

I watched Maxon; and maybe I only imagined it, but it looked like panic flickered briefly behind his eyes.

"Or," the king offered, "I could simply talk to her." He gestured over to me.

"No," Maxon said quickly, holding up a hand in protest.

"That won't be necessary. Ladies," he added, turning to us, "why don't you all head upstairs? We'll have dinner sent to you tonight." He paused. "America, maybe you should go ahead and collect your things. Just in case."

The king smiled, an eerie action after his recent explosion. "Excellent idea. After you, *son*."

I looked at Maxon, who seemed defeated. I felt ashamed. Maxon opened his mouth to say something, but in the end he shook his head and walked away.

Kriss was wringing her hands, looking after Maxon. I couldn't blame her. Something about all of this seemed menacing.

"Clarkson?" Queen Amberly said quietly. "What about the other matter?"

"What?" he asked in irritation.

"The news?" she reminded him.

"Oh, yes." He walked back toward us. I was close enough that I decided to retreat into my chair, afraid of being out there alone again. King Clarkson's voice was steady and calm. "Natalie, we didn't want to tell you before the *Report*, but we've received some bad news."

"Bad news?" she asked, fiddling with her necklace, already too anxious.

The king came closer. "Yes. I'm very sorry for your loss, but it appears the rebels took your sister this morning."

"What?" she whispered.

"Her remains were found this afternoon. We're sorry." To his credit, there was something close to sympathy in his voice, though it sounded more like training than genuine emotion.

He quickly returned to Maxon, escorting him forcefully out the door as Natalie broke into an ear-shattering scream. The queen rushed over to her, smoothing her hair and trying to calm her down. Celeste, never too sisterly, quietly left the room, with an overwhelmed Elise close behind. Kriss stayed and tried to comfort Natalie, but once it was clear that she couldn't do much, she left as well. The queen told Natalie there would be guards with her parents for good measure and that she would be able to leave for the funeral if she wanted to, holding on to her the whole time.

Everything had gotten so dark so quickly, I found myself frozen in my seat.

When the hand appeared in front of my face, I was so startled, I shied away.

"I won't hurt you," Gavril said. "Just want to help you up." His lapel pin shimmered, reflecting the light.

I gave him my hand, surprised by how shaky my legs were.

"He must love you very much," Gavril said once I had my footing.

I couldn't look at him. "What makes you say that?"

Gavril sighed. "I've known Maxon since he was a child. He's never stood up to his father like that."

Gavril walked away then, talking to the crew about keeping all that they had heard tonight quiet.

I went to Natalie. It wasn't like I knew everything about her, but I was sure she loved her sister the way I loved May;

and I couldn't imagine the ache she must be feeling.

"Natalie, I'm so sorry," I whispered. She nodded. That was the most she could manage.

The queen looked up at me sympathetically, not sure how to convey all her sadness. "And . . . I'm sorry to you, too. I wasn't trying to . . . I just . . ."

"I know, dear."

With how Natalie was doing, asking for more of a goodbye was too selfish, so I gave the queen a final, deep curtsy and slowly left the room, wallowing in the disaster I'd created.

CHAPTER 28

THE LAST THING I WAS expecting when I walked in my door-way was the smattering of applause from my maids.

I stood there for a moment, genuinely moved by their support and comforted by the shining pride in their faces. Once they were done making me blush, Anne took me by the hands.

"Well said, miss." She gave a gentle squeeze, and I saw in her eyes so much joy over my words, for a second I didn't feel so awful.

"I can't believe you did that! No one ever stands up for us!" Mary added.

"Maxon has to pick you," Lucy cried. "You're the only one who gives me hope."

Hope.

I needed to think, and the one place I could really do

that was the gardens. Though my maids were insistent that I stay, I left, taking the long way, down a back stairwell on the other end of the hall. Besides the occasional guard, the first floor was empty and quiet. It felt like the palace should be bustling with activity, given how much had happened in the last half hour or so.

As I passed the hospital wing, the door flew open and I ran right into Maxon, who dropped a sealed metal box. He groaned after we collided, even though it really wasn't that hard.

"What are you doing out of your room?" he asked, slowly bending to pick up the box. I noticed it had his name on the side. I wondered what he was storing in the hospital wing.

"I was going to the gardens. I'm trying to figure out if I did something stupid or not."

Maxon appeared to be having a difficult time standing. "Oh, I can assure you it was stupid."

"Do you need help?"

"No," he answered quickly, avoiding my eyes. "Just heading to my room. And I suggest you do the same."

"Maxon." The quiet plea in my voice made him look at me. "I'm so sorry. I was mad, and I wanted to . . . I don't even know anymore. And you were the one who said there were perks to being a One, that you could change things."

He rolled his eyes. "You're not a One." There was a silence between us. "Even if you were, did you not pay attention at all to the way I'm doing things? It's quiet and small. That's how it has to be for now. You can't go on television complaining about the way things are run and expect to have my father's, or anyone's, support."

"I'm sorry!" I cried. "I'm so, so sorry."

He paused for a moment. "I'm not sure that—"

We heard the shouting at the same time. Maxon turned and started walking, and I followed, trying to make sense of the sound. Was someone fighting? As we got closer to the intersection of the main hallway and the doors to the gardens, we saw guards come flooding toward the area.

"Sound the alarm!" someone called. "They're through the gates!"

"Guns at the ready!" another guard yelled over the shouts.

"Alert the king!"

And then, like bees intent on landing, small, quick things buzzed into the hall. A guard was struck and fell back, his head hitting the marble with a disturbing crack. The blood pouring from his chest made me scream.

Maxon instinctively pulled me away, but not very quickly. Perhaps he was in shock as well.

"Your Majesty!" a guard called, racing over to us. "You have to get downstairs now!"

He gruffly turned Maxon around and shoved him away. Maxon cried out and dropped the metal box again. I looked over at the guard's hand on Maxon, expecting to see that he'd driven a knife into his back based on the sound Maxon had made. All I saw was a thick, pewter ring around his thumb. I picked up the box by the handle on the side, hoping that didn't mess up anything inside, and ran in the direction the guard was trying to move us.

"I won't make it," Maxon said.

I turned back to him and saw that he was sweating. Something was really wrong with him.

"Yes, sir," the guard said grimly. "This way."

He pulled Maxon around a corner to what appeared to be a dead end. I wondered if he was going to leave us there when he hit some invisible trigger on the wall and another one of the palace's mysterious doors opened. It was so dark inside, I couldn't see where it went; but Maxon walked in, hunched over, without a second thought.

"Tell my mother that America and I are safe. Do that before anything else," he said.

"Absolutely, sir. I'll come back for you myself when this is over."

The siren sounded. I hoped that was fast enough to save everyone.

Maxon nodded and the door closed, leaving us in complete darkness. The seal was so secure, I couldn't even make out the sound of the alarm. I heard Maxon's hand rubbing against the wall, and he eventually came upon a switch that dimly lit the room. I looked around and surveyed the space.

There were some shelves that held a bunch of dark, plastic packages and a different shelf that held a few thin blankets. In the middle of the tiny space was one wooden bench big enough to seat maybe four people, and in the opposite corner was a small sink and what looked like a very crude toilet. Hooks lined one wall, but there was nothing on them; and the whole room smelled like the metal that appeared to make up the walls.

"At least this is one of the good ones," Maxon said, and hobbled over to the bench to sit.

"What's wrong?"

"Nothing," he said quietly, and propped up his head on his arms.

I sat beside him, placing the metal box on the bench and looking around the room again.

"I'm guessing those were Southern rebels?"

Maxon nodded. I tried to slow my breathing and erase what I'd just seen from my mind. Would that guard survive? Could anyone survive something like that?

I wondered how far the rebels had gotten in the time it took us to hide. Was the alarm fast enough?

"Are we safe here?"

"Yes. This is one of the places for servants. If they happen to be down in the kitchen and storage area, they're pretty safe as it is. But the ones running about doing chores might not be able to get there quickly enough. It's not quite as safe as the big room for the royal family, and we have supplies to survive down there for quite some time; but these work in a pinch."

"Do the rebels know?"

"They might," he said, wincing as he sat up a bit straighter. "But they can't get in once the rooms are in use. There are only three ways out. Someone with a key has to activate it from the outside, someone with a key can activate it from the inside"—Maxon patted his pocket, implying that he could get us out if he had to—"or you have to wait for two days. After forty-eight hours, the doors automatically open. The guards check every safe room once the danger has passed, but there's always a chance they could miss one; and without the delayed-unlocking mechanism, someone could be stuck in here forever."

It took him awhile to get all this out. He was clearly in pain, but it seemed that he was trying to distract himself with the words. He leaned forward and then hissed when the action added to whatever was hurting him.

"Maxon?"

"I can't . . . I can't take it anymore. America, help with my coat?"

He held out his arm, and I jumped up to help him slide his coat down his back. He let it drop behind him and moved to his buttons. I started helping him, but he stopped me, holding my hands in his.

"Your record for keeping secrets isn't that impressive right now. But this is one that goes to your grave. And mine. Do you understand?"

I nodded, though I wasn't sure what he meant. Maxon released my hands, and I slowly unbuttoned his shirt. I wondered if he'd ever imagined me doing this. I could admit that I had. Halloween night, I had lain in bed and dreamed of this very second in our future. I thought it would be much different. Still, a thrill went through me.

I had been raised a musician, but I was surrounded by

artists. I'd once seen a sculpture that was hundreds of years old of an athlete throwing a disk. I'd thought to myself at the time that only an artist could do that, make someone's body look so beautiful. Maxon's chest was as sculpted as any piece of art I'd ever seen.

But everything changed as I went to slide the shirt down his back. It stuck to him, making a slippery, sticky sound as I tried to get it to move.

"Slowly," he said. I nodded and went behind him to try from there.

The back of Maxon's shirt was soaked with blood.

I gasped, immobile for a moment. But then, sensing that my staring made things worse, I kept working. Once I got the shirt off, I threw it on one of the hooks, giving myself a moment to gain my composure.

I turned around and got a good look at Maxon's back. A bleeding gash on his shoulder tore down to his waist and crossed over another one that was also dripping blood, which crossed over another one that had been healed for a while, which crossed over yet another one that was puckered from age. It looked like there were maybe six fresh slashes across Maxon's back piled on top of too many more to count.

How could this have happened? Maxon was the prince. He was royal, sovereign, set apart from everyone. He was above everything, sometimes including the law, so how had he come to be covered with scars?

Then I remembered the look in the king's eyes tonight.

And Maxon's effort to hide his fear. How could any man do this to his son?

I turned away again, hunting until I found a small washcloth. I went to the sink, glad to find that it worked even though the water was ice-cold.

I steadied myself and walked over, trying to be calm for his sake. "This might sting a little," I warned.

"It's okay," he whispered. "I'm used to it."

I took the wet washcloth and dabbed at the long gouge in his shoulder, deciding that I'd work from the top down. He pulled away a bit but took it all silently. When I moved on to the second gash, Maxon started talking.

"I've been preparing for tonight for years, you know? I've been waiting for the day when I was strong enough to take him on."

Maxon was silent for a moment, and some things made sense: why a person who sat at a desk had such serious muscles, why he always seemed half dressed and ready to go, why a girl calling him a child and pushing him would make him angry.

I cleared my throat. "Why didn't you?"

He paused. "I was afraid that if he didn't have me, he'd want you."

I had to stop for a moment, too overcome even to speak. Tears threatened to spill over, but I tried to hold it together. I was sure it would only make things worse.

"Does anyone know?" I asked.

"No."

"Not the doctor? Or your mother?"

"The doctor must, but he's quiet. And I would never tell my mother or even give her a reason to suspect. She knows Father is stern with me, but I don't want her to worry. And I can take it."

I kept dabbing.

"He's not like this with her," he promised quickly. "She gets mistreated in her own ways, I suppose, but not like this."

"Hmm," I said, not sure of what else to say.

I wiped again, and Maxon hissed. "Damn, that stings."

I pulled away for a minute while he slowed down his breathing. After a moment, he made a small nod, so I started again.

"I have more sympathy for Carter and Marlee than you know," he said, trying to sound light. "These things take awhile to stop hurting, especially if you're determined to take care of them on your own."

I paused for a moment, shocked. Marlee got caned fifteen times at once. I think if I had to, I'd pick that over them coming at times you weren't prepared.

"What are the others for?" I asked, then shook my head. "Never mind. That's rude."

He shrugged his uninjured shoulder. "Things I said or did. Things I know."

"Things *I* know," I added. "Maxon, I'm so . . ." My breathing hitched, threatening to send me over the edge. I might as well have caned him myself.

He didn't turn around, but his hand searched and found my knee. "How are you going to finish fixing me up if you're crying?"

I laughed weakly through the tears and wiped my face. I got everything cleaned, trying to stay gentle.

"Do you think there are any bandages in here?" I asked, looking around the room.

"The box," he said.

As he sat there, steadying his breathing, I opened the clasps on the box, looking at the abundance of supplies.

"Why don't you have bandages in your room?"

"Sheer pride. I was determined never to need them again."

I sighed quietly. I read the labels, finding a disinfectant solution, something that looked like it would help soothe the pain, and bandages.

I moved behind him, preparing to apply the medication. "This might hurt."

He nodded. When it made contact with his skin, he grunted once and then reverted to silence. I tried to be quick and thorough, ready to make him as comfortable as possible.

I started putting ointment on his wounds, and it was clear that whatever I was using helped. The tension in his shoulders eased as I worked, and I was glad; it felt in a way like I was making up for some of the trouble I'd caused.

He snorted out a light laugh. "I knew my secret would come out eventually. I've been trying to come up with a good story for years. I was hoping to find something believable before the wedding since I knew my wife would see them, but I'm still stumped. Any ideas?"

I thought a moment. "The truth works."

He nodded. "Not my favorite option. Not for this anyway."

"I think I'm done."

Maxon twisted and bent a little bit, moving gingerly. He turned to look at me, his expression thankful. "That's great, America. Better than any job I ever did."

"Anytime."

He looked at me a moment, and the silence grew. What was there to say now?

My eyes kept darting to his chest, and I needed to stop that.

"I'm going to wash your shirt." I buried myself in the corner, rubbing his shirt against itself, watching the water turn rust colored before it escaped down the drain. I knew all the blood wouldn't come out, but at least it gave me something to do.

When I finished, I wrung it out and placed it back on a hook. I turned around, and Maxon was staring at me.

"Why don't you ever ask questions I actually want to answer?"

I didn't think I could sit next to him on the bench without being tempted to touch him. Instead I settled on the floor across from him.

"I didn't know I did that."

"You do."

"Well, what am I not asking that you want me to?"

He let out a long breath and gently leaned forward, resting his elbows on his knees.

"Don't you want me to explain Kriss and Celeste? Don't you think you deserve that?"

CHAPTER 29

I CROSSED MY ARMS. "I'VE heard Kriss's version of what happened, and I don't think she's exaggerating anything. As for Celeste, I'd rather never talk about her ever again."

He laughed. "So stubborn. I'll miss that."

I was quiet for a minute. "So it's done then? I'm out?"

Maxon thought it over. "I'm not sure I could stop it now. Isn't that what you wanted?"

I shook my head. "I was mad," I whispered. "I was so mad."

I looked away, not wanting to cry. Apparently Maxon decided that I needed to listen to what he had to say, whether I wanted to or not. Finally he had me trapped, and I would hear everything he'd been waiting to tell me.

"I thought you were mine," he said. I peeked over and found him staring at the ceiling. "If I could have proposed to you at the Halloween party, I would have. I'm supposed to do something official with my parents and guests and cameras, but I got special permission to ask you privately when we were ready and have a reception afterward. I never told you about that, did I?"

Maxon looked over to me, and I gave a small shake of my head. He smiled bitterly, remembering.

"I had this speech prepared, all these promises I wanted to make. I probably would have forgotten it and made an idiot of myself. Though . . . I can remember it now." He sighed. "I'll spare you."

He paused briefly. "When you pushed me away, I panicked. I had thought that I was done with this insane contest, and I found myself feeling like it was the very first day of the Selection all over again, only this time my options were far more limited. And just the week before, I'd spent time with all those girls trying to find someone who outshone you, who I thought I could want more, and failed. I felt hopeless.

"And then Kriss came to me, so very humble, only wanting to see me happy, and I wondered how I'd missed that in her. I knew she was nice, and she's very attractive; but there was something more to her this whole time.

"I think I simply wasn't really looking. What reason did I have when there was you?"

I wrapped my arms around myself, trying to hide from the ache. There was no me anymore. I'd ruined all that.

"Do you love her?" I asked meekly. I didn't want to see his face, but the long pause let me know that there was something deep between the two of them.

"It's different than what you and I had. It's quieter, maybe friendlier. But it's steady. I can depend on Kriss, and I know without question that she is devoted to me. As you can see, there is very little certainty in my world. She's refreshing in that way."

I nodded, still avoiding eye contact. All I could think about was how he spoke of him and me in the past tense and had nothing but praise for Kriss. I wished I had something bad to say about her, something that would bring her down a notch; but I didn't. Kriss was a lady. From the beginning she'd done everything well, and I was surprised that he had ever favored me over her anyway. She was perfect for him.

"Then why Celeste?" I asked, finally facing him. "If Kriss is so wonderful . . ."

Maxon nodded his head, seeming embarrassed about this subject. It was his idea to talk about this in the first place, though, so he must already have had something in mind to say. He stood, giving his back another tentative stretch, and started pacing the small space.

"As you now know, my life is full of stresses that I prefer not to share. I live in a constant state of tension. I'm always being watched, judged. My parents, our advisers . . . there are always cameras in my life, and now you're all here," he said, motioning to me. "I'm sure you've felt trapped at least once because of your caste, but imagine how I feel. There are things I've seen, America, and things I know; and I don't think I'll ever be able to change them.

"You're aware, I'm sure, that technically my father is supposed to retire in my twenties, when he feels I'm ready to lead; but do you think he'll ever stop pulling the strings? That's not going to happen so long as he lives; and I know he's terrible, but I don't want him to die. . . . He *is* my father."

I nodded.

"Speaking of which, he's had his hand in the Selection from very early on. If you look at who's left, it's pretty clear." He started ticking off the girls on his fingers. "Natalie is extremely pliable, and that makes her my father's favorite, as I am too willful in his opinion. The fact that he's so fond of her makes me have to fight the urge to hate her.

"Elise has allies in New Asia, but I'm not sure if that's of any use at all. That war . . ." Maxon debated something and shook his head. There was some detail about this war that he didn't want to share with me. "And she's so . . . I don't even know the word for it. I knew from the beginning that I didn't want some girl who would agree with everything I said or just roll over and adore me. I try to contradict her, and she concedes the point. Every time! It's infuriating. It's like she doesn't have a spine."

He took a steadying breath. I didn't realize how much she got under his skin. He was always so patient with us. Finally he looked at me.

"You were my pick. My only pick. My father wasn't enthusiastic; but at that point you hadn't done anything to upset him. So long as you were quiet, he didn't mind me keeping you. In fact, he was fine with me choosing you, if you were well behaved. He's used your recent actions to point out the flaws in my judgment and is insisting that he have the final say now."

He shook his head. "That's beside the point. The others—Marlee, Kriss, and Celeste—were chosen by advisers. Marlee was a favorite, as is Kriss." He sighed. "Kriss would be a fine choice. I wish she would let me closer, if only for the fact that I don't know if we have . . . chemistry. I'd like to at least have an idea.

"And Celeste. She is very influential, a celebrity in her own right. It looks good on TV. It sounds right for someone who is close to being on the same level as me to be the final choice. I like her if only for her tenacity. She at least has a backbone. But I can tell that she's got a manipulative streak and that she's working this whole situation for everything she can get out of it. I know when she holds me, it's the crown she pulls close to her heart."

He closed his eyes, as if what he was about to say was the worst of all. "She's using me, so I don't feel guilty using her. I wouldn't be surprised if she'd been encouraged to throw herself at me. I can respect Kriss's boundaries. And I'd much prefer to be in your arms, but you've barely spoken to me. . . .

"Is it so awful of me to want fifteen minutes of my life not to matter? To feel good? To pretend for a little while that someone loves me? You can judge me if you want, but I can't apologize for needing something normal in my life."

He stared deep into my eyes, waiting for me to reproach

him and hoping I wouldn't at the same time.

"I get that."

I thought of Aspen, holding me tight and making his promises. Hadn't I done the very same thing? I could see the wheels turning in Maxon's head, wondering how literally I meant that. This was one secret I couldn't share. Even if it was all over for me, I couldn't let Maxon think of me that way.

"Would you ever pick her? Celeste, I mean?"

He came to sit beside me, making his moves carefully. I couldn't imagine how much his back was hurting him.

"If I had to, I'd take her over Elise or Natalie. But that won't happen unless Kriss decides she wants to go."

I nodded. "Kriss is a good choice. She'd make a much better princess than I ever would have."

He chuckled. "She is less of an instigator. Lord knows what would happen to the country with you at the helm."

I laughed along because he was right. "I'd probably ruin it."

Maxon continued to smile when he spoke. "But maybe it needs ruining."

We sat there in silence for a little while. I wondered what our world would look like ruined. We couldn't get rid of the royal family—how could we possibly transition it out?—but maybe we could change the way some things were run. Offices could be elected instead of inherited. And the castes . . . I really would love to see those dead and gone.

"Would you indulge me?" Maxon asked.

"What do you mean?"

"Well, I've shared a lot of things with you tonight that are very difficult for me to admit. I was wondering if you could answer one question for me."

His face was so sincere, I didn't want to deny him. I hoped I wouldn't regret whatever this was about, but he had been more honest than I deserved at this point.

"Yes. Anything."

He swallowed. "Did you ever love me?"

Maxon looked into my eyes, and I wondered if he could see it there. All the emotions I'd fought because I thought he was something he wasn't, all the feelings I never wanted to put a name on. I ducked my head.

"I know that when I thought you were responsible for hurting Marlee, it crushed me. Not just because it happened, but because I didn't want to think of you as that kind of person. I know that when you talk about Kriss or when I think about you kissing Celeste . . . I'm so jealous I can hardly breathe. And I know that when we talked on Halloween, I was thinking about our future. And I was happy. I know if you had asked, I would have said yes." Those last words were a whisper, almost too difficult to think about.

"I also know that I never knew how to feel about you dating other people or being a prince. Even with everything you told me tonight, I think there are pieces of yourself that you will always guard. . . .

"But, with all that . . ." I nodded. I couldn't say the words aloud. If I did, how would I be able to leave?

"Thank you," he whispered. "At least I can know for certain that, for one brief moment of our time together, you and I felt the same thing."

My eyes stung, threatening to spill over with more tears. He'd never actually told me he loved me, and he wasn't exactly saying it now. But the words were so, so very close.

"I've been so foolish," I said, my breath catching. I'd fought hard against the tears, but I couldn't anymore. "I kept letting the crown scare me out of wanting you. I told myself that you didn't really matter to me. I kept thinking that you had lied to me or tricked me, that you didn't trust me or care about me enough. I let myself believe that I wasn't important to you."

I stared at his handsome face. "One look at your back says you'd do damn near anything for me. And I threw it away. I just threw it away. . . ."

He opened his arms, and I fell into them. Maxon held me silently, running his hands through my hair. I wished I could erase everything else and hold on to this moment, this brief second when he and I knew how much we meant to each other.

"Please don't cry, darling. I'd spare you tears for the rest of your life if I could."

My breathing was uneven as I spoke. "I'll never see you again. It's all my fault."

He held me closer. "No, I should have been more open."

"I should have been more patient."

"I should have proposed that night in your room."

"I should have let you."

He chuckled. I looked up at his face, unsure of how many more of his smiles I'd have. Maxon's fingers swept away the tears from my cheeks, and he sat there gazing into my eyes. I did the same to him, wanting to remember this so badly.

"America . . . I don't know how much time we have left together, but I don't want to spend it regretting things we didn't do."

"Me either." I turned my face into his palm, kissing it. Then I kissed the tips of each of his fingers. He slid that hand deep into my hair and pulled my lips to his.

I had missed these kisses, so quiet, so sure. I knew that, in my whole life, if I married Aspen or someone else, no one would ever make me feel this way. It wasn't like I made his world better. It was like I *was* his world. It wasn't some explosion; it wasn't fireworks. It was a fire, burning slowly from the inside out.

We shifted, sliding so I was on the floor and Maxon was above me. He ran his nose along my jawline, down my neck, across my shoulder, and kissed the same path back to my lips. I kept running my fingers through his hair. It was so soft, it almost tickled my palms.

After a while we pulled out the blankets and built a makeshift bed. He held me for the longest time, looking into my eyes. We could have spent years doing this if not for me.

Once Maxon's shirt was dry, he put it on, covering the dried stains with his coat, and curled up next to me again. When we both got tired, we started talking. I didn't want to sleep through a second of this, and I sensed he didn't either.

"Do you think you'll go back to him? Your ex?"

I didn't want to talk about Aspen right now, but I considered this. "He's a good choice. Smart, brave, maybe the only person on the planet more stubborn than me."

Maxon laughed lightly. My eyes were closed, but I kept talking. "It would be awhile before I could think about that though."

"Mmm."

The silence stretched. Maxon rubbed his thumb along the hand he was holding.

"Could I write you?" he asked.

I thought about that. "Maybe you should wait a few months. You might not even miss me."

He gave an almost-laugh.

"If you do write . . . you have to tell Kriss."

"You're right."

He didn't clarify whether that meant he would tell her or simply not write me, but I didn't really want to know at the moment.

I couldn't believe that all this was happening because of a stupid book.

I gasped, and my eyes shot open. A book!

"Maxon, what if the Northern rebels are looking for the diaries?"

He shifted, still not quite alert. "What do you mean?"

"When I was chased that day in the gardens, I saw them as they passed me. A girl dropped a bag full of books. The guy

299

with her had bunches, too. They're stealing books. What if they're looking for a specific one?"

Maxon opened his eyes, squinting in thought. "America . . . what exactly was in that diary?"

"A lot. About how Gregory basically stole the country, how he forced the castes on people. It was awful, Maxon."

"But the *Report* was cut off," he insisted. "Even if that is what they're looking for, there's no way they could know that was it or what's inside it. Trust me, after that little display, my father is making sure those things are even more protected than usual."

"That's it." I covered my face, stifling a yawn. "I know it."

"Don't," he said. "Don't get worked up. For all we know, they just really, really like to read."

I moaned at his attempt at humor.

"I seriously thought I couldn't make this any worse."

"Shh," he said, coming closer. His strong arms grounded me to the earth. "Don't worry now. You should probably sleep."

"But I don't want to," I whispered, though I curled closer into him.

Maxon closed his eyes again, still holding on to me. "Me either. Even on a good day, sleeping makes me nervous."

It made my heart ache. I couldn't imagine his constant state of worry, especially considering that the person keeping him on edge was his own father.

He let go of my hand and reached into his pocket. My eyelids parted a bit, but he was doing all this with his eyes closed. We were both so close to sleep. He found my hand again and started tying something on my wrist. I recognized the feeling of the bracelet he got me in New Asia as it slid into place.

"I've been carrying it in my pocket. I'm a pitiful romantic, right? I was going to keep it, but I want you to have something from me."

He'd put the bracelet on over Aspen's, and I felt the button pressing into my skin underneath it.

"Thank you. It makes me happy."

"Then I'm happy, too."

We didn't say anything else.

CHAPTER 30

THE SOUND OF THE CREAKING door woke me, and the light streaming in was so bright, I had to block my eyes.

"Your Majesty?" someone asked. "Oh, God! I've found him," he screamed. "He's alive!"

There was a sudden flurry around us as guards and butlers stormed to our location.

"Were you not able to get downstairs, Your Majesty?" one of the guards asked. I looked at his name. Markson. I wasn't sure, but he seemed to be one of the higher-ups in the guard.

"No. An officer was supposed to tell my parents. I told him to go there first," Maxon explained, trying to straighten his hair. Only once did his face give away that the movement pained him.

"Which officer?"

Maxon sighed. "I didn't get his name." He looked to me for confirmation.

"Me either. But he was wearing a ring on his thumb. It was gray, like pewter or something."

Officer Markson nodded. "That was Tanner. He didn't make it. We lost about twenty-five of the guards and a dozen staff."

"What?" I covered my mouth.

Aspen.

I prayed that he was safe. I'd been so consumed last night, it hadn't occurred to me to worry.

"What about my parents? The other Elite?"

"All fine, sir. Your mother has been hysterical though."

"Is she out yet?" We started moving, Maxon leading the way.

"Everyone is. We missed a few of the small safe rooms and were doing a second sweep, hoping to find you and Lady America."

"Oh, God," Maxon said. "I'll go to her first." But then he stopped dead in his tracks.

I followed his eyes and saw the destruction. That same line, the one from last time, was scrawled across the wall.

WE'RE COMING

Over and over, by any means they could find, the warning covered the halls. Beyond that, the level of destruction was elevated yet again. I'd never seen what the rebels managed to do to the first floor, only to the hallways near my room. Huge stains in the carpet announced where someone, perhaps a helpless maid or fearless guard, had died. Windows were shattered, leaving jagged teeth of glass in their place.

Lights were broken, some flickering as they refused to give up. Terrifyingly, there were massive gouges in the walls; and it made me wonder if they had seen people going into the safe rooms, if they had been hunting. How close were Maxon and I to death last night?

"Miss?" a guard said, bringing me back to the moment. "We've taken the liberty of contacting all the families. It appears the attack on Lady Natalie's family was a direct attempt to end the Selection. They're targeting your relatives to get you to leave."

I covered my mouth. "No."

"We're already sending palace guards out to protect them. The king was adamant that none of the girls should go."

"What if they want to?" Maxon challenged. "We can't hold them here against their will."

"Of course, sir. You'll need to speak with the king." The guard seemed embarrassed, not quite sure how to handle the difference of opinions.

"You won't have to guard my family long," I said, hoping to break some tension. "Let them know I'll be home soon."

The guard's eyes flickered between Maxon and me, looking to confirm that I'd been eliminated. Maxon simply nodded once.

"Yes, miss," the guard said with a bow.

Maxon interjected. "Is my mother in her room?"

"Yes, sir."

"Tell her I'm coming. You're dismissed."

We were alone again.

Maxon took my hand in his. "Don't rush away. Say good-bye to your maids and any of the girls if you want. And eat something. I know how you love the food."

I smiled. "I will."

Maxon wet his lips, almost fidgeting. This was it. This was good-bye.

"You've changed me forever. And I'll never forget you."

I ran my free hand down his chest, straightening his coat. "Don't tug your ear with anyone else. That's mine." I gave him a tight smile.

"A lot of things are yours, America."

I swallowed. "I need to go."

He nodded.

Maxon kissed me once, quickly, on the lips, and ran down the hall. I watched until he was out of sight and then made my way back to my room.

Each step up the main stairwell was torture, both because of what I had left and what I feared was coming. What if I rang the bell and Lucy didn't come? Or Mary? Or Anne? What if I looked at every face of every guard I passed and not a single one was Aspen's?

I made my way to the second floor, passing destruction at every turn. It was still recognizable, the most beautiful place I'd ever seen, even in ruins. But the time and money it would take to restore this was beyond my imagination. The rebels were very thorough. As I got closer to my room, I heard the distinct sound of crying. Lucy.

I let out a breath, happy she was alive but terrified of what was making her cry. I braced myself and turned the corner into my room.

Working with red faces and swollen eyes, Mary and Anne were collecting the shattered glass from the doors to my balcony. I watched as Mary had to stop midsweep to exhale and calm herself. In a corner, Lucy was weeping into Aspen's chest.

"Shh," he said, comforting her. "They'll find her, I know it."

I was so relieved, I burst into tears. "You're okay. You're all okay."

Aspen let out a huge sigh, his tight shoulders slumping as they relaxed.

"My lady?" Lucy said. A second later she was running for me. Not too far behind, Mary and Anne came, enveloping me in hugs.

"Oh, this isn't proper," Anne said as she held me.

"For goodness' sake, give it a rest," Mary retorted.

And we were so happy to be alive and safe that we laughed about it all.

Behind them, Aspen stood, watching with a quiet smile, so clearly grateful to see me there.

"Where were you? They looked everywhere." Mary pulled me over to the bed to sit, though it was a terrible mess, with the comforter shredded, the pillows stabbed and leaking feathers.

"In one of the safe rooms they missed. Maxon's okay, too," I said.

"Thank God," Anne said.

"He saved my life. I was on my way to the gardens when they came. If I'd been outside . . ."

"Oh, my lady," Mary cried.

"Don't you worry about a thing," Anne said. "We'll get this room fixed up in no time, and we have a fantastic new dress once you're ready. And we can—"

"That won't be necessary. I'm going home today. I'll put on something simple and leave in a few hours."

"What?" Mary gasped. "But why?"

I shrugged. "It didn't work out." I looked up at Aspen but was unable to read his face. All I could see was relief that I was alive.

"I really thought it would be you," Lucy said. "From the start. And after everything you said last night . . . I can't believe you're going home."

"That's very sweet, but it'll be all right. From here on out, anything you can do to help Kriss, please do that. For me."

"Of course," Anne said.

"Anything for you," Mary seconded.

Aspen cleared his throat. "Ladies, maybe you could give

me a moment. If Lady America is leaving today, I need to go over some security measures. We didn't get her this far only to let someone hurt her now.

"Anne, maybe you could go get some fresh towels and things. She should go home like a lady. Mary, some food?" They both nodded. "And Lucy, do you need to rest?"

"No!" she cried, standing tall. "I can work."

Aspen smiled. "Very well."

"Lucy, go to the workroom and finish that dress. We'll come help soon. I don't care what anyone says, Lady America. You're leaving in style," Anne said, addressing me at the end.

"Yes, ma'am," I answered. They left, closing the door behind them.

Aspen walked over, and I stood to face him.

"I thought you were dead. I thought I'd lost you."

"Not today," I said, smiling weakly. Now that I saw how bad it was, the only way to stay calm was to joke about it.

"I got your letter. I can't believe you didn't tell me about the diary."

"I couldn't."

He bridged the space between us and ran his hand down my hair. "Mer, if you couldn't show it to me, you really shouldn't have tried to show it to the country. And the caste thing . . . You're crazy, you know that?"

"Oh, I know." I looked at the ground, thinking over all the insanity of the last day.

"So Maxon kicked you out because of that?"

I sighed. "Not exactly. The king's the one sending me

home. If Maxon proposed to me this very second, it wouldn't matter. The king says no, so I'm going."

"Oh," he said simply. "It's going to be strange without you here."

"I know," I said with a sigh.

"I'll write," he promised quickly. "And I can send you money if you want. I've got plenty. We can get married right when I come home. I know it's going to be awhile—"

"Aspen," I said, cutting him off. I didn't know how to explain that my heart had just been crushed. "When I leave, I want some peace, okay? I need to recover from all this."

He stepped back, offended. "So, what, do you not want me to write or call?"

"Maybe not right away," I said, trying to make it sound like it wasn't a big deal. "I just want to spend some time with my family and get my bearings again. After everything I've felt here, I can't—"

"Wait," he said, holding up a hand. He was silent for a moment, reading my face. "You still want him," he accused. "After everything he's done—after Marlee—and even when there's absolutely no hope, you're still thinking about him."

"He never did anything, Aspen. I wish I could explain about Marlee to you, but I gave my word. I have no hard feelings toward Maxon. And I know it's over, but it's the same way I felt when you broke up with me."

He scoffed incredulously, rolling his head back like he couldn't believe what he was hearing.

"I'm serious. When you ended it, the Selection became

my lifeline because I knew I'd at least have some time to get past what I felt for you. And then you showed up here, and everything shifted. You were the one who changed us when you left me in the tree house; and you keep thinking that if you push hard enough, you can make everything go back to before that moment. It doesn't work that way. Give me a chance to *choose* you."

As the words came out of my mouth, I knew that this was so much of what was wrong. I'd loved Aspen for so long, we'd just assumed a lot of things. But everything was different now. It wasn't like we were still two nobodies from Carolina. We'd seen too much to pretend we would ever happily be those people again.

"Why wouldn't you choose me, Mer? Aren't I your only choice?" he asked, sadness dripping into his voice.

"Yes. Doesn't that bother you? I don't want to be the girl you end up with because my only other option isn't available and you never looked at anyone else. Do you really want to get me by default?"

He spoke intensely. "I don't care how I get you, Mer."

Suddenly he charged at me, taking my face in his hands. Aspen kissed me fiercely, willing me to remember what he was to me.

I couldn't kiss him back.

When he finally gave up, he pulled back my head, trying to read my face.

"What's happening here, America?"

"My heart is breaking! That's what's happening! How do

you think this feels? I'm so confused right now, and you're the only thing I have left, and you don't love me enough to let me breathe."

I started crying, and he finally calmed down.

"I'm sorry, Mer," he whispered. "It's just, I keep thinking I've lost you for some reason or another, and it's my instinct to fight for you. It's all I know to do."

I looked at the floor, trying to pull myself together.

"I can wait," he promised. "When you're ready, write me. I do love you enough to let you breathe. After last night, that's all I need you to do. Please breathe."

I walked into him, letting him hold me, but it felt different. I'd thought I would always have Aspen in my life, and for the first time I wondered if that was completely true.

"Thank you," I whispered. "Stay safe here. Don't be a hero, Aspen. Take care of yourself."

He stepped away, giving me a nod but no words. He kissed my forehead and made his way to the door.

I stood there for a long time, not sure what to do with myself, waiting for my maids to come and pull me together one last time.

CHAPTER 31

I TUGGED AT MY DRESS. "Isn't this a bit grand for the occasion?"

"Not at all!" Mary insisted.

It was late afternoon, but they'd put me in an evening gown. It was purple, and very regal. The sleeves went to my elbows, as it was colder back in Carolina; and a sweeping hooded cape was draped over my arm for when I landed. A high collar would protect my neck from any wind that might come, and they'd pulled up my hair so elegantly, I was positive this was the prettiest I'd ever looked at the palace. I wished that I could go see Queen Amberly, sure that even she would be impressed.

"I don't want to linger," I insisted. "It's hard enough to go as it is. I just want you all to know that I'm so grateful for everything you've done for me. Not only for keeping me clean and dressed, but for spending time with me and caring about me. I'll never forget you."

"And we'll always remember you, miss," Anne promised.

I nodded and started fanning my face. "Okay, okay, I've had enough tears for one day. If you could tell the driver I'll be right down, I'm going to take a moment."

"Of course, miss."

"Is it still improper for us to hug?" Mary asked, looking at me and then Anne.

"Who cares?" she said, and they crowded around me one last time.

"Take care of yourselves."

"You, too, miss," Mary said.

"You were always a lady," Anne added.

They stepped away, but Lucy held on. "Thank you," she breathed, and I could tell she was crying. "I'll miss you."

"Me, too."

She let me go, and they walked to the door, standing together in a group. They gave me one last curtsy, and I waved as they left me alone.

So many times in the last few weeks I had wished I could leave. Now that it was here, seconds away, I was dreading it. I walked onto the balcony. I looked down at the gardens, gazing at the bench, the spot where Maxon and I had met. I didn't know why, but I suspected he'd be there.

He wasn't though. He had more important things to do than to sit around thinking about me. I touched the bracelet on my wrist. He *would* think about me, though, from time to time, and that comforted me. No matter what, this was real.

I backed away, closing the door and heading to the hallway. I moved slowly, taking in the beauty of the palace one last time, even though it was slightly marred by broken mirrors and chipped frames.

I remembered walking down this grand stairwell the first day, feeling confused and grateful at the same time. There were so many girls then.

When I reached the front doors, I paused for a moment. I'd gotten so used to being behind those massive blocks of wood that it almost felt wrong to go through them.

I took a deep breath and reached for the handle.

"America?"

I turned. Maxon was standing at the other end of the corridor.

"Hey," I said lamely. I hadn't thought I'd get to see him again.

He walked over to me quickly. "You look absolutely breathtaking."

"Thank you." I touched the fabric of my last dress.

There was a breath of silence as we stood there, watching each other. Maybe that's all this was: a last chance to see.

Suddenly he cleared his throat, remembering his purpose. "I've spoken with my father."

"Oh?"

"Yes. He was quite happy that I wasn't killed last night. As you might have guessed, carrying on the royal line is very important to him. I explained to him that I nearly died because of his temper and attributed my finding a hiding place to you."

"But I didn't—"

"I know. But he needn't."

I smiled.

"I then told him that I set you straight on some behavioral things. Again, he needn't know that's untrue; but you could act like it happened, if you wanted."

I didn't know why I would need to act like anything happened when I would be on the other side of the country, but I nodded.

"Considering that I owe my life to you as far as he knows, he agreed that my desire to keep you here might be somewhat justified, so long as you were on your best behavior and could learn your place."

I stared at him, not completely sure I was hearing this right.

"Really, the fair thing to do is let Natalie go. She's not cut out for this; and with her family grieving right now, her home is the best place for her. We've already spoken."

I was still dumbstruck.

"Shall I explain?"

"Please."

Maxon reached for my hand. "You would stay here as a member of the Selection and still be a part of the competition, but things will be different. My father will probably be harsh toward you and do whatever he can to make you fail. I think there are some ways to fight that, but it will take time.

You know how ruthless he is. You have to prepare yourself."

I nodded. "I think I can do that."

"There's more." Maxon looked to the carpet, trying to align his thoughts. "America, there's no question that you've had my heart from the beginning. By now you have to know that."

When he brought his eyes up to mine, I could see it in every part of him and feel it in every piece of me. "I do."

"But what you do not have right now is my trust."

I was stricken. "What?"

"I've shown you so many of my secrets, defended you in every way I can. But when you aren't pleased with me, you act rashly. You shut me out, blame me, or, most impressively, try to change the entire country."

Ouch. That was pretty rough.

"I need to know that I can depend on you. I need to know that you can keep my secrets, trust my judgment, and not hold things back from me. I need you to be completely honest with me and to stop questioning every decision I make. I need you to have faith in me, America."

It hurt to hear all of that, but he was right. What had I done to prove to him that he could trust me? Everyone around him was pulling or pushing him into something. Could I just be there for him?

I fiddled with my hands. "I do have faith in you. And I hope you can see that I want to be with you. But you could have been more honest with me, too."

He nodded. "Perhaps. And there are things I want to tell

you, but many of the things I know are of such a nature that they cannot be shared if there's even a minuscule chance that you can't keep them to yourself. I need to know that you can do that. And I need you to be wholly open with me."

I inhaled to respond, but it never came out.

"Maxon, there you are." Kriss called, rounding the corner. "I didn't get to ask you earlier if we were still on for dinner tonight."

Maxon looked at me as he spoke. "Of course. We'll eat in your room."

"Wonderful!"

That hurt.

"America? Are you really leaving?" she asked, coming up to us. I could see the spark of hope in her eyes. I looked to Maxon, whose expression seemed to say *This is what I'm talking about. I need you to accept the consequences of your actions, to trust me to make my own choice.*

"No, Kriss, not today."

"Good." She sighed, coming to hug me. I wondered how much of this embrace was for Maxon's sake; but, really, it didn't matter. Kriss was my toughest competition, but she was also the closest friend I had here. "I was really worried about you last night. I'm glad you're okay."

"Thanks, it was lucky—" I almost said that it was lucky I had Maxon to keep me company, but bragging would have probably ruined what little bit of trust I'd built in the last ten seconds. I cleared my throat. "Lucky the guards got there so fast."

"Thank goodness. Well, I'll see you later." She turned to Maxon. "And I'll see you tonight."

Kriss skipped down the hall, giddier than I'd ever seen her. I guess if I saw the guy I loved put me above his former favorite, I'd feel like skipping, too.

"I know you don't like that, but I need her. If you let me down, she's my best bet."

"It doesn't matter," I said with a shrug. "I won't let you down."

I gave him a quick kiss on the cheek and headed upstairs without looking back. A few hours ago, I thought I'd lost Maxon for good; and now that I knew what he meant to me, I was going to fight for him. The other girls wouldn't know what hit them.

As I made my way up the grand stairwell, I felt encouraged. I probably should have been more worried about the challenge that was ahead of me, but all I could think of was how I'd eventually overcome it.

Perhaps the king sensed my joy, or maybe he was just waiting; but as I stepped onto the second floor, he was there, halfway down the hall.

He approached me slowly, a clear display of control. When he stopped in front of me, I curtsied.

"Your Majesty," I said.

"Lady America. It seems you're still with us."

"So it does."

A pack of guards passed us, bowing as they did so. "Let's

talk business," he said sternly. "What do you think of my wife?"

I pursed my forehead, surprised at the direction of the conversation. Still, I answered honestly. "I think the queen is amazing. I don't know enough words to say how wonderful I think she is."

He nodded. "She's a rare woman. Beautiful, obviously, and also humble. Timid, but not to the point of being cowardly. Obedient, good-humored, an excellent conversationalist. It seems that even though she was born into poverty, she was meant to be a queen."

He paused and looked at me, taking in the clear admiration on my face. "The same cannot be said of you."

I tried to stay calm as he continued. "Your looks are average. Red hair, a bit pale, and I suppose a decent figure; but you're nothing next to Celeste. As far as your temper . . ." He inhaled sharply. "You're rude, jocular; and the one time you do something serious, it tears at the fabric of our nation. Completely thoughtless. And that's not even counting your poor posture and gait. Kriss is far lovelier and more agreeable."

I pushed my lips together, willing myself not to cry. I reminded myself that I already knew all this.

"And, of course, there is absolutely no political advantage to having you in the family. Your caste isn't low enough to be inspiring, and your connections are nonexistent. Elise, however, was very helpful with our trip to New Asia."

I wondered how true that could be if they never actually made contact with her family. Maybe there was something going on that I simply didn't know about. Or maybe all of this was being exaggerated to make me feel worthless. If that was the goal, he'd done an excellent job.

His cold eyes focused on mine. "What are you doing here?"

I swallowed. "I suppose you would have to ask Maxon."

"I'm asking you."

"He wants me here," I said firmly. "And I want to be here. As long as both of those things are true, I'm staying."

The king grinned. "You're what, sixteen? Seventeen?"

"Seventeen."

"I suspect you don't know very much about men, which you shouldn't if you're here. Let me say, they can be very fickle. You might not want to hold on to your affection for him so tightly when a single moment could take his heart away for good."

I squinted, unsure of what he meant.

"I have eyes all over this palace. I know there are girls offering him more than you'd dream. Do you think someone as plain as you could stand a chance next to them?"

Girls? As in plural? Was he saying that more than what I'd seen in the hall between Maxon and Celeste was happening? Were our hours of kisses last night tame compared to everything else he was experiencing?

Maxon had said he wanted to be honest with me. Was he keeping this a secret?

I had to decide in my heart that I trusted Maxon.

"If that's true, then Maxon will let me go in his own time, and you have nothing to worry about."

"But I do!" he bellowed, then dropped his voice. "If by some act of stupidity, Maxon actually chooses you, your little stunts would cost us everything. Decades, generations of work gone because you thought you were being a hero!"

He got in my face to the point that I actually took a step back, but he came closer, leaving very little space between us. His voice was low and harsh, and far more frightening than when he was yelling.

"You're going to need to learn to hold your tongue. If not, you and I will be enemies. Trust me when I say that you do not want to be my enemy."

His angry finger was pointing into my cheek. He could rip me to shreds right now. Even if there was someone nearby, what would they do? No one was going to protect me from the king.

I tried to sound calm. "I understand."

"Excellent," he said, suddenly turning cheerful. "Then I'll leave you to settle back in. Good afternoon."

I stood there, only realizing once he left that I was shaking. When he said to keep my mouth shut, I assumed that meant not even *thinking* of mentioning this to Maxon. So, for now I wouldn't. I was betting this was a test to see how far he could push me. I willed myself to be unbreakable.

As I thought it, something in me changed. I was nervous, yes, but I was also angry.

Who was this man to order me around? Yes, he was king; but, really, he was just a tyrant. Somehow he'd convinced himself that by keeping everyone around him oppressed and quiet, he was doing us all a favor. How was it a blessing to be forced to live in a corner of society? How was it good that there were limits for everyone in Illéa but him?

I thought of Maxon sneaking Marlee into the depths of the kitchens. Even if I wasn't here for very long, I knew he would do a better job than his father. Maxon at least had the capacity for compassion.

I continued to breathe slowly, and once I felt composed, I carried on.

I walked into my room and scurried over to press the button that sent for my maids. Faster than I could have imagined, Anne, Mary, and Lucy came running breathlessly into my room.

"My lady?" Anne said. "Is something wrong?"

I smiled. "Not unless you think me staying is a bad thing."

Lucy squealed. "Really?"

"Absolutely."

"But how?" Anne asked. "I thought you said—"

"I know, I know. It's hard to explain. All I can say is that I've been given a second chance. Maxon matters to me, and I'm going to fight for him."

"That's so romantic!" Mary cried, and Lucy started clapping her hands.

"Hush, hush!" Anne called out sternly. I thought she would be excited and didn't understand her sudden seriousness.

"If she's going to win, we need a plan." Her smile was diabolical, and I grinned with her. I'd never met anyone as organized as these girls. If I had them, there was no way I could lose.

END OF BOOK TWO

ACKNOWLEDGMENTS

WELL, HELLO THERE, SASSY READER. Thank you for reading my book! I hope it made you have unbearable feelings that you find yourself tweeting about at 3:00 a.m. That's what it does to me, so . . .

To Callaway, the sweetest hubby a girl could have. Thank you for your support of and pride in what I do. You make it so much better. Lurve you.

To Guyden and Zuzu, Mommy loves you bunches! I'm crazy about the stories I write, but you'll always be the best things I ever made.

To Mom, Dad, and Jody, thanks for being the weirdest family possible, and for loving me just like I am.

To Mimi, Papa, and Chris, thanks for your love and support, and for being so excited every step of the way.

To the rest of my family—too many names to even think about listing—thank you! I know that, wherever you are, you're always bragging about your niece/granddaughter/ cousin who writes books, and it means a lot to me to know you're behind me all the way.

To Elana, thanks for pretty much everything under the sun. This wouldn't have happened without you.*awkward hug*

To Erica, thanks for letting me call you a zillion times and for being as excited as I am about this story and for just generally being awesome.

To Kathleen, thank you for making it so people in Brazil and China and Indonesia and wherever else get to read these books, too! Still blows my mind.

To the gang at HarperTeen, you guys are unendingly rad, and I love you.

To FTW . . . *throws ham in celebration*

To Northstar, thanks for being home for the Cass family.

To Athena, Rebeca, and the gang at the Christiansburg Panera for making me great hot chocolates and being awkward in the background while I did phone interviews. Thanks!

To Jessica and Monica . . . basically because a promise is a promise, and you guys make me laugh.

To you for sticking with America (and with me) while this all unfolds. Also, you rock my face off.

To God for the mercy that is writing. I'd be lost otherwise.

To naps . . . which is where I'm going now. And to cake, just because.

Turn the page for a sneak peek
at the thrilling third book in
THE SELECTION SERIES

35 GIRLS ENTERED THE SELECTION. ONLY 1 CAN WIN.

THE
ONE
BOOK THREE OF
THE SELECTION SERIES
KIERA CASS
#1 *New York Times* BESTSELLING AUTHOR

CHAPTER 1

THIS TIME WE WERE IN the Great Room enduring another etiquette lesson when bricks came flying through the window. Elise immediately hit the ground and started crawling for the side door, whimpering as she went. Celeste let out a high-pitched scream and bolted toward the back of the room, barely escaping a shower of glass. Kriss grabbed my arm, pulling me, and I broke into a run alongside her as we made our way to the exit.

"Hurry, ladies!" Silvia cried.

Within seconds, the guards had lined up at the windows and were firing, and the bursts of sound echoed in my ears as we fled. Whether they came with guns or stones, anyone showing the smallest level of aggression within sight of the palace would die. There was no more patience left for these attacks.

"I hate running in these shoes," Kriss muttered, a heap of dress draped over her arm, eyes focused on the end of the hall.

"One of us is going to have to get used to it," Celeste said, her breath labored.

I rolled my eyes. "If it's me, I'll wear sneakers every day. I'm already over this."

"Less talking, more moving!" Silvia yelled.

"How do we get downstairs from here?" Elise asked.

"What about Maxon?" Kriss huffed.

Silvia didn't answer. We followed her through a maze of hallways, looking for a path to the basement, watching as guard after guard ran in the opposite direction. I found myself admiring them, wondering at the courage it took to run *toward* danger for the sake of other people.

The guards passing us were completely indistinguishable from one another until a set of green eyes locked with mine. Aspen didn't look afraid or even startled. There was a problem, and he was on his way to fix it. That was simply who he was.

Our gaze was brief, but it was enough. It was like that with Aspen. In a split second, without a word, I could tell him *Be careful and stay safe*. And saying nothing, he'd answer *I know, just take care of yourself.*

While I could easily be at peace with the things we didn't need to say, I had no such luck with the things we'd said out loud. Our last conversation wasn't exactly a happy one. I had been about to leave the palace and had asked him to give me some space to get over the Selection. And then I'd ended up staying and had given him no explanation as to why.

Maybe his patience with me was falling short, his ability to see only the best in me running dry. Somehow I would have to fix that. I couldn't see a life for me that didn't include Aspen. Even now, as I hoped Maxon would choose me, a world without Aspen felt unimaginable.

"Here it is!" Silvia called, pushing a mysterious panel in a wall.

We started down the stairs, Elise and Silvia heading the charge.

"Damn it, Elise, pick up the pace!" Celeste yelled. I wanted to be irritated that she said it, but I knew we were all thinking the same thing.

As we descended into the darkness, I tried to reconcile myself to the hours that would be wasted, hiding like mice. We continued on, the sound of our escape covering the shouts until one man's voice rang out right on top of us.

"Stop!" he yelled.

Kriss and I turned together, watching as the uniform became clear. "Wait," she called to the girls below. "It's a guard."

We stood on the steps, breathing heavily. He finally reached us, gasping himself.

"Sorry, ladies. The rebels ran as soon as the shots were fired. Weren't in the mood for a fight today, I guess."

Silvia, running her hands over her clothes to smooth them, spoke for us. "Has the king deemed it safe? If not, you're putting these girls in a very dangerous position."

"The head of the guard cleared it. I'm sure His Majesty—"

"You don't speak for the king. Come on, ladies, keep moving."

"Are you serious?" I asked. "We're going down there for nothing."

She fixed me with a stare that might have stopped a rebel in his tracks, and I shut my mouth. Silvia and I had built a friendship of sorts as she unknowingly helped me distract myself from Maxon and Aspen with her extra lessons. After my little stunt on the *Report* a few days ago, it seemed that had dissolved into nothing. Turning to the guard, she continued. "Get an official order from the king, and we'll return. Keep walking, ladies."

The guard and I shared an exasperated look and parted ways.

Silvia showed absolutely no remorse when, twenty minutes later, a different guard came, telling us we were free to go upstairs.

I was so irritated by the whole situation, I didn't wait for Silvia or the other girls. I climbed the stairs, exiting somewhere on the first floor, and continued to my room with my shoes still hooked on my fingers. My maids were missing, but a small silver platter holding an envelope was waiting on the bed.

I recognized May's handwriting instantly and tore open the envelope, devouring her words.

> *Ames,*
> *We're aunts! Astra is perfect. I wish you were here to meet her in person, but we all understand you need to be at the palace right now. Do you think we'll be together for Christmas? Not that far away! I've got to get back to helping Kenna and James. I can't believe how pretty she is! Here's a picture for you. We love you!*
> *May*

I slipped the glossy photo from behind the note. Everyone was there except for Kota and me. James, Kenna's husband, was beaming, standing over his wife and daughter with puffy eyes. Kenna sat upright in the bed, holding a tiny pink bundle, looking equal parts thrilled and exhausted. Mom and Dad were glowing with pride, while May's and Gerad's enthusiasm jumped from the image. Of course Kota wouldn't have gone; there was nothing for him to gain from being present. But I should have been there.

I wasn't though.

I was here. And sometimes I didn't understand why. Maxon was still spending time with Kriss, even after all he'd done to get me to stay. The rebels unrelentingly attacked our safety from the outside, and inside, the king's icy words did just as much damage to my confidence. All the while, Aspen orbited me, a secret I had to keep. And the cameras came and went, stealing pieces of our lives to entertain the people. I was being pushed into a corner from every angle, and I was missing out on all the things that had always mattered to me.

I choked back angry tears. I was so tired of crying.

Instead I went into planning mode. The only way to set things right was to end the Selection.

Though I still occasionally questioned my desire to be the princess, there was no doubt in my mind that I wanted to be Maxon's. If that was going to happen, I couldn't sit back and wait for it. Remembering my last conversation with the king, I paced as I waited for my maids.

I could hardly breathe, so I knew eating would be a waste. But it would be worth the sacrifice. I needed to make some progress, and I needed to do it fast. According to the king, the other girls were making advances toward Maxon—physical advances—and he'd said I was far too plain to have a chance of matching them in that department.

As if my relationship with Maxon wasn't complicated enough, there was a whole new issue of rebuilding trust. And I wasn't sure if that meant I wasn't supposed to ask questions or not. While I felt pretty sure he hadn't gone that far physically with the other girls, I couldn't help but wonder. I'd never tried to be seductive before—pretty much every intimate moment I'd had with Maxon came about without intention—but I had to hope that if I was deliberate, I could make it clear that I was just as interested in him as the others.

I took a deep breath, raised my chin, and walked into the dining hall. I was purposely a minute or two late, hoping everyone would already be seated. I was right on that count. But the reaction was better than I'd hoped.

I curtsied, swinging my leg around so the slit in the dress fell open, leading nearly all the way up my thigh. The dress was a deep red, strapless and practically backless, and I was almost positive my maids had used magic to make it stay up at all. I rose, locking eyes with Maxon, who I noticed had stopped chewing. Someone dropped a fork.

Lowering my gaze, I walked to my seat, settling in next to Kriss.

"Seriously, America?" she whispered.

I tilted my head in her direction. "I'm sorry?" I replied, feigning confusion.

She put her silverware down, and we stared at each other. "You look trashy."

"Well, you look jealous."

I'd hit pretty close to the mark, because she flushed a bit before returning to her food. I took limited bites of my own, already miserably constricted. As dessert was being set in front of me, I chose to stop ignoring Maxon, and as I had hoped, his eyes were on me. He reached up and grabbed his ear immediately, and I demurely did the same. My gaze flickered quickly toward King Clarkson, and I tried not to smile. He was irritated, another trick I'd managed to get away with.

I excused myself first, giving Maxon a chance to admire the back of the dress, and scurried to my room. I closed the door to my room behind me and unzipped the gown immediately, desperate for a breath.

"How'd it go?" Mary asked, rushing over.

"He seemed stunned. They all did."

Lucy squealed, and Anne came to help Mary. "We'll hold it up. Just walk," she ordered. I did as I was told. "Is he coming tonight?"

"Yes. I'm not sure when, but he'll definitely be here." I perched on the edge of my bed, arms folded around my stomach to keep the open dress from falling down.

Anne gave me a sad face. "I'm sorry you'll have to be uncomfortable for a few more hours. I'm sure it'll be worth it though."

I smiled, trying to look like I was fine dealing with the pain. I'd told my maids I wanted to get Maxon's attention. I'd left out my hope that, with any luck, this dress would be on the floor pretty soon.

"Do you want us to stay until he arrives?" Lucy asked, her enthusiasm bubbling over.

"No, just help me zip this thing back up. I need to think some things through," I answered, standing so they could help me.

Mary took hold of the zipper. "Suck it in, miss." I obeyed, and as the dress cinched me in again, I thought of a soldier going to war. Different armor but the same idea.

Tonight I was taking down a man.

CHAPTER 2

I OPENED THE BALCONY DOORS, letting the air sweeten my room. Even though it was December, the breeze was light and tickled my skin. We weren't allowed to go outside at all anymore, not without guards by our sides, so this would have to do.

I scurried around the room, lighting candles, trying to make the space inviting. The knock came at the door, and I blew out the match, bolted over to the bed, picked up a book, and fanned out my dress. *Why yes, Maxon, this is how I always look when I read.*

"Come in," I offered, barely loud enough to be heard.

Maxon entered, and I lifted my head delicately, catching the wonder in his eyes as he surveyed my dimly lit room. Finally he focused on me, his gaze traveling up my exposed leg.

"There you are," I said, closing the book and standing to greet him.

He shut the door and came in, his eyes locked on my curves. "I wanted to tell you that you look fantastic tonight."

I flicked my hair over my shoulder. "Oh, this thing? It was just sitting in the back of the closet."

"I'm glad you pulled it out."

I laced my fingers through his. "Come sit with me. I haven't seen you much lately."

He sighed and followed. "I'm sorry about that. Things have been a bit tense since we lost so many people in that rebel attack, and you know how my father is. We sent several guards to protect your families, and our forces are stretched thin, so he's worse than usual. And he's pressuring me to end the Selection, but I'm holding my ground. I want to have some time to think this through."

We sat on the edge of the bed, and I settled close to him. "Of course. You should be in charge of this."

He nodded. "Exactly. I know I've said it a thousand times, but when people push me, it makes me crazy."

I gave him a little pout. "I know."

He paused, and I couldn't read his face. I was trying to figure out how to move this forward without being pushy, but I wasn't sure how to manufacture a romantic moment.

"I know this is silly, but my maids put this new perfume on me today. Is it too strong?" I asked, tilting my neck so he could lean in and breathe.

He came near, his nose hitting a soft patch of skin. "No,

dear, it's lovely," he said into the curve that led to my shoulder. Then he kissed me there. I swallowed, trying to focus. I needed to have some level of control.

"I'm glad you like it. I've really missed you."

I felt his hand snake around my back, and I brought my face down. There he was, eyes looking into mine, our lips millimeters apart.

"How much have you missed me?" he breathed.

His stare, combined with his voice being so low, was doing funny things to my heartbeat. "So much," I whispered back. "So, so much."

I leaned forward, aching to be kissed. Maxon was confident, pulling me closer with one hand and stringing the other through my hair. My body wanted to melt into the kiss, but the dress stopped me. Then, suddenly nervous again, I remembered my plan.

Sliding my hands down Maxon's arms, I guided his fingers to the zipper on the back of my dress, hoping that would be enough.

His hands lingered there for a moment, and I was seconds away from just asking him to unzip it when he burst out laughing.

The sound sobered me up pretty quickly.

"What's so funny?" I asked, horrified, trying to think of an inconspicuous way to check my breath.

"Of everything you've done, this is by far the most entertaining!" Maxon bent over, hitting his knee as he laughed.

"Excuse me?"

He kissed me hard on my forehead. "I always wondered what it would be like to see you try." He started laughing again. "I'm sorry; I have to go." Even the way he stood held a sense of amusement. "I'll see you in the morning."

And then he left. He just left!

I sat there, completely mortified. Why in the world did I think I could pull that off? Maxon may not know everything about me, but at the very least he knew my character—and this? It wasn't me.

I looked down at the ridiculous dress. It was way too much. Even Celeste wouldn't have gone this far. My hair was too perfect, my makeup too heavy. He knew what I was trying to do from the second he walked through the doorway. Sighing, I went around the room, blowing out candles and wondering how I was supposed to face him tomorrow.

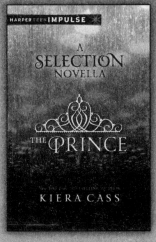